One Brave Thing

by K.M. Creamer

INTRODUCTION

Ellen Datlow

What is it about cats? Why do they lend themselves to fiction so easily? There have been numerous anthologies of cat stories, several of them multi-volume series. There is no other animal about which writers from all genres seem to be obsessed. Mystery, horror, science fiction, and fantasy stories have been written about cats.

It's possible that felines, thought to be domesticated by happenstance rather than intent, are considered more mysterious, and thus more interesting to write about than other animals. Canines are pretty up front about their feelings—they're considered to be loyal, obedient, and cheerful. Dogs, the oldest domesticated animal, have anthropomorphized themselves—become more like people. Cats have done very little of that. They are still strangers in the house. The cat does what it wants and goes its own way, which conjures up the darker images of willfulness, self-interest, and mystery.

It's said that one is a dog person or a cat person. I've been both. I grew up with a wonderful cocker spaniel I adored and took "exploring" in the suburban woods across from where I lived. I don't recall seeing many cats. All I knew of these mysterious creatures was that they chased and ate mice in the weird, silent, black and white, very primitive "Farmer Grey" cartoons of my childhood, and that my aunt living in West Germany would write regular letters to me reporting on her cat's antics. It, and as a result she, were always in trouble with the neighbors for its skill at killing birds.

It wasn't until I moved to Manhattan that I acquired (through a roommate) my first cat. The roommate moved in, immediately brought home two kittens, and then fled Manhattan after a couple of months, leaving me with one kitten because her parents wouldn't let her take both back to Ann Arbor. I was suddenly a cat owner, soon acquiring a second, older cat (who lived to be twenty-three plus), and was soon faced with my own dead or dying birds—a roof adjoining my apartment allowed my cats limited roaming area.

Since then I've always owned cats. Or have they owned me?

The stories herein are culled from anthologies, magazines, and collections, most published from 1980–2009, a few (such as the Lewis Carroll excerpt and

1

the John Crowley and Stephen King stories) in the late 70s. There are stories in which cats are the heroes and some in which they're the villains. There are domestic cats, tigers, lions, mythical part-cat beings, people transformed into cats, and cats transformed into people. There's science fiction, fantasy, mystery, horror, and even one mainstream cat story. And yes, a few cute cats.

This is not my first cat anthology. I edited *Twists of the Tale* in 1996—it consisted of mostly original horror stories, three of them reprinted in this book.

THROUGH THE LOOKING GLASS (EXCERPT)

Lewis Carroll

One thing was certain, that the *white* kitten had had nothing to do with it—it was the black kitten's fault entirely. For the white kitten had been having its face washed by the old cat for the last quarter of an hour (and bearing it pretty well, considering); so you see that it *couldn't* have had any hand in the mischief.

The way Dinah washed her children's faces was this: first she held the poor thing down by its ear with one paw, and then with the other paw she rubbed its face all over, the wrong way, beginning at the nose; and just now, as I said, she was hard at work on the white kitten, which was lying quite still and trying to purr—no doubt feeling that it was all meant for its good.

But the black kitten had been finished with earlier in the afternoon, and so, while Alice was sitting curled up in a corner of the great armchair, half talking to herself and half asleep, the kitten had been having a grand game of romps with the ball of worsted Alice had been trying to wind up, and had been rolling it up and down till it had all come undone again; and there it was, spread over the hearth-rug, all knots and tangles, with the kitten running after its own tail in the middle.

"Oh, you wicked little thing!" cried Alice, catching up the kitten, and giving it a little kiss to make it understand that it was in disgrace. "Really, Dinah ought to have taught you better manners! You *ought*, Dinah, you know you ought!" she added, looking reproachfully at the old cat, and speaking in as cross a voice as she could manage—and then she scrambled back into the armchair, taking the kitten and the worsted with her, and began winding up the ball again. But she didn't get on very fast, as she was talking all the time, sometimes to the kitten, and sometimes to herself. Kitty sat very demurely on her knee, pretending to watch the progress of the winding, and now and then putting out one paw and gently touching the ball, as if it would be glad to help, if it might.

"Do you know what to-morrow is, Kitty?" Alice began. "You'd have guessed if you'd been up in the window with me—only Dinah was making you tidy, so you couldn't. I was watching the boys getting in sticks for the bonfire—and it wants plenty of sticks, Kitty! Only it got so cold, and it snowed so, they had to leave off. Never mind, Kitty, we'll go and see the bonfire to-morrow." Here Alice wound two or three turns of the worsted round the kitten's neck, just to see how it would look; this led to a scramble, in which the ball rolled down upon the floor, and yards and yards of it got unwound again.

"Do you know, I was so angry, Kitty," Alice went on as soon as they were comfortably settled again, "when I saw all the mischief you had been doing, I was very nearly opening the window, and putting you out into the snow! And you'd have deserved it, you little mischievous darling! What have you got to say for yourself? Now don't interrupt me!" she went on, holding up one finger. "I'm going to tell you all your faults. Number one: you squeaked twice while Dinah was washing your face this morning. Now you can't deny it, Kitty, I heard you! What's that you say?" (pretending that the kitten was speaking.) "Her paw went into your eye? Well, that's *your* fault, for keeping your eyes open—if you'd shut them tight up, it wouldn't have happened. Now don't make any more excuses, but listen! Number two: you pulled Snowdrop away by the tail just as I had put down the saucer of milk before her! What, you were thirsty, were you? How do you know she wasn't thirsty too? Now for number three: you unwound every bit of the worsted while I wasn't looking!

"That's three faults, Kitty, and you've not been punished for any of them yet. You know I'm saving up all your punishments for Wednesday week—Suppose they had saved up all *my* punishments!" she went on, talking more to herself than the kitten. "What *would* they do at the end of a year? I should be sent to prison, I suppose, when the day came. Or—let me see—suppose each punishment was to be going without a dinner: then, when the miserable day came, I should have to go without fifty dinners at once! Well, I shouldn't mind *that* much! I'd far rather go without them than eat them!

"Do you hear the snow against the window-panes, Kitty? How nice and soft it sounds! Just as if someone was kissing the window all over outside. I wonder if the snow *loves* the trees and fields, that it kisses them so gently? And then it covers them up snug, you know, with a white quilt; and perhaps it says, 'Go to sleep, darlings, till the summer comes again.' And when they wake up in the summer, Kitty, they dress themselves all in green, and dance about—whenever the wind blows—oh, that's very pretty!" cried Alice, dropping the ball of worsted to clap her hands. "And I do so *wish* it was true! I'm sure the woods look sleepy in the autumn, when the leaves are getting brown.

"Kitty, can you play chess? Now, don't smile, my dear, I'm asking it seriously. Because, when we were playing just now, you watched just as if you understood it: and when I said 'Check!' you purred! Well, it *was* a nice check, Kitty, and really I might have won, if it hadn't been for that nasty Knight, that came wiggling down among my pieces. Kitty, dear, let's pretend—" And here I wish I could tell you half the things Alice used to say, beginning with her favourite phrase "Let's pretend." She had had quite a long argument with her sister only the day before—all because Alice had begun with "Let's pretend we're kings and queens;" and her sister, who liked being very exact, had argued that they couldn't, because there were only two of them, and Alice had been reduced at last to say, "Well, *you* can be one of them then, and *I'll* be all the rest." And once she had really frightened her old nurse by shouting suddenly in her ear, "Nurse! Do let's pretend that I'm a hungry hyaena, and you're a bone."

But this is taking us away from Alice's speech to the kitten. "Let's pretend that you're the Red Queen, Kitty! Do you know, I think if you sat up and folded your arms, you'd look exactly like her. Now do try, there's a dear!" And Alice got the Red Queen off the table, and set it up before the kitten as a model for it to imitate; however, the thing didn't succeed, principally, Alice said, because the kitten wouldn't fold its arms properly. So, to punish it, she held it up to the Looking-glass, that it might see how sulky it was—"and if you're not good directly," she added, "I'll put you through into Looking-glass House. How would you like *that*?"

"Now, if you'll only attend, Kitty, and not talk so much, I'll tell you all my ideas about Looking-glass House. First, there's the room you can see through the glass—that's just the same as our drawing room, only the things go the other way. I can see all of it when I get upon a chair—all but the bit behind the fireplace. Oh! I do so wish I could see *that* bit! I want so much to know whether they've a fire in the winter; you never *can* tell, you know, unless our fire smokes, and then smoke comes up in that room too—but that may be only pretence, just to make it look as if they had a fire. Well then, the books are something like our books, only the words go the wrong way; I know that, because I've held up one of our books to the glass, and then they hold up one in the other room.

"How would you like to live in Looking-glass House, Kitty? I wonder if they'd give you milk in there? Perhaps Looking-glass milk isn't good to drink—But oh, Kitty! now we come to the passage. You can just see a little *peep* of the passage in Looking-glass House, if you leave the door of our drawing-room wide open; and it's very like our passage as far as you can see, only you know it may be quite different on beyond. Oh, Kitty! how nice it would be if we could only get through into Looking-glass House! I'm sure it's got, oh! such beautiful things in it! Let's pretend there's a way of getting through into it, somehow, Kitty. Let's pretend the glass has got all soft like gauze, so that we can get through. Why, it's turning into a sort of mist now, I declare! It'll be easy enough to get through—" She was up on the chimney-piece while she said this, though she hardly knew how she had got there. And certainly the glass *was* beginning to melt away, just like a bright, silvery mist.

NO HEAVEN WILL NOT EVER HEAVEN BE...

A. R. Morlan

A.R. Morlan's short fiction (under her own name and three pen names) has been published or is forthcoming in over one hundred twenty different magazines, anthologies, and webzines in the United States, Canada, and parts of Europe. Her stories are collected in *Smothered Dolls*. She lives in the Midwest with a house full of cat "children."

Morlan's love of cats shows in her portrait of a man and his cats. When I first read the story (I originally bought it for my cat horror anthology *Twists of the Tale*), I was so taken by Hobart Gurney and Katz's cats that I called the author to ask if Gurney was based on a real person: the answer is yes and no. Morlan says that the character was inspired by a real barn advertising painter (who only painted text, not pictures of cats). All of the cats depicted in the story are based on actual cats the author has owned.

> *There are no ordinary cats.*
> —COLETTE

Not too long ago, it wasn't too uncommon for someone driving down Little Egypt way, where southern Illinois merges into Kentucky close to the Cumberland River, to see oh, maybe five-six Katz's Chewing Tobacco barn advertisements within a three- or four-hour drive; in his prime, Hobart Gurney was a busy man. Now, if a person wants to see Gurney's handiwork, they have to drive or fly out to New York City, or—if they're lucky—catch one of the traveling exhibitions of his work. *If* the exhibitors can get insurance—after all, Gurney was sort of the Jackson Pollock of the barn-art world; he worked with what paints he had, with an eye toward getting the job done fast and getting his pay even quicker once he was finished, so those cut-out chunks of barn wall need to be babied like they were fashioned out of spun sugar and spider webs—and not just flaking paint on sometimes-rotting planks. Someone once told me that the surviving Katz's barn signs had to be treated with the same sort of preservation methods as the relics unearthed from Egyptian tombs—now *that* would've tickled old Hobart Gurney's fancy, as he might've put it.

Oh, not so much the preservation part, but the Egyptian aspect of it all, for Gurney did far more than paint Katz's Chewing Tobacco signs for a living (not to mention for a good part of his life, period); he *lived* for his "Katz's cats."

Died for them, too. But that's another story... one you won't read about in any of those books filled with photographs of Gurney's barn signs, or hear about on those PBS or Arts & Entertainment specials on his life and work. But the story rivals any ever told about the cat-worshiping Egyptians... especially since Hobart knew his cats weren't gods but loved them anyhow. And because they loved *him* back....

When I first met Hobart Gurney, I thought he was just another one of those old men you see in just about every small town in the rural heartland; you've seen them—old men of less than average height, wearing pants that are too big in the waist and too long in the leg, held up by suspenders or belts snugged up so tight they can hardly breathe, with spines like shallow Cs and shoulders pinched protectively around their collarbones, the kind of old men who wear too-clean baseball caps or maybe tam-o-shanters topped with fluffy pom-poms, and no matter how often they shave, they always seem to have an eighth-inch-long near-transparent stubble dusting their parchment cheeks. The kind who shuffle and pause near curbs, then stop and stand there, lost in thought, once they step off the curb. The kind of old man who's all but invisible until he hawks phlegm on the sidewalk not out of spite but because men *did* that sort of thing without thinking years ago.

I was adjusting the shutter speed on my camera when I heard him hawk and spit not two feet away from me—making that irritating noise that totally blows one's concentration. And it was one of those days when the clouds kept moving in front of the sun every few seconds, totally changing the amount of available natural light hitting the side of the barn whose painted side I was trying to capture... without thinking, I looked back over my shoulder and grumped, "You *mind*? I'm trying to adjust my camera—"

The old man just stood there, hands shoved past the wrists into his trouser pockets, a fine dark dribble of tobacco spittle still clinging to the side of his stubbled chin, staring mildly at me with hat bill-shaded pale-blue eyes. After a few false fluttering starts of his chapped-lipped mouth, he said, "No self-respectin' cat ever wants to be a model... you have to sorta sneak up on 'em, when they ain't payin' *you* no mind."

"Uh-huh," I said, turning my attention back to the six-foot-tall cat painted next to the neatly lettered legend: KATZ'S CHEWING TOBACCO—IT'S THE KATZ'S MEOW. This Katz's cat was one of the finest I'd seen yet—unlike other cat-logo signs, like the Chessie railroad cat, for instance, every Katz's cat was different: different color, different pose, sometimes even more than one cat per barn sign. And this one was a masterpiece: a gray tiger, the kind of animal whose fur you *know* would be soft to the touch, with each multi-hued hair tipped with just enough white to give the whole cat an aura-like sheen, and a softly thick neck that told the world that this cat was an unneutered male, old enough to have sired a few litters of kittens but not old enough to be piss-mean or battle-scarred. A young male, maybe two, three years old. And his eyes were gentle, too; trusting eyes, of hazy green touched with a hint of yellow along the oval pupils, over a grayish-pink nose and a mouth covering barely visible fang tips. He was resting on his side, so all four of his paw pads were visible, each one colored that between gray and pink color that's a bit of each yet something not at all on the artist's color wheel. And his ombre-ringed tail was curled up and over his hind feet, resting in a relaxed curl over his hind paws. But something in his sweet face told a person that this cat would jump right up into your arms if you only patted your chest and said "Come 'ere—"

But… considering that this cat was mostly gray, and the barn behind him was weathering fast, I had to make sure the shutter speed was adjusted *so,* or I'd never capture this particular Katz's cat. Not the way the clouds were rolling in faster and faster—

"Don't look like Fella wants his picture took today," the tobacco-spitting old man said helpfully, as I missed yet another split-second-of-sun opportunity to capture the likeness of the reclining cat. That did it. Letting my camera flop down against my chest by the strap, I turned around and asked, "Do you own this barn? Am I supposed to pay you for taking a picture or what?"

The old man looked at me meekly, his bill-shaded eyes wide with hurt as he said around a glob of chaw, "I already got my pay for that 'un, but I 'spose you could say it's my *cat*—"

When he said that, all my irritation and impatience melted into a soggy feeling of shame mingled with heart-thumping awe—this baggy-trousered old man had to be Hobart Gurney, the sign painter responsible for all of the Katz's Tobacco signs dotting barns throughout southern Illinois and western Kentucky, the man who was still painting such signs up until a couple of years ago, stopping only when old age made it difficult for him to get up and down the ladders.

I'd seen that profile about him on CNN a few years ago, when he was painting his last or next-to-last Katz's sign, but most old men tend to look alike, especially when decked out in the ubiquitous uniform of a baseball cap and paint-splattered overalls, and at any rate, the work had impressed me more than the man who created it…

Putting out my hand, I said, "Hey, sorry about what I said… I—I didn't mean it like that, it's just that I only have so many days of vacation left, and the weather hasn't exactly been cooperative—"

Gurney's hand was dry and firm; he shook hands until I had to withdraw my aching hand, as he replied, "No offense meant, no offense taken. I 'spect Fella will wait awhiles until the clouds see fit to cooperate with you. He's a patient one, is Fella, but shy 'round strangers." The way he said "Fella," I knew the name should be capitalized, instead of it being a generic nomenclature for the animal at hand.

Judging from the way the clouds scudded across the sun, I figured that Fella was in for a good long wait, so I motioned to the rental car parked a few yards away from the barn, inviting Gurney to share one of the cans of Pepsi in my backseat cooler. Gurney's trousers made a raspy rubbing noise when he walked, not unlike the sound a cat's tongue makes when it licks your bare arm. And when he was speaking in close quarters, his tobacco-laced breath was sort of cat fetid, too, all wild-smelling and warm. The old man positioned himself half in and half out of my car, so he could see his Fella clearly, while still keeping his body in the relative warmth of my car. Between noisy slurps of soda, he told me, "Like I said, no self-respectin' cat aims to model for you, so's the only way to get around it is to make your *own* cat. Memory's the best model they is—"

I almost choked on my Pepsi when he said that; all along, I'd assumed that Gurney had used whatever barn cats were wandering around him for his inspiration... but to create such accurate, personable cats from memory and imagination—

"Funny thing is, when I was hired on to work for Katz, back in the thirties, all they was interested in was gettin' their name out in front of the public, in as big letters as possible. That I added cats to the Katz's signs was my idea—didn't get paid no extra for doin' it, neither. But it seemed natural, you see? And it did get folks' attention. 'Sides, them cats, they kept me company, while I was workin'—gets mighty lonely up on that ladder, with the wind snaking down your shirt collar and no one to talk to up that high. Was sorta like when I was a boy, muckin' out my pa's barn, and the barn cats, they'd come snaking 'round my legs purrin' and sometimes jumpin' straight up onto my shoulders, so they'd hitch a free ride while I was workin'—only I didn't get 'round to givin' too many of them cats names, you see, 'cause they was always comin' or goin', or gettin' cow-crushed—oh, them cows didn't mean no harm, see, it's just they was so big and them cats too small when they'd try snuggling up wi'em on cold winter nights. But I sure did enjoy their company. Now you may laugh at this, but—" Here Gurney lowered his voice, even though there was no one else around to hear him but me and the huge painted Fella resting on the side of the abandoned barn. "—when I was a young'un, and even a *not* so young'un, I had me this dream. I wanted to be small, like a cat, for oh, maybe a night or so. Just long enough for me to snuggle down with a whole litterful of cats, four-five of 'em, all of us same-sized and warm in the hay, and we'd tangle our legs and whatnot in a warm pile, and they'd lick my face and then burrow their heads under my chin, or mine under theirs, and we'd sleep for a time. Nothing better for the insomnia than to rest with a cat purring in your ears. 'Tis true. Don't need none of them sleeping pills when you gots yourself a cat.

"That's why I took the Katz's Tobacco job when I heard of it, even though I wasn't too keen on heights. Course, it bein' the Depression was a powerful motivator, too, but the *name* Katz was just too good to pass by... and them not minding when I dickied with their adverts was heaven-made for me, too.

Struck me funny, when them television-fellers interviewed me and all, when I was paintin' the little girls—"

Gurney's words made me remember the album of Katz's signs I kept locked in the trunk of the car (not my only set, but a spare album I used for reference, especially when coming across a barn I may have photographed before, under different lighting or seasonal circumstances); too excited to speak, I got out of the backseat and hurried for the trunk, while Gurney kept on talking about the "pup reporter" who'd interviewed him for that three-minute interview.

"—and he didn't even ask me what the cats' names was, like it didn't matter none to—"

"Were these the 'little girls'?" I asked as I flipped through the album pages until I found the dry-mounted snapshot of one of the most elaborate Katz's signs: four kittens snuggled together in a hollowed-out bed of straw, their pointed little faces curious yet subtly wary, as if they'd all burrow into the straw if you took one step closer to them. Clearly a litter of barn kittens, even if you discounted the straw bedding; these weren't Christmas-card-and-yarn-balls kittens, cavorting like live Dakin kittens for a Madison Avenue artist, but feral-type kittens, the kind you'd be lucky to coax close enough to sniff your fingers before they'd run off to hide in the farthest corners of the manure-scented barn where they were born. The kind of kitten who'd grow up slat-thin and long-tailed, slinking around corners like a fleshed-out shadow, or coming up to you from behind, as if sizing up whether or not to take a sharp-clawed swipe at your shoe before running for cover. The kind of cat you know will get kittened out before she's three years old, winding up saggy-bellied and defensive by the time she's four.

But when Gurney saw the eight-by-ten enlargement, his face lit up and his puckered lips stretched out into a broad grin, exposing what my own grandfather used to call "dime-store choppers" of an astonishing Chiclets gum uniform squareness and off-whiteness.

"You took a picture of my little girls! Usually they're tricky ones, on 'count of Prissy and Mish-Mish lookin' so much alike, but you caught 'em, by gummy, got them in just the right light—"

"Wait, wait, let me get this down," I said, reaching over the seat for the notebook and pen resting on the front passenger seat. "Now, which one is which?"

His face glowing with the kind of pride most men his age took in showing off pictures of their grandchildren (or even great-grandkids), Gurney pointed at each kitten in turn, stroking their chemically captured images with a tender, affectionate forefinger, as if chucking each under her painted chin. "This 'un's Smokey, the tiger gray, and here's Prissy—see how dainty she looks, with them fox-narrow eyes and little points on her ears?—and right next to her is Mish-Mish, even though they're both calicos, Mishy's a little more patchy-colored than usual—"

"'Mish-Mish'?" I asked, not knowing how he'd come up with that name; Gurney's answer surprised—and touched—me.

"Got that name from the *Milwaukee Journal* Green Sheet, where they put all their funnies and little offbeat articles... was an article about the Middle East, and it mentioned how them A-rabs like cats so much, and how their version of 'Kitty-kitty' was 'Mish-Mish,' which is their lingo for peach color, on 'count of most of their strays bein' sorta peachy-orange. See how Mish-Mish's face is got that big splotch of peach on it? Oh, I know we're not 'sposed to care what them A-rab folks think, on 'count of them bein' the enemy or whatnot, but you can't fault a people who care so much for their cats too much. Heard tell the Egyptians worshiped their cats, like gods... done up their pets as mummies, the whole shebang. So's I don't even mind when their descendants says they hate us, long as they take care of their cats—'cause a man who can hate a cat can't much like hisself, *I* says."

I had to laugh at that; before Gurney could go on, I quoted Mark Twain from memory: "If man could be crossed with the cat, it would improve the man but deteriorate the cat—"

Now it was Gurney's turn to laugh, until he spittle-flecked his shirt collar before he went on, "Anyhows, next to Mish-Mish is Tinker, only you can't tell from lookin' at her that she's a girl, on 'count of her only bein' two colors and all, but from personal experience, most gray cats with white feet I've seen's been girls. Don't know why that is... sorta like how you never see a white cat with black feet and chest, like you see black cats with white socks and bibs. Funny how nature works that way, ain't it?"

Having told me the names of the "little girls" (which I duly wrote down in my notebook), Gurney began paging through the rest of the album, matching heretofore anonymous painted felines with the names that somehow made them real—at least to the man who created them: black-bodied and white-socked Ming, with his clear, clear green eyes and luxurious long fur with a couple of mats along the chest; calico Beanie with her rounded gray chin and owl-like yellow-green eyes; dandelion-fuzzy Stan and Ollie, black-and-white tuxedo-patterned kittens, one obviously fatter, but both still too wobbly-limbed and tiny-eared to look anything but pick-me-up adorable; and too many more to remember offhand (thank goodness I had many clean pages left in my notebook that afternoon). But once each cat was named, I could never again look at it as just another Katz's Tobacco cat; for instance, knowing that Beanie was *Beanie* made her *into* a cat, one with a history and a personality... you just knew that she was full of beans when she was a kitten, getting into things, playing with her tail until she'd spun herself like a dime-store top... And for a moment, Gurney's cats became more than pigment and imagination. Not unlike the work of regular canvas-easels-and-palette artists, or those natural-born billboard painters, the legendary ones who never needed to use those gridlike blue-prints to create the advertisements.

It was sad, really, how that reporter had missed out on the essence of Gurney's work; all the "pup reporter" seemed to be interested in was how *long* Gurney had been at it.

As Gurney looked at the last of the barn pictures I'd taken and enlarged, he said shyly, "I feel sorta humbled by this and all... it's like I was one of them art-fart painter guys, in a gallery 'stead of a regular workin' Joe... Oh, not that I'm not pleased... it's just... oh, I dunno. It just seems funny to have my cats all put in a book form, 'stead of them just *bein'* out where they are, in the open and all. Like they was suddenly domesticated 'stead of bein' regular barn kitties."

I didn't know how to answer that; I realized that Gurney must be astute enough to realize that his signs *were* works of art—he may have been slightly inarticulate, and most likely unschooled, but he wasn't ignorant by any means—he was obviously in a quandary; on the one hand, he was from a time when work was simply something you got paid for, period; yet on the other hand, the fact that he'd been interviewed on TV and caught me taking pictures of his efforts must have been an indication that his work *was* something special. He couldn't quite cope with having a fuss being made over something he'd considered to be paid labor.

I gently lifted the book off his lap and placed it on the seat between us before saying, "I can empathize with you there... I work as an advertising photographer, taking pictures of products for clients, and when someone praises me for my composition, or whatever, it can be a strange feeling... especially since I'm just a go-between when it comes to the product and the consumer—"

Gurney's watery pale-blue eyes were darting around as I spoke, and for a moment I was afraid that I was losing his attention, but instead he surprised me by saying, "I think Fella's lost his shyness... the sun's been shining for a good minute now."

Quickly, I got out of the car and positioned myself in front of the barn; true to Gurney's word, Fella was no longer shy, but exposed in all his sunlit perfection against the sun-weathered barn. It's funny, but even though the lettering next to the cat was badly flaked, I could almost see every individual hair of the tomcat's fur.

And behind me, Hobart Gurney took a noisy slurp of soda as he repeated, in the way of old men you find in every small town, "Yessirree, my Fella's not shy anymore..."

I said good-bye to Gurney a couple of hours later, outside the adult day-care center and seniors apartment where he lived; without going in, I knew what his room must be like—single bed, with a worn ripcord bedspread, some issues of *Reader's Digest* large-print edition on the bed-stand, and a doorless closet filled with not too many clothes hanging from those crochet-covered hangers, and—most depressing of all—no animals at all to keep him company. It was the sort of place where they only bring in some puppies or kittens when the local newspaper editor wants a set of human interest pictures for the inner spread during a dull news week—"Oldsters with Animals" on their afghan-covered laps.

Not the sort of place where suddenly-small men snuggle with litters of barn cats in a bed of straw...

With an almost comic formality, Gurney thanked me for the Pepsi and for "letting me see the kitties" in my album. I asked him if he got out much, to see the signs in person, but instantly regretted my words when he nonchalantly spit at his feet before saying, "Don't get 'round much since I turned in my driver's license… my hands aren't as steady as they used to be, be it with a brush or with a steering wheel. Once I almost run over a cat crossing a back road and tol' myself, 'This is it, Hobart' even though the cat, she got away okay. Wasn't worth the risk…"

Not knowing what else to do, I opened the back door of the car and brought out the album; Gurney didn't want to take it at first, even though I assured him that I had another set of prints plus the negatives back in my studio in New York City. The way he brushed the outside of the album with his fingers, as if the imitation leather was soft tiger-stripe fur, was almost too much for me; knowing that I couldn't stay, couldn't see any more of this, I bid him farewell and left him standing in front of the oldsters' home, album of kitties in his hands. I know I should've done more, but what could I do? Really? I'd given him back his cats; I couldn't give him back his old life… and what he'd shared with me already hurt too much, especially his revelation of the smallness fantasy. I mean, how often do even people who are close to each other, like old friends, or family, reveal such intimate, deeply *need*ing things like that—especially without being asked to? Once you know things like that about a person, it gets a little hard to face them without feeling like you have a bought-from-a-comic-book-ad pair of X-ray glasses capable of peering into their soul. Nobody should be that vulnerable to another living being.

Especially one they hardly know…

A few days after I met Hobart Gurney my vacation in the Midwest was over, and I returned to my studio, to turn lifeless sample products into… something potentially essential to people who didn't know they needed that thing until that month's issue of *Vanity Fair* or *Cosmopolitan* arrived in the mail, and they finally got around to paging through the magazine after getting home from work. Not that I felt responsible for turning the unknown *into* the essential; even when I got to keep what I photographed, it didn't mean squat to me. I could appreciate my work, respect my better efforts… but I never gave a pet name to a bottle of men's cologne, if you get my drift. And I envied Hobart for being able to love what he did, because he had the freedom to *do* it the way he wanted to. And because the now-defunct Katz's Chewing Tobacco people could've cared less what he painted next to their logo. (Oh, for such benign indifference when it came to *my* work!)

But I also pitied Hobart, because letting go of what you've come to love is a hard, hard thing, which makes the lending of that creative, *loving* process all the harder to take, especially when the ending is an involuntary thing. What had the old man said in the TV interview? That he was too old to climb the ladder anymore? That had to have been as bad as him realizing that he couldn't drive safely anymore…

And the funny thing was, I got the feeling that if he could have climbed those ladders, he would've still been putting those man-sized cats on barns, whether Katz's paid him or not.

I honestly couldn't say the same about what *I* did for a living.

I was in the middle of shooting a series of pictures of a new women's cologne, which happened to come in a bottle that resembled a piece of industrial flotsam more than a container for a fragrance boasting "top notes of green, with cinnamon undercurrents"—whatever *that* meant, since the stuff smelled like dime-store deodorant, when my studio phone rang. I had the answering machine on Call Screening, so I could hear it while not missing out on my next shot... but I hurried to the phone when a tentative-sounding voice asked, "Uhm... are you the one who dropped Mr. Gurney off at the home a couple of months ago?"

"Yeah, you're speaking to me, not the machine—"

The woman on the other end began without preamble, "Sorry to bother you, but we found your card in Mr. Gurney's room... the last anyone saw of him he was carrying that album you give him under his arm, before he went for his walk, only he never went for a walk for a week before—"

The sick feeling began in my stomach and soon fanned out all over my body; as the woman in charge of the old people's home rambled on, telling me that no one in the area had seen the old man after he'd accepted a lift from someone with Canadian plates on his car, which naturally meant that he could be anywhere, but maybe headed for New York. I shook my head, even though the woman couldn't possibly see me, as I cut in "No, ma'am, don't even try looking here. He's not far away... I'm sure of it. If he's not still in Little Egypt, he's across the border in Kentucky... just look for the Katz's Tobacco signs—"

"The what?"

I pressed the receiver against my chest, muttered *You stupid old biddy* just to make myself feel better, then told her, "He painted signs, on barns... he's saying good-bye to the signs," and as I said the last few words, I wondered at my own choice of words... even as my own artist's instincts—instincts Gurney and I shared—told me that I had, indeed, chosen my words correctly.

Despite the fact that the woman from the rest home had gotten her information from me, she never bothered to call me back when Hobart Gurney's body was found, half buried in the unmown grass surrounding one of the abandoned barns bearing his loving handiwork; I found out about his death along with all the other people watching CNN that late-fall evening—the network reran the piece about his last or next-to-last sign-painting job, along with an oddly sentimental obituary that ended with a close-up of the "little girls," whose particular sign the old man's body had been found under. The camera zoomed in for a close-up of Mish-Mish, with her patchwork face of mixed tan and gray and white, with that peach-colored blotch over one eye, and she looked so poignant yet so *real* that no one watching her—be they a cat lover or not—could fail to realize what may've been more difficult to realize during that warts-and-all initial CNN interview, which plainly showed how unsophisticated and gauche Hobart Gurney may have seemed to be on the outside (so much so, perhaps, that it made underestimating his work all the easier): that Gurney was more than a great artist: He was a genius, easily on the par of Grandma Moses or anyone of her ilk.

J. C. Suarès was the first person to put out a book devoted to Katz's Cats, as Gurney's creations were to become popularly known. Many famous photographers, including Herb Ritts, Annie Leibovitz, and Avedon, took in that collection; I wasn't one of them, but I did get on that other collection put together for one of the AIDS charities. Then came the specials on what Gurney would've called the "art-fart" stations, and there's even been word of a postage stamp bearing his likeness, along with one of the Katz's Cats.

The irony was, I seriously doubt Gurney would've truly enjoyed all the fuss made about his work; what he'd created was too private for all *that*. Not when he'd so lovingly stroked the images of his "little girls" faces in that rental car of mine, and not when he'd so spontaneously shared that cat-size dream of his from his barn-mucking boyhood so many years—and barn cats—ago. But at least for me, there was one benefit from his life, and his work, becoming so public: It gave me an opportunity to find out what really happened to him, without my needing to visit that depressing small town where I'd met him or to actually see his all-but-empty cell-like adult day-care bedroom.

Some policemen found his body, almost covered by long, dead grass, just below the barn where he'd painted the "little girls"; he was curled on his left side, almost in a fetal position, with both hands covering his face, not unlike a cat at sleep or rest. Supposedly it was a heart attack, but that didn't account for the abrasions on his exposed face and hands; a rough, red, rash-like disruption on his flesh, which was eventually dismissed as fire-ant bites. Nor did the "official" cause of death account for the blissful look on his face that the policeman in one A&E special described; you don't have to be a doctor to know that heart attacks are painful.

Nor do you need to be an expert on cats—especially *big* cats—to know what a cat's tongue can do to unprotected flesh, especially when they get it into their heads to keep licking and licking while snuggled together in a pile of warm, furry flesh.

Maybe Hobart Gurney didn't mean to say good-bye per se during that self-prescribed tour of his creations; maybe he'd just grown nostalgic after seeing the pictures I'd given to him. Funny how he took the album with him, when he'd never forgotten a single cat he'd created, but then again, no one will ever know what drove him to turn a Depression-era job taken despite an aversion to heights into something more than his life's work. Perhaps *my* decision to collect photographs of his work ultimately led to his death, which I heard about on the CNN news. But if that is so, I can't quite feel guilty about it—after all, Gurney hadn't painted cats in years; true, nothing stopped him from painting them on canvas, but I don't think that was Gurney's way at all.

Hadn't he said that what he was doing was work, something he was supposed to be doing? I doubt that the notion of painting for himself applied to his practical mind, just as I doubt that he could have foreseen a day when his cats would be severed from the very barns on which they lived, to be taken in wall-size chunks and "domesticated" in museums and art galleries all over the country.

Or… maybe he *did* have an inkling of what would happen, and knew that he wouldn't have his cats to himself for very much longer…

And, considering what was written on his tombstone—by whom, I don't know—I don't think I'm the only person who *maybe* knows what really happened to Hobart Gurney, down in the long, dead, flattened grass below the "little girls"… for this is what is carved on his barn-gray tombstone:

> No Heaven will not ever Heaven be,
> Unless my Cats are there to Welcome me.

All I can say is, I hope it was warm, and soft, and *loving*, there in the long, dead grass, with the little girls…

In memory of:

Beanie, Ming, Fella, Ollie, Stan, Puddin', Blackie, Cupcake, Smokie, Prissy, Mish-Mish, Dewie, Rusty, Precious, Puff, Lucky, Eric, Sweetheart, Jack, Early Grey, Charlie, Dolly, Maynard, Willie, Gwen, Laya, Spunky, Belle, Stripes, Boo, Moo-Moo, Bruiser, Monkey, Goldie, Poco, Butterball, Spooky, Silky, Ladybug, Orangey, Ko-Ko, Frosty, Simba, Rosie, Mrs. T., Mister, Muffin (Bubba), Speedy, Whiskers, Bitsy, Purr-Bear, Kay-Tu, Chloe, Bippy, Brutis, Teddy, Amelia, Elmo, Alphie, Gloria, Woody, Jezebel, Tigger, Pansy, Oscar, April, Peokoe, Meg, Adrian, Sylvester, Baby, Marco Polo, Lovey, Candy, Lola, Lacy, Poopie (Violet), Queenie, Otto, Babykins, Momma Cat, Cutie Pie, Sandy, Beauty, Sean, Chewie, Scooter, Mittens, Taffy, Boo Boo, Clyde, Bailey, Gummitch, Dundee, Chatty, Princess, Pinky, Apollo, Amber, Denise, Callie, Bijou, Squeeky, Cee-Cee, Felix, Boogie, Little Boy, Sugarplum, Tweetie Pie, Ruby, Penny, Fluffy (II), Pumpkin, Casper, Boots, Jet, Honey, Beau, Angel, Mack, Bugsy, Miss Kitty, Katie, June Bug, Cinnamon, Tippi, Gracie, Quinn, Grady, Trudy, Baby Biscuit, May, and Mongo.

THE PRICE
Neil Gaiman

Neil Gaiman is the Newbery-winning author of *The Graveyard Book* and a *New York Times* bestseller, whose books have been made into major motion pictures including the recent *Coraline*. He is also famous for the "Sandman" graphic novel series, and for numerous other books and comics for adult, young adult, and younger readers. He has won the Hugo, Nebula, Mythopoeic, World Fantasy, and other awards. He is also the author of powerful short stories and poems.

"The Price" is a lovely mystical, powerful, and moving tale that Gaiman admits is also more or less true. At least, the narrator in this story "is pretty much me, the house is my house, the cats my cats, and the family is my family. The black cat was just as I have described him."

Tramps and vagabonds have marks they make on gateposts and trees and doors, letting others of their kind know a little about the people who live at the houses and farms they pass on their travels. I think cats must leave similar signs; how else to explain the cats who turn up at our door through the year, hungry and flea-ridden and abandoned?

We take them in. We get rid of the fleas and the ticks, feed them and take them to the vet. We pay for them to get their shots, and, indignity upon indignity, we have them neutered or spayed.

And they stay with us, for a few months, or for a year, or for ever.

Most of them arrive in summer. We live in the country, just the right distance out of town for the city-dwellers to abandon their cats near us.

We never seem to have more than eight cats, rarely have less than three. The cat population of my house is currently as follows: Hermione and Pod, tabby and black respectively, the mad sisters who live in my attic office, and do not mingle; Princess, the blue-eyed long-haired white cat, who lived wild in the woods for years before she gave up her wild ways for soft sofas and beds; and, last but largest, Furball, Princess's cushion-like calico long-haired daughter, orange and black and white, whom I discovered as a tiny kitten in our garage one day, strangled and almost dead, her head poked through an old badminton net, and who surprised us all by not dying but instead growing up to be the best-natured cat I have ever encountered.

And then there is the black cat. Who has no other name than the Black Cat, and who turned up almost a month ago. We did not realize he was going to be living here at first: he looked too well-fed to be a stray, too old and jaunty to have been abandoned. He looked like a small panther, and he moved like a patch of night.

One day, in the summer, he was lurking about our ramshackle porch: eight or nine years old, at a guess, male, greenish-yellow of eye, very friendly, quite unperturbable. I assumed he belonged to a neighboring farmer or household.

I went away for a few weeks, to finish writing a book, and when I came home he was still on our porch, living in an old cat-bed one of the children had found for him. He was, however, almost unrecognizable. Patches of fur had gone, and there were deep scratches on his grey skin. The tip of one ear was chewed away. There was a gash beneath one eye, a slice gone from one lip. He looked tired and thin.

We took the Black Cat to the vet, where we got him some antibiotics, which we fed him each night, along with soft cat food.

We wondered who he was fighting. Princess, our white, beautiful, near-feral queen? Raccoons? A rat-tailed, fanged possum?

Each night the scratches would be worse—one night his side would be chewed-up; the next, it would be his underbelly, raked with claw marks and bloody to the touch.

When it got to that point, I took him down to the basement to recover, beside the furnace and the piles of boxes. He was surprisingly heavy, the Black Cat, and I picked him up and carried him down there, with a cat-basket, and a litter bin, and some food and water. I closed the door behind me. I had to wash the blood from my hands, when I left the basement.

He stayed down there for four days. At first he seemed too weak to feed himself: a cut beneath one eye had rendered him almost one-eyed, and he limped and lolled weakly, thick yellow pus oozing from the cut in his lip.

I went down there every morning and every night, and I fed him, and gave him antibiotics, which I mixed with his canned food, and I dabbed at the worst of the cuts, and spoke to him. He had diarrhea, and, although I changed his litter daily, the basement stank evilly.

The four days that the Black Cat lived in the basement were a bad four days in my house: the baby slipped in the bath, and banged her head, and might have drowned; I learned that a project I had set my heart on—adapting Hope Mirrlees' novel *Lud in the Mist* for the BBC—was no longer going to happen, and I realized that I did not have the energy to begin again from scratch, pitching it to other networks, or to other media; my daughter left for Summer Camp, and immediately began to send home a plethora of heart-tearing letters and cards, five or six each day, imploring us to take her away; my son had some kind of fight with his best friend, to the point that they were no longer on speaking terms; and returning home one night, my wife hit a deer, who ran out in front of the car. The deer was killed, the car was left undriveable, and my wife sustained a small cut over one eye.

By the fourth day, the cat was prowling the basement, walking haltingly but impatiently between the stacks of books and comics, the boxes of mail and cassettes, of pictures and of gifts and of stuff. He mewed at me to let him out and, reluctantly, I did so.

He went back onto the porch, and slept there for the rest of the day.

The next morning there were deep, new gashes in his flanks, and clumps of black cat hair—his—covered the wooden boards of the porch.

Letters arrived that day from my daughter, telling us that Camp was going better, and she thought she could survive a few days; my son and his friend sorted out their problem, although what the argument was about—trading cards, computer games, Star Wars or a Girl—I would never learn. The BBC Executive who had vetoed *Lud in the Mist* was discovered to have been taking bribes (well, "questionable loans") from an independent production company, and was sent home on permanent leave: his successor, I was delighted to learn, when she faxed me, was the woman who had initially proposed the project to me before leaving the BBC.

I thought about returning the Black Cat to the basement, but decided against it. Instead, I resolved to try and discover what kind of animal was coming to our house each night, and from there to formulate a plan of action—to trap it, perhaps.

For birthdays and at Christmas my family gives me gadgets and gizmos, pricy toys which excite my fancy but, ultimately, rarely leave their boxes. There is a food dehydrator and an electric carving knife, a bread-making machine, and, last year's present, a pair of see-in-the-dark binoculars. On Christmas Day I had put the batteries into the binoculars, and had walked about the basement in the dark, too impatient even to wait until nightfall, stalking a flock of imaginary Starlings. (You were warned not to turn it on in the light: that would have damaged the binoculars, and quite possibly your eyes as well.) Afterwards I had put the device back into its box, and it sat there still, in my office, beside the box of computer cables and forgotten bits and pieces.

Perhaps, I thought, if the creature, dog or cat or raccoon or what-have-you, were to see me sitting on the porch, it would not come, so I took a chair into the box-and-coat-room, little larger than a closet, which overlooks the porch, and, when everyone in the house was asleep, I went out onto the porch, and bade the Black Cat goodnight.

That cat, my wife had said, when he first arrived, is a person. And there was something very person-like in his huge, leonine face: his broad black nose, his greenish-yellow eyes, his fanged but amiable mouth (still leaking amber pus from the right lower lip).

I stroked his head, and scratched him beneath the chin, and wished him well.

Then I went inside, and turned off the light on the porch.

I sat on my chair, in the darkness inside the house, with the see-in-the-dark binoculars on my lap. I had switched the binoculars on, and a trickle of greenish light came from the eyepieces.

Time passed, in the darkness.

I experimented with looking at the darkness with the binoculars, learning to focus, to see the world in shades of green. I found myself horrified by the number of swarming insects I could see in the night air: it was as if the night world were some kind of nightmarish soup, swimming with life. Then I lowered the binoculars from my eyes, and stared out at the rich blacks and blues of the night, empty and peaceful and calm.

Time passed. I struggled to keep awake, found myself profoundly missing cigarettes and coffee, my two lost addictions. Either of them would have kept my eyes open. But before I had tumbled too far into the world of sleep and dreams a yowl from the garden jerked me fully awake. I fumbled the binoculars to my eyes, and was disappointed to see that it was merely Princess, the white cat, streaking across the front garden like a patch of greenish-white light. She vanished into the woodland to the left of the house, and was gone.

I was about to settle myself back down, when it occurred to me to wonder what exactly had startled Princess so, and I began scanning the middle distance with the binoculars, looking for a huge raccoon, a dog, or a vicious possum. And there was indeed something coming down the driveway, towards the house. I could see it through the binoculars, clear as day.

It was the Devil.

I had never seen the Devil before, and, although I had written about him in the past, if pressed would have confessed that I had no belief in him, other than as an imaginary figure, tragic and Miltonion. The figure coming up the driveway was not Milton's Lucifer. It was the Devil.

My heart began to pound in my chest, to pound so hard that it hurt. I hoped it could not see me, that, in a dark house, behind window-glass, I was hidden.

The figure flickered and changed as it walked up the drive. One moment it was dark, bull-like, minotaurish, the next it was slim and female, and the next it was a cat itself, a scarred, huge grey-green wildcat, its face contorted with hate.

There are steps that lead up to my porch, four white wooden steps in need of a coat of paint (I knew they were white, although they were, like everything else, green through my binoculars). At the bottom of the steps, the Devil stopped, and called out something that I could not understand, three, perhaps four words in a whining, howling language that must have been old and forgotten when Babylon was young; and, although I did not understand the words, I felt the hairs raise on the back of my head as it called.

And then I heard, muffled through the glass, but still audible, a low growl, a challenge, and, slowly, unsteadily, a black figure walked down the steps of the house, away from me, toward the Devil. These days the Black Cat no longer moved like a panther, instead he stumbled and rocked, like a sailor only recently returned to land.

The Devil was a woman, now. She said something soothing and gentle to the cat, in a tongue that sounded like French, and reached out a hand to him. He sank his teeth into her arm, and her lip curled, and she spat at him.

The woman glanced up at me, then, and if I had doubted that she was the Devil before, I was certain of it now: the woman's eyes flashed red fire at me; but you can see no red through the night-vision binoculars, only shades of a green. And the Devil saw me, through the window. It saw me. I am in no doubt about that at all.

The Devil twisted and writhed, and now it was some kind of jackal, a flat-faced, huge-headed, bull-necked creature, halfway between a hyena and a dingo. There were maggots squirming in its mangy fur, and it began to walk up the steps.

The Black Cat leapt upon it, and in seconds they became a rolling, writhing thing, moving faster than my eyes could follow.

All this in silence.

And then a low roar—down the country road at the bottom of our drive, in the distance, lumbered a late-night truck, its blazing headlights burning bright as green suns through the binoculars. I lowered them from my eyes, and saw only darkness, and the gentle yellow of headlights, and then the red of rear lights as it vanished off again into the nowhere at all.

When I raised the binoculars once more there was nothing to be seen. Only the Black Cat, on the steps, staring up into the air. I trained the binoculars up, and saw something flying away—a vulture, perhaps, or an eagle—and then it flew beyond the trees and was gone.

I went out onto the porch, and picked up the Black Cat, and stroked him, and said kind, soothing things to him. He mewled piteously when I first approached him, but, after a while, he went to sleep on my lap, and I put him into his basket, and went upstairs to my bed, to sleep myself. There was dried blood on my tee shirt and jeans, the following morning.

That was a week ago.

The thing that comes to my house does not come every night. But it comes most nights: we know it by the wounds on the cat, and the pain I can see in those leonine eyes. He has lost the use of his front left paw, and his right eye has closed for good.

I wonder what we did to deserve the Black Cat. I wonder who sent him. And, selfish and scared, I wonder how much more he has to give.

DARK EYES, FAITH, AND DEVOTION
Charles de Lint

Charles de Lint is a full-time writer and musician who presently makes his home in Ottawa, Canada, with his wife MaryAnn Harris, an artist and musician. His most recent books are *Widdershins*, *Promises to Keep*, *Dingo*, and *The Mystery of Grace*. Other recent publications include the collections *The Hour Before Dawn*, *Triskell Tales 2*, and *Muse and Reverie*. For more information about his work, visit his website at www.charlesdelint.com.

Many of de Lint's short stories take place in the fictional city of Newford and "Dark Eyes, Faith, and Devotion" is one of them. In it, an atypical taxi driver provides an atypical favor for one of his fares, with unexpected results.

I've just finished cleaning the vomit my last fare left in the back seat—his idea of a tip, I guess, since he actually short-changed me a couple of bucks—and I'm back cruising when the woman flags me down on Gracie Street, outside one of those girl-on-girl clubs. I'll tell you, I'm as open-minded as the next guy, but it breaks my heart when I see a looker like this playing for the other team. She's enough to give me sweet dreams for the rest of the week, and this is only Monday night.

She's about five-seven or five-eight and dark-skinned—Hispanic, maybe, or Indian. I can't tell. I just know she's gorgeous. Jet black hair hanging straight down her back and she's all decked out in net stockings, spike heels, and a short black dress that looks like it's been sprayed on and glistens like satin. Somehow she manages to pull it off without looking like a hooker. It's got to be her babydoll face—made up to a T, but so innocent all you want to do is keep her safe and take care of her. After you've slept with her, mind.

I watch her in the rearview mirror as she gets into the backseat—showing plenty of leg with that short dress of hers and not shy about my seeing it. We both know that's all I'm getting and I'm lucky to get that much. She wrinkles her nose and I can't tell if it's some linger of l'eau de puke or the Lysol I sprayed on the seat after I cleaned up the mess my last fare left behind.

Hell, maybe it's me.

"What can I do for you, ma'am?" I ask.

She's got these big, dark eyes and they fix on mine in the rearview mirror, just holding on to my gaze like we're the only two people in the world.

"How far are you willing to go?" she asks.

Dressed like she is, you'd be forgiven for thinking it was a come-on. Hell, that was my first thought anyway, doesn't matter she's playing on that other team. But there's that cherub innocence thing she's got going for her and, well, take a look at a pug like me and you know the one thing that isn't going to happen is some pretty girl's going to make a play for me from the back seat of my cab.

"I can take you any place you need to go," I tell her, playing it safe.

"And if I need something else?" she asks.

I shake my head. "I don't deal with anything that might put me inside."

I almost said "back inside," but that's not something she needs to know. Though maybe she already does. Maybe when I pulled over she saw the prison tattoos on my arms—you know, you put them on with a pin and the ink from a ballpoint so they always come out looking kind of scratchy and blue.

"Someone has stolen my cat," she says. "I was hoping you might help me get her back."

I turn right around in my seat to look at her straight on. I decide she's Hispanic from her accent. I like the Spanish warmth it puts on her words.

"Your cat," I say. "You mean like a pet?"

"Something like that. I really do need someone to help me steal her back."

I laugh. I can't help it.

"So what, you flag down the first cab you see and figure whoever's driving it'll take a short break from cruising for fares to help you creep some joint?"

"Creep?" she asks.

"Break in. But quietly, you know, because you're hoping you won't get caught."

She shakes her head.

"No," she says. "I just thought *you* might."

"And that would be because…?"

"You've got kind eyes."

People have said a lot of things about me over the years, but that's something I've never heard before. It's like telling a wolf he's got a nice smile. I've been told I've got dead eyes, or a hard stare, but no one's ever had anything nice to say about them before. I don't know if it's because of that, or if it's because of that innocence she carries that just makes you want to take care of her, but I find myself nodding.

"Sure," I tell her. "Why not? It's a slow night. Where can we find this cat of yours?"

"First I need to go home and get changed," she says. "I can't go—what was the word you used?" She smiles. "Creep a house wearing this."

Well, she could, I think, and it would sure make it interesting for me if I was hoisting her up to a window, but I just nod again.

"No problem," I tell her. "Where do you live?"

This whole situation would drive Hank crazy.

We did time together a while back—we'd each pulled a stretch and they ran in tandem for a few years. It's all gangs inside now and since we weren't either of us black or Indian or Hispanic, and we sure as hell weren't going to run with the Aryans, we ended up passing a lot of the time with each other. He told me to look him up when I got out and he'd fix me up. A lot of guys say that, but they don't mean it. You're trying to do good and you want some hardcase showing up at your home or place of employment? I don't think so.

So I wouldn't have bothered, but Hank never said something unless he meant it, and since I really did want to take a shot at walking the straight and narrow this time out, I took him up on it.

He hooked me up with this guy named Moth who runs a Gypsy cab company out of a junkyard—you know, the wheels aren't licensed but so long as no one looks too hard at the piece of bureaucratic paper stuck on the back of the driver's seat, it's the kind of thing you can get away with. You just make a point of cruising for fares in the parts of town that the legit cabbies prefer to stay out of.

So Hank gave me the break to make good, and Moth laid one piece of advice on me—"Don't get involved with your fares"—and I've been doing okay, keeping my nose clean, making enough to pay for a room in a boarding house, even stashing a little extra cash away on the side.

Funny thing is, I like this gig. I'm not scared to take the rough fares and I'm big enough that the freaks don't mess with me. Occasionally I even get someone like the woman I picked up on Gracie Street.

None of which explains why I'm parked outside a house across town on Marett Street, getting ready to bust in and rescue a cat.

My partner-in-crime is sitting in the front with me now. Her name's Luisa Jaramillo. She's changed into a tight black T-shirt with a pair of baggy faded jean overalls, black hightops on her feet. Most of her make-up's gone and her hair's hidden under a baseball cap turned backwards. She still looks gorgeous. Maybe more than she did before.

"What's your cat's name?" I ask.

"Patience."

I shrug. "That's okay. You don't have to tell me."

"No, that's her name," Luisa says. "Patience."

"And this guy that stole her is…?"

"My ex-boyfriend. My very recent ex-boyfriend."

That's what I get for jumping to conclusions, I think. Hell, *I* was cruising Gracie Street. That doesn't automatically put me on the other team either. Only don't get me wrong. I'm not getting my hopes up or anything. I know I'm just a pug and all she's doing is using me for this gig because I'm handy and I said I'd do it. There's not going to be any fairy tale reward once we get kitty back from her ex. I'll be lucky to get a handshake.

So why am I doing it?

I'll lay it out straight: I'm bored. I've got a head that never stops working. I'm always considering the percentages, making plans. When I said I'd come to enjoy driving a cab, I was telling the truth. I do. But you're talking to a guy who's spent the better part of his life working out deals, and when the deals didn't pan out, he just went in and took what he needed. That's what put me inside.

They don't put a whole lot of innocent people in jail. I'm not saying they aren't biased towards what most people think of as the dregs of society—the homeboys and Indians and white trash I was raised to be—but most of us doing our time, we did the crime.

Creeping some stranger's house gives me a buzz like a junkie getting a fix. I don't get the shakes when I go cold turkey like I've been doing these past couple of months, but the jones is still there. Tonight I'm just cozying it up with a sugar coating of doing the shiny white knight bit, that's all.

I never even stopped to ask her why we were stealing a cat. I just thought, let's do it. But when you think about it, who steals cats? You lose your cat, you just go get another one. We never had pets when I was a kid, so maybe that's why I don't get it. In our house the kids were the pets, only we weren't so well-treated as I guess Luisa's cat is. Somebody ever took one of us, the only thing Ma'd regret is the cut in her cheque from social services.

You want another reason? I don't often get a chance to hang out with a pretty girl like this.

"So what's the plan?" I ask.

"The man who lives in that house is very powerful," Luisa says.

"Your ex."

She nods.

"So he's what? A politician? A lawyer? A drug dealer?"

"No, no. Much more powerful than that. He's a brujo—a witch man. That is not a wrong thing in itself, but his medicine is very bad. He is an evil man."

I give her the same blank look I'm guessing anybody would.

"I can see you don't believe me," she says.

"It's more like I don't understand," I tell her.

"It doesn't matter. I tell you this only so that you won't look into his eyes. No matter what, do not meet his gaze with your own."

"Or what? He'll turn me into a pumpkin?"

"Something worse," she says in all seriousness.

She gets out of the car before I can press her on it, but I'm not about to let it go. I get out my side and join her on the sidewalk. She takes my hand and leads me quickly into the shadows cast by a tall hedge that runs the length of the property, separating her ex's house from its neighbours. I like the feel of her skin against mine. She lets go all too soon.

"What's really going on here?" I ask her. "I mean, I pick you up outside a girl bar on Gracie Street where you're dressed like a hooker, and now we're about to creep some magic guy's house to get your cat back. None of this is making a whole lot of sense."

"And yet you are here."

I give her a slow nod. "Maybe I should never have looked in your eyes," I say. I'm joking, but she's still all seriousness when she answers.

"I would never do such a thing to another human being," she tells me. "Yes, I went out looking the way I did in hopes of attracting a man such as you, but there was no magic involved."

I focus on the "a man such as you," not sure I like what it says about what she thinks of me. I may not look like much, which translates into a lot of nights spent on my own, but I've never paid for it.

"You looked like a prostitute, trying to pick up a john or some freak."

She actually smiles, her teeth flashing in the shadows, white against her dark skin.

"No, I was searching for a man who would desire me enough to want to be close to me, but who had the heart to listen to my story and the compassion to want to help once he knew the trouble I was in."

"I think you've got the wrong guy," I tell her. "Neither of those are things I'm particularly known for."

"And yet you are here," she says again. "And you shouldn't sell yourself short. Sometimes we don't fulfill our potential only because there is no one in our life to believe in us."

I've got an idea where she's going with that—Hank and Moth have talked about that kind of thing some nights when we're sitting around a campfire in the junkyard, not to mention every damn social worker who's actually trying to do their job—but I don't want to go there with her any more than I do with them. It's a nice theory, but I've never bought it. Your life doesn't go a certain way just because other people think that's the way it will.

"You were taking a big chance," I say instead. "You could've picked up some freak with a knife who wasn't going to stop to listen."

She shakes her head. "No one would have troubled me."

"But you need my help with your ex."

"That is different. I have looked in his eyes. He has sewn black threads in my soul and without a champion at my side, I'm afraid he would pull me back under his influence."

This I understand. I've helped a couple of women get out of a bad relationship by pounding a little sense into their ex-boyfriend's head. It's amazing how the threat of more of the same is so much more effective than a restraining order.

"So you're looking for some muscle to pound on your ex."

"I'm hoping that won't be necessary. You wouldn't want him for an enemy."

"Some people say you're judged by your enemies."

"Then you would be considered a powerful man, too," she says.

"So the get-up you had on was like a costume."

She nods, but even in the shadows I can see the bitter look that comes into her eyes.

"I have many 'costumes' such as that," she says. "My boyfriend insists I wear them in order to appear attractive. He likes it that men would desire me, but could not have me."

"Boy, what planet is he from?" I say. "You could wear a burlap sack and you'd still be drop-dead gorgeous."

"You did not like the dress?"

I shrug. "What can I say? I'm a guy. Of course I liked it. I'm just saying you don't need it."

"You are very sweet."

Again with the making nice. Funny thing is, I don't want to argue it with her anymore. I find I like the idea that someone'd say these kinds of things to me. But I don't pretend there's a hope in hell that it'll ever go past this. Instead I focus on the holes in her story. There are things she isn't telling me and I say as much, but while she can't help but look a little guilty, she doesn't share them either.

"Look," I tell her. "It doesn't matter what they are. I just need to know, are they going to get in the way of our getting the job done?"

"I don't think so."

I wait a moment but she's still playing those cards pretty much as close to her vest as she can. I wonder how many of them are wild.

"Okay," I say. "So we'll just do it. But we need to make a slight detour first. Do you think your cat can hold out for another hour or so?"

She nods.

She doesn't ask any questions when I pull up behind a plant nursery over on East Kelly Street. I jimmy the lock on the back door like it's not even there—hey, it's what I do; or at least used to do—and slip inside. It takes me a moment to track down what I'm looking for, using the beam of a cheap key-ring flashlight to read labels. Finally, I find the shelf I need.

I cut a hole in a small bag of diatomaceous earth and carefully pour a bit of it into each of my jacket's pockets. When I replace the bag, I leave a five-spot on the shelf beside it as payment. See, I'm learning. Guys back in prison would be laughing their asses off if they ever heard about this, but I don't care. I may still bust into some guy's house to help his ex-girlfriend steal back her cat, but I'm done with taking what I haven't earned.

"You figure he's home?" I ask when we pull back up outside the house on Marett.

She nods. "He would not leave her alone—not so soon after stealing her from me."

"You know where his bedroom is?"

"At the back of the house, on the second floor. He is a light sleeper."

Of course he would be.

"And your cat," I say. "Would she have the run of the house, or would he keep her in a cage?"

"He would have… other methods of keeping her docile."

"The magic eyes business."

"His power is not a joking matter," she says.

"I'm taking it seriously," I tell her.

Though I'm drawing the line at magic. Thing is, I know guys who can do things with their eyes. You see it in prison all the time—whole conversations taking place without a word being exchanged. It's all in the eyes. Some guys are like a snake, mesmerizing its prey. The eyes lock onto you and before you know what's going on, he's stuck a shiv in your gut and you're down on the floor, trying to keep your life from leaking out of you, your own blood pouring over your hands.

But I'm pretty good with the thousand-yard stare myself.

I get out of the car and we head for the side door in the carport. I'd have had Luisa stay behind in the cab, except I figure her cat's going to be a lot more docile if she's there to carry it back out again.

I give the door a visual check for an alarm. There's nothing obvious, but that doesn't mean anything, so I ask Luisa about it.

"A man such as he does not need a security system," she tells me.

"The magic thing again."

When she nods, I shrug and take a couple of pairs of surgical gloves out of my back pocket. I hand her one pair and put the other on, then get out my picks.

This door takes a little longer than the one behind the nursery did. For a guy who's got all these magic chops, he's still sprung for a decent lock. That makes me feel a little better. I'm not saying that Luisa's gullible or anything, but with guys like this—doesn't matter what scam they're running, magic mumbo-jumbo's not a whole lot different from the threat of a beating—it's the fear factor that keeps people in line. All you need is for your victim to believe that you can do what you say you'll do if they don't toe the line. You don't actually need magic.

The lock gives up with a soft click. I put my picks away and take out a small can of W-30, spraying each of the hinges before I let the door swing open. Then I lean close to Luisa, my mouth almost touching her ear.

"Where should we start looking?" I say.

My voice is so soft you wouldn't hear me a few steps away. She replies as quietly, her breath warm against my ear. This close to her I realize that a woman like her smells just as good as she looks. That's something I just never had the opportunity to learn before.

"The basement," Luisa says. "If she is not hiding from him there, then he will have her in his bedroom with him. There is a door leading downstairs, just past that cupboard."

I nod and start for the door she pointed to, my sneakers silent on the tiled floor. Luisa whispers along behind me. I do the hinges on this door, too, and I'm cautious on the steps going down, putting my feet close to the sides of the risers where they're less liable to wake a creak.

There was a light switch at the top of the stairs. Once I get to the bottom, I stand silent, listening. There's nothing. I feel along the wall and come across the other switch I was expecting to find.

"Close your eyes," I tell Luisa.

I do the same thing and flick the switch. There's a blast of light behind my closed lids. I crack them slightly and take a quick look around. The basement is furnished, casually, like an upscale rec room. There's an entertainment center against one wall, a wet bar against another. Nice couch set up in front of the TV. I count three doors, all of them slightly ajar. I'm not sure what they lead to. Furnace room, laundry room, workshop. Who knows?

By the time I'm finished looking around my eyes have adjusted to the light. The one thing I don't see is a cat.

"You want to try calling her?" I ask.

Luisa shakes her head. "I can feel her. She is hiding in there." She points to one of the mystery doors. "In the storage room."

I let her go ahead of me, following after. Better the cat see her first than my ugly mug.

We're halfway across the room when someone speaks from behind us.

<I knew you would return,> a man's voice says, speaking in Spanish. <And look what you have brought me. A peace offering.>

I turn slowly, not letting on that I know what he's said. I picked up a lot of Spanish on the street, more in jail. So I just look surprised, which isn't a stretch. I can't believe I didn't feel him approach. When I'm creeping a joint I carry a sixth sense inside me that stretches out throughout the place, letting me know when there's a change in the air.

Hell, I should at least have heard him on the stairs.

"I have brought you nothing," Luisa says, speaking English for my benefit, I guess.

<And yet I will have you and your champion. I will make you watch as I strip away his flesh and sharpen my claws on his bones.>

"Please. I ask only for our freedom."

<You can never be free from me.>

I have to admit he's a handsome devil. Same dark hair and complexion as Luisa, but there's no warmth in his eyes.

Oh, I know what Luisa said. Don't look in his eyes. But the thing is, I don't play that game. You learn pretty quickly when you're inside that the one thing you don't do is back down. Show even a hint of weakness and your fellow inmates will be on you like piranha.

So I just put a hand in the pocket of my jacket and look him straight in the eye, give him my best convict stare.

He smiles. "You are a big one, aren't you?" he says. "But your size means nothing in this game we will play."

You ever get into a staring contest? I can see that starting up here, except dark eyes figures he's going to mesmerize me in seconds, he's so confident. The funny thing is, I can feel a pull in that gaze of his. His pupils seem to completely fill my sight. I hear a strange whispering in the back of my head and can feel that thousand-yard stare of mine already starting to fray at the edges.

So maybe he's got some kind of magical power. I don't know and I don't care. I take my hand out of my pocket and I'm holding a handful of that diatomaceous earth I picked up earlier in the nursery.

Truth is, I never thought I'd use it. I picked it up as a back-up, nothing more. Like insurance just in case, crazy as it sounded, Luisa really knew what she was talking about. I mean, you hear stories about every damn thing you can think of. I never believed most of what I heard, but a computer's like magic to someone who's never seen one before—you know what I'm saying? The world's big enough and strange enough that pretty much anything can be out there in it, somewhere.

So I've got that diatomaceous earth in my hand and I throw it right in his face, because I'm panicking a little at the way those eyes of his are getting right into my head and starting to shut me down inside.

You know anything about that stuff? It's made of ground up shells and bones that are sharp as glass. Gardeners use it to make barriers for various kinds of insects. The bug crawls over it and gets cut to pieces. It's incredibly fine—so much so that it doesn't come through the latex of my gloves—but eyes don't have that kind of protection.

Imagine what it would do if it got in them.

Tall, dark and broody over there doesn't have to use his imagination. He lifts his hand as the cloud comes at him, but he's too late. Too late to wave it away. Too late to close his eyes like I've done as I back away from any contact with the stuff.

His eyelids instinctively do what they're supposed to do in a situation like this—they blink rapidly and the pressure cuts his eyes all to hell and back again.

It doesn't help when he reaches up with his hands to try to wipe the crap away.

He starts to make this horrible mewling sound and falls to his knees.

I'm over by the wall now, well out of range of the rapidly settling cloud. Looking at him I start to feel a little queasy, thinking I did an overkill on this. I don't know what went on between him and Luisa—how bad it got, what kind of punishment he deserves—but I think maybe I crossed a line here that I really shouldn't have.

He lifts his bloodied face, sightless eyes pointed in our direction, and manages to say something else. This time he's talking in some language I never heard before, ending with some Spanish that I do understand.

<Be so forever,> he cries.

I'm turning to Luisa just then, so I see what happens.

Well, I see it, but it doesn't register as real. One moment there's this beautiful dark-haired woman standing there, then she vanishes and there's only the heap of her clothes left lying on the carpet. I'm still staring slack-jawed when the clothing moves and a sleek black cat wriggles out from under the overalls and darts into the room where Luisa said *her* cat was.

As I take a step after her, the man starts in with something else in that unrecognizable language. I don't know if it's still aimed at Luisa, or if he's planning to turn me into something, too—hell, I'm a dyed-in-the-wool believer at this point—but I don't take any chances. I take a few quick steps in his direction and give him a kick in the side of the head. When that doesn't completely stop him, I give him a couple more.

He finally goes down and stays down.

I turn back to go after Luisa, but before I can, that black cat comes soft-stepping out of the room once more, this time carrying a kitten in its mouth.

"Luisa?" I find myself saying.

I swear, even with that kitten in its mouth, the cat nods. But I don't even need to see that. I only have to look into her eyes. The cat has Luisa's eyes, there's no question in my mind about that.

"Is this... permanent?" I ask.

The cat's response is to trot by me, giving her unconscious ex's body a wide berth as she heads for the stairs.

I stand there, looking at the damage I've done to her ex for a long, unhappy moment, then I follow her up the stairs. She's sitting by the door with the kitten, but I can't leave it like this. I look around the kitchen, not ready to leave yet.

The cat makes a querulous sound, but I ask her to wait and go prowling through the house. I don't know what I'm looking for, something to justify what I did downstairs, I guess. I don't find anything, not really. There are spooky masks and icons and other weird magical-looking artifacts scattered throughout the house, but he's not going to be the first guy that likes to collect that kind of thing. Nothing explains why he needed to have this hold over Luisa and her—I'm not thinking of the kitten as a cat anymore. After what I saw downstairs, I'm sure it's her kid.

I go upstairs and poke through his office, his bedroom. Still nothing. But then it's often like that. Too often the guy you'd never suspect of having a bad thought turns out to beating on his family, or goes postal where he works, or some damn crazy thing.

It really makes you wonder—especially with a guy like Luisa's ex. You find yourself with power like he's got, why wouldn't you use it to put something good into the world?

I know, I know. Look who's talking. But I'm telling you straight, I might have robbed a lot of people, but I never hurt them. Not intentionally. And never a woman or a kid.

I go back downstairs and find the cat still waiting by the kitchen door for me. She's got a paw on the kitten, holding it in place.

"Let's go," I say.

I haven't even started to think about how a woman can be changed into a cat, or when and if and how she'll change back again. I can only deal with one thing at a time.

My first impulse is to burn the place to the ground with him in it, but playing the cowboy like that's just going to put me back inside and it won't prove anything. I figure I've done enough damage and it's not like he's going to call the cops. But the first thing I'm going to do when I get home is change the plates on the cab and dig out the spare set of registration papers that Moth provides for all his vehicles.

For now I follow the cats down the driveway. I open the passenger door to the cab. The mama cat grabs her kitten by the skin at the nape of her neck and jumps in. I close the door and walk around to the driver's side.

I take a last look at the house, remembering the feel of the guy's eyes inside my head, the relief I felt when the diatomaceous earth got in his eyes and cut them all to hell. There was a lot of blood, but I don't know how permanent the damage'll be. Maybe he'll come after us, but I doubt it. Nine out of ten times, a guy like that just folds his hand when someone stands up to him.

Besides, the city's so big, he's never going to find us, even if he does come looking. It's not like we run in the same circles or anything.

So I get in the cab, say something that I hope sounds calming to the cats, and we drive away.

I've got a different place now, a one-bedroom, ground-floor apartment which gives me access to a backyard. It's not much, just a jungle of weeds and flowers gone wild, but the cats seem to like it.

I sit on the back steps sometimes and watch them romp around like… well, like the cats they are, I guess. I know I hurt the man who had them under his power, hurt him bad. And I know I walked into his house with a woman and came out with a cat. But it still feels like a dream.

It's true the cat seems to understand everything I say, and acts smarter than I think a cat would normally act, but what do I know? I never had a pet before. And anybody I talk to seems to think the same thing about their own cat or dog.

I haven't told anybody about any of this, though I did come at it from a different angle, sitting around the fire in the junkyard with Hank one night. There were a half-dozen of us. Moth, Hank's girlfriend Lily, and some of the others from their extended family of choice. The junkyard's in the middle of the city, but it backs onto the Tombs and it gets dark out there. As we sit in deck chairs, nursing beers and coffees, we watch the sparks flicker above the flames in the cut-down steel barrel Moth uses for his fires.

"Did you ever hear any stories about people that can turn into animals?" I ask during a lull in the conversation.

We have those kinds of talks. We can go from carbs and engine torques to what's wrong with social services or the best kind of herbal tea for nausea. That'd be ginger tea.

"You mean like a werewolf?" Moth says.

Sitting beside him, Paris grins. She's as dark-haired as Luisa was and her skin's pretty much covered with tattoos that seem to move on their own in the flickering light.

"Nah," she says. "Billy Joe's just looking for a way to turn himself into a raccoon or a monkey so he can get into houses again but without getting caught."

"I gave that up," I tell her.

She smiles at me, eyes still teasing. "I know that. But I still like the picture it puts in my head."

"There are all kinds of stories," Hank says, "and we know one or two. The way they go, the animal people were here first and some of them are still living among us, not looking any different from you or me."

They tell a few then—Hank and Lily and Katy, this pretty red-haired girl who lives on her own in a school bus not far from the junkyard. They all tell the stories like they've actually met the people they're talking about, but Katy's are the best. She's got the real storyteller's gift, makes you hang onto every word until she's done.

"But what about if someone's put a spell on someone?" I say after a few of their stories, because they're mostly about people who were born that way, part-animal, part-human, changing their skins as they please. "You know any stories like that? How it works? How they get changed back?"

I've got a lot of people looking at me after I come out with that.

Nobody has an answer.

Moth gives me a look—but it's curious, not demanding. "Why are you asking?" he says.

I just shrug. I don't know that it's my story to tell. But as the weeks go by I bring it up again and this time I tell them what happened, or at least what I think happened. Funny thing is, they just take me at my word. They start looking in on it for me, but nobody comes up with an answer.

Maybe there isn't one.

So I just drive my cab and spend time with these new families of mine—both the one in the junkyard and the cats I've got back home. I find it gets easier to walk the straight-and-narrow, the longer you do it. Gets so that doing the right thing, the honest thing, comes like second nature to me.

But I never stop wondering about what happened that night. I don't even know if they're really cats who were pretending to be human, or humans that got turned into cats. I guess I'm always going to be waiting to see if they'll change back.

But I don't think about it twenty-four/seven. Mostly I just figure it's my job to make a home for them and keep them safe. And you know what? Turns out I'm pretty good at doing that.

NOT WAVING
Michael Marshall Smith

Michael Marshall Smith is a bestselling novelist and screenwriter, writing under several different names, including Michael Marshall. His first novel, *Only Forward*, won the August Derleth and Philip K. Dick awards. *Spares* and *One of Us* were optioned for film by DreamWorks and Warner Brothers, and the Straw Men trilogy—*The Straw Men*, *The Lonely Dead*, and *Blood of Angels*—were international bestsellers. His Steel Dagger-nominated novel *The Intruders* is currently in series development with the BBC.

Smith is also a three-time winner of the British Fantasy Award for short fiction, and his stories are collected in two volumes—*What You Make It* and *More Tomorrow and Other Stories* (which won the International Horror Guild Award). His most recent novels are *Bad Things* and *The Servants* (a short novel published under the new pseudonym M. M. Smith).

"Not Waving" is a story about love, guilt, and the choices that sometimes trap us. Smith comments on the story's most unusual—and one of its most painful—aspects, "I wrote about bulimia because a friend of mine was a sufferer—though I stress she bore no relationship whatsoever to the character in the story. I guess I wanted to try to capture the strange combination of strength and weakness that the condition seems to confer on people, without making it the sole focus of the story; not least because that combination of strength and weakness is in all of us. Also, that it is the condition of which one appears to be trapped—much like the relationship of the narrator."

Sometimes when we're in a car, driving country roads in autumn, I see sparse poppies splashed in among the grasses and it makes me want to cut my throat and let the blood spill out of the window to make more poppies, many more, until the roadside is a blaze of red.

Instead I light a cigarette and watch the road, and in a while the poppies will be behind us, as they always are.

On the morning of 10th October I was in a state of reasonably high excitement. I was at home, and I was supposed to be working. What I was mainly doing, however, was sitting thrumming at my desk, leaping to my feet whenever I heard the sound of traffic outside the window. When I wasn't doing that I was peeking at the two large cardboard boxes that were sitting in the middle of the floor.

The two large boxes contained, respectively, a new computer and a new monitor. After a year or so of containing my natural wirehead need to own the brightest and best in high-specification consumer goods, I'd finally succumbed and upgraded my machine. Credit card in hand, I'd picked up the phone and ordered myself a piece of science fiction, in the shape of a computer that not only went like a train but also had built-in telecommunications and *speech recognition.* The future was finally here, and sitting on my living room floor.

However.

While I had £3000 worth of Mac and monitor, what I didn't have was the £15 cable that connected the two together. The manufacturer, it transpired, felt it constituted an optional extra despite the fact that without it the two system components were little more than bulky white ornaments of a particularly tantalizing and frustrating kind. The cable had to be ordered separately, and there weren't any in the country at the moment. They were all in Belgium.

I was only told this a week after I ordered the system, and I strove to make my feelings on the matter clear to my supplier, during the further week in which they playfully promised to deliver the system first on one day, then another, all such promises evaporating like the morning dew. The two boxes had finally made it to my door the day before and, by a bizarre coincidence, the cables had today crawled tired and overwrought into the supplier's warehouse. My contact at Callhaven Direct knew just how firmly one of those cables had my name on it and had phoned to grudgingly admit they were available. I'd immediately called my courier firm, which I occasionally used to send design roughs to clients. Callhaven had offered, but I somehow sensed that they wouldn't quite get round to it *today,* and I'd waited long enough. The bike firm I used specializes in riders who look as if they've been chucked out of the Hell's Angels for being too tough. A large man in leathers turning up in Callhaven's offices, with instructions not to leave without my cable, was just the sort of incentive I felt they needed. And so I was waiting, drinking endless cups of coffee, for such a person to arrive at the flat, brandishing said component above his head in triumph.

When the buzzer finally went I nearly fell off my chair. The entry phone in our building was fashioned with waking the dead in mind, and I swear the walls vibrate. Without bothering to check who it was I left the flat and pounded down the stairs to the front door, swinging it open with, I suspect, a look of joy upon my face. I get a lot of pleasure out of technology. It's a bit sad, I know—God knows Nancy has told me so often enough—but hell, it's my life.

Standing on the step was a leather convention, topped with a shining black helmet. The biker was a lot slighter than their usual type, but quite tall. Tall enough to have done the job, evidently.

"Bloody marvelous," I said. "Is that a cable?"

"Sure is," the biker said indistinctly. A hand raised the visor on the helmet, and I saw with some surprise that it was a woman. "They didn't seem too keen to let it go."

I laughed and took the package from her. Sure enough, it said AV adapter cable on the outside.

"You've made my day," I said a little wildly, "and I'm more than tempted to kiss you."

"That seems rather forward," the girl said, reaching up to her helmet. "But a cup of coffee would be nice. I've been driving since five this morning and my tongue feels like it's made of brick."

Slightly taken aback, I hesitated for a moment. I'd never had a motorcycle courier in for tea before. Also, it meant a delay before I could ravage through the boxes and start connecting things up. But it was still only eleven in the morning, and another fifteen minutes wouldn't harm. I was also, I guess, a little pleased at the thought of such an unusual encounter.

"You would be," I said with Arthurian courtliness, "most welcome."

"Thank you, kind sir," the courier said, and pulled her helmet off. A great deal of dark brown hair spilled out around her face, and she swung her head to clear it. Her face was strong, with a wide mouth and vivid green eyes that had a smile already in them. The morning sun caught chestnut gleams in her hair as she stood with extraordinary grace on the doorstep. Bloody hell, I thought, the cable unregarded in my hand. Then I stood to one side to let her into the house.

It turned out her name was Alice, and she stood looking at the books on the shelves as I made a couple of cups of coffee.

"Your girlfriend's in Personnel," she said.

"How did you guess?" I said, handing her a cup. She indicated the raft of books on Human Resource Development and Stating the Bleeding Obvious in 5 Minutes a Day, which take up half our shelves.

"You don't look the type. Is this it?" She pointed her mug at the two boxes on the floor. I nodded sheepishly. "Well," she said, "aren't you going to open them?"

I glanced up at her, surprised. Her face was turned toward me, a small smile at the corners of her mouth. Her skin was the pale tawny color that goes with rich hair, I noticed, and flawless. I shrugged, slightly embarrassed.

"I guess so," I said noncommittally. "I've got some work I ought to do first."

"Rubbish," she said firmly. "Let's have a look."

And so I bent down and pulled open the boxes, while she settled down on the sofa to watch. What was odd was that I didn't mind doing it. Normally, when I'm doing something that's very much to do with me and the things I enjoy, I have to do it alone. Other people seldom understand the things that give you the most pleasure, and I for one would rather not have them around to undermine the occasion.

But Alice seemed genuinely interested, and ten minutes later I had the system sitting on the desk. I pressed the button and the familiar tone rang out as the machine set about booting up. Alice was standing to one side of me, sipping the remains of her coffee, and we both took a startled step back at the vibrancy of the tone ringing from the monitor's stereo speakers. In the meantime I'd babbled about voice recognition and video output, the half-gigabyte hard disk and CD-ROM. She'd listened, and even asked questions, questions that followed from what I was saying rather than to simply set me up to drivel on some more. It wasn't that she knew a vast amount about computers. She just understood what was exciting about them.

When the screen threw up the standard message saying all was well we looked at each other.

"You're not going to get much work done today, are you?" she said.

"Probably not," I agreed, and she laughed.

Just then a protracted squawking noise erupted from the sofa, and I jumped. The courier rolled her eyes and reached over to pick up her unit. A voice of stunning brutality informed her that she had to pick something up from the other side of town, urgently, like five minutes ago, and why wasn't she there already, darlin'?

"Grr," she said, like a little tiger, and reached for her helmet. "Duty calls."

"But I haven't told you about the telecommunications yet," I said, joking.

"Some other time," she said.

I saw her out, and we stood for a moment on the doorstep. I was wondering what to say. I didn't know her, and would never see her again, but wanted to thank her for sharing something with me. Then I noticed one of the local cats ambling past the bottom of the steps. I love cats, but Nancy doesn't, so we don't have one. Just one of the little compromises you make, I guess. I recognized this particular cat and had long since given up hope of appealing to it. I pointlessly made the sound universally employed for gaining cats' attention, with no result. It glanced up at me wearily and then continued to cruise on by.

After a look at me Alice sat down on her heels and made the same noise. The cat immediately stopped in its tracks and looked at her. She made the noise again and the cat turned, glanced down the street for no apparent reason, and then confidently made its way up the steps to weave in and out of her legs.

"That is truly amazing," I said. "He is not a friendly cat."

She took the cat in her arms and stood up.

"Oh, I don't know," she said. The cat sat up against her chest, looking around benignly. I reached out to rub its nose and felt the warm vibration of a purr. The two of us made a fuss of him for a few moments, and then she put him down. She replaced her helmet, climbed on her bike, and then, with a wave, set off.

Back in the flat I tidied away the boxes, anal-retentive that I am, before settling down to immerse myself in the new machine. On impulse I called Nancy, to let her know the system had finally arrived.

I got one of her assistants instead. She didn't put me on hold, and I heard Nancy say "Tell him I'll call him hack" in the background. I said good-bye to

Trish with fairly good grace, trying not to mind.

Voice recognition software hadn't been included, it turned out, nor anything to put in the CD-ROM drive. The telecommunications functions wouldn't work without an expensive add-on, which Callhaven didn't expect for four to six weeks. Apart from that, it was great.

Nancy cooked that evening. We tended to take it in turns, though she was much better at it than me. Nancy is good at most things. She's accomplished.

There's a lot of infighting in the world of Personnel, it would appear, and Nancy was in feisty form that evening, having outmaneuvered some coworker. I drank a glass of red wine and leaned against the counter while she whirled ingredients around. She told me about her day, and I listened and laughed. I didn't tell her much about mine, only that it had gone okay. Her threshold for hearing about the world of freelance graphic design was pretty low. She'd listen with relatively good grace if I really had to get something out of my system, but she didn't understand it and didn't seem to want to. No reason why she should, of course. I didn't mention the new computer sitting on my desk, and neither did she.

Dinner was very good. It was chicken, but she'd done something intriguing to it with spices. I ate as much as I could, but there was a little left. I tried to get her to finish it, but she wouldn't. I reassured her that she hadn't eaten too much, in the way that sometimes seemed to help, but her mood dipped and she didn't have any dessert. I steered her toward the sofa and took the stuff out to wash up and make some coffee.

While I was standing at the sink, scrubbing the plates and thinking vaguely about the mountain of things I had to do the next day, I noticed a cat sitting on a wall across the street. It was a sort of very dark brown color, almost black, and I hadn't seen it before. It was crouched down, watching a twittering bird with that catty concentration that combines complete attention with the sense that they might at any moment break off and wash their foot instead. The bird eventually fluttered chaotically off and the cat watched it for a moment before sitting upright, as if drawing a line under that particular diversion.

Then the cat's head turned, and it looked straight at me. It was a good twenty yards away, but I could see its eyes very clearly. It kept looking, and after a while I laughed, slightly taken aback. I even looked away for a moment, but when I looked back it was still there, still looking.

The kettle boiled and I turned to tip water into a couple of mugs of Nescafé. When I glanced out of the window on the way out of the kitchen the cat was gone.

Nancy wasn't in the lounge when I got there, so I settled on the sofa and lit a cigarette. After about five minutes the toilet flushed upstairs, and I sighed.

My reassurances hadn't done any good at all.

A couple of days came and went, with the usual flurry of deadlines and redrafts. I went to a social evening at Nancy's office and spent a few hours being ignored and patronized by her power-dressed colleagues, while she stood and sparkled in the center. I messed up a print job and had to cover the cost of doing it again. Good things happened, too, I guess, but it's the others that stick in your mind.

One afternoon the buzzer went and I wandered absentmindedly downstairs to get the door. As I opened it I saw a flick of brown hair and saw that it was Alice.

"Hello there," I said, strangely pleased.

"Hello yourself." She smiled. "Got a parcel for you." I took it and looked at the label. Color proofs from the repro house. Yawn. She must have been looking at my face, because she laughed. "Nothing very exciting, then."

"Hardly." After I'd signed the delivery note, I looked up at her. She was still smiling, I think, though it was difficult to tell. Her face looked as if it always was.

"Well," she said, "I can either go straight to Peckham to pick up something else that's dull, or you can tell me about the telecommunications features."

Very surprised, I stared at her for a moment, then stepped back to let her in.

"Bastards," she said indignantly when I told her about the things that hadn't been shipped with the machine, and she looked genuinely annoyed. I told her about the telecoms stuff anyway, as we sat on the sofa and drank coffee. Mainly we just chatted, but not for very long, and when she got to the end of the road on her bike she turned and waved before turning the corner.

That night Nancy went to Sainsbury's on the way home from work. I caught her eye as she unpacked the biscuits and brownies, potato chips and pastries, but she just stared back at me, and I looked away. She was having a hard time at work. Deflecting my gaze to the window, I noticed the dark cat was sitting on the wall opposite. It wasn't doing much, simply peering vaguely this way and that, watching things I couldn't see. It seemed to look up at the window for a moment, but then leapt down off the wall and wandered away down the street.

I cooked dinner and Nancy didn't eat much, but she stayed in the kitchen when I went into the living room to finish off a job. When I made our cups of tea to drink in bed I noticed that the bin had been emptied, and the gray bag stood, neatly tied, to one side. When I nudged it with my foot it rustled, full of empty packets. Upstairs the bathroom door was pulled shut, and the key turned in the lock.

I saw Alice a few more times in the next few weeks. A couple of major jobs were reaching crisis point at the same time, and there seemed to be a semi-constant flurry of bikes coming up to the house. On three or four of those occasions it was Alice whom I saw when I opened the door.

Apart from one, when she had to turn straight around on pain of death, she came in for a coffee each time. We'd chat about this and that, and when the voice recognition software finally arrived I showed her how it worked. I had a rip-off copy, from a friend who'd sourced it from the States. You had to do an impersonation of an American accent to get the machine to understand anything you said, and my attempts to do so made Alice laugh a lot. Which is curious, because it made Nancy merely sniff and ask me whether I'd put the new computer on the insurance.

Nancy was having a bit of a hard time, those couple of weeks. Her so-called boss was dumping more and more responsibility onto her while stalwartly refusing to give her more credit. Nancy's world was very real to her, and she relentlessly kept me up to date on it: the doings of her boss were more familiar to me by then than the activities of most of my friends. She got her company car upgraded, which was a nice thing. She screeched up to the house one evening in something small and red and sporty, and hollered up to the window. I scampered down and she took us hurtling around North London, driving with her customary verve and confidence. On impulse we stopped at an Italian restaurant we sometimes went to, and they miraculously had a table. Over coffee we took each other's hands and said we loved one another, which we hadn't done for a while.

When we parked outside the house I saw the dark cat sitting under a tree on the other side of the street. I pointed it out to Nancy but, as I've said, she doesn't really like cats, and merely shrugged. She went in first and as I turned to close the door I saw the cat was still sitting there, a black shape in the half-light. I wondered who it belonged to, and wished that it was ours.

A couple of days later I was walking down the street in the late afternoon when I noticed a motorbike parked outside Sad Café. I seemed to have become sensitized to bikes over the previous few weeks: Probably because I'd used so many couriers. "Sad" wasn't the café's real name, but what Nancy and I used to call it, when we used to traipse hung-over down the road on Sunday mornings on a quest for a cooked breakfast. The first time we'd slumped over a Formica table in there we had been slowly surrounded by middle-aged men in zip-up jackets and beige bobble hats, a party of mentally subnormal teenagers with broken glasses, and old women on the verge of death. The pathos attack we'd suffered had nearly finished us off, and it had been Sad Café ever since. We hadn't been there in a while: Nancy usually had work in the evenings in those days, even at weekends, and fried breakfasts appeared to be off the map again.

The bike resting outside made me glance inside the window, and with a shock of recognition I saw Alice in there, sitting at a table nursing a mug of something or other. I nearly walked on, but then thought what the hell, and stepped inside. Alice looked startled to see me, but then relaxed, and I sat down and ordered a cup of tea.

She'd finished for the day, it turned out, and was killing time before heading off for home. I was at a loose end myself: Nancy was out for the evening, entertaining clients. It was very odd seeing Alice for the first time outside the flat, and strange seeing her not in working hours. Possibly it was that which made the next thing coalesce in front of us.

Before we knew how the idea had arisen, we were wheeling her bike down the road to prop it up outside the Bengal Lancer, Kentish Town's bravest stab in the direction of a decent restaurant. I loitered awkwardly to one side while she stood in the street, took off her leathers, and packed them into the bike's carrier. She was wearing jeans and a green sweatshirt underneath, a green that matched her eyes. Then she ran her hands through her hair, said "Close enough for rock and roll," and strode toward the door. Momentarily reminded of Nancy's standard hour and a half preparation before going out, I followed her into the restaurant.

We took our time and had about four courses, and by the end were absolutely stuffed. We talked of things beyond computers and design, but I can't remember what. We had a bottle of wine, a gallon of coffee, and smoked most of a packet of cigarettes. When we were done I stood outside again, more relaxed this time, as she climbed back into her work clothes. She waved as she rode off, and I watched her go, and then turned and walked for home.

It was a nice meal. It was also the big mistake. The next time I rang for a bike, I asked for Alice by name. After that, it seemed the natural thing to do. Alice also seemed to end up doing more of the deliveries to me, more than you could put down to chance.

If we hadn't gone for that meal, perhaps it wouldn't have happened. Nothing was said, and no glances exchanged: I didn't note the date in my diary.

But we were falling in love.

The following night Nancy and I had a row, the first full-blown one in a while. We rarely argued. She was a good manager.

This one was short, and also very odd. It was quite late and I was sitting in the lounge, trying to work up the energy to turn on the television. I didn't have much hope for what I would find on it but was too tired to read. I'd been listening to music before and was staring at the stereo, half mesmerized by the green and red points of LEDs. Nancy was working at the table in the kitchen, which was dark apart from the lamp that shed yellow light over her papers.

Suddenly she marched into the living room, already at maximum temper, and shouted incoherently at me. Shocked, I half stood, brow furrowed as I tried to work out what she was saying. In retrospect I was probably slightly asleep, and her anger frightened me with its harsh intensity, seeming to fill the room.

She was shouting at me for getting a cat. There was no point me denying it, because she'd seen it. She'd seen the cat under the table in the kitchen, it was in there still, and I was to go and throw it out. I knew how much she disliked cats, and anyway, how could I do it without asking her, and the whole thing was a classic example of what a selfish and hateful man I was.

It took me a while to get to the bottom of this and start denying it. I was too baffled to get angry. In the end I went with her into the kitchen and looked under the table. By then I was getting a little spooked, to be honest. We also looked in the hallway, the bedroom, and the bathroom. Then we looked in the kitchen again and in the living room.

There was, of course, no cat.

I sat Nancy on the sofa and brought in a couple of hot drinks. She was still shaking, though her anger was gone. I tried to talk to her, to work out what exactly was wrong. Her reaction was disproportionate, misdirected: I'm not sure even she knew what it was about. The cat, of course, could have been nothing more than a discarded shoe seen in near darkness, maybe even her own foot moving in the darkness. After leaving my parents' house, where there had always been a cat, I'd often startled myself by thinking I saw them in similar ways.

She didn't seem especially convinced but did calm a little. She was so timid and quiet, and as always I found it difficult to reconcile her as she was then with her as Corporate Woman, as she was for so much of the time. I turned the fire on and we sat in front of it and talked, and even discussed her eating. Nobody else knew about that, apart from me. I didn't understand it, not really. I sensed that it was something to do with feelings of lack of control, of trying to shape herself and her world, but couldn't get much closer than that. There appeared to be nothing I could do except listen, but I suppose that was better than nothing.

We went to bed a little later and made careful, gentle love. As she relaxed toward sleep, huddled in my arms, I caught myself for the first time feeling for her something that was a little like pity.

Alice and I had dinner again about a week later. This time it was less of an accident and took place farther from home. I had an early-evening meeting in town, and by coincidence Alice would be in the area at around about the same time. I told Nancy I might end up having dinner with my client, but she didn't seem to hear. She was preoccupied, some new power struggle at work edging toward resolution.

Though it was several weeks since the previous occasion, it didn't feel at all strange seeing Alice in the evening, not least because we'd talked to each other often in the meantime. She'd started having two cups of coffee, rather than one, each time she dropped something off, and had once phoned me for advice on computers. She was thinking of getting one herself, I wasn't really sure what for.

While it didn't feel odd, I was aware of what I was doing. Meeting another woman for dinner, basically, and looking forward to it. When I talked to her, my feelings and what I did seemed more important, as if they were a part of someone worth talking to. Some part of me felt that was more important than a little economy with the truth. To be honest, I tried not to think too hard about it.

When I got home Nancy was sitting in the living room, reading.

"How was your meeting?" she asked.

"Fine," I replied. "Fine."

"Good," she said, and went back to scanning her magazine. I could have tried to make conversation, but knew it would have come out tinny and forced. In the end I went to bed and lay tightly curled on my side, wide awake.

I was just drifting off to sleep when I heard a low voice in the silence, speaking next to my ear.

"Go away," it said. "Go away."

I opened my eyes, expecting I don't know what. Nancy's face, I suppose, hanging over mine. There was no one there. I was relaxing slightly, prepared to believe it had been a fragment of a dream, when I heard her voice again, saying the same words in the same low tone.

Carefully I climbed out of bed and crept toward the kitchen. Through it I could see into the living room, where Nancy was standing in front of the main window in the darkness. She was looking out at something in the street.

"Go away," she said again, softly.

I turned round and went back to bed.

A couple of weeks passed. Time seemed to do that, that autumn. I was very immersed, what with one thing and another. Each day held something that fixed my attention and pulled me through it. I'd look up, and a week would have gone by, with me having barely noticed.

One of the things that held my attention, and became a regular part of most days, was talking to Alice. We talked about things that Nancy and I never touched upon, things Nancy simply didn't understand or care about. Alice read, for example. Nancy read, too, in that she studied memos, and reports, and boned up on the current corporate claptrap being imported from the States. She didn't read books, though, or paragraphs even. She read sentences, to strip from them what she needed to do her job, find out what was on television, or hold her own on current affairs. Every sentence was a bullet point, and she read to acquire information.

Alice read for its own sake. She wrote, too, hence her growing interest in computers. I mentioned once that I'd written a few articles, years back, before I settled on being a barely competent graphic designer instead. She said she'd written some stories and, after regular nagging from me, diffidently gave me copies. I don't know anything about fiction from a professional point of view, so I don't know how innovative or clever they were. But they gripped my attention, and I read them more than once, and that's good enough for me. I told her so, and she seemed pleased.

We spoke most days and saw each other a couple of times a week. She delivered things to me, or picked them up, and sometimes I chanced by Sad Café when she was sipping a cup of tea. It was all very low key, very friendly.

Nancy and I got on with each other, in an occasional, space-sharing sort of way. She had her friends, and I had mine. Sometimes we saw them together, and performed, as a social pair. We looked good together, like a series of stills from a lifestyle magazine. Life, if that's what it was, went on. Her eating vacillated between not good and bad, and I carried on being bleakly accepting of the fact that there didn't seem much I could do to help. So much of our lives seemed geared up to perpetuating her idea of how two young people should live that I somehow didn't feel that I could call our bluff, point out what was living beneath the stones in our house. I also didn't mention the night I'd seen her in the lounge. There didn't seem any way of bringing it up.

Apart from having Alice to chat to, the other good news was the new cat in the neighborhood. When I glanced out of the living room window sometimes it would be there, ambling smoothly past or plonked down on the pavement, watching movement in the air. It had a habit of sitting in the middle of the road, daring traffic to give it any trouble, as if the cat knew what the road was for but was having no truck with it. This was a field once, the twitch of her tail seemed to say, and as far as I'm concerned it still is.

One morning I was walking back from the corner shop, clutching some cigarettes and milk, and came upon the cat, perched on a wall. If you like cats there's something rather depressing about having them run away from you, so I approached cautiously. I wanted to get to at least within a yard of this one before it went shooting off into hyperspace.

To my delight, it didn't move away at all. When I got up next to her she stood up, and I thought that was it, but it turned out to be just a recognition that I was there. She was quite happy to be stroked and to have the fur on her head runkled, and responded to having her chest rubbed with a purr so deep it was almost below the threshold of hearing. Now that I was closer I could see the chestnut gleams in the dark brown of her fur. She was a very beautiful cat.

After a couple of minutes of this I moved away, thinking I ought to get on, but the cat immediately jumped off the wall and wove in figure eights about my feet, pressing up against my calves. I find it difficult enough to walk away from a cat at the best of times. When they're being ultra-friendly it's impossible. So I bent down and tickled, and talked fond nonsense. I finally got to my door and looked back to see her, still sitting on the pavement. She was looking around as if wondering what to do next, after all that excitement. I had to fight down the impulse to wave.

I closed the door behind me, feeling for a moment very lonely, and then went back upstairs to work.

Then one Friday night Alice and I met again, and things changed.

Nancy was out at yet another work get-together. Her organization seemed to like running the social lives of its staff, like some rabid church, intent on infiltrating every activity of its disciples. Nancy mentioned the event in a way that made it clear that my attendance was far from mandatory, and I was quite happy to oblige. I do my best at these things but doubt I look as if I'm having the time of my life.

I didn't have anything else on, so I just flopped about the house for a while, reading and watching television. It was easier to relax when Nancy wasn't there, when we weren't busy being a Couple. I couldn't settle, though. I kept thinking how pleasant it would be not to feel that way, that it would be nice to want your girlfriend to be home so you could laze about together. It didn't work that way with Nancy, not anymore. Getting her to consider a lie-in on one particular Saturday was a major project in itself. I probably hadn't tried very hard in a while, either. She got up, I got up. I'd been developed as a human resource.

My reading grew fitful and in the end I grabbed my coat and went for a walk down streets that were dark and cold. A few couples and lone figures floated down the roads, in mid-evening transit between pubs and Chinese restaurants.

The very formlessness of the activity around me, its random wandering, made me feel quietly content. The room in which Nancy and her colleagues stood, robotically passing business catchphrases up and down the hierarchy, leapt into my mind, though I'd no idea where it was. I thought quietly to myself that I would much rather be here than there.

Then for a moment I felt the whole of London spread out around me, and my contentment faded away. Nancy had somewhere to go. All I had was miles of finite roads in winter light, black houses leaning in toward each other. I could walk, and I could run, and in the end I would come to the boundaries, the edge of the city. When I reached them there would be nothing I could do except turn around and come back into the city. I couldn't feel anything beyond the gates, couldn't believe anything was there. It wasn't some yearning for the countryside or far climes: I like London, and the great outdoors irritates me. It was more a sense that a place that should hold endless possibilities had been tamed by something, bleached out by my lack of imagination, by the limits of my life.

I headed down the Kentish Town Road toward Camden, so wrapped up in heroic melancholy that I nearly got myself run over at the junction with Prince of Wales Road. Rather shaken, I stumbled back onto the curb, dazed by a passing flash of yellow light and a blurred obscenity. Fuck that, I thought, and crossed at a different place, sending me down a different road, toward a different evening.

Camden was, as ever, trying to prove that there was still a place for hippie throwback losers in the 1990s, and I skirted the purposeful crowds and ended up in a back road instead.

And it was there that I saw Alice. When I saw her I felt my heart lurch, and I stopped in my tracks. She was walking along the road, dressed in a long skirt and dark blouse, hands in pockets. She appeared to be alone and was wandering down the street much as I was, looking around but in a world of her own. It was too welcome a coincidence not to take advantage of and, careful not to surprise her, I crossed the road and met her on the other side.

We spent the next three hours in a noisy, smoky pub. The only seats were very close together, crowded round one corner of a table in the center of the room. We drank a lot, but the alcohol didn't seem to function in the way it usually did. I didn't get drunk but simply felt warmer and more relaxed. The reeling crowds of locals gave us ample ammunition to talk about, until we were going fast enough not to need any help at all. We just drank, and talked, and talked and drank, and the bell for last orders came as a complete surprise.

When we walked out of the pub some of the alcohol kicked suddenly in, and we stumbled in unison on an unexpected step, to fall together laughing and shh-ing. Without even discussing it we knew that neither of us felt like going home yet, and we ended up down by the canal instead. We walked slowly past the backs of houses and speculated what might be going on beyond the curtains, we looked up at the sky and pointed out stars, we listened to the quiet splashes of occasional ducks coming into land. After about fifteen minutes we found a bench and sat down for a cigarette.

When she'd put her lighter back in her pocket Alice's hand fell near mine. I was very conscious of it being there, of the smallness of the distance mine would have to travel, and I smoked left-handed so as not to move it. I wasn't forgetting myself. I still knew Nancy existed, knew how my life was set up. But I didn't move my hand.

Then, like a chess game of perfect simplicity and naturalness, the conversation took us there.

I said that work seemed to be slackening off, after the busy period of the last couple of months. Alice said that she hoped it didn't drop off too much. So that I can continue to afford expensive computers that don't do quite what I expect? I asked.

"No," she replied, "so that I can keep coming to see you." I turned and looked at her. She looked nervous but defiant, and her hand moved the inch that put it on top of mine.

"You might as well know," she said. "If you don't already. There are three important things in my life at the moment. My bike, my stories, and you."

People don't change their lives: evenings do. There are nights that have their own momentum, their own purpose and agenda. They come from nowhere and take people with them. That's why you can never understand, the next day, quite how you came to do what you did. Because it wasn't you who did it. It was the evening.

My life stopped that evening, and started up again, and everything was a different color.

We sat on the bench for another two hours, wrapped up close to each other. We admitted when we'd first thought about each other, and laughed quietly about the distance we'd kept. After weeks of denying what I felt, of simply not realizing, I couldn't let go of her hand now that I had it. It felt so extraordinary to be that close to her, to feel the texture of her skin on mine and her nails against my palm. People change when you get that near to them, become much more real. If you're already in love with them then they expand to fill the world.

In the end we got on to Nancy. We were bound to, sooner or later. Alice asked how I felt about her, and I tried to explain, tried to understand myself. In the end we let the topic lapse.

"It's not going to be easy," I said, squeezing her hand. I was thinking glumly to myself that it might not happen at all. Knowing the way Nancy would react, it looked like a very high mountain to climb. Alice glanced at me and then turned back toward the canal.

A big cat was sitting there, peering out over the water. First moving myself even closer to Alice, so that strands of her hair tickled against my face, I made a noise at the cat. It turned to look at us and then ambled over toward the bench.

"I do like a friendly cat," I said, reaching out to stroke its head.

Alice smiled and then made a noise of her own. I was a bit puzzled that she wasn't looking at the cat when she made it, until I saw that another was making its way out of the shadows. This one was smaller and more lithe, and walked right up to the bench. I was, I suppose, still a little befuddled with drink, and when Alice turned to look in a different direction it took me a moment to catch up. A third cat was coming down the canal walk in our direction, followed by another.

When a fifth emerged from the bushes behind our bench, I turned and stared at Alice. She was already looking at me, a smile on her lips like the first one of hers I'd seen. She laughed at the expression on my face and then made her noise again. The cats around us sat to attention, and two more appeared from the other direction, almost trotting in their haste to join the collection. We were now so outnumbered that I felt rather beset.

When the next one appeared I had to ask.

"Alice, what's going on?"

She smiled very softly, like a painting, and leaned her head against my shoulder.

"A long time ago," she said, as if making up a story for a child, "none of this was here. There was no canal, no streets and houses, and all around was trees, and grass." One of the cats round the bench briefly licked one of its paws, and I saw another couple padding out of the darkness toward us. "The big people have changed all of that. They've cut down the trees, and buried the grass, and they've even leveled the ground. There used to be a hill here, a hill that was steep on one side but gentle on the other. They've taken all that away, and made it look like this. It's not that it's so bad. It's just different. The cats still remember the way it was."

It was a nice story, and yet another indication of how we thought in the same way. But it couldn't be true, and it didn't explain all the cats around us. There were now about twenty, and somehow that was too many. Not for me, but for common sense. Where the hell were they all coming from?

"But they didn't have cats in those days," I said nervously. "Not like this. This kind of cat is modern, surely. An import, or crossbreed."

She shook her head. "That's what they say," she said, "and that's what people think. They've always been here. It's just that people haven't always known."

"Alice, what are you talking about?" I was beginning to get really spooked by the number of cats milling softly around. They were still coming, in ones and twos, and now surrounded us for yards around. The stretch of canal was dark apart from soft glints of moonlight off the water, and the lines of the banks and walkway seemed somehow stark, sketched out, as if modeled on a computer screen. They'd been rendered well and looked convincing, but something wasn't quite right about the way they sat together, as if some angle was one degree out.

"A thousand years ago cats used to come to this hill, because it was their meeting place. They would come and discuss their business, and then they would go away. This was their place, and it still is. But they don't mind us."

"Why?"

"Because I love you," she said, and kissed me for the first time.

It was ten minutes before I looked up again. Only two cats were left. I pulled my arm tighter around Alice and thought how simply and unutterably happy I was.

"Was that all true?" I asked, pretending to be a child.

"No," she said, and smiled. "It was just a story." She pushed her nose up against mine and nuzzled, and our heads melted into one.

At two o'clock I realized I was going to have to go home, and we got up and walked slowly back to the road. I waited shivering with her for a minicab, and endured the driver's histrionic sighing as we said good-bye. I stood on the corner and waved until the cab was out of sight, and then turned and walked home.

It wasn't until I turned into our road and saw that the lights were still on in our house that I realized just how real the evening had been. As I walked up the steps the door opened. Nancy stood there in a dressing gown, looking angry and frightened.

"Where the hell have you *been?*" she said. I straightened my shoulders and girded myself up to lie.

I apologized. I told her I'd been out drinking with Howard, lying calmly and with a convincing determination. I didn't even feel bad about it, except in a self-serving, academic sort of way.

Some switch had been finally thrown in my mind, and as we lay in bed afterward I realized that I wasn't in bed with my girlfriend anymore. There was just someone in my bed. When Nancy rolled toward me, her body open in a way that suggested that she might not be thinking of going to sleep, I felt my chest tighten with something that felt like dread. I found a way of suggesting that I might be a bit drunk for anything other than unconsciousness, and she curled up beside me and went to sleep instead. I lay awake for an hour, feeling as if I were lying on a slab of marble in a room open to the sky.

Breakfast the next morning was a festival of leaden politeness. The kitchen seemed very bright, and noise rebounded harshly off the walls. Nancy was in a good mood, but there was nothing I could do except smile tight smiles and talk much louder than usual, waiting for her to go to work.

The next ten days were both dismal and the best days of my life. Alice and I managed to see each other every couple of days, occasionally for an evening but more often just for a cup of coffee. We didn't do any more than talk, and hold hands, and sometimes kiss. Our kisses were brief, a kind of sketching out of the way things could be. Bad starts always undermine a relationship, for fear it could happen again. So we were restrained and honest with each other and it was wonderful, but it was also difficult.

Being home was no fun at all. Nancy hadn't changed, but I had, and so I didn't know her anymore. It was like having a complete stranger living in your house, a stranger who was all the worse for reminding you of someone you once loved. The things that were the closest to the way they used to be were the things that made me most irritable, and I found myself avoiding anything that might promote them.

Something had to be done, and it had to be done by me. The problem was gearing myself up to it. Nancy and I had been living together for four years. Most of our friends assumed we'd be engaged before long; I'd already heard a few jokes. We knew each other very well, and that does count for something. As I moved warily around Nancy during those weeks, trying not to seem too close, I was also conscious of how much we had shared together, of how affectionate a part of me still felt toward her. She was a friend, and I cared about her. I didn't want her to be hurt.

My relationship with Nancy wasn't completely straightforward. I wasn't just her boyfriend, I was her brother and father, too. I knew some of the reasons her eating was as bad as it was, things no one else would ever know. I'd talked it through with her, and knew how to live with it, knew how to not make her feel any worse. She needed support, and I was the only person there to give it. Ripping that away when she was already having such a bad time would be very difficult to forgive.

And so things went on, for a little while. I saw Alice when I could, but always in the end I would have to go, and we would part, and each time it felt more and more arbitrary and I found it harder to remember why I should have to leave. I grew terrified of saying her name in my sleep, or of letting something slip, and felt as if I were living my life on stage in front of a predatory audience waiting for a mistake. I'd go out for walks in the evening and walk as slowly up the road as possible, stopping to talk to the cat, stroking her for as long as she liked and walking up and down the pavement with her, doing anything to avoid going back into the house.

I spent most of the second week looking forward to the Saturday. At the beginning of each week Nancy announced she would be going on a team-building day at the weekend. She explained to me what was involved, the chasm of evangelical corporate vacuity into which she and her colleagues were cheerfully leaping. She was talking to me a lot more at the time, wanting to share her life. I tried, but I couldn't really listen. All I could think about was that I was due to be driving up to Cambridge that day, to drop work off at a client's. I'd assumed that I'd be going alone. With Nancy firmly occupied somewhere else, another possibility sprang to mind.

When I saw Alice for coffee that afternoon I asked if she'd like to come. The warmth of her reply helped me through the evenings of the week, and we talked about it every day. The plan was that I'd ring home early evening, when Nancy was back from her day, and say that I'd run into someone up there and wouldn't be back until late. It was a bending of our unspoken doing-things-by-the-book rule, but it had to be done. Alice and I needed a longer period with each other, and I needed to build myself up to what had to be done.

By midevening on Friday I was at fever pitch. I was pacing round the house not settling at anything, so much in my own little world that it took me a while to notice that something was up with Nancy, too.

She was sitting in the living room, going over some papers, but kept glancing angrily out of the window as if expecting to see someone. When I asked her about it, slightly irritably, she denied she was doing it, and then ten minutes later I saw her do it again. I retreated to the kitchen and did something dull to a shelf that I'd been putting off for months. When Nancy stalked in to make some more coffee she saw what I was doing and seemed genuinely touched that I'd finally got around to it. My smile of self-deprecating good-naturedness felt as if it were stretched across the lips of a corpse.

Then she was back out in the lounge again, glaring nervously out of the window, as if fearing imminent invasion from a Martian army. It reminded me of the night I'd seen her standing by the window, which I had found rather spooky. She was looking very flaky that evening, and I'd run out of pity. I simply found it irritating, and hated myself for that.

Eventually, finally, at long last, it was time for bed. Nancy went ahead and I volunteered to close windows and tidy ashtrays. It's funny how you seem most solicitous and endearing when you don't want to be there at all.

What I actually wanted was a few moments to wrap a present I was going to give to Alice. When I heard the bathroom door shut I leapt for the filing cabinet and took out the book. I grabbed tape and paper from a drawer and started wrapping. As I folded I glanced out of the window and saw the cat sitting outside in the road, and smiled to myself. With Alice I'd be able to have a cat of my own, could work with furry company and doze with a warm bundle on my lap. The bathroom door opened again and I paused, ready for instant action. When Nancy's feet had padded safely into the bedroom, I continued wrapping. When it was done I slipped the present in a drawer and took out the card I was going to give with it, already composing in my head the message for the inside.

"Mark?"

I nearly died when I heard Nancy's voice. She was striding through the kitchen toward me, and the card was still lying on my desk. I quickly drew a sheaf of papers toward me and covered it, but only just in time. Heart beating horribly, feeling almost dizzy, I turned to look at her, trying to haul an expression of bland normality across my face.

"What's this?" she demanded, holding her hand up in front of me. It was dark in the room, and I couldn't see at first. Then I saw. It was a hair. A dark brown hair.

"It looks like a hair," I said carefully, shuffling papers on the desk.

"I know what it fucking is," she snapped. "It was in the bed. I wonder how it got there."

Jesus Christ, I thought. She knows.

I stared at her with my mouth clamped shut and wavered on the edge of telling the truth, of getting it over with. I thought it would happen some other, calmer, way, but you never know. Perhaps this was the pause into which I had to drop the information that I was in love with someone else.

Then, belatedly, I realized that Alice had never been in the bedroom. Even since the night of the canal she'd only ever been in the living room and the downstairs hall. Maybe the kitchen, but certainly not the bedroom. I blinked at Nancy, confused.

"It's that bloody cat," she shouted, instantly livid in the way that always disarmed and frightened me. "It's been on our fucking bed."

"What cat?"

"The cat who's always fucking outside. Your little *friend*." She sneered violently, face almost unrecognizable. "You've had it in here."

"I haven't. What are you talking about?"

"Don't you deny, don't you—"

Unable to finish, Nancy simply threw herself at me and smashed me across the face. Shocked, I stumbled backward and she whacked me across the chin, and then pummeled her fists against my chest as I struggled to grab hold of her hands. She was trying to say something but it kept breaking up into furious sobs. In the end, before I could catch her hands, she took a step backward and stood very still. She stared at me for a moment, and then turned and walked quickly out of the room.

I spent the night on the sofa and was awake long after the last long, moaning sound had floated out to me from the bedroom. It may sound like selfish evasion, but I really felt I couldn't go to comfort her. The only way I could make her feel better was by lying, so in the end I stayed away.

I had plenty of time to finish writing the card to Alice, but found it difficult to remember exactly what I'd been going to say. In the end I struggled into a shallow, cramped sleep, and when I woke Nancy was already gone for the day.

I felt tired and hollow as I drove to meet Alice in the center of town. I still didn't actually know where she lived, or even her phone number. She hadn't volunteered the information, and I could always contact her via the courier firm. I was content with that until I could enter her life without any skulking around.

I remember very clearly the way she looked, standing on the pavement and watching out for my car. She was wearing a long black woolen skirt and a thick sweater of various chestnut colors. Her hair was backlit by morning light, and when she smiled as I pulled over toward her I had a moment of plunging doubt. I don't have any right to be with her, I thought. I already have someone, and Alice is far and away too wonderful. But she put her arms around me, and kissed my nose, and the feeling went away.

I have never driven so slowly on a motorway as that morning with Alice. I'd put some tapes in the car, music I knew we both liked, but they never made it out of the glove compartment. They simply weren't necessary. I sat in the slow lane and pootled along at sixty miles an hour, and we talked or sat in silence, sometimes glancing across at each other and grinning.

The road cuts through several hills, and when we reached the first cutting we both gasped at once. The embankment was a blaze of poppies, nodding in a gathering wind, and when we'd left them behind I turned to Alice and for the first time said I loved her. She stared at me for a long time, and in the end I had to glance away at the road. When I looked back she was looking straight ahead and smiling, her eyes shining with held-back tears.

My meeting took just under fifteen minutes. I think my client was rather taken aback, but who cares. We spent the rest of the day walking around the shops, picking up books and looking at them, stopping for two cups of tea. As we came laughing out of a record store she slung her arm around my back, and very conscious of what I was doing, I put mine around her shoulders. Though she was tall it felt comfortable, and there it stayed.

By about five I was getting tense, and we pulled into another café to have more tea, and so I could make my phone call. I left Alice sitting at the table waiting to order and went to the other side of the restaurant to use the booth. As I listened to the phone ringing I willed myself to be calm, and turned my back on the room to concentrate on what I was saying.

"Hello?"

When Nancy answered I barely recognized her. Her voice was like that of a querulously frightened old woman who'd not been expecting a call. I nearly put the phone down, but she realized who it was and immediately started crying.

It took me about twenty minutes to calm her even a little. She'd left the team-building at lunchtime, claiming illness. Then she'd gone to Sainsbury's. She had eaten two Sara Lee chocolate cakes, a fudge roll, a packet of cereal, and three packets of biscuits. She'd gone to the bathroom, vomited, and then started again. I think she'd been sick again at least once, but I couldn't really make sense of part of what she said. It was so mixed up with abject apologies to me that the sentences became confused, and I couldn't tell whether she was talking about the night before or about the half-eaten packet of Jell-O she still had in her hand.

Feeling a little frightened and completely unaware of anything outside the cubicle I was standing in, I did what I could to focus her until what she was saying made a little more sense. I gave up trying to say that no apology was needed for last night and in the end just told her everything was all right. She promised to stop eating for a while and to watch television instead. I said I'd be back as soon as I could.

I had to. I loved her. There was nothing else I could do.

When the last of my change was gone I told her to take care and slowly replaced the handset. I stared at the wood paneling in front of me and gradually became aware of the noise from the restaurant on the other side of the glass door behind me. Eventually I turned and looked out.

Alice was sitting at the table, watching the passing throng. She looked beautiful, and strong, and about two thousand miles away.

We drove back to London in silence. Most of the talking was done in the restaurant. It didn't take very long. I said I couldn't leave Nancy in the state that she was in, and Alice nodded once, tightly, and put her cigarettes in her bag.

She said that she'd sort of known, perhaps even before we'd got to Cambridge. I got angry then, and said she couldn't have done, because I hadn't known myself.

She got angry back when I said we'd still be friends, and she was in the right, I suppose. It was a stupid thing for me to say.

Awkwardly I asked if she'd be all right, and she said, yes, in the sense that she'd survive. I tried to explain that was the difference, that Nancy might not be able to. She shrugged and said that was the other difference: Nancy would never have to find out if she could. The more we talked the more my head felt it was going to explode, the more my eyes felt as if they could burst with the pain and run in bloody lines down my cold cheeks. In the end she grew businesslike and paid the bill, and we walked slowly back to the car.

Neither of us could bring ourselves to small talk in the car, and for the most part the only sound was that of the wheels upon the road. It was dark by then, and rain began to fall before we'd been on the motorway for very long. When we passed through the first cut in the hillside, I felt the poppies all around us, heads battered down by the falling water. Alice turned to me.

"I did know."

"How," I said, trying not to cry, trying to watch what the cars behind me were doing.

"When you said you loved me, you sounded so unhappy."

I dropped her in town, on the corner where I'd picked her up. She said a few things to help me, to make me feel less bad about what I'd done. Then she walked off around the corner, and I never saw her again.

When I'd parked outside the house I sat for a moment, trying to pull myself together. Nancy would need to see me looking whole and at her disposal. I got out and locked the door, looking around halfheartedly for the cat. It wasn't there.

Nancy opened the door with a shy smile, and I followed her into the kitchen. As I hugged her and told her everything was all right, I gazed blankly over her shoulder around the room. The kitchen was immaculate, no sign left of the afternoon's festivities. The rubbish had been taken out, and something was bubbling on the stove. She'd cooked me dinner.

She didn't eat but sat at the table with me. The chicken was okay, but not up to her usual standard. There was a lot of meat but it was tough, and for once there was a little too much spice. It tasted odd, to be honest. She noticed a look on my face and said she'd gone to a different butcher. We talked a little about her afternoon, but she was feeling much better. She seemed more interested in discussing the way her office reorganization was shaping up.

Afterward she went through into the lounge and turned the television on, and I set about making coffee and washing up, moving woodenly around the kitchen as if on abandoned rails. As Nancy's favorite inanity boomed out from the living room I looked around for a bin bag to shovel the remains of my dinner into, but she'd obviously used them all. Sighing with a complete lack of feeling, I opened the back door and went downstairs to put it directly into the bin.

There were two sacks by the bin, both tied with Nancy's distinctive knot. I undid the nearest and opened it a little. Then, just before I pushed the bones off my plate, something in the bag caught my eye. A patch of darkness amid the garish wrappers of high-calorie comfort foods. An oddly shaped piece of thick fabric, perhaps. I pulled the edge of the bag back a little farther to look, and the light from the kitchen window above fell across the contents of the bag.

The darkness changed to a rich chestnut brown flecked with red, and I saw it wasn't fabric at all.

We moved six months later, after we got engaged. I was glad to move. The flat never felt like home again. Sometimes I go back and stand in that street, remembering the weeks in which I stared out of the window, pointlessly watching the road. I called the courier firm after a couple of days. I was expecting a stonewall and knew it was unlikely they'd give an address. But they denied she'd ever worked there at all.

After a couple of years Nancy and I had our first child, and she'll be eight this November. She has a sister now. Some evenings I'll leave them with their mother and go out for a walk. I'll walk with heavy calm through black streets beneath featureless houses and sometimes go down to the canal. I sit on the bench and close my eyes, and sometimes I think I can see it. Sometimes I think I can feel the way it was when a hill was there and meetings were held in secret.

In the end I always stand up slowly and walk the streets back to the house. The hill has gone and things have changed, and it's not like that anymore. No matter how long I sit and wait, the cats will never come.

CATCH

Ray Vukcevich

Ray Vukcevich's fiction has appeared in many magazines including *The Maga-zine of Fantasy & Science Fiction*, *Lady Churchill's Rosebud Wristlet*, *SmokeLong Quarterly*, *Night Train*, *Polyphony*, and *Hobart*, and has been collected in *Meet Me in the Moon Room*. He also works as a programmer in a couple of brain labs at the University of Oregon. Read more about him at www.sff.net/people/rayv.

I asked the author how he came up with the preposterous germ of his story and this is what he relates: "The story, I remember, came from a jumble of images. I remembered throwing my son up in the air when he was a baby. He loved it. Those might have been his first giggles. But one time, I nearly missed. It was a close call, he was so slippery for some reason, and I might have dropped him. He might have hit his head on the edge of the coffee table on the way down. It might have been a disaster. My wife was sitting across the room, reading, smiling up at us now and then. She didn't realize what had happened, and I didn't tell her, and now it's too late, but the kid seemed to know, or maybe it was the look on my face. He clutched at my shirt. I hugged him in close rather than go for one more toss.

"Oddly, the other image was of a kitten who had put her paw through a hole in a cardboard box to swat at the turtle inside, and the turtle had grabbed the paw. Much drama. Once I got the cat loose, I tossed her to my wife who caught her neatly.

"The story didn't come together for more than twenty years after those two incidents."

Your face, I say, is a wild animal this morning, Lucy, and I'm glad it's caged. Her scowl is so deep I can't imagine she's ever been without it. Her yellow hair is a frumpy halo around her wire mask. My remark doesn't amuse her.

55

I know what I did. I just don't know why it pissed her off, and if I don't know, insensitive bastard that I am, she certainly isn't going to tell me.

She lifts the cat over her head and hurls it at me. Hurls it hard. I catch it and underhand it back to her. The cat is gray on top and snowy white below and mostly limp, its eyes rolled back in its head and its coated tongue hanging loose out of one side of its mouth. I know from experience that it will die soon, and its alarm collar will go off, and one of us will toss it into the ditch that runs between us. A fresh angry bundle of teeth and claws will drop from the hatch in the ceiling, and we'll toss the new cat back and forth between us until our staggered breaks and someone takes our places. The idea is to keep the animals in motion twenty-four hours a day.

In this profession, we wear canvas shirts and gloves and wire cages over our faces. I sometimes dream we've lost our jobs, Lucy and me. What a nightmare. What else do we know?

My replacement comes in behind me. He takes up the straw broom and dips it into the water in the ditch that runs through the toss-box and sweeps at the smeared feces and urine staining the floor and walls. A moment later, the buzzer sounds, and he puts the broom back in the corner. I step aside, and Lucy tosses the cat to him. I slip out of the box and into the catacomb for my fifteen-minute break before moving on to the next box.

Lucy and I work an hour on and fifteen minutes off all day long. As we move from toss-box to toss-box, our paths cross and recross. I'll be out of phase with her for half an hour, probably just long enough for her to work up a real rage.

The catacomb is a labyrinth of wide tunnels dotted with concrete boxes. There is a metal chute running from the roof to the top of each box. The boxes are evenly spaced, and there is a light bulb for every box, but not all the bulbs are alive so there are gaps in the harsh light. The boxes are small rooms, and there is a wooden door on each side so catchers can be replaced without interrupting the tossing. The concrete walls of the tunnels, like the concrete walls of the boxes, are streaked black and white and beaded with moisture. The floors are roughened concrete. Everything smells like wet rocks and dead things.

So what did I do?

While Lucy dressed for work this morning, I played with our infant daughter, Megan, tossing her into the air and catching her again, blowing bubbles into her stomach while she pulled my hair and giggled until she got the hiccups.

When Lucy came in, I tossed the baby in a high arc across the room to her. Megan tumbled in a perfect backward somersault in the air. Lucy went dead white. She snatched Megan out of the air and hugged the child to her chest.

"Nice catch," I said.

"Don't you ever," Lucy said, her voice all husky and dangerous, "ever do that again, Desmond! Not ever."

Then she stomped out, taking Megan with her.

What the hell? I'd known there was no chance whatever that Lucy would miss. She's a professional. My trusting her to catch the love of my life, the apple of my eye, Daddy's little girl, was, I thought, a pretty big compliment. Lucy didn't buy it. In fact, she didn't even let me explain at all, said instead, oh shut up, Desmond, just shut up, and off we went to work, silent, stewing, our hurt feelings like a sack of broken toys between us.

Now she's not speaking to me. It's going to be a long day.

The buzzer sounds, and I move into the next box. I do my duty with the broom, and when the buzzer sounds again I replace the catcher. The cat here is a howling orange monster, and I have my hands full. When the animal is this fresh, the tossing technique looks a lot like volleyball. You don't want to be too close to the thing for very long.

By the time Lucy takes her place across from me, I've established a rhythm and am even able to put a little spin on the cat now and then. I have to hand it to Lucy. She catches up quickly, and soon we have the animal sailing smoothly between us.

The animals go through stages as we toss and catch them. First defiance, then resistance, followed by resignation, then despair, and finally death. This one is probably somewhere in the resistance stage, not fighting wildly, but watching for an opening to do some damage. I put one hand on the cat's chest and the other under its bottom and send it across to Lucy in a sitting position. Not to be outdone she sends it back still sitting but upside down now. Maybe the silly positions have done the trick. Whatever. I can feel the animal slip into the resignation stage.

I toss the cat tumbling head over heels, a weak howl and a loose string of saliva trailing behind it. Is Lucy ever going to talk to me again?

"Okay, I'm sorry," I say, giving in to the idea that I might never know exactly why I should be sorry.

I see tears come to her eyes, and she falters, nearly drops the cat. I want to go to her. I want to comfort her, but it will be some time before we're both on a break at the same time, and I see suddenly that it will be too late by then. It simply won't matter anymore.

My replacement comes in and sweeps up. Then the buzzer sounds. I step aside.

Lucy isn't crying anymore.

I reach for the door.

THE MANTICORE SPELL

Jeffrey Ford

Jeffrey Ford is the author of the novels *The Physiognomy, Memoranda, The Beyond, The Portrait of Mrs. Charbuque, The Girl in the Glass,* and *The Shadow Year.* His short fiction has been published in three collections: *The Fantasy Writer's Assistant, The Empire of Ice Cream,* and *The Drowned Life.* His fiction has won the World Fantasy Award, the Nebula Award, the Edgar Allan Poe Award, and Grand Prix de l'Imaginaire. He lives in New Jersey with his wife and two sons and teaches literature and writing at Brookdale Community College.

Ford has said that his use of the Manticore as the center of a story was influenced by his having read a number of old and modern bestiaries, and by the Pre-Raphaelite paintings of fantastic creatures: harpies, unicorns, mermaids, and the Sphinx. In addition, his fellow teacher and author—William Jon Watkins, a sort of wizard in his own right—had just retired. Watkins taught Ford so much about writing and teaching, two strange, chimerical beasts, that he was given a place in the story as well.

The first reports of the creature, mere sightings, were absurd—a confusion of parts; a loss of words to describe the smile. The color, they said, was a flame, a hot coal, a flower, and each of the witnesses tried to mimic the thing's song but none could. My master, the wizard Watkin, bade me record in word and image every thing each one said. We'd been put to it by the king, whose comment was, "Give an ear to their drollery. Make them think you're thinking about it at my command. It's naught but bad air, my old friend." My master nodded and smiled, but after the king had left the room, the wizard turned to me and whispered, "Manticore."

"It's the last one, no doubt," said Watkin. We watched from the balcony in late afternoon when the king's hunters returned from the forest across the wide green lawn to the palace, the blood of the Manticore's victims trailing bright red through the grass. "It's a very old one," he said. "You can tell by the fact that it devours the horses but the humans often return with a limb or two intact."

He cast a spell of protection around the monster, threading the eye of a needle with a hummingbird feather.

"You want it to survive?" I asked.

"To live till it dies naturally," was his answer. "The king's hunters must not kill it."

Beneath the moon and stars at the edge of autumn, we sat with the rest of the court along the ramparts of the castle and listened for the creature's flute-like trill, descending and ascending the scale, moving through the distant darkness of the trees. Its sound set the crystal goblets to vibrating. The ladies played hearts by candle light, their hair up and powdered. The gentlemen leaned back, smoking their pipes, discussing how they'd fell the beast if the job was theirs.

"Wizard," the king said. "I thought you'd taken measures."

"I did," said Watkin. "It's difficult, though. Magic against magic, and I'm an old man."

A few moments later, the King's engineer appeared at his side. The man carried a mechanical weapon that shot an arrow made of elephant ivory. "The tip is dipped in acid that will eat the creature's flesh," said the engineer. "Aim anywhere above the neck. Keep the gear work within the gun well-oiled." His highness smiled and nodded.

A week later, just prior to dinner, at the daily ritual in which the king assessed the state of his kingdom, it was reported that the creature devoured two horses and a hunter, took the right leg of the engineer's assistant and so twisted and crumpled the new weapon of the engineer that the poison arrow set to strike the beast turned round and stabbed its inventor in the ear, the lobe of which dripped off his head like a lit candle.

"We fear the thing may lay eggs," said the engineer. "I suggest we burn the forest."

"We're not burning down the forest," said the king. He turned and looked at the wizard. Watkin faked sleep.

I helped the old man out of his chair and accompanied him down the stone steps to the corridor that led to our chambers. Before I let him go, he took me by the collar and whispered, "The spell's weakening, I can feel it in my gums." I nodded, and he brushed me aside, walking the rest of the way to his rooms unassisted. Following behind, I looked over my shoulder almost positive the king was aware that his wizard's art had been turned against him.

I lay down in my small space off the western side of the work room. I could see the inverted, hairless pink corpse of the hunch monkey swinging from the ceiling in the other room. The wizard had written away for it to Palgeria five years earlier, or so said his records. When it arrived, I could see by his reaction that he could no longer remember what he'd meant to do with it. Two days later, he came to me and said, "See what you can make of this hunch monkey." I had no idea, so I hung the carcass in the work room.

From the first day of my service to Watkin he insisted that I tell him my dreams each morning. "Dreams are the manner in which those who mean you harm infiltrate the defenses of you existence," he told me during a thunderstorm. It was mid-august, and we stood, dry, beneath the spreading branches of a hemlock one afternoon as a hard rain fell in curtains around us. That night, in sleep, I followed a woman through a field of purple flowers that eventually sloped down to the edge of a cliff. Below, an enormous mound of black rock heaved as if breathing, and when it expanded I could see through cracks and fissures red and orange light radiating out from within. The dream woman looked over her shoulder and said, "Do you remember the day you came to serve the wizard?"

Then the light was in my eyes and I was surprised to find I was awake. Watkin, holding a lantern up to my face said, "It's perished. Come quickly." He spun away from the bed, casting me in shadow again. I trembled as I dressed. I'd seen the old man pull, with his teeth, the spirit of a spitting demon from the nostril of one of the ladies of court. Unfathomable. His flowered robe was a brilliant design of peonies in the snow, but I no longer trusted the sun.

I stepped into the work room as Watkin was clearing things from the huge table at which he mixed his powders and dissected the reptiles whose small brains had a region that when mashed and dried quickened his potions. "Fetch your pen and paper," he said. "We will record everything." I did as I was told and then helped him. At one point he tried to lift a large crystal globe of blue powder and his thin wrists shook with the exertion. I took it from him just as it slipped from his fingers.

Suddenly, everywhere, the scent of roses and cinnamon. The wizard sniffed the air, and warned me that its arrival was imminent. Six hunters carried the corpse, draped across three battle stretchers, and covered by the frayed tapestry of the War of the Willows which had hung in the corridor that ran directly from the Treasury to the Pity Fountain. Watkin and I stood back as the dark bearded men grunted, gritted their teeth, and hoisted the stretchers onto the table. As they filed out of our chambers, my master handed each of them a small packet of powder tied up with a ribbon—an aphrodisiac, I suspected. Before collecting his reward and leaving, the last of the hunters took the edge of the tapestry, and lifting the corner high, walked swiftly around the table, unveiling the Manticore.

I glanced for a mere sliver and instinctually looked away. While my eyes were averted, I heard the old man purr, squeal, chitter. The thick cloud of the creature's scent was a weight on my shoulders, and then I noticed the first buzz of the flies. The wizard slapped my face and forced me to look. His grip on the back of my neck could not be denied.

It was crimson and shades of crimson. And after I noted the color, I saw the teeth and looked at nothing else for a time. Both a wince and a smile. I saw the lion paws, the fur, the breasts, that long beautiful hair. The tail of shining segments led to a smooth, sharp stinger—a green bubble of venom at its tip. "Write this down," said Watkin. I fumbled for my pen. "*Female Manticore*," he said. I wrote at the top of the page.

The wizard took one step that seemed to last for minutes. Then he took another and another, until he was pacing slowly around the table, studying the creature from all sides. In his right hand he held the cane with the wizard's head carved into the head of it. Its tip was not touching the floor. "Draw it," he commanded. I set to the task, but this was a skill I was deficient at. Still, I drew it—the human head and torso, the powerful body of a lion, the tail of the scorpion. It turned out to be my best drawing, but it too was terrible.

"The first time I saw one of these," Watkin said, "I was with my class as a boy. We'd gone on a walk to the lake, and we'd just passed through an orchard and onto a large meadow with yellow flowers. My teacher, a woman named Levu, with a mole beside her lip, pointed into the distance, one hand on my shoulder, and whispered, 'A husband and wife Manticore, look.' I saw them, blurs of crimson, grazing the low hanging fruit by the edge of the meadow. On our way back to town that evening, we heard their distinctive trill and then were attacked by two of them. They each had three rows of teeth chewing perfectly in sync. I watched them devour the teacher as she frantically confessed to me. While I prayed for her, the monsters recited poems in an exotic tongue and licked the blood from their lips."

I wrote down all of what Watkin said, although I wasn't sure it was to the point. He never looked me in the eye, but moved slowly, slowly, around the thing, lightly prodding it with his cane, squinting with one eye into the darkness of its recesses. "Do you see the face?" he asked me. I told him I did. "But for that fiendish smile, she's beautiful," he said. I tried to see her without the smile and what I saw in my mind was the smile without her. Suffice to say, her skin was crimson as was her fur, her eyes yellow diamonds. Her long hair had its own mind, deep red-violet whips at her command. And then that smile.

"She lived next to me, with hair as long as this but golden," Watkin said, pointing. "I, a little younger than you, she a little older. Only once we went out together into the desert and climbed down into the dunes. Underground there, in the ruins, we saw the stone carved face of the hunch monkey. We lay down in front of it together, kissed, and went to sleep. Our parents and neighbors were looking for us. Late in the night while she slept, a wind blew through the pursed lips of the stone face, warning me of *treachery* and *time*. When she woke, she said in sleep she'd visited the ocean and gone fishing with a Manticore. The next time we kissed was at our wedding."

"Draw that," he shouted. I did my best, but didn't know whether to depict the Manticore or the wizard with her at the beach. "One more thing about the smile," he said. "It continually, perpetually grinds with the organic rotary mechanism of a well-lubricated jaw and three sets of teeth—even after death, in the grave, it masticates the pitch black."

"Should I draw that?" I asked.

He'd begun walking. A few moments later, he said, "No."

He laid down his cane on the edge of the table and took one of the paws in both his hands. "Look here at this claw," he said. "How many heads do you think it's taken off?" "Ten," I said. "Ten thousand," he said, dropping the paw and retrieving his cane. "How many will it take off now?" he asked. I didn't answer.

"The lion is fur, muscle, tendon, claw and speed, five important ingredients of the unfathomable. Once a king of Dreesha captured and tamed a brood of Manticore. He led them into battles on long, thousand link, iron chains. They cut through the forward ranks of the charging Igridots with the artful tenacity his royal highness reserves for only the largest pastries."

"Take this down?" I asked.

"To the last dribbling vowel," he said, nodding and slowly moving. His cane finally tapped the floor. "Supposedly," he said, "there's another smaller organ floating within their single chambered heart. At the center of this small organ is a smaller ball of gold—the purest gold imaginable. So pure it could be eaten. And if it were, I am told the result is one million beautiful dreams of flying.

"I had an uncle," said the wizard, "who hunted the creature, bagged one, cut out its ball of gold, and proceeded to eat the entire thing in one bound. After that, my uncle was sane only five times a day. Always, he had his hands up. His tongue was always wagging, his eyes shivering. He walked away from home one night when no one was watching. He wandered into the forest. There were reports for a while of a ragged holy man but then a visitor returned his ring and watch and told us his head had been found. Once it was safely under glass, I performed my first magic on it and had it tell me about its final appointment with a Manticore.

"Take a lock of this hair, boy, when we're done," he said. "When you get old, tie it into a knot and wear it in your vest pocket. It will ward off danger… to an extent."

"How fast do they run?" I asked.

"How fast?" he said, and then he stopped walking. A breeze blew through the windows and porticos of the work room. He turned quickly and looked over his shoulder out the window. Storm clouds, lush hedge, and a humidity of roses and cinnamon. The flies now swarmed. "That fast," he said. "Draw it."

"Notice," he said, "there is no wound. The hunters didn't kill it. It died of old age and they found it." He stood very silent, his hands behind his back. I wondered if he'd run out of things to say. Then he cleared his throat and said, "There's a point at which a wince and a smile share the same shape and intensity, almost but not quite the same meaning. It's at that point and that point alone that you can begin to understand the beast's scorpion tail. Sleek, black, poisonous, and needle sharp, it moves like lightening, piercing flesh and bone, depositing a chemical that halts all memory. When stung you want to scream, to run, to aim your crossbow at its magenta heart, but alas… you forget."

"I'm drawing it," I said. "Excellent," he said and ran his free hand over one of the smooth sections of the scorpion tail. "Don't forget to capture the forgetting." He laughed to himself. "The Manticore venom was at one time used to cure certain cases of melancholia. There's very often some incident from the past at the heart of depression. The green poison, measured judiciously, and administered with a long syringe to the corner of the eye, will instantly paralyze memory, negating the cause of sorrow. There was one fellow, I'd heard, who took too much of it and forgot to forget—he remembered everything and could let nothing go. His head filled up with every second of every day and it finally exploded.

"The poison doesn't kill you, though. It only dazes you with the inability to remember, so those teeth can have their way. There are those few who'd been stung by the beast but not devoured. In every case, they described experiencing the same illusion—an eye-blink journey to an old summer home, with four floors of guest rooms, sunset, mosquitoes. For the duration of the poison's strength, around two days, the victim lives at this retreat… in the mind, of course. There are cool breezes as the dark comes on, moths against the screen, the sound of waves far off, and the victim comes to the conclusion that he or she is alone. I suppose to die while in the throes of the poison, is to stay alone at that beautiful place by the sea for eternity."

I spoke without thinking, "Every aspect of the beast brings you to eternity—the smile, the purest gold, the sting."

"Write that down," said Watkin. "What else can you say of it?"

"I remember that day I came to serve you," I said, "and on the long stretch through the poplars, my carriage was stopped due to a dead body in the road. As the carriage passed, I peered out to see a bloody mess on the ground. You were one of the people in the crowd."

"You can't understand my invisible connection to these creatures—a certain symbiosis. I feel it in my lower back. Magic becomes a pin hole shrinking into the future," he said.

"Can you bring the monster back to life?" I asked him.

"No," he said. "It doesn't work that way. I have something else in mind." He stepped over to a work bench, left the cane there and lifted a hatchet. Returning to the body of the creature, he walked slowly around it to the tail. "That was my wife you saw in the road that day. Killed by a Manticore—by this very Manticore."

"I'm sorry," I said. "I'd think you'd have tried harder to kill it."

"Don't try to understand," he said. He lifted the hatchet high above his head, and then with one swift chop, severed the stinger from the tail of the creature. "Under the spell of the poison, I will go to the summer house and rescue her from eternity."

"I'll go with you," I said.

"You can't go. You could be stranded in eternity with my wife and me—think of that," said Watkin. "No, there's something else I need you to do for me while I'm under the effects of the venom. You must take the head of the Manticore into the forest and bury it. Their heads turn into the roots of trees, the fruit of which are Manticore pups. You'll carry the last seed." He used the hatchet to sever the creature's head while I dressed for the outdoors.

I'd learned to ride a horse before I went to serve the wizard, but the forest at night frightened me. I couldn't shake the image of Watkin's palm impaled on the tip of the black stinger and him rapidly accruing dullness, gagging, his eyes rolling back behind their lids. I carried the Manticore head in a woolen sac tied to the saddle and trembled at the prospect that perhaps Watkin was wrong and the one sprawled on the work table, headless and tailless, was not the last. For my protection, he'd given me a spell to use if it became necessary—a fistful of yellow powder and a half dozen words I no longer remembered.

I rode through the dark for a few minutes and had quickly had enough of it. I dismounted and dug a hole at the side of the path, standing my torch upright in it. It made a broad circle of light on the ground. I retrieved the shovel I'd brought and the head. After nearly a half hour of digging, I began to hear a slight murmuring sound coming from somewhere close by me. I thought someone was spying from a darker part of the forest, and then I took it for the whirring of a Manticore's tri-toothed jaws and was paralyzed by fear. Two minutes later, I realized the voice was coming from inside the sack. When I looked, the smile was facing out. The Manticore's eyes went wide, that chasm of a mouth opened, flashing three-way ivory, and she spoke in a foreign language.

I took her out of the sack, set her head up at the center of the circle of torch light, brushed back her hair, and listened to the beautiful sing-song language. Later, after waking from a kind of trance brought on by the flow of words, I remembered the spell Watkin had given me. Laying the powder out on the upturned palm of my hand, I aimed it carefully and blew it into the creature's face. She coughed. I'd forgotten the words, so said anything that I recalled them sounding like. Then she spoke to me, and I understood her.

"Eternity," she said and then repeated it, methodically, with the precise same intonation again and again and again…

I grabbed the shovel and started digging. By the time I had dug a deep enough hole, my nerves were frayed by her repetition, and I couldn't fill the dirt in fast enough. When the head was thoroughly buried, its endless phrase still sounding, muffled, beneath the ground, I tamped the soil down and then found an odd looking green rock, like a fist, to mark the spot for future reference.

Watkin never returned from the place by the sea. After the venom wore off, his body was lifeless. I then became the wizard. No one seemed to care that I knew nothing about magic. "Make it up till you've got it," said the King. "Then spread it around." I thanked him for his insight, but was aware he'd eaten pure gold and now, when not soaring in his dreams, was rarely sane. The years came and went, and I did my best to learn the devices, potions, phenomena, that Watkin had bothered to record. I suppose there was something of magic in it, but it wasn't readily recognizable.

I was able to witness Watkin's fate by use of a magic looking glass I'd found in his bedroom and learned to command. It was a tall mirror that stood on the back of his writing desk. In it I could see anywhere in existence with a simple command. I chose the quiet place by the sea, and there before me were the clean swept pathways, the blossoming wisteria, the gray and splintering fence board. Darkness was coming on. The woman with golden hair sat on the screened porch in a wicker rocker, listening to the floor boards creak. The twilight breeze was cool against sunburn. The day seemed endless. As night came on, she rocked herself to sleep. I ordered the mirror to show me her dream.

She dreamed that she was at the beach. The surf rolled gently up across the sand. There was a Manticore—her crimson resplendent against the clear blue day—fishing at the shoreline with a weighted net. Without fear, the woman with bright hair approached the creature. The Manticore politely asked, with smile upon smile, if the woman would like to help hoist the net. She nodded. The net was flung far out and they waited. Finally there was a tug. The woman with the golden hair and the Manticore both pulled hard to retrieve their catch. Eventually they dragged Watkin ashore, tangled in the webbing, seaweed in his hair. She ran to him and helped him out of the net. They put their arms around each other and kissed.

Now I keep my ears pricked up for descriptions of strange beasts in the heart of the forest. If a horse or a human goes missing, I must get to the bottom of it before I can rest. I try to speak to the hunters every day. Reports of the creature are vague but growing, and I realize now I have some invisible connection to it, as if its muffled, muted voice is enclosed within a chamber of my heart, relentlessly whispering, "Eternity."

CATSKIN
Kelly Link

Kelly Link is the author of three collections: *Stranger Things Happen*, *Magic for Beginners*, and *Pretty Monsters* (the last, for young adults). Her short stories have recently been published in *Tin House*, *Firebirds Rising*, *Noisy Outlaws*, *The Restless Dead*, *The Starry Rift*, and *Troll's Eye View*. Her work has won three Nebulas, a Hugo, four Locus Awards, The British Science Fiction Association Award, and a World Fantasy Award. She and her husband Gavin J. Grant run Small Beer Press, and twice-yearly produce the 'zine *Lady Churchill's Rosebud Wristlet*.

Link has said that the inspiration for "Catskin" was a conversation she had with fellow-writer Christopher Rowe, about whether or not a picture of his cat was a real feline, or a spooky cat-impersonator. Rowe produced a 'zine, *Say... is this a cat?*, on the subject.

Cats went in and out of the witch's house all day long. The windows stayed open, and the doors, and there were other doors, cat-sized and private, in the walls and up in the attic. The cats were large and sleek and silent. No one knew their names, or even if they had names, except for the witch.

Some of the cats were cream-colored and some were brindled. Some were black as beetles. They were about the witch's business. Some came into the witch's bedroom with live things in their mouths. When they came out again, their mouths were empty.

The cats trotted and slunk and leapt and crouched. They were busy. Their movements were catlike, or perhaps clockwork. Their tails twitched like hairy pendulums. They paid no attention to the witch's children.

The witch had three living children at this time, although at one time she had had dozens, maybe more. No one, certainly not the witch, had ever bothered to tally them up. But at one time the house had bulged with cats and babies.

Now, since witches cannot have children in the usual way—their wombs are full of straw or bricks or stones, and when they give birth, they give birth to rabbits, kittens, tadpoles, houses, silk dresses, and yet even witches must have heirs, even witches wish to be mothers—the witch had acquired her children by other means: she had stolen or bought them.

She'd had a passion for children with a certain color of red hair. Twins she had never been able to abide (they were the wrong kind of magic), although she'd sometimes attempted to match up sets of children, as though she had been putting together a chess set, and not a family. If you were to say a witch's chess set, instead of a witch's family, there would be some truth in that. Perhaps this is true of other families as well.

One girl she had grown like a cyst, upon her thigh. Other children she had made out of things in her garden, or bits of trash that the cats brought her: aluminum foil with strings of chicken fat still crusted to it, broken television sets, cardboard boxes that the neighbors had thrown out. She had always been a thrifty witch.

Some of these children had run away and others had died. Some of them she had simply misplaced, or accidentally left behind on buses. It is to be hoped that these children were later adopted into good homes, or reunited with their natural parents. If you are looking for a happy ending in this story, then perhaps you should stop reading here and picture these children, these parents, their reunions.

Are you still reading? The witch, up in her bedroom, was dying. She had been poisoned by an enemy, a witch, a man named Lack. The child Finn, who had been her food taster, was dead already and so were three cats who'd licked her dish clean. The witch knew who had killed her and she snatched pieces of time, here and there, from the business of dying, to make her revenge. Once the question of this revenge had been settled to her satisfaction, the shape of it like a black ball of twine in her head, she began to divide up her estate between her three remaining children.

Flecks of vomit stuck to the corners of her mouth, and there was a basin beside the foot of the bed, which was full of black liquid. The room smelled like cats' piss and wet matches. The witch panted as if she were giving birth to her own death.

"Flora shall have my automobile," she said, "and also my purse, which will never be empty, so long as you always leave a coin at the bottom, my darling, my spendthrift, my profligate, my drop of poison, my pretty, pretty Flora. And when I am dead, take the road outside the house and go west. There's one last piece of advice."

Flora, who was the oldest of the witch's living children, was redheaded and stylish. She had been waiting for the witch's death for a long time now, although she had been patient. She kissed the witch's cheek and said, "Thank you, Mother."

The witch looked up at her, panting. She could see Flora's life, already laid out, flat as a map. Perhaps all mothers can see as far.

"Jack, my love, my birdsnest, my bite, my scrap of porridge," the witch said, "you shall have my books. I won't have any need of books where I am going. And when you leave my house, strike out in an an easterly direction and you won't be any sorrier than you are now."

Jack, who had once been a little bundle of feathers and twigs and eggshell all tied up with a tatty piece of string, was a sturdy lad, almost full grown. If he knew how to read, only the cats knew it. But he nodded and kissed his mother's gray lips.

"And what shall I leave to my boy Small?" the witch said, convulsing. She threw up again in the basin. Cats came running, leaning on the lip of the basin to inspect her vomitus. The witch's hand dug into Small's leg.

"Oh it is hard, hard, so very hard, for a mother to leave her children (though I have done harder things). Children need a mother, even such a mother as I have been." She wiped at her eyes, and yet it is a fact that witches cannot cry.

Small, who still slept in the witch's bed, was the youngest of the witch's children. (Perhaps not as young as you think.) He sat upon the bed, and although he didn't cry, it was only because witch's children have no one to teach them the use of crying. His heart was breaking.

Small could juggle and sing and every morning he brushed and plaited the witch's long, silky hair. Surely every mother must wish for a boy like Small, a curly-headed, sweet-breathed, tenderhearted boy like Small, who can cook a fine omelet, and who has a good strong singing voice as well as a gentle hand with a hairbrush.

"Mother," he said, "if you must die, then you must die. And if I can't come along with you, then I'll do my best to live and make you proud. Give me your hairbrush to remember you by, and I'll go make my own way in the world."

"You shall have my hairbrush, then," said the witch to Small, looking, and panting, panting. "And I love you best of all. You shall have my tinderbox and my matches, and also my revenge, and you will make me proud, or I don't know my own children."

"What shall we do with the house, Mother?" said Jack. He said it as if he didn't care.

"When I am dead," the witch said, "this house will be of no use to anyone. I gave birth to it—that was a very long time ago—and raised it from just a dollhouse. Oh, it was the most dear, most darling dollhouse ever. It had eight rooms and a tin roof, and a staircase that went nowhere at all. But I nursed it and rocked it to sleep in a cradle, and it grew up to be a real house, and see how it has taken care of me, its parent, how it knows a child's duty to its mother. And perhaps you can see how it is now, how it pines, how it grows sick to see me dying like this. Leave it to the cats. They'll know what to do with it."

All this time the cats have been running in and out of the room, bringing things and taking things away. It seems as if they will never slow down, never come to rest, never nap, never have the time to sleep, or to die, or even to mourn. They have a certain proprietary look about them, as if the house is already theirs.

The witch vomits up mud, fur, glass buttons, tin soldiers, trowels, hat pins, thumbtacks, love letters (mislabeled or sent without the appropriate amount of postage and never read), and a dozen regiments of red ants, each ant as long and wide as a kidney bean. The ants swim across the perilous stinking basin, clamber up the sides of the basin, and go marching across the floor in a shiny ribbon. They are carrying pieces of Time in their mandibles. Time is heavy, even in such small pieces, but the ants have strong jaws, strong legs. Across the floor they go, and up the wall, and out the window. The cats watch, but don't interfere. The witch gasps and coughs and then lies still. Her hands beat against the bed once and then are still. Still the children wait, to make sure that she is dead, and that she has nothing else to say.

In the witch's house, the dead are sometimes quite talkative.

But the witch has nothing else to say at this time.

The house groans and all the cats begin to mew piteously, trotting in and out of the room as if they have dropped something and must go and hunt for it—they will never find it—and the children, at last, find they know how to cry, but the witch is perfectly still and quiet. There is a tiny smile on her face, as if everything has happened exactly to her satisfaction. Or maybe she is looking forward to the next part of the story.

The children buried the witch in one of her half-grown dollhouses. They crammed her into the downstairs parlor, and knocked out the inner walls so that her head rested on the kitchen table in the breakfast nook, and her ankles threaded through a bedroom door. Small brushed out her hair, and, because he wasn't sure what she should wear now that she was dead, he put all her dresses on her, one over the other over the other, until he could hardly see her white limbs at all beneath the stack of petticoats and coats and dresses. It didn't matter: once they'd nailed the dollhouse shut again, all they could see was the red crown of her head in the kitchen window, and the worn-down heels of her dancing shoes knocking against the shutters of the bedroom window.
Jack, who was handy, rigged a set of wheels for the dollhouse, and a harness so that it could be pulled. They put the harness on Small, and Small pulled and Flora pushed, and Jack talked and coaxed the house along, over the hill, down to the cemetery, and the cats ran along beside them.

The cats are beginning to look a bit shabby, as if they are molting. Their mouths look very empty. The ants have marched away, through the woods, and down into town, and they have built a nest on your yard, out of the bits of Time. And if you hold a magnifying glass over their nest, to see the ants dance and burn,

Time will catch fire and you will be sorry.

Outside the cemetery gates, the cats had been digging a grave for the witch. The children tipped the dollhouse into the grave, kitchen window first. But then they saw that the grave wasn't deep enough, and the house sat there on its end, looking uncomfortable. Small began to cry (now that he'd learned how, it seemed he would spend all his time practicing), thinking how horrible it would be to spend one's death, all of eternity, upside down and not even properly buried, not even able to feel the rain when it beat down on the exposed shingles of the house, and seeped down into the house and filled your mouth and drowned you, so that you had to die all over again, every time it rained.

The dollhouse chimney had broken off and fallen on the ground. One of the cats picked it up and carried it away, like a souvenir. That cat carried the chimney into the woods and ate it, a mouthful at a time, and passed out of this story and into another one. It's no concern of ours.

The other cats began to carry up mouthfuls of dirt, dropping it and mounding it around the house with their paws. The children helped, and when they'd finished, they'd managed to bury the witch properly, so that only the bedroom window was visible, a little pane of glass like an eye at the top of a small dirt hill.

On the way home, Flora began to flirt with Jack. Perhaps she liked the way he looked in his funeral black. They talked about what they planned to be, now that they were grown up. Flora wanted to find her parents. She was a pretty girl: someone would want to look after her. Jack said he would like to marry someone rich. They began to make plans.

Small walked a little behind, slippery cats twining around his ankles. He had the witch's hairbrush in his pocket, and his fingers slipped around the figured horn handle for comfort.

The house, when they reached it, had a dangerous, grief-stricken look to it, as if it was beginning to pull away from itself. Flora and Jack wouldn't go back inside. They squeezed Small lovingly, and asked if he wouldn't want to come along with them. He would have liked to, but who would have looked after the witch's cats, the witch's revenge? So he watched as they drove off together. They went north. What child has ever heeded a mother's advice?

Jack hasn't even bothered to bring along the witch's library: he says there isn't space in the trunk for everything. He'll rely on Flora and her magic purse.

Small sat in the garden, and ate stalks of grass when he was hungry, and pretended that the grass was bread and milk and chocolate cake. He drank out of the garden hose. When it began to grow dark, he was lonelier than he had ever been in his life. The witch's cats were not good company. He said nothing to them and they had nothing to tell him, about the house, or the future, or the witch's revenge, or about where he was supposed to sleep. He had never slept anywhere except in the witch's bed, so at last he went back over the hill and down to the cemetery.

Some of the cats were still going up and down the grave, covering the base of the mound with leaves and grass and feathers, their own loose fur. It was a soft sort of nest to lie down on. The cats were still busy when Small fell asleep—cats are always busy—cheek pressed against the cool glass of the bedroom window, hand curled in his pocket around the hairbrush, but in the middle of the night, when he woke up, he was swaddled, head to foot, in warm, grass-scented cat bodies.

A tail is curled around his chin like a rope, and all the bodies are soughing breath in and out, whiskers and paws twitching, silky bellies rising and falling. All the cats are sleeping a frantic, exhausted, busy sleep, except for one, a white cat who sits near his head, looking down at him. Small has never seen this cat before, and yet he knows her, the way that you know the people who visit you in dreams: she's white everywhere, except for reddish tufts and frills at her ears and tail and paws, as if someone has embroidered her with fire around the edges.

"What's your name?" Small says. He's never talked to the witch's cats before.

The cat lifts a leg and licks herself in a private place. Then she looks at him. "You may call me Mother," she says.

But Small shakes his head. He can't call the cat that. Down under the blanket of cats, under the windowpane, the witch's Spanish heel is drinking in moonlight.

"Very well, then, you may call me The Witch's Revenge," the cat says. Her mouth doesn't move, but he hears her speak inside his head. Her voice is furry and sharp, like a blanket made of needles. "And you may comb my fur."

Small sits up, displacing sleeping cats, and lifts the brush out of his pocket. The bristles have left rows of little holes indented in the pink palm of his hand, like some sort of code. If he could read the code, it would say: Comb my fur.

Small combs the fur of The Witch's Revenge. There's grave dirt in the cat's fur, and one or two red ants, who drop and scurry away. The Witch's Revenge bends her head down to the ground, snaps them up in her jaws. The heap of cats around them is yawning and stretching. There are things to do.

"You must burn her house down," The Witch's Revenge says. "That's the first thing."

Small's comb catches a knot, and The Witch's Revenge turns and nips him on the wrist. Then she licks him in the tender place between his thumb and his first finger. "That's enough," she says. "There's work to do."

So they all go back to the house, Small stumbling in the dark, moving farther and farther away from the witch's grave, the cats trotting along, their eyes lit like torches, twigs and branches in their mouths, as if they plan to build a nest, a canoe, a fence to keep the world out. The house, when they reach it, is full of lights, and more cats, and piles of tinder. The house is making a noise, like an instrument that someone is breathing into. Small realizes that all the cats are mewing, endlessly, as they run in and out the doors, looking for more kindling. The Witch's Revenge says, "First we must latch all the doors."

So Small shuts all the doors and windows on the first floor, leaving open only the kitchen door, and The Witch's Revenge shuts the catches on the secret doors, the cat doors, the doors in the attic, and up on the roof, and the cellar doors. Not a single secret door is left open. Now all the noise is on the inside, and Small and The Witch's Revenge are on the outside.

All the cats have slipped into the house through the kitchen door. There isn't a single cat in the garden. Small can see the witch's cats through the windows, arranging their piles of twigs. The Witch's Revenge sits beside him, watching. "Now light a match and throw it in," says The Witch's Revenge.

Small lights a match. He throws it in. What boy doesn't love to start a fire?

"Now shut the kitchen door," says The Witch's Revenge, but Small can't do that. All the cats are inside. The Witch's Revenge stands on her hindpaws and pushes the kitchen door shut. Inside, the lit match catches something on fire. Fire runs along the floor and up the kitchen walls. Cats catch fire, and run into the other rooms of the house. Small can see all this through the windows. He stands with his face against the glass, which is cold, and then warm, and then hot. Burning cats with burning twigs in their mouths press up against the kitchen door, and the other doors of the house, but all the doors are locked. Small and The Witch's Revenge stand in the garden and watch the witch's house and the witch's books and the witch's sofas and the witch's cooking pots and the witch's cats, her cats, too, all her cats burn.

You should never burn down a house. You should never set a cat on fire. You should never watch and do nothing while a house is burning. You should never listen to a cat who says to do any of these things. You should listen to your mother when she tells you to come away from watching, to go to bed, to go to sleep. You should listen to your mother's revenge.

You should never poison a witch.

In the morning, Small woke up in the garden. Soot covered him in a greasy blanket. The Witch's Revenge was curled up asleep on his chest. The witch's house was still standing, but the windows had melted and run down the walls.

The Witch's Revenge woke and stretched and licked Small clean with her small sharkskin tongue. She demanded to be combed. Then she went into the house and came out, carrying a little bundle. It dangled, boneless, from her mouth, like a kitten.

It is a catskin, Small sees, only there is no longer a cat inside it. The Witch's Revenge drops it in his lap.

He picked it up and something shiny fell out of the loose light skin. It was a piece of gold, sloppy, slippery with fat. The Witch's Revenge brought out dozens and dozens of catskins, and there was a gold piece in every skin. While Small counted his fortune, The Witch's Revenge bit off one of her own claws, and pulled one long witch hair out of the witch's comb. She sat up, like a tailor, cross-legged in the grass, and began to stitch up a bag, out of the many catskins.

Small shivered. There was nothing to eat for breakfast but grass, and the grass was black and cooked.

"Are you cold?" said The Witch's Revenge. She put the bag aside and picked up another catskin, a fine black one. She slit a sharp claw down the middle. "We'll make you a warm suit."

She used the coat of a black cat, and the coat of a calico cat, and she put a trim around the paws, of grey-and-white-striped fur.

While she did this, she said to Small, "Did you know that there was once a battle, fought on this very patch of ground?"

Small shook his head no.

"Wherever there's a garden," The Witch's Revenge said, scratching with one paw at the ground, "I promise you there are people buried somewhere beneath it. Look here." She plucked up a little brown clot, put it in her mouth, and cleaned it with her tongue.

When she spat the little circle out again, Small saw it was an ivory regimental button. The Witch's Revenge dug more buttons out of the ground—as if buttons of ivory grew in the ground—and sewed them onto the catskin. She fashioned a hood with two eyeholes and a set of fine whiskers, and sewed four fine cat tails to the back of the suit, as if the single tail that grew there wasn't good enough for Small. She threaded a bell on each one. "Put this on," she said to Small.

Small put on the suit and the bells chime. The Witch's Revenge laughs. "You make a fine-looking cat," she says. "Any mother would be proud."

The inside of the cat suit is soft and a little sticky against Small's skin. When he puts the hood over his head, the world disappears. He can see only the vivid corners of it through the eyeholes—grass, gold, the cat who sits cross-legged, stitching up her sack of skins—and air seeps in, down at the loosely sewn seam, where the skin droops and sags over his chest and around the gaping buttons. Small holds his tails in his clumsy fingerless paw, like a handful of eels, and swings them back and forth to hear them ring. The sound of the bells and the sooty, cooked smell of the air, the warm stickiness of the suit, the feel of his new fur against the ground: he falls asleep and dreams that hundreds of ants come and lift him and gently carry him off to bed.

When Small tipped his hood back again, he saw that The Witch's Revenge had finished with her needle and thread. Small helped her fill the bag with gold. The Witch's Revenge stood up on her hind legs, took the bag, and swung it over her shoulders. The gold coins went sliding against each other, mewling and hissing. The bag dragged along the grass, picking up ash, leaving a trail of green behind it. The Witch's Revenge strutted along as if she were carrying a sack of air.

Small put the hood on again, and he got down on his hands and knees. And then he trotted after The Witch's Revenge. They left the garden gate wide open and went into the forest, towards the house where the witch Lack lived.

The forest is smaller than it used to be. Small is growing, but the forest is shrinking. Trees have been cut down. Houses have been built. Lawns rolled, roads laid. The Witch's Revenge and Small walked alongside one of the roads. A school bus rolled by: The children inside looked out their windows and laughed when they saw The Witch's Revenge walking on her hind legs, and at her heels, Small, in his cat suit. Small lifted his head and peered out of his eyeholes after the school bus.

"Who lives in these houses?" he asked The Witch's Revenge.

"That's the wrong question, Small," said The Witch's Revenge, looking down at him and striding along.

Miaow, the catskin bag says. Clink.

"What's the right question, then?" Small said.

"Ask me who lives under the houses," The Witch's Revenge said.

Obediently, Small said, "Who lives under the houses?"

"What a good question!" said The Witch's Revenge. "You see, not everyone can give birth to their own house. Most people give birth to children instead. And when you have children, you need houses to put them in. So children and houses: most people give birth to the first and have to build the second. The houses, that is. A long time ago, when men and women were going to build a house, they would dig a hole first. And they'd make a little room—a little, wooden, one-room house—in the hole. And they'd steal or buy a child to put in the house in the hole, to live there. And then they built their house over that first little house."

"Did they make a door in the lid of the little house?" Small said.

"They did not make a door," said The Witch's Revenge.

"But then how did the girl or the boy climb out?" Small said.

"The boy or the girl stayed in that little house," said The Witch's Revenge. "They lived there all their life, and they are living in those houses still, under the other houses where the people live, and the people who live in the houses above may come and go as they please, and they don't ever think about how there are little houses with little children, sitting in little rooms, under their feet."

"But what about the mothers and fathers?" Small asked. "Didn't they ever go looking for their boys and girls?"

"Ah," said The Witch's Revenge. "Sometimes they did and sometimes they didn't. And after all, who was living under their houses? But that was a long time ago. Now people mostly bury a cat when they build their house, instead of a child. That's why we call cats house-cats. Which is why we must walk along smartly. As you can see, there are houses under construction here."

And so there are. They walk by clearings where men are digging little holes.

First Small puts his hood back and walks on two legs, and then he puts on his hood again, and goes on all fours: He makes himself as small and slinky as possible, just like a cat. But the bells on his tails jounce and the coins in the bag that The Witch's Revenge carries go clink, miaow, and the men stop their work and watch them go by.

How many witches are there in the world? Have you ever seen one? Would you know a witch if you saw one? And what would you do if you saw one? For that matter, do you know a cat when you see one? Are you sure?

Small followed The Witch's Revenge. Small grew calluses on his knees and the pads of his fingers. He would have liked to carry the bag sometimes, but it was too heavy. How heavy? You would not have been able to carry it, either.

They drank out of streams. At night they opened the catskin bag and climbed inside to sleep, and when they were hungry they licked the coins, which seemed to sweat golden fat, and always more fat. As they went, The Witch's Revenge sang a song:

> I had no mother
> and my mother had no mother
> and her mother had no mother
> and her mother had no mother
> and her mother had no mother
> and you have no mother
> to sing you
> this song

The coins in the bag sang too, miaow, miaow, and the bells on Small's tails kept the rhythm.

Every night Small combs The Witch's Revenge's fur. And every morning The Witch's Revenge licks him all over, not neglecting the places behind his ears, and at the backs of his knees. And then he puts the catsuit back on, and she grooms him all over again.

Sometimes they were in the forest, and sometimes the forest became a town, and then The Witch's Revenge would tell Small stories about the people who lived in the houses, and the children who lived in the houses under the houses. Once, in the forest, The Witch's Revenge showed Small where there had once been a house. Now there was only the stones of the foundation, upholstered in moss, and the chimney stack, propped up with fat ropes and coils of ivy.

The Witch's Revenge rapped on the grassy ground, moving clockwise around the foundation, until both she and Small could hear a hollow sound; The Witch's Revenge dropped to all fours and clawed at the ground, tearing it up with her paws and biting at it, until they could see a little wooden roof. The Witch's Revenge knocked on the roof, and Small lashed his tails.

"Well, Small," said The Witch's Revenge, "shall we take off the roof and let the poor child go?"

Small crept up close to the hole she had made. He put his ear to it and listened, but he heard nothing at all. "There's no one in there," he said.

"Maybe they're shy," said The Witch's Revenge. "Shall we let them out, or shall we leave them be?"

"Let them out!" said Small, but what he meant to say was, "Leave them alone!" Or maybe he said Leave them be! although he meant the opposite. The Witch's Revenge looked at him, and Small thought he heard something then—beneath him where he crouched, frozen—very faint: a scrabbling at the dirty, sunken roof.

Small sprang away. The Witch's Revenge picked up a stone and brought it down hard, caving the roof in. When they peered inside, there was nothing except blackness and a faint smell. They waited, sitting on the ground, to see what might come out, but nothing came out. After a while, The Witch's Revenge picked up her catskin bag, and they set off again.

For several nights after that, Small dreamed that someone, something, was following them. It was small and thin and bleached and cold and dirty and afraid. One night it crept away again, and Small never knew where it went. But if you come to that part of the forest, where they sat and waited by the stone foundation, perhaps you will meet the thing that they set free.

No one knew the reason for the quarrel between the witch Small's mother and the witch Lack, although the witch Small's mother had died for it. The witch Lack was a handsome man and he loved his children dearly. He had stolen them out of the cribs and beds of palaces and manors and harems. He dressed his children in silks, as befitted their station, and they wore gold crowns and ate off gold plates. They drank from cups of gold. Lack's children, it was said, lacked nothing.

Perhaps the witch Lack had made some remark about the way the witch Small's mother was raising her children, or perhaps the witch Small's mother had boasted of her children's red hair. But it might have been something else. Witches are proud and they like to quarrel.

When Small and The Witch's Revenge came at last to the house of the witch Lack, The Witch's Revenge said to Small, "Look at this monstrosity! I've produced finer turds and buried them under leaves. And the smell, like an open sewer! How can his neighbors stand the stink?"

Male witches have no wombs, and must come by their houses in other ways, or else buy them from female witches. But Small thought it was a very fine house. There was a prince or a princess at each window staring down at him, as he sat on his haunches in the driveway, beside The Witch's Revenge. He said nothing, but he missed his brothers and sisters.

"Come along," said The Witch's Revenge. "We'll go a little ways off and wait for the witch Lack to come home."

Small followed The Witch's Revenge back into the forest, and in a while, two of the witch Lack's children came out of the house, carrying baskets made of gold. They went into the forest as well and began to pick blackberries.

The Witch's Revenge and Small sat in the briar and watched.

There was a wind in the briar. Small was thinking of his brothers and sisters. He thought of the taste of blackberries, the feel of them in his mouth, which was not at all like the taste of fat.

The Witch's Revenge nestled against the small of Small's back. She was licking down a lump of knotted fur at the base of his spine. The princesses were singing.

Small decided that he would live in the briar with The Witch's Revenge. They would live on berries and spy on the children who came to pick them, and The Witch's Revenge would change her name. The word Mother was in his mouth, along with the sweet taste of the blackberries.

"Now you must go out," said The Witch's Revenge, "and be kittenish. Be playful. Chase your tail. Be shy, but don't be too shy. Don't talk too much. Let them pet you. Don't bite."

She pushed at Small's rump, and Small tumbled out of the briar and sprawled at the feet of the witch Lack's children.

The Princess Georgia said, "Look! It's a dear little cat!"

Her sister Margaret said doubtfully, "But it has five tails. I've never seen a cat that needed so many tails. And its skin is done up with buttons and it's almost as large as you are."

Small, however, began to caper and prance. He swung his tails back and forth so that the bells rang out and then he pretended to be alarmed by this. First he ran away from his tails and then he chased his tails. The two princesses put down their baskets, half-full of blackberries, and spoke to him, calling him a silly puss.

At first he wouldn't go near them. But, slowly, he pretended to be won over. He allowed himself to be petted and fed blackberries. He chased a hair ribbon and he stretched out to let them admire the buttons up and down his belly. Princess Margaret's fingers tugged at his skin; then she slid one hand in between the loose catskin and Small's boy skin. He batted her hand away with a paw, and Margaret's sister Georgia said knowingly that cat's didn't like to be petted on their bellies.

They were all good friends by the time The Witch's Revenge came out of the briar, standing on her hind legs and singing

> I have no children
> and my children have no children
> and their children
> have no children
> and their children

have no whiskers
and no tails

At this sight, the Princesses Margaret and Georgia began to laugh and point. They had never heard a cat sing, or seen a cat walk on its hind legs. Small lashed his five tails furiously, and all the fur of the catskin stood up on his arched back, and they laughed at that too.

When they came back from the forest, with their baskets piled with berries, Small was stalking close at their heels, and The Witch's Revenge came walking just behind. But she left the bag of gold hidden in the briar.

That night, when the witch Lack came home, his hands were full of gifts for his children. One of his sons ran to meet him at the door and said, "Come and see what followed Margaret and Georgia home from the forest! Can we keep them?"

And the table had not been set for dinner, and the children of the witch Lack had not sat down to do their homework, and in the witch Lack's throne room, there was a cat with five tails, spinning in circles, while a second cat sat impudently upon his throne, and sang,

Yes!
your father's house
is the shiniest
brownest largest
the most expensive
the sweetest-smelling
house
that has ever
come out of
anyone's
ass!

The witch Lack's children began to laugh at this, until they saw the witch, their father, standing there. Then they fell silent. Small stopped spinning.

"You!" said the witch Lack.

"Me!" said The Witch's Revenge, and sprang from the throne. Before anyone knew what she was about, her jaws were fastened about the witch Lack's neck, and then she ripped out his throat. Lack opened his mouth to speak and his blood fell out, making The Witch's Revenge's fur more red now than white. The witch Lack fell down dead, and red ants went marching out of the hole in his neck and the hole of his mouth, and they held pieces of Time in their jaws as tightly as The Witch's Revenge had held Lack's throat in hers. But she let Lack go and left him lying in his blood on the floor, and she snatched up the ants and ate them, quickly, as if she had been hungry for a very long time.

While this was happening, the witch Lack's children stood and watched and did nothing. Small sat on the floor, his tails curled about his paws. Children, all of them, they did nothing. They were too surprised. The Witch's Revenge, her belly full of ants, her mouth stained with blood, stood up and surveyed them.

"Go and fetch me my catskin bag," she said to Small.

Small found that he could move. Around him, the princes and princesses stayed absolutely still. The Witch's Revenge was holding them in her gaze.

"I'll need help," Small said. "The bag is too heavy for me to carry."

The Witch's Revenge yawned. She licked a paw and began to pat at her mouth. Small stood still.

"Very well," she said. "Take those big strong girls the Princesses Margaret and Georgia with you. They know the way."

The Princesses Margaret and Georgia, finding that they could move again, began to tremble. They gathered their courage and they went with Small, the two girls holding each other's hands, out of the throne room, not looking down at the body of their father, the witch Lack, and back into the forest.

Georgia began to weep, but the Princess Margaret said to Small: "Let us go!"

"Where will you go?" said Small. "The world is a dangerous place. There are people in it who mean you no good." He threw back his hood, and the Princess Georgia began to weep harder.

"Let us go," said the Princess Margaret. "My parents are the King and Queen of a country not three days' walk from here. They will be glad to see us again."

Small said nothing. They came to the briar and he sent the Princess Georgia in to hunt for the catskin bag. She came out scratched and bleeding, the bag in her hand. It had caught on the briars and torn open. Gold coins rolled out, like glossy drops of fat, falling on the ground.

"Your father killed my mother," said Small.

"And that cat, your mother's devil, will kill us, or worse," said Princess Margaret. "Let us go!"

Small lifted the catskin bag. There were no coins in it now. The Princess Georgia was on her hands and knees, scooping up coins and putting them into her pockets.

"Was he a good father?" Small asked.

"He thought he was," Princess Margaret said. "But I'm not sorry he's dead. When I grow up, I will be Queen. I'll make a law to put all the witches in the kingdom to death, and all their cats as well."

Small became afraid. He took up the catskin bag and ran back to the house of the witch Lack, leaving the two princesses in the forest. And whether they made their way home to the Princess Margaret's parents, or whether they fell into the hands of thieves, or whether they lived in the briar, or whether the Princess Margaret grew up and kept her promise and rid her kingdom of witches and cats, Small never knew, and neither do I, and neither shall you.

When he came back into the witch Lack's house, The Witch's Revenge saw at once what had happened. "Never mind," she said.

There were no children, no princes and princesses, in the throne room. The witch Lack's body still lay on the floor, but The Witch's Revenge had skinned it like a coney, and sewn up the skin into a bag. The bag wriggled and jerked, the sides heaving as if the witch Lack were still alive somewhere inside. The Witch's Revenge held the witchskin bag in one hand, and with the other, she was stuffing a cat into the neck of the skin. The cat wailed as it went into the bag. The bag was full of wailing. But the discarded flesh of the witch Lack lolled, slack.

There was a little pile of gold crowns on the floor beside the flayed corpse, and transparent, papery things that blew about the room, on a current of air, surprised looks on the thin, shed faces.

Cats were hiding in the corners of the room, and under the throne. "Go catch them," said The Witch's Revenge. "But leave the three prettiest alone."

"Where are the witch Lack's children?" Small said.

The Witch's Revenge nodded around the room. "As you see," she said. "I've slipped off their skins, and they were all cats underneath. They're cats now, but if we were to wait a year or two, they would shed these skins as well and become something new. Children are always growing."

Small chased the cats around the room. They were fast, but he was faster. They were nimble, but he was nimbler. He had worn his cat suit longer. He drove the cats down the length of the room, and The Witch's Revenge caught them and dropped them into her bag. At the end there were only three cats left in the throne room and they were as pretty a trio of cats as anyone could ask for. All the other cats were inside the bag.

"Well done and quickly done, too," said The Witch's Revenge, and she took her needle and stitched shut the neck of the bag. The skin of the witch Lack smiled up at Small, and a cat put its head through Lack's stained mouth, wailing. But The Witch's Revenge sewed Lack's mouth shut too, and the hole on the other end, where a house had come out. She left only his earholes and his eyeholes and his nostrils, which were full of fur, rolled open so that the cats could breathe.

The Witch's Revenge slung the skin full of cats over her shoulder and stood up.

"Where are you going?" Small said.

"These cats have mothers and fathers," The Witch's Revenge said. "They have mothers and fathers who miss them very much."

She gazed at Small. He decided not to ask again. So he waited in the house with the two princesses and the prince in their new cat suits, while The Witch's Revenge went down to the river. Or perhaps she took them down to the market and sold them. Or maybe she took each cat home, to its own mother and father, back to the kingdom where it had been born. Maybe she wasn't so careful to make sure that each child was returned to the right mother and father. After all, she was in a hurry, and cats look very much alike at night.

No one saw where she went—but the market is closer than the palaces of the Kings and Queens whose children had been stolen by the witch Lack, and the river is closer still.

When The Witch's Revenge came back to Lack's house, she looked around her. The house was beginning to stink very badly. Even Small could smell it now.

"I suppose the Princess Margaret let you fuck her," said The Witch's Revenge, as if she had been thinking about this while she ran her errands. "And that is why you let them go. I don't mind. She was a pretty puss. I might have let her go myself."

She looked at Small's face and saw that he was confused. "Never mind," she said.

She had a length of string in her paw, and a cork, which she greased with a piece of fat she had cut from the witch Lack. She threaded the cork on the string, calling it a good, quick, little mouse, and greased the string as well, and she fed the wriggling cork to the tabby who had been curled up in Small's lap. And when she had the cork back again, she greased it again and fed it to the little black cat, and then she fed it to the cat with two white forepaws, so that she had all three cats upon her string.

She sewed up the rip in the catskin bag, and Small put the gold crowns in the bag, and it was nearly as heavy as it had been before. The Witch's Revenge carried the bag, and Small took the greased string, holding it in his teeth, so the three cats were forced to run along behind him as they left the house of the witch Lack.

Small strikes a match, and he lights the house of the dead witch, Lack, on fire, as they leave. But shit burns slowly, if at all, and that house might be burning still, if someone hasn't gone and put it out. And maybe, someday, someone will go fishing in the river near that house, and hook their line on a bag full of princes and princesses, wet and sorry and wriggling in their catsuit skins—that's one way to catch a husband or a wife.

Small and The Witch's Revenge walked without stopping and the three cats came behind them. They walked until they reached a little village very near where the witch Small's mother had lived and there they settled down in a room The Witch's Revenge rented from a butcher. They cut the greased string, and bought a cage and hung it from a hook in the kitchen. They kept the three cats in it, but Small bought collars and leashes, and sometimes he put one of the cats on a leash and took it for a walk around the town.

Sometimes he wore his own catsuit and went out prowling, but The Witch's Revenge used to scold him if she caught him dressed like that. There are country manners and there are town manners and Small was a boy about town now.

The Witch's Revenge kept house. She cleaned and she cooked and she made Small's bed in the morning. Like all of the witch's cats, she was always busy. She melted down the gold crowns in a stewpot, and minted them into coins.

The Witch's Revenge wore a silk dress and gloves and a heavy veil, and ran her errands in a fine carriage, Small at her side. She opened an account in a bank, and she enrolled Small in a private academy. She bought a piece of land to build a house on, and she sent Small off to school every morning, no matter how he cried. But at night she took off her clothes and slept on his pillow and he combed her red and white fur.

Sometimes at night she twitched and moaned, and when he asked her what she was dreaming, she said, "There are ants! Can't you comb them out? Be quick and catch them, if you love me."

But there were never any ants.

One day when Small came home, the little cat with the white front paws was gone. When he asked The Witch's Revenge, she said that the little cat had fallen out of the cage and through the open window and into the garden and before The Witch's Revenge could think what to do, a crow had swooped down and carried the little cat off.

They moved into their new house a few months later, and Small was always very careful when he went in and out the doorway, imagining the little cat, down there in the dark, under the doorstep, under his foot.

Small got bigger. He didn't make any friends in the village, or at his school, but when you're big enough, you don't need friends.

One day while he and The Witch's Revenge were eating their dinner, there was a knock at the door. When Small opened the door, there stood Flora and Jack. Flora was wearing a drab, thrift-store coat, and Jack looked more than ever like a bundle of sticks.

"Small!" said Flora. "How tall you've become!" She burst into tears, and wrung her beautiful hands. Jack said, looking at The Witch's Revenge, "And who are you?"

The Witch's Revenge said to Jack, "Who am I? I'm your mother's cat, and you're a handful of dry sticks in a suit two sizes too large. But I won't tell anyone if you won't tell, either."

Jack snorted at this, and Flora stopped crying. She began to look around the house, which was sunny and large and well appointed.

"There's room enough for both of you," said The Witch's Revenge, "if Small doesn't mind."

Small thought his heart would burst with happiness to have his family back again. He showed Flora to one bedroom and Jack to another. Then they went downstairs and had a second dinner, and Small and The Witch's Revenge listened, and the cats in their hanging cage listened, while Flora and Jack recounted their adventures.

A pickpocket had taken Flora's purse, and they'd sold the witch's automobile, and lost the money in a game of cards. Flora found her parents, but they were a pair of old scoundrels who had no use for her. (She was too old to sell again. She would have realized what they were up to.) She'd gone to work in a department store, and Jack had sold tickets in a movie theater. They'd quarreled and made up, and then fallen in love with other people, and had many disappointments. At last they had decided to go home to the witch's house and see if it would do for a squat, or if there was anything left, to carry away and sell.

But the house, of course, had burned down. As they argued about what to do next, Jack had smelled Small, his brother, down in the village. So here they were.

"You'll live here, with us," Small said.

Jack and Flora said they could not do that. They had ambitions, they said. They had plans. They would stay for a week, or two weeks, and then they would be off again. The Witch's Revenge nodded and said that this was sensible.

Every day Small came home from school and went out again, with Flora, on a bicycle built for two. Or he stayed home and Jack taught him how to hold a coin between two fingers, and how to follow the egg, as it moved from cup to cup. The Witch's Revenge taught them to play bridge, although Flora and Jack couldn't be partners. They quarreled with each other as if they were husband and wife.

"What do you want?" Small asked Flora one day. He was leaning against her, wishing he were still a cat, and could sit in her lap. She smelled of secrets. "Why do you have to go away again?"

Flora patted Small on the head. She said, "What do I want? That's easy enough! To never have to worry about money. I want to marry a man and know that he'll never cheat on me, or leave me." She looked at Jack as she said this.

Jack said, "I want a rich wife who won't talk back, who doesn't lie in bed all day, with the covers pulled up over her head, weeping and calling me a bundle of twigs." And he looked at Flora when he said this.

The Witch's Revenge put down the sweater that she was knitting for Small. She looked at Flora and she looked at Jack and then she looked at Small.

Small went into the kitchen and opened the door of the hanging cage. He lifted out the two cats and brought them to Flora and Jack. "Here," he said. "A husband for you, Flora, and a wife for Jack. A prince and a princess, and both of them beautiful, and well brought up, and wealthy, no doubt."

Flora picked up the little tomcat and said, "Don't tease at me, Small! Who ever heard of marrying a cat!"

The Witch's Revenge said, "The trick is to keep their catskins in a safe hiding place. And if they sulk, or treat you badly, sew them back into their catskin and put them into a bag and throw them in the river."

Then she took her claw and slit the skin of the tabby-colored cat suit, and Flora was holding a naked man. Flora shrieked and dropped him on the ground. He was a handsome man, well made, and he had a princely manner. He was not a man that anyone would ever mistake for a cat. He stood up and made a bow, very elegant, for all that he was naked. Flora blushed, but she looked pleased.

"Go fetch some clothes for the Prince and the Princess," The Witch's Revenge said to Small. When he got back, there was a naked princess hiding behind the sofa, and Jack was leering at her.

A few weeks after that, there were two weddings, and then Flora left with her new husband, and Jack went off with his new princess. Perhaps they lived happily ever after.

The Witch's Revenge said to Small, "We have no wife for you."

Small shrugged. "I'm still too young," he said.

But try as hard as he can, Small is getting older now. The catskin barely fits across his shoulders. The buttons strain when he fastens them. His grown-up fur—his people fur—is coming in. At night he dreams.

The witch his mother's Spanish heel beats against the pane of glass. The princess hangs in the briar. She's holding up her dress, so he can see the catfur down there. Now she's under the house. She wants to marry him, but the house will fall down if he kisses her. He and Flora are children again, in the witch's house. Flora lifts up her skirt and says, see my pussy? There's a cat down there, peeking out at him, but it doesn't look like any cat he's ever seen. He says to Flora, I have a pussy too. But his isn't the same.

At last he knows what happened to the little, starving, naked thing in the forest, where it went. It crawled into his catskin, while he was asleep, and then it climbed right inside him, his Small skin, and now it is huddled in his chest, still cold and sad and hungry. It is eating him from the inside, and getting bigger, and one day there will be no Small left at all, only that nameless, hungry child, wearing a Small skin.

Small moans in his sleep.

There are ants in The Witch's Revenge's skin, leaking out of her seams, and they march down into the sheets and pinch at him, down under his arms, and between his legs where his fur is growing in, and it hurts, it aches and aches. He dreams that The Witch's Revenge wakes now, and comes and licks him all over, until the pain melts. The pane of glass melts. The ants march away again on their long, greased thread.

"What do you want?" says The Witch's Revenge.

Small is no longer dreaming. He says, "I want my mother!"

Light from the moon comes down through the window over their bed. The Witch's Revenge is very beautiful—she looks like a Queen, like a knife, like a burning house, a cat—in the moonlight. Her fur shines. Her whiskers stand out like pulled stitches, wax and thread. The Witch's Revenge says, "Your mother is dead."

"Take off your skin," Small says. He's crying and The Witch's Revenge licks his tears away. Small's skin pricks all over, and down under the house, something small wails and wails. "Give me back my mother," he says.

"Oh, my darling," says his mother, the witch, The Witch's Revenge, "I can't do that. I'm full of ants. Take off my skin, and all the ants will spill out, and there will be nothing left of me."

Small says, "Why have you left me all alone?"

His mother the witch says, "I've never left you alone, not even for a minute. I sewed up my death in a catskin so I could stay with you."

"Take it off! Let me see you!" Small says. He pulls at the sheet on the bed, as if it were his mother's catskin.

The Witch's Revenge shakes her head. She trembles and beats her tail back and forth. She says, "How can you ask me for such a thing, and how can I say no to you? Do you know what you're asking me for? Tomorrow night. Ask me again, tomorrow night."

And Small has to be satisfied with that. All night long, Small combs his mother's fur. His fingers are looking for the seams in her catskin. When The Witch's Revenge yawns, he peers inside her mouth, hoping to catch a glimpse of his mother's face. He can feel himself becoming smaller and smaller. In the morning he will be so small that when he tries to put his catskin on, he can barely do up the buttons. He'll be so small, so sharp, you might mistake him for an ant, and when The Witch's Revenge yawns, he'll creep inside her mouth, he'll go down into her belly, he'll go find his mother. If he can, he'll help his mother cut her catskin open so that she can get out again and come and live in the world with him, and if she won't come out, then he won't, either. He'll live there, the way that sailors learn to live, inside the belly of fish who have eaten them, and keep house for his mother inside the house of her skin.

This is the end of the story. The Princess Margaret grows up to kill witches and cats. If she doesn't, then someone else will have to do it. There is no such thing as witches, and there is no such thing as cats, either, only people dressed up in catskin suits. They have their reasons, and who is to say that they might not live that way, happily ever after, until the ants have carried away all of the time that there is, to build something new and better out of it?

MIEZE CORRECTS AN INCOMPLETE REPRESENTATION OF REALITY

Michaela Roessner

Michaela Roessner has had four novels, assorted fiction and nonfiction published. She is also an exhibiting visual artist. Her most recently published and upcoming publications include "The Fisherman's Wife," in *Room* magazine, "The Klepsydra" in the anthology *Polyphony 7,* and "The Fishes Speak," in the winter 2009/2010 *Postscripts* anthology. A graduate of the Stonecoast MFA in Creative Writing program, she teaches online for Gotham Writers' Workshop and Axia College. She has practiced Aikido for over twenty-five years and has been known to fall down with great mastery.

Roessner explains her inspiration for this story: "As someone who has always been owned by cats, the whole Schrödinger's Cat paradox always drove me bonkers. Even if it was supposed to be just a *gedankan*, a thought experiment, why would Erwin Schrödinger pick a *cat* to hypothetically lock in a box and put in peril? It's not like there aren't plenty of other critters, like cockroaches, flies and mosquitoes, that would have made for a better fit, both literally and figuratively.

"It seemed clear to me that Schrödinger bore a passive-aggressive hostility towards felines. And what a silly choice, as well, for an *observer effect* experiment. Because who is a more focused observer than a cat? I felt that it was *more* than time to give a voice to the cat jammed in the deadly box, and to turn the tables in a duel of observer one-up-manship."

Zurich, 1935.
Mieze flattens her ears to her skull and thrashes her tail about in the manner of irritated cats everywhere. She opens her jaws so that she can smell with the

86

inside of her mouth, a motion humans take for nervous panting.

Humans, who think they know so much. Who know so little.

Mieze needs the extra olfactory sense to track her surroundings in the airtight, light-tight box, where even *her* enormous, luminous golden eyes cannot see.

But there are many ways of seeing. Many ways of observing.

Eye-blind inside the box, Mieze still knows her surroundings well. She's been here before. She's endured many sessions in this container.

As soon as her human pet, Felicie, leaves for school, Felicie's father, the great Herr Professor Erwin Schrödinger, is prone to pop Mieze in the box.

With the sensitive organs in her oral tissues, Mieze breathes in the smell of the sweet-honey heavy-lead walls of her prison; the acid metal taste and tick of the Geiger counter; the slick glassine odor of the bottle containing and masking, for now, the cyanide gas; the wood and steel of the trip-hammer poised to crash down on the cyanide bottle.

But even more than these, Mieze tastes/smells/observes/*knows* the pulse of electrons and trembling of nuclei in the little case that contains the radioactive isotope. This smaller box is surrounded by a cage to prevent her from dislodging it in the fit of fear or fury that Herr Erwin seems to expect of her. Does Herr Erwin think she hasn't noticed that he hasn't similarly secured the bottle of cyanide?

Well, that's the crux of the matter, isn't it? Not the great scientific experiment, the one Herr Erwin's friend, the renowned Doktor Einstein, called the "prettiest way" to show that the wave representation of matter is an incomplete representation of reality.

No, the true reality, the *real* representation of reality, is that Herr Erwin, father Mieze's beloved Felicie, detests cats.

So if Mieze, in the process of this to-be-famous experiment, should inadvertently bump into the cyanide instead of waiting for the statistical judgment of nuclei, what will Herr Erwin say? He will say, "I am a Swiss scientist. I am not responsible for the non-precision of felines."

Yet for all the innocence Mieze knows Herr Erwin would profess, she notices how gingerly he lifts the lid at the end of each experiment, the gloves he has donned, the air-filter mask he wears over nose and mouth.

In spite of her anger, Mieze is drawn to and fascinated by the cage around the box of radioactive matter. It reminds her of the cage that secures Felicie's brother's white mice and the wire prison that confines Felicie's mother's canary.

Inside *this* cell too, the atomic particles tremble, hop and spin, watching her watch them. Just like the mice and the bird. Sometimes (Mieze cannot help herself) she feels one paw curling out towards the caged box. Her hindquarters begin their rhythmic pre-pounce twitch.

At these moments she sympathizes briefly with Herr Erwin Schrödinger. Is this not the same twitch she has observed in him as he sets up his experiments?

When he pounces upon and captures the elusive, fluttering bits of knowledge, she has seen in him the sharp spark of the thrill of a successful hunt. She believes he may even experience a brief, atavistic sensation as of soft fur or feathers against the inside of his mouth; a rush of the sweet warmth of blood.

But after a while of such conjecture Mieze grows bored and tired and wishes she could sleep. Then she again becomes irritated with Herr Erwin. She is not stupid. If she dozes, if she suspends her observations, she could die.

At some point in the time she spends in here, Herr Erwin Schrödinger believes there is a fifty percent chance (in *his* mind, at least) that one of the nuclei in the case will decay and trigger the Geiger counter, causing the hammer to descend on the bottle containing the cyanide. Herr Erwin lives for a brief moment's delusion of immortality and omnipotence. He hypothesizes that as long as *he* does not open the box that Mieze is neither dead nor alive. Or she is both. During that indeterminate moment he believes himself to be her deity—that it is his paltry act of lifting the lid that determines her survival.

Yet Mieze has noticed that he has at times left her in the box far longer than necessary to make this determination. At first she thought he might have lost track of the time in his addictive immersion into godhood. Later she accepted the possibility that his hatred of cats might be stronger than his egomania. If he "forgot" and left her in the box long enough, she would suffocate. Then he would say, "I am a Swiss *physicist*. What would I know of feline lung capacity and oxygen requirements?"

So the moment he places her in the enclosure, Mieze shallows her breathing, shuns the desire to sleep.

Poor Herr Erwin, Mieze thinks. He congratulates himself on his scientific prowess, yet he lacks the most rudimentary observational skills. Take, as an example, how he initiates this experiment. Anyone who observes cats for the briefest length of time knows that to entice a cat into a box, one has only to leave it invitingly open. The cat's own scientific fervor (mislabeled by humans as mere curiosity) will lead it unerringly to investigate.

Yet time and time again, Herr Erwin—ignorant, sadistic, and completely untalented—has picked her up and jammed her into this container. Always with the same results. It is her only satisfaction, she thinks as she licks his blood from between her claws.

No, Herr Professor Erwin Schrödinger sees and understands nothing. Even the mice and the canary know more than he. Even *they* would be capable of scrutinizing the subatomic particles studying them and be able to control the atomic assassins with their own watching. Creatures, being more intelligent than men, know that all the games of life and death, existence and non-existence, are determined by one-upmanship in observation. The cat sits and waits at the mousehole. The mouse sits and waits on the other side. Each by its watching determines the other's reality.

Sad, pathetic Herr Erwin does not understand how much his own existence is determined by the watchful vigilance of cats, of small birds and rodents, even of atomic particles—all watching *him*. Herr Erwin, who neither sees nor tastes/smells/observes the imprisoning box of his own reality.

Mieze yawns. She wishes the canary or one of the mice were here instead. Stalemating nuclei is too easy. She's had plenty of time, too much time, to think of all the ramifications of her situation.

Oh yes, yes, she knows that by imposing her will to live that in a parallel reality another Mieze (she assumes a sub-intelligent version of herself) is dying. But Mieze is pragmatic. She is only concerned with her consciousness continuing along this particular lifeline.

She's imagined so many other possibilities, all of which she knows must be happening at this very moment in an "else-when." In another universe Herr Erwin's daughter is not called Felicie and does not like cats. There Mieze chose to be mistress to a dairyman's family. She lives on cream by a warm hearth.

In other continuums, Herr Erwin:

Has only sons, no daughters, and kidnaps his feline victims from alleys.

Is married, but has no children.

Is not married and has no children.

Only *proposes* the experiment as an idea, leaving others to follow through with it, if they will. But he doesn't fool the cats in that reality for an instant. After all, if he truly meant no malice, why didn't he suggest another animal for the experiment? Say, for example, a dog?

Mieze conjectures other, earlier realities she knows must exist. A continuum where before he receives his doctorate in 1910, Herr Erwin Schrödinger is drummed out of the university for a sexual scandal involving a middle-aged whore, a baron's wife and daughter, and copious amounts of cherry strudel.

Whole universes where at the age of eight young master Erwin trips over a black cat while on his way to school and is run over by a passing carriage, his skull crushed!

But still, Mieze considers, later would not be too late. She meditates on a universe where Herr Professor Erwin Schrödinger—woefully ignorant of the extent to which his very existence depends on the adroit observation of certain four-legged adepts—mysteriously disappears after a hard day of experimenting in his lab. His dear little daughter Felicie comes by to see him after her lessons, discovers him gone and in the nick of time rescues her beloved, golden-eyed silver tabby from a diabolical box.

Mieze lingers over the potential of this universe. She likes it. A great deal. Yes, it will do nicely.

After all, she has held back from meddling up until now. She has endured session after session in this box, thinking with a softened heart of Felicie, who slips her morsels of chicken livers; who knows how to sleep in just the right alignment of curves for ideal cat nestling. Mieze *does* know the anguish Felicie would suffer if anything should happen to her father, Herr Erwin, who the child believes to be perfect.

Yet Herr Erwin cares not a whit for the grief that *Mieze's* death would cause Felicie. How heartbroken Felicie would be to discover what a monster her father truly was. Far better to save the child that trauma.

Mieze stretches in the confines of the box. It is decided. She cannot be like the mice and the canary, even if she wished it. She is an observer extraordinaire—a hunter far superior to Herr Erwin. Which means she has been patient. But a cat can be patient *too* long.

A deep voluptuous purr fills Mieze's throat. The moment has come. It is time to open the box on Herr Professor Erwin Schrödinger.

GUARDIANS
George R. R. Martin

George R.R. Martin is best known today for his epic fantasy series "A Song of Ice and Fire," which began with *A Game of Thrones* in 1996. Before that, he was already a multi-award-winning science fiction and horror writer, having won Hugo Awards, Nebula Awards, Locus Awards, the Bram Stoker Award, and the World Fantasy award for his work. His earlier novels range from science fiction, with *Dying of the Light* and science fantasy *Windhaven* (with Lisa Tuttle), to the historical vampire novel *Fevre Dream*, and the rock n roll apocalyptic novel *Armageddon Rag*, all written between 1977 and 1983.

Martin became story editor for *The New Twilight Zone* in 1986 and later was Executive Story Consultant for the television series *Beauty and the Beast*, on which he worked for several years. He also helped create and edit the "Wild Cards" shared world series of anthologies in 1987, which continue to be published today.

"Guardians" is one of a series of darkly comic science fiction space adventures about a cat-loving trader who sells his services as he travels the galaxy. Martin likes cats, and has said that Dax, Tuf's companion in most of the stories, was actually a cat he owned back in the 70s, around the time he started writing the Tuf stories. A picture of the cat appears on Martin's website.

Haviland Tuf thought the Six Worlds Bio-Agricultural Exhibition a great disappointment.

He had spent a long wearying day on Brazelourn, trooping through the cavernous exhibition halls, pausing now and then to give a cursory inspection to a new grain hybrid or a genetically improved insect. Although the *Ark's* cell library held cloning material for literally millions of plant and animal species from an uncounted number of worlds, Haviland Tuf was nonetheless always alert for any opportunity to expand his stock-in-trade.

But few of the displays on Brazelourn seemed especially promising, and as the hours passed Tuf grew bored and uncomfortable in the jostling, indifferent crowds. People swarmed everywhere—Vagabonder tunnel-farmers in deep maroon furs, plumed and perfumed Areeni landlords, somber nightsiders and brightly garbed evernoons from New Janus, and a plethora of the native Brazeleen. All of them made excessive noise and favored Tuf with curious stares as he passed among them. Some even brushed up against him, bringing a frown to his long face.

Ultimately, seeking escape from the throngs, Tuf decided he was hungry. He pressed his way through the fairgoers with dignified distaste, and emerged from the vaulting five-story Ptolan Exhibit Hall. Outside, hundreds of vendors had set up booths between the great buildings. The man selling pop-onion pies seemed least busy of those nearby, and Tuf determined that a pop-onion pie was the very thing he craved.

"Sir," he said to the vendor, "I would have a pie."

The pieman was round and pink and wore a greasy apron. He opened his hotbox, reached in with a gloved hand, and extracted a hot pie. When he pushed it across the counter at Tuf, he stared. "Oh," he said, "you're a big one."

Indeed, sir," said Haviland Tuf. He picked up the pie and bit into it impassively.

"You're an offworlder," the pieman observed. "Not from no place nearby, neither."

Tuf finished his pie in three neat bites, and cleaned his greasy fingers on a napkin. "You belabor the obvious, sir," he said. He held up a long, calloused finger. "Another," he said.

Rebuffed, the vendor fetched out another pie without further observations, letting Tuf eat in relative peace. As he savored the flaky crust and tartness within, Tuf studied the milling fairgoers, the rows of vendors' booths, and the five great halls that loomed over the landscape. When he had done eating, he turned back to the pieman, his face as blank as ever. "Sir, if you will, a question."

"What's that?" the other said gruffly.

"I see five exhibition halls," said Haviland Tuf. "I have visited each in turn." He pointed. "Brazelourn, Vale Areen, New Janus, Vagabond, and here Ptola." Tuf folded his hands together neatly atop his bulging stomach. "Five, sir. Five halls, five worlds. No doubt, being a stranger as I am, I am unfamiliar with some subtle point of local usage, yet I am perplexed. In those regions where I have heretofore traveled, a gathering calling itself the Six Worlds Bio-Agricultural Exhibition might be expected to include exhibits from six worlds. Plainly that is not the case here. Perhaps you might enlighten me as to why?"

"No one came from Namor."

"Indeed," said Haviland Tuf.

"On account of the troubles," the vendor added.

"All is made clear," said Tuf. "Or, if not all, at least a portion. Perhaps you would care to serve me another pie, and explain to me the nature of these troubles. I am nothing if not curious, sir. It is my great vice, I fear."

The pieman slipped on his glove again and opened the hotbox. "You know what they say. Curiosity makes you hungry."

"Indeed," said Tuf. "I must admit I have never heard them say that before."

The man frowned. "No, I got it wrong. Hunger makes you curious, that's what it is. Don't matter. My pies will fill you up."

"Ah," said Tuf. He took up the pie. "Please proceed."

So the pie-seller told him, at great rambling length, about the troubles on the world Namor. "So you can see," he finally concluded, "why they didn't come, with all this going on. Not much to exhibit."

"Of course," said Haviland Tuf, dabbing his lips. "Sea monsters can be most vexing."

Namor was a dark green world, moonless and solitary, banded by wispy golden clouds. The *Ark* shuddered out of drive and settled ponderously into orbit around it. In the long, narrow communications room, Haviland Tuf moved from seat to seat, studying the planet on a dozen of the room's hundred viewscreens. Three small grey kittens kept him company, bounding across the consoles, pausing only to slap at each other. Tuf paid them no mind.

A water world, Namor had only one landmass decently large enough to be seen from orbit, and that none too large. But magnification revealed thousands of islands scattered in long, crescent-shaped archipelagoes across the deep green seas, earthen jewels strewn throughout the oceans. Other screens showed the lights of dozens of cities and towns on the nightside, and pulsing dots of energy outlay where settlements sat in sunlight.

Tuf looked at it all, and then seated himself, flicked on another console, and began to play a war game with the computer. A kitten bounded up into his lap and went to sleep. He was careful not to disturb it. Some time later, a second kitten vaulted up and pounced on it, and they began to tussle. Tuf brushed them to the floor.

It took longer than even Tuf had anticipated, but finally the challenge came, as he had known it would. "*Ship in orbit,*" came the demand, "ship in orbit, this is Namor Control. State your name and business. State your name and business, please. Interceptors have been dispatched. State your name and business."

The transmission was coming from the chief landmass. The *Ark* tapped into it. At the same time, it found the ship that was moving toward them—there was only one—and flashed it on another screen.

"I am the *Ark*," Haviland Tuf told Namor Control.

Namor Control was a round-faced woman with close-cropped brown hair, sitting at a console and wearing a deep green uniform with golden piping. She frowned, her eyes flicking to the side, no doubt to a superior or another console. "*Ark,*" she said, "state your homeworld. State your homeworld and your business, please."

The other ship had opened communications with the planet, the computer indicated. Two more viewscreens lit up. One showed a slender young woman with a large, crooked nose on a ship's bridge, the other an elderly man before a console. They both wore green uniforms, and they were conversing animatedly in code. It took the computer less than a minute to break it, so Tuf could listen in. "...damned if I know what it is," the woman on the ship was saying. "There's never been a ship that big. My God, just look at it. Are you getting all this? Has it answered?"

"*Ark*," the round-faced woman was still saying, "state your homeworld and your business, please. This is Namor Control."

Haviland Tuf cut into the other conversation, to talk to all three of them simultaneously. "This is the *Ark*," he said. "I have no homeworld, sirs. My intentions are purely peaceful—trade and consultation. I learned of your tragic difficulties, and moved by your plight, I have come to offer you my services."

The woman on the ship looked startled. "What are *you*..." she started. The man was equally nonplussed, but he said nothing, only gaped open-mouthed at Tuf's blank white visage.

"This is Namor Control, *Ark*," said the round-faced woman. "We are closed to trade. Repeat, we are closed to trade. We are under martial law here."

By then the slender woman on the ship had composed herself. "*Ark*, this is Guardian Kefira Qay, commanding NGS *Sunrazor*. We are armed, *Ark*. Explain yourself. You are a thousand times larger than any trader I have ever seen, *Ark*. Explain yourself or be fired upon."

"Indeed," said Haviland Tuf. "Threats will avail you little, Guardian. I am most sorely vexed. I have come all this long way from Brazelourn to offer you my aid and solace, and you meet me with threats and hostility." A kitten leapt up into his lap. Tuf scooped it up with a huge white hand, and deposited it on the console in front of him, where the viewer would pick it up. He gazed down at it sorrowfully. "There is no trust left in humanity," he said to the kitten.

"Hold your fire, *Sunrazor*," said the elderly man. "*Ark*, if your intentions are truly peaceful, explain yourself. What are you? We are hard-pressed here, *Ark*, and Namor is a small, undeveloped world. We have never seen your like before. Explain yourself."

Tuf stroked the kitten. "Always I must truckle to suspicion," he told it. "They are fortunate that I am so kind-hearted, or else I would simply depart and leave them to their fate." He looked up, straight into the viewer. "Sir," he said. "I am the *Ark*. I am Haviland Tuf, captain and master here, crew entire. You are troubled by great monsters from the depths of your seas, I have been told. Very well. I shall rid you of them."

"*Ark*, this is *Sunrazor*. How do you propose doing that?"

"The *Ark* is a seedship of the Ecological Engineering Corps," said Haviland Tuf with stiff formality. "I am an ecological engineer and a specialist in biological warfare."

"Impossible," said the old man. "The EEC was wiped out a thousand years ago, along with the Federal Empire. None of their seedships remain."

"How distressing." said Haviland Tuf. "Here I sit in an illusion. No doubt, now that you have told me my ship does not exist, I shall sink right through it and plunge into your atmosphere, where I shall burn up as I fall."

"Guardian," said Kefira Qay from the *Sunrazor*, "these seedships may indeed no longer exist, but I am fast closing on something that my scopes tell me is almost thirty kilometers long. It does not appear to be an illusion."

"I am not yet falling," admitted Haviland Tuf.

"Can you truly help us?" asked the round-faced woman at Namor Control.

"Why must I always be doubted?" Tuf asked the small grey kitten.

"Lord Guardian, we must give him the chance to prove what he says," insisted Namor Control.

Tuf looked up. "Threatened, insulted, and doubted as I have been, nonetheless my empathy for your situation bids me to persist. Perhaps I might suggest that *Sunrazor* dock with me, so to speak. Guardian Qay may come aboard and join me for an evening meal, while we converse. Surely your suspicions cannot extend to mere conversation, that most civilized of human pastimes."

The three Guardians conferred hurriedly with each other and with a person or persons offscreen, while Haviland Tuf sat back and toyed with the kitten. "I shall name you Suspicion," he said to it, "to commemorate my reception here. Your siblings shall be Doubt, Hostility, Ingratitude and Foolishness."

"We accept your proposal, Haviland Tuf," said Guardian Kefira Qay from the bridge of the *Sunrazor*. "Prepare to be boarded."

"Indeed," said Tuf. "Do you like mushrooms?"

The shuttle deck of the *Ark* was as large as the landing field of a major starport, and seemed almost a junkyard for derelict space craft. The *Ark*'s own shuttles stood trim in their launch berths, five identical black ships with rakish lines and stubby triangular wings angling back, designed for atmospheric flight and still in good repair. Other craft were less impressive. A teardrop-shaped trading vessel from Avalon squatted wearily on three extended landing legs, next to a driveshift courier scored by battle, and Karaleo lionboat whose ornate trim was largely gone. Elsewhere stood vessels of stranger, more alien design.

Above, the great dome cracked into a hundred pie-wedge segments, and drew back to reveal a small yellow sun surrounded by stars, and a dull green manta-shaped ship of about the same size as one of Tuf's shuttles. The *Sunrazor* settled, and the dome closed behind it. When the stars had been blotted out again, atmosphere came swirling back in to the deck, and Haviland Tuf arrived soon after.

Kefira Qay emerged from her ship with her lips set sternly beneath her big, crooked nose, but no amount of control could quite conceal the awe in her eyes. Two armed men in golden coveralls trimmed with green followed her.

Haviland Tuf drove up to them in an open three-wheeled cart. "I am afraid that my dinner invitation was only for one, Guardian Qay," he said when he saw her escort. "I regret any misunderstanding, yet I must insist."

"Very well," she said. She turned to her guard. "Wait with the others. You have your orders." When she got in next to Tuf she told him, "The *Sunrazor* will tear your ship apart if I am not returned safely within two standard hours."

Haviland Tuf blinked at her. "Dreadful," he said. "Everywhere my warmth and hospitality is met with mistrust and violence." He set the vehicle into motion.

They drove in silence through a maze of interconnected rooms and corridors, and finally entered a huge shadowy shaft that seemed to extend the full length of the ship in both directions. Transparent vats of a hundred different sizes covered walls and ceiling as far as the eye could see, most empty and dusty, a few filled with colored liquids in which half-seen shapes stirred feebly. There was no sound but a wet, viscous dripping somewhere off behind them. Kefira Qay studied everything and said nothing. They went at least three kilometers down the great shaft, until Tuf veered off into a blank wall that dilated before them. Shortly thereafter they parked and dismounted.

A sumptuous meal had been laid out in the small, spartan dining chamber to which Tuf escorted the Guardian Kefira Qay. They began with iced soup, sweet and piquant and black as coal, followed by neograss salads with a gingery topping. The main course was a breaded mushroom top full as large as the plate on which it was served, surrounded by a dozen different sorts of vegetables in individual sauces. The Guardian ate with great relish.

"It would appear you find my humble fare to your taste," observed Haviland Tuf.

"I haven't had a good meal in longer than I care to admit," replied Kefira Qay. "On Namor, we have always depended on the sea for our sustenance. Normally it is bountiful, but since our troubles began…" She lifted a forkful of dark, misshapen vegetables in a yellow-brown sauce. "What am I eating? It's delightful."

"Rhiannese sinners' root, in a mustard sauce," Haviland Tuf said.

Qay swallowed and set down her fork. "But Rhiannon is so far, how do you…" She stopped.

"Of course," Tuf said, steepling his fingers beneath his chin as he watched her face. "All this provender derives from the *Ark*, though originally it might be traced back to a dozen different worlds. Would you like more spiced milk?"

"No," she muttered. She gazed at the empty plates. "You weren't lying, then. You are what you claim, and this is a seedship of the… what did you call them?"

"The Ecological Engineering Corps, of the long-defunct Federal Empire. Their ships were few in number, and all but one destroyed by the vicissitudes of war. The *Ark* alone survived, derelict for a millennium. The details need not concern you. Suffice it to say that I found it, and made it functional."

"You *found* it?"

"I believe I just said as much, in those very same words. Kindly pay attention. I am not partial to repeating myself. Before finding the *Ark*, I made a humble living from trade. My former ship is still on the landing deck. Perhaps you chanced to see it."

"Then you're really just a trader."

"Please!" said Tuf with indignation. "I am an ecological engineer. The *Ark* can remake whole planets, Guardian. True, I am but one man, alone, when once this ship was crewed by two hundred, and I do lack the extensive formal training such as was given centuries ago to those who wore the golden theta, the sigil of the Ecological Engineers. Yet, in my own small way, I contrive to muddle through. If Namor would care to avail itself of my services, I have no doubt that I can help you."

"Why?" the slender Guardian asked warily. "Why are you so anxious to help us?"

Haviland Tuf spread his big white hands helplessly. "I know, I might appear a fool. I cannot help myself. I am a humanitarian by nature, much moved by hardship and suffering. I could no more abandon your people, beset as they are, than I could harm one of my cats. The Ecological Engineers were made of sterner stuff, I fear, but I am helpless to change my sentimental nature. So here I sit before you, prepared to do my best."

"You want nothing?"

"I shall labor without recompense," said Tuf. "Of course, I will have operating expenses. I must charge a small fee to offset them. Say, three million standards. Do you think that fair?"

"Fair," she said sarcastically. "Fairly high, I'd say. There have been others like you, Tuf—arms merchants and soldiers of fortune who have come to grow rich off our misery."

"Guardian," said Tuf, reproachfully, "you do me grievous wrong. I take little for myself. The *Ark* is so large, so costly. Perhaps two million standards would suffice? I cannot believe you would grudge me this pittance. Is your world worth less?"

Kefira Qay sighed, a tired look etched on her narrow face. "No," she admitted. "Not if you can do all you promise. Of course, we are not a rich world. I will have to consult my superiors. This is not my decision alone." She stood up abruptly. "Your communications facilities?"

"Through the door and left down the blue corridor. The fifth door on the right." Tuf rose with ponderous dignity, and began cleaning up as she left.

When the Guardian returned he had opened a decanter of liquor, vividly scarlet, and was stroking a black-and-white cat who had made herself at home on the table. "You're hired, Tuf," said Kefira Qay, seating herself. "Two million standards. *After* you win this war."

"Agreed," said Tuf. "Let us discuss your situation over glasses of this delightful beverage."

"Alcoholic?"

"Mildly narcotic."

"A Guardian uses no stimulants or depressants. We are a fighting guild. Substances like that pollute the body and slow the reflexes. A Guardian must be vigilant. We guard and protect."

"Laudable," said Haviland Tuf. He filled his own glass.

"*Sunrazor* is wasted here. It has been recalled by Namor Control. We need its combat capabilities below."

"I shall expedite its departure, then. And yourself?"

"I have been detached," she said, wrinkling up her face. "We are standing by with data on the situation below. I am to help brief you, and act as your liaison officer."

The water was calm, a tranquil green mirror from horizon to horizon.

It was a hot day. Bright yellow sunlight poured down through a thin bank of gilded clouds. The ship rested still on the water, its metallic sides flashing silver-blue, its open deck a small island of activity in an ocean of peace. Men and women small as insects worked the dredges and nets, bare-chested in the heat. A great claw full of mud and weeds emerged from the water, dripping, and was sluiced down an open hatchway. Elsewhere bins of huge milky jellyfish baked in the sun.

Suddenly there was agitation. For no apparent reason, people began to run. Others stopped what they were doing and looked around, confused. Still others worked on, oblivious. The great metal claw, open and empty now, swung back out over the water and submerged again, even as another one rose on the far side of the ship. More people were running. Two men collided and went down.

Then the first tentacle came curling up from beneath the ship.

It rose and rose. It was longer than the dredging claws. Where it emerged from the dark green sea, it looked as thick as a big man's torso. It tapered to the size of an arm. The tentacle was white, a soft slimy sort of white. All along its underside were vivid pink circles big as dinner plates, circles that writhed and pulsed as the tentacle curled over and about the huge farming ship. The end of the tentacle split into a rat's nest of smaller tentacles, dark and restless as snakes.

Up and up it went, and then over and down, pinioning the ship. Something moved on the other side, something pale stirring beneath all that green, and the second tentacle emerged. Then a third, and a fourth. One wrestled with a dredging claw. Another had the remains of a net draped all about it, like a veil, which didn't seem to hinder it. Now all the people were running—all but those the tentacles had found. One of them had curled itself around a woman with an axe. She hacked at it wildly, thrashing in the pale embrace, until her back arched and suddenly she fell still. The tentacle dropped her, white fluid pulsing feebly from the gashes she had left, and seized someone else.

Twenty tentacles had attached themselves when the ship abruptly listed to starboard. Survivors slid across the deck and into the sea. The ship tilted more and more. Something was pushing it over, pulling it down. Water sloshed across the side, and into the open hatchways. Then the ship began to break up.

Haviland Tuf stopped the projection, and held the image on the large viewscreen: the green sea and golden sun, the shattered vessel, the pale embracing tentacles. "This was the first attack?" he asked.

"Yes and no," replied Kefira Qay. "Prior to this, one other harvester and two passenger hydrofoils had vanished mysteriously. We were investigating, but we did not know the cause. In this case, a news crew happened to be on the site, making a recording for an educational broadcast. They got more than they bargained for."

"Indeed," said Tuf.

"They were airborne, in a skimmer. The broadcast that night almost caused a panic. But it was not until the next ship went down that things began to get truly serious. That was when the Guardians began to realize the full extent of the problem."

Haviland stared up at the viewscreen, his heavy face impassive, expressionless, his hands resting on the console. A black-and-white kitten began to bat at his fingers. "Away, Foolishness," he said, depositing the kitten gently on the floor.

"Enlarge a section of one of the tentacles," suggested the Guardian beside him.

Silently, Tuf did as she bid him. A second screen lit up, showing a grainy close-up of a great pale rope of tissue arching over the deck.

"Take a good look at one of the suckers," said Qay. "The pink areas, there, you see?"

"The third one from the end is dark within. And it appears to have teeth."

"Yes," said Kefira Qay. "All of them do. The outer lips of those stickers are a kind of hard, fleshy flange. Slapped down, they spread and create a vacuum seal of sorts, virtually impossible to tear loose. But each of them is a mouth, too. Within the flange is a soft pink flap that falls back, and then the teeth come sliding out—a triple row of them, serrated, and sharper than you'd think. Now move down to the tendrils at the end, if you would."

Tuf touched the console, and put another magnification up on a third screen, bringing the twisting snakes into easy view.

"Eyes," said Kefira Qay. "At the end of every one of those tendrils. Twenty eyes. The tentacles don't need to grope around blindly. They can *see* what they are doing."

"Fascinating," said Haviland Tuf. "What lies beneath the water? The source of these terrible arms?"

"There are cross-sections and photographs of dead specimens later on, as well as some computer simulations. Most of the specimens we took were quite badly mangled. The main body of the thing is sort of an inverted cup, like a half-inflated bladder, surrounded by a great ring of bone and muscle that anchors these tentacles. The bladder fills and empties with water to enable the creature to rise to the surface, or descend far below—the submarine principle. By itself it doesn't weigh much, although it is amazingly strong. What it does, it empties its bladder to rise to the surface, grabs hold, and then begins to fill again. The capacity of the bladder is astounding, and as you can see, the creature is *huge*. If need be, it can even force water *up* those tentacles and out of its mouths, in order to flood the vessel and speed things along. So those tentacles are arms, mouths, eyes, and living hoses all at once."

"And you say that your people had no knowledge of such creatures until this attack?"

"Right. A cousin of this thing, the Namorian man-of-war, was well-known in the early days of colonization. It was sort of a cross between a jellyfish and an octopus, with twenty arms. Many native species are built along the same lines—a central bladder, or body, or shell, or what have you, with twenty legs or tendrils or tentacles in a ring around it. The men-of-war were carnivores, much like this monster, although they had a ring of eyes on the central body instead of at the end of the tentacles. The arms couldn't function as hoses, either. And they were much smaller—about the size of a human. They bobbed about on the surface above the continental shelves, particularly above mud-pot beds, where fish were thick. Fish were their usual prey, although a few unwary swimmers met a bloody awful death in their embrace."

"Might I ask what became of them?" said Tuf.

"They were a nuisance. Their hunting grounds were the same areas we need-ed—shallows rich with fish and seagrass and waterfruit, over mud-pot beds and scrabbler runs full of chameleon-clams and bobbing freddies. Before we could harvest or farm safely, we had to pretty much clean out the men-of-war. We did. Oh, there are still a few around, but they are rare now."

"I see," said Haviland Tuf. "And this most formidable creature, this living sub-marine and ship-eater that plagues you so dreadfully, does it have a name?"

"The Namorian dreadnaught," said Kefira Qay. "When it first appeared, we theorized it was an inhabitant of the great deeps that had somehow wandered to the surface. Namor has been inhabited for barely a hundred standard years, after all. We have scarcely begun to explore the deeper regions of the seas, and we have little knowledge of the things that might live down there. But as more and more ships were attacked and sunk, it became obvious that we had an army of dreadnaughts to contend with."

"A navy," corrected Haviland Tuf.

Kefira Qay scowled. "Whatever. A *lot* of them, not one lost specimen. At that point the theory was that some unimaginable catastrophe had taken place deep under the ocean, driving forth this entire species."

"*You* give no credit to this theory," Tuf said.

"No one does. It's been disproved. The dreadnaughts wouldn't be able to withstand the pressures at those depths. So now we don't know where they came from." She made a face. "Only that they are here."

"Indeed," said Haviland Tuf. "No doubt you fought back."

"Certainly. A game but losing fight. Namor is a young planet, with neither the population nor the resources for the sort of struggle we have been plunged into. Three million Namorians are scattered across our seas, on more than seventeen thousand small islands. Another million huddle on New Atlantis, our single small continent. Most of our people are fisherfolk and sea-farmers. When this all began, the Guardians numbered barely fifty thousand. Our guild is descended from the crews of the ships who brought the colonists from Old Poseidon and

Aquarius here to Namor. We have always protected them, but before the coming of the dreadnaughts our task was simple. Our world was peaceful, with little real conflict. There was some ethnic rivalry between Poseidonites and Aquarians, but it was good-natured. The Guardians provided planetary defense, with *Sunrazor* and two similar craft, but most of our work was in fire and flood control, disaster relief, police work, that sort of thing. We had about a hundred armed hydrofoil patrol boats, and we used them for escort duty for a while, and inflicted some casualties, but they were really no match for the dreadnaughts. It soon became clear that there were more dreadnaughts than patrol boats, anyway."

"Nor do patrolboats reproduce, as I must assume these dreadnaughts do," Tuf said. Foolishness and Doubt were tussling in his lap.

"Exactly. Still, we tried. We dropped depth charges on them when we detected them below the sea, we torpedoed them when they came to the surface. We killed hundreds. But there were hundreds more, and every boat we lost was irreplaceable. Namor has no technological base to speak of. In better days, we imported what we needed from Brazelourn and Vale Areen. Our people believed in a simple life. The planet couldn't support industry anyway. It is poor in heavy metals and has almost no fossil fuel."

"How many Guardian patrolboats remain to you?" asked Haviland Tuf.

"Perhaps thirty. We dare not use them anymore. Within a year of the first attack, the dreadnaughts were in complete command of our sea lanes. All of the great harvesters were lost, hundreds of sea-farms had been abandoned or destroyed, half of the small fisherfolk were dead, and the other half huddled fearfully in port. Nothing human dared move on the seas of Namor."

"Your islands were isolated from one another?"

"Not quite," Kefira Qay replied. "The Guardians had twenty armed skimmers, and there were another hundred-odd skimmers and aircars in private hands. We commandeered them, armed them. We also had our airships. Skimmers and aircars are difficult and expensive to maintain here. Parts are hard to come by, and we have few trained techs, so most of the air traffic before the troubles was carried by airships—solar-powered, helium-filled, large. There was quite a sizable fleet, as many as a thousand. The airships took over the provisioning of some of the small islands, where starvation was a very real threat. Other airships, as well as the Guardian skimmers, carried on the fight. We dumped chemicals, poisons, explosives and such from the safety of the air and destroyed thousands of dreadnaughts, although the cost was frightful. They clustered thickest about our best fishing grounds and mud-pot beds, so we were forced to blow up and poison the very areas we needed most. Still, we had no choice. For a time, we thought we were winning the fight. A few fishing boats even put out and returned safely, with a Guardian skimmer flying escort."

"Obviously, this was not the ultimate result of the conflict," said Haviland Tuf, "or we would not be sitting here talking." Doubt batted Foolishness soundly across the head, and the smaller kitten fell off Tuf's knee to the floor. Tuf bent and scooped him up. "Here," he said, handing him to Kefira Qay, "hold him, if you please. Their small war is distracting me from your larger one."

"I—why, of course." The Guardian took the small black-and-white kitten in hand gingerly. He fit snugly into her palm. "What is it?" she asked.

"A cat," said Tuf. "He will jump out of your hand if you continue to hold him as if he were a diseased fruit. Kindly put him in your lap. I assure you he is harmless."

Kefira Qay, appearing very uncertain, shook the kitten out of her hand onto her knees. Foolishness yowled, almost tumbling to the floor again before sinking his small claws into the fabric of her uniform. "Ow," said Kefira Qay. "It has talons."

"Claws," corrected Tuf. "Tiny and harmless."

"They aren't poisoned, are they?"

"I think not," said Tuf. "Stroke him, front to back. It will make him less agitated."

Kefira Qay touched the kitten's head uncertainly.

"Please," said Tuf. "I said *stroke,* not pat."

The Guardian began to pet the kitten. Instantly, Foolishness began to purr. She stopped and looked up in horror. "It's trembling," she said, "and making a noise."

"Such a response is considered favorable," Tuf assured her. "I beg you to continue your ministrations, and your briefing. If you will."

"Of course," said Qay. She resumed petting Foolishness, who settled down comfortably on her knee. "If you would go on to the next tape," she prompted.

Tuf wiped the stricken ship and the dreadnaught off the main screen. Another scene took their place—a winter's day, windy and chill by the look of it. The water below was dark and choppy, flecked with white foam as the wind pushed against it. A dreadnaught was afloat the unruly sea, its huge white tentacles extended all around it, giving it the look of some vast swollen flower bobbing on the waves. It reached up as they passed overhead, two arms with their writhing snakes lifting feebly from the water, but they were too far above to be in danger. They appeared to be in the gondola of some long silver airship, looking down through a glass-bottomed viewport, and as Tuf watched, the vantage point shifted and he saw that they were part of a convoy of three immense airships, cruising with stately indifference above the war-torn waters.

"The *Spirit of Aquarius,* the *Lyle D.,* and the *Skyshadow,*" said Kefira Qay, "on a relief mission to a small island grouping in the north where famine had been raging. They were going to evacuate the survivors and take them back to New Atlantis." Her voice was grim. "This record was made by a news crew on the *Skyshadow,* the only airship to survive. Watch."

On and on the airships sailed, invincible and serene. Then, just ahead of the silver-blue *Spirit of Aquarius,* there was motion in the water, something stirring beneath that dark green veil. Something big, but not a dreadnaught. It was dark, not pale. The water grew black and blacker in a great swelling patch, then bulged upward. A great ebony dome heaved into view and grew, like an island emerging from the depths, black and leathery and immense, and surrounded by twenty long black tentacles. Larger and higher it swelled, second by second, until it burst from the sea entirely. Its tentacles hung below it, dripping water, as it rose. Then they began to lift and spread. The thing was fully as large as the airship moving toward it. When they met, it was as if two vast leviathans of the sky had come together to mate. The black immensity settled atop the long silver-blue dirigible, its arms curling about in a deadly embrace. They watched the airship's outer skin tear asunder, and the helium cells rip and crumple. The Spirit of Aquarius twisted and buckled like a living thing, and shriveled in the black embrace of its lover. When it was over, the dark creature dropped the remains into the sea.

Tuf froze the image, staring with solemn regard at the small figures leaping from the doomed gondola.

"Another one got the *Lyle D.* on the way home," said Kefira Qay. "The *Skyshadow* survived to tell the story, but it never returned from its next mission. More than a hundred airships and twelve skimmers were lost in the first week the fire-balloons emerged."

"Fire-balloons?" queried Haviland Tuf. He stroked Doubt, who was sitting on his console. "I saw no fire."

"The name was coined the first time we destroyed one of the accursed things. A Guardian skimmer put a round of explosive shot into it, and it went up like a bomb, then sank, burning, into the sea. They are extremely inflammable; one laser burst, and they go up spectacularly."

"Hydrogen," said Haviland Tuf.

"Exactly," the Guardian confirmed. "We've never taken one whole, but we've puzzled them out from bits and pieces. The creatures can generate an electric current internally. They take on water, and perform a sort of biological electrolysis. The oxygen is vented into the water or the air, and helps push the things around. Air jets, so to speak. The hydrogen fills the balloon sacs and gives them lift. When they want to retreat to the water, they open a flap on top—see, up there—and all the gas escapes, so the fire-balloon drops back into the sea. The outer skin is leathery, very tough. They're slow, but clever. At times they hide in cloud banks and snatch unwary skimmers flying below. And we soon discovered, to our dismay, that they breed just as fast as the dreadnaughts."

"Most intriguing," said Haviland Tuf. "So, I might venture to suggest, with the emergence of these fire-balloons, you lost the sky as well as the sea."

"More or less," admitted Kefira Qay. "Our airships were simply too slow to risk. We tried to keep things going by sending them out in convoys, escorted by Guardian skimmers and aircars, but even that failed. The morning of the Fire Dawn… I was there, commanding a nine-gun skimmer… it was terrible…"

"Continue," said Tuf

"The Fire Dawn," she muttered bleakly. "We were… we had thirty airships, *thirty,* a great convoy, protected by a dozen armed skimmers. A long trip, from New Atlantis to the Broken Hand, a major island grouping. Near dawn on the second day, just as the east was turning red, the sea beneath us began to… seethe. Like a pot of soup that has begun to boil. It was *them,* venting oxygen and water, rising. Thousands of them, Tuf, thousands. The waters churned madly, and they rose, all those vast black shadows coming up at us, as far as the eye could see in all directions. We attacked with lasers, with explosive shells, with everything we had. It was like the sky itself was ablaze. All those things were bulging with hydrogen, and the air was rich and giddy with the oxygen they had vented. The Fire Dawn, we call it. It was terrible. Screaming everywhere, balloons burning, our airships crushed and falling around us, bodies afire. There were dreadnaughts waiting below, too. I saw them snatching swimmers who had fallen from the airships, those pale tentacles coiling around them and yanking them under. Four skimmers escaped from that battle. Four. Every airship was lost, with all hands."

"A grim tale," said Tuf.

Kefira Qay had a haunted look in her eyes. She was petting Foolishness with a blind rhythm, her lips pressed tightly together, her eyes fixed on the screen, where the first fire-balloon floated above the tumbling corpse of the *Spirit of Aquarius.* "Since then," she said at last, "life has been a continuing nightmare. We have lost our seas. On three-fourths of Namor, hunger and even starvation hold sway. Only New Atlantis still has surplus food, since only there is land-farming practiced extensively. The Guardians have continued to fight. The *Sunrazor* and our two other spacecraft have been pressed into service—bombing runs, clumping poison, evacuating some of the smaller islands. With aircars and fast skimmers, we have maintained a loose web of contact with the outer islands. And we have radio, of course. But we are barely hanging on. Within the last year, more than twenty islands have fallen silent. We sent patrols out to investigate in a half-dozen of those cases. Those that returned all reported the same things. Bodies everywhere, rotting in the sun. Buildings crushed and ruined. Scrabblers and crawling maggies feasting on the corpses. And on one island they found something else, something even more frightful. The island was Seastar. Almost forty thousand people lived there, and it was a major spaceport as well, before trade was cut off. It was a terrible shock when Seastar suddenly stopped broadcasting. Go to the next exhibit, Tuf. Go on."

Tuf pressed a series of lights on the console.

A dead thing was lying on a beach, rotting on indigo sands.

It was a still picture, this one, not a tape. Haviland Tuf and Guardian Kefira Qay had a long time to study the dead thing where it sprawled, rich and rotten. Around and about it was a litter of human corpses, lending it scale by their proximity. The dead thing was shaped like an inverted bowl, and it was as big as a house. Its leathery flesh, cracked and oozing pustulence now, was a mottled grey-green. Spread on the sand around it, like spokes from a central wheel, were the thing's appendages—ten twisted green tentacles, puckered with pinkish-white mouths and, alternately, ten limbs that looked stiff and hard and black, and were obviously jointed.

"*Legs,*" said Kefira Qay bitterly. "It was a walker, Tuf, before they killed it. We have only found that one specimen, but it was enough. We know why our islands fall silent now. They come from out of the sea, Tuf. Things like that. Larger, smaller, walking on ten legs like spiders and grabbing and eating with the other ten, the tentacles. The carapace is thick and tough. A single explosive shell or laser burst won't kill one of these the way it would a fire-balloon. So now you understand. First the sea, then the air, and now it has begun on the land as well. The *land*. They burst from the water in thousands, striding up onto the sand like some terrible tide. Two islands were overrun last week alone. They mean to wipe us from this planet. No doubt a few of us will survive on New Atlantis, in the high inland mountains, but it will be a cruel life and a short one. Until Namor throws something new at us, some new thing out of nightmare." Her voice had a wild edge of hysteria.

Haviland Tuf turned off his console, and the telescreens all went black. "Calm yourself, Guardian," he said, turning to face her. "Your fears are understandable but unnecessary. I appreciate your plight more fully now. A tragic one indeed, yet not hopeless."

"You still think you can help?" she said. "Alone? You and this ship? Oh, I'm not discouraging you, by any means. We'll grasp at any straw. But…"

"But you do not believe," Tuf said. A small sigh escaped his lips. "Doubt," he said to the grey kitten, hoisting him up in a huge white hand, "you are indeed well named." He shifted his gaze back to Kefira Qay. "I am a forgiving man, and you have been through many cruel hardships, so I shall take no notice of the casual way you belittle me and my abilities. Now, if you might excuse me, I have work to do. Your people have sent up a great many more detailed reports on these creatures, and on Namorian ecology in general. It is vital that I peruse these, in order to understand and analyze the situation. Thank you for your briefing."

Kefira Qay frowned, lifted Foolishness from her knee and set him on the ground, and stood up. "Very well," she said. "How soon will you be ready?"

"I cannot ascertain that with any degree of accuracy," Tuf replied, "until I have had a chance to run some simulations. Perhaps a day and we shall begin. Perhaps a month. Perhaps longer."

"If you take too long, you'll find it difficult to collect your two million," she snapped. "We'll all be dead."

"Indeed," said Tuf. "I shall strive to avoid that scenario. Now, if you would let me work. We shall converse again at dinner. I shall serve vegetable stew in the fashion of Anon, with plates of Thorite fire mushrooms to whet our appetites."

Qay sighed loudly. "Mushrooms again?" she complained. "We had stir-fried mushrooms and peppers for lunch, and crisped mushrooms in bitter cream for breakfast."

"I am fond of mushrooms," said Haviland Tuf.

"I am weary of mushrooms," said Kefira Qay. Foolishness rubbed up against her leg, and she frowned down at him. "Might I suggest some meat? Or seafood?" She looked wistful. "It has been years since I've had a mud-pot. I dream of it sometimes. Crack it open and pour butter inside, and spoon out the soft meat, you can't imagine how fine it was. Or sabrefin. Ah, I'd kill for a sabrefin on a bed of seagrass!"

Haviland Tuf looked stern. "We do not eat animals here," he said. He set to work, ignoring her, and Kefira Qay took her leave. Foolishness went bounding after her. "Appropriate," muttered Tuf, "indeed."

Four days and many mushrooms later, Kefira Qay began to pressure Haviland Tuf for results. "What are you *doing?*" she demanded over dinner. "When are you going to act? Every day you seclude yourself and every day conditions on Namor worsen. I spoke to Lord Guardian Harvan an hour ago, while you were off with your computers. Little Aquarius and the Dancing Sisters have been lost while you and I are up here dithering, Tuf."

"Dithering?" said Haviland Tuf. "Guardian, I do not dither. I have never dithered, nor do I intend to begin dithering now. I work. There is a great mass of information to digest."

Kara Qay snorted. "A great mass of mushrooms to digest, you mean," she said. She stood up, tipping Foolishness from her lap. The kitten and she had become boon companions of late. "Twelve thousand people lived on little Aquarius," she said, "and almost as many on the Dancing Sisters. Think of that while you're digesting, Tuf." She spun and stalked out of the room.

"Indeed," said Haviland Tuf. He returned his attention to his sweet-flower pie.

A week passed before they clashed again. "Well?" the Guardian demanded one day in the corridor, stepping in front of Tuf as he lumbered with great dignity down to his work room.

"Well," he repeated. "Good day, Guardian Qay."

"It is not a good day," she said querulously. "Namor Control tells me the Sunrise Islands are gone. Overrun. And a dozen skimmers lost defending them, along with all the ships drawn up in those harbors. What do you say to that?"

"Most tragic," replied Tuf. "Regrettable."

"When are you going to be ready?"

He gave a great shrug. "I cannot say. This is no simple task you have set me. A most complex problem. Complex. Yes, indeed, that is the very word. Perhaps I might even say mystifying. I assure you that Namor's sad plight has fully engaged my sympathies, however, and this problem has similarly engaged my intellect."

"That's all it is to you, Tuf, isn't it? A problem?"

Haviland Tuf frowned slightly, and folded his hands before him, resting them atop his bulging stomach. "A problem indeed," he said.

"No. It is not just a problem. This is no game we are playing. Real people are dying down there. Dying because the Guardians are not equal to their trust, and because you do nothing. *Nothing.*"

"Calm yourself. You have my assurance that I am laboring ceaselessly on your behalf. You must consider that my task is not so simple as yours. It is all very well and good to drop bombs on a dreadnaught, or fire shells into a fire-balloon and watch it burn. Yet these simple, quaint methods have availed you little, Guardian. Ecological engineering is a far more demanding business. I study the reports of your leaders, your marine biologists, your historians. I reflect and analyze. I devise various approaches, and run simulations on the *Ark*'s great computers. Sooner or later I shall find your answer."

"Sooner," said Kefira Qay, in a hard voice. "Namor wants results, and I agree. The Council of Guardians is impatient. Sooner, Tuf. Not later. I warn you." She stepped aside, and let him pass.

Kefira Qay spent the next week and a half avoiding Tuf as much as possible. She skipped dinner and scowled when she saw him in the corridors. Each day she repaired to the communications room, where she had long discussions with her superiors below, and kept up on all the latest news. It was bad. All the news was bad.

Finally, things came to a head. Pale-faced and furious, she stalked into the darkened chamber Tuf called his "war room," where she found him sitting before a bank of computer screens, watching red and blue lines chase each other across a grid. "*Tuf!*" she roared. He turned off the screen and swung to face her, batting away Ingratitude. Shrouded by shadows, he regarded her impassively. "The Council of Guardians has given me an order," she said.

"How fortunate for you," Tuf replied. "I know you have been growing restless of late from inactivity."

"The Council wants immediate action, Tuf. *Immediate.* Today. Do you understand?"

Tuf steepled his hands beneath his chin, almost in an attitude of prayer. "Must I tolerate not only hostility and impatience, but slurs on my intelligence as well? I understand all that needs understanding about your Guardians, I assure you. It is only the peculiar and perverse ecology of Namor that I do not understand. Until I have acquired that understanding, I cannot act."

"You *will* act," said Kefira Qay. Suddenly a laser pistol was in her hand, aimed at Tuf's broad paunch. "You will act now."

Haviland Tuf reacted not at all. "Violence," he said, in a voice of mild reproach. "Perhaps, before you burn a hole in me and thereby doom yourself and your world, you might give me the opportunity to explain?"

"Go on," she said. "I'll listen. For a little while."

"Excellent," said Haviland Tuf. "Guardian, something very odd is happening on Namor."

"You've noticed," she said drily. The laser did not move.

"Indeed. You are being destroyed by an infestation of creatures that we must, for want of a better term, collectively dub sea monsters. Three species have appeared, in less than half a dozen standard years. Each of these species is apparently new, or at least unknown. This strikes me as unlikely in the extreme. Your people have been on Namor for one hundred years, yet not until recently have you had any knowledge of these things you call dreadnaughts, fire-balloons, and walkers. It is almost as if some dark analogue of my *Ark* were waging biowar upon you, yet obviously that is not the case. New or old, these sea monsters are native to Namor, a product of local evolution. Their close relatives fill your seas—the mud-pots, the bobbing freddies, the jellydancers and men-of-war. So. Where does that leave us?"

"I don't know," said Kefira Qay.

"Nor do I," Tuf said. "Consider further. These sea monsters breed in vast numbers. The sea teems with them, they fill the air, they overrun populous islands. They kill. Yet they do not kill each other, nor do they seem to have any other natural enemies. The cruel checks of a normal ecosystem do not apply. I have studied the reports of your scientists with great interest. Much about these sea monsters is fascinating, but perhaps most intriguing is the fact that you know nothing about them except in their full adult form. Vast dreadnaughts prowl the seas and sink ships, monstrous fire-balloons swirl across your skies. Where, might I ask, are the little dreadnaughts, the baby balloons? Where indeed."

"Deep under the sea."

"Perhaps, Guardian, perhaps. You cannot say for certain, nor can I. These monsters are most formidable creatures, yet I have seen equally formidable predators on other worlds. They do not number in hundreds or thousands. Why? Ah, because the young, or the eggs, or the hatchlings, they are less formidable than the parents, and most die long before reaching their terrible maturity. This does not appear to happen on Namor. It does not appear to happen at all. What can it all mean? What indeed." Tuf shrugged. "I cannot say, but I work on, I think, I endeavor to solve the riddle of your overabundant sea."

Kefira Qay grimaced. "And meanwhile, we die. We die, and you don't care."

"I protest!" Tuf began.

"Silence," she said, waving the laser. "I'll talk now, you've given your speech. Today we lost contact with the Broken Hand. Forty-three islands, Tuf. I'm afraid to even think how many people. All gone now, in a single day. A few garbled radio transmissions, hysteria, and silence. And you sit and talk about riddles. No more. You *will* take action now. I insist. Or threaten, if you prefer. Later, we will solve the whys and hows of these things. For the moment, we will kill them, without pausing for questions."

"Once," said Haviland Tuf, "there was a world idyllic but for a single flaw—an insect the size of a dust mote. It was a harmless creature, but it was everywhere. It fed on the microscopic spores of a floating fungus. The folk of this world hated the tiny insect, which sometimes flew about in clouds so thick they obscured the sun. When citizens went outdoors, the insects would land on them by the thousands, covering their bodies with a living shroud. So a would-be ecological engineer proposed to solve their problem. From a distant world, he introduced another insect, larger, to prey on the living dust motes. The scheme worked admirably. The new insects multiplied and multiplied, having no natural enemies in this ecosystem, until they had entirely wiped out the native species. It was a great triumph. Unfortunately, there were unforeseen side effects. The invader, having destroyed one form of life, moved on to other, more beneficial sorts. Many native insects became extinct. The local analogue of bird life, deprived of its customary prey and unable to digest the alien bug, also suffered grievously. Plants were not pollinated as before. Whole forests and jungles changed and withered. And the spores of the fungus that had been the food of the original nuisance were left unchecked. The fungus grew everywhere—on buildings, on food crops, even on living animals. In short, the ecosystem was wrenched entirely askew. Today, should you visit, you would find a planet dead but for a terrible fungus. Such are the fruits of hasty action, with insufficient study. There are grave risks should one move without understanding."

"And certain destruction if one fails to move at all," Kefira Qay said stubbornly. "No, Tuf. You tell frightening tales, but we are a desperate people. The Guardians accept whatever risks there may be. I have my orders. Unless you do as I bid, I will use this." She nodded at her laser.

Haviland Tuf folded his arms. "If you use that," he said, "you will be very foolish. No doubt you could learn to operate the *Ark* in time. The task would take years, which by your own admission you do not have. I shall work on in your behalf, and forgive you your crude bluster and your threats, but I shall move only when I deem myself ready. I am an ecological engineer. I have my personal and professional integrity. And I must point out that, without my services, you are utterly without hope. Utterly. So, since you know this and I know this, let us dispense with further drama. You will not use that laser."

For a moment, Kefira Qay's face looked stricken. "You…" she said in confusion; the laser wavered just a bit. Then her look hardened once again. "You're wrong, Tuf," she said. "I will use it."

Haviland Tuf said nothing.

"Not on you," she said. "On your cats. I will kill one of them every day, until you take action." Her wrist moved slightly, so the laser was trained not on Tuf, but on the small form of Ingratitude, who was prowling hither and yon about the room, poking at shadows. "I will start with this one," the Guardian aid. "On the count of three."

Tuf's face was utterly without emotion. He stared.

"One," said Kefira Qay.

Tuf sat immobile.

"Two," she said.

Tuf frowned, and there were wrinkles in his chalk-white brow.

"Three," Qay blurted.

"No," Tuf said quickly. "Do not fire. I shall do as you insist. I can begin cloning within the hour."

The Guardian holstered her laser.

So Haviland Tuf went reluctantly to war.

On the first clay he sat in his war room before his great console, tight-lipped and quiet, turning dials and pressing glowing buttons and phantom holographic keys. Elsewhere on the *Ark*, murky liquids of many shades and colors spilled and gurgled into the empty vats along the shadowy main shaft, while specimens from the great cell Library were shifted and sprayed and manipulated by tiny waldoes as sensitive as the hands of a master surgeon. Tuf saw none of it. He remained at his post, starting one clone after another.

On the second day he did the same.

On the third day he rose and strolled slowly down the kilometers-long shaft where his creations had begun to grow, indistinct forms that stirred feebly or not at all in the tanks of translucent liquid. Some tanks were fully as large as the *Ark*'s shuttle deck, others as small as a fingernail. Haviland Tuf paused by each one, studied the dials and meters and glowing spyscopes with quiet intensity, and sometimes made small adjustments. By the end of the day he had progressed only half the length of the long, echoing row.

On the fourth day he completed his rounds.

On the fifth day he threw in the chronowarp. "Time is its slave," he told Kefira Qay when she asked him. "It can hold it slow, or bid it hurry. We shall make it run, so the warriors I breed can reach maturity more quickly than in nature."

On the sixth day he busied himself on the shuttle deck, modifying two of his shuttles to carry the creatures he was fashioning, adding tanks great and small and filling them with water.

On the morning of the seventh day he joined Kefira for breakfast and said, "Guardian, we are ready to begin."

She was surprised. "So soon?"

"Not all of my beasts have reached full maturity, but that is as it should be. Some are monstrous large, and must be transshipped before they have attained adult growth. The cloning shall continue, of course. We must establish our creatures in sufficient numbers so they will remain viable. Nonetheless, we are now at the stage where it is possible to begin seeding the seas of Namor."

"What is your strategy?" asked Kefira Qay.

Haviland Tuf pushed aside his plate and pursed his lips. "Such strategy as I have is crude and premature, Guardian, and based on insufficient knowledge. I take no responsibility for its success or failure. Your cruel threats have impelled me to unseemly haste."

"Nonetheless," she snapped. "What are you doing?"

Tuf folded his hands atop his stomach. "Biological weaponry, like other sorts of armament, comes in many forms and sizes. The best way to slay a human enemy is a single laser burst planted square in the center of the forehead. In biological terms, the analogue might be a suitable natural enemy or predator, or a species-specific pestilence. Lacking time, I have had no opportunity to devise such an economical solution.

"Other approaches are less satisfactory. I might introduce a disease that would cleanse your world of dreadnaughts, fire-balloons, and walkers, for example. Several likely candidates exist. Yet your sea monsters are close relatives of many other kinds of marine life, and those cousins and uncles would also suffer. My projections indicate that fully three-quarters of Namor's oceangoing life would be vulnerable to such an attack. Alternatively, I have at my disposal fast-breeding fungi and microscopic animals who would literally fill your seas and crowd out all other life. That choice too is unsatisfactory. Ultimately it would make Namor incapable of sustaining human life. To pursue my analogy of a moment ago, these methods are the biological equivalent of killing a single human enemy by exploding a low-yield thermonuclear device in the city in which he happens to reside. So I have ruled them out.

"Instead, I have opted for what might be termed a scattershot strategy, introducing many new species into your Namorian ecology in the hopes that some of them will prove effective natural enemies capable of winnowing the ranks of your sea monsters. Some of my warriors are great deadly beasts, formidable enough to prey even on your terrible dreadnaughts. Others are small and fleet, semi-social pack hunters who breed quickly. Still others are tiny things. I have hope that they will find and feed on your nightmare creatures in their younger, less potent stages, and thereby thin them out. So you see, I pursue many strategies. I toss down the entire deck rather than playing a single card. Given your bitter ultimatum, it is the only way to proceed." Tuf nodded at her. "I trust you will be satisfied, Guardian Qay."

She frowned and said nothing.

"If you are finished with that delightful sweet-mushroom porridge," Tuf said, "we might begin. I would not have you think that I was dragging my feet. You are a trained pilot, of course?"

"Yes," she snapped.

"Excellent!" Tuf exclaimed. "I shall instruct you in the peculiar idiosyncrasies of my shuttle craft, then. By this hour, they are already fully stocked for our first run. We shall make long low runs across your seas, and discharge our cargoes into your troubled waters. I shall fly the *Basilisk* above your northern hemisphere. You shall take the *Manticore* to the south. If this plan is acceptable, let us go over the routes I have planned for us." He rose with great dignity.

For the next twenty days, Haviland Tuf and Kefira Qay crisscrossed the dangerous skies of Namor in a painstaking grid pattern, seeding the seas. The Guardian flew her runs with elan. It felt good to be in action again, and she was filled with hope as well. The dreadnaughts and fire-balloons and walkers would have their own nightmares to contend with now—nightmares from half-a-hundred scattered worlds.

From Old Poseidon came vampire eels and nessies and floating tangles of web-weed, transparent and razor-sharp and deadly.

From Aquarius Tuf cloned black raveners, the swifter scarlet raveners, poisonous puff-puppies, and fragrant, carnivorous lady's bane.

From Jamison's World the vats summoned sand-dragons and dreerhants and a dozen kinds of brightly colored water snakes, large and small.

From Old Earth itself the cell library provided great white sharks, barracuda, giant squid, and clever semi-sentient orcas.

They seeded Namor with the monstrous grey kraken of Lissador and the smaller blue kraken of Ance, with water-jelly colonies from Noborn, Daronnian spinnerwhips, and bloodlace out of Cathaday, with swimmers as large as the fortress-fish of Dam Tullian, the mockwhale of Gulliver, and the ghrin'da of Hruun-2, or as small as the blisterfins of Avalon, the parasitical caesni from Ananda, and the deadly nest-building, egg-laying Deirdran waterwasps. To hunt the drifting fire-balloons they brought forth countless fliers: lashtail mantas, bright red razorwings, flocks of scorn, semi-aquatic howlers, and a terrible pale blue thing—half-plant and half-animal and all but weightless—that drifted with the wind and lurked inside clouds like a living, hungry spiderweb. Tuf called it the-weed-that-weeps-and-whispers, and advised Kefira Qay not to fly through clouds.

Plants and animals and things that were both and neither, predators and parasites, creatures dark as night or bright and gorgeous or entirely colorless, things strange and beautiful beyond words or too hideous even for thought, from worlds whose names burned bright in human history and from others seldom heard of. And more and more. Day after day the *Basilisk* and the *Manticore* flashed above the seas of Namor, too swift and deadly for the fire-balloons that drifted up to attack them, dropping their living weapons with impunity.

After each day's run they would repair to the *Ark*, where Haviland Tuf and one or more of his cats would seek solitude, while Kefira Qay habitually took Foolishness with her to the communications room so she could listen to the reports.

Guardian Smitt reports the sighting of strange creatures in the Orange Strait. No sign of dreadnaughts.

"A dreadnaught has been seen off Batthern, locked in terrible combat with some huge tentacled thing twice its size. A grey kraken, you say? Very well. We shall have to learn these names, Guardian Qay."

"Mullidor Strand reports that a family of lashtail mantas has taken up residence on the offshore rocks. Guardian Horn says they slice through fire-balloons like living knives—that the balloons flail and deflate and fall helplessly. Wonderful!"

"Today we heard from Indigo Beach, Guardian Qay. A strange story. Three walkers came rushing out of the water, but it was no attack. They were crazed, staggering about as if in great pain, and ropes of some pale scummy substance dangled from every joint and gap. What is it?"

"A dead dreadnaught washed up on New Atlantis today. Another corpse was sighted by the *Sunrazor* on its western patrol, rotting atop the water. Various strange fishes were picking it to pieces."

"*Starsword* swung out to Fire Heights yesterday, and sighted less than a half-dozen fire-balloons. The Council of Guardians is thinking of resuming short airship flights to the Mud-Pot Pearls, on a trial basis. What do you think, Guardian Qay? Would you advise that we risk it, or is it premature?"

Each day the reports flooded in, and each day Kefira Qay smiled more broadly as she made her runs in the *Manticore*. But Haviland Tuf remained silent and impassive.

Thirty-four days into the war, Lord Guardian Lysan told her, "Well, another dead dreadnaught was found today. It must have put up quite a battle. Our scientists have been analyzing the contents of its stomachs, and it appears to have fed exclusively on orcas and blue kraken." Kefira Qay frowned slightly, then shrugged it off.

"A grey kraken washed upon Boreen today," Lord Guardian Moen told her a few days later. "The residents are complaining of the stink. It has gigantic round bite-marks, they report. Obviously a dreadnaught, but even larger than the usual kind." Guardian Qay shifted uncomfortably.

"All the sharks seem to have vanished from the Amber Sea. The biologists can't account for it. What do you think? Ask Tuf about it, will you?" She listened, and felt a faint trickle of alarm.

"Here's a strange one for you two. Something has been sighted moving back and forth across the Coherine Deep. We've had reports from both *Sunrazor* and *Skyknife,* and various confirmations from skimmer patrols. A huge thing, they say, a veritable living island, sweeping up everything in its path. Is that one of yours? If it is, you may have miscalculated. They say it is eating barracuda and blister-fins and lander's needles by the thousands." Kefira Qay scowled.

"Fire-balloons sighted again off Mullidor Strand—hundreds of them. I can hardly give credence to these reports, but they say the lashtail mantas just carom off them, now. Do you..."

"Men-of-war again, can you believe it? We thought they were all nearly gone. So many of them, and they are gobbling up Tuf's smaller fish like nobody's business. You have to..."

"Dreadnaughts spraying water to knock howlers from the sky..."

"Something new, Kefira, a *flyer,* or a glider rather, swarms of them launch from the tops of these fire-balloons. They've gotten three skimmers already, and the mantas are no match for them... all over, I tell you, that thing that hides in the clouds... the balloons just rip them loose, the acid doesn't bother them anymore, they fling them down..."

"...more dead waterwasps, hundreds of them, thousands, where are they all..."

"...walkers again. Castle Dawn has fallen silent, must be overrun. We can't understand it. The island was ringed by bloodlace and water-jelly colonies. It ought to have been safe unless..."

"...no word from Indigo Beach in a week..."

"...thirty, forty fire-balloons seen just off Cabben. The Council fears..."

"...nothing from Lobbadoon..."

"...dead fortress-fish, half as big as the island itself... dreadnaughts came right into the harbor..."

"...walkers..."

"...Guardian Qay, the *Starsword* is lost, gone down over the Polar Sea. The last transmission was garbled, but we think..."

Kefira Qay pushed herself up, trembling, and turned to rush out of the communications room, where all the screens were babbling news of death, destruction, defeat. Haviland Tuf was standing behind her, his pale white face impassive, Ingratitude sitting calmly on his broad left shoulder.

"What is *happening?*" the Guardian demanded.

"I should think that would be obvious, Guardian, to any person of normal intelligence. We are losing. Perhaps we have lost already."

Kefira Qay fought to keep from shrieking. "Aren't you going to *do* anything? Fight back? This is all your fault, Tuf. You aren't an ecological engineer—you're a trader who doesn't know what he's doing. That's why this is..."

Haviland Tuf raised up a hand for silence. "Please," he said. "You have already caused me considerable vexation. Insult me no further. I am a gentle man, of kindly and benevolent disposition, but even one such as myself can be provoked to anger. You press close to that point now. Guardian, I take no responsibility for this unfortunate course of events. This hasty biowar we have waged was none of my idea. Your uncivilized ultimatum forced me to unwise action in order to placate you. Fortunately, while you have spent your nights gloating over transient and illusory victories, I have continued with my work. I have mapped out your world on my computers and watched the course of your war shudder and flow across it in all its manifold stages. I've duplicated your biosphere in one of my great tanks and seeded it with samples of Namorian life cloned from dead specimens—a bit of tentacle here, a piece of carapace there. I have observed and analyzed and at last I have come to conclusions. Tentative, to be sure, although this late sequence of events on Namor tends to confirm my hypothesis. So defame me no further, Guardian. After a refreshing night's sleep I shall descend to Namor and attempt to end this war of yours."

Kefira Qay stared at him, hardly daring to believe, her dread turning to hope once again. "You have the answer, then?"

"Indeed. Did I not just say as much?"

"What is it?" she demanded. "Some new creatures? That's it—you've cloned something else, haven't you? Some plague? Some monster?"

Haviland Tuf held up his hand. "Patience. First I must be certain. You have mocked me and derided me with such unflagging vigor that I hesitate to open myself to further ridicule by confiding my plans to you. I shall prove them valid first. Now, let us discuss tomorrow. You shall fly no war run with the *Manticore*. Instead, I would have you take it to New Atlantis and convene a full meeting of the Council of Guardians. Fetch those who require fetching from outlying islands, please."

"And you?" Kefira Qay asked.

"I shall meet with the council when it is time. Prior to that, I shall take my plans and my creature to Namor on a mission of our own. We shall descend in the *Phoenix*, I believe. Yes. I do think the *Phoenix* most appropriate, to commemorate your world rising from its ashes. Markedly wet ashes, but ashes nonetheless."

Kefira Qay met Haviland Tuf on the shuttle deck just prior to their scheduled departure. *Manticore* and *Phoenix* stood ready in their launch berths amidst the scatter of derelict spacecraft. Haviland Tuf was punching numbers into a mini-computer strapped to the inside of his wrist. He wore a long grey vinyl greatcoat with copious pockets and flaring shoulderboards. A green and brown duckbilled cap decorated with the golden theta of the Ecological Engineers perched rakishly atop his bald head.

"I have notified Namor Control and Guardian Headquarters," Qay said. "The Council is assembling. I will provide transportation for a half-dozen Lords Guardian from outlying districts, so all of them will be on hand. How about you, Tuf? Are you ready? Is your mystery creature on board?"

"Soon," said Haviland Tuf, blinking at her.

But Kefira Qay was not looking at his face. Her gaze had gone lower. "Tuf," she said, "there is something in your pocket. Moving." Incredulous, she watched the ripple creep along beneath the vinyl.

"Ah," said Tuf. "Indeed." And then the head emerged from his pocket, and peered around curiously. It belonged to a kitten, a tiny jet-black kitten with lambent yellow eyes. "A cat," muttered Kefira Qay sourly.

"Your perception is uncanny," said Haviland Tuf. He lifted the kitten out gently, and held it cupped in one great white hand while scratching behind its ear with a finger from the other. "This is Dax," he said solemnly. Dax was scarcely half the size of the older kittens who frisked about the *Ark*. He looked like nothing but a ball of black fur, curiously limp and indolent.

"Wonderful," the Guardian replied. "Dax, eh? Where did this one come from? No, don't answer that. I can guess. Tuf, don't we have more important things to do than play with cats?"

"I think not," said Haviland Tuf. "You do not appreciate cats sufficiently, Guardian. They are the most civilized of creatures. No world can be considered truly cultured without cats. Are you aware that all cats, from time immemorial, have had a touch of psi? Do you know that some ancient societies of Old Earth worshipped cats as gods? It is true."

"Please," said Kefira Qay irritably. "We don't have time for a discourse on cats. Are you going to bring that poor little thing down to Namor with you?"

Tuf blinked. "Indeed. This poor little thing, as you so contemptuously call him, is the salvation of Namor. Respect might be in order."

She stared at him as if he had gone mad. "What? That? Him? I mean, Dax? Are you serious? What are you talking about? You're joking, aren't you? This is some kind of insane jest. You've got some thing loaded aboard the *Phoenix*, some huge leviathan that will cleanse the sea of those dreadnaughts—something, anything, I don't know. But you can't mean... you can't... not that."

"Him," said Haviland Tuf. "Guardian, it is so wearisome to have to state the obvious, not once but again and again. I have given you raveners and krakens and lashtail mantas, at your insistence. They have not been efficacious. Accordingly, I have done much hard thinking, and I have cloned Dax."

"A kitten," she said. "You're going to use a *kitten* against the dreadnaughts and the fire-balloons and the walkers. One. Small. *Kitten.*"

"Indeed," said Haviland Tuf. He frowned down at her, slid Dax back into the roomy confines of his great pocket, and turned smartly toward the waiting *Phoenix.*

Kefira Qay was growing very nervous. In the council chambers high atop Breakwater Tower on New Atlantis, the twenty-five Lords Guardian who commanded the defense of all Namor were restive. All of them had been waiting for hours. Some had been there all day. The long conference table was littered with personal communicators and computer printouts and empty water glasses. Two meals had already been served and cleared away. By the wide curving window that dominated the far wall, portly Lord Guardian Alis was talking in low urgent tones to Lord Guardian Lysan, thin and stern, and both of them were giving meaningful glances to Kefira Qay from time to time. Behind them the sun was going down, and the great bay was turning a lovely shade of scarlet. It was such a beautiful scene that one scarcely noticed the small bright dots that were Guardian skimmers, flying patrol.

Dusk was almost upon them, the council members were grumbling and stirring impatiently in their big cushioned chairs, and Haviland Tuf had still failed to make an appearance. "When did he say he would be here?" asked Lord Guardian Khem, for the fifth time.

"He wasn't very precise, Lord Guardian," Kefira Qay replied uneasily, for the fifth time.

Khem frowned and cleared his throat.

Then one of the communicators began to beep, and Lord Guardian Lysan strode over briskly and snatched it up. "Yes?' he said. "I see. Quite good. Escort him in." He set clown the communicator and rapped its edge on the table for order. The others shuffled to their seats, or broke off their conversations, or straightened. The council chamber grew silent. "That was the patrol. Tuf's shuttle has been sighted. He is on his way, I am pleased to report." Lysan glanced at Kefira Qay. "At last."

The Guardian felt even more uneasy then. It was bad enough that Tuf had kept them waiting, but she was dreading the moment when he came lumbering in, Dax peering out of his pocket. Qay had been unable to find the words to tell her superiors that Tuf proposed to save Namor with a small black kitten. She fidgeted in her seat and plucked at her large crooked nose. This was going to be bad, she feared.

It was worse than anything she could have dreamed.

All of the Lords Guardian were waiting, stiff and silent and attentive, when the doors opened and Haviland Tuf walked in, escorted by four armed guards in golden coveralls. He was a mess. His boots made a squishing sound as he walked, and his greatcoat was smeared with mud. Dax was visible in his left pocket all right, paws hooked over its edge and large eyes intent. But the Lords Guardian weren't looking at the kitten. Beneath his other arm, Haviland Tuf was carrying a muddy rock the size of a big man's head. A thick coating of green-brown slime covered it, and it was dripping water onto the plush carpet.

Without so much as a word, Tuf went directly to the conference table and set the rock down in the center of it. That was when Kefira Qay saw the fringe of tentacles, pale and fine as threads, and realized that it wasn't a rock after all. "A mud-pot," she said aloud in surprise. No wonder she hadn't recognized it. She had seen many a mud-pot in her time, but not until after they had been washed and boiled and the tendrils trimmed away. Normally they were served with a hammer and chisel to crack the bony carapace, and a dish of melted butter and spices on the side.

The Lords Guardian looked on in astonishment, and then all twenty-five began talking at once, and the council chamber became a blur of overlapping voices.

"…it *is* a mud-pot, I don't understand…"

"What is the meaning of this?"

"He makes us wait all day and then comes to council as filthy as a mudgrubber. The dignity of the council is…"

"…haven't eaten a mud-pot in, oh, two, three…"

"…can't be the man who is supposed to save…"

"…insane, why just look at…"

"…what is that thing in his pocket? Look at it! My God, it *moved!* It's alive, I tell you, I saw it…"

"*Silence!*" Lysan's voice was like a knife cutting through the hubbub. The room quieted as, one by one, the Lords Guardian turned toward him. "We have come together at your beck and call," Lysan said acidly to Tuf. "We expected you to bring us an answer. Instead you appear to have brought us dinner."

Someone snickered.

Haviland Tuf frowned down at his muddy hands, and wiped them primly on his greatcoat. Taking Dax from his pocket, Tuf deposited the lethargic black kitten on the table. Dax yawned and stretched, and ambled toward the nearest of the Lords Guardian, who stared in horror and hurriedly inched her chair back a bit. Shrugging out of his wet, muddy greatcoat, Tuf looked about for a place to put it, and finally hung it from the laser rifle of one of his escort. Only then did he turn back to the Lords Guardian. "Esteemed Lords Guardian," he said, "this is not dinner you see before you. In that very attitude lies the root of all your problems. This is the ambassador of the race that shares Namor with you, whose name, regrettably, is far beyond my small capabilities. His people will take it quite badly if you eat him."

Eventually someone brought Lysan a gavel, and he rapped it long and loud enough to attract everyone's attention, and the furor slowly ebbed away. Haviland Tuf had stood impassively through all of it, his face without expression, his arms folded against his chest. Only when silence was restored did he say, "perhaps I should explain."

"You are mad," Lord Guardian Harvan said, looking from Tuf to the mud-pot and back again. "Utterly mad."

Haviland Tuf scooped up Dax from the table, cradled him in one arm, and began to pet him. "Even in our moment of victory, we are mocked and insulted," he said to the kitten.

"Tuf," said Lysan from the head of the long table, "what you suggest is impossible. We have explored Namor quite sufficiently in the century we have been here so as to be certain that no sentient races dwell upon it. There are no cities, no roads, no signs of any prior civilization or technology, no ruins or artifacts—*nothing*, neither above nor below the sea."

"Moreover," said another councilor, a beefy woman with a red face, "the mud-pots cannot possibly be sentient. Agreed, they have brains the size of a human brain. But that is about *all* they have. They have no eyes, ears, noses, almost no sensory equipment whatever except for touch. They have only those feeble tendrils as manipulative organs, scarcely strong enough to lift a pebble. And in fact, the tendrils are only used to anchor them to their spot on the seabed. They are hermaphroditic and downright primitive, mobile only in the first month of life, before the shell hardens and grows heavy. Once they root on the bottom and cover themselves with mud, they never move again. They stay there for hundreds of years."

"Thousands," said Haviland. "They are remarkably long-lived creatures. All that you say is undoubtedly correct. Nonetheless, your conclusions are in error. You have allowed yourself to be blinded by belligerence and fear. If you had removed yourself from the situation and paused long enough to think about it in depth, as I did, no doubt it would become obvious even to the military mind that your plight was no natural catastrophe. Only the machinations of some enemy intelligence could sufficiently explain the tragic course of events on Namor."

"You don't expect us to believe—" someone began.

"Sir," said Haviland Tuf, "I expect you to listen. If you will refrain from interrupting me, I will explain all. Then you may choose to believe or not, as suits your peculiar fancy. I shall take my fee and depart." Tuf looked at Dax. "Idiots, Dax. Everywhere we are beset by idiots." Turning his attention back to the Lords Guardian, he continued, "As I have stated, intelligence was clearly at work here. The difficulty was in finding that intelligence. I perused the work of your Namorian biologists, living and dead, read much about your flora and fauna, recreated many of the native lifeforms aboard the *Ark*. No likely candidate for sentience was immediately forthcoming. The traditional hallmarks of intelligent life include a large brain, sophisticated biological sensors, mobility, and some sort of manipulative organ, such as an opposable thumb. Nowhere on Namor could I find a creature with all of these attributes. My hypothesis, however, was still correct. Therefore I must needs move on to unlikely candidates, as there were no likely ones.

"To this end I studied the history of your plight, and at once some things suggested themselves. You believed that your sea monsters emerged from the dark oceanic depths, but where did they first appear? In the offshore shallows—the areas where you practiced fishing and sea-farming. What did all these areas have in common? Certainly an abundance of life, that must be admitted. Yet not the *same* life. The fish that habituated the waters off New Atlantis did not frequent those of the Broken Hand. Yet I found two interesting exceptions, two species found virtually everywhere—the mud-pots, lying immobile in their great soft beds through the long slow centuries and, originally, the things you called Namorian men-of-war. The ancient native race has another term for those. They call them guardians.

"Once I had come this far, it was only a matter of working out the details and confirming my suspicions. I might have arrived at my conclusion much earlier, but for the rude interruptions of liaison officer Qay, who continually shattered my concentration and finally, most cruelly, forced me to waste much time sending forth grey krakens and razorwings and sundry other such creatures. In the future I shall spare myself such liaisons."

"Yet, in a way, the experiment was useful, since it confirmed my theory as to the true situation on Namor. Accordingly I pressed on. Geographic studies showed that all of the monsters were thickest near mud-pot beds. The heaviest fighting had been in those selfsame areas, my Lords Guardian. Clearly, these mud-pots you find so eminently edible were your mysterious foes. Yet how could that be? These creatures had large brains, to be sure, but lacked all the other traits we have come to associate with sentience, as we know it. And that was the very heart of it! Clearly they were sentient as we do no know it. What sort of intelligent being could live deep under the sea, immobile, blind, deaf, bereft of all input? I pondered that question. The answer, sirs, is obvious. Such an intelligence must interact with the world in ways we cannot, must have its own modes of sensing and communicating. Such an intelligence must be telepathic. Indeed. The more I considered it, the more obvious it became.

"Thereupon it was only a matter of testing my conclusions. To that end, I brought forth Dax. All cats have some small psionic ability, Lords Guardian. Yet long centuries ago, in the days of the Great War, the soldiers of the Federal Empire struggled against enemies with terrible psi powers; Hrangan Minds and githyanki soulsucks. To combat such formidable foes, the genetic engineers worked with felines, and vastly heightened and sharpened their psionic abilities, so they could esp in unison with mere humans. Dax is such a special animal."

"You mean that thing is reading our minds?" Lysan said sharply.

"Insofar as you have minds to read," said Haviland Tuf, "yes. But more importantly, through Dax, I was able to reach that ancient people you have so ignominiously dubbed *mud-pots*. For they, you see, are entirely telepathic.

"For millennia beyond counting they have dwelled in tranquility and peace beneath the seas of this world. They are a slow, thoughtful, philosophic race, and they lived side by side in the billions, each linked with all the others, each an individual and each a part of the great racial whole. In a sense they were deathless, for all shared the experiences of each, and the death of one was as nothing. Experiences were few in the unchanging sea, however. For the most part their long lives are given over to abstract thought, to philosophy, to strange green dreams that neither you nor I can truly comprehend. They are silent musicians, one might say. Together they have woven great symphonies of dreams, and those songs go on and on.

"Before humanity came to Namor, they had had no real enemies for millions of years. Yet that had not always been the case. In the primordial beginnings of this wet world, the oceans teemed with creatures who relished the taste of the dreamers as much as you do. Even then, the race understood genetics, understood evolution. With their vast web of interwoven minds, they were able to manipulate the very stuff of life itself, more skillfully than any genetic engineers. And so they evolved their guardians, formidable predators with a biological imperative to protect those you call mud-pots. These were your men-of-war. From that time to this they guarded the beds, while the dreamers went back to their symphony of thought.

"Then you came, from Aquarius and Old Poseidon. Indeed you did. Lost in the reverie, the dreamers hardly noticed for many years, while you farmed and fished and discovered the taste of mud-pots. You must consider the shock you gave them, Lords Guardian. Each time you plunged one of them into boiling water, all of them shared the sensations. To the dreamers, it seemed as though some terrible new predator had evolved upon the landmass, a place of little interest to them. They had no inkling that you might be sentient, since they could no more conceive of a nontelepathic sentience than you could conceive of one blind, deaf, immobile, and edible. To them, things that moved and manipulated and ate flesh were animals, and could be nothing else.

"The rest you know, or can surmise. The dreamers are a slow people lost in their vast songs, and they were slow to respond. First they simply ignored you, in the belief that the ecosystem itself would shortly check your ravages. This did not appear to happen. To them it seemed you had no natural enemies. You bred and expanded constantly, and many thousands of minds fell silent. Finally they returned to the ancient, almost-forgotten ways of their dim past, and woke to protect themselves. They sped up the reproduction of their guardians until the seas above their beds teemed with their protectors, but the creatures that had once sufficed admirably against other enemies proved to be no match for you. Finally they were driven to new measures. Their minds broke off the great symphony and ranged out, and they sensed and understood. At last they began to fashion new guardians, guardians formidable enough to protect them against this great new nemesis. Thus it went. When I arrived upon the *Ark*, and Kefira Qay forced me to unleash many new threats to their peaceful dominion, the dreamers were initially taken aback. But the struggle had sharpened them and they responded more quickly now, and in only a very short time they were dreaming newer guardians still, and sending them forth to battle to oppose the creatures I had loosed upon them. Even as I speak to you in this most imposing tower of yours, many a terrible new lifeform is stirring beneath the waves, and soon will emerge to trouble your sleep in years to come—unless, of course, you come to a peace. That is entirely your decision. I am only a humble ecological engineer. I would not dream of dictating such matters to the likes of you. Yet I do suggest it, in the strongest possible terms. So here is the ambassador plucked from the sea—at great personal discomfort to myself, I might add. The dreamers are now in much turmoil, for when they felt Dax among them and through him touched me, their world increased a millionfold. They learned of the stars today, and learned moreover that they are not alone in this cosmos. I believe they will be reasonable, as they have no use for the land, nor any taste for fish. Here is Dax as well, and myself. Perhaps we might commence to talk?"

But when Haviland Tuf fell silent at last, no one spoke for quite a long time. The Lords Guardian were all ashen and numb. One by one they looked away from Tuf's impassive features, to the muddy shell on the table.

Finally Kefira Qay found her voice. "What do they *want?*" she asked nervously.

"Chiefly," said Haviland Tuf, "they want you to stop eating them. This strikes me as an eminently sensible proposal. What is your reply?"

"Two million standards is insufficient," Haviland Tuf said some time later, sitting in the communications room of the *Ark*. Dax rested calmly in his lap, having little of the frenetic energy of the other kittens. Elsewhere in room Suspicion and Hostility were chasing each other hither and yon.

Up on the telescreen, Kefira Qay's features broke into a suspicious scowl. "What do you mean? This was the price we agreed upon, Tuf. If you are trying to cheat us…"

"Cheat?" Tuf sighed. "Did you hear her, Dax? After all we have done, such grim accusations are still flung at us willy-nilly. Yes. Willy-nilly indeed. An odd phrase, when one stops to mull on it." He looked back at the telescreen. "Guardian Qay, I am fully aware of the agreed-on price. For two million standards, I solved your difficulties. I analyzed and pondered and provided the insight and the translator you so sorely needed. I have even left you with twenty-five telepathic cats, each linked to one of your Lords Guardian, to facilitate further communications after my departure. That too is included within the terms of our initial agreement, since it was necessary to the solution of your problem. And, being at heart more a philanthropist than a businessman, and deeply sentimental as well, I have even allowed you to retain Foolishness, who took a liking to you for some reason that I am entirely unable to fathom. For that, too, there is no charge."

"Then why are you demanding an additional three million standards?" demanded Kefira Qay.

"For unnecessary work which I was cruelly compelled to do," Tuf replied. "Would you care for an itemized accounting?"

"Yes, I would," she said.

"Very well. For sharks. For barracuda. For giant squid. For orcas. For grey kraken. For blue kraken. For bloodlace. For water jellies. Twenty thousand standards per item. For fortress-fish, fifty thousand standards. For the-weed-that-weeps-and-whispers, eight…" he went on for a long, long time.

When he was done, Kefira Qay set her lips sternly. "I will submit your bill to the Council of Guardians," she said. "But I will tell you straight out that your demands are unfair and exorbitant, and our balance of trade is not sufficient to allow for such an outflow of hard standards. You can wait in orbit for a hundred years, Tuf, but you won't get any five million standards."

Haviland Tuf raised his hands in surrender. "Ah," he said. "So, because of my trusting nature, I must take a loss. I will not be paid, then?"

"Two million standards," said the Guardian. "As we agreed."

"I suppose I might accept this cruel and unethical decision, and take it as one of life's hard lessons. Very well then. So be it." He stroked Dax. "It has been said that those who do not learn from history are doomed to repeat it. I can only blame myself for this wretched turn of events. Why, it was only a few scant months past that I chanced to view a historical drama on this very sort of situation. It was about a seedship such as my own that rid one small world of an annoying pest, only to have the ungrateful planetary government refuse payment. Had I been wiser, that would have taught me to demand my payment in advance." He sighed. "But I was not wise, and now I must suffer." Tuf stroked Dax again, and paused. "Perhaps your Council of Guardians might be interested in viewing this particular tape, purely for recreational purposes. It is holographic, fully dramatized, and well-acted, and moreover, it gives a fascinating insight into the workings and capabilities of a ship such as this one. Highly educational. The title is *Seedship of Hamelin*."

They paid him, of course.

LIFE REGARDED AS A JIGSAW PUZZLE OF HIGHLY LUSTROUS CATS

Michael Bishop

Michael Bishop has been publishing stories, novels, poetry, and criticism for forty years (starting at age two). His novel *No Enemy but Time* won the Nebula Award, *Unicorn Mountain* won the Mythopoeic Fantasy Award, and *Brittle Innings* won the Locus Award for Best Fantasy Novel. He has published seven volumes of short fiction, and his stories have won the Nebula, two Southeastern Science Fiction Association short-fiction awards, and, most recently, the Shirley Jackson Award for Best Short Story ("The Pile," based on notes left behind by his late son, Jamie). His most recent book, this time as editor, is the anthology *A Cross of Centuries: Twenty-Five Imaginative Tales about the Christ,* and his most recent story is a Lovecraftian science-fiction tale, "The City Quiet as Death," written with Steven Utley and published at Tor.com.

Bishop says that he "borrowed" one image in the story from Annie Dillard's *Pilgrim at Tinker Creek*, a passage in which she describes a cat of hers—walking across her bed and unclothed body, leaving rose-like red paw prints behind as a result of having earlier stalked through wet red clay.

Your father-in-law, who insists that you call him Howie, even though you prefer Mr. Bragg, likes jigsaw puzzles. If they prove harder than he has the skill or the patience for, he knows a sneaky way around the problem.

During the third Christmas season after your marriage to Marti, you find Howie at a card table wearing a parka, a blue watch cap with a crown of burgundy leather, and fur-lined shoes. (December through February, it is freezing in the Braggs' Tudor-style house outside Spartanburg.) He is assembling a huge jigsaw puzzle, for the Braggs give him one every Christmas. His challenge is to put it together, unaided by drop-in company or any other family member, before the Sugar Bowl kick-off on New Year's Day.

This year, the puzzle is of cats.

The ESB procedure being administered to you by the Zoo Cop and his associates is keyed to cats. When they zap your implanted electrodes, cat-related memories parachute into your mind's eye, opening out like fireworks.

The lid from the puzzle's box is Mr. Bragg's—Howie's—blueprint, and it depicts a population explosion of stylized cats. They are both mysterious beasts and whimsical cartoons. The puzzle lacks any background, it's so full of cats. They run, stalk, lap milk, tussel, tongue-file their fur, snooze, etc., etc. There are no puzzle areas where a single color dominates, a serious obstacle to quick assembly.

Howie has a solution. When only a handful of pieces remain in the box, he uses a razor blade to shave any piece that refuses to fit where he wants it to. This is cheating, as even Howie readily acknowledges, but on New Year's Eve, with Dick Clark standing in Times Square and the Sugar Bowl game only hours away, a man can't afford to screw around.

"Looking good," you say as the crowd on TV starts its rowdy countdown to midnight. "You're almost there."

Howie confesses—complains?—that this puzzle has been a "real mindbender." He appreciates the challenge of a thousand-plus pieces and a crazy-making dearth of internal clues, but why this particular puzzle? He usually receives a photographic landscape or a Western painting by Remington.

"I'm not a cat fancier," he tells you. "Most of 'em're sneaky little bastards, don't you think?"

Marti likes cats, but when you get canned at Piedmont Freight in Atlanta, she moves back to Spartanburg with your son, Jacob, who may be allergic to cats. Marti leaves in your keeping two calico mongrels that duck out of sight whenever you try to feed or catch them. You catch them eventually, of course, and drive them to the pound in a plastic animal carrier that Marti bought from Delta, or Eastern, or some other airline out at Hartsfield.

Penfield, a.k.a. the Zoo Cop, wants to know how you lost your job. He gives you a multiple-choice quiz:

A. Companywide lay-off
B. Neglect of duty and/or unacceptable job performance
C. Personality conflict with a supervisor
D. Suspicion of disloyalty
E. All, or none, of the above

You tell him that there was an incident of (alleged) sexual harassment involving a female secretary whose name, even under the impetus of electrical stimulation of the brain (ESB), you cannot now recall. All you can recall is every cat, real or imaginary, ever to etch its image into your consciousness.

After your firing, you take the cats, Springer and Ossie (short for Ocelot), to the pound. When you look back from the shelter's doorway, a teen-age attendant is giving you, no doubt about it, the evil eye. Springer and Ossie are doomed. No one in the big, busy city wants a mixed-breed female. The fate awaiting nine-year-old Jacob's cats—never mind their complicity in his frightening asthma—is the gas chamber, but, today, you are as indifferent to the cats' fate as a latter-day Eichmann. You are numb from the molecular level upward.

"We did have them spayed," you defend yourself. "Couldn't you use that to pitch them to some nice family?"

You begin to laugh.

Is this, another instance of Inappropriate Affect? Except for the laughing gas given to you to sink the electrodes, you've now been off all medication for... you don't know how long.

On the street only three years after your dismissal, you wept at hoboes' bawdy jokes, got up and danced if the obituaries you'd been sleeping under reported an old friend's death.

Once, you giggled when a black girl bummed a cigarette in the parking lot of Trinity United Methodist: "I got AIDS, man. Hain't no smoke gonna kill me. Hain't time enough for the old lung cee to kick in, too."

Now that Penfield's taken you off antipsychotics, is Ye Olde Inappropriate Affect kicking in again? Or is this fallout from the ESB? After all, one gets entirely different responses (rage and affection; fear and bravado) from zapping hypothalamic points less than 0.02 inches from each other.

Spill it, Adolf, Penfield says. What's so funny?

Cat juggling, you tell him. (Your name has never been Adolf.)

What?

Steve Martin in *The Jerk*. An illegal Mexican sport. A joke, you know. Cat juggling.

You surrender to jerky laughter. It hurts, but your glee isn't inappropriate. The movie was a comedy. People were *supposed* to laugh. Forget that when you close your eyes, you see yourself as the outlaw juggler. Forget that the cats in their caterwauling orbits include Springer, Ossie, Thai Thai, Romeo, and an anonymous albino kitten from your dead grandparents' grain crib on their farm outside Montgomery....

As a boy in Hapeville, the cat you like best is Thai Thai, a male Siamese that your mama and you inherit from the family moving out. His name isn't Thai Thai before your mama starts calling him that, though. It's something fake Chinese, like Lung Cee or Mouser Tung. The folks moving out don't want to take him with them, their daddy's got a job with Otero Steel in Pueblo, Colorado. Besides,

Mouser Tung's not likely to appreciate the ice and snow out there. He's a Deep South cat, Dixie-born and -bred.

"You are who you are," Mama tells the Siamese while he rubs her laddered nylons, "but from here on out your *name* is Thai Thai."

"Why're you calling him that?" you ask her.

"Because it *fits* a cracker Siamese," she says.

It's several years later before you realize that Thailand is Siam's current name and that there's a gnat-plagued town southeast of Albany called, yeah, Ty Ty.

Your mama's a smart gal, with an agile mind and a quirky sense of humor. How Daddy ever got it into his head that she wasn't good enough for him is a mystery.

It's her agile mind and her quirky sense of humor that did her in, the Zoo Cop says, pinching back your eyelid.

Anyway, Daddy ran off to a Florida dog-track town with a chunky bottle-blonde ex-hairdresser who dropped a few pounds and started a mail-order weight-loss-tonic business. He's been gone nine weeks and four days.

Thai Thai, when you notice him, is pretty decent company. He sheathes his claws when he's in your lap. He purrs at a bearable register. He eats leftover vegetables—peas, lima beans, spinach—as readily as he does bacon rinds or chicken scraps. A doll, Mama calls him. A gentleman.

This ESB business distorts stuff. It flips events, attitudes, preferences upsidedown. The last shall be first, the first shall be last. This focus on cats, for example, is a *major* distortion, a misleading reenvisioning of the life that you lived before getting trapped by Rockdale Biological Supply Company.

Can't Penfield see this? Uh-uh, no way. He's too hot to screw Rockdale Biological's bigwigs. The guy may have right on his side, but to him—for the moment, anyway—you're just another human oven-cake. If you crumble when the heat's turned up, great, zip-a-dee-zoo-cop, pop me a cold one, justice is served.

Thing is, you prefer dogs. Even as a kid, you like them more. You bring home flea-bitten strays and beg to keep them. When you live in Alabama, you covet the liony chow, Simba, that waits every afternoon in the Notasulga schoolyard for Wesley Duplantier. Dogs, not cats. Until Mouser Tung—Thai Thai—all the cats you know prowl on the edges of your attention. Even Thai Thai comes to you and Mama, over here in Georgia, as a kind of offhand house-warming gift. Dogs, Mister Zoo Cop, not cats.

Actually, Penfield says, I'm getting the idea that what was in the *forefront* of your attention, Adolf, was women….

After puberty, your attention never *has* a forefront. You are divebombed by stimuli. Girls' faces are billboards. Their bodies are bigger billboards. Jigsawed ad signs. A piece here. A piece there. It isn't just girls. It's everything. Cars, buildings,

TV talking heads, mosquito swarms, jet contrails, interchangeable male callers at suppertime, battle scenes on the six o'clock news, rock idols infinitely glitterized, the whole schmear fragmenting as it feeds into you, Mr. Teen-age Black Hole of the Spirit. Except when romancing a sweet young gal, your head's a magnet for all the flak generated by the media-crazed twentieth century.

"You're tomcatting, aren't you?" Mama says. "You're tomcatting just like Webb did. God."

It's a way to stay focused. With their faces and bodies under you, they cease to be billboards. You're a human being again, not a radio receiver or a gravity funnel. The act imposes a fleeting order on the ricocheting chaos working every instant to turn you, the mind cementing it all together, into a flimsy cardboard box of mismatched pieces.

Is that tomcatting? Resisting, by a tender union of bodies, the consequences of dumping a jigsaw puzzle of cats into a box of pieces that, assembled, would depict, say, a unit of embattled flak gunners on Corregidor?

Christ, the Zoo Cop says, a more highfalutin excuse for chasing tail I've never heard.

Your high school is crawling with cats. Cool cats, punk cats, stray cats, dead cats. Some are human, some aren't.

You dissect a cat in biology lab. On a plaster-of-Paris base, guyed upright by wires, stands the bleached skeleton of a quadruped that Mr. Osteen—he's also the track and girls' softball coach—swears was a member of *Felis catus*, the common house cat.

With its underlying gauntness exposed and its skull gleaming brittle and grotesque, this skeleton resembles that of something prehistoric. Pamela van Rhyn and two or three other girls want to know where the cats in the lab came from.

"A scientific supply house," Coach Osteen says. "Same place we get our bullfrogs, our microscope slides, the insects in that there display case." He nods at it.

"Where does the supply house get them?" Pamela says.

"I don't know, Pammie. Maybe they raise 'em. Maybe they round up strays. You missing a kitty?"

In fact, rumor holds that Mr. Osteen found the living source of his skeleton behind the track field's south bleachers, chloroformed it, carried it home, and boiled the fur off it in a pot on an old stove in his basement. Because of the smell, his wife spent a week in Augusta with her mother. Rumor holds that cat lovers hereabouts would be wise to keep their pets indoors.

Slicing into the chest cavity of the specimen provided by the supply house, you find yourself losing it. You are the only boy in Coach Osteen's lab to contract nausea and an overwhelming uprush of self-disgust; the only boy, clammy-palmed and light-headed, to have to leave the room. The ostensible shame of your departure is lost on Pamela, who agrees, in Nurse Mayhew's office, to rendezvous with you later that afternoon at the Huddle House.

"This is the heart," you can still hear Osteen saying. "Looks like a wet rubber strawberry, don't it?"

As a seven-year-old, you wander into the grain crib of the barn on the Powell farm. A one-eyed mongrel queen named Sky has dropped a litter on the deer hides, today stiff and rat-eaten, that Gramby Powell stowed there twenty or more years ago. Sky one-eyes you with real suspicion, all set to bolt or hiss, as you lean over a rail to study the blind quintet of her kittening.

They're not much, mere lumps. "Turds with fur," Gramby called them last night, to Meemaw Anita's scandalized dismay and the keen amusement of your daddy. They hardly move.

One kitten gleams white on the stiff hide, in the nervous curl of Sky's furry belly. You spit at Sky, as another cat would spit, but louder—*sssphh! sssphh!*—so that eventually, intimidated, she gets up, kittens falling from her like bombs from the open bay of a B-52, and slinks to the far wall of the crib.

You climb over the rail and pick up the white kitten, the Maybe Albino as Meemaw Anita dubbed it. "Won't know for sure," she said, "till its eyes're open."

You turn the kitten in your hands. Which end is which? It's sort of hard to say. Okay, here's the starchy white potato print of its smashed-in pug of a face: eyes shut, ears a pair of napkin folds, mouth a miniature crimson gap.

You rub the helpless critter on your cheek. Cat smells. Hay smells. Hide smells. It's hard not to sneeze.

It occurs to you that you could throw this Maybe Albino like a baseball. You could wind up like Denny McLain and fling it at the far wall of the grain crib. If you aim just right, you may be able to hit the wall so that the kitten rebounds and lands on Sky. You could sing a funny song, "Sky's being fallen on, / Oh, Sky's being fallen on, / Whatcha think 'bout that?" And nobody'll ever know if poor little Maybe Albino has pink eyes or not....

This sudden impulse horrifies you, even as a kid, especially as a kid. You can see the white kitten dead. Trembling, you set the kitten back down on the cardboardy deer hide, climb back over the crib rail, and stand away from the naked litter while Sky tries to decide what to do next.

Unmanfully you start to cry. "S-sorry, k-kitty. S-s-sorry, Sk-sky. I'm r-r-really s-sorry." You almost want Gramby or Meemaw Anita to stumble in on you, in the churchly gloom and itch of their grain crib, to see you doing this heartfelt penance for a foul deed imagined but never carried out. It's okay to cry a bit in front of your mama's folks.

I'm touched, Penfield says. But speak up. Stop mumbling.

For several months after your senior year, you reside in the Adolescent Wing of the Quiet Harbor Psychiatric Center in a suburb of Atlanta. You're there to neutralize the disorienting stimuli—flak, you call it—burning out your emotional wiring, flying at you from everywhere. You're there to relearn how to live with no despairing recourse to disguises, sex, drugs.

Bad drugs, the doctors mean.

At QHPC, they give you good drugs. This is actually the case, not sarcastic bullshit. Kim Yaughan, one of the psychotherapists in the so-called Wild Child Wing, assures you that this is so; that antipsychotics aren't addictive. You get twenty milligrams a day of haloperidol. You take it in liquid form in paper cups shaped like doll-house-sized coffee filters.

"You're not an addict," Kim says. (Everyone at QHPC calls her Kim.) "Think of yourself as a diabetic, of Haldol as insulin. You don't hold a diabetic off insulin, that'd be criminal."

Not only do you get Haldol, you get talk therapy, recreational therapy, family therapy, crafts therapy. Some of the residents of the Wild Child Wing are druggies and sexual-abuse victims as young as twelve. They get these same therapies, along with pet therapy. The pets brought in on Wednesdays often include cats.

At last, Penfield tells an associate. That last jolt wasn't a mis-hit, after all.

The idea is that hostile, fearful, or withdrawn kids who don't interact well with other people will do better with animals. Usually, they do. Kittens under a year, tumbling with one another, batting at yarn balls, exploring the pet room with their tails up like the radio antennas on cars, seem to be effective four-legged therapists.

One teen-age girl, a manic-depressive who calls herself Eagle Rose, goes ga-ga over them. "Oh," she says, holding up a squirmy smoke-colored male and nodding at two kittens wrestling in an empty carton of Extra Large Tide, "they're so soft, so neat, so... so *highly lustrous*."

Despite Kim Yaughan's many attempts to involve you, you stand aloof from everyone. It's Eagle Rose who focuses your attention, not the kittens, and E.R.'s an untouchable. Every patient here is an untouchable, that way. It would be a terrible betrayal to think anything else. So, mostly, you don't.

The year before you marry, Marti is renting a house on North Highland Avenue. A whole house. It's not a big house, but she has plenty of room. She uses one bedroom as a studio. In this room, on the floor, lies a large canvas on which she has been painting, exclusively in shades of blue, the magnified heart of a magnolia. She calls the painting—too explicitly, you think—*Magnolia Heart in Blue*. She's worked on it all quarter, often appraising it from a stepladder to determine how best to continue.

Every weekend, you sleep with Marti in the bedroom next to the studio. Her mattress rests on the floor, without box springs or bedstead. You sometimes feel that you're lying in the middle of a painting in progress, a strange but gratifying sensation that you may or may not carry into your next week of classes at GSU.

One balmy Sunday, you awake to find Marti's body stenciled with primitive blue flowers, a blossom on her neck, more on her breasts, an indigo bouquet on the milky plane of her abdomen. You gape at her in groggy wonderment. The woman you plan to marry has become, overnight, an arabesque of disturbing floral bruises.

Then you see the cat, Romeo, a neighbor's gray Persian, propped in the corner, belly exposed, so much like a hairy little man in a recliner that you laugh. Marti stirs. Romeo preens. Clearly, he entered through a studio window, walked all over *Magnolia Heart in Blue,* then came in here and violated Marti.

My wife-to-be as a strip of *fin de siècle* wallpaper, you muse, kissing her chastely on one of the paw-print flowers.

You sleep on the streets. You wear the same stinking clothes for days on end. You haven't been on haloperidol for months. The city could be Lima, or Istanbul, or Bombay, as easily as Atlanta. Hell, it could be a boulder-littered crater on the moon. You drag from one place to another like a zombie, and the people you hit up for hamburgers, change, MARTA tokens, old newspapers, have no more substance to you than you do to them, they could all be holograms or ghosts. They could be androids programmed to keep you dirty and hungry by dictating your behavior with remote-control devices that look like wristwatches and key rings.

Cats mean more to you than people do. (The people may not *be* people.) Cats are fellow survivors, able to sniff out nitrogenous substances from blocks away. Food.

You follow a trio of scrawny felines down Ponce de Leon to the rear door of a catfish restaurant where the Dumpster overflows with greasy paper and other high refuse. The cats strut around on the mounded topography of this debris while you balance on an upturned trash barrel, mindlessly picking and choosing.

Seven rooms away from Coach Osteen's lab, Mr. Petty is teaching advanced junior English. Poetry. He stalks around the room like an actor doing Hamlet, even when the poem's something dumb by Ogden Nash, or something beat and surface-sacrilegious by Ferlinghetti, or something short and puzzling by Carlos Williams.

The Williams piece is about a cat that climbs over a cabinet—a "jamcloset"—and steps into a flowerpot. Actually, Mr. Petty says, it's about the *image* created by Williams's purposely simple diction. Everyone argues that it isn't a poem at all. It's even less a poem, lacking metaphors, than that Carl Sandberg thing about the fog coming on little, for Christ's sake, cat's feet.

You like it, though. You can see the cat stepping cautiously into the flowerpot. The next time you're in Coach Osteen's class, trying to redeem yourself at the dissection table, you recite the poem for Pamela van Rhyn, Jessie Faye Culver, Kathy Margenau, and Cynthia Spivy.

Coach Osteen, shaking his head, makes you repeat the lines so that he can say them, too. Amazing.

"Cats are digitigrade critters," he tells the lab. "That means they walk on their toes. Digitigrade."

Cynthia Spivy catches your eye. *Well, I'll be a pussywillow,* she silently mouths. *Who'd've thunk it?*

"Unlike the dog or the horse," Coach Osteen goes on, "the cat walks by moving the front and back legs on one side of its body and then the front and back legs on the other. The only other animals to move that way are the camel and the giraffe."

And naked crazy folks rutting on all fours, you think, studying Cynthia's lips and wondering if there was ever a feral child raised by snow leopards or jaguars...

Thai Thai develops a urinary tract infection. Whenever he has to pee, he looks for Mama pulling weeds or hanging out clothes in the backyard, and squats to show her that he's not getting the job done. It takes Mama two or three days to realize what's going on. Then you and she carry Thai to the vet.

Mama waits tables at a Denny's near the expressway. She hasn't really got the money for the operation that Thai needs to clear up the blockage, a common problem in male Siamese. She tells you that you can either forfeit movie money for the next few months or help her pay to make Thai well. You hug Mama, wordlessly agreeing that the only thing to do is to help your cat. The operation goes okay, but the vet telephones a day later to report that Thai took a bad turn overnight and died near morning.

Thai's chocolate and silver body has a bandage cinched around his middle, like a wraparound saddle.

You're the one who buries Thai because Mama can't bring herself to. You put him in a Siamese-sized cardboard box, dig a hole under the holly in the backyard, and lay him to rest with a spank of the shovel blade and a prayer consisting of grief-stricken repetitions of the word please.

Two or three months later, you come home from school to find a pack of dogs in the backyard. They've dug Thai Thai up. You chase the dogs away, screeching from an irate crouch. Thai's corpse is nothing but matted fur and protruding bones. Its most conspicuous feature is the bandage holding the maggoty skeleton together at its cinched-in waist.

This isn't Thai, you tell yourself. I buried Thai a long, long time ago, and this isn't him.

You carry the remains, jacketed in the editorial section of the *Atlanta Constitution,* to a trash can and dump them with an abrupt, indifferent thunk. Pick-up is tomorrow.

One Sunday afternoon in March, you're standing with two hundred other homeless people at the entrance to Trinity United Methodist's soup kitchen, near the state capitol. It's drizzling. A thin but gritty-looking young woman in jeans and sweatshirt, her hair lying in dark strands against her forehead, is passing out hand-numbered tickets to every person who wants to get into the basement. At the head of the outside basement steps is a man in pleated slacks and a plaid shirt. He won't let anyone down the steps until they have a number in the group of ten currently being admitted. He has to get an okay from the soup-kitchen staff downstairs before he'll allow a new group of ten to pass.

Your number, on a green slip of paper already drizzle-dampened, is 126. The last group down held numbers 96 to 105. You think. Hard to tell with all the shoving, cursing, and bantering on the line. One angry black man up front doesn't belong there. He waves his ticket every time a new group of ten is called, hoping, even though his number is 182, to squeeze past the man set there to keep order.

"How many carahs yo ring?" he asks. "I sick. Lemme in fo I fall ouw. Damn disere rain."

When the dude holding number 109 doesn't show, the stair guard lets number 182 pass, a good-riddance sort of charity.

You shuffle up with the next two groups. How many of these people are robots, human machines drawn to the soup kitchen, as you may have been, on invisible tractor beams? The stair guard isn't wearing a watch or shaking a key ring. It's probably his wedding band that's the remote-control device....

"My God," he cries when he sees you. "Is that really you? It is, isn't it?"

The stair guy's name is Dirk Healy. He says he went to school with you in Hapeville. Remember Pamela van Rhyn? Remember Cynthia What's-her-name? When you go down into the basement, and get your two white-bread sandwiches and a Styrofoam cup of vegetable soup, Dirk convinces another volunteer to take over his job and sits down next to you at one of the rickety folding tables where your fellow street folk are single-mindedly eating. Dirk—who, as far as you're concerned, could be the Man in the Moon—doesn't ask you how you got in this fix, doesn't accuse, doesn't exhort.

"You're off your medication, aren't you?" Your hackles lift.

"Hey," he soothes, "I visited you at Quiet Harbor. The thing to do is, to get you back on it."

You eat, taking violent snatches of the sandwiches, quick sips of the soup. You one-eye Dirk over the steam the way that, years ago, Sky one-eyed you from her grain-crib nest.

"I may have a job for you," Dirk says confidentially. "Ever hear of Rockdale Biological?"

One summer, for reasons you don't understand, Mama sends you to visit your father and his ex-hairdresser floozie—whose name is Carol Grace—in the Florida town where they live off the proceeds of her mail-order business and sometimes bet the dogs at the local greyhound track.

Carol Grace may bet the greyhounds at the track, but, at home, she's a cat person. She owns seven: a marmalade-colored tom, a piebald tom, three tricolor females, an orange Angora of ambiguous gender, and a Manx mix with a tail four or five inches long, as if someone shortened it with a cleaver.

"If Stub was pure Manx," Carol Grace says, "he wouldn't have no tail. Musta been an alley tom in his mama's Kitty Litter."

Stroking Stub, she chortles happily. She and your mother look a little alike. They have a similar feistiness, too, although it seems coarser in Carol Grace, whom your balding father—she calls him Webby, for Pete's sake—unabashedly dotes on.

A few days into your visit, Carol Grace and you find one of her females, Hedy

Lamarr, lying crumpled under a pecan tree shading the two-story house's south side. The cat is dead. You kneel to touch her. Carol Grace kneels beside you.

"Musta fell," she says. "Lotsa people think cats are too jack-be-nimble to fall, but they can slip up, too. Guess my Hedy didn't remember that, pretty thing. Now look."

You are grateful that, today, Carol Grace does the burying and the prayer-saying. Her prayer includes the melancholy observation that anyone can fall. Anyone.

Enough of this crap, Penfield says. Tell me what you did, and for whom, and why, at Rockdale Biological.

Givin whah I can, you mumble, working to turn your head into the uncompromising rigidity of the clamps.

Adolf, Penfield says, what you're giving me is cat juggling.

Alone in the crafts room with Kim Yaughan while the other kids in Blue Group (QHPC's Wild Child Wing has two sections, Blue and Gold) go on a field trip, you daub acrylics at a crude portrayal of a cat walking upside down on a ceiling. Under the cat, a woman and a teen-age boy point and make hateful faces.

"Are they angry at the cat or at each other?" Kim asks.

You give her a look: What a stupid question.

Kim comes over, stands at your shoulder. If she were honest, she'd tell you that you're no artist at all. The painting may be psychologically revealing, but it refutes the notion that you have any talent as a draftsman or a colorist.

"Ever hear of British artist Louis Wain?" Kim says. "He lived with three unmarried sisters and a pack of cats. His schizophrenia didn't show up until he was almost sixty. That's late."

"Lucky," you say. "He didn't have so long to be crazy."

"Listen, now. Wain painted only cats. He must've really liked them. At first, he did smarmy, realistic kitties for calandars and postcards. Popular crap. Later, thinking jealous competitors were zapping him with X-rays or something, the cats in his paintings got weird, really hostile and menacing."

"Weirder than mine?" You jab your brush at it.

"Ah, that's a mere puddy-tat." Then: "In the fifteen years he was institutionalized, Wain painted scads of big-eyed, spiky-haired cats. He put bright neon auras and electrical fields around them. His backgrounds got geometrically rad. Today, you might think they were computer-generated. Anyhow, Wain's crazy stuff was better—fiercer, stronger—than the crap he'd done sane."

"Meaning I'm a total loss unless I get crazier?" you say.

"No. What I'm trying to tell you is that the triangles, stars, rainbows, and repeating arabesques that Wain put into his paintings grew from a desperate effort to... well, to impose order on the chaos *inside* him. It's touching, really touching. Wain was trying to confront and reverse, the only way he could, the disintegration of his adult personality. See?"

But you don't. Not exactly.

Kim taps your acrylic cat with a burgundy fingernail. "You're not going to be the new Picasso, but you aren't doomed to suffer as terrifying a schizophrenia as Wain suffered, either. The bizarre thing in your painting is the cat on the ceiling. The colors, and the composition itself, are reassuringly conventional. A good sign for your mental health. Another thing is, Wain's doctors couldn't give him antipsychotic drugs. You, though, have access."

"Cheers." You pantomime knocking back a little cup of Haldol.

Kim smiles. "So why'd you paint the cat upside-down?"

"Because *I'm* upside-down," you say.

Kim gives you a peck on the cheek. "You're not responsible for a gone-awry brain chemistry or an unbalanced metabolism, hon. Go easy on yourself, okay?" Dropping your brush, you pull Kim to you and try to nuzzle her under the jaw. Effortlessly, she bends back your hand and pushes you away. "But that," she says, "you're going to have to control. Friends, not lovers. Sorry if I gave you the wrong idea. Really. Really."

"If the pieces toward the end don't fit," Howie tells you, "you can always use a razor blade." He holds one up.

You try to take it. Double-edged, it slices your thumb. Some of your blood spatters on the cat puzzle.

A guy in a truck drives up to the specimen-prep platform and loading dock behind Rockdale Biological Medical Supply. It's an unmarked panel truck with no windows behind the cab. The guys who drive the truck change, it seems, almost every week, but you're a two-month fixture on the concrete platform with the slide cages and the euthanasia cabinet. Back here, you're Dirk Healy's main man, especially now that he's off on a business trip somewhere.

Your job is both mindless and strength-sapping. The brick wall around the rear of the RBMS complex, and the maple trees shielding the loading dock, help you keep your head together. Healy has you on a lower dosage of haloperidol than you took while you and Marti were still married. Says you were overmedicated before. Says you were, ha ha, "an apathetic drug slave." He should know. He's been a hotshot in national medical supply for years.

"We'll have you up in the front office in no time," he assured you a couple weeks ago. "The platform job's a kind of trial."

The guy in the truck backs up and starts unloading. Dozens of cats in slide cages. You wear elbow-length leather gloves, and a heavy apron, and feel a bit like an old-timey Western blacksmith. The cats are pieces of scrap iron to be worked in the forge. You slide the door end of each cage into the connector between the open platform and the euthanasia cabinet, then poke the cats in the butt or the flank with a long metal rod until they duck into the cabinet to escape your prod-ding. When the cabinet's full, you drop the safety door, check the gauges, turn on the gas. It hisses louder than the cats climbing over one another, louder than their yowling and tumbling, which noises gradually subside and finally stop.

By hand, you unload the dead cats from the chamber, slinging them out by their tails or their legs. You cease feeling like a blacksmith. You imagine yourself as a nineteenth-century trapper, stacking fox, beaver, rabbit, wolf, and muskrat pelts on a travois for a trip to the trading post. The pelts are pretty, though many are blemished by vivid skin diseases and a thick black dandruff of gassed fleas. How much could they be worth?

"Nine fifty a cat," Dirk Healy has said. That seems unlikely. They're no longer moving. They're no longer—if they ever were—highly lustrous. They're floppy, anonymous, and dead, their fur contaminated by a lethal gas.

A heavy-duty wheelbarrow rests beside the pile of cats on the platform. You unwind a hose and fill the barrow with water. Dirk has ordered you to submerge the gassed cats to make certain they're dead. Smart. Some of the cats are plucky boogers. They'll mew at you or swim feebly in the cat pile even before you pick them up and sling them into the wheelbarrow. The water in the wheelbarrow ends it. Indisputably. It also washes away fleas and the worst aspects of feline scabies. You pull a folding chair over and sort through the cats for the ones with flea col-lars, ID collars, rabies tags. You take these things off. You do it with your gloves on, a sodden cat corpse hammocked in your apron. It's not easy, given your wet glove fingers.

If it's sunny, you take the dead cats to the bright part of the platform and lay them out in neat rows to dry.

Can't you get him to stop mumbling? Penfield asks someone in the room. His testimony's almost unintelligible.

He's replaying the experience inwardly, an indistinct figure says. But he's starting to go autistic on us.

Look, Penfield says. We've got to get him to verbalize clearly—or we've wasted our time.

Two months after the divorce, you drive to Spartanburg, to the Braggs' house, to see Jacob. Mr. Bragg—Howie—intercepts you at the front gate, as if appraised of your arrival by surveillance equipment.

"I'm sorry," he says, "but Marti doesn't want to see you, and she doesn't want *you* to see Jake. If you don't leave, I'll have to call the police to, ah, you know, remove you."

You don't contest this. You walk across the road to your car. From there, you can see that atop the brick post on either side of Mr. Bragg's ornate gate reposes a roaring granite lion. You can't remember seeing these lions before, but the crazed and reticulated state of the granite suggests they've been there a while.

It's a puzzle ....

As you lay out the dead cats, you assign them names. The names you assign are always Mehitabel, Felix, Sylvester, Tom, Heathcliff, Garfield, and Bill. These seven names must serve for all the cats on the platform. Consequently, you add Roman numerals to the names when you run out of names before you do cats:

Mehitabel II, Felix II, Sylvester Tom II, and so on. It's a neat, workable system. Once, you cycled all the way to Sylvester VII before running out of specimens.

As a fifth grader in Notasulga, you sit and watch a film about the American space program.

An old film clip shows a cat—really more a kitten than a cat—suspended from a low ceiling by its feet. It's a metal ceiling, and the scientist who devised the experiment (which has something to do with studying the kitten's reactions to upside-downness, then applying these findings to astronauts aboard a space station) has fastened magnets to the cat's feet so that they will adhere to the metal surface.

The scientist has also rigged up a pair of mice in the same odd way, to see if they will distract, entice, or frighten the hanging kitten. They don't. The kitten is terrified not of the mice (who seem to be torpid and unimaginative representatives of their kind), but of the alien condition in which it finds itself. Insofar as it is able, the kitten lurches against the magnets, its ears back, its mouth wide open in a silent cry. On the sound track, a male voice explains the import and usefulness of this experiment.

No one can hear him, though, because most of the other kids in Miss Beischer's class are laughing uproariously at the kitten. You look around in a kind of sick stupefaction.

Milly Heckler, Agnes Lee Terrance, and a few other girls appear to be as appalled as you, but the scene doesn't last long—it's probably shorter than your slow-motion memory of it—and it seems for a moment that you *are* that kitten, that everything in the world has been wrenchingly upended.

I know it *seemed* to you that evil people were trying to invade and control your thoughts," Dr. Hall, the director of Quiet Harbor, tells you. He pets a neutered male just back from a visit to the Gerontological Wing. "But that was just a symptom of the scrambled condition of your brain chemistry. The truth is…

Fatigued, you slouch out the rear gate of Rockdale Biological. Your apartment—the three-roomer that Healy provided—is only a short distance away. A late-model Lincoln Town Car pulls alongside you as you walk the weed-grown sidewalk. The tinted window on the front-seat passenger's side powers down, and you catch your first glimpse of the raw-complexioned man who introduces himself as David Penfield. An alias? Why do you think so?

"If you like," he says, "think of me as the Zoo Cop."

It's a permission you don't really want. Why would you choose to think of a well-dressed, ordinary-featured man with visible acne scarring as something as *déclassé* as, Jesus, the Zoo Cop. Is he a detective of some sort? What does he want?

The next thing you know you're in the car with Penfield and two other tight-lipped men.

The next thing you know you're on the expressway and one of the Zoo Cop's associates—goons?—has locked the suction-cup feet of one of those corny Garfield toys on his tinted window as a kind of—what?—mockery? rebuke? warning?

The next thing you know you're in a basement that clearly isn't the soup kitchen of Trinity United Methodist. The next thing you know you're flat on your back on a table. The next thing you know you don't know anything....

Marti's body is stenciled with primitive blue flowers, a blossom on her neck, more on her breasts, an indigo bouquet on the milky plane of her abdomen. You gaze at her in groggy wonderment. The woman you one day marry has become, overnight, an arabesque of disturbing floral bruises.

"Marti," you whisper. "Marti, don't leave me. Marti, don't take my son away."

Penfield, a.k.a. the Zoo Cop (you realize during your descent into the puzzle box), isn't a real cop. He hates you because what you've been doing for Healy is vile, contemptible, evil. So it is, so it is. He wants to get Healy, who hasn't been around this last week at all, who's maybe skipped off to Barbados or the Yucatan or Saint-Tropez.

Penfield is an animal-rights eco-terrorist, well-financed and determined, and the ESB zappings to which he and his associates are subjecting you are designed to incriminate, pinpoint, and doom old Dirk and *his* associates, who obviously deserve it. You, too. You deserve it, too. No argument there. None.

Christ, Penfield says, unhook the son of a bitch and carry him upstairs. Dump him somewhere remote, somewhere rural.

You visit the pound for a replacement for Springer and Ossie, gassed three or four years ago. The attendant tells you there are plenty of potential adoptees at the shelter. You go down the rows of cages to select one. The kittens in the fouled sawdust tumble, paw, and miaow, putting on a dispirited show.

"This one," you finally say.

"Cute." The attendant approves. Well, they'd fire her if she didn't. The idea is to adopt these creatures out, not to let them lapse into expendability.

"It's for Jake, my son," you tell her. "His asthma isn't that bad. I think he may be growing out of it."

"Look at my puzzle," Howie says, yanking the razor blade away from you. "You've bled all over it...."

—*For Jeanne Schinto*

GORDON,
THE SELF-MADE CAT
Peter S. Beagle

Peter S. Beagle was born in Manhattan in 1939 and raised in the Bronx. He originally proclaimed he would be a writer when ten years old, and is now acknowledged as an American fantasy icon. In addition to being an acclaimed novelist and writer of short stories and nonfiction, Peter also has written numerous plays, teleplays, and screenplays, and is a gifted poet, librettist, lyricist, and singer/songwriter. For more information about *The Last Unicorn*, *A Fine and Private Place*, *Summerlong*, *I'm Afraid You've Got Dragons*, *I See By My Outfit*, "Two Hearts," and the rest of his work, visit www.peterbeagle.com.

"Gordon, the Self-Made Cat" started life in the late 1960s when Beagle was asked by a relatively small (and now defunct) animation company to submit ideas for possible feature-length development. Nothing came of it and the story languished until late 2001, when a friend discovered the manuscript while hunting through a rusty filing cabinet in the author's garage. After several revisions, "Gordon" was published in Beagle's email newsletter *The Raven* as a freebie and then reprinted in his collection *The Line Between*. He is now expanding the story into a standalone children's book.

Beagle had a Persian cat named Princess Grace (the original of Miss Sophia Brown in his novel *Tamsin*), who hung out entirely with the dogs—she never once looked at another cat—and was a fully-accepted member of the pack. "Gordon" is an outgrowth of his speculation on what a mouse equivalent of Princess Grace ("the Hussy," as his kids called her) might be like.

Once upon a time to a family of house mice there was born a son named Gordon. He looked very much like his father and mother and all his brothers and sisters, who were gray and had bright, twitchy, black eyes, but what went on inside Gordon was very different from what went on inside the rest of his family. He was forever asking why everything had to be the way it was, and never satisfied with the answer. Why did mice eat cheese? Why did they live in the dark and only go out when it was dark? Where did mice come from, anyway? *What were people?* Why did people smell so funny? Suppose mice were big and people were tiny? Suppose mice could fly? Most mice don't ask many questions, but Gordon never stopped.

One evening, when Gordon was only a few weeks old, his next-to-eldest sister was sent out to see if anything interesting had been left open in the pantry. She never returned. Gordon's father shrugged sadly and spread his front paws, and said, "The cat."

"What's a cat?" Gordon asked.

His mother and father looked at one another and sighed. "They have to know sometime," his father said. "Better he learns it at home than on the streets."

His mother sniffled a little and said, "But he's so young," and his father answered, "Cats don't care." So they told Gordon about cats right then, expecting him to start crying and saying that there weren't any such things. It's a hard idea to get used to. But Gordon only asked, "Why do cats eat mice?"

"I guess we taste very good," his father said.

Gordon said, "But cats don't have to eat mice. They get plenty of other food that probably tastes as good. Why should anybody eat anybody if he doesn't have to?"

"Gordon," said his father. "Listen to me. There are two kinds of creatures in the world. There are animals that hunt, and animals that are hunted. We mice just happen to be the kind of animal that gets hunted, and it doesn't really matter if the cat *is* hungry or not. It's the way life is. It's really a great honor to be the hunted, if you just look at it the right way."

"Phooey on that," said Gordon. "Where do I go to learn to be a cat?"

They thought he was joking, but as soon as Gordon was old enough to go places by himself, he packed a clean shirt and some peanut butter, and started off for cat school. "I love you very much," he said to his parents before he left, "but this business of being hunted for the rest of my life just because I happened to be born a mouse is not for me." And off he went, all by himself.

All cats go to school, you know, whether you ever see them going or not. Dogs don't, but cats always have and always will. There are a great many cat schools, so Gordon found one easily enough, and he walked bravely up the front steps and knocked at the door. He said that he wanted to speak to the Principal.

He almost expected to be eaten right there, but the cats—students and teachers alike—were so astonished that they let him pass through, and one of the teachers took him to the Principal's office. Gordon could feel the cats looking at him, and hear the sounds their noses made as they smelled how good he was, but he held on tight to the suitcase with his shirt and the peanut butter, and he never looked back.

The Principal was a fat old tiger cat who chewed on his tail all the time he was talking to Gordon. "You must be out of your mind," he said when Gordon told him he wanted to be a cat. "I'd smack you up this minute, but it's bad luck to eat crazies. Get out of here! The day mice go to cat school…"

"Why not?" said Gordon. "Is it in writing? Where does it say that I can't go to school here if I want?"

Well, of course there's nothing in the rules of cat schools that says mice can't enroll. Nobody ever thought of putting it in.

The Principal folded his paws and said, "Gordon, look at it this way—"

"You look at it *my* way," said Gordon. "I want to be a cat, and I bet I'd make a better one than the dopey-looking animals I've seen in this school. Most of them look as if they wouldn't even make good mice! So let's make a deal. You let me come to school here and study for one term, and if at the end of that time I'm not doing better than any cat in the school—if even one cat has better grades than I have—then you can eat me and that'll be the end of it. Is that fair?"

No cat can resist a challenge like that. But before agreeing, the Principal insisted on one small change: at the end of the term, if Gordon didn't have the very best marks in the school, then the privilege of eating him would go to the cat that did.

"Ought to encourage some of those louts to work harder," the Principal said to himself, as Gordon left his office. "He's crazy, but he's right—most of them wouldn't even make good mice. I almost hope he does it."

So Gordon went to cat school. Every day he sat at his special little desk, surrounded by a hundred kittens and half-grown cats who would have liked nothing better than to leap on him and play games with him for a while before they gobbled him. He learned how to wash himself, and what to do to keep his claws sharp, and how to watch everything in the room while pretending to be asleep. There was a class on Dealing With Dogs, and another on Getting Down From Trees, which is much harder than climbing up, and also a particularly scholarly seminar on the various meanings of "Bad Kitty!" Gordon's personal favorite was the Visions class, which had to do with the enchanting things all cats can see that no one else ever does—the great, gliding ancestors, and faraway castles, and mysterious forests full of monsters to chase. The Professor of Visions told his colleagues that he had never had such a brilliant student. "It would be a crime to eat such a mouse!" he proclaimed everywhere. "An absolute, shameful, yummy crime."

The class in Mouse-Hunting was a bit awkward at first, because usually the teacher asks one of the students to be the mouse, and in Gordon's case the Principal felt that would be too risky. But Gordon insisted on being chased like everyone else, and not only was he never caught (well, *almost* never; there was one blue Persian who could turn on a dime), but when he took his own turn at chasing, he proved to be a natural expert. In fact his instant mastery of the Flying Pounce caused his teacher and the entire class to sit up and applaud. Gordon took three bows and an encore.

There was also a class where the cats learned the necessities of getting along with people: how to lie in laps, how to keep from scratching furniture even when you feel you have to, what to do when children pick you up, and how to ask for food or affection in such a sweet manner that people call other people to look at you. These classes always made Gordon a little sad. He didn't suppose that he would ever be a real "people" cat, for who would want to hold a mouse on his lap, or scratch it behind the ears while it purred? Still, he paid strict attention in People Class, as he did in all the others, for all the cats knew that whoever did best in school that term would be the one who ate him, and they worked harder than they ever had in their lives. The Principal said that they were becoming the best students in the school's history, and he talked openly about making this a regular thing, one mouse to a term.

When all the marks were in, and all the grades added up, two students led the rankings: Gordon and the blue Persian. Their scores weren't even a whisker's thickness apart. In the really important classes, like Running And Pouncing, Climbing, Stalking, and Waiting For The Prey To Forget You're Still There; and in matters of feline manners such as Washing, Tail Etiquette, The Elegant Yawn, Sleeping In Undignified Positions, and Making Sure You Get Enough Food Without Looking Greedy (101 *and* 102)—in all of these Gordon and the blue Persian were first, and the rest nowhere. Besides that, both could meow in five different dialects: Persian, Abyssinian, Siamese, Burmese (which almost no cat who isn't Burmese ever learns), and basic tiger.

But there can only be one Top Cat to a term; no ties allowed. In order to decide the matter once and for all between them, the Principal announced that Gordon and the blue Persian would have to face one another in a competitive mouse roundup.

The Persian and Gordon got along quite well, all things considered, so they shook paws—carefully—and the Persian purred, "No hard feelings."

"None at all," Gordon answered. "If anyone here got to eat me, I'd much rather it was you."

"Very sporting of you," the Persian said. "I hope so too."

"But it won't happen," Gordon said.

The blue Persian never had a chance. Once he and Gordon were set on their marks in a populous mouse neighborhood, Gordon ambushed and outsmarted and cornered all but a handful of the very quickest mice, and did it in a style so smooth, so effortlessly elegant—so *catlike*—that the Persian finally threw up his paws and surrendered. In front of the entire faculty and student body of the cat school, he announced, "I yield to Gordon. He's a better cat than I am, and I'm not ashamed to admit it. If all mice were like him, we cats would be vegetarians." (Persians are *very* dramatic.)

The cheering was so wild and thunderous that no one objected in the least when Gordon freed all the mice he had captured. Cats can appreciate a grand gesture, and everyone had already had lunch.

Gordon had won his bet, and, like the blue Persian, the Principal was cat enough to accept it graciously. He scheduled a celebration, which the whole school attended, and at the end of the party he announced that Gordon was now to be considered as much a cat as any student in the school, if not more so. He gave Gordon a little card to show that he was a cat in good standing, and all the students cheered, and Gordon made another speech that began, "Fellow cats...." As he spoke, he wished very much that his parents could be there to see what he had accomplished, and just how different things could be if you just asked questions and weren't afraid of new ideas.

Being acknowledged the best cat in the school didn't make Gordon let up in his studies. Instead, he worked even harder, and did so well that he graduated with the special degree of *felis maximus*, which is Latin for *some cat!* He stayed on at the school to teach a seminar in Evasive Maneuvers, which proved very popular, and a course in the Standing Jump (for a bird that comes flying over when you weren't looking).

The story of his new life spread everywhere among all mice, and grew very quickly into a myth more terrifying than any cat could have been. They whispered of "Gordon the Terrible," "Gordon, the Self-Made Cat," and, simply, "The Unspeakable," and told midnight tales of a gigantic mouse who lashed his tail and sprang at them with his razor claws out and his savage yellow eyes blazing; a mouse without pity who hunted them out in their deepest hiding places, walking without a sound. They believed unquestioningly that he ate mice like gingersnaps, and laughingly handed over to his cat friends those he was too full to devour. There was even a dreadful legend that Gordon had eaten his own family, and that he frequently took kittens from the school on field trips in order to teach them personally the secret mouse ways that no mere cat could ever have known.

These stories made Gordon deeply unhappy when he heard them, because he believed with absolute conviction that what he had achieved was for the good of all mice everywhere. Whether he trapped a lone mouse or cornered a dozen trembling in an attic or behind a refrigerator, he would say the same thing to them: "Look at me. *Look at me!* I am a mouse like you—nothing more, nothing less—and yet I walk with cats every day, and I am not eaten! I am respected, I am admired, I am even powerful among cats—and every one of you could be like me! Do not believe that we mice are born only to be hunted, humiliated, tormented, and finally gobbled up. It is not true! Instead of huddling in the shadows, in constant lifelong terror, pitiful little balls of fur, we too can be sleek, fierce hunters, fearing nothing and no one. Run now and spread the word! You must spread the word!"

Saying that, he would step back and let the mice scatter, hoping each time that they would finally understand what he was trying to show them. But it simply never happened. The mice always scurried away, convinced that they had escaped only by great good fortune, and myths and legends of the terrible Self-Made Cat were all that spread among them, growing ever more horrifying, ever more chilling. It didn't matter that not one mouse had ever actually seen Gordon doing any of the frightful things he was supposed to have done. That's the way it is with legends.

Now it happened that Gordon was walking down the street one day, on his way to a faculty meeting, padding along like a leopard, twitching his tail like a lion, and making the eager little noises in his throat that a tiger makes when he smells food. Quite suddenly an enormous shadow fell across his path, so big that he looked up to see if he were going through a tunnel. What he saw was a dog. What he actually saw was a leg, for this dog was huge, too big for even a full-grown cat to have understood his real size without looking twice. The dog rumbled, "Oh, goody! I love mice. Lots of phosphorus in mice. Yummy."

Gordon crouched, tail lashing, and lifted the fur along his spine. "Watch it, dog," he said warningly. "Don't mess with me, I'm telling you."

"Oh, how cute," the dog said. "He's playing he's a cat. I'm a cat too. Meow."

"I *am* a cat!" Gordon arched his back until it ached, hissing and spitting and growling in his throat, all more or less at the same time. "I *am!* You want to see my card? Look, right here."

"A crazy," the dog said wonderingly. "They say it's bad luck to eat a crazy. Good thing I'm not superstitious."

Having given the proper First Warning, exactly as he'd been taught, Gordon moved quickly to the Second—the lightning-swift slash of the right paw across the nose. Gordon had to leap straight up to reach the dog's big wet nose, but even with that handicap, he executed the Second Warning in superb style.

Instead of yelping and retreating in a properly humbled state, however, the dog only sneezed.

This, Gordon thought, is the difference between theory and practice.

But there was a reason that Gordon's seminar in Evasive Maneuvers was always so well attended. With astonishing daring, he went directly from the Second Warning right into the Fourth Avoidance, which involves a double feint—head looking *this* way, tail jerking *that* way—followed by a quick, threatening charge directly at the attacker, and *then* a leap to the side, which, done correctly, leaves one perfectly poised either for escape or the Flying Pounce, depending on the situation.

But the big dog had no idea that a classic Evasive Maneuver had just been performed upon him, leaving him looking like an idiot. He was used to looking like an idiot. He gave a delighted bounce, wuffed, "*Tag*—you're it!" and went straight for Gordon, who responded by going up a tree with the polished grace that always left his students too breathless to cheer. He found a comfortable branch and rested there, thinking ruefully that a real cat wouldn't have been so proud of being a cat as to waste time arguing about it.

The dog sat down too, grinning. "Be a bird now," he called to Gordon. "Let's see you be a bird and fly away."

Normally, Gordon could easily have stayed up in the tree longer than the dog felt like waiting below, but he was tired and rather thirsty, not to mention annoyed at the thought of being late for the faculty meeting. Something had to be done. But what?

He was bravely considering an original plan of leaping straight down at the dog, when three young mice happened along. They had been out shopping for their mother.

They were really very young, and as they had never seen Gordon the Terrible—though they had heard about him since they were blind babies—they didn't know who it was in the tree. All they saw was a fellow mouse in danger, and, being at the age when they didn't know any better than to do things like that, they carefully put down their packages and began luring the dog away from the tree. First one mouse would rush in at him and make the dog chase him a little way, and then another would come scampering from somewhere else, so that the dog would leave off chasing the first mouse and go after him.

The dog, who was actually quite good-natured, and not very hungry, had a fine time running after them all. He followed them farther and farther away from the tree, and had probably forgotten all about Gordon by the time the Unspeakable was able to spring down from the tree and vanish into the bushes.

Gordon would have waited to thank the three mice, but they had disappeared, along with the dog. Anxious not to miss his meeting, he dashed back to the school, slowing down before he got there to catch his breath and smooth his whiskers. "It could happen to anyone," he told himself. "There's nothing to be ashamed of." Yet there was something fundamentally troubling to Gordon about having run away. Feeling uncertain for the first time since he had marched up the front steps, he washed himself all over and stalked on into the school, outwardly calm and proud, the best cat anyone there would ever see, Gordon the Terrible, the Unspeakable—yes, the Self-Made Cat.

But another cat—the Assistant Professor of Tailchasing, in fact—had seen the whole incident, and had already interrupted the faculty meeting with the shocking tale.

The Principal tried to brush the news aside. "When it's time to climb a tree, you climb a tree," he said. "Any cat knows that." (He had become quite fond of Gordon, in his way.)

It wasn't enough. The Assistant Professor of Tailchasing (a chocolate-point Siamese who dreamed of one day heading the school himself) led the opposition. As the Assistant Professor saw it, Gordon was plainly a fraud, a pretender, a cat in card only, so friendly with his fellow mice that they had rushed to help him when he was in danger. In light of that, who could say what Gordon's *real* plans might be? Why had he come to the school in the first place? What if more like him followed? What if the mice were plotting to attack the cat school, all cat schools?

This thought rattled everyone at the table. With a mouse like Gordon in their midst, a mouse who knew far more about being a cat than the cats themselves, was any feline safe?

Just that quickly, fear replaced reason. Within minutes everyone but the Principal forgot how much they had liked and admired Gordon. Admitting him to the school had been a catastrophic mistake, one that must be set right without a moment's delay!

The Principal groaned and covered his eyes and sent for Gordon. He was almost crying as he took Gordon's cat card away.

Gordon protested like mad, of course. He spoke of Will and Choice, and Freedom, and the transforming power of Questioning Assumptions. But the Principal said sadly, "We just can't trust you, Gordon. Go away now, before I eat you myself. I always wondered what you'd taste like." Then he put his head down on his desk and really did begin to cry.

So Gordon packed his clean shirt and his leftover peanut butter and left the cat school. All the cats formed a double line to let him pass, their faces turned away, and nobody said a word. The Assistant Professor of Tailchasing was poised to pounce at the very last, but the Principal stepped on his tail.

Nobody ever heard of Gordon again. There were stories that he'd gone right on being a cat, even without his card; and there were other tales that said he had been driven out of the country by the mice themselves. But only the Principal knew for sure, because only the Principal had heard the words that Gordon was muttering to himself as he walked away from the cat school with his head held high.

"Woof," Gordon was murmuring thoughtfully. "Woof. Bow-wow. Shouldn't be too hard."

THE JAGUAR HUNTER

Lucius Shepard

Lucius Shepard was born in Lynchburg Virginia, grew up in Daytona Beach, Florida, and lives in Portland, Oregon. His short fiction has won the Nebula Award, the Hugo Award, the International Horror Guild Award, the National Magazine Award, the Locus Award, the Theodore Sturgeon Award, and the World Fantasy Award. His most recent books are a short fiction collection, *Viator Plus* and a short novel, *The Taborin Scale*. Forthcoming are another short fiction collection, *Five Autobiographies*, and two novels, tentatively titled *The Piercefields* and *The End Of Life As We Know It*, and a short novel, *The House of Everything and Nothing*.

"The Jaguar Hunter" is based on a story told to Shepard in a bar in Telas, Honduras by an old and very drunk man.

It was his wife's debt to Onofrio Esteves, the appliance dealer, that brought Esteban Caax to town for the first time in almost a year. By nature he was a man who enjoyed the sweetness of the countryside above all else; the placid measures of a farmer's day invigorated him, and he took great pleasure in nights spent joking and telling stories around a fire, or lying beside his wife, Incarnación. Puerto Morada, with its fruit-company imperatives and sullen dogs and cantinas that blared American music, was a place he avoided like the plague; indeed, from his home atop the mountain whose slopes formed the northernmost enclosure of Bahía Onda, the rusted tin roofs ringing the bay resembled a dried crust of blood such as might appear upon the lips of a dying man.

On this particular morning, however, he had no choice but to visit the town. Incarnación had—without his knowledge—purchased a battery-operated television set on credit from Onofrio, and he was threatening to seize Esteban's three milk cows in lieu of the eight hundred lempiras that was owed; he refused to accept the return of the television, but had sent word that he was willing to discuss an alternate method of payment. Should Esteban lose the cows, his income would drop below a subsistence level and he would be forced to take up his old

146

occupation, an occupation far more onerous than farming.

As he walked down the mountain, past huts of thatch and brushwood poles identical to his own, following a trail that wound through sun-browned thickets lorded over by banana trees, he was not thinking of Onofrio but of Incarnación. It was in her nature to be frivolous, and he had known this when he had married her; yet the television was emblematic of the differences that had developed between them since their children had reached maturity. She had begun to put on sophisticated airs, to laugh at Esteban's country ways, and she had become the doyenne of a group of older women, mostly widows, all of whom aspired to sophistication. Each night they would huddle around the television and strive to outdo one another in making sagacious comments about the American detective shows they watched; and each night Esteban would sit outside the hut and gloomily ponder the state of his marriage. He believed Incarnación's association with the widows was her manner of telling him that she looked forward to adopting the black skirt and shawl, that—having served his purpose as a father—he was now an impediment to her. Though she was only forty-one, younger by three years than Esteban, she was withdrawing from the life of the senses; they rarely made love anymore, and he was certain that this partially embodied her resentment to the fact that the years had been kind to him. He had the look of one of the Old Patuca—tall, with chiseled features and wide-set eyes; his coppery skin was relatively unlined and his hair jet black. Incarnación's hair was streaked with gray, and the clean beauty of her limbs had dissolved beneath layers of fat. He had not expected her to remain beautiful, and he had tried to assure her that he loved the woman she was and not merely the girl she had been. But that woman was dying, infected by the same disease that had infected Puerto Morada, and perhaps his love for her was dying, too.

The dusty street on which the appliance store was situated ran in back of the movie theater and the Hotel Circo del Mar, and from the inland side of the street Esteban could see the bell towers of Santa María del Onda rising above the hotel roof like the horns of a great stone snail. As a young man, obeying his mother's wish that he become a priest, he had spent three years cloistered beneath those towers, preparing for the seminary under the tutelage of old Father Gonsalvo. It was the part of his life he most regretted, because the academic disciplines he had mastered seemed to have stranded him between the world of the Indian and that of contemporary society; in his heart he held to his father's teachings—the principles of magic, the history of the tribe, the lore of nature—and yet he could never escape the feeling that such wisdom was either superstitious or simply unimportant. The shadows of the towers lay upon his soul as surely as they did upon the cobbled square in front of the church, and the sight of them caused him to pick up his pace and lower his eyes.

Farther along the street was the Cantina Atómica, a gathering place for the well-to-do youth of the town, and across from it was the appliance store, a one-story building of yellow stucco with corrugated metal doors that were lowered at night. Its façade was decorated by a mural that supposedly represented the merchandise within: sparkling refrigerators and televisions and washing machines, all given the impression of enormity by the tiny men and women painted below them, their hands upflung in awe. The actual merchandise was much less imposing, consisting mainly of radios and used kitchen equipment. Few people in Puerto Morada could afford more, and those who could generally bought elsewhere. The majority of Onofrio's clientele were poor, hard-pressed to meet his schedule of payments, and to a large degree his wealth derived from selling repossessed appliances over and over.

Raimundo Esteves, a pale young man with puffy cheeks and heavily lidded eyes and a petulant mouth, was leaning against the counter when Esteban entered; Raimundo smirked and let out a piercing whistle, and a few seconds later his father emerged from the back room: a huge slug of a man, even paler than Raimundo. Filaments of gray hair were slicked down across his mottled scalp, and his belly stretched the front of a starched *guayabera*. He beamed and extended a hand.

"How good to see you," he said. "Raimundo! Bring us coffee and two chairs."

Much as he disliked Onofrio, Esteban was in no position to be uncivil: He accepted the handshake. Raimundo spilled coffee in the saucers and clattered the chairs and glowered, angry at being forced to serve an Indian.

"Why will you not let me return the television?" asked Esteban after taking a seat; and then, unable to bite back the words, he added, "Is it no longer your policy to swindle my people?"

Onofrio sighed, as if it were exhausting to explain things to a fool such as Esteban. "I do not swindle your people. I go beyond the letter of the contracts in allowing them to make returns rather than pursuing matters through the courts. In your case, however, I have devised a way whereby you can keep the television without any further payments and yet settle the account. Is this a swindle?"

It was pointless to argue with a man whose logic was as facile and self-serving as Onofrio's. "Tell me what you want," said Esteban.

Onofrio wetted his lips, which were the color of raw sausage. "I want you to kill the jaguar of Barrio Carolina."

"I no longer hunt," said Esteban.

"The Indian is afraid," said Raimundo, moving up behind Onofrio's shoulder. "I told you."

Onofrio waved him away and said to Esteban, "That is unreasonable. If I take the cows, you will once again be hunting jaguars. But if you do this, you will have to hunt only one jaguar."

"One that has killed eight hunters." Esteban set down his coffee cup and stood. "It is no ordinary jaguar."

Raimundo laughed disparagingly, and Esteban skewered him with a stare.

"Ah!" said Onofrio, smiling a flatterer's smile. "But none of the eight used your method."

"Your pardon, *don* Onofrio," said Esteban with mock formality. "I have other business to attend."

"I will pay you five hundred lempiras in addition to erasing the debt," said Onofrio.

"Why?" asked Esteban. "Forgive me, but I cannot believe it is due to a concern for the public welfare."

Onofrio's fat throat pulsed, his face darkened.

"Never mind," said Esteban. "It is not enough."

"Very well. A thousand." Onofrio's casual manner could not conceal the anxiety in his voice.

Intrigued, curious to learn the extent of Onofrio's anxiety, Esteban plucked a figure from the air. "Ten thousand," he said. "And in advance."

"Ridiculous! I could hire ten hunters for this much! Twenty!"

Esteban shrugged. "But none with my method."

For a moment Onofrio sat with hands enlaced, twisting them, as if struggling with some pious conception. "All right," he said, the words squeezed out of him. "Ten thousand!"

The reason for Onofrio's interest in Barrio Carolina suddenly dawned on Esteban, and he understood that the profits involved would make his fee seem pitifully small. But he was possessed by the thought of what ten thousand lempiras could mean: a herd of cows, a small truck to haul produce, or—and as he thought it, he realized this was the happiest possibility—the little stucco house in Barrio Clarín that Incarnación had set her heart on. Perhaps owning it would soften her toward him. He noticed Raimundo staring at him, his expression a knowing smirk; and even Onofrio, though still outraged by the fee, was beginning to show signs of satisfaction, adjusting the fit of his *guayabera*, slicking down his already-slicked-down hair. Esteban felt debased by their capacity to buy him, and to preserve a last shred of dignity, he turned and walked to the door.

"I will consider it," he tossed back over his shoulder. "And I will give you my answer in the morning."

"Murder Squad of New York," starring a bald American actor, was the featured attraction on Incarnación's television that night, and the widows sat cross-legged on the floor, filling the hut so completely that the charcoal stove and the sleeping hammock had been moved outside in order to provide good viewing angles for the latecomers. To Esteban, standing in the doorway, it seemed his home had been invaded by a covey of large black birds with cowled heads, who were receiving evil instruction from the core of a flickering gray jewel. Reluctantly, he pushed between them and made his way to the shelves mounted on the wall behind the set; he reached up to the top shelf and pulled down a long bundle wrapped in oil-stained newspapers. Out of the corner of his eye, he saw Incarnación watching him, her lips thinned, curved in a smile, and that cicatrix of a smile branded its mark on Esteban's heart. She knew what he was about, and she was delighted! Not in the least worried! Perhaps she had known of Onofrio's plan to kill the jaguar, perhaps she had schemed with Onofrio to entrap him. Infuriated, he barged through the widows, setting them to gabbling, and walked out into his banana grove and sat on a stone amidst it. The night was cloudy, and only a handful of stars showed between the tattered dark shapes of the leaves; the wind sent the leaves slithering together, and he heard one of his cows snorting and smelled the ripe odor of the corral. It was as if the solidity of his life had been reduced to this isolated perspective, and he bitterly felt the isolation. Though he would admit to fault in the marriage, he could think of nothing he had done that could have bred Incarnación's hateful smile.

After a while, he unwrapped the bundle of newspapers and drew out a thin-bladed machete of the sort used to chop banana stalks, but which he used to kill jaguars. Just holding it renewed his confidence and gave him a feeling of strength. It had been four years since he had hunted, yet he knew he had not lost the skill. Once he had been proclaimed the greatest hunter in the province of Nueva Esperanza, as had his father before him, and he had not retired from hunting because of age or infirmity, but because the jaguars were beautiful, and their beauty had begun to outweigh the reasons he had for killing them. He had no better reason to kill the jaguar of Barrio Carolina. It menaced no one other than those who hunted it, who sought to invade its territory, and its death would profit only a dishonorable man and a shrewish wife, and would spread the contamination of Puerto Morada. And besides, it was a black jaguar.

"Black jaguars," his father had told him, "are creatures of the moon. They have other forms and magical purposes with which we must not interfere. Never hunt them!"

His father had not said that the black jaguars lived on the moon, simply that they utilized its power; but as a child, Esteban had dreamed about a moon of ivory forests and silver meadows through which the jaguars flowed as swiftly as black water; and when he had told his father of the dreams, his father had said that such dreams were representations of a truth, and that sooner or later he would discover the truth underlying them. Esteban had never stopped believing in the dreams, not even in face of the rocky, airless place depicted by the science programs on Incarnación's television: That moon, its mystery explained, was merely a less enlightening kind of dream, a statement of fact that reduced reality to the knowable.

But as he thought this, Esteban suddenly realized that killing the jaguar might be the solution to his problems, that by going against his father's teaching, that by killing his dreams, his Indian conception of the world, he might be able to find accord with his wife's; he had been standing halfway between the two conceptions for too long, and it was time for him to choose. And there was no real choice. It was this world he inhabited, not that of the jaguars; if it took the death of a magical creature to permit him to embrace as joys the television and trips to the movies and a stucco house in Barrio Clarín, well, he had faith in this method. He swung the machete, slicing the dark air, and laughed. Incarnación's frivolousness, his skill at hunting, Onofrio's greed, the jaguar, the television … all these things were neatly woven together like the elements of a spell, one whose products would be a denial of magic and a furthering of the unmagical doctrines that had corrupted Puerto Morada. He laughed again, but a second later he chided himself: It was exactly this sort of thinking he was preparing to root out.

Esteban waked Incarnación early the next morning and forced her to accompany him to the appliance store. His machete swung by his side in a leather sheath, and he carried a burlap sack containing food and the herbs he would need for the hunt. Incarnación trotted along beside him, silent, her face hidden by a shawl. When they reached the store, Esteban had Onofrio stamp the bill PAID IN FULL, then he handed the bill and the money to Incarnación.

"If I kill the jaguar or if it kills me," he said harshly, "this will be yours. Should I fail to return within a week, you may assume that I will never return."

She retreated a step, her face registering alarm, as if she had seen him in a new light and understood the consequences of her actions; but she made no move to stop him as he walked out the door.

Across the street, Raimundo Esteves was leaning against the wall of the Cantina Atómica, talking to two girls wearing jeans and frilly blouses; the girls were fluttering their hands and dancing to the music that issued from the cantina, and to Esteban they seemed more alien than the creature he was to hunt. Raimundo spotted him and whispered to the girls; they peeked over their shoulders and laughed. Already angry at Incarnación, Esteban was washed over by a cold fury. He crossed the street to them, rested his hand on the hilt of the machete, and stared at Raimundo; he had never before noticed how soft he was, how empty of presence. A crop of pimples straggled along his jaw, the flesh beneath his eyes was pocked by tiny indentations like those made by a silversmith's hammer, and, unequal to the stare, his eyes darted back and forth between the two girls.

Esteban's anger dissolved into revulsion. "I am Esteban Caax," he said. "I have built my own house, tilled my soil, and brought four children into the world. This day I am going to hunt the jaguar of Barrio Carolina in order to make you and your father even fatter than you are." He ran his gaze up and down Raimundo's body, and, letting his voice fill with disgust, he asked, "Who are you?"

Raimundo's puffy face cinched in a knot of hatred, but he offered no response. The girls tittered and skipped through the door of the cantina; Esteban could hear them describing the incident, laughter, and he continued to stare at Raimundo. Several other girls poked their heads out the door, giggling and whispering. After a moment Esteban spun on his heel and walked away. Behind him there was a chorus of unrestrained laughter, and a girl's voice called mockingly, "Raimundo! Who are you?" Other voices joined in, and it soon became a chant.

Barrio Carolina was not truly a barrio of Puerto Morada; it lay beyond Punta Manabique, the southernmost enclosure of the bay, and was fronted by a palm hammock and the loveliest stretch of beach in all the province, a curving slice of white sand giving way to jade-green shallows. Forty years before, it had been the headquarters of the fruit company's experimental farm, a project of such vast scope that a small town had been built on the site: rows of white frame houses with shingle roofs and screen porches, the kind you might see in a magazine illustration of rural America. The company had touted the project as being the keystone of the country's future and had promised to develop high-yield crops that would banish starvation; but in 1947 a cholera epidemic had ravaged the coast, and the town had been abandoned. By the time the cholera scare had died down, the company had become well entrenched in national politics and no longer needed to maintain a benevolent image; the project had been dropped and the property abandoned until—in the same year that Esteban had retired from hunting—developers had bought it, planning to build a major resort. It was then the jaguar had appeared. Though it had not killed any of the workmen, it had terrorized them to the point that they had refused to begin the job. Hunters had been sent, and these the jaguar *had* killed. The last party of hunters had been equipped with automatic rifles, all manner of technological aids; but the jaguar had picked them off one by one, and this project, too, had been abandoned. Rumor had it that the land had recently been resold (now Esteban knew to whom), and that the idea of a resort was once more under consideration.

The walk from Puerto Morada was hot and tiring, and upon arrival Esteban sat beneath a palm and ate a lunch of cold banana fritters. Combers as white as toothpaste broke on the shore, and there was no human litter, just dead fronds and driftwood and coconuts. All but four of the houses had been swallowed by the jungle, and only sections of those four remained visible, embedded like moldering gates in a blackish green wall of vegetation. Even under the bright sunlight, they were haunted looking: their screens ripped, boards weathered gray, vines cascading over their façades. A mango tree had sprouted from one of the porches, and wild parrots were eating its fruit. He had not visited the barrio since childhood; the ruins had frightened him then, but now he found them appealing, testifying to the dominion of natural law. It distressed him that he would help transform it all into a place where the parrots would be chained to perches and the jaguars would be designs on tablecloths, a place of swimming pools and tourists sipping from coconut shells. Nonetheless, after he had finished lunch, he set out to explore the jungle and soon discovered a trail used by the jaguar: a narrow path that wound between the vine-matted shells of the houses for about a half mile and ended at the Rio Dulce. The river was a murkier green than the sea, curving away through the jungle walls; the jaguar's tracks were everywhere along the bank, especially thick upon a tussocky rise some five or six feet above the water. This baffled Esteban. The jaguar could not drink from the rise, and it certainly would not sleep there. He puzzled over it awhile, but eventually shrugged it off, returned to the beach, and, because he planned to keep watch that night, took a nap beneath the palms.

Some hours later, around midafternoon, he was started from his nap by a voice hailing him. A tall, slim, copper-skinned woman was walking toward him, wearing a dress of dark green—almost the exact color of the jungle walls—that exposed the swell of her breasts. As she drew near, he saw that though her features had a Patucan cast, they were of a lapidary fineness uncommon to the tribe; it was as if they had been refined into a lovely mask: cheeks planed into subtle hollows, lips sculpted full, stylized feathers of ebony inlaid for eyebrows, eyes of jet and white onyx, and all this given a human gloss. A sheen of sweat covered her breasts, and a single curl of black hair lay over her collarbone, so artful-seeming it appeared to have been placed there by design. She knelt beside him, gazing at him impassively, and Esteban was flustered by her heated air of sensuality. The sea breeze bore her scent to him, a sweet musk that reminded him of mangoes left ripening in the sun.

"My name is Esteban Caax," he said, painfully aware of his own sweaty odor.

"I have heard of you," she said. "The jaguar hunter. Have you come to kill the jaguar of the barrio?"

"Yes," he said, and felt shame at admitting it.

She picked up a handful of sand and watched it sift through her fingers.

"What is your name?" he asked.

"If we become friends, I will tell you my name," she said. "Why must you kill the jaguar?"

He told her about the television set, and then, to his surprise, he found himself describing his problems with Incarnación, explaining how he intended to adapt to her ways. These were not proper subjects to discuss with a stranger, yet he was lured to intimacy; he thought he sensed an affinity between them, and that prompted him to portray his marriage as more dismal than it was, for though he had never once been unfaithful to Incarnación, he would have welcomed the chance to do so now.

"This is a black jaguar," she said. "Surely you know they are not ordinary animals, that they have purposes with which we must not interfere?"

Esteban was startled to hear his father's words from her mouth, but he dismissed it as coincidence and replied, "Perhaps. But they are not mine."

"Truly, they are," she said. "You have simply chosen to ignore them." She scooped up another handful of sand. "How will you do it? You have no gun. Only a machete."

"I have this as well," he said, and from his sack he pulled out a small parcel of herbs and handed it to her.

She opened it and sniffed the contents. "Herbs? Ah! You plan to drug the jaguar."

"Not the jaguar. Myself." He took back the parcel. "The herbs slow the heart and give the body a semblance of death. They induce a trance, but one that can be thrown off at a moment's notice. After I chew them, I will lie down in a place that the jaguar must pass on its nightly hunt. It will think I am dead, but it will not feed unless it is sure that the spirit has left the flesh, and to determine this, it will sit on the body so it can feel the spirit rise up. As soon as it starts to settle, I will throw off the trance and stab it between the ribs. If my hand is steady, it will die instantly."

"And if your hand is unsteady?"

"I have killed nearly fifty jaguars," he said. "I no longer fear unsteadiness. The method comes down through my family from the Old Patuca, and it has never failed, to my knowledge."

"But a black jaguar…"

"Black or spotted, it makes no difference. Jaguars are creatures of instinct, and one is like another when it comes to feeding."

"Well," she said, "I cannot wish you luck, but neither do I wish you ill." She came to her feet, brushing the sand from her dress.

He wanted to ask her to stay, but pride prevented him, and she laughed as if she knew his mind.

"Perhaps we will talk again, Esteban," she said. "It would be a pity if we did not, for more lies between us than we have spoken of this day."

She walked swiftly down the beach, becoming a diminutive black figure that was rippled away by the heat haze.

That evening, needing a place from which to keep watch, Esteban pried open the screen door of one of the houses facing the beach and went onto the porch. Chameleons skittered into the corners, and an iguana slithered off a rusted lawn chair sheathed in spiderweb and vanished through a gap in the floor. The interior of the house was dark and forbidding, except for the bathroom, the roof of which was missing, webbed over by vines that admitted a gray-green infusion of twilight. The cracked toilet was full of rainwater and dead insects. Uneasy, Esteban returned to the porch, cleaned the lawn chair, and sat.

Out on the horizon the sea and sky were blending in a haze of silver and gray; the wind had died, and the palms were as still as sculpture; a string of pelicans flying low above the waves seemed to be spelling a sentence of cryptic black syllables. But the eerie beauty of the scene was lost on him. He could not stop thinking of the woman. The memory of her hips rolling beneath the fabric of her dress as she walked away was repeated over and over in his thoughts, and whenever he tried to turn his attention to the matter at hand, the memory became more compelling. He imagined her naked, the play of muscles rippling her haunches, and this so enflamed him that he started to pace, unmindful of the fact that the creaking boards were signaling his presence. He could not understand her effect upon him. Perhaps, he thought, it was her defense of the jaguar, her calling to mind of all he was putting behind him… and then a realization settled over him like an icy shroud.

It was commonly held among the Patuca that a man about to suffer a solitary and unexpected death would be visited by an envoy of death, who—standing in for family and friends—would prepare him to face the event; and Esteban was now very sure that the woman had been such an envoy, that her allure had been specifically designed to attract his soul to its imminent fate. He sat back down in the lawn chair, numb with the realization. Her knowledge of his father's words, the odd flavor of her conversation, her intimation that more lay between them: It all accorded perfectly with the traditional wisdom. The moon rose three-quarters full, silvering the sands of the barrio, and still he sat there, rooted to the spot by his fear of death.

He had been watching the jaguar for several seconds before he registered its presence. It seemed at first that a scrap of night sky had fallen onto the sand and was being blown by a fitful breeze; but soon he saw that it was the jaguar, that it was inching along as if stalking some prey. Then it leaped high into the air, twisting and turning, and began to race up and down the beach: a ribbon of black water flowing across the silver sands. He had never before seen a jaguar at play, and this alone was cause for wonder; but most of all, he wondered at the fact that here were his childhood dreams come to life. He might have been peering out onto a silvery meadow of the moon, spying on one of its magical creatures. His fear was eroded by the sight, and like a child he pressed his nose to the screen, trying not to blink, anxious that he might miss a single moment.

At length the jaguar left off its play and came prowling up the beach toward the jungle. By the set of its ears and the purposeful sway of its walk, Esteban recognized that it was hunting. It stopped beneath a palm about twenty feet from the house, lifted its head, and tested the air. Moonlight frayed down through the fronds, applying liquid gleams to its haunches; its eyes, glinting yellow-green, were like peepholes into a lurid dimension of fire. The jaguar's beauty was heart-stopping—the embodiment of a flawless principle—and Esteban, contrasting this beauty with the pallid ugliness of his employer, with the ugly principle that had led to his hiring, doubted that he could ever bring himself to kill it.

All the following day he debated the question. He had hoped the woman would return, because he had rejected the idea that she was death's envoy—that perception, he thought, must have been induced by the mysterious atmosphere of the barrio—and he felt that if she was to argue the jaguar's cause again, he would let himself be persuaded. But she did not put in an appearance, and as he sat upon the beach, watching the evening sun decline through strata of dusky orange and lavender clouds, casting wild glitters over the sea, he understood once more that he had no choice. Whether or not the jaguar was beautiful, whether or not the woman had been on a supernatural errand, he must treat these things as if they had no substance. The point of the hunt had been to deny mysteries of this sort, and he had lost sight of it under the influence of old dreams.

He waited until moonrise to take the herbs, and then lay down beneath the palm tree where the jaguar had paused the previous night. Lizards whispered past in the grasses, sand fleas hopped onto his face; he hardly felt them, sinking deeper into the languor of the herbs. The fronds overhead showed an ashen green in the moonlight, lifting, rustling; and the stars between their feathered edges flickered crazily as if the breeze were fanning their flames. He became immersed in the landscape, savoring the smells of brine and rotting foliage that were blowing across the beach, drifting with them; but when he heard the pad of the jaguar's step, he came alert. Through narrowed eyes he saw it sitting a dozen feet away, a bulky shadow craning its neck toward him, investigating his scent. After a moment it began to circle him, each circle a bit tighter than the one before, and whenever it passed out of view he had to repress a trickle of fear. Then, as it passed close on the seaward side, he caught a whiff of its odor.

A sweet, musky odor that reminded him of mangoes left ripening in the sun.

Fear welled up in him, and he tried to banish it, to tell himself that the odor could not possibly be what he thought. The jaguar snarled, a razor stroke of sound that slit the peaceful mesh of wind and surf, and realizing it had scented his fear, he sprang to his feet, waving his machete. In a whirl of vision he saw the jaguar leap back, then he shouted at it, waved the machete again, and sprinted for the house where he had kept watch. He slipped through the door and went staggering into the front room. There was a crash behind him, and turning, he had a glimpse of a huge black shape struggling to extricate itself from a moonlit tangle of vines and ripped screen. He darted into the bathroom, sat with his back against the toilet bowl, and braced the door shut with his feet.

The sound of the jaguar's struggles subsided, and for a moment he thought it had given up. Sweat left cold trails down his sides, his heart pounded. He held his breath, listening, and it seemed the whole world was holding its breath as well. The noises of wind and surf and insects were a faint seething; moonlight shed a sickly white radiance through the enlaced vines overhead, and a chameleon was frozen among peels of wallpaper beside the door. He let out a sigh and wiped the sweat from his eyes. He swallowed.

Then the top panel of the door exploded, shattered by a black paw. Splinters of rotten wood flew into his face, and he screamed. The sleek wedge of the jaguar's head thrust through the hole, roaring. A gateway of gleaming fangs guarding a plush red throat. Half-paralyzed, Esteban jabbed weakly with the machete. The jaguar withdrew, reached in with its paw, and clawed at his leg. More by accident than design, he managed to slice the jaguar, and the paw, too, was withdrawn. He heard it rumbling in the front room, and then, seconds later, a heavy thump against the wall behind him. The jaguar's head appeared above the edge of the wall; it was hanging by its forepaws, trying to gain a perch from which to leap down into the room. Esteban scrambled to his feet and slashed wildly, severing vines. The jaguar fell back, yowling. For a while it prowled along the wall, fuming to itself. Finally there was silence.

When sunlight began to filter through the vines, Esteban walked out of the house and headed down the beach to Puerto Morada. He went with his head lowered, desolate, thinking of the grim future that awaited him after he returned the money to Onofrio: a life of trying to please an increasingly shrewish Incarnación, of killing lesser jaguars for much less money. He was so mired in depression that he did not notice the woman until she called to him. She was leaning against a palm about thirty feet away, wearing a filmy white dress through which he could see the dark jut of her nipples. He drew his machete and backed off a pace.

"Why do you fear me, Esteban?" she called, walking toward him.

"You tricked me into revealing my method and tried to kill me," he said. "Is that not reason for fear?"

"I did not know you or your method in that form. I knew only that you were hunting me. But now the hunt has ended, and we can be as man and woman."

He kept his machete at point. "What are you?" he asked.

She smiled. "My name is Miranda. I am Patuca."

"Patucas do not have black fur and fangs."

"I am of the Old Patuca," she said. "We have this power."

"Keep away!" He lifted the machete as if to strike, and she stopped just beyond his reach.

"You can kill me if that is your wish, Esteban." She spread her arms, and her breasts thrust forward against the fabric of her dress. "You are stronger than I, now. But listen to me first."

He did not lower the machete, but his fear and anger were being overridden by a sweeter emotion.

"Long ago," she said, "there was a great healer who foresaw that one day the Patuca would lose their place in the world, and so, with the help of the gods, he opened a door into another world where the tribe could flourish. But many of the tribe were afraid and would not follow him. Since then, the door has been left open for those who would come after." She waved at the ruined houses. "Barrio Carolina is the site of the door, and the jaguar is its guardian. But soon the fevers of this world will sweep over the barrio, and the door will close forever. For though our hunt has ended, there is no end to hunters or to greed." She came a step nearer. "If you listen to the sounding of your heart, you will know this is the truth."

He half-believed her, yet he also believed her words masked a more poignant truth, one that fitted inside the other the way his machete fitted into its sheath.

"What is it?" she asked. "What troubles you?"

"I think you have come to prepare me for death," he said, "and that your door leads only to death."

"Then why do you not run from me?" She pointed toward Puerto Morada. "That is death, Esteban. The cries of the gulls are death, and when the hearts of lovers stop at the moment of greatest pleasure, that, too, is death. This world is no more than a thin covering of life drawn over a foundation of death, like a scum of algae upon a rock. Perhaps you are right, perhaps my world lies beyond death. The two ideas are not opposed. But if I am death to you, Esteban, then it is death you love."

He turned his eyes to the sea, not wanting her to see his face. "I do not love you," he said.

"Love awaits us," she said. "And someday you will join me in my world."

He looked back to her, ready with a denial, but was shocked to silence. Her dress had fallen to the sand, and she was smiling. The litheness and purity of the jaguar were reflected in every line of her body; her secret hair was so absolute a black that it seemed an absence in her flesh. She moved close, pushing aside the machete. The tips of her breasts brushed against him, warm through the coarse cloth of his shirt; her hands cupped his face, and he was drowning in her heated scent, weakened by both fear and desire.

"We are of one soul, you and I," she said. "One blood and one truth. You cannot reject me."

Days passed, though Esteban was unclear as to how many. Night and day were unimportant incidences of his relationship with Miranda, serving only to color their lovemaking with a spectral or a sunny mood; and each time they made love, it was as if a thousand new colors were being added to his senses. He had never been so content. Sometimes, gazing at the haunted façades of the barrio, he believed that they might well conceal shadowy avenues leading to another world; however, whenever Miranda tried to convince him to leave with her, he refused: He could not overcome his fear and would never admit—even to himself—that he loved her. He attempted to fix his thoughts on Incarnación, hoping this would undermine his fixation with Miranda and free him to return to Puerto Morada; but he found that he could not picture his wife except as a black bird hunched before a flickering gray jewel. Miranda, however, seemed equally unreal at times. Once as they sat on the bank of the Rio Dulce, watching the reflection of the moon—almost full—floating upon the water, she pointed to it and said, "My world is that near, Esteban. That touchable. You may think the moon above is real and this is only a reflection, but the thing most real, that most illustrates the real, is the surface that permits the illusion of reflection. Passing through this surface is what you fear, and yet it is so insubstantial, you would scarcely notice the passage."

"You sound like the old priest who taught me philosophy," said Esteban. "His world—his Heaven—was also philosophy. Is that what your world is? The idea of a place? Or are there birds and jungles and rivers?"

Her expression was in partial eclipse, half-moonlit, half-shadowed, and her voice revealed nothing of her mood. "No more than there are here," she said.

"What does that mean?" he said angrily. "Why will you not give me a clear answer?"

"If I were to describe my world, you would simply think me a clever liar." She rested her head on his shoulder. "Sooner or later you will understand. We did not find each other merely to have the pain of being parted."

In that moment her beauty—like her words—seemed a kind of evasion, obscuring a dark and frightening beauty beneath; and yet he knew that she was right, that no proof of hers could persuade him contrary to his fear.

One afternoon, an afternoon of such brightness that it was impossible to look at the sea without squinting, they swam out to a sandbar that showed as a thin curving island of white against the green water. Esteban floundered and splashed, but Miranda swam as if born to the element; she darted beneath him, tickling him, pulling at his feet, eeling away before he could catch her. They walked along the sand, turning over starfish with their toes, collecting whelks to boil for their dinner, and then Esteban spotted a dark stain hundreds of yards wide that was moving below the water beyond the bar: a great school of king mackerel.

"It is too bad we have no boat," he said. "Mackerel would taste better than whelks."

"We need no boat," she said. "I will show you an old way of catching fish."

She traced a complicated design in the sand, and when she had done, she led him into the shallows and had him stand facing her a few feet away.

"Look down at the water between us," she said. "Do not look up, and keep perfectly still until I tell you."

She began to sing with a faltering rhythm, a rhythm that put him in mind of the ragged breezes of the season. Most of the words were unfamiliar, but others he recognized as Patuca. After a minute he experienced a wave of dizziness, as if his legs had grown long and spindly, and he was now looking down from a great height, breathing rarefied air. Then a tiny dark stain materialized below the expanse of water between him and Miranda. He remembered his grandfather's stories of the Old Patuca, how—with the help of the gods—they had been able to shrink the world, to bring enemies close and cross vast distances in a matter of moments. But the gods were dead, their powers gone from the world. He wanted to glance back to shore and see if he and Miranda had become coppery giants taller than the palms.

"Now," she said, breaking off her song, "you must put your hand into the water on the seaward side of the school and gently wiggle your fingers. Very gently! Be sure not to disturb the surface."

But when Esteban made to do as he was told, he slipped and caused a splash. Miranda cried out. Looking up, he saw a wall of jade-green water bearing down on them, its face thickly studded with the fleeting dark shapes of the mackerel. Before he could move, the wave swept over the sandbar and carried him under, dragging him along the bottom and finally casting him onto shore. The beach was littered with flopping mackerel; Miranda lay in the shallows, laughing at him. Esteban laughed, too, but only to cover up his rekindled fear of this woman who drew upon the powers of dead gods. He had no wish to hear her explanation; he was certain she would tell him that the gods lived on in her world, and this would only confuse him further.

Later that day as Esteban was cleaning the fish, while Miranda was off picking bananas to cook with them—the sweet little ones that grew along the riverbank—a Land Rover came jouncing up the beach from Puerto Morada, an orange fire of the setting sun dancing on its windshield. It pulled up beside him, and Onofrio climbed out the passenger side. A hectic flush dappled his cheeks, and he was dabbing his sweaty brow with a handkerchief. Raimundo climbed out the driver's side and leaned against the door, staring hatefully at Esteban.

"Nine days and not a word," said Onofrio gruffly. "We thought you were dead. How goes the hunt?"

Esteban set down the fish he had been scaling and stood. "I have failed," he said. "I will give you back the money."

Raimundo chuckled—a dull, cluttered sound—and Onofrio grunted with amusement. "Impossible," he said. "Incarnación has spent the money on a house in Barrio Clarín. You must kill the jaguar."

"I cannot," said Esteban. "I will repay you somehow."

"The Indian has lost his nerve, Father." Raimundo spat in the sand. "Let me and my friends hunt the jaguar."

The idea of Raimundo and his loutish friends thrashing through the jungle was so ludicrous that Esteban could not restrain a laugh.

"Be careful, Indian!" Raimundo banged the flat of his hand on the roof of the car.

"It is you who should be careful," said Esteban. "Most likely the jaguar will be hunting you." Esteban picked up his machete. "And whoever hunts this jaguar will answer to me as well."

Raimundo reached for something in the driver's seat and walked around in front of the hood. In his hand was a silvered automatic. "I await your answer," he said.

"Put that away!" Onofrio's tone was that of a man addressing a child whose menace was inconsequential, but the intent surfacing in Raimundo's face was not childish. A tic marred the plump curve of his cheek, the ligature of his neck was cabled, and his lips were drawn back in a joyless grin. It was, thought Esteban—strangely fascinated by the transformation—like watching a demon dissolve its false shape: the true lean features melting up from the illusion of the soft.

"This son of a whore insulted me in front of Julia!" Raimundo's gun hand was shaking.

"Your personal differences can wait," said Onofrio. "This is a business matter." He held out his hand. "Give me the gun."

"If he is not going to kill the jaguar, what use is he?" said Raimundo.

"Perhaps we can convince him to change his mind." Onofrio beamed at Esteban. "What do you say? Shall I let my son collect his debt of honor, or will you fulfill our contract?"

"Father!" complained Raimundo; his eyes flicked sideways. "He…"

Esteban broke for the jungle. The gun roared, a white-hot claw swiped at his side, and he went flying. For an instant he did not know where he was; but then, one by one, his impressions began to sort themselves. He was lying on his injured side, and it was throbbing fiercely. Sand crusted his mouth and eyelids. He was curled up around his machete, which was still clutched in his hand. Voices above him, sand fleas hopping on his face. He resisted the urge to brush them off and lay without moving. The throb of his wound and his hatred had the same red force behind them.

"…carry him to the river," Raimundo was saying, his voice atremble with excitement. "Everyone will think the jaguar killed him!"

"Fool!" said Onofrio. "He might have killed the jaguar, and you could have had a sweeter revenge. His wife…"

"This was sweet enough," said Raimundo.

A shadow fell over Esteban, and he held his breath. He needed no herbs to deceive this pale, flabby jaguar who was bending to him, turning him onto his back.

"Watch out!" cried Onofrio.

Esteban let himself be turned and lashed out with the machete. His contempt for Onofrio and Incarnación, as well as his hatred of Raimundo, was involved in the blow, and the blade lodged deep in Raimundo's side, grating on bone. Raimundo shrieked and would have fallen, but the blade helped to keep him upright; his hands fluttered around the machete as if he wanted to adjust it to a more comfortable position, and his eyes were wide with disbelief. A shudder vibrated the hilt of the machete—it seemed sensual, the spasm of a spent passion—and Raimundo sank to his knees. Blood spilled from his mouth, adding tragic lines to the corners of his lips. He pitched forward, not falling flat but remaining kneeling, his face pressed into the sand: the attitude of an Arab at prayer.

Esteban wrenched the machete free, fearful of an attack by Onofrio, but the appliance dealer was squirming into the Land Rover. The engine caught, the wheels spun, and the car lurched off, turning through the edge of the surf and heading for Puerto Morada. An orange dazzle flared on the rear window, as if the spirit who had lured it to the barrio was now harrying it away.

Unsteadily, Esteban got to his feet. He peeled his shirt back from the bullet wound. There was a lot of blood, but it was only a crease. He avoided looking at Raimundo and walked down to the water and stood gazing out at the waves; his thoughts rolled in with them, less thoughts than tidal sweeps of emotion.

It was twilight by the time Miranda returned, her arms full of bananas and wild figs. She had not heard the shot. He told her what had happened as she dressed his wounds with a poultice of herbs and banana leaves. "It will mend," she said of the wound. "But this"—she gestured at Raimundo—"this will not. You must come with me, Esteban. The soldiers will kill you."

"No," he said. "They will come, but they are Patuca… except for the captain, who is a drunkard, a shell of a man. I doubt he will even be notified. They will listen to my story, and we will reach an accommodation. No matter what lies Onofrio tells, his word will not stand against theirs."

"And then?"

"I may have to go to jail for a while, or I may have to leave the province. But I will not be killed."

She sat for a minute without speaking, the whites of her eyes glowing in the half-light. Finally she stood and walked off along the beach.

"Where are you going?" he called.

She turned back. "You speak so casually of losing me…" she began.

"It is not casual!"

"No!" She laughed bitterly. "I suppose not. You are so afraid of life, you call it death and would prefer jail or exile to living it. That is hardly casual." She stared at him, her expression a cipher at that distance. "I will not lose you, Esteban," she said. She walked away again, and this time when he called she did not turn.

Twilight deepened to dusk, a slow fill of shadow graying the world into negative, and Esteban felt himself graying along with it, his thoughts reduced to echoing the dull wash of the receding tide. The dusk lingered, and he had the idea that night would never fall, that the act of violence had driven a nail through the substance of his irresolute life, pinned him forever to this ashen moment and deserted shore. As a child he had been terrified by the possibility of such magical isolations, but now the prospect seemed a consolation for Miranda's absence, a remembrance of her magic. Despite her parting words, he did not think she would be back—there had been sadness and finality in her voice—and this roused in him feelings of both relief and desolation, feelings that set him to pacing up and down the tidal margin of the shore.

The full moon rose, the sands of the barrio burned silver, and shortly there-after four soldiers came in a jeep from Puerto Morada. They were gnomish copper-skinned men, and their uniforms were the dark blue of the night sky, bearing no device or decoration. Though they were not close friends, he knew them each by name: Sebastian, Amador, Carlito, and Ramón. In their headlights Raimundo's corpse—startlingly pale, the blood on his face dried into intricate whorls—looked like an exotic creature cast up by the sea, and their inspection of it smacked more of curiosity than of a search for evidence. Amador unearthed Raimundo's gun, sighted along it toward the jungle, and asked Ramón how much he thought it was worth.

"Perhaps Onofrio will give you a good price," said Ramón, and the others laughed.

They built a fire of driftwood and coconut shells, and sat around it while Esteban told his story; he did not mention either Miranda or her relation to the jaguar, because these men—estranged from the tribe by their government service—had grown conservative in their judgments, and he did not want them to consider him irrational. They listened without comment; the firelight burnished their skins to reddish gold and glinted on their rifle barrels.

"Onofrio will take his charge to the capital if we do nothing," said Amador after Esteban had finished.

"He may in any case," said Carlito. "And then it will go hard with Esteban."

"And," said Sebastian, "if an agent is sent to Puerto Morada and sees how things are with Captain Portales, they will surely replace him, and it will go hard with us."

They stared into the flames, mulling over the problem, and Esteban chose the moment to ask Amador, who lived near him on the mountain, if he had seen Incarnación.

"She will be amazed to learn you are alive," said Amador. "I saw her yester-day in the dressmaker's shop. She was admiring the fit of a new black skirt in the mirror."

It was as if a black swath of Incarnación's skirt had folded around Esteban's thoughts. He lowered his head and carved lines in the sand with the point of his machete.

"I have it," said Ramón. "A boycott!"

The others expressed confusion.

"If we do not buy from Onofrio, who will?" said Ramon. "He will lose his business. Threatened with this, he will not dare involve the government. He will allow Esteban to plead self-defense."

"But Raimundo was his only son," said Amador. "It may be that grief will count more than greed in this instance."

Again they fell silent. It mattered little to Esteban what was decided. He was coming to understand that without Miranda, his future held nothing but uninteresting choices; he turned his gaze to the sky and noticed that the stars and the fire were flickering with the same rhythm, and he imagined each of them ringed by a group of gnomish copper-skinned men, debating the question of his fate.

"Aha!" said Carlito. "I know what to do. We will occupy Barrio Carolina—the entire company—and *we* will kill the jaguar. Onofrio's greed cannot withstand this temptation."

"That you must not do," said Esteban.

"But why?" asked Amador. "We may not kill the jaguar, but with so many men we will certainly drive it away."

Before Esteban could answer, the jaguar roared. It was prowling down the beach toward the fire, like a black flame itself, shifting over the glowing sand. Its ears were laid back, and silver drops of moonlight gleamed in its eyes. Amador grabbed his rifle, came to one knee, and fired: The bullet sprayed sand a dozen feet to the left of the jaguar.

"Wait!" cried Esteban, pushing him down.

But the rest had begun to fire, and the jaguar was hit. It leaped high as it had that first night while playing, but this time it landed in a heap, snarling, snapping at its shoulder; it regained its feet and limped toward the jungle, favoring its right foreleg. Excited by their success, the soldiers ran a few paces after it and stopped to fire again. Carlito dropped to one knee, taking careful aim.

"No!" shouted Esteban, and as he hurled his machete at Carlito, desperate to prevent further harm to Miranda, he recognized the trap that had been sprung and the consequences he would face.

The blade sliced across Carlito's thigh, knocking him onto his side. He screamed, and Amador, seeing what had happened, fired wildly at Esteban and called to the others. Esteban ran toward the jungle, making for the jaguar's path. A fusillade of shots rang out behind him, bullets whipped past his ears. Each time his feet slipped in the soft sand, the moonstruck façades of the barrio appeared to lurch sideways as if trying to block his way. And then, as he reached the verge of the jungle, he was hit.

The bullet seemed to throw him forward, to increase his speed, but somehow he managed to keep his feet. He careened along the path, arms waving, breath shrieking in his throat. Palmetto fronds swatted his face, vines tangled his legs. He felt no pain, only a peculiar numbness that pulsed low in his back; he pictured the wound opening and closing like the mouth of an anemone. The soldiers were shouting his name. They would follow, but cautiously, afraid of the jaguar, and he thought he might be able to cross the river before they could catch up. But when he came to the river, he found the jaguar waiting.

It was crouched on the tussocky rise, its neck craned over the water, and below, half a dozen feet from the bank, floated the reflection of the full moon, huge and silvery, an unblemished circle of light. Blood glistened scarlet on the jaguar's shoulder, like a fresh rose pinned in place, and this made it look even more an embodiment of principle: the shape a god might choose, that some universal constant might assume. It gazed calmly at Esteban, growled low in its throat, and dove into the river, cleaving and shattering the moon's reflection, vanishing beneath the surface. The ripples subsided, the image of the moon re-formed. And there, silhouetted against it, Esteban saw the figure of a woman swimming, each stroke causing her to grow smaller and smaller until she seemed no more than a character incised upon a silver plate. It was not only Miranda he saw, but all mystery and beauty receding from him, and he realized how blind he had been not to perceive the truth sheathed inside the truth of death that had been sheathed inside her truth of another world. It was clear to him now. It sang to him from his wound, every syllable a heartbeat. It was written by the dying ripples, it swayed in the banana leaves, it sighed on the wind. It was everywhere, and he had always known it: If you deny mystery—even in the guise of death—then you deny life and you will walk like a ghost through your days, never knowing the secrets of the extremes. The deep sorrows, the absolute joys.

He drew a breath of the rank jungle air, and with it drew a breath of a world no longer his, of the girl Incarnación, of friends and children and country nights … all his lost sweetness. His chest tightened as with the onset of tears, but the sensation quickly abated, and he understood that the sweetness of the past had been subsumed by a scent of mangoes, that nine magical days—a magical number of days, the number it takes to sing the soul to rest—lay between him and tears. Freed of those associations, he felt as if he were undergoing a subtle refinement of form, a winnowing, and he remembered having felt much the same on the day when he had run out the door of Santa María del Onda, putting behind him its dark geometries and cobwebbed catechisms and generations of swallows that had never flown beyond the walls, casting off his acolyte's robe and racing across the square toward the mountain and Incarnación: It had been she who had lured him then, just as his mother had lured him to the church and as Miranda was luring him now, and he laughed at seeing how easily these three women had diverted the flow of his life, how like other men he was in this.

The strange bloom of painlessness in his back was sending out tendrils into his arms and legs, and the cries of the soldiers had grown louder. Miranda was a tiny speck shrinking against a silver immensity. For a moment he hesitated, experiencing a resurgence of fear; then Miranda's face materialized in his mind's eye, and all the emotion he had suppressed for nine days poured through him, washing away the fear. It was a silvery, flawless emotion, and he was giddy with it, light with it; it was like thunder and fire fused into one element and boiling up inside him, and he was overwhelmed by a need to express it, to mold it into a form that would reflect its power and purity. But he was no singer, no poet. There was but a single mode of expression open to him. Hoping he was not too late, that Miranda's door had not shut forever, Esteban dove into the river, cleaving the image of the full moon; and—his eyes still closed from the shock of the splash—with the last of his mortal strength, he swam hard down after her.

ARTHUR'S LION

Tanith Lee

Tanith Lee has written nearly one hundred books and over two hundred and seventy short stories, as well as radio plays and TV scripts. Her genre-crossing combines fantasy, SF, horror, young adult, historical, detective, and contemporary fiction. Her latest publications include the Lionwolf Trilogy: *Cast a Bright Shadow, Here in Cold Hell,* and *No Flame but Mine,* and the three Piratica novels for young adults. She has also recently published several short stories and novellas in *Asimov's Science Fiction, Weird Tales, Realms of Fantasy, The Ghost Quartet* and *Wizards.* Norilana Books is reprinting all of her Flat Earth series, with two new volumes to follow. Lethe Press will be reprinting the Esther Garber lesbian fiction, plus a new collection of gay/lesbian short stories, including all new tales by "Esther, her brother Judas and even myself."

She lives on the Sussex Weald with her husband, writer/artist John Kaiine, and two omnipresent cats. More information can be found at www.TanithLee.com.

About the story, Lee says: "'Arthur's Lion' arrived from a sort of semi-waking dream I experienced one morning. The background scenario, including the narrator, had also arrived by breakfast time. The direction of the story too, though, was ultimately a surprise."

That year I had some business to see to in Kent, and it wasn't long after arranging this that I received the letter from my uncle. It came as a surprise; at first I hadn't the faintest idea who was writing to me so familiarly. When I realized, I was in two minds. But curiosity got the upper hand.

I had better explain that I was nephew only to one uncle, Arthur, the brother of my then-deceased male parent. Arthur had made a lot of money in the north of England, as my mother had been wont to say: "By exploiting the workers and putting them into marmalade." This had always been the joke, that Uncle Arthur had made a fortune in marmalade, some exotic variety which, I'm pretty certain, never appeared on our table. Frankly, once I'd grown up and moved into my own life, I may well, here and there, have eaten the fabulous spread—and not known it. Basically, Arthur had removed himself from the family early on, and never afterwards himself maintained any contact. My father had seen his brother last in childhood. "I was only five when he took himself off. But I always remember, he was a funny chap," said my father. "Peculiar things stick in your mind, even when you can't recall what they were all about." The peculiar Arthurian thing which had stuck, apparently, concerned an Arthur then sixteen years of age, letting out a loud cry and promptly fainting to the ground.

"We were in some sort of park—I think it was a park. We were going somewhere, but there was such a fuss, we didn't go. I've no memory as to where. All I recollect is Arthur yelling at the top of his lungs and sprawling on the gravel path."

"Perhaps," postulated my mother, "it was the first time making a fortune in marmalade occurred to him."

In fact, though Arthur did become extremely rich, it formed a dark mark on his escutcheon that none of this wealth was ever put in the way either of my grandparents, or my father's family, of which it seemed Arthur had been told.

Arthur's contemporary letter, however, when it reached me, was friendly and warm in tone. He said that he had come across my name in a promotion in the local newspapers, relating to the theatrical performance because of which I was going down to Kent. Since our name is rather unusual, he had decided it must be me, and an inquiry at a London theatre provided him my address. The substance of his letter was to invite me to stay with him at his house. This was, he assured me, only three miles from my business venue, and his chauffeur would, of course, drive me in each day and retrieve me in the evening. Arthur was sure, besides, I would appreciate the comforts of a house over an "inn," and added that he sincerely hoped I would visit him, we had been "estranged" too long.

Initially I tossed the letter in the waste-paper bin. But then, as I say, curiosity won me round. By that era of my life, I was involved in work I found both fascinating and highly remunerative, so Arthur's fortune had no allure. But I'd heard of the house, which I will call Blue Firs, a place, it seemed, of luxury. And I confess I wondered very much what Arthur would be like—and if at all like my father, or even myself.

I therefore rescued his letter, and replied in the affirmative. The next morning, I travelled down to Kent.

It was a mild October afternoon when I arrived at Kesslington Station. Arthur's huge shining car, complete with respectful driver, picked me up and bore me away down autumnal lanes thick with yellow foliage and cows peering across gates.

Blue Firs was a large house, if by no means a mansion. It had been built in the 1800s for someone or other's mistress. Enormous trees framed the views as we drove up through the grounds, and there gradually appeared a cream-and-rose façade with pillarings and tall windows. Long roofs, with sun-gilded red tiles, had put up the periscopes of rather charming ornamental chimneys, modelled on an earlier design. I could imagine my mother saying, "Ah, the house built of marmalade."

When I'd got inside, I found myself in one of those polished echoing halls, whose acoustics are normally so bad for actors—a whisper carries like an unintelligible roar, and a roar like a rumble.

I asked the housekeeper if my uncle was about. She told me he was lying down but would meet me at the drinks hour. I went to unpack. It seemed Arthur hadn't after all lost his social gracelessness, at least where it could be applied to relatives.

But my room was large and airy, with a fire laid ready for later, and the great bed comfortable, and the bathroom well-appointed. Someone had also supplied gin, whisky and soda, and a bowl of hot-house oranges. Not so bad.

When I went down at six, a butler showed me at once into the long, narrow drawing-room that looked out across the lawn. No one else was there.

"Is my uncle coming down?" I asked, rather impatiently.

"Yes, sir. He'll be here directly."

"Are there other guests for dinner?"

"No, sir."

Left alone, I sat by the fireside, watching the brown shadows gather over the room, and the bluer ones fill in the sweep of grass and trees outside.

I felt—and now for the first I admitted it—distinctly uneasy. Was I worried then, to be confronting my "peculiar" uncle? Or was it the big quaint house? I thought not. Already once or twice I had stayed with various theatrical royalty and been in buildings far more eccentric and grandly expanded. Besides, I have never been the nervous type. Even First Nights move me only to extra diligence. A cool head: I've been mocked for it.

The shadows thickened. I got up and switched on a pair of lamps, and turning again, saw the light reflecting on a short stocky man, formally dressed for dinner, standing in the wide doorway, and staring at me with enormous eyes. It struck me, extraordinarily, he was most like a child, an anxious child. I had the urge to put him at his ease. And too the wild notion he was truly frightened, scared at meeting at last this alien nephew, son to a brother he had barely troubled to know.

What did I call him?

I decided on mundane family courtesy. "Uncle Arthur?"

"Oh," he said, "Arthur. We're both past the age of needing 'uncle' shoved in. And you must be—" he named me.

And I found myself saying kindly, "Oh, please call me Jack. It's what I generally answer to with friends."

"I hope we shall be," he said.

"I hope so too."

He stole forward—no other way to describe it. We shook hands. His was warm enough, but slightly stiff and swiftly withdrawn. He then came to the fire and stood there, lit by the flames and the lamps, his melancholy gaze now on the hearth and now, in fleeting glimpses, on me. Neither of us sat down.

Finally he glanced at the drink in my hand, but didn't seem to want one for himself. Suddenly he said, "You must think it odd, my contacting you like that, out of the blue."

"It was a pleasant surprise."

He looked away from me then, discounting, I thought, the shallowness of my reply. He looked instead at the dark lawn beyond the window, and the trees heavy with a new night.

"Don't you think," he said, "this lighted room is like a camp in some jungle place, or on some open plain? A fire, a pair of lamps. Anything might be there," he said, strangely, "beyond the light."

"Do you mean in your grounds? I suppose—"

"No, not in the grounds. Nothing's there."

Somewhere from the depths of the house there came at that moment a long, indefinite sound. It was, I thought, the timbers shifting at the chill of evening. But Arthur looked round now at it, scanning the doorway, as if he expected some-one—something—to appear. He seemed less startled, though a little startled, than apprehensively resigned.

At that second moment too, something did move into or over the doorway. It was a large bulky shadow, reeling across the duller lighting of the hall. And it was instantly followed by its cause. The butler filled the doorframe.

"Have you locked up?" asked Arthur, rather breathlessly, I thought.

"Yes, sir. All but the usual door."

"Good. That's good."

The butler then spoke about the dinner arrangements, which sounded ordinary enough that a report seemed unnecessary. Arthur must be a very pedantic and unsettled man. I pondered also why the house had been locked so early, and why the "usual door" was not. Perhaps to let particular servants, who didn't sleep over at the house, return to the village?

When the butler again went out, he left the drawing-room door wide open. Looking after him quite idly, I saw that flowing shadow veer again along the hallway. This time it seemed not to match his movements, nor that of anything in the room. But firelight can play tricks.

In any case Arthur now sat down, and I with him. He helped himself to a drink and me to another. And then at last, in the expected way of relatives, he began to question me about my father and mother, our past life, my present one, and so on, until a maid came to call us to dine.

The meal was very good, with local fish and roast, and a wonderful sugary dessert concocted by Arthur's cook. All through the courses he seemed fairly relaxed, and only once got the jitters, for some reason I couldn't fathom at all. But he swallowed another glass of wine and cheered up again.

We went into an old-fashioned smoking-room after dinner, with the brandy and cigarettes—it was a tradition of Arthur's, because smoking otherwise was permitted everywhere about the house.

The velvet curtains were drawn, and another fire sparkled. Everything all told was very appealing and comfortable. Had it not been for the constant sense of unease and alertness—most like a vague, almost undetectable smell—that also hung over virtually every instant. Even Arthur's relaxed periods had begun to seem forced. What was bothering him? I had come to the conclusion, whatever it was, it would be the very same matter that had prompted him to invite me to his home. I'm afraid I felt quite irritable at this. Once tomorrow dawned, I would have my hands full with the theatrical event in the town, and little time for sudden extra dramas.

Throughout dinner we'd spoken only of trivial things, mostly to do with the family. Arthur had remarked that I resembled my grandfather, when young, which I valued. In him, although I didn't say so, I could see no likeness to any of our tribe.

Once in the smoking-room, a silence drifted down. We sat in armchairs, and Arthur stared long into the fire. And I thought, by now highly apprehensive myself, any minute and he'll come out with it. Whatever the hell it is. And then let's hope it can be put right very simply. Otherwise it must wait until the play is done.

Arthur said, again, "Yes, I can see my father in you. My brother must have grown to be a strong, well set-up young man. I know he can have been afraid of absolutely nothing. As a little child, even, he was fearless. I remember his nanny, the very woman who had terrified me as a child with her ghost stories, having no effect on him whatsoever."

I said, "Yes, he was a brave man. I've seen as much myself from his war record."

"Indeed. But I suppose," said Arthur softly, "we are all of us, in the end, afraid of something. Otherwise, could we be human?"

"Certainly, I'm terrified of several things. The British tax system for one thing. Oh, and I admit, a certain well-known actress who shall be nameless."

Arthur smiled, but the smile slipped off like water.

His face was closed-in, bent to the fire, his eyes viewing, it seemed, only that.

"Yes, but there are other fears, aren't there? Inner fears. Fears located—how do they say it now—within the Id."

I said nothing. This promised to be more weird and much more time-consuming than I'd supposed.

Arthur stirred the fire slowly with a poker. Then he sat there, holding the poker loosely in his hand.

"Since I was a boy," he said, "since then, about six years of age. Something. I saw it first in a book, one of those stupid highly-coloured old illustrated books for children. Though I'd guess now it was meant for a much older child than I then was. It was on a low table, in the library. Thinking back, I believe it must have been my father's property, when he was little. Had it terrified him? Apparently not. And why anyway was it lying out open where I could find it? I've often wondered that. I'd think, really, almost any child might have been frightened by it. The drawn picture—was very crude, all reds, yellows, blacks—horrible—" He raised his eyes straight up to mine. And they were full of utter terror, that glowed like tears. "I know now it was a book about Ancient Rome. And this picture concerned the Emperor Nero's habit of having Christians thrown into the arena, and savage hungry animals let loose on them. An awful subject to illustrate. Probably meant to be improving. But *me* it did *not* improve. I rather think," he lowered the poker slowly back into its place, "it ruined me."

I was then, and am, no psychiatrist. I said, no doubt with inappropriate foolishness, "Of course, as a child, you might be afraid at it. But—how can it have ruined you?"

"I'd been quite a bold little boy. Always in scrapes. Brave. I used to lead a little local gang. We had some piratical name. But after I saw in that book—after I saw that picture, a change came over me. I used to dream, you see. I used to dream over and over about the picture."

"The Christians being killed in the arena by the animals."

"Killed, and devoured. Yes. They were—" he hesitated, and the oddest small twist of a smile distorted his lips, "they were lions," he said. And then again, "Lions." As if to repeat the name took a great effort of will, which he *must* exert.

Something in how he had stirred the fire had upset the logs. It sank and darkened, and the room seemed to darken too, despite the electric lamps.

I said, encouragingly, "Well, what you describe could be enough to give any kid nightmares."

"Perhaps. But I must explain. My dreams were very specific. I was in the arena, you see. I, as a child. And I was alone. Alone that was but for a huge, formless, faceless crowd shouting and baying all around me from the seats. And I would stand there on the sand, naked, shivering and afraid—sickeningly afraid—and then a kind of black hole would come in the side of the arena, and a lion would come out. Only one, you see. Only one." Arthur stopped. He put his head into his hands, but not before I'd seen his face was now almost green.

"Don't go on if it distresses—"

"I *must* go on," he said. He lifted his head and brought his brandy to his mouth and gulped the lot. "One lion," he said. "I know him so well. A huge ochre beast, with a vast black-ruffed head. There were bloody welts on his side—they must have whipped him up from the cages below—that filthy book showed all that too… Each of his eyes were like yellow-red coals. He stank. I could smell him. He stank of butcher's meat. And then he ran towards me—right at me—and I stood there screaming—and as he leapt his great claws flashed like silver hooks—and I woke—always I woke—just before his weight could come down and his talons and teeth could go into me. Always. And always, screaming. It happened every night, yet only ever once—once every night. It happened once every night for a whole year. I was afraid to go to bed. I would make myself keep awake, sitting up in the darkness—but in the end always I fell asleep. And then

I'd be in the arena, alone but for the crowd, and he would come, the lion. And he would run and leap and in that split second, when the rush of his stinking flesh and his claws already felt like a boiling wind across my body—I'd wake up. I would *escape* him."

"My God," I said. Finally, I thought, the elements of his fear had truly communicated themselves to me. As with a powerful acting performance, the catharsis of empathically induced emotion. I was shaken.

"Well," Arthur said presently. "I must tell you why the dreams stopped. First my parents tried to laugh and tease me out of them. Then they tried to bully me out. You perhaps have wondered why I've been a stranger to my own family all these years. Partly it began there. I never forgave them for it, their crass lack of understanding. And though in later years I could grasp almost perfectly that it came not from cruelty, but from a genuine, if entirely misplaced, conception of how best to deal with me—the rift had widened and was too enormous to heal. However, long before that, when I was seven years old, I met a gypsy in our garden. He'd just walked in at the gate, and was going round to the back of the house with some tinker's stuff he'd got for the kitchen. But seeing me, he pulled a face, and then called to me, quite politely and gently. *Come here, young master.* That was what he said. And for some reason, to him I went. I was by then a thin, pale-faced child, with rings under my eyes from never sleeping well. I must have looked haunted enough; our doctor had already apparently warned my father I might be in the early stages of some incurable malady—which idea alarmed mother, but my father scoffed at it, saying I was just in a silly mood, trying still to be a baby, and waking everyone by yelling every night. But the gypsy man stared into my face, and then he said, 'I can make him go away. One day he will come back. But you'll be a man then, and perhaps a man will have the strength to turn him off for good.' I gaped at him, and because I'd been brought up a certain way, I feebly said to him, 'What do you mean?' 'Hush now,' he answered. Then he put his hand on my head. It felt scalding hot, his hand, and he breathed in my face, and his breath was bad, because I suppose, poor fellow, his teeth weren't up to much. But somehow that didn't repulse me. When he lifted his hand away, I felt something go with it. He said, 'Done now. Not till you're a man will it come back. Go and tell the cook you took a toy off me from my sack, and I'm owed half a shilling.' I did what he said, and later I received a smacking from my father, who told me off for making the cook pay for a paltry toy for me. He asked where the toy was. I said it had broken, and my father said that served me right. He would have broken it if I had not. That night I crept up to bed, and sat there in the dark as usual, my back sore from the blows, and biting my hand to keep awake. But I kept thinking of the gypsy, too. And in the end I let go. I let go and I slept. I slept right through. It was the first night in a year I didn't have the dream. But after that, night followed night without it. Gradually then my general health improved. I was soon at school, and began to lead my own boy's life again. Although I was never as I had been before I saw the book. I hadn't the stamina I had had, even though I'd grown older and bigger. I tended to weight rather than muscle, I had headaches and once or twice fainted, if I was too hot or cold, and sometimes in church. But the dream was entirely gone. Gone till I should *be a man* and have the strength to face it once more, and then be able to send it away, to *turn it off for good.* Nevertheless—I could never be reconciled to that word, that name, or if I saw any picture of them, even a fine painting. Or if it was in a lesson. In Latin, for example. I even fainted then, too. Something in Suetonius, I think it was, about the Roman Circus."

The fire was dying. I took it on myself to poke at the logs and drop on another one. Arthur poured us more brandy, but said nothing. His face was less pallid, but had the greasy look of light sweating.

When I straightened up I said, "What happened then, when you were sixteen?"

"Oh," said Arthur, "your father remembered that, did he? Yes. It was nothing really. Nothing for them. We were to visit a garden. A zoological garden. By that time I'd got much better at suppressing my fear. Or I told myself I had. I'd been nerving myself to the excursion, thinking it might be a test I could overcome. But then—I heard them roaring, you see. In the distance. Over the trees. Lions. I knew instantly what the noise was. I screamed, as I had in my nightmares, and screaming is all I recollect after this, until I found myself at home again. I left my father's house as soon as I was well enough to do so. I led then a quite unadventurous life. I won't bore you with the details. They bore me, too, you see. Until that piece of luck with the recipe, the marmalade—more an orange jam, you understand. An old Scottish formula. Pure luck. Idiotic. But it made us rich, my partners and I. I can assure you, however, such good fortune doesn't hold off loneliness. I have always found it awkward, to mix with people, to find companions. And so I have been a lonely man. Unmarried—childless—I can't imagine such things as wedlock or paternity, for myself. Even so, I have got by. I have lived. And now," he said. Arthur leant back in his chair as I sat down again in mine. "And now," he repeated.

Though never having myself walked out on the boards, save in the most administrative capacity, I found myself responding as if we two, he and I, were spot-lit now at the centre of a stage. Faultless on my cue I announced, "And now it has returned."

Arthur met my eyes. His had changed to flat dark stones. "Yes. It has come back."

"As the gypsy said it would."

"As he said."

"Do you know why?"

"Oh yes. Something very ordinary."

I leant forward. "Which *is?*"

"I saw the damnable picture again."

"Good lord—where? Where did you see it?"

"Oh, not in that vile little book. No, it was reproduced in a catalogue. It seems the ghastly work is now something of an antique, and this illustration, the particular one, the one I think was fashioned in Hell, for me alone, that picture had been reproduced in the brightest, gaudiest detail. Leafing carelessly through the catalogue in the house of a business associate, suddenly it was all before me again. I had to leave the house immediately, making some incredible excuse, I can't remember what. That night I tried to reason with myself. But it was no use whatsoever. I found myself at 2 a.m., wandering about with the whisky decanter. Afraid to go to bed, just as I had been, night after night, when a child. In the end, of course, adult common-sense propelled me to my room. I downed a final glass of whisky and fell instantly asleep. Half an hour later I woke half the servants with my shrieks. My poor housekeeper believed criminals had broken in and were murdering me. It might have been amusing, if this state of affairs hadn't, then, continued for six further months. Yes, naturally, my doctor, and then several specialists, were summoned. They could do nothing, only drug me to a deathly moribund slumber from which—despite all the muck I had swallowed—I still woke once a night screaming in terror. The lion—" Arthur spoke the name now in a loud clear stroke, like the movement of a surgeon's knife, "— the lion came for me, as he always had. Out of the dark hole in the arena wall, over the dirty sand, leaping, his claws raking the air, just missing me as I sprang awake."

I too lifted my glass and drained it.

"But," I said, "six further months, I heard you say. Do you mean you found a way again to stop the dreams?"

"In a manner of speaking." Arthur stared downwards into nothingness. "A last specialist arrived here two months ago. In his demeanour he reminded me once more of my father, though he was younger than I am now. A strong-minded, bullying man, himself brave as—I was going to say, brave as a lion. He told me roundly I was a nervous wreck, and that the fault lay only with me. I had let this literary phantasm prey on me, and had offered no resistance. To drug myself with morphine or liquor was past the point. I must instead lie down to sleep and face the beast, in the knowledge that it was *nothing*. Nothing at all. It was only, he told me sternly, *my own fear* which had birthed, and subsequently sustained the nightmare. Forgivable, he admitted, in a very young child but in a grown man nauseating and absurd. 'It is your cowardice,' he bluntly said, 'which is destroying your sleep, your health and your life. You and you alone can be rid of it. You must cast it out. Then you will be free.' When he'd quite done with me, I was trembling like a boy. But I could see, as I can see now, that he was fundamentally in the right. My terrors had formed this curse. I must turn my back on them. And so I ate a light supper, had a couple of drinks, and went to bed. I stayed awake about half an hour, during which time I refused myself a single thought of the nightmare, and fell asleep abruptly. I dreamed of nothing at all. Since then too, the dream hasn't plagued me once. Indeed, I can sleep at any hour of day or night without any inconvenience."

I sat looking at him. His hands were folded down, one on each arm of his chair. He stared on into the abyss, invisible to me, which opened at his feet.

Arthur said, "I think you'll be both too mature and too young to know the fears and nervousness, in their way not unlike those of infancy, which can come on with increasing age. I suspect, too, being so like my own father in appearance, that you yourself may never succumb to this form of trepidation, even in old age. Death may never tap you on the shoulder to expound his prologue. You may never think about it. Your kind, and please do not think I insult you, I am only very jealous, can stay impervious to most horrors and frights. Your nerve holds in battle, and if there are ever such things as ghosts or demons, you would confront them, face them down. Or produce a revolver and shoot them, perhaps, back to mortal life."

Embarrassed by his accuracy, I too lowered my gaze. Where my glance fell then, I saw, across the fine Aubussin carpet, a curious baroque shadow, thick and black, lying oddly sidelong from the lamps. What was it? Puzzled, I turned my head and looked straight up into the corner of the room. There was a slice of darkness there also, and in the dark, something—no, two things—glittered in a sudden crushed flicker of brilliancy, now yellowish, now red.

"Ah," he said, in a quiet, cracked little voice, almost sarcastic, almost bitter. "Is it there? Can you see it?"

I turned back and glared at Arthur. "See what, precisely?"

"Don't you know?"

"No, frankly. Of course I'm sympathetic to what's happened to you. But even you yourself are now calling it a form of neurasthenia. So what is there to gain from dramatizing any of it further?"

"I can't help myself, it seems. When that clever specialist rehearsed my case before me, he mercilessly showed me exactly what I had most to fear: my own fear itself. My terrors, whether real or groundless, are my worst enemies. But I have to tell you, for such a person as myself, terror is now basic to my personality. And by refusing to let it visit me in sleep, it seems—it seems—I've let it out into the concrete world, at last. Where, having had me consistently elude it for so long, it has always yearned to follow me. My nightmare—has become a reality, and my terror feeds it every hour. Perhaps not even only terror, either. My *accustomedness*."

"Rubbish," I said. "Utter rot."

Behind me, some entity stirred, a velvet sound, edged with something rasping and barbed. Like the noise of a cat, amplified.

I stood up and looked round again. Something was there. No doubt of it. In deep shadow, between the top of a wooden cupboard and the cornice of the ceiling. It looked most like a large full trunk. It hadn't, I thought, been there previously.

My conclusion was that my Uncle Arthur had become insane, and was playing some type of bizarre, possibly dangerous, trick on me. I've had dealings with the unstable before—the profession on whose perimeter I work has presented to me some fine examples. To humour Arthur therefore seemed the best course.

Reluctant to stay with my back to whatever it was which had manifested in the corner, I moved my chair to a different angle, before sitting back down.

"Very well," I said. "But you've got your answer to it, haven't you? Cast out fear. Then it will go."

"I try," he said. "I try. It's a war that never stops. That gypsy man who helped me in my childhood, he thought I might eventually prove the stronger, and the victory be mine. Or maybe that was only his pretense, because he could foresee what was more likely. I try, and try, and try. But the fear never goes. How can it? The evidence of what there is to fear is frequently in front of me. Besides, by now, I believe it is less fear—than how mighty that fear it has already fed on has made the—creature. How else has it done what it has? Perversely, at last, it's only in sleep I ever evade it. Others here," he said, with a weary, flat, matter-of-factness, "see the thing too. Oh yes, that's how actual, despite my resistance, it has become. They see it. As you just did over there, up by the ceiling. And look now, the shadow on the carpet moving, the tail of it wagging slowly to and fro."

I stared resolutely into the fire. Behind me, far off, vague, I heard a kind of soft grumbling guttural, that might only be some freak sound of the autumn wind in the chimneys.

"You should pack up and leave this house," I said, lighting another cigarette.

"It would go with me," he said. "By now it goes with me always. Sometimes it disappears, as if it has other little tasks it likes to see to about the place. Then it's there again. My housekeeper has seen it. You can ask her. She's decided it's the ghost of a dog that once lived here. And my butler. The cook and maids somehow generally refuse to see it. Those that do sometimes complain of a large cat that has got into the main house from the kitchen."

There was a long, slipping, heavy noise.

Arthur's eyes went over above me. I saw him watch something move quickly across the upper air. His face was green again, but again he smiled. He nodded. He said, "It's gone for the moment. I could see them then, the welts on its side. Poor thing. It must suffer. Poor damnable thing."

I'd had enough. I got up again and said, "Sir, I have a very busy schedule, which begins quite early tomorrow. I understood you were aware of that when you invited me here. This matter, whatever it is, is beyond me. I don't know what you expect me to do."

"Only to listen. What else is feasible? I'd ask you to shoot it, if that were any good. But how could it be? It came out of the dark inside me. The dark where we go in dreams. It wants to take me back there, to keep me, to play with perhaps, or only to fulfill its function. Rend me. Devour me. Like the hapless Christians in the book."

"You'll have to excuse me," I said. "It's midnight. Perhaps I could ring for your man… Do you have any opiates to help you sleep?"

"Yes, go to bed," Arthur replied. His face was icy with disgust.

I stood in the doorway of the smoking-room. The hall outside was rosily low-lit from a single lamp standing on a table. At the curve of the staircase, one of the maids was crossing, with an armful of what looked like table linen, to the baise door giving on the servants' area. I looked at her, her trim brisk figure, and how, just before she reached the baise, something loped across her path, from shade to shadow, and she hesitated, as if to check the fall of one of the pile of linens she held, which were not slipping at all.

I saw its eyes gleam, fitfully. It glanced at me, indifferent. In its half-seen, solid shape was all the intangible presence of the night. But as he had said, it was an indoor beast, a beast of locked houses that left only one door open for it, in the frantic hope it might go out and lose itself. A beast too of the indoors of the brain, the psyche. A beast of the indoors of the human soul.

Like a scene from a play, I saw it, his dream, and how the beast leapt at him, missed him, always missing, as he fled outward to the world. And then his fear coming out of him, rejected, but still inextricably attached. Externalized.

The lion had gone around the corner and the maid passed through the servants' door and the hall was empty.

I walked back into the smoking-room. He was sitting quietly crying, poor old child, with the welts of horror blistering on his side.

"All right, old chap," I said. "All right."

"I don't," he said, apologetically, "want to be alone."

"Then you shan't be. Hang the theatre. I'll deal with it tomorrow."

After a while, we went upstairs, and along one of the corridors to his room. Nothing was about, all was silence, and in the cracks of windows, where curtains didn't quite meet, a low moon floated on a cloud.

We had another brandy, and he went to bed, or at least lay down with the coverlet over him. His round fallen face on the pillows stared at me.

"Nothing can be done. I know that," he said. "When it comes back—"

"I'll wake you," I said. "Sleep for now."

I'd asked myself if it *could* come in when he slept, but of course it could, that was the whole point to it now. It was in the world, and outside of him. And his former fear of meeting it in his mind had been replaced, not unreasonably, by the fear it would eventually seize him while he slept.

The electric light on the upper floors was dimmer. I sat in an armchair in this duller glow, and midnight passed into one, and so on through two. I smoked, and watched the clock, and wished I'd thought to bring some coffee upstairs.

But even so, I was wide awake. Arthur slept, deep and dumb. He might have been dead, I couldn't help thinking that. I had no inspiration of what I could do. Keep the creature off him, then in the morning drive him somewhere, look up any one of a number of people who dealt in fractured minds and halluci- nations—God knows. The brain ticks away in its backrooms often, and we're unaware of its secret progress. I sincerely hoped it might offer me a plan, but hadn't much faith it could.

For I knew too, of course I did, this now was more than a dream or mirage. I'd seen it. I'm prosaic enough, and it was merely pragmatic now to *admit* to having seen it. To deny the situation further would be to enter myself the lists of the fanciful or mad.

It returned when the clock said a quarter past three.

It came up through the floor.

That was like a stage effect, something clever with traps and levers, but involving no dry ice to mask it.

Arrived, it shook itself. The housekeeper had convinced herself it was a phantom dog, and there was something doglike about it certainly, as there often is with the big cats; tigers, panthers, and the rest. But its face was savage and evil, its eyes two mindless sumps of decayed fire that seemed to have given off the smoke of its mane. It did faintly stink, as he'd said. How had he known, as a child, what it might smell of? But perhaps lions don't smell of meat; it was only something he'd heard and so made this one do it. For it was all his own work—his, and that of the artist who first so luridly depicted it and its kind, in the arena of Nero.

I'd promised him I would wake him when it came back. I called his name sharply, and Arthur opened his eyes, instantly fully conscious. "Is it there?"

"Across the room by the window."

The moon had gone, but the low-burning electric light illustrated the lion as accurately as its initial paint.

It did not look at him or me. It looked about itself at the massively furnished room. Then it padded away, across the floor, and nudging open the bathroom door, went inside.

In the total noiselessness of the night, Arthur and I listened as it drank from some trickle of water, real or etheric, issuing from the taps of the bath.

When it had finished, it returned, not through the door, but simply out of the wall. It stood, its heavy head lowered, its tail swinging.

Something struck me then. I couldn't have described it. But abruptly I saw the cruelty in its face was only instinct, and perhaps the pain from the stripes on its side, which anyway looked partly cured. It was an animal of sorts, at least. It was hungry, and had been thirsty, and chose sometimes to use a door rather than pass through a blank floor or wall.

So then I spoke to it, by its name. "Lion."

It made a snorting noise, and turned, and looked at me, that terrible look, the hellish eyes that were really only reflecting light.

"There he is," I said to it. "There. Look *there*."

And the head again turned as if it grasped my meaning. And I saw Arthur brace himself. I said to Arthur then, "It's yours. You made it. You gave it life. You're—you're like a father to the damn thing, Arthur. Stop resisting it, do you hear? It's your belonging now, whatever it was to start with. It doesn't want to drag you back into the shadows—if did it would lose all this new territory you've given it. I'm fairly sure it knows that, or it would have done it by now. After all, it's had a couple of months to try. First you gave it the Roman arena to play in. But now its got a whole house—and anything outside it fancies too. Why do you think it goes off and leaves you? It goes exploring like a bloody cat. And why do you think it follows you, comes back to you? If it isn't for violence, it must be something else. Maybe that's where it *is* like a dog. It knows, if you don't, it belongs to you."

The lion, with no warning, sprang. It was too quick for Arthur even to cry out, even to register his fear. It landed, and balanced on his bed, at the foot of it, gazing at him, breathing.

I crossed the room in three strides and pushed it hard in its unmarked side—except there was nothing, nothing substantial to push—but with a grunt it dropped, and flopped down. It lay there sprawled.

It blinked at me, growling.

"Be quiet," I said. "You must do as you're told. If you want to stay, you must behave yourself." The growl changed to a yawn.

We remained watching it, Arthur bolt upright on the pillows, I standing at the bedside, and after a while it lowered its head on to the coverlet. The horror of its eyes shut.

After that, we kept vigil till first light, talking slowly and methodically, discussing it, over its sleeping form, Arthur not moving an inch, I static in a chair. When dawn began to seep in, the lion woke and rose. It kicked its paws and jumped off the bed—and vanished.

At ten to seven some tea was brought up by a maid, and I went down to telephone the town, reporting my absence as due to food-poisoning.

The lion was standing in the echoing hallway when I turned, looking off along a corridor to a narrow, opened door. The morning smelled enticingly there, of trees and mist, and bonfires. While the open door, since the lion could utilize blank walls for exits and entrances, was presumably an aesthetic choice. Outside lay the grounds, with plenty of game—mice and squirrels, birds, rabbits and hares. Any big animal could hunt for itself if it wanted, although I doubted any of the hunted things would suffer much worse than a nasty shock. The lion, though it was visible and could create smell and sound, had no actual substance. But, like the bath-taps, which didn't leak but had provided water, an idea was conceivably enough for it to feed from. A beast of imagination in more than one way. Arthur's beast, very apparently. Even as I watched, it made a decision and bounded off along the corridor and out of the open door. Hungry—well, it had had to wait several decades for a meal.

Needless to say, I recounted nothing of any of this when I reached the theatre the next day. My assistant had managed pretty ably without me, and all was soon put in order. I meanwhile secured myself a room in the local hotel.

Arthur survived another twenty-five years, and died without warning, but peacefully, during a fishing holiday in Scotland with one of his partners in the marmalade venture. There had been some talk of a large ghost dog, I believe, being seen often about Blue Firs, and also in other houses where Arthur visited. A slight mythology had connected itself to my uncle, who, apparently, was once or twice spotted, as witnesses thought, throwing sticks for some large hound, in a selection of rural retreats. In Scotland, years before he died, there was a strange story of something lying on the foot of his bed, purring—but it had disappeared by the time others came to investigate. After Arthur's death, the beast vanished completely, at least according to his housekeeper. Blue Firs is now, I rather ashamedly admit, mine, but I am seldom there. Nevertheless, those who rent the property relate nothing either of dogs, cats or lions.

From Arthur, in the years before his death, I heard very little of anything, and less of his creature. With his renewed sense of safety, our "estrangement" had recurred, which seemed to suit us both. Only a postscript appeared now and then to a rare letter: *The lion is in good spirits.* Anyone reading this correspondence might take it that Arthur referred sportively to himself. People told me afterwards my solitary visit had done him a power of good.

He had thrown off at once his old timidity and depression, and the recent bad nerves. Instead he took to long, hale walks, and large cuts of meat served almost raw at dinner—though these were barely touched. Sometimes, when alone, he would, it seems, laugh aloud. He informed anybody who asked him, it was at something he had read in a newspaper.

Naturally I have no knowledge of where either of them is now For myself, I assume life ends with the body. But then again, perhaps there are some mind-fashioned heavens in which certain mentally creative people continue to exist. If so, I don't think for a moment Arthur and his lion are now locked back in any Roman arena. He freed the lion, and ultimately was set free by it. Trite in the paucity of my own imaginative knack, I see them bounding along a seaside, Arthur a gleeful kid of seven, wiry, healthy and tough, and with a great, black-maned dog, scarred a little on one flank, whose claws flash like silver hooks, and leave starry markers on the clean, unearthly sand of the shore.

PRIDE

Mary A. Turzillo

Mary Turzillo's fiction has recently appeared in *Analog, Year's Best Lesbian Fiction 2008, Cat Tales, Space and Time, The Vampire Archives*, and *Sky Whales and Other Wonders*. She has published about fifty stories in magazines and anthologies and her poetry is collected in *Your Cat & Other Space Aliens*. Her Nebula winning "Mars Is No Place for Children," and her novel *An Old-Fashioned Martian Girl* have been selected as recreational reading on the International Space Station.

Turzillo says: "Like many of my stories, 'Pride' comes out of my life as a professor at Trumbull branch of Kent State University. Residents of Trumbull County, Ohio, love their exotic pets. Two sisters in one of my classes told me they had adopted a lion cub which liked to bask in the middle of their residential street, forcing traffic to drive around it. A philosophy professor had to give up his pet python to get custody of his young son. A little girl was mauled by a tiger cub at the county fair. A friend of my son always dreaded the part of his paper route that took him past a caged animal he never saw, but that roared terrifyingly. And of course there was Iron Mike Tyson's fruitless suit to keep Kenya, his white Bengal tiger, plus other big cats, on his sixty-acre estate in rural Southington, only a few miles from where I lived.

"To understand Jonesy, I've watched countless bored, scary big cats in Busch Gardens, the Cleveland Zoo, and other zoological gardens, contemplating their casual menace. Jonesy's roll-and-strike attack is based on speculations of the way sabertooth cats tore out the throats of their prey, but the truth is, I've observed my kitten, Mahasamatman, make the same move play-attacking another cat."

The hot fur thing under Kevin's shirt clawed at his chest. *Nice going*, he thought. *First the bum rap for weed, and now if I don't get caught stealing lab animals, I'll get rabies from this freak.*

181

Frankenlab, at Franken U, AKA Franklin Agricultural College, was messing with animals, electrodes in their brains, cloning them like Dolly the Sheep, except not regular animals. Dead animals from frozen meat. And they were going to kill the animals.

He couldn't save them all. Those fuzzy orange-furred mice, most wouldn't make it. Those guys from Animals Our Brethren had pried open cages, and when the mice wouldn't come out, they shook them out, and when the mice squeed, cowering under lab tables, they kicked them until they ran into corners, and from there may God have mercy on their itty souls.

Kevin petted the little monster through his shirt, but it writhed around and gummed him. "I'm saving your life, dumb-ox!" He dashed out of the building minutes before alarms brought the fire department.

Kevin had been in trouble before. A year ago, his girl friend's cousin Ed and he had been cruising around in Ed's van, which had expired plates. Kevin didn't know about the baggie of pot under the driver's seat. When the state patrol started following, Ed asked Kevin to switch places. His license, like the plates, was expired, he said. They switched, veering madly, on a lonely stretch of 422. When they finally stopped and the cops asked to search the van, Kevin shrugged and said okay.

"And whose is this?" Ed said, not me. Kevin was too surprised to look properly surprised, and this was a zero-tolerance state. So Ed got off with a warning, and Kevin, stuck with court-appointed counsel, served thirty days.

Kevin had been looking for a job to pay for college, when local papers broke the story that some thousand-odd animals (mostly, admittedly, mice) would be killed because their experiment was over. What was he thinking of? He wasn't an animal-rights kind of dude. Still, he felt panicked exultation fleeing the scene of the crime.

He struggled to control his Pinto while driving with the squirming thing scratching inside his shirt. He fumbled the back door key and pounded downstairs to the basement, where he pulled the light cord above the laundry tub and took the furball out of his shirt.

"Oh God, what have they done to you?" It was deformed: big head, chopped-off tail. Cat? Dog? A mix?

He deposited it in the laundry tub. Boggling at the size of its mouth, he realized it needed food. Now.

Forward pointing eyes. Meat-eater. He ran upstairs and grabbed a raw chicken breast from the fridge. He held it out to the cub.

The cub flopped down on its belly in the tub, and tried to howl. All that came out was a squeak.

He tried to stuff the meat into its mouth, but it flinched away and lay looking at him, sides heaving.

Maybe the mother chewed the food up for it. Mother? Not hardly. This thing didn't have a mother. It was fucking hatched in Frankenlab.

Raised in farm country, Kevin liked animals. He sometimes even petted Rosebud, the town pit bull, when Rosebud wasn't into tearing people's arms off. If his parents had been rich, he'd be pre-veterinary at Franken U. Or a cattle rancher, or a discoverer of rare snakes.

He retrieved a knife from upstairs, hacked tidbits off the chicken breast, and put them in the cub's mouth. The cub sucked on them, famished. It got to its feet and seized his finger with its front paws. Head held sideways, it chomped down on his finger. It did have a few teeth, it seemed.

He jerked away. "Stop it, you little monster!" Then he realized he might wake his mother.

Kevin, it's a baby. Duh.

Where would he get a baby bottle?

He opened a can of condensed milk from the pantry, dipped a chicken chunk in it, and let the monster suck milk off the meat. Twenty minutes later it either got satisfied, or gave up. Its little belly looked marginally bigger, and the can was empty, mostly spilled on the laundry tub or his shirt.

It stretched and unsheathed claws way too big for a little guy the size of a raccoon.

Kevin thought, *It'll purr now.* Instead, it washed its face, running front paws over those deformed big jaws.

And then, just when Kevin decided it was almost cute, it reached out a claw and pricked his arm, not enough to hurt, just to say, *More?*

"You're beginning to tick me off," he said. The cub's gaze radiated adoration. It licked his hand, nearly rasping his skin off.

Its fur was golden retriever blonde, its eyes the color of river moss. Green-eyed blonde, like Sara. Dappled coat, like freckles on Sara's sweet shoulders. Sara Jones: they were almost a couple before his arrest; now she acted distant.

The monster leapt out of the tub and landed on the floor. It shook itself, surprised at the fall.

He lay down and stared at it, eye to eye. "You need a name."

He was furious that they planned to kill it. It was harmless. Uh, maybe not harmless. Planning to get big, judging from those paws, each the size of cheeseburgers. But innocent.

"What the hell have I got myself into?" he asked it.

Its grotesque little face shone with trust.

With the knife he'd used to cut the chicken, and thinking of Sara Jones, he tapped the little monster on each shoulder, and said, "I dub thee Sir Jonesy."

For a week, he kept Jonesy locked in the root cellar. His mom either didn't know, or pretended not to. Rosebud, Mr. Trumbull's pitbull, kept getting off his chain and sneaking over to paw at the basement door. There was an article in the paper about the lab fire, but the lab animals were hardly mentioned.

The scientists downplayed it all. The animals had been slated for "sacrifice," Dr. Betty Hartley said. Federal regulations required that animals be euthanized at the end of an experiment, she said, plus the money had run out. Cold. "Sacrifice": nice euphemism. Like "put to sleep." Like anything ever woke up from that sleep. Sacrifice? What, were they going to dance around an altar and beg God to protect them from weird-ass animal zombies?

Dr. Hartley said she was sad that the animals had all died in the fire, but accidents will happen.

So now he couldn't let anybody in on his secret. It would be insane to let the scientists find the cub again and kill it. But Jonesy (the cub was female, he discovered) whined and shivered in the root cellar, so he brought it upstairs.

His mother was not pleased.

"Look, Mom. I know it's humongous for a kitten, but that's all it is. Pet it?"

She refused to touch it. "I don't care what it is, I don't want it in my house."

"Listen, they'll kill it if I take it back. It's cute, see?" He held it to his chest to minimize her view of the monstrous head. Its fur was rough, not silky like a kitten's. But it was warm and happy to snuggle.

"Cute? Kevin, I'll show you cute. I know you stole it from Frankenlab. It'll probably get up in the night and suck our blood."

"Shit, mom. It eats milk, not blood. You can't just kick it out on the street like a—like a broken TV."

"Kevin, get a job. And get that thing out of my house."

But Kevin's mother was too tired to put her foot down.

The cub's teeth started coming in. On a diet of ground meat that Kevin got from dumpster-diving, it had loads of energy. It used the energy stalking Kevin and shredding everything in Kevin's room.

The eye teeth erupted. And erupted. And erupted. Not domestic cat teeth. Long as the fishing knife the cops had taken away from him when he was caught with the pot.

He woke up one morning to find the monster sitting on his chest, hungry or affectionate, as if you could tell even with a tame cat.

"Man," said Kevin, peering closer. "Your mom should have sued your orthodontist."

The cub did not laugh.

Not a vampire, but those sharp, sharp teeth—

And then his mind chewed through a bunch of information and farted out the truth. Rumors of ice age frozen flesh? Cloning? Bingo.

The damn thing, scrutinizing him with gold-green eyes, opening its huge mouth in a silent howl, was a sabertooth tiger.

"Woo, dude. I thought you were trouble before."

It would need lots more meat.

At first he bought cheap cuts, then when he realized his money from mowing lawns wasn't cutting it, he abstracted food from his own meals and from the refrigerator. And dumpster-dove the local supermarket.

One day, he found his mother in the kitchen, her hand bandaged. He hoped the bite was from Rosebud, but if Rosebud had bitten her, she'd probably be a mangled corpse.

He sank into a chair, while the sabertooth attacked the stinky mess he'd brought home for it.

"That's it, Kevin. You're my only son, the light of my life, a good smart boy although way too trusting, but that cat is out by tonight or I call the cops." She blew her nose on a crumpled tissue. "I know where he came from."

Kevin didn't blame her. She was tired from overwork, just wanted to be left alone and sleep more than five hours at a time. They'd been moderately affluent before Kevin's dad left. But Dad had a really good lawyer. The measly child support had stopped when Kevin turned eighteen. Dad still sent birthday cards with a two-dollar bill in each.

"If the boy wants a college education, a job will make him appreciate it more."

Jobs, yeah, well. Jobs for twenty-one year old guys who've done even a little time aren't easy to come by. Odd jobs, maybe shoveling walks in winter. Kevin wasn't a drinker, so he didn't have AA networking to fall back on.

Also, the damn cub was too mischievous to leave alone for long.

The week before the cat nipped Mom, he'd come home from helping a neighbor get her hay in and found the cub playing with a large rat. When the sabertooth saw him, she grabbed the rat in her mouth and tried to run away. Thank God it had been a rat and not those ratty-looking poodles the Parks owned.

So Mom was right. The cat needed a home

Sara. Their beginning romance had aborted, but he ran into to her sometimes at the feed store. She'd understood Kevin didn't know about the pot. But she always said, "It's not a good time," if he wanted to come over to the farm, or ask her out, not that he had much money for dates.

Guess she didn't want to be with a loser.

But, hell, he could rise again. Many great men, millionaires, politicians, had a shady past.

Sara didn't hate him.

He put the cub in an appliance carton (it whimpered, but complied), wrapped it with pink and ivory paper and gold ribbon, and lugged it to the Pinto. The cub thrashed around inside the box on his front seat, while he drove like a maniac to Sara's farm. Sara's parents hadn't really worked the family farm much since her granddad died, just kept geese and a big garden, and when they moved south to escape the winters, Sara kept the farm. Kevin used to help out, before he went to jail.

He lost his nerve and left the gyrating package on her paint-peeled porch.

The phone was ringing when he got back.

"Kevin, what is this? It nearly took my arm off."

He breathed slowly. He'd enrolled in an anger management class while in jail, not because he had problems with anger, but because the textbook looked interesting, and he found the breathing helped calm him. "Sara, it's a sabertooth tiger."

"They're extinct."

"Yeah, yeah, yeah, so's the Bill of Rights. But this thing is a clone. From frozen meat."

"And this concerns me how?"

"It's, uh—"

"Look, Kevin, I remember the Maine Coon kittens you gave me. I love those cats. But this is different, no? You must have stolen this thing from the college. And that's not all. It's going to grow up and be really aggressive. And, well, also—"

"Sorry. I'll come and get her back. Don't let her out, though. I'm not sure she knows how to defend herself."

When he got to the farm, Sara acted nervous, but she kissed him, and they sat on the couch and talked, about Ed, about jail. They didn't have sex, but he got his hopes up they could reconnect. Jonesy, meantime, tried to shred everything in her living room. She had put out a bowl of hamburger, otherwise the cub might have started shredding their clothes.

"It's not exactly *cute*," she said.

Jonesy's whiskers were almost as amazing as her teeth. Long and delicate. She stalked everything in the room, even shadows.

Kevin watched. The cub would hunker down and wriggle her backside, then dart forward and roll upside down. The hunker/wriggle part looked like any cat, but he'd never seen an animal do a half roll while attacking. Did that have anything to do with the sword-like canines?

"Kevin, you know I love animals."

Kevin said nothing. Their shoulders touched, and he put his hand on hers.

She left it there. "Okay. Until you get a place of your own. Don't come visiting without calling, though." She withdrew her hand.

Somebody was living with her. Of course.

The arrangement lasted three weeks.

When he drove over in answer to her phone call, Sara was crying. Jonesy had killed one of her geese, a real achievement, since even Rosebud was loathe to fool with the geese. But when Kevin opened the door, he boggled at how much the sabertooth had grown. Jonesy had to weigh as much Rosebud now.

Oops. What if Jonesy had attacked Sara?

"I let her run," she said. "You can't keep an animal like this cooped up. And it killed Emily Dickinson." Emily Dickinson was one of her geese. She named her geese after women poets.

"What have you been feeding her? "He felt shame that he hadn't offered to pay for Jonesy's food. As if he could. He had a sudden panic over the welfare of the two Maine Coon cats, but they were dozing on the sofa. The sofa was shredded, but the cats were fine.

"I feed her canned dogfood, but she's always hungry. I haven't seen a raccoon in the neighborhood for two weeks. Kevin, I don't know where you can take her but she can't stay here."

Was Jonesy grown enough to survive on her own, on garbage, raccoons, and people's geese? "How did she learn to eat the raccoons?"

"When I separated them, Emily kind of—split open, you know—and Jonesy stood over Emily, and then, as if she was sorry for the poor goose, she bent over and started licking her feathers, and she tasted the blood, and all of a sudden—"

Kevin had seen barn cats experience this epiphany. They discover their toy tastes good. Most learned from the mother cat, but get them hungry enough—

"She doesn't bother the geese any more. They run away. But then there's the deer."

Kevin looked at his baby monster. "Jonesy couldn't take down a deer."

"Maybe not, but she sure knows how to chase them. And I worry about Mr. Trumbull's cows."

Kevin stood. "Thanks for taking care of her."

She took his hand, then moved closer. They gazed at each other. Could he kiss her?

She stepped back. "Take her somewhere. Hey, what about your dad's old trailer?"

The trailer featured scarcely more than a bed and a mini-dinette, abandoned on the lot near his mom's apartment. Roof leaked, plumbing wasn't connected. No trailer park would let him in with that wreck.

Nor with an "exotic animal." Even if he could pass Jonesy off as a rescued bobcat or lion cub.

"I'll call around." He had brought a collar and leash, and he snapped these on Jonesy. Jonesy had been on leash before and didn't like it, but she trusted Kevin enough not to fight.

Kevin was becoming an expert on smilodons. They weren't even from the same branch of the Felidae family as lions and tigers, but still might live in families. He must seem to Jonesy like her mother or the leader of her—what did they call lion families?—pride.

He smiled at Sara, eyes full of hope.

"Go!" she said, shoving him playfully. The sabertooth bared huge teeth at Sara until she smoothed its back fur. "You can come back. Bring Jonesy if you can control her. Just call first."

He led the sabertooth to his car. His mind roiled with possibility. *Ask her!* he thought. *She's got a new guy, or she doesn't. Ask!*

Too many secrets in Kevin's life: an animal he couldn't give up and couldn't keep, and a girl he wanted and whose life had become a mystery.

"Cat," he said. "We ain't neither of us got no pride."

Kevin's uncle owned some unworked farmland twenty miles out of town center. He got permission to park the trailer there, planning to haul water and use cartridges for gas heat. He bought a generator and parked the trailer well back from the road.

Odd jobs weren't enough. His mom's restaurant needed a dishwasher. Since the owner knew him—and about the jail time—there was no background check problem. Kevin bought a cellphone that didn't require a credit card, and the modern man out of his time and Ice Age cat went there to live their hard life.

College plans receded into mist. Maybe someday Kevin could write a book about this. He bought a cheap digital camera and started a journal of the Jonesy's growth and behavior.

The sabertooth soon learned to paw open the refrigerator. Kevin was forced to keep only vegetables in it. To supplement the dogfood, he brought home a cut-up chicken or a chuck steak every night. Jonesy tore into these, sometimes before Kevin could get the wrapper off. Sometimes the wrapper would get impaled on the four inch-long canines, and she would run around the room trying to scrape them off. Kevin fell down laughing the first time that happened.

Kevin's own meals were either vegetarian or eaten at the restaurant.

He bought a used copy of *Born Free* at a yard sale. Jonesy wasn't any kind of modern cat, but it was a start. The librarian found him treatises on the smilodons of North America, though he wasn't even sure that's what Jonesy was. He had to play it cool when the librarian got nosy about his interest in cloning.

Jonesy shredded any book he brought home. To her, books, like everything else, were toys. So his reading was restricted to the library and their internet computers, and since he didn't like leaving the cat alone when she was awake, he kept all his research in his head.

He couldn't keep the sabertooth penned up, any more than Sara could. So, after a few weeks, he let her off the long line he'd tied to the trailer, and watched her lope the perimeter of the mowed area, where the demolished farmhouse had set. The line wouldn't hold her anyway, if she wanted to get away. She would chew through chain, though it might damage her beautiful teeth.

She stopped periodically to smell things, and her ears perked at the passage of a bird.

Then she saw the fox, and he thought he'd have to change her name to Turbo.

Did she eat the fox? No doubt she'd caught it. No bloody carcass in the trampled down area where the chase had ended. But for two days later, Jonesy looked quite pleased with herself.

The rest of that summer, the winter, and spring. The sabertooth grew sleek and menacing, muscles moving smoothly under short tawny fur. One of her magnificent eyeteeth loosened. When it fell out, she let Kevin feel inside her mouth, and underneath where it had been, he felt a new sharp point under the gum. Which grew and grew and grew. The other side did the same, and one morning he awoke to her heavy paws on his chest and opened his eyes to see her monstrous white glistening sabers new and sharp and creamy white, each as long as the knife they used in the restaurant kitchen to hack apart beef joints.

Her inscrutable face and hot moist breath made his heart jump with terror. But she was his companion; he had held her under his shirt. He had fed her milk.

He reached up and stroked her ears, which alone of her fur retained kittenish silkiness. Then, with the greatest caution, he touched her saber fangs. Smooth, like ivory knives. This meant she was—Smilodon fatalis? Smilodon neogaeus? Or the other genus—Megantereon? He couldn't tell: he was no paleontologist.

He called Sara, to share this experience. She picked up after two rings, and hung up. But not even Sara's rejection could spoil that moment.

He was the first man ever to touch a living smilodon's teeth, and survive.

Sara would call now and then to ask about Jonesy, or tell him about a job opening. He could leave the sabertooth with her during the day, she said.

But when he called, employers always knew he was the kid who went to jail for drugs. Such is rural town gossip.

Jonesy and he walked the perimeter of the farm every night, out of sight of the road. He'd been four years out of high school. College seemed much further away now. He thought, *Some would say I have no life. A dumbass job. Had good grades, could gone to college, married a beautiful woman who owned land. Lost all that because I trusted the wrong person, didn't fight the system hard enough. Could have done better. But I've touched the saber teeth of a smilodon, and if no other gift is given me in this life, that might be enough.*

If Jonesy missed anything, she never said so.

Then Jonesy came into heat.

As she came insinuating up to him, dragging her butt against the floor, trying to hump the ragged sofa arm, beseeching him to do something, anything, he just said, "Kitten, I'd write you a personals ad, but your kind don't subscribe to the *Country Cryer*."

Neutering, but how the hell would he pass her off as anything but what she was? The vet would remember the incident at Frankenlab, and all would be up. Another jail sentence for Kevin. Worse for Jonesy: "sacrifice" at the hands of the scientists.

He tried penning her in the trailer while he slept in the Pinto, but she started chewing through the metal window frame. He let her out, and she howled to get inside with him.

Next night, his cell phone rang.

"Kevin, Keith, whatever your name is. People hear that howling, don't know what it is. But I do."

Kevin's heart lurched. Caller ID said: *B. Hartley*. The scientist. "Doctor Hartley. You plan to 'sacrifice' her now?"

"No, you dolt. Do I have to spell it out for you? I incited your stupid Animals Our Brethren people to start that fire so she'd get away."

He took it in. "She's in heat. What should—"

"She'll either go out of heat, or she'll attack somebody. She may even decide you're the lucky tom. Give her back to me."

"Was there another sabertooth? A male?"

"Of course not, you idiot."

He snapped the cellphone shut and threw it against a wall.

Jonesy disappeared into the woods behind French Lick Creek.

A week later she slunk back. Kevin waited, but she was not knocked up. How could she be?

He was pretty sure Jonesy was keeping down the deer and raccoon population, but nobody mentioned missing any dogs. Cats, maybe.

When he needed to go to work, he had to lock her in the trailer, and she gnawed at the door and chewed the knob. Thank God she didn't have opposable thumbs; she was smarter than most dogs and cats. And some people.

But heaven, even Kevin and Jonesy's twisted heaven, can never last.

He had to run an errand. The feed store, which closed in the evening, was the cheapest place to get her dogfood.

How she got out and trailed him wasn't that hard to reconstruct. He'd been careless. As he walked out of the store, he nearly tripped over her sunning herself on the front steps.

And across the square was Rosebud. Rosebud wasn't supposed to be out, either, but Mr. Trumbull was pretty lax too.

Rosebud hated cats. And Jonesy smelled like a big, unneutered cat. Rosebud killed cats. Smart cat owners in French Creek Township kept their pets indoors. As to farm cats, thank God Rosebud couldn't climb trees.

Rosebud was across the square, urinating on a post. He stopped abruptly and put his leg down, tiny ears perked, nose twitching. Then he charged.

Halfway across the square, he suddenly changed his mind. Uncertain, he froze, then turned tail.

Jonesy wasn't a long distance runner, but she was fast on a sprint.

What Kevin saw next was that weird smilodon leap. Jonesy charged and without stopping, rolled to her back, hugged Rosebud's neck, then sank her saber teeth into the dog's throat. The dog heaved into the air, Jonesy rolled over on top of him, and the two struggled. Rosebud had no offensive weapons but his jaws, and he'd never had to defend himself before, so his struggles turned to spasms and in seconds, he lay still.

Jonesy straddled the dog and raised her bloodied jaws in a terrifying roar. Everybody ran out of the feed store, the diner, and the gift shop.

Jonesy lowered her jaws and began to tear pieces out of the dog's belly.

Kevin fought vertigo and nausea. Somebody yelled, "Anybody catch that on video?"

He charged across the square, screaming at Jonesy. Three guys tried to stop him, yelling, "It'll kill you!" but he slid to a stop by the scene of carnage and yanked on Jonesy's collar.

"He's crazy!" somebody yelled.

Kevin realized he *was* crazy. Jonesy weighed maybe five hundred pounds by now. He'd read plenty of accounts of people mauled by previously docile big cats. Why did he assume Jonesy was different?

But he had to get the cat away, before somebody with a gun thought to use it.

A small, strong hand gripped his wrist.

Sara. Sara had the rifle her grandfather always carried in her truck. It had been a fixture in the truck for so long he'd forgotten about it. Nor did he wonder why she happened to be in town that day.

She gave him a serious look, then handed him the rifle. "It's under control," she yelled at the gathering crowd. "Back off before somebody gets hurt."

The dog was mangled meat. Jonesy had ripped open its throat and its belly and was standing over it, sides heaving with desire, jaws quivering with hunger and triumph.

The crowd all took a step back.

"Get her in the truck," Sara said. "You can still control her, can't you?"

Jonesy roared again, a softer roar.

Very deliberately—he believed that crap about animals being able to sense fear, but also knew he could fake courage pretty well—he took a handful of the loose flesh at the back of Jonesy's neck and said in a low growl, "Into the truck, bad girl."

And it was over. Jonesy lowered her head and her stump of a tail and climbed into Sara's truck. Kevin slammed the door.

Which left Sara and Kevin standing outside.

Sara was shaking. She reached up and grabbed Kevin's ears and kissed him hard, tongue and all. Breaking loose, she said, "You're an idiot! But, God almighty, you've got guts!"

What now? Kevin couldn't leave Jonesy inside the truck; first, the sabertooth would demolish the inside. Second, it was a nice spring day, sunny, and heat would eventually build up and kill her.

But he could no longer predict the cat's behavior. Jonesy's blood was up; she might boil over.

"We have to get her out of here before the cops come," said Kevin. He shrugged, grabbed Sara's keys, and sprang into the truck.

Jonesy didn't kill him. The rest of his life, he would wonder why. Because he was dominant? Because she loved him? Do top predators know love?

He let Jonesy out of the truck outside his trailer. She lingered, licking his hand and making begging grunts, so he opened one of the dogfood cans. She took it away from him and rasped the horse meat out, then lay down in the grass.

He went inside and wept.

Yes, somebody had videotaped it. Not the two animals running toward each other, not Jonesy's karate-like attack, but the dog underneath Jonesy, thrashing, then still, and Jonesy pulling out intestines. The video played several times, always zooming on the dead pitbull, then panning to Kevin pulling the cat away. He lay on the bed staring at the ceiling

Thank God the cat looked like a female lion in the video. Some bystanders remarked on its teeth, but nobody connected it with the break-in and fire at the lab a couple years previous.

In the evening, Sara brought his car back. He didn't know how she started it, but she came in uninvited and lay beside him on the bed.

They kissed. She said, "Lock the door."

He did, obediently. "It won't stop Jonesy, if that's what you're thinking."

Hours later, they dressed and talked about hunting for Jonesy. Did anybody recognize them from the video? It was really jerky. Nobody was knocking on the door. But Kevin's mind roiled with possibilities: if somebody recognized Sara's truck, they'd go to her house, then figure she was here. They'd come with guns for Jonesy. Jonesy was tame; she wouldn't know to run.

Hellfire. Maybe Jonesy *should* be put down.

He said, "I always thought you still loved me a little. Unless this is just a stress reaction."

She leaned into him, then grabbed and shook him, hard enough that he thought, she's going to slug me next. She said, "I loved you, you jerk, but I couldn't keep on loving somebody who was stupid enough to go to jail for what he didn't do."

"Ed is your cousin. I couldn't rat out your cousin. And I never was sure the pot was his, anyway."

"Idiot!" And she did slap him, not enough to hurt, then turned away, hiding tears. "Ed is a goddamn jerk. He got you in trouble, you shielded him. He's my blood, but nobody I'd ever choose for family. Kevin, Kevin. I can't be with a man who spent time in jail and who—who lives with this monster."

"You like animals."

She sobered. "I do. I'm not sure what you should do with Jonesy. Maybe we could get rid of her somehow? Not kill her. Find somebody who would take her and keep her safe. Would you do that if I asked?"

"And we'd be like before?" He didn't say, *And you'll marry me*, but he hoped she'd know that's what he meant.

"We'd at least solve a problem. I have a friend who knows how to sell things on the Internet. Remember those people who tried to sell their kid on e-Bay?"

"They got caught."

"They were stupid. E-bay's not the option I had in mind. Listen, Ed isn't the only shady character we know. Maybe we can find a place for her."

He was reluctant. "Sara, don't get her killed."

He stayed up drinking cola after she left, but fell asleep in his lounge chair and awoke to early light and his cell phone ringtone.

"It's happened," said Hartley.

"What?" He thought she was talking about the attack on Rosebud.

"Sara Jones, that's your girl, right? The cat's over at her farm."

"Yeah, but Sara will be okay. Jonesy loves Sara."

"Judas Priest, boy, that cat is a top predator. Her definition of love is different from yours and mine. Big cats seem okay for years, then go off like a bomb and eviscerate somebody for no reason. For hunger. For a mate. Because a fly bit them on the nose."

"She loves Sara—"

"Yeah, she loves you, too. And maybe she thinks Sara is a rival in love."

That sounded crazy. But Kevin pulled his clothes back on and ran to his car.

He beat the police cruisers to the farm.

Jonesy was bashing the front door, roaring her earsplitting roar, not the roar of triumph she'd roared over Rosebud, not the roar of desire she'd yowled in heat. This was rage. And she was destroying the door.

As the first cruiser threw open its door and a cop sprang out with weapon drawn, the door imploded and Jonesy bounded inside.

Why had he thought Sara was safe? For some reason—oh God maybe it *was* sexual rivalry—Jonesy was after her.

Kevin bolted out of his car and up the porch stairs.

Inside, he smelled the fury of big, enraged cat.

"I'm up here!" Sara screamed.

He pounded up the stairs three at a time.

Sara's voice came from the upstairs bedroom. Outside that closed door, Jonesy reared on her back feet, head scraping the ceiling. She clawed at the door knob, chewed at the door panels.

One door panel split and fell inward. Jonesy threw herself with renewed rage, and the door splintered.

"Here girl! Bad girl!" Why hadn't he thought of bringing meat?

No. Meat wouldn't work.

Sara was screaming, punching at the jammed window.

He raced up and grabbed the cat's collar, but she turned and knocked him flat.

As he lay gasping from the blow, Jonesy lunged for Sara.

He crawled, dizzy, trying to rise despite the agony in his chest. He just reached the door when Jonesy rolled across the floor, sprang up, and sank her teeth into Sara's throat.

Sara's eyes went wide, green as Jonesy's eyes. Her head snapped back. The cat ripped out her flesh together with a piece of her tee shirt, then howled, head thrown back, whiskered black nose grazing the ceiling light fixture.

Then the cat leapt through the window, splintering the frame.

Kevin crawled over to Sara. Her head was nearly separated from her body, blood gushing everywhere, in her beautiful golden hair, on her torn shirt, the cracked linoleum floor. More blood than he had ever seen.

He buried his face in the hollow between her breasts and sobbed.

Then he rose and looked out the window. Jonesy was loping into the barn.

He felt his way down the stairs, shattered. Sara was so beautiful. And Jonesy, his charge, his responsibility, his pet, had killed her. Pet? Oh, no. Not a pet. No more than an astronaut would call the moon a pet. No more than a composer would call his greatest symphony a pet. No more than a mountain climber would call Everest a pet.

He stumbled out into the light. Five police cruisers ringed the house now, and a paramedic van. One of the paramedics had the rifle from Sara's truck.

"Cat still in there?" one cop yelled.

"Sara's upstairs. She's dead," Kevin said. He sank to his knees and sobbed.

Hartley appeared. "The cat ran into the barn. I saw it."

The paramedic raised the rifle, and another cop hauled open the barn door. He had a German shepherd with him on a short leash. Kevin pulled himself erect.

The dog strained forward, then turned to cower behind the cop. The cop broke into a run, at the same time trying to unholster his service revolver.

Jonesy exploded out of the barn. The cop with the dog fell down and Jonesy vaulted over them.

Kevin heard the sound of the rifle being cocked.

Kevin screamed, "No!" He launched himself at the rifleman.

The rifleman stumbled and the shot went wild.

A tawny streak—Jonesy—broke into the woods behind the barn and coursed out of sight.

Hartley screamed, "Why did you do that?"

"Killing the cat won't make Sara be alive again."

"You're in denial! The smilodon will kill again."

Kevin was silent. Hartley was right. He had no idea why he had pushed the rifleman. He felt his arms being jerked back, cuffs cut his wrists. But the sabertooth, the miracle from another world, was free.

"You were involved with Sara Jones," Hartley said. "I thought you loved her."

"I did. Not what matters."

"This monster kills the woman you love, and you protect it?"

How could he explain?

Jonesy was never found, though attacks on domestic animals and deer increased in the county for a few weeks. Maybe the sabertooth died, maybe she went north, where the woods were thicker and the game larger.

Kevin went to jail. He got most of a college degree in there, gratis the state. He wasn't street smart, that was obvious, but he had a talent for book learning.

His life had changed forever. He got out of jail, went to university, studied paleontology, but studiously avoided Franklin U and Hartley, though she begged him for his photos of the smilodon.

He never married.

But he had companioned a smilodon, brought back from the deeps of time. It had been like stepping on the moon. He had touched its white, saber-like teeth. And it made him immortal.

It was enough.

THE BURGLAR TAKES A CAT

Lawrence Block

Lawrence Block is a multiple winner of the Edgar Allan Poe, Shamus, and Maltese Falcon awards, is a Mystery Writers of America Grand Master, and has received Life Achievement awards from France and the UK. He's a devoted New Yorker and an ardent world traveler.

In "The Burglar Takes a Cat," an excerpt from Block's novel *The Burglar Who Traded Ted Williams,* the protagonist, Bernie Rhodenbarr, is a bookstore owner/burglar who features in a series of ten (so far) comic novels by Block. The author does not have a cat.

Look, it wasn't my idea.

And it happened very quickly. One day back in early June Carolyn brought pastrami sandwiches and celery tonic to the bookstore, and I showed her a couple of books, an Ellen Glasgow novel and the collected letters of Evelyn Waugh. She took a look at the spines and made a sound somewhere between a *tssst* and a cluck. "You know what did that," she said.

"I have a haunting suspicion."

"Mice, Bern."

"That's what I was afraid you were going to say."

"Rodents," she said. "Vermin. You can throw those books right in the garbage."

"Maybe I should keep them. Maybe they'll eat these and leave the others alone."

"Maybe you should leave a quarter under your pillow," she said, "and the Tooth Fairy'll come in the middle of the night and chew their heads off."

"That doesn't seem very realistic, Carolyn."

"No," she said. "It doesn't. Bern, you wait right here."

"Where are you going?"

"I won't be long," she said. "Don't eat my sandwich."

"I won't, but—"

"And don't leave it where the mice can get it, either."

"Mouse," I said. "There's no reason to assume there's more than one."

"Bern," she said, "take my word for it. There's no such thing as one mouse."

I might have figured out what she was up to, but I opened the Waugh volume while I knocked off the rest of my own sandwich, and one letter led to another. I was still at it when the door opened and there she was, back again. She was holding one of those little cardboard satchels with air holes, the kind shaped like a New England salt box house.

The sort of thing you carry cats in.

"Oh, no," I said.

"Bern, give me a minute, huh?"

"No."

"Bern, you've got mice. Your shop is infested with rodents. Do you know what that means?"

"It doesn't mean I'm going to be infested with cats."

"Not cats," she said. "There's no such thing as one mouse. There is such a thing as one cat. That's all I've got in here, Bern. One cat."

"That's good," I said. "You came in here with one cat, and you can leave with one cat. It makes it easy to keep track that way."

"You can't just live with the mice. They'll do thousands of dollars worth of damage. They won't sit back and settle down with one volume and read it from cover to cover, you know. No, it's a bite here and a bite there, and before you know it you're out of business."

"Don't you think you're overdoing it?"

"No way. Bern, remember the Great Library at Alexandria? One of the seven wonders of the ancient world, and then a single mouse got in there."

"I thought you said there was no such thing as a single mouse."

"Well, now there's no such thing as the Great Library at Alexandria, and all because the pharaoh's head librarian didn't have the good sense to keep a cat."

"There are other ways to get rid of mice," I said.

"Name one."

"Poison."

"Bad idea, Bern."

"What's so bad about it?"

"Forget the cruelty aspect of it."

"Okay," I said. "It's forgotten."

"Forget the horror of gobbling down something with Warfarin in it and having all your little blood vessels burst. Forget the hideous spectre of one of God's own little warmblooded creatures dying a slow, agonizing death from internal bleeding. Forget all that, Bern. If you possibly can."

"All forgotten. The memory tape's a blank."

"Instead, focus on the idea of dozens of mice dying in the walls around you, where you can't see them or get at them."

"Ah, well. Out of sight, out of mind. Isn't that what they say?"

"Nobody ever said it about dead mice. You'll have a store with hundreds of them decomposing in the walls."

"Hundreds?"

"God knows the actual number. The poisoned bait's designed to draw them from all over the area. You could have mice scurrying here from miles around, mice from SoHo to Kips Bay, all of them coming here to die."

I rolled my eyes.

"Maybe I'm exaggerating a tiny bit," she allowed. "But all you need is one dead mouse in the wall and you're gonna smell a rat, Bern."

"A mouse, you mean."

"You know what I mean. And maybe your customers won't exactly cross the street to avoid walking past the store—"

"Some of them do that already."

"—but they won't be too happy spending time in a shop with a bad odor to it. They might drop in for a minute, but they won't browse. No book lover wants to stand around smelling rotting mice."

"Traps," I suggested.

"Traps? You want to set mousetraps?"

"The world will beat a path to my door."

"What kind will you get, Bern? The kind with a powerful spring, that sooner or later you screw up while you're setting it and it takes off the tip of your finger? The kind that breaks the mouse's neck, and you open up the store and there's this dead mouse with its neck broken, and you've got to deal with that first thing in the morning?"

"Maybe one of those new glue traps. Like a Roach Motel, but for mice."

"'Mice check in, but they can't check out.'"

"That's the idea."

"Great idea. There's the poor little mousie with its feet caught, whining piteously for hours, maybe trying to gnaw off its own feet in a pathetic attempt to escape, like a fox in a leg-hold trap in one of those animal-rights commercials."

"Carolyn—"

"It could happen. Who are you to say it couldn't happen? Anyway, you come in and open the store and there's the mouse, still alive, and then what do you do? Stomp on it? Get a gun and shoot it? Fill the sink and drown it?"

"Suppose I just drop it in the garbage, trap and all."

"Now *that's* humane," she said. "Poor thing's half-suffocated in the dark for days, and then the garbage men toss the bag into the hopper and it gets ground up into mouseburger. That's terrific, Bern. While you're at it, why not drop the trap into the incinerator? Why not burn the poor creature alive?"

I remembered something. "You can release the mice from glue traps," I said. "You pour a little baby oil on their feet and it acts as a solvent for the glue. The mouse just runs off, none the worse for wear."

"None the worse for wear?"

"Well—"

"Bern," she said. "Don't you realize what you'd be doing? You'd be releasing a psychotic mouse. Either it would find its way back into the store or it would get into one of the neighboring buildings, and who's to say what it would do? Even if you let it go miles from here, even if you took it clear out to Flushing, you'd be unleashing a deranged rodent upon the unsuspecting public. Bern, forget traps. Forget poison. You don't need any of that." She tapped the side of the cat carrier. "You've got a friend," she said.

"You're not talking friends. You're talking cats."

"What have you got against cats?"

"I haven't got anything against cats. I haven't got anything against elk, either, but that doesn't mean I'm going to keep one in the store so I'll have a place to hang my hat."

"I thought you liked cats."

"They're okay."

"You're always sweet to Archie and Ubi. I figured you were fond of them."

"I *am* fond of them," I said. "I think they're fine in their place, and their place happens to be your apartment. Carolyn, believe me, I don't want a pet. I'm not the type. If I can't even keep a steady girlfriend, how can I keep a pet?"

"Pets are easier," she said with feeling. "Believe me. Anyway, this cat's not a pet."

"Then what is it?"

"An employee," she said. "A working cat. A companion animal by day, a solitary night watchman when you're gone. A loyal, faithful, hard-working servant."

"Miaow," the cat said.

We both glanced at the cat carrier, and Carolyn bent down to unfasten its clasps. "He's cooped up in there," she said.

"Don't let him out."

"Oh, come on," she said, doing just that. "We're not talking Pandora's Box here, Bern. I'm just letting him get some air."

"That's what the air holes are for."

"He needs to stretch his legs," she said, and the cat emerged and did just that, extending his front legs and stretching, then doing the same for his rear legs. You know how cats do, like they're warming up for a dance class.

"He," I said. "It's a male? Well, at least it won't be having kittens all the time."

"Absolutely not," she said. "He's guaranteed not to have kittens."

"But won't he run around peeing on things? Like books, for instance. Don't male cats make a habit of that sort of thing?"

"He's post-op, Bern."

"Poor guy."

"He doesn't know what he's missing. But he won't have kittens, and he won't father them, either, or go nuts yowling whenever there's a female cat in heat somewhere between Thirty-fourth Street and the Battery. No, he'll just do his job, guarding the store and keeping the mice down."

"And using the books for a scratching post. What's the point of getting rid of mice if the books all wind up with claw marks?"

"No claws, Bern."

"Oh."

"He doesn't really need them, since there aren't a lot of enemies to fend off in here. Or a whole lot of trees to climb."

"I guess." I looked at him. There was something strange about him, but it took me a second or two to figure it out. "Carolyn," I said, "what happened to his tail?"

"He's a Manx."

"So he was born tailless. But don't Manx cats have a sort of hopping gait, almost like a rabbit? This guy just walks around like your ordinary garden-variety cat. He doesn't look much like any Manx I ever saw."

"Well, maybe he's only part Manx."

"Which part? The tail?"

"Well—"

"What do you figure happened? Did he get it caught in a door, or did the vet get carried away? I'll tell you, Carolyn, he's been neutered and declawed and his tail's no more than a memory. When you come right down to it, there's not a whole lot of the original cat left, is there? What we've got here is the stripped-down economy model. Is there anything else missing that I don't know about?"

"No."

"Did they leave the part that knows how to use a litter box? That's going to be tons of fun, changing the litter every day. Does he at least know how to use a box?"

"Even better, Bern. He uses the toilet."

"Like Archie and Ubi?" Carolyn had trained her own cats, first by keeping their litter pan on top of the toilet seat, then by cutting a hole in it, gradually enlarging the hole and finally getting rid of the pan altogether. "Well, that's something," I said. "I don't suppose he's figured out how to flush it."

"No. And don't leave the seat up."

I sighed heavily. The animal was stalking around my store, poking his head into corners. Surgery or no surgery, I kept waiting for him to cock a leg at a shelf full of first editions. I admit it, I didn't trust the little bastard.

"I don't know about this," I said. "There must be a way to mouseproof a store like this. Maybe I should talk it over with an exterminator."

"Are you kidding? You want some weirdo skulking around the aisles, spraying toxic chemicals all over the place? Bern, you don't have to call an exterminator. You've got a live-in exterminator, your own personal organic rodent control division. He's had all his shots, he's free of fleas and ticks, and if he ever needs grooming you've got a friend in the business. What more could you ask for?"

I felt myself weakening, and I hated that. "He seems to like it here," I admitted. "He acts as though he's right at home."

"And why not? What could be more natural than a cat in a bookstore?"

"He's not bad-looking," I said. "Once you get used to the absence of a tail. And that shouldn't be too hard, given that I was already perfectly accustomed to the absence of an entire cat. What color would you say he was?"

"Gray tabby."

"It's a nice functional look," I decided. "Nothing flashy about it, but it goes with everything, doesn't it? Has he got a name?"

"Bern, you can always change it."

"Oh, I bet it's a pip."

"Well, it's not horrendous, at least I don't think it is, but he's like most cats I've known. He doesn't respond to his name. You know how Archie and Ubi are. Calling them by name is a waste of time. If I want them to come, I just run the electric can opener."

"What's his name, Carolyn."

"Raffles," she said. "But you can change it to anything you want. Feel free."

"Raffles," I said.

"If you hate it—"

"Hate it?" I stared at her. "Are you kidding? It's got to be the perfect name for him."

"How do you figure that, Bern?"

"Don't you know who Raffles was? In the books by E. W. Hornung back around the turn of the century, and in the stories Barry Perowne's been doing recently? Raffles the amateur cracksman? World-class cricket player and gentleman burglar? I can't believe you never heard of the celebrated A. J. Raffles."

Her mouth fell open. "I never made the connection," she said. "All I could think of was like raffling off a car to raise funds for a church. But now that you mention it—"

"Raffles," I said. "The quintessential burglar of fiction. And here he is, a cat in a bookstore, and the bookstore's owned by a former burglar. I'll tell you, if I were looking for a name for the cat I couldn't possibly do better than the one he came with."

Her eyes met mine, "Bernie," she said solemnly, "it was meant to be."

"Miaow," said Raffles.

At noon the following day it was my turn to pick up lunch. I stopped at the falafel stand on the way to the Poodle Factory. Carolyn asked how Raffles was doing.

"He's doing fine," I said. "He drinks from his water bowl and eats out of his new blue cat dish, and I'll be damned if he doesn't use the toilet just the way you said he did. Of course I have to remember to leave the door ajar, but when I forget he reminds me by standing in front of it and yowling."

"It sounds as though it's working out."

"Oh, it's working out marvelously," I said. "Tell me something. What was his name before it was Raffles?"

"I don't follow you, Bern."

"'I don't follow you, Bern.' That was the crowning touch, wasn't it? You waited until you had me pretty well softened up, and then you tossed in the name as a sort of *coup de foie gras*. 'His name's Raffles, but you can always change it.' Where did the cat come from?"

"Didn't I tell you? A customer of mine, he's a fashion photographer, he has a really gorgeous Irish water spaniel, and he told me about a friend of his who developed asthma and was heartbroken because his allergist insisted he had to get rid of his cat."

"And then what happened?"

"Then you developed a mouse problem, so I went and picked up the cat, and—"

"No."

"No?"

I shook my head. "You're leaving something out. All I had to do was mention the word mouse and you were out of here like a cat out of hell. You didn't even have to think about it. And it couldn't have taken you more than twenty minutes to go and get the cat and stick it in a carrying case and come back with it. How did you spend those twenty minutes? Let's see—first you went back to the Poodle Factory to look up the number of your customer the fashion photographer, and then you called him and asked for the name and number of his friend with the allergies. Then I guess you called the friend and introduced yourself and arranged to meet him at his apartment and take a look at the animal, and then—"

"Stop it."

"Well?"

"The cat was at my apartment."

"What was he doing there?"

"He was living there, Bern."

I frowned. "I've met your cats," I said. "I've known them for years. I'd recognize them, with or without tails. Archie's a sable Burmese and Ubi's a Russian Blue. Neither one of them could pass for a gray tabby, except maybe in a dark alley."

"He was living *with* Archie and Ubi," she said.

"Since when?"

"Oh, just for a little while."

I thought for a moment. "Not for just a little while," I said, "because he was there long enough to learn the toilet trick. You don't learn something like that overnight. Look how long it takes with human beings. That's how he learned, right? He picked it up from your cats, didn't he?"

"I suppose so."

"And he didn't pick it up overnight, either. Did he?"

"I feel like a suspect," she said. "I feel as though I'm being grilled."

"Grilled? You ought to be char-broiled. You set me up and euchred me, for heaven's sake. How long has Raffles been living with you?"

"Two and a half months."

"Two and a half *months*!"

"Well, maybe it's more like three."

"Three months! That's unbelievable. How many times have I been over to your place in the past three months? It's got to be eight or ten at the very least. Are you telling me I looked at the cat and didn't even notice him?"

"When you came over," she said, "I used to put him in the other room."

"What other room? You live in one room."

"I put him in the closet."

"In the closet?"

"Uh-huh. So you wouldn't see him."

"But why?"

"The same reason I never mentioned him."

"Why's that? I don't get it. Were you ashamed of him? What's wrong with him, anyway?"

"There's nothing wrong with him."

"Because if there's something shameful about the animal, I don't know that I want him hanging around my store."

"There's nothing shameful about him," she said. "He's a perfectly fine cat. He's trustworthy, he's loyal, he's helpful and friendly—"

"Courteous, kind," I said. "Obedient, cheerful, thrifty. He's a regular Boy Scout, isn't he? So why the hell were you keeping him a secret from me?"

"It wasn't just you, Bern. Honest. I was keeping him a secret from everybody."

"But *why*, Carolyn?"

"I don't even want to say it."

"Come on, for God's sake."

She took a breath. "Because," she said darkly, "he was the Third Cat."

"You lost me."

"Oh, God. This is impossible to explain. Bernie, there's something you have to understand. Cats can be very dangerous for a woman."

"What are you talking about?"

"You start with one," she said, "and that's fine, no problem, nothing wrong with that. And then you get a second one and that's even better, as a matter of fact, because they keep each other company. It's a curious thing, but it's actually easier to have two cats than one."

"I'll take your word for it."

"Then you get a third, and that's all right, it's still manageable, but before you know it you take in a fourth, and then you've gone and done it."

"Done what?"

"You've crossed the line."

"What line, and how have you crossed it?"

"You've become a Woman With Cats." I nodded. Light was beginning to dawn. "You know the kind of woman I mean," she went on. "They're all over the place. They don't have any friends, and they hardly ever set foot outdoors, and when they die people discover thirty or forty cats in the house. Or they're cooped up in an apartment with thirty or forty cats and the neighbors take them to court to evict them because of the filth and the smell. Or they seem perfectly normal, and then there's a fire or a break-in or something, and the world finds them out for what they are. They're Women With Cats, Bernie, and that's not what I want to be."

"No," I said, "and I can see why. But—"

"It doesn't seem to be a problem for men," she said. "There are lots of men with two cats, and probably plenty with three or four, but when did you ever hear anything about a Man With Cats? When it comes to cats, men don't seem to have trouble knowing when to stop." She frowned. "Funny, isn't it? In every other area of their lives—"

"Let's stick to cats," I suggested. "How did you happen to wind up with Raffles hanging out in your closet? And what was his name before it was Raffles?"

She shook her head. "Forget it, Bern. It was a real pussy name, if you ask me. Not right for the cat at all. As far as how I got him, well, it happened pretty much the way I said, except there were a few things I left out. George Brill is a customer of mine. I groom his Irish water spaniel."

"And his friend is allergic to cats."

"No, George is the one who's allergic. And when Felipe moved in with George, the cat had to go. The dog and cat got along fine, but George was wheezing and red-eyed all the time, so Felipe had to give up either George or the cat."

"And that was it for Raffles."

"Well, Felipe wasn't all that attached to the cat. It wasn't his cat in the first place. It was Patrick's."

"Where did Patrick come from?"

"Ireland, and he couldn't get a green card and he didn't like it here that much anyway, so when he went back home he left the cat with Felipe, because he couldn't take him through Immigration. Felipe was willing to give the cat a home, but when he and George got together, well, the cat had to go."

"And how come you were elected to take him?"

"George tricked me into it."

"What did he do, tell you the Poodle Factory was infested with mice?"

"No, he used some pretty outrageous emotional blackmail on me. Anyway, it worked. The next thing I knew I had a Third Cat."

"How did Archie and Ubi feel about it?"

"They didn't actually say anything, but their body language translated into something along the lines of, 'There goes the neighborhood.' I don't think it broke their hearts yesterday when I packed him up and took him out of there."

"But in the meantime he spent three months in your apartment and you never said a word."

"I was planning on telling you, Bern."

"When?"

"Sooner or later. But I was afraid."

"Of what I would think?"

"Not only that. Afraid of what the Third Cat signified." She heaved a sigh.

"All those Women With Cats," she said. "They didn't plan on it, Bern. They got a first cat, they got a second cat, they got a third cat, and all of a sudden they were gone."

"You don't think they might have been the least bit odd to begin with?"

"No," she said. "No, I don't. Oh, once in a while, maybe, you get a slightly wacko lady, and next thing you know she's up to her armpits in cats. But most of the Cat Ladies start out normal. By the time you get to the end of the story they're nuts, all right, but having thirty or forty cats'll do that to you. It sneaks up on you, and before you know it you're over the edge."

"And the Third Cat's the charm, huh?"

"No question. Bern, there are primitive cultures that don't really have numbers, not in the sense that we do. They have a word that means 'one,' and other words for 'two' and 'three,' and after that there's a word that just means 'more than three.' And that's how it is in our culture with cats. You can have one cat, you can have two cats, you can even have three cats, but after that you've got 'more than three.'"

"And you're a Woman With Cats."

"You got it."

"I've got it, all right. I've got your third cat. Is that the real reason you never mentioned it? Because you were planning all along to palm the little bugger off on me?"

"No," she said quickly. "Swear to God, Bern. A couple of times over the years the subject of a dog or cat has come up, and you've always said you didn't want a pet. Did I ever once press you?"

"No."

"I took you at your word. It sometimes crossed my mind that you might have a better time in life if you had an animal to love, but I managed to keep it to myself. It never even occurred to me that you could use a working cat. And then when I found out about your rodent problem—"

"You knew just how to solve it."

"Well, sure. And it's a great solution, isn't it? Admit it, Bern. Didn't it do your heart good this morning to have Raffles there to greet you?"

"It was all right," I admitted. "At least he was still alive. I had visions of him lying there dead with his paws in the air, and the mice forming a great circle around his body."

"See? You're concerned about him, Bern. Before you know it you're going to fall in love with the little guy."

"Don't hold your breath. Carolyn? What was his name before it was Raffles."

"Oh, forget it. It was a stupid name."

"Tell me."

"Do I have to?" She sighed. "Well, it was Andro."

"Andrew? What's so stupid about that? Andrew Jackson, Andrew Johnson, Andrew Carnegie—they all did okay with it."

"Not Andrew, Bern. An*dro*."

"Andrew Mellon, Andrew Gardner… *not* Andrew? Andro?"

"Right."

"What's that, Greek for Andrew?"

She shook her head. "It's short for Androgenous."

"Oh."

"The idea being that his surgery had left the cat somewhat uncertain from a sexual standpoint."

"Oh."

"Which I gather was also the case for Patrick, although I don't believe surgery had anything to do with it."

"Oh."

"I never called him 'Andro' myself," she said. "Actually, I didn't call him anything. I didn't want to give him a new name because that would mean I was leaning toward keeping him, and—"

"I understand."

"And then on the way over to the bookstore it just came to me in a flash. Raffles."

"As in raffling off a car to raise money for a church, I think you said."

"Don't hate me, Bern."

"I'll try not to."

"It's been no picnic, living a lie for the past three months. Believe me."

"I guess it'll be easier for everybody now that Raffles is out of the closet."

"I know it will. Bern, I didn't want to trick you into taking the cat."

"Of course you did."

"No, I didn't. I just wanted to make it as easy as possible for you and the cat to start off on the right foot. I knew you'd be crazy about him once you got to know him, and I thought anything I could do to get you over the first hurdle, any minor deception I might have to practice—"

"Like lying your head off."

"It was in a good cause. I had only your best interests at heart, Bern. Yours and the cat's."

"And your own."

"Well, yeah," she said, and flashed a winning smile. "But it worked out, didn't it? Bern, you've got to admit it worked out."

"We'll see," I said.

THE WHITE CAT
Joyce Carol Oates

Joyce Carol Oates is one of the most prolific and respected writers in the United States today. Oates has written fiction in almost every genre and medium. Her keen interest in the Gothic and psychological horror has spurred her to write dark suspense novels under the name Rosamond Smith, to write enough stories in the genre to have published five collections of dark fiction, the most recent being *The Museum of Dr. Moses: Tales of Mystery and Suspense* and *Wild Nights!: Stories about the Last Days of Poe, Dickinson, Twain, James, and Hemingway*, and to edit *American Gothic Tales*. Oates's short novel *Zombie* won the Bram Stoker Award, and she has been honored with the Stoker Award for Lifetime Achievement by the Horror Writers Association.

Oates's most recent novels are *Blood Mask, The Gravedigger's Daughter* and *My Sister, My Love: The Intimate Story of Skyler Rampike*. She teaches creative writing at Princeton and with her late husband, Raymond J. Smith, ran the small press and literary magazine *The Ontario Review* for many years.

Oates is a cat lover and has written several dark stories about cats. This one could be seen as the inverse of Edgar Allan Poe's "The Black Cat."

There was a gentleman of independent means who, at about the age of fifty-six, conceived of a passionate hatred for his much-younger wife's white Persian cat.

His hatred for the cat was all the more ironic, and puzzling, in that he himself had given the cat to his wife as a kitten, years ago, when they were first married. And he himself had named her Miranda—after his favorite Shakespearean heroine.

It was ironic, too, in that he was hardly a man given to irrational sweeps of emotion. Except for his wife (whom he'd married late—his first marriage, her second) he did not love anyone very much, and would have thought it beneath his dignity to hate anyone. For whom should he take that seriously? Being a gentleman of independent means allowed him that independence of spirit unknown to the majority of men.

Julius Muir was of slender build, with deep-set, somber eyes of no distinctive color; thinning, graying, baby-fine hair; and a narrow, lined face to which the adjective *lapidary* had once been applied, with no vulgar invention of mere flattery. Being of old American stock he was susceptible to none of the fashionable tugs and sways of "identity": He knew who he was, who his ancestors were, and thought the subject of no great interest. His studies both in America and abroad had been undertaken with a dilettante's rather than a scholar's pleasure, but he would not have wished to make too much of them. Life, after all, is a man's primary study.

Fluent in several languages, Mr. Muir had a habit of phrasing his words with inordinate care, as if he were translating them into a common vernacular. He carried himself with an air of discreet self-consciousness that had nothing in it of vanity, or pride, yet did not bespeak a pointless humility. He was a collector (primarily of rare books and coins), but he was certainly not an obsessive collector; he looked upon the fanaticism of certain of his fellows with a bemused disdain. So his quickly blossoming hatred for his wife's beautiful white cat surprised him, and for a time amused him. Or did it frighten him? Certainly he didn't know what to make of it!

The animosity began as an innocent sort of domestic irritation, a half-conscious sense that being so respected in public—so recognized as the person of quality and importance he assuredly was—he should warrant that sort of treatment at home. Not that he was naively ignorant of the fact that cats have a way of making their preferences known that lacks the subtlety and tact devised by human beings. But as the cat grew older and more spoiled and ever more choosy it became evident that she did not, for affection, choose *him.* Alissa was her favorite, of course; then one or another of the help; but it was not uncommon for a stranger, visiting the Muirs for the first time, to win or to appear to win Miranda's capricious heart. "Miranda! Come here!" Mr. Muir might call—gently enough, yet forcibly, treating the animal in fact with a silly sort of deference—but at such times Miranda was likely to regard him with indifferent, unblinking eyes and make no move in his direction. What a fool, she seemed to be saying, to court someone who cares so little for you!

If he tried to lift her in his arms—if he tried, with a show of playfulness, to subdue her—in true cat fashion she struggled to get down with as much violence as if a stranger had seized her. Once as she squirmed out of his grasp, she accidentally raked the back of his hand and drew blood that left a faint stain on the sleeve of his dinner jacket. "Julius, dear, are you hurt?" Alissa asked. "Not at all," Mr. Muir said, dabbing at the scratches with a handkerchief. "I think Miranda is excited because of the company," Alissa said. "You know how sensitive she is." "Indeed I do," Mr. Muir said mildly, winking at their guests. But a pulse beat hard in his head and he was thinking he would like to strangle the cat with his bare hands—were he the kind of man who was capable of such an act.

More annoying still was the routine nature of the cat's aversion to him. When he and Alissa sat together in the evening, reading, each at an end of their sofa, Miranda would frequently leap unbidden into Alissa's lap—but shrink fastidiously from Mr. Muir's very touch. He professed to be hurt. He professed to be amused. "I'm afraid Miranda doesn't like me any longer," he said sadly. (Though in truth he could no longer remember if there'd been a time the creature *had* liked him. When she'd been a kitten, perhaps, and utterly indiscriminate in her affections?) Alissa laughed and said apologetically, "Of course she likes you, Julius," as the car purred loudly and sensuously in her lap. "But—you know how cats are."

"Indeed, I am learning," Mr. Muir said with a stiff little smile.

And he felt he *was* learning—something to which he could give no name.

What first gave him the idea—the fancy, really—of killing Miranda, he could not have afterward said. One day, watching her rubbing about the ankles of a director-friend of his wife's, observing how wantonly she presented herself to an admiring little circle of guests (even people with a general aversion to cats could not resist exclaiming over Miranda—petting her, scratching her behind the ears, cooing over her like idiots), Mr. Muir found himself thinking that, as he had brought the cat into his household of his own volition and had paid a fair amount of money for her, she was his to dispose of as he wished. It was true that the full-blooded Persian was one of the prize possessions of the household—a household in which possessions were not acquired casually or cheaply—and it was true that Alissa adored her. But ultimately she belonged to Mr. Muir. And he alone had the power of life or death over her, did he not?

"What a beautiful animal! Is it a male or a female!"

Mr. Muir was being addressed by one of his guests (in truth, one of Alissa's guests; since returning to her theatrical career she had a new, wide, rather promiscuous circle of acquaintances) and for a moment he could not think how to answer. The question lodged deep in him as if it were a riddle: *Is it a male* or *a female?*

"Female, of course," Mr. Muir said pleasantly. "Its name after all is Miranda."

He wondered: Should he wait until Alissa began rehearsals for her new play—or should he act quickly, before his resolution faded? Alissa, a minor but well-regarded actress, was to be an understudy for the female lead in a Broadway play opening in September.) And how should he do it? He could not strangle the cat—could not bring himself to act with such direct and unmitigated brutality—nor was it likely that he could run over her, as if accidentally, with the car. (Though *that* would have been fortuitous, indeed.) One midsummer evening when sly, silky Miranda insinuated herself onto the lap of Alissa's new friend Alban (actor, writer, director; his talents were evidently lavish) the conversation turned to notorious murder cases —to poisons—and Mr. Muir thought simply, *Of course. Poison.*

Next morning he poked about in the gardener's shed and found the remains of a ten-pound sack of grainy white "rodent" poison. The previous autumn they'd had a serious problem with mice, and their gardener had set out poison traps in the attic and basement of the house. (With excellent results, Mr. Muir surmised. At any rate, the mice had certainly disappeared.) What was ingenious about the poison was that it induced extreme thirst—so that after having devoured the bait the poisoned creature was driven to seek water, leaving the house and dying outside. Whether the poison was "merciful" or not, Mr. Muir did not know.

He was able to take advantage of the servants' Sunday night off—for as it turned out, though rehearsals for her play had not yet begun, Alissa was spending several days in the city. So Mr. Muir himself fed Miranda in a corner of the kitchen where she customarily ate—having mashed a generous teaspoon of the poison in with her usual food. (How spoiled the creature was! From the very first, when she was a seven-weeks' kitten, Miranda had been fed a special high-protein, high-vitamin cat food, supplemented by raw chopped liver, chicken giblets, and God knows what all else. Though as he ruefully had to admit, Mr. Muir had had a hand in spoiling her, too.)

Miranda ate the food with her usual finicky greed, not at all conscious of, or grateful for, her master's presence. He might have been one of the servants; he might have been no one at all. If she sensed something out of the ordinary—the fact that her water dish was taken away and not returned, for instance—like a true aristocrat she gave no sign. Had there ever been any creature of his acquaintance, human or otherwise, so supremely complacent as this white Persian cat

Mr. Muir watched Miranda methodically poison herself with an air not of elation as he'd anticipated, nor even with a sense of satisfaction in a wrong being righted, in justice being (however ambiguously) exacted—but with an air of profound regret. That the spoiled creature deserved to die he did not doubt; for after all, what incalculable cruelties, over a lifetime, must a cat inflict on birds, mice, and rabbits! But it struck him as a melancholy thing, that *he*, Julius Muir—who had paid so much for her, and who in fact had shared in the pride of her—should find himself out of necessity in the role of executioner. But it was something that had to be done, and though he had perhaps forgotten why it had to be done, he knew that he and he alone was destined to do it.

The other evening a number of guests had come to dinner, and as they were seated on the terrace Miranda leapt whitely up out of nowhere to make her way along the garden wall—plumelike tail erect, silky ruff floating about her high-held head, golden eyes gleaming—quite as if on cue, as Alissa said. "This is Miranda, come to say hello to you! *Isn't* she beautiful!" Alissa happily exclaimed. (For she seemed never to tire of remarking upon her cat's beauty—an innocent sort of narcissism, Mr. Muir supposed.) The usual praise, or flattery, was aired; the cat preened herself—fully conscious of being the center of attention—then leapt away with a violent sort of grace and disappeared down the steep stone steps to the river embankment. Mr. Muir thought then that he understood why Miranda was so uncannily *interesting* as a phenomenon: She represented a beauty that was both purposeless and necessary; a beauty that was (considering her pedigree) completely an artifice, and yet (considering she *was a* thing of flesh and blood) completely natural: Nature.

Though was Nature always and invariably—*natural?*

Now, as the white cat finished her meal (leaving a good quarter of it in the dish, as usual), Mr. Muir said aloud, in a tone in which infinite regret and satisfaction were commingled, "But beauty won't save you."

The car paused to look up at him with her flat, unblinking gaze. He felt an instant's terror: Did she know? Did she know—already? It seemed to him that she had never looked more splendid: fur so purely, silkily white; ruff full as if recently brushed; the petulant pug face; wide, stiff whiskers; finely shaped ears so intelligently erect. And, of course, the eyes…

He'd always been fascinated by Miranda's eyes, which were a tawny golden hue, for they had the mysterious capacity to flare up, as if at will. Seen at night, of course—by way of the moon's reflection, or the headlights of the Muirs' own homebound car—they were lustrous as small beams of light. "Is that Miranda, do you think?" Alissa would ask, seeing the twin flashes of light in the tall grass bordering the road. "Possibly," Mr. Muir would say. "Ah, she's waiting for us! Isn't that sweet! She's waiting for us to come home!" Alissa would exclaim with childlike excitement. Mr. Muir—who doubted that the cat had even been aware of their absence, let alone eagerly awaited their return—said nothing.

Another thing about the cat's eyes that had always seemed to Mr. Muir somehow perverse was the fact that, while the human eyeball is uniformly white and the iris colored, a cat eyeball is colored and the iris purely black. Green, yellow, gray, even blue—the entire eyeball! And the iris so magically responsive to gradations of light or excitation, contracting to razor-thin slits, dilating blackly to fill almost the entire eye… As she stared up at him now her eyes were so dilated their color was nearly eclipsed.

"No, beauty can't save you. It isn't enough." Mr. Muir said quietly. With trembling fingers he opened the screen door to let the cat our into the night. As she passed him—perverse creature, indeed!—she rubbed lightly against his leg as she had not done for many months. Or had it been years?

Alissa was twenty years Mr. Muir's junior but looked even younger: a petite woman with very large, very pretty brown eyes; shoulder-length blond hair; the upbeat if sometimes rather frenetic manner of a well-practiced ingenue. She was a minor actress with a minor ambition—as she freely acknowledged—for alter all, serious professional acting is brutally hard work, even if one somehow manages to survive the competition.

"And then, of course, Julius takes such good care of me," she would say, linking her arm through his or resting her head for a moment against his shoulder. "I have everything I want, really, right here…" By which she meant the country place Mr. Muir had bought for her when they were married. (Of course they also kept an apartment in Manhattan, two hours to the south. But Mr. Muir had grown to dislike the city—it abraded his nerves like a cat's claws raking against a screen—and rarely made the journey in any longer.) Under her maiden name, Howth, Alissa had been employed intermittently for eight years before marrying Mr. Muir; her first marriage—contracted at the age of nineteen to a well-known (and notorious) Hollywood actor, since deceased—had been a disaster of which she cared not to speak in any detail. (Nor did Mr. Muir care to question her about those years. It was as if, for him, they had not existed.)

At the time of their meeting Alissa was in temporary retreat, as she called it, from her career. She'd had a small success on Broadway but the success had not taken hold. And was it worth it, really, to keep going, to keep trying? Season after season, the grinding round of auditions, the competition with new faces, "promising" new talents… Her first marriage had ended badly and she'd had a number of love affairs of varying degrees of worth (precisely how many Mr. Muir was never to learn), and now perhaps it was time to ease into private life. And there was Julius Muir: not young, not particularly charming, but well-to-do, and well-bred, and besotted with love for her, and—*there.*

Of course Mr. Muir was dazzled by her; and he had the time and the re-sources to court her more assiduously than any man had ever courted her. He seemed to see in her qualities no one else saw; his imagination, for so reticent and subdued a man, was rich, lively to the point of fever, immensely flattering. And he did not mind, he extravagantly insisted, that he loved her more than she loved him—even as Alissa protested she *did* love him—would she consent to marry him otherwise?

For a few years they spoke vaguely of "starting a family," but nothing came of it. Alissa was too busy, or wasn't in ideal health; or they were traveling; or Mr. Muir worried about the unknown effect a child would have upon their marriage. (Alissa would have less time for him, surely?) As time passed he vexed himself with the thought that he'd have no heir when he died—that is, no child of his own—but there was nothing to be done.

They had a rich social life; they were wonderfully *busy* people. And they had, after all, their gorgeous white Persian cat. "Miranda would be traumatized if there was a baby in the household," Alissa said. "We really couldn't do that to her."

"Indeed we couldn't," Mr. Muir agreed.

And then, abruptly, Alissa decided to return to acting. To her "career" as she gravely called it—as if it were a phenomenon apart from her, a force not to be resisted. And Mr. Muir was happy for her—very happy for her. He took pride in his wife's professionalism, and he wasn't at all jealous of her ever-widening circle of friends, acquaintances, associates. He wasn't jealous of her fellow ac-tors and actresses—Rikka, Mario, Robin, Sibyl, Emile, each in turn—and now Alban of the damp, dark, shiny eyes and quick sweet smile; nor was he jealous of the time she spent away from home; nor, if home, of the time she spent sequestered away in the room they called her studio, deeply absorbed in her work. In her maturity Alissa Howth had acquired a robust sort of good-heartedness that gave her more stage presence even as it relegated her to certain sorts of roles—the roles inevitable, in any case, for older actresses, regardless of their physical beauty. And she'd become a far better, far more subtle actress—as everyone said.

Indeed, Mr. Muir *was* proud of her, and happy for her. And if he felt, now and then, a faint resentment—or, if not quite resentment, a tinge of regret at the way their life had diverged into lives—he was too much a gentleman to show it.

"Where is Miranda? Have you seen Miranda today?"

It was noon, it was four o'clock, it was nearly dusk, and Miranda had not returned. For much of the day Alissa had been preoccupied with telephone calls—the phone seemed always to be ringing—and only gradually had she become aware of the cat's prolonged absence. She went outside to call her; she sent the servants out to look for her. And Mr. Muir, of course, gave his assistance, wandering about the grounds and for some distance into the woods, his hands cupped to his mouth and his voice high-pitched and tremulous: *"Kitty-kitty-kitty-kitty-kitty! Kitty-kitty-kitty—"* How pathetic, how foolish—how futile! Yet it had to he performed since it was what, in innocent circumstances, would be performed. Julius Muir, that most solicitous of husbands, tramping through the underbrush looking for his wife's Persian cat....

Poor Alissa! he thought. She'll be heartbroken for days—or would it be weeks?

And he, too, would miss Miranda—as a household presence at the very least. They would have had her, after all, for ten years this autumn.

Dinner that night was subdued, rather leaden. Not simply because Miranda was missing (and Alissa did seem inordinately and genuinely worried), but because Mr. Muir and his wife were dining alone; the table, set for two, seemed almost aesthetically wrong. And how unnatural, the quiet... Mr. Muir tried to make conversation but his voice soon trailed off into a guilty silence. Midmeal Alissa rose to accept a telephone call (from Manhattan, of course—her agent, or her director, or Alban, or a female friend—an urgent call, otherwise Mrs. Muir did not accept calls at this intimate hour) and Mr. Muir—crestfallen, hurt—finished his solitary meal in a kind of trance, tasting nothing. He recalled the night before—the pungent-smelling cat food, the grainy white poison, the way the shrewd animal had looked up at him, and the way she'd brushed against his leg in a belated gesture of... was it affection? Reproach? Mockery? He felt a renewed stab of guilt, and an even more powerful stab of visceral satisfaction. Then, glancing up, he chanced to see something white making its careful way along the top of the garden wall....

Of course it was Miranda come home.

He stared, appalled. He stared, speechless—waiting for the apparition to vanish.

Slowly, in a daze, he rose to his feet. In a voice meant to be jubilant he called out the news to Alissa in the adjoining room: "Miranda's come home!"

He called out: "Alissa! Darling! Miranda's come home!"

And there Miranda was, indeed; indeed it was Miranda, peering into the dining room from the terrace, her eyes glowing tawny gold. Mr. Muir was trembling, but his brain worked swiftly to absorb the fact, and to construe a logic to accommodate it. She'd vomited up the poison, no doubt. Ah, no doubt! Or, after a cold, damp winter in the gardener's shed, the poison had lost its efficacy.

He had yet to bestir himself, to hurry to unlatch the sliding door and let the white cat in, but his voice fairly quavered with excitement: "Alissa! Good news! Miranda's come home!"

Alissa's joy was so extreme and his own initial relief so genuine that Mr. Muir—stroking Miranda's plume of a tail as Alissa hugged the cat ecstatically in her arms—thought he'd acted cruelly, selfishly—certainly he'd acted out of character—and decided that Miranda, having escaped death at her master's hands, should be granted life. He would *not* try another time.

Before his marriage at the age of forty-six Julius Muir, like most never-married men and women of a certain temperament—introverted, self-conscious; observers of life rather than participants—had believed that the marital state was unconditionally *marital;* he'd thought that husband and wife were one flesh in more than merely the metaphorical sense of that term. Yet it happened that his own marriage was a marriage of a decidedly diminished sort. Marital relations had all but ceased, and there seemed little likelihood of their being resumed. He would shortly be fifty-seven years old, after all. (Though sometimes he wondered: Was that truly *old?*)

During the first two or three years of their marriage (when Alissa's theatrical career was, as she called it, in eclipse), they had shared a double bed like any married couple—or so Mr. Muir assumed. (For his own marriage had not enlightened him to what "marriage" in a generic sense meant.) With the passage of time, however, Alissa began to complain gently of being unable to sleep because of Mr. Muir's nocturnal "agitation"—twitching, kicking, thrashing about, exclaiming aloud, sometimes even shouting in terror. Wakened by her he would scarcely know, for a moment or two, where he was; he would then apologize profusely and shamefully, and creep away into another bedroom to sleep, if he could, for the rest of the night. Though unhappy with the situation, Mr. Muir was fully sympathetic with Alissa; he even had reason to believe that the poor woman (whose nerves were unusually sensitive) had suffered many a sleepless night on his account without telling him. It was like her to be so considerate; so loath to hurt another's feelings.

As a consequence they developed a cozy routine in which Mr. Muir spent a half-hour or so with Alissa when they first retired for the night; then, taking care not to disturb her, he would tiptoe quietly away into another room, where he might sleep undisturbed. (If, indeed, his occasional nightmares allowed him undisturbed sleep. He rather thought the worst ones, however, were the ones that failed to wake him.)

Yet a further consequence had developed in recent years: Alissa had acquired the habit of staying awake late—reading in bed, or watching television, or even, from time to time, chatting on the telephone—so it was most practical for Mr. Muir simply to kiss her good-night without getting in bed beside her, and then to go off to his own bedroom. Sometimes in his sleep he imagined Alissa was calling him back—awakened, he would hurry out into the darkened corridor to stand by her door for a minute or two, eager and hopeful. At such times he dared not raise his voice above a whisper: "Alissa? Alissa, dearest? Did you call me?"

Just as unpredictable and capricious as Mr. Muir's bad dreams were the nighttime habits of Miranda, who at times would cozily curl up at the foot of Alissa's bed and sleep peacefully through to dawn, but at other times would insist upon being let outside, no matter that Alissa loved her to sleep on the bed. There was comfort of a kind—childish, Alissa granted—in knowing the white Persian was there through the night, and feeling at her feet the cat's warm, solid weight atop the satin coverlet.

But of course, as Alissa acknowledged, a cat can't be forced to do anything against her will. "It seems almost to be a law of nature," she said solemnly.

A few days after the abortive poisoning Mr. Muir was driving home in the early dusk when, perhaps a mile from his estate, he caught sight of the white cat in the road ahead—motionless in the other lane, as if frozen by the car's headlights. Unbidden, the thought came to him: *This is just to frighten her*—and he turned his wheel and headed in her direction. The golden eyes flared up in a blaze of blank surprise—or perhaps it was terror, or recognition—*This is just to redress the balance*, Mr. Muir thought as he pressed down harder on the accelerator and drove directly at the white Persian—and struck her, just as she started to bolt toward the ditch, with the front left wheel of his car. There was a thud and a cat's yowling, incredulous scream—and it was done.

My God! It *was* done!

Dry mouthed, shaking, Mr. Muir saw in his rearview mirror the broken white form in the road; saw a patch of liquid crimson blossoming out around it. He had not meant to kill Miranda, and yet he had actually done it this time—without premeditation, and therefore without guilt.

And now the deed was done forever.

"And no amount of remorse can undo it," he said in a slow, wondering voice.

Mr. Muir had driven to the village to pick up a prescription for Alissa at the drugstore—she'd been in the city on theater matters; had returned home late on a crowded commuter train and gone at once to lie down with what threatened to be a migraine headache. Now he felt rather a hypocrite, a brute, presenting headache tablets to his wife with the guilty knowledge that if she knew what he'd done, the severity of her migraine would be tenfold. Yet how could he have explained to her that he had not meant to kill Miranda this time, but the steering wheel of his car had seemed to act of its own volition, wresting itself from his grip! For so Mr. Muir—speeding home, still trembling and excited as though he himself had come close to violent death—remembered the incident.

He remembered the cat's hideous scream, cut off almost at once by the impact of the collision—but not quite at once.

And was there a dent in the fender of the handsome, English-built car? There was not.

And were there bloodstains on the left front tire? There were not.

Was there in fact any sign of a mishap, even of the mildest, most innocent sort? There was not.

"No proof! No proof!" Mr. Muir told himself happily, taking the stairs to Alissa's room two at a time. It was a matter of some relief as well when he raised his hand to knock at the door to hear that Alissa was evidently feeling better. She was on the telephone, talking animatedly with someone; even laughing in her light, silvery way that reminded him of nothing so much as wind chimes on a mild summer's night. His heart swelled with love and gratitude. "Dear Alissa—we will be so happy from now on!"

Then it happened, incredibly, that at about bedtime the white cat showed up again. *She had not died after all.*

Mr. Muir, who was sharing a late-night brandy with Alissa in her bedroom, was the first to see Miranda: she had climbed up onto the roof—by way, probably, of a rose trellis she often climbed for that purpose—and now her pug face appeared at one of the windows in a hideous repetition of the scene some nights ago. Mr. Muir sat paralyzed with shock, and it was Alissa who jumped out of bed to let the cat in.

"Miranda! What a trick! What *are* you up to?'

Certainly the cat had not been missing for any worrisome period of time, yet Alissa greeted her with as much enthusiasm as if she had. And Mr. Muir—his heart pounding in his chest and his very soul convulsed with loathing—was obliged to go along with the charade. He hoped Alissa would not notice the sick terror that surely shone in his eyes.

The cat he'd struck with his car must have been another cat, not Miranda... Obviously it had not been Miranda. Another white Persian with tawny eyes, and not his own.

Alissa cooed over the creature, and petted her, and encouraged her to settle down on the bed for the night, but after a few minutes Miranda jumped down and scratched to be let out the door: she'd missed her supper; she was hungry; she'd had enough of her mistress's affection. Not so much as a glance had she given her master, who was staring at her with revulsion. He knew now that he *must* kill her—if only to prove he could do it.

Following this episode the cat shrewdly avoided Mr. Muir—not out of lazy indifference, as in the past, but out of a sharp sense of their altered relations. She could not be conscious, he knew, of the fact that he had tried to kill her—but she must have been able to sense it. Perhaps she had been hiding in the bushes by the road and had seen him aim his car at her unfortunate doppelganger, and run it down....

This was unlikely, Mr. Muir knew. Indeed, it was highly improbable. But how otherwise to account for the creature's behavior in his presence—her demonstration, or simulation, of animal fear? Leaping atop a cabinet when he entered a room, as if to get out of his way; leaping atop a fireplace mantel (and sending, it seemed deliberately, one of his carved jade figurines to the hearth, where it shattered into a dozen pieces); skittering gracelessly through a doorway, her sharp toenails clicking against the hardwood floor. When, without intending to, he approached her out-of-doors, she was likely to scamper noisily up one of the rose trellises, or the grape arbor, or a tree; or run off into the shrubbery like a wild creature. If Alissa happened to be present she was invariably astonished, for the cat's behavior *was* senseless. "Do you think Miranda is ill?" she asked. "Should we take her to the veterinarian?" Mr. Muir said uneasily that he doubted they would be able to catch her for such a purpose—at least, he doubted *he* could.

He had an impulse to confess his crime, or his attempted crime, to Alissa. He had killed the hateful creature and *she had not died.*

One night at the very end of August Mr. Muir dreamt of glaring, disembodied eyes. And in their centers those black, black irises like old-fashioned keyholes: slots opening into the Void. He could not move to protect himself. A warm, furry weight settled luxuriantly upon his chest... upon his very face! The cat's whiskery white muzzle pressed against his mouth in a hellish kiss and in an instant the breath was being sucked from him...

"Oh, no! Save me! Dear God—"

The damp muzzle against his mouth, sucking his life's breath from him, and he could not move to tear it away—his arms, leaden at his sides; his entire body struck dumb, paralyzed...

"Save me... *save me!*"

His shouting, his panicked thrashing about in his bedclothes, woke him. Though he realized at once it had been only a dream, his breath still came in rapid, shallow gasps, and his heart hammered so violently he was in terror of dying: had not his doctor only the other week spoken gravely to him of imminent heart disease, the possibility of heart failure? And how mysterious it was, his blood pressure being so very much higher than ever before in his life....

Mr. Muir threw himself out of the damp, tangled bedclothes and switched on a lamp with trembling fingers. Thank God he was alone and Alissa had not witnessed this latest display of nerves!

"Miranda?" he whispered. "Are you in here?"

He switched on an overhead light. The bedroom shimmered with shadows and did not seem, for an instant, any room he knew.

"Miranda...?"

The sly, wicked creature! The malevolent beast! To think that cat's muzzle had touched his very lips, the muzzle of an animal that devoured mice, rats—any sort of foul filthy thing out in the woods! Mr. Muir went into his bathroom and rinsed out his mouth even as he told himself calmly that the dream had been only a dream, and the cat only a phantasm, and that of course Miranda was *not* in his room.

Still, she had settled her warm, furry, unmistakable weight on his chest. She had attempted to suck his breath from him, to choke him, suffocate him, stop his poor heart. *It was within her power* "Only a dream," Mr. Muir said aloud, smiling shakily at his reflection in the mirror. (Oh! To think that pale, haggard apparition was indeed *his...*) Mr. Muir raised his voice with scholarly precision. "A foolish dream. A child's dream. A woman's dream."

Back in his room he had the fleeting sense that something—a vague white shape—had just now scampered beneath his bed. But when he got down on his hands and knees to look, of course there was nothing.

He did, however, discover in the deep-pile carpet a number of cat hairs. White, rather stiff—quite clearly Miranda's. Ah, quite clearly. "Here's the evidence!" he said excitedly. He found a light scattering of them on the carpet near the door and, nearer his bed, a good deal more—as if the creature had lain there for a while and had even rolled over (as Miranda commonly did out on the terrace in the sun) and stretched her graceful limbs in an attitude of utterly pleasurable abandon. Mr. Muir had often been struck by the cat's remarkable *luxuriance* at such times: a joy of flesh (and fur) he could not begin to imagine. Even before relations between them had deteriorated, he had felt the impulse to hurry to the cat and bring the heel of his shoe down hard on that tender, exposed, pinkish-pale belly....

"Miranda? Where are you? Are you still in here?" Mr. Muir said. He was breathless, excited. He'd been squatting on his haunches for some minutes, and when he tried to straighten up his legs ached.

Mr. Muir searched the room, but it was clear that the white cat had gone. He went out onto his balcony, leaned against the railing, blinked into the dimly moonlit darkness, but could see nothing—in his fright he'd forgotten to put on his glasses. For some minutes he breathed in the humid, sluggish night air in an attempt to calm himself, but it soon became apparent that something was wrong. Some vague murmurous undertone of—was it a voice? Voices?

Then he saw it: the ghostly white shape down in the shrubbery. Mr. Muir blinked and stared, but his vision was unreliable. "Miranda...?" A scuttling noise rustled above him and he turned to see another white shape on the sharp-slanted roof making its rapid way over the top. He stood absolutely motionless—whether out of terror or cunning, he could not have said. That there was more than one white cat, more than one white Persian—more, in fact, than *merely one Miranda*—was a possibility he had not considered! "Yet perhaps that explains it," he said. He was badly frightened, but his brain functioned as clearly as ever.

It was not so very late, scarcely 1:00 a.m. The undertone Mr. Muir heard was Alissa's voice, punctuated now and then by her light, silvery laughter. One might almost think there was someone in the bedroom with her—but of course she was merely having a late-night telephone conversation, very likely with Alban—they would be chatting companionably, with an innocent sort of malice, about their co-actors and -actresses, mutual friends and acquaintances. Alissa's balcony opened out onto the same side of the house that Mr. Muir's did, which accounted for her voice (or *was* it voices? Mr. Muir listened, bemused) carrying so clearly. No light irradiated from her room; she must have been having her telephone conversation in the dark.

Mr. Muir waited another few minutes, but the white shape down in the shrubbery had vanished. And the slate-covered roof overhead was empty, reflecting moonlight in dull, uneven patches. He was alone. He decided to go back to bed but before doing so he checked carefully to see that he *was* alone. He locked all the windows, and the door, and slept with the lights on—but so deeply and with such grateful abandon that in the morning, it was Alissa's rapping on the door that woke him. "Julius? Julius? Is something wrong, dear?" she cried. He saw with astonishment that it was *nearly noon;* he'd slept four hours past his usual rising time!

Alissa said good-bye to him hurriedly. A limousine was coming to carry her to the city; she was to be away for several nights in succession; she was concerned about him, about his health, and hoped there was nothing wrong…"Of course there is nothing wrong," Mr. Muir said irritably. Having slept so late in the day left him feeling sluggish and confused; it had not at all refreshed him. When Alissa kissed him good-bye he seemed rather to suffer the kiss than to participate in it, and after she had gone he had to resist an impulse to wipe his mouth with the back of his hand.

"God help us!" he whispered.

By degrees, as a consequence of his troubled mind, Mr. Muir had lost interest in collecting. When an antiquarian bookdealer offered him a rare octavo edition of the *Directorium Inquisitorum* he felt only the mildest tinge of excitement, and allowed the treasure to be snatched up by a rival collector. Only a few days afterward he responded with even less enthusiasm when offered the chance to bid on a quarto Gothic edition of Machiavelli's *Belfagor*. "Is something wrong, Mr. Muir?" the dealer asked him. (They had been doing business together for a quarter of a century.) Mr. Muir said ironically, "*Is* something wrong?" and broke off the telephone connection. He was never to speak to the man again.

Yet more decisively, Mr. Muir had lost interest in financial affairs. He would not accept telephone calls from the various Wall Street gentlemen who managed his money; it was quite enough for him to know that the money was there and would always be there. Details regarding it struck him as tiresome and vulgar.

In the third week of September the play in which Alissa was an understudy opened to superlative reviews, which meant a good, long run. Though the female lead was in excellent health and showed little likelihood of ever missing a performance, Alissa felt obliged to remain in the city a good deal, sometimes for a full week at a time. (What she did there, how she busied herself day after day, evening after evening, Mr. Muir did not know and was too proud to ask.) When she invited him to join her for a weekend (why didn't he visit some of his antiquarian dealers, as he used to do with such pleasure?) Mr. Muir said simply, "But why, when I have all I require for happiness here in the country?"

Since the night of the attempted suffocation Mr. Muir and Miranda were yet more keenly aware of each other. No longer did the white cat flee his presence; rather, as if in mockery of him, she held her ground when he entered a room. If he approached her she eluded him only at the last possible instant, often flattening herself close against the floor and scampering, snakelike, away. He cursed her; she bared her teeth and hissed. He laughed loudly to show her how very little he cared; she leapt atop a cabinet, out of his reach, and settled into a cat's blissful sleep. Each evening Alissa called at an appointed hour; each evening she inquired after Miranda, and Mr. Muir would say, "Beautiful and healthy as ever! A pity you can't see her!"

With the passage of time Miranda grew bolder and more reckless—misjudging, perhaps, the quickness of her master's reflexes. She sometimes appeared underfoot, nearly tripping him on the stairs or as he left the house; she dared approach him as he stood with a potential weapon in hand—a carving knife, a poker, a heavy, leatherbound book. Once or twice, as Mr. Muir sat dreaming through one of his solitary meals, she even leapt onto his lap and scampered across the dining room table, upsetting dishes and glasses.

"Devil!" he shrieked, swiping in her wake with his fists. "What do you want of me!"

He wondered what tales the servants told of him, whispered backstairs. He wondered if any were being relayed to Alissa in the city.

One night, however, Miranda made a tactical error, and Mr. Muir did catch hold of her. She had slipped into his study—where he sat examining some of his rarest and most valuable coins (Mesopotamian, Etruscan) by lamplight—having calculated, evidently, on making her escape by way of the door. But Mr. Muir, leaping from his chair with extraordinary, almost feline swiftness, managed to kick the door shut. And now what a chase! What a struggle! What a mad frolic! Mr. Muir caught hold of the animal, lost her, caught hold of her again, lost her; she raked him viciously on the backs of both hands and on his face; he managed to catch hold of her again, slamming her against the wall and closing his bleeding fingers around her throat. He squeezed, he squeezed! He had her now and no force on earth could make him release her! As the cat screamed and clawed and kicked and thrashed and seemed to be suffering the convulsions of death, Mr. Muir crouched over her with eyes bulging and mad as her own. The arteries in his forehead visibly throbbed. "Now! Now I have you! Now!" he cried. And at that very moment when, surely, the white Persian was on the verge of extinction, the door to Mr. Muir's study was flung open and one of the servants appeared, white faced and incredulous: "Mr. Muir? What is it? We heard such—" the fool was saying; and of course Miranda slipped from Mr. Muir's loosened grasp and bolted from the room.

After that incident Mr. Muir seemed resigned to the knowledge that he would never have such an opportunity again. The end was swiftly approaching.

It happened quite suddenly, in the second week of November, that Alissa returned home.

She had quit the play; she had quit the "professional stage"; she did not even intend, as she told her husband vehemently, to visit New York City for a long time.

He saw to his astonishment that she'd been crying. Her eyes were unnaturally bright and seemed smaller than he recalled. And her prettiness looked worn, as if another face—harder, of smaller dimensions—were pushing through. Poor Alissa! She had gone away with such hope! When Mr. Muir moved to embrace her, however, meaning to comfort her, she drew away from him; her very nostrils pinched as if she found the smell of him offensive. "Please," she said, not looking him in the eye. "I don't feel well. What I want most is to be alone... just to be alone."

She retired to her room, to her bed. For several days she remained sequestered there, admitting only one of the female servants and, of course, her beloved Miranda, when Miranda condescended to visit the house. (To his immense relief Mr. Muir observed that the white cat showed no sign of their recent struggle. His lacerated hands and face were slow to heal, but in her own grief and self-absorption, Alissa seemed not to have noticed.)

In her room, behind her locked door, Alissa made a number of telephone calls to New York City. Often she seemed to be weeping over the phone, but so far as Mr. Muir could determine—being forced, under these special circumstances, to eavesdrop on the line—none of her conversations were with Alban.

Which meant ? He had to confess he had no idea; nor could he ask Alissa. For that would give away the fact that he'd been eavesdropping, and she would be deeply shocked.

Mr. Muir sent small bouquets of autumn flowers to Alissa's sickroom; bought her chocolates and bonbons, slender volumes of poetry, a new diamond bracelet. Several times he presented himself at her door, ever the eager suitor, but she explained that she was not prepared to see him just yet—not just yet. Her voice was shrill and edged with a metallic tone Mr. Muir had not heard before.

"Don't you love me, Alissa?" he cried suddenly.

There was a moment's embarrassed silence. Then: "Of course I do. But please go away and leave me alone."

So worried was Mr. Muir about Alissa that he could no longer sleep for more than an hour or two at a time, and these hours were characterized by tumultuous dreams. The white cat! The hideous smothering weight! Fur in his very mouth! Yet awake he thought only of Alissa and of how, though she had come home to him, it was not in fact to *him.*

He lay alone in his solitary bed, amidst the tangled bedclothes, weeping hoarsely. One morning he stroked his chin and touched bristles: He'd neglected to shave for several days.

From his balcony he chanced to see the white cat preening atop the garden wall, a larger creature than he recalled. She had fully recovered from his attack. (If, indeed, she had been injured by it. If indeed, the cat on the garden wall was the selfsame cat that had blundered into his study.) Her white fur very nearly blazed in the sun; her eyes were miniature golden-glowing coals set deep in her skull. Mr. Muir felt a mild shock seeing her: What a beautiful creature!

Though in the next instant, of course, he realized what she was.

One rainy, gusty evening in late November Mr. Muir was driving on the narrow blacktop road above the river, Alissa silent at his side—stubbornly silent, he thought. She wore a black cashmere cloak and a hat of soft black felt that fitted her head tightly, covering most of her hair. These were items of clothing Mr. Muir had not seen before, and in their stylish austerity they suggested the growing distance between them. When he had helped her into the car she'd murmured "thank you" in a tone that indicated "Oh! Must you touch me?" And Mr. Muir had made a mocking little bow, standing bare-headed in the rain.

And I had loved you so much.

Now she did not speak. Sat with her lovely profile turned from him. As if she were fascinated by the lashing rain, the river pocked and heaving below, the gusts of wind that rocked the English-built car as Mr. Muir pressed his foot ever harder on the gas pedal. "It will be better this way, my dear wife," Mr. Muir said quietly. "Even if you love no other man, it is painfully clear that you do not love me." At these solemn words Alissa started guiltily, but still would not face him. "My dear? Do you understand? It will be better this way—do not be frightened." As Mr. Muir drove faster, as the car rocked more violently in the wind, Alissa pressed her hands against her mouth as if to stifle any protest; she was staring transfixed—as Mr. Muir stared transfixed at the rushing pavement.

Only when Mr. Muir bravely turned the car's front wheels in the direction of a guardrail did her resolve break: she emitted a series of breathless little screams, shrinking back against the seat, but made no effort to seize his arm or the wheel. And in an instant all was over, in any case—the car crashed through the railing, seemed to spin in midair, dropped to the rock-strewn hillside and bursting into flame, turned end over end...

He was seated in a chair with wheels—a wheeled chair! It seemed to him a remarkable invention and he wondered whose ingenuity lay behind it.

Though he had not the capacity, being almost totally paralyzed, to propel it of his own volition.

And, being blind, he had no volition in any case! He was quite content to stay where he was, so long as it was out of the draft. (The invisible room in which he now resided was, for the most part, cozily heated—his wife had seen to that—but where yet remained unpredictable currents of cold air that assailed him from time to time. His bodily temperature, he feared, could not maintain its integrity against any sustained onslaught.)

He had forgotten the names for many things and felt no great grief. Indeed, not knowing *names* relaxes one's desire for the *things* that, ghostlike, forever unattainable, dwell behind them. And of course his blindness had much to do with this—for which he was grateful! Quite grateful!

Blind, yet not wholly blind: for he could see (indeed, could not *not* see) washes of white, gradations of white, astonishing subtleties of white like rivulets in a stream perpetually breaking and filling about his head, not distinguished by any form or outline or vulgar suggestion of an object in space….

He had had, evidently, a number of operations. How many he did not know; nor did he care to know. In recent weeks they had spoken earnestly to him of the possibility of yet another operation on his brain, the (hypothetical) object being, if he understood correctly, the restoration of his ability to move some of the toes on his left foot. Had he the capacity to laugh he would have laughed, but perhaps his dignified silence was preferable.

Alissa's sweet voice joined with the others in a chorus of bleak enthusiasm, but so far as he knew the operation had never taken place. Or if it had, it had not been a conspicuous success. The toes of his left foot were as remote and lost to him as all the other parts of his body.

"How lucky you were, Julius, that another car came along! Why, you might have *died!*"

It seemed that Julius Muir had been driving alone in a violent thunderstorm on the narrow River Road, high above the embankment; uncharacteristically, he'd been driving at a high speed; he'd lost control of his car, crashed through the inadequate guardrail, and over the side… "miraculously" thrown clear of the burning wreckage. Two-thirds of the bones in his slender body broken, skull severely fractured, spinal column smashed, a lung pierced… So the story of how Julius had come to this place, his final resting place, this place of milk-white peace, emerged, in fragments shattered and haphazard as those of a smashed windshield.

"Julius, dear? Are you awake, or—?" The familiar, resolutely cheerful voice came to him out of the mist, and he tried to attach a name to it, *Alissa?* or, no, *Miranda?*—which?

There was talk (sometimes in his very hearing) that, one day, some degree of his vision might be restored. But Julius Muir scarcely heard, or cared. He lived for those days when, waking from a doze, he would feel a certain furry, warm weight lowered into his lap—"Julius, dear, someone very special has come to visit!"—soft, yet surprisingly heavy; heated, yet not disagreeably so; initially a bit restless (as a cat must circle fussily about, trying to determine the ideal position before she settles herself down), yet within a few minutes quite wonderfully relaxed, kneading her claws gently against his limbs and purring as she drifted into a companionable sleep. He would have liked to see, beyond the shimmering watery whiteness of his vision, her particular whiteness; certainly he would have liked to feel once again the softness, the astonishing silkiness, of that fur. But he could hear the deep-throated melodic purring. He could feel, to a degree, her warmly pulsing weight, the wonder of her mysterious *livingness* against his—for which he was infinitely grateful.

"My love!"

RETURNS

Jack Ketchum

Jack Ketchum is the author of eleven novels, four of which have recently been filmed: *The Lost, The Girl Next Door, Red*, and *Offspring*. His short story "The Box" won a 1994 Bram Stoker Award and "Gone" won again in 2000. In 2003 he won two Stokers: best collection for *Peaceable Kingdom* and best long fiction for "Closing Time." His stories are collected in *The Exit at Toledo Blade Boulevard, Peaceable Kingdom, Sleep Disorder* (with Edward Lee) and *Closing Time and Other Stories. Old Flames* was cited by Stephen King in *Entertainment Weekly* as one of the ten best books of 2008.

Ketchum's novels are often graphically violent. His stories are usually less visceral but no less powerful. Ketchum fittingly says that "…where I can dependably get all warm and fuzzy myself is when it comes to animals. Hence, the novel *Red* and stories like 'Returns.' Harm an animal in one of my stories and you're going straight to hell, brother."

"I'm here."
"You're what?"
"I said I'm here."
"Aw, don't start with me. Don't get started."
Jill's lying on the stained expensive sofa with the TV on in front of her tuned to some game show, a bottle of Jim Beam on the floor and a glass in her hand. She doesn't see me but Zoey does. Zoey's curled up on the opposite side of the couch waiting for her morning feeding and the sun's been up four hours now, it's ten o'clock and she's used to her Friskies at eight.
I always had a feeling cats saw things that people didn't. Now I know.
She's looking at me with a kind of imploring interest. Eyes wide, black nose twitching. I know she expects something of me. I'm trying to give it to her.
"You're supposed to feed her for godsakes. The litter box needs changing."
"What? Who?"
"The cat. Zoey. Food. Water. The litter box. Remember?"

She fills the glass again. Jill's been doing this all night and all morning, with occasional short naps. It was bad while I was alive but since the cab cut me down four days ago on 72nd and Broadway it's gotten immeasurably worse. Maybe in her way she misses me. I only just returned last night from god knows where knowing there was something I had to do or try to do and maybe this is it. Snap her out of it.

"Jesus! Lemme the hell *alone*. You're in my goddamn head. *Get outa my goddamn head!*"

She shouts this loud enough for the neighbors to hear. The neighbors are at work. She isn't. So nobody pounds the walls. Zoey just looks at her, then back at me. I'm standing at the entrance to the kitchen. I know that's where I am but I can't see myself at all. I gesture with my hands but no hands appear in front of me. I look in the hall mirror and there's nobody there. It seems that only my seven-year-old cat can see me.

When I arrived she was in the bedroom asleep on the bed. She jumped off and trotted over with her black-and-white tail raised, the white tip curled at the end. You can always tell a cat's happy by the tail-language. She was purring. She tried to nuzzle me with the side of her jaw where the scent-glands are, trying to mark me as her own, to confirm me in the way cats do, the way she's done thousands of times before but something wasn't right. She looked up at me puzzled. I leaned down to scratch her ears but of course I couldn't and that seemed to puzzle her more. She tried marking me with her haunches. No go.

"I'm sorry," I said. And I was. My chest felt full of lead.

"Come on, Jill. Get up! You need to feed her. Shower. Make a pot of coffee. Whatever it takes."

"This is fuckin' crazy," she says.

She gets up though. Looks at the clock on the mantle. Stalks off on wobbly legs toward the bathroom. And then I can hear the water running for the shower. I don't want to go in there. I don't want to watch her. I don't want to see her naked anymore and haven't for a long while. She was an actress once. Summer stock and the occasional commercial. Nothing major. But god, she was beautiful. Then we married and soon social drinking turned to solo drinking and then drinking all day long and her body slid fast into too much weight here, too little there. Pockets of self-abuse. I don't know why I stayed. I'd lost my first wife to cancer. Maybe I just couldn't bear to lose another.

Maybe I'm just loyal.

I don't know.

I hear the water turn off and a while later she walks back into the living room in her white terry robe, her hair wrapped in a pink towel. She glances at the clock. Reaches down to the table for a cigarette. Lights it and pulls on it furiously. She's still wobbly but less so. She's scowling. Zoey's watching her carefully. When she gets like this, half-drunk and half-straight, she's dangerous. I know.

"You still here?

"Yes."

She laughs. It's not a nice laugh.

"Sure you are."

"I am."

"Bullshit. You fuckin' drove me crazy while you were alive. Fuckin' driving me crazy now you're dead."

"I'm here to help you, Jill. You and Zoey."

She looks around the room like finally she believes that maybe, maybe I really *am* here and not some voice in her head. Like she's trying to locate me, pin down the source of me. All she has to do, really, is to look at Zoey, who's staring straight at me.

But she's squinting in a way I've seen before. A way I don't like.

"Well, you don't have to worry about Zoey," she says.

I'm about to ask her what she means by that when the doorbell rings. She stubs out the cigarette, walks over to the door and opens it. There's a man in the hall I've never seen before. A small man, shy and sensitive looking, mid-thirties and balding, in a dark blue windbreaker. His posture says he's uncomfortable.

"Mrs. Hunt?"

"Un-huh. Come on in," she says. "She's right over there."

The man stoops and picks up something off the floor and I see what it is.

A cat-carrier. Plastic with a grated metal front. Just like ours. The man steps inside.

"Jill, *what are you doing*? What the hell are you *doing*, Jill?"

Her hands flutter to her ears as though she's trying to bat away a fly or a mosquito and she blinks rapidly but the man doesn't see that at all. The man is focused on my cat who *remains focused on me*, when she should be watching the man, *when she should be seeing the cat-carrier, she knows damn well what they mean for godsakes, she's going somewhere, somewhere she won't like.*

"Zoey! Go! Get out of here! *Run!*"

I clap my hands. They make no sound. But she hears the alarm in my voice and sees the expression I must be wearing and at the last instant turns toward the man just as he reaches for her, reaches down to the couch and snatches her up and shoves her head-first inside the carrier. Closes it. Engages the double-latches.

He's fast. He's efficient.

My cat is trapped inside.

The man smiles. He doesn't quite pull it off.

"That wasn't too bad," he says.

"No. You're lucky. She bites. She'll put up a hell of a fight sometimes."

"You lying bitch," I tell her.

I've moved up directly behind her by now. I'm saying this into her ear. I can *feel* her heart pumping with adrenalin and I don't know if it's me who's scaring her or what she's just done or allowed to happen that's scaring her but she's all actress now, she won't acknowledge me at all. I've never felt so angry or useless in my life.

"You sure you want to do this, ma'am?" he says. "We could put her up for adoption for a while. We don't *have* to euthanize her. 'Course, she's not a kitten anymore. But you never know. Some family…"

"I *told* you," my wife of six years says. "*She bites.*"

And now she's calm and cold as ice.

Zoey has begun meowing. My heart's begun to break. Dying was easy compared to this.

Our eyes meet. There's a saying that the soul of a cat is seen through its eyes and I believe it. I reach inside the carrier. My hand passes *through* the carrier. I can't see my hand but she can. She moves her head up to nuzzle it. And the puzzled expression isn't there anymore. It's as though this time she can actually *feel* me, feel my hand and my touch. I wish I could feel her too. I petted her just this way when she was only a kitten, a street-waif, scared of every horn and siren. And I was all alone. She begins to purr. I find something out. Ghosts can cry.

The man leaves with my cat and I'm here with my wife.

I can't follow. Somehow I know that.

You can't begin to understand how that makes me feel. I'd give anything in the world to follow.

My wife continues to drink and for the next three hours or so I do nothing but scream at her, tear at her. Oh, she can hear me, all right. I'm putting her through every torment as I can muster, reminding her of every evil she's ever done to me or anybody, reminding her over and over of what she's done *today* and I think, so this is my purpose, this is why I'm back, the reason I'm here is to get this bitch to end herself, end her miserable fucking life and I think of my cat and how Jill never really cared for her, cared for her wine-stained furniture more than my cat and I urge her toward the scissors, I urge her toward the window and the seven-story drop, toward the knives in the kitchen and she's crying, she's screaming, too bad the neighbors are all at work, they'd at least have her arrested. And she's hardly able to walk or even stand and I think, *heart attack maybe, maybe stroke* and I stalk my wife and urge her to die, *die* until it's almost one o'clock and something begins to happen.

She's calmer.

Like she's not hearing me as clearly.

I'm losing something.

Some power drifting slowly away like a battery running down.

I begin to panic. I don't understand. *I'm not done yet.*

Then I feel it. I feel it reach out to me from blocks and blocks away far across the city. I feel the breathing slow. I feel the heart stopping. I feel the quiet end of her. I feel it more clearly than I felt my own end.

I feel it grab my own heart and *squeeze.*

I look at my wife, pacing, drinking. And I realize something. And suddenly it's not so bad anymore. It still hurts, but in a different way.

I haven't come back to torment Jill. Not to tear her apart or to shame her for what she's done. She's tearing herself apart. She doesn't need me for that. She'd have done this terrible thing anyway, with or without my being here. She'd planned it. It was in motion. My being here didn't stop her. My being here afterwards didn't change things. Zoey was mine. And given who and what Jill was, what she'd done was inevitable.

And I think, *to hell with Jill. Jill doesn't matter a bit.* Not one bit. *Jill is zero.*

It was Zoey I was here for. Zoey all along. That awful moment.

I was here for my cat.

That last touch of comfort inside the cage. The nuzzle and purr. Reminding us both of all those nights she'd comforted me and I her. The fragile brush of souls.

That was what it was about.

That was what we needed.

The last and the best of me's gone now.

And I begin to fade.

PUSS-CAT

Reggie Oliver

Reggie Oliver has been a professional playwright, actor, and theatre director since 1975. His biography of Stella Gibbons, *Out of the Woodshed,* was published by Bloomsbury in 1998. Besides plays and his novel *Virtue in Danger,* his publications include four volumes of stories: *The Dreams of Cardinal Vittorini, The Complete Symphonies of Adolf Hitler, Masques of Satan,* and *Madder Mysteries.* An omnibus edition of his stories entitled *Dramas from the Depths* is forthcoming from Centipede Press. His stories have been published in *Strange Tales, Shades of Darkness, Exotic Gothic, The Year's Best Fantasy and Horror, The Black Book of Horror,* and the *Mammoth Book of Best New Horror.*

Oliver says: "As with all of my stories, there are elements of autobiography and personal experience woven into the fabric of 'Puss-Cat,' though I am definitely not Godfrey in the story. He is older and much drunker than I am. On the other hand I am an actor, have worked on tour and in the West End, and did once understudy a famous theatrical knight who used to… But that would be giving the plot away.

"As for the cats, when I married my wife who is also an actress, I enthusiastically adopted her love of these wonderful animals. I am particularly interested in the way they are as attached to places as they are to people, perhaps more so. Every self-respecting theatre has its cat who is as vital to its well-being as the stage doorman or the box office manager. The theatre cat's sense of proprietorship is quite remarkable. I remember one at a seaside repertory theatre I worked in who used to regularly saunter casually on stage during a performance, usually through the unglazed frame of a French Window; then, just as insouciantly, he would exit through the fireplace. A warm round of applause from the audience always greeted this feat. You will meet several theatre cats in this story, and one who is not quite a theatre cat."

So, you want to know about Sir Roderick Bentley, do you? Well, you've come to the right department, as they say. Thank you, I'll have a large Bell's Whisky, if I may. Plenty of soda. Ice? Good God, no! Yes, Roddy and I went back a long way, to the Old Vic days just after the war. No. No resentment. Roddy was always destined for great things, me for the supporting roles.

"Godders," Roddy said to me once. He always called me "Godders" for some reason, but I prefer to be called Godfrey, if you don't mind. That's my name. "Godders, you're a good actor. Devilish good, and you'll always be in work. I'll tell you why. You're good but you haven't enough personality to worry a leading man." I'll never forget that. Of course, I suppose I knew he was right, but that doesn't mean to say it wasn't an almighty sock in the jaw.

Well, when Roddy formed his own company, Navigator Productions, he asked me to be in it. Played some good parts—not leads or anything, of course—but I did understudy him quite a bit. In fact I understudied him in his last two productions, and thereby hangs a tale, as they say.

Want to know a funny thing about Roddy? He couldn't stand cats. No, I know on it's own that's not particularly strange, but it is odd when you consider that in spite of that he always used to call his girlfriends "puss-cat."

You don't know about the girlfriends? Oh, perhaps I shouldn't have said, but you were bound to find out in the end, weren't you? But you won't mention, will you, in this biography of yours that it was I who told you? I'd hate it to get back to Lady Margery that I said such a thing. I rather doubt that she knows, you see. Or perhaps she does and won't admit it. Women are queer cattle. Ah, the drinks! Well, here's to your book, eh?

Let me make it quite clear: Roddy was devoted to Lady Margery. Devoted. But, you know, when Margery started to have the kids she gave up the theatre. They had this lovely home down in Kent and she didn't like to leave it just to go on tour with him or off to some godforsaken film location in Spain or California. So Roddy had his little adventures, but he always came home.

Now, I know what's going through your mind. I'm not quite the drink-sodden old idiot you think I am, you see. You've got the neat psychological explanation all lined up, haven't you? You think he despised these girlfriends of his, and as he hated cats he called them "puss-cat" out of some subconscious urge to put them down. But it's rather more complicated than that. You see Roddy had three passions in life: the theatre, women and sailing. He had an absolute mania for messing about in boats and when he became rich and famous he bought this yacht which was his pride and joy. It was a catamaran, and do you know what he called it? Yes. "Puss-Cat." So you see it wasn't that simple. Roddy did a lot for his girls one way and another: he brought them on professionally, encouraged them. Some of them have had very good careers thanks to him. No, I'm not going to tell all you their names—you'll have to find that out for yourself—but I'll mention a couple of them perhaps, because they're relevant to what you came to me for. I assume it was the last months of Roddy's life that you wanted me to tell you about?

Thank you. Just another double Bell's with soda and that's my lot. I've always known my limit: key to success, knowing your limits, believe me. By the way,

I'll say it just once: this is my version of what happened. Others will tell you different, and it's up to you to decide what the truth of the matter is, because at the end of the day your guess is as good as mine. Probably better actually. After all, you're the writer, aren't you?

Well, the year after Roddy got his "K" and became Sir Roderick, he took out a tour of Pinero's *The Magistrate* and, of course, I was in it. I understudied him and played the nice little role of Wormington. Gets some good laughs in the third act, but you don't want to hear about that, do you? Well naturally Roddy plays the title role of the Magistrate, Posket, and he was superb, believe me.

Do you know *The Magistrate*? It's a good old-fashioned farce. No smut. Never fails: except with the critics who think it's a bit dusty and dated. That's why we didn't come into the West-End with it, I'm convinced. Well, anyway, in this play there's a rather nice part of a young music teacher called Beatie, and for it Roddy hires a young unknown actress, name of Yolande Carey. You've heard about her? Well, hold your horses, because believe me, you don't know the half.

Yolande was a sweet little thing, just Roddy's type as it happens. His type? Well, she was slender—"petite," I suppose is the word—blonde with delicate features and a little turned-up nose. Looked as if she'd blow away in a light gale. That was Roddy's type. Attraction of opposites, I suppose, because Roddy, as you know, was a big man with one hell of a physique. He was sixty-three at the time I'm talking about but if it wasn't for the grey hair he could have passed for forty-five. Don't get the idea though that Roddy picked Yolande just because he fancied her. He wasn't like that. Yolande had talent, believe me, a bit raw, perhaps, and underpowered in the vocal department, but definitely there, and Roddy had spotted it at the audition.

I knew Roddy and I could tell from the start of rehearsals that he fancied her because he gave her such a hard time. Incidentally, Roddy was directing as well as playing the lead. That was not the usual practice, rather archaic, but still done, like the soloist conducting a piano concerto from the keyboard. But, dammit, Gielgud did it, Olivier did it, why not Roddy? He could be a bit of a bully, but, on the other hand, he always bullied the ones he cared about most, because he knew they had it in them to give more. Sometimes younger actors found that hard to understand; just as *he* failed to understand that some people just don't respond well to bullying, Yolande being one of them. He kept on at her to project more, throw herself more into the role, until once or twice I could see she was close to tears.

I did my best to reassure Yolande but she thought I was just taking pity on her. When I tried a quiet word with Roddy about it he was very sharp with me, told me to mind my own something something business. I got the impression that he suspected me of being sweet on Yolande, but this wasn't the case. Just to make things clear at the start, I'm gay: not a word I like terribly but the only one available these days. It was a fact about my life that Roddy always chose to ignore. You see, though I don't deny it, I'm not open or obvious about it, and I was actually once married. She left me for a dentist: I won't bore you with the details. Cheers!

Where was I? Yes, well, the Yolande-Roddy situation was resolved in a rather odd way. We were rehearsing for the tour in a run-down old Church Hall in Lambeth. It was a gruesome place, but it was cheap to hire. Roddy, like nearly all theatrical managements I've worked with, could be both very mean and very extravagant in the most unexpected directions, and the Church Hall was one of his false economies. It had Biblical texts on the walls; its windows were dirty; it got us down. It also had a resident cat, an ancient ginger Tom, called Charlie—God knows why I remember that, but I do!—the mangiest old bruiser you ever saw. Charlie had a habit of trotting into rehearsals at odd moments, and standing or sitting very still while he stared at proceedings; then he would start to howl. I think Charlie just wanted to be fed, but we all called him "The Critic", because he did sometimes seem to be commenting on our attempts at comedy.

Needless to say, Roddy loathed Charlie, and one afternoon the animal started howling at a particularly tense moment in rehearsals. Roddy, who was trying to remember lines, lost his temper completely, rushed at Charlie and gave him the most almighty kick. Charlie let out an awful screech and Yolande, who was standing nearby, ran to pick him up. She was the only one of us who had shown any sort of soft spot for Charlie, the Critic. She cuddled the wretched old beast in her arms and absolutely tore a strip off Roddy for what he had done. Roddy stared at her in amazement. He said nothing, and I could see his mind working. Once I saw his mouth twitch into a smile, but he controlled himself. Having heard her out in silence he simply and graciously apologised to her. He said that what he had done was "unpardonable." Yolande released Charlie, who had been clawing and struggling in her arms in the most ungrateful way. He dashed off and was never seen again.

That incident marked a turning point in relations between Roddy and Yolande. Her acting became bolder and more confident; Roddy's criticisms became more muted. They ceased to be boss and junior employee and became colleagues. It was a great relief all round.

I don't exactly know when their affair started, but I think it was fairly early on in the tour, and I suspect it was our second week which was at the Theatre Royal, Newcastle. Do you know it? Lovely old theatre.

On the Tuesday morning Yolande and I happened to meet Roddy at the stage door. We had just been in to see if there was any mail for us and, as it was a fine April day, we were standing outside talking about nothing in particular when Roddy appeared. I could see he was in one of his restless moods, and on the spur of the moment he proposed to take us out on a jaunt. He was going to show us Hadrian's Wall, an idea which seemed to thrill Yolande, me less so. I'd been. However I went because it was clear from Roddy's look that he wanted me there. I wasn't quite sure why, but, you know, Roddy was a compulsive performer and liked an audience for practically everything he did, even seduction.

We drove out of Newcastle and followed the wall. It was one of those soft, mild days of spring, full of haze and new bird song when the pale green of the hills blended with the grey ribs and ridges of Roman wall and fortress. Yolande listened to Roddy with the rapt wonder of a schoolgirl as he explained the wall to her. We got out at Housesteads, the best preserved fort on the wall, and wandered about, almost the only people there. At one point Yolande asked about Hadrian himself, what sort of man was he? Roddy who, outside military history and dates, was less well informed, hesitated. So I gave them an account of the only thing I knew about Hadrian, his passion for the glamorous youth Antinous whose mysterious death blighted the Emperor's later years. Yolande was puzzled.

"I didn't know they had gays in those days," she said. Roddy, who was standing behind her, looked at me and winked. I ignored him and went into some rubbish about the Greeks and Plato and Socrates. For the rest of the time we were out I felt very uneasy. Roddy was flirting with Yolande and completely ignoring me, while she was laughing at everything he said in that way people do when they meet Royalty or fall in love.

He drove us back to the theatre. At the stage door I noticed that the theatre cat, a black, green-eyed streak of feline cunning, had stretched out its lean body on the door step to catch the weak Newcastle sun. When he saw it, Roddy did a thing I'd never seen him do before. He crouched down and tentatively tickled the animal's stomach.

"Hello, puss-cat," he said with a rather unconvincing show of bonhomie. The cat ignored him, and Roddy looked up at Yolande.

He said: "I wonder, old thing. I'm going back to my hotel. I've got to look over that bit in the third act where I got in such a tangle last night. Remember? You wouldn't be an absolute brick and come back with me for a cuppa and test me on my lines, would you?"

There was a little pause, just long enough for it to be made obvious that she knew what he meant and he knew that she knew, and, well, you know the rest. I thought for a moment she was going to turn him down rather huffily, but she didn't; she simply said: "Okay," and off they went.

I'm pretty sure that was the beginning of things, because after that one would often see them together in the wings or in the dressing room corridors, just talking. They weren't touching or anything obvious like that and I'm sure they thought they were being incredibly discreet, but very soon the rumours were flying around. You know how these things are picked up amazingly quickly by a company on tour with nothing much to do except gossip about each other.

One thing that one of the other actresses in the company said stuck in my mind. She said: "I wonder what would happen if Bel knew." Bel of course was Belinda Courteney. Yes, *the* Belinda Courteney. Yes, she was one of Roddy's girls at one time, but don't tell her I told you. I'm up for an interview for the National next week and you know how her writ runs there. As a matter of fact I thought the Bel Courteney affair was over, but apparently some thought otherwise.

Yolande occasionally confided in me. I suppose I was a safe pair of hands, and she knew I knew, so to speak. I tried to sound kindly and wise: you know how one slips into these roles, especially if one is an actor. I was dear old Uncle Godfrey to her, and, I'm afraid, to me too in those moments. Yolande was a sweet thing, but such a child. She had become obsessed by Roddy and used to ask me about every detail of his career, the books he liked, the food he preferred, everything. I honestly think she thought he was going to leave Lady Margery for her. She said: "You know he hasn't slept with her for eight years." I refrained from saying that that was what he told all the girls, because it was only a guess, but perhaps I should have done.

Well, the tour wound up fairly successfully in October at the Theatre Royal Richmond, traditionally one of those "last date before the West End" venues, but it was not to be. There had been talk of a West End Theatre several times in the tour, but it came to nothing. With such a huge cast we needed a thousand-seater-plus just to break even and all the big houses were stubbornly full of American musicals that year.

So the company disbanded, but Yolande and I kept in touch, partly because I sensed she needed someone to talk to about Roddy. Most of her other friends wouldn't have understood. They were non-theatrical and, frankly, just a bit odd. They tended to call themselves "aromatherapists," "Feng Shui consultants," "musicians," "spiritual healers": all those euphemisms by which the barely employable salve the wound of their uselessness. Forgive me, my prejudice is showing; it must be the Bell's.

She had a little flat above a patisserie in the St John's Wood High Street. She'd ask me round at odd times of the day for a cup of herb tea and, if I was lucky, a slice of carrot cake, but the subject of conversation was always the same: Roddy. They were still seeing each other, and he occasionally used to take her away for weekends in Paris or Torquay—his boat was down at Torquay, you see—but after one or two visits he wouldn't come to her flat any more. The excuse he gave was that he was allergic to her cat, and one can't altogether blame him. I'm not myself averse to cats, but this one of Yolande's, a rescued stray, was not a notably attractive specimen. It was an elderly, neutered Tom, brindled, with a sagging belly and a passion for tinned sardines. Yolande, you see, was one of those people who is instantly drawn to anything even more defenceless than herself.

Rather unwisely I think, Yolande called the cat Roddy. I don't know whether she actually addressed the cat as such in the other Roddy's presence, but it would explain his allergy if she did.

I was managing to keep myself alive by the odd voice-over, and a beer commercial, but by the end of November Yolande was beginning to be rather uncomfortably out of work. She had some sort of part-time employment at a nearby book shop which didn't bring in much, but it wasn't just the money. Acting is a drug: once you become addicted, you need a regular fix. Yolande told me that Roddy had offered to "lend" her some money which she had indignantly refused, and he was beginning to see less of her. In December he went away for some filming in Spain; then just before Christmas something happened which lifted her out of the gloom she was falling into. She had a Christmas Card from Roddy, and there was a message in it.

Excitedly she asked me round for herb tea to see the card. She wouldn't say anything more on the phone, so I came. I had barely taken a sip of Dandelion and Chamomile—a filthy concoction, take my word, don't go near the stuff—before she had thrust the Actor's Benevolent Fund card into my hand. Inside it read as follows:

"Darling Puss-Cat,

"Filming here nearly over. Shan't be sorry. Ghastly Spanish food swimming in oil. Fell off a horse yesterday in full armour. No joke. Puss-Cat, I'm taking out a Spring Tour of King Lear next year and I've done a deal which guarantees us a West End Theatre. The long and the short of it is I want you to be my Cordelia. What say you?

"Your ever loving,

"Roddy"

I have to confess that my first reaction was a typical actor's one: jealousy. He was taking out a tour of King Lear and there were plenty of parts for me—Kent, perhaps even Gloucester—why hadn't Roddy been in touch about it? But this was no time to feel hurt; Yolande was asking me what she should do. I said it was obvious. She should get her agent to contact the Navigator Productions office and accept the offer. Yolande said she had already done that.

Then there was a long laborious discussion in which she went on about her utter inadequacy for the role—she had never done Shakespeare profession-ally—and I, as I was expected to do, reassured her that she would make a splendid Cordelia. I thought it might be tactless to remark that one of her main qualifica-tions for the part was the fact that she was a light girl, only just over seven stone. The elderly actor playing Lear, you see, must carry Cordelia on stage at the end of the play, so weight is a consideration, especially in a long run, and it was one of which I am sure Roddy had been mindful.

Well, that seemed to be that. I didn't hear much from Yolande till after Christmas. Then she began to be a bit worried because Roddy had not been in touch with her. This was the arrangement, you see. She was not allowed to ring him in case Lady Margery answered the phone: he would always call her. More worrying perhaps than that, there had been no response from the Navigator Productions office about her acceptance of Cordelia. This puzzled me because by this time my agent had been notified that Roddy was "interested" in me for the part of Kent.

Early in January Roddy asked me over to the Navigator Offices just off the Charing Cross Road to "talk about Kent." I knew this amounted to a firm offer, so I went eagerly and found him welcoming and friendly as always, but, I thought, a little distracted. We discussed the production and my part which he described as "hell's important" and "absolutely key." We also discussed the salary he was offering. He apologised profusely that it couldn't be higher; in fact he seemed so distressed about it that in the end I began to feel guilty, as if I had gone in asking for more money than he could afford which, of course, I hadn't. In the end, to relieve the tension, I said:

"I gather Yolande is going to be your Cordelia."

Roddy's reaction was most unexpected. He looked at me with a shocked, almost fearful expression, as if something poisonous had just bitten him.

"What the hell are you on about, Godders?" he said.

Now, I didn't want to admit that I'd read a private Christmas card so I was a bit vague at first, but Roddy simply didn't understand. In the end I had to tell him explicitly that she had shown me the message from him. Even then, it was quite some time before he reacted. Then it was as if a flash from a bolt of lightning had suddenly bleached his face.

Roddy said: "Oh, my God! Oh, my Christ! Oh, my golly gosh!" Then, after a long pause, he said in a quiet, thoughtful sort of a way: "Oh, fuck!"

I waited patiently for the explanation. At last he sighed, as if these things had been sent to try him and he told me:

"I wrote all my bloody Christmas cards in Spain. I thought it would be something to do. You know the waiting around that goes on, especially when you're filming one of these ghastly Hollywood Epics. I can remember writing all the cards, then I got a tummy bug from some fearful Spanish muck they served us. Well, the doc, under instructions from the director of course, just drugged me up to the eyeballs so I could get onto that bloody horse again. It was while I was under the influence that I did the envelopes for the cards. I do vaguely remember doing Bel Courteney's at the same time as Yolande's—"

I got his drift. "You mean the offer of Cordelia was meant for Belinda Courteney? You put the card in the wrong envelope?"

"Yes. Dammit! Yes! I've been wondering why Bel hadn't responded. In fact… Oh, buggeration and hell!"

He seemed even more upset than before and I asked him what was the matter. At last I got it out of him that the card he had intended for Yolande contained a suggestion, couched in the gentlest possible terms, that perhaps in future they might be seeing rather less of each other than before.

I said: "You mean, you might have sent the brush-off for Yolande to Belinda by mistake as well?" Roddy started rubbing his face with his hands so he wouldn't have to look at me. By this time, I was almost as upset as he was. I said: "But you called her puss-cat."

"Who?"

"Yolande—I mean Belinda."

"Yes. Yes! They're all called puss-cat." He seemed very irritated that I had brought the matter up. Then he became all abject and apologetic which was almost worse. He said: "Look, Godfrey, dear old thing, would you do me the most enormous favour? Would you try to break all this to Yolande? And do it gently, won't you, dear old boy. I know you will. You're such a brick. The fact is I just can't face it at the moment. I'm up to here with Lear, as you can imagine, and I've got to try and sort things out with Belinda."

I said: "Are you sure you wouldn't like me to tackle *her* as well?"

Roddy didn't react; he just shook his head solemnly. "No, thanks. That's awfully decent, but I have to do that myself." My attempts at irony have always fallen on deaf ears. Not so much *esprit de l'escalier* as *esprit de corpse*, eh? Oh, never mind. So I agreed to see Yolande for him. Of course I agreed. You can't just fall out of love with someone after forty years. At least, I can't.

I thought of telling Yolande by phone or even a letter, but in the end I decided to go to see her: it seemed the only decent thing to do. Well, we got sat down with the herb tea and everything and the cat Roddy purring on her lap and I began to explain. It was horrible because she found it so hard to take it in. I had to say everything twice. She didn't rage, or throw things, or spit with hatred or anything—I would have preferred that—she just listened with a baffled expression on her face. There were no sobs, but her eyes were wet with tears. She kept saying: "But why? Does he hate me or something?" And I said "No," very loudly and firmly, because I was sure he didn't. Then she asked me to explain about the card yet again, so I did.

She nodded a few times before she said: "So he doesn't want me to be his Cordelia?"

I shook my head. There was a bit of a pause, then she came out with something which jolly nearly broke me up. She said: "I'd started learning the lines."

Oh, God! You wouldn't understand, would you? You're not an actor.

Well, we began work on Lear and I rather lost touch with Yolande. Rehearsals were engrossing and I had the feeling she would not want to hear about them. Incidentally, Belinda Courteney did not play Cordelia—it was the year of her groundbreaking Hedda Gabler at the National—and the girl who did was no better and no worse than Yolande might have been. Roddy was on top form as Lear and I think everyone who saw him agrees that he gave the performance of his life. The rest of the cast was good, the set was functional and, though the costumes belonged to the then-fashionable "Ruritanian Stalinist" school, they did at least fit. We opened fairly triumphantly in, of all places, Blackpool.

There was a six week pre-West End tour and I must admit that I completely forgot about Yolande until the last week at Cardiff when, half an hour before curtain up on the Thursday I was summoned through the loudspeaker in my dressing room to the phone at the stage door. There was a call for me.

It was one of Yolande's odd friends—the aromatherapist, I think—and how she had managed to track me down to the Theatre Royal Cardiff, I do not know. She told me that the previous day the couple in the flat above Yolande's had heard this howling and scratching on the door of Yolande's flat, obviously the wretched cat Roddy in some distress. They tried calling Yolande but got no reply. To cut a long story short, the police were summoned and when they broke down the door they found Yolande lying on the bed, dead. She'd taken enough barbiturates to kill a horse. Roddy the cat had gone frantic with hunger and everything and the place stank of his poo, but he hadn't touched Yolande's body.

I went through the performance that night in a daze, wondering when and how I should tell Roddy. In the end I funked it altogether. The following evening I was standing in the wings waiting to go on and begin the play when I became aware of Roddy lurking behind me.

He said: "You've heard about Yolande?" I nodded. He said: "I've been rather knocked endways by it all. The Company Office rang and told me this afternoon. Someone there had seen a paragraph in the Evening Standard. I can't understand it, can you?"

I shook my head.

"I mean, I know she was out of work and all that, but… She must have had some sort of mental trouble. A breakdown. Terrible. She was a dear, sweet thing. Not without talent." There was a pause, then he said: "You know, Godders, I hate to say it, but young people today, they don't seem to have the backbone. They give up too easily. I mean, we've all had our bad patches in this profession, God knows, but you need a bit of grit and spunk to stick to it. Don't you agree?" To my shame I nodded and Roddy gave me a great bear hug.

The next minute the lights had gone up on stage and I was striding into another world as Kent and uttering the first words of the play: "I thought the King had more affected the Duke of Albany than Cornwall."

Roddy never mentioned Yolande again in my presence, but I believe there was a moment that night at the end of the play when perhaps he remembered her. It came in the final scene when he is on the ground, lamenting over the dead body of Cordelia and I am in attendance, and he says the words:

"A plague upon you, murderers, traitors all!

I might have saved her; now she's gone for ever."

At that moment he did something he'd never done before, he looked up at me. There were tears in his eyes, and they were not stage tears. I like to think they weren't.

So we moved to our London venue, the Irving Theatre in The Strand, for a limited run of three months, and the critics fortunately decided that Roddy was a great Lear. All the same, after the exhilaration of the tour when we were all discovering how good the show was, the West End run seemed to be a bit flat, and, of course, because in London most of the cast had their own homes to go to and their own lives to lead, some of the camaraderie in the company went too.

I didn't particularly like the Irving. It's big, draughty old Victorian building, perhaps even a little sinister, and it had, of course, a theatre cat. They're vital things you know, because theatres get rats, and rats gnaw cables, and gnawed electric cables start fires, especially in theatres. The Irving cat was a black Tom called Nimrod, not a very sociable beast, but, as befitted his name, a "mighty hunter before the Lord" who kept the rats and mice down very effectively. But here's a funny thing: about a week into our run Nimrod disappeared.

The theatre manager was very distressed and offered a reward for his discovery and return. There was even a bit in the papers about it. I wouldn't have mentioned this only it may have a bearing on what happened next.

Fortunately, the disappearance of Nimrod did not result in a rodent invasion. In fact—and this was something that puzzled many of us—the odd half-eaten rat or mouse could still be found in odd corners of the theatre, if anything with more frequency than before Nimrod's vanishing act. These grisly remains, which had been left around by Nimrod as tokens of his prowess, were now nearly always to be found either in the wings or in the corridor leading to Dressing Room Number 1, Roddy's of course. In fact Roddy came in one day for a matinee to find a headless rat carefully placed on the very threshold of Number 1. He made a terrific fuss about that, as he had every right to, of course, but I thought there was a touch of hysteria in his manner which was uncharacteristic. He didn't usually play the Prima Donna.

A couple of days later Roddy happened to meet me back stage in the interval and invited me to his dressing room for a whisky. The one he poured himself was unusually large. He'd never been a boozer, and certainly not during a show. He seemed to be under some sort of strain.

Having sat me down, he said: "Now, then, Godders, what are we going to do about this cat business?" I looked blank. He said: "Don't tell me you haven't noticed this damned cat which keeps following me around the theatre?"

I said that I hadn't seen any cat and anyway—didn't he know?—Nimrod had disappeared. Roddy banged his glass impatiently down on the dressing table.

"Yes! Yes! I know all about Nimrod. That damn theatre manager is obsessed with Nimrod. I didn't mind Nimrod. He kept out of your way and did his job. This is a different cat altogether. It won't leave me alone. It keeps coming up to me just as I'm going on stage and purring, and doing that thing that cats do, you know, curling itself round your legs. It nearly tripped me up the other day just as I was going on for 'Blow Winds!' It's a blasted nuisance. And it keeps leaving these offerings for me in my dressing room. You know, bits of disemboweled rat and mouse. I trod on an intestine with my bare foot the other day as I was changing. Ugh! I can't think how the bugger gets in. I always lock my dressing room when I go. I suppose it must be the cleaners. I've spoken to the manager about it but he hasn't a clue. He's so obsessed about Nimrod I don't think he believes in this other cat."

I asked what it looked like.

"Funny sort of colour. I don't know. Greyish, I think, but these sort of yellow eyes which look as if they light up in the dark. You know how some cats seem to have luminous eyes. It's difficult to tell exactly what it looks like because I haven't seen it in full light. It usually turns up in the wings, just outside the glare of the stage lights. I wouldn't mind only—I know this is a funny thing to say—it's so damned fond of me. It's obsessed. It's like, you know, some creepy sort of stalker. Godders, you must have seen it."

There was pleading in his voice, but I had to confess that I hadn't. To reassure him I said I said I would keep "a weather eye" open for it. He liked that: a nautical expression, you see, "weather eye."

In the final scene that night an odd thing happened. Lear has come on with the dead body of Cordelia and we're standing around. Roddy was doing pretty well, but not on top form, I thought. He kept looking off-stage. Then comes his final speech when he is lamenting over the dead Cordelia and he says:

"Why should a dog, a horse, a rat have life,
And thou no breath at all?"
Except that this night he doesn't quite say that, he says:
"Why should a dog, a horse, a *cat* have life,
And thou no breath at all?"

And his eyes are fixed on something off-stage right in the wings. Well, I couldn't resist looking there myself. I was half-dazzled by the stage lights so I can't be sure, but do you know for a second or two somewhere in the gloom I thought I did catch sight of two yellow cat's eyes staring at the action on stage. Well, I can't be sure because I had to get back to my job. I still had lines to say, but when I'd said my last ones—you remember—

"I have a journey, sir, shortly to go;
My master calls me, I must not say no."—I look back into the wings, and there's nothing there. The eyes had gone.

Next day was a matinee day and before the first house Roddy summoned me to his dressing room. He seemed very excited.

He said: "I think I've got a way to nail the little bugger. You see this?" He held up a transparent plastic phial, the kind you pee into for doctors. It had about a centimetre of white powder in it. "Know what that is?" He didn't wait for my answer. "Strychnine. Don't ask me how I got it. Had to pull a few strings. One of the few advantages of being 'Sir Roderick' is that you can occasionally pull a string or two. I'm going to put it in some milk and put the milk in a saucer in my dressing room and when that damn cat comes, it is going to drink that milk. All cats like milk, don't they?"

I said I was no expert, but I understood that cats liked milk.

He said: "Right! That damn cat's going to die and all our troubles are over!"

I couldn't help feeling that Roddy had got things rather out of proportion, but he seemed exhilarated and that afternoon a slightly sparse audience got the performance of a lifetime. By the end of it Roddy was clearly exhausted, which worried me, but something was keeping him alight. He seemed—what's the word I'm looking for?—febrile, that's it, and it worried me.

That was why I decided to look in on him in his dressing room just before the half-hour call for the evening show. I knocked on the door which was slightly ajar but got no reply, so I looked in.

Roddy had not got out of his last act costume or his make-up. He was lying on the floor of his dressing room, arms outstretched. He didn't look to me as if he was breathing. Beside him on the floor was an empty bowl. At the corners of his half-open mouth were little droplets of liquid which looked to me like milk.

But that was not the worst of it. Crouched on his chest was the biggest damned cat I've ever seen in my life. Its fur was shaggy and grey—it looked like a great ball of dirty smoke—and its angry eyes were a bright sulphur yellow. Slowly it arched its back and gave me a low, stertorous hiss like the sudden escape of steam from an engine under pressure.

You don't believe me? Well, that's my story and I'm sticking to it.

I ran to get the Company Stage Manager and when we got back to Number One dressing room, Roddy was still there on the floor, but the cat had gone. We phoned for an ambulance and they carted him off to hospital but it wasn't any good. He was dead as mutton: heart failure apparently. I said nothing about the strychnine business because I thought it would only muddy the waters, and it probably wasn't relevant.

That night, for the first and last time in my life, I went on for Roddy as King Lear. Did I tell you I was his understudy? Made a pretty good fist of it too, though I says it as shouldn't. Standing ovation and all that.

"Godders," Roddy used to say to me, "you're a good actor. Devilish good, but you haven't enough personality to worry a leading man." Well, he should have seen me *that* night! What? Another Bell's? Oh, all right, just this once, since you're twisting my arm. Cheers!

CAT IN GLASS
Nancy Etchemendy

Nancy Etchemendy lives in Northern California and has been publishing fiction and poetry for twenty-five years. Though she is best known for her children's books, she has also published several dozen stories for adults, mainly dark fantasy and horror. Her work has won three Bram Stoker Awards (two for children's horror), a Golden Duck Award for excellence in children's science fiction, and an International Horror Guild Award. *Cat in Glass and Other Tales of the Unnatural*, her collection of dark fantasy for young adults, was on the American Library Association's *Best Books for Young Adults* list for 2003.

She says: "When my sister, Cecily, and I were three or four years old, my dad brought a male kitten home from the auto shop where he worked. We named it Ralph. At first Ralph was a nice little kitten who liked to be cuddled. But as he grew to un-neutered adulthood, he became enormous and wild, and spent more and more of his time outdoors hunting and fighting with other cats. He only came home to eat and sleep, and he frequently had large, suppurating wounds. His fur stuck out in tufts. He smelled terrible, and if we tried to pet him, he would hiss.

"One day Cecily and I decided we were going to get back at him for being so mean. Each of us took one end of a spool of crochet thread. We ran in opposite directions around poor old Ralph until he was wrapped in thread, hissing, growling and spitting. We were between him and the open door, so when he finally got loose, he came right at us. The sight, sound, and stink of that huge, ugly tom cat fighting his way free of the thread was truly terrifying. I'm half scared of cats to this day. Even though I've given good homes to a couple of them over the years, I've never gotten over the feeling that if the mood struck, a cat would happily scratch off its master's face. I much prefer dogs."

I was once a respectable woman. Oh, yes, I know that's what they all say when they've reached a pass like mine: I was well educated, well traveled, had lovely children and a nice husband with a good financial mind. How can anyone have fallen so far, except one who deserved to anyway? I've had time aplenty to consider the matter, lying here eyeless in this fine hospital bed while the stench of my wounds increases. The matrons who guard my room are tight-lipped. But I heard one of them whisper yesterday, when she thought I was asleep, "Jesus, how could anyone do such a thing?" The answer to all these questions is the same. I have fallen so far, and I have done what I have done, to save us each and every one from the *Cat in Glass*.

My entanglement with the cat began fifty-two years ago, when my sister Delia was attacked by an animal. It happened on an otherwise ordinary spring afternoon. There were no witnesses. My father was still in his office at the college, and I was dawdling along on my way home from first grade at Chesly Girls' Day School, counting cracks in the sidewalk. Delia, younger than I by three years, was alone with Fiona, the Irish woman who kept house for us. Fiona had just gone outside for a moment to hang laundry. She came in to check on Delia and discovered a scene of almost unbelievable carnage. Oddly, she had heard no screams.

As I ran up the steps and opened our door, I heard screams indeed. Not Delia's—for Delia had nothing left to scream with—but Fiona's, as she stood in the front room with her hands over her eyes.

She couldn't bear the sight. Unfortunately, six-year-olds have no such compunction. I stared long and hard, sick and trembling, yet entranced.

From the shoulders up, Delia was no longer recognizable as a human being. Her throat had been shredded and her jaw ripped away. Most of her hair and scalp were gone. There were long, bloody furrows in the creamy skin of her arms and legs. The organdy pinafore in which Fiona had dressed her that morning was clotted with blood, and the blood was still coming. Some of the walls were even spattered with it where the animal, whatever it was, had worried her in its frenzy. Her fists and heels banged jerkily against the floor. Our pet dog, Freddy, lay beside her, also bloody, but quite limp. Freddy's neck was broken.

I remember slowly raising my head—I must have been in shock by then—and meeting the bottomless gaze of the glass cat that sat on the hearth. Our father, a professor of art history, was very proud of this sculpture, for reasons I did not understand until many years later. I only knew it was valuable and we were not allowed to touch it. A chaotic feline travesty, it was not the sort of thing you would want to touch anyway. Though basically catlike in shape, it bristled with transparent threads and shards. There was something at once wild and vaguely human about its face. I had never liked it much, and Delia had always been downright frightened of it. On this day, as I looked up from my little sister's ruins, the cat seemed to glare at me with bright, terrifying satisfaction.

I had experienced, a year before, the thing every child fears most: the death of my mother. It had given me a kind of desperate strength, for I thought, at the tender age of six, that I had survived the worst life had to offer. Now, as I returned the mad stare of the glass cat, it came to me that I was wrong. The world was a much more evil place than I had ever imagined, and nothing would ever be the same again.

Delia died officially in the hospital a short time later. After a cursory investigation, the police laid the blame on Freddy. I still have the newspaper clipping, yellow now, and held together with even yellower cellophane tape. "The family dog lay dead near the victim, blood smearing its muzzle and forepaws. Sergeant Morton theorizes that the dog, a pit bull terrier and member of a breed specifically developed for vicious fighting, turned killer and attacked its tragic young owner. He also suggests that the child, during the death struggle, flung the murderous beast away with enough strength to break its neck."

Even I, a little girl, knew that this "theory" was lame; the neck of a pit bull is an almost impossible thing to break, even by a large, determined man. And Freddy, in spite of his breeding, had always been gentle, even protective, with us. Simply stated, the police were mystified, and this was the closest thing to a rational explanation they could produce. As far as they were concerned, that was the end of the matter. In fact, it had only just begun.

I was shipped off to my Aunt Josie's house for several months. What Father did during this time, I never knew, though I now suspect he spent those months in a sanitarium. In the course of a year, he had lost first his wife and then his daughter. Delia's death alone was the kind of outrage that might permanently have unhinged a lesser man. But a child has no way of knowing such things. I was bitterly angry at him for going away. Aunt Josie, though kind and good-hearted, was a virtual stranger to me, and I felt deserted. I had nightmares in which the glass cat slunk out of its place by the hearth and across the countryside. I would hear its hard claws ticking along the floor outside the room where I slept. At those times, half awake and screaming in the dark, no one could have comforted me except Father.

When he did return, the strain of his suffering showed. His face was thin and weary and his hair dusted with new gray, as if he had stood outside too long on a frosty night. On the afternoon of his arrival, he sat with me on Aunt Josie's sofa, stroking my cheek while I cuddled gladly, my anger at least temporarily forgotten in the joy of having him back.

His voice, when he spoke, was as tired as his face. "Well, my darling Amy, what do you suppose we should do now?"

"I don't know," I said. I assumed that, as always in the past, he had something entertaining in mind—that he would suggest it and then we would do it.

He sighed. "Shall we go home?"

I went practically rigid with fear. "Is the cat still there?"

Father looked at me, frowning slightly. "Do we have a cat?"

I nodded. "The big glass one."

He blinked, then made the connection. "Oh, the Chelichev, you mean? Well… I suppose it's still there. I hope so, in fact."

I clung to him, scrambling halfway up his shoulders in my panic. I could not manage to speak. All that came out of my mouth was an erratic series of whimpers.

"Shhhh, shhhh," said Father. I hid my face in the starched white cloth of his shirt, and heard him whisper, as if to himself, "How can a glass cat frighten a child who's seen the things you've seen?"

"I hate him! He's glad Delia died. And now he wants to get *me*."

Father hugged me fiercely. "You'll never see him again. I promise you," he said. And it was true, at least as long as he lived.

So the Chelichev *Cat in Glass* was packed away in a box and put into storage with the rest of our furnishings. Father sold the house, and we traveled for two years. When the horror had faded sufficiently, we returned home to begin a new life. Father went back to his professorship, and I to my studies at Chesly Girls' Day School. He bought a new house. The glass cat was not among the items he had sent up from storage. I did not ask him why. I was just as happy to forget about it, and forget it I did.

I neither saw the glass cat nor heard of it again until many years later. I was a grown woman by then, a school teacher in a town far from the one in which I'd spent my childhood. I was married to a banker, and had two lovely daughters and even a cat, which I finally permitted in spite of my abhorrence for them, because the girls begged so hard for one. I thought my life was settled, that it would progress smoothly toward a peaceful old age. But this was not to be. The glass cat had other plans.

The chain of events began with Father's death. It happened suddenly, on a snowy afternoon, as he graded papers in the tiny snug office he had always had on campus. A heart attack, they said. He was found seated at his desk, Erik Satie's Dadaist composition, "La Belle Excentrique," still spinning on the turntable of his record player.

I was not at all surprised to discover that he had left his affairs in some disarray. It's not that he had debts or was a gambler. Nothing so serious. It's just that order was slightly contrary to his nature. I remember once, as a very young woman, chiding him for the modest level of chaos he preferred in his life. "Really, Father," I said. "Can't you admire Dadaism without living it?" He laughed and admitted that he didn't seem able to.

As Father's only living relative, I inherited his house and other property, including his personal possessions. There were deeds to be transferred, insurance reports to be filed, bills and loans to be paid. He did have an attorney, an old school friend of his who helped me a great deal in organizing the storm of paperwork from a distance. The attorney also arranged for the sale of the house and hired someone to clean it out and ship the contents to us. In the course of the winter, a steady stream of cartons containing everything from scrapbooks to Chinese miniatures arrived at our doorstep. So I thought nothing of it when a large box labeled "fragile" was delivered one day by registered courier. There was a note from the attorney attached, explaining that he had just discovered it in a storage warehouse under Father's name, and had had them ship it to me unopened.

It was a dismal February afternoon, a Friday. I had just come home from teaching. My husband, Stephen, had taken the girls to the mountains for a weekend of skiing, a sport I disliked. I had stayed behind and was looking forward to a couple of days of quiet solitude. The wind drove spittles of rain at the windows as I knelt on the floor of the front room and opened the box. I can't explain to you quite what I felt when I pulled away the packing paper and found myself face-to-face with the glass cat. Something akin to uncovering a nest of cockroaches in a drawer of sachet, I suppose. And that was swiftly followed by a horrid and minutely detailed mental recreation of Delia's death.

I swallowed my screams, struggling to replace them with something rational. "It's merely a glorified piece of glass." My voice bounced off the walls in the lonely house, hardly comforting.

I had an overpowering image of something inside me, something dark and featureless except for wide, white eyes and scrabbling claws. *Get us out of here!* it cried, and I obliged, seizing my coat from the closet hook and stumbling out into the wind.

I ran in the direction of town, slowing only when one of my shoes fell off and I realized how I must look. Soon, I found myself seated at a table in a diner, warming my hands in the steam from a cup of coffee, trying to convince myself that I was just being silly. I nursed the coffee as long as I could. It was dusk by the time I felt able to return home. There I found the glass cat, still waiting for me.

I turned on the radio for company and made a fire in the fireplace. Then I sat down before the box and finished unpacking it. The sculpture was as horrible as I remembered, truly ugly and disquieting. I might never have understood why Father kept it if he had not enclosed this letter of explanation, neatly handwritten on his college stationery:

To whom it may concern:

This box contains a sculpture, *Cat in Glass*, designed and executed by the late Alexander Chelichev. Because of Chelichev's standing as a noted forerunner of Dadaism, an historical account of *Cat's* genesis may be of interest to scholars.

I purchased *Cat* from the artist himself at his Zürich loft in December, 1915, two months before the violent rampage which resulted in his confinement in a hospital for the criminally insane, and well before his artistic importance was widely recognized. (For the record, the asking price was forty-eight Swiss francs, plus a good meal with wine.) It is known that Chelichev had a wife and two children elsewhere in the city at that time, though he lived with them only sporadically. The following is the artist's statement about *Cat in Glass*, transcribed as accurately as possible from a conversation held with me during dinner.

"I have struggled with the devil all my life. He wants no rules. No order. His presence is everywhere in my work. I was beaten as a child, and when I became strong enough, I killed my father for it. I see you are skeptical, but it is true. Now I am a grown man and I find my father in myself. I have a wife and children, but I spend little time with them because I fear the father-devil in me. I do not beat my children. Instead I make this cat. Into the glass I have poured this madness of mine. Better there than in the eyes of my daughters."

It is my belief that *Cat in Glass* was Chelichev's last finished creation.

Sincerely,
Lawrence Waters
Professor of Art History

I closed the box, sealed it with the note inside, and spent the next two nights in a hotel, pacing the floor, sleeping little. The following Monday, Stephen took the cat to an art dealer for appraisal. He came home late that afternoon excited and full of news about the great Alexander Chelichev.

He made himself a gin and tonic as he expounded. "That glass cat is priceless, Amy. Did you realize? If your father had sold it, he'd have been independently wealthy. He never let on."

I was putting dinner on the table. The weekend had been a terrible strain. This had been a difficult day on top of it—snowy, and the children in my school class were wild with pent-up energy. So were our daughters, Eleanor and Rose, aged seven and four respectively. I could hear them quarreling in the play room down the hall.

"Well, I'm glad to hear the horrid thing is worth something," I said. "Why don't we sell it and hire a maid?"

Stephen laughed as if I'd made an incredibly good joke. "A maid? You could hire a thousand maids for what that cat would bring at auction. It's a fascinating piece with an extraordinary history. You know, the value of something like this will increase with time. I think we'll do well to keep it awhile."

My fingers grew suddenly icy on the hot rim of the potato bowl. "I wasn't trying to be funny, Stephen. It's ugly and disgusting. If I could, I would make it disappear from the face of the Earth."

He raised his eyebrows. "What's this? Rebellion? Look, if you really want a maid, I'll get you one."

"That's not the point. I won't have the damned thing in my house."

"I'd rather you didn't swear, Amelia. The children might hear."

"I don't care if they do."

The whole thing degenerated from there. I tried to explain the cat's connection with Delia's death. But Stephen had stopped listening by then. He sulked through dinner. Eleanor and Rose argued over who got which spoonful of peas. And I struggled with a steadily growing sense of dread that seemed much too large for the facts of the matter.

When dinner was over, Stephen announced with exaggerated brightness, "Girls. We'd like your help in deciding an important question."

"Oh goody," said Rose.

"What is it?" said Eleanor.

"Please don't," I said. It was all I could do to keep from shouting.

Stephen flashed me the boyish grin with which he had originally won my heart. "Oh, come on. Try to look at it objectively. You're just sensitive about this because of an irrational notion from your childhood. Let the girls be the judge. If they like it, why not keep it?"

I should have ended it there. I should have insisted. Hindsight is always perfect, as they say. But inside me a little seed of doubt had sprouted. Stephen was always so logical and so right, especially about financial matters. Maybe he was right about this, too.

He had brought the thing home from the appraiser without telling me. He was never above a little subterfuge if it got him his own way. Now he carried the carton in from the garage and unwrapped it in the middle of our warm, hardwood floor, with all the lights blazing. Nothing had changed. I found it as frightening as ever. I could feel cold sweat collecting on my forehead as I stared at it, all aglitter in a rainbow of refracted lamplight.

Eleanor was enthralled with it. She caught our real cat, a calico named Jelly, and held it up to the sculpture. "See, Jelly? You've got a handsome partner now." But Jelly twisted and hissed in Eleanor's arms until she let her go. Eleanor laughed and said Jelly was jealous.

Rose was almost as uncooperative as Jelly. She shrank away from the glass cat, peeking at it from between her father's knees. But Stephen would have none of that.

"Go on, Rose," he said. "It's just a kitty made of glass. Touch it and see." And he took her by the shoulders and pushed her gently toward it. She put out one hand, hesitantly, as she would have with a live cat who did not know her. I saw her finger touch a nodule of glass shards that might have been its nose. She drew back with a little yelp of pain. And that's how it began. So innocently.

"He bit me!" she cried.

"What happened?" said Stephen. "Did you break it?" He ran to the sculpture first, the brute, to make sure she hadn't damaged it.

She held her finger out to me. There was a tiny cut with a single drop of bright red blood oozing from it. "Mommy, it burns, it burns." She was no longer just crying. She was screaming.

We took her into the bathroom. Stephen held her while I washed the cut and pressed a cold cloth to it. The bleeding stopped in a moment, but still she screamed. Stephen grew angry. "What's this nonsense? It's a scratch.

Just a scratch."

Rose jerked and kicked and bellowed. In Stephen's defense, I tell you now it was a terrifying sight, and he was never able to deal well with real fear, especially in himself. He always tried to mask it with anger. We had a neighbor who was a physician. "If you don't stop it, Rose, I'll call Doctor Pepperman. Is that what you want?" he said, as if Doctor Pepperman, a jolly septuagenarian, were anything but charming and gentle, as if threats were anything but asinine at such a time.

"For God's sake, get Pepperman! Can't you see something's terribly wrong?" I said.

And for once he listened to me. He grabbed Eleanor by the arm. "Come with me," he said, and stomped across the yard through the snow without so much as a coat. I believe he only took Eleanor, also without a coat, because he was so unnerved that he didn't want to face the darkness alone.

Rose was still screaming when Dr. Pepperman arrived fresh from his dinner, specks of gravy clinging to his mustache. He examined Rose's finger, and looked mildly puzzled when he had finished. "Can't see much wrong here. I'd say it's mostly a case of hysteria." He took a vial and a syringe from his small, brown case and gave Rose an injection, "…to help settle her down," he said. It seemed to work. In a few minutes, Rose's screams had diminished to whimpers. Pepperman swabbed her finger with disinfectant and wrapped it loosely in gauze. "There, Rosie. Nothing like a bandage to make it feel better." He winked at us. "She should be fine in the morning. Take the gauze off as soon as she'll let you."

We put Rose to bed and sat with her till she fell asleep. Stephen unwrapped the gauze from her finger so the healing air could get to it. The cut was a bit red, but looked all right. Then we retired as well, reassured by the doctor, still mystified at Rose's reaction.

I awakened sometime after midnight. The house was muffled in the kind of silence brought by steady, soft snowfall. I thought I had heard a sound. Something odd. A scream? A groan? A snarl? Stephen still slept on the verge of a snore; whatever it was, it hadn't been loud enough to disturb him.

I crept out of bed and fumbled with my robe. There was a short flight of stairs between our room and the rooms where Rose and Eleanor slept. Eleanor, like her father, often snored at night and I could hear her from the hallway now, probably deep in dreams. Rose's room was silent.

I went in and switched on the night light. The bulb was very low wattage. I thought at first that the shadows were playing tricks on me. Rose's hand and arm looked black as a bruised banana. There was a peculiar odor in the air, like the smell of a butcher shop on a summer day. Heart galloping, I turned on the overhead light. Poor Rosie. She was so very still and clammy. And her arm was so very rotten.

They said Rose died from blood poisoning—a rare type most often associated with animal bites. I told them over and over again that it fit, that our child had indeed been bitten, by a cat, a most evil glass cat. Stephen was embarrassed. His own theory was that, far from blaming an apparently inanimate object, we ought to be suing Pepperman for malpractice. The doctors patted me sympathetically at first. Delusions brought on by grief, they said. It would pass. I would heal in time.

I made Stephen take the cat away. He said he would sell it, though in fact he lied to me. And we buried Rose. But I could not sleep. I paced the house each night, afraid to close my eyes because the cat was always there, glaring his satis-fied glare, and waiting for new meat. And in the daytime, everything reminded me of Rosie. Fingerprints on the woodwork, the contents of the kitchen draw-ers, her favorite foods on the shelves of grocery stores. I could not teach. Every child had Rosie's face and Rosie's voice. Stephen and Eleanor were first kind, then gruff, then angry.

One morning, I could find no reason to get dressed or to move from my place on the sofa. Stephen shouted at me, told me I was ridiculous, asked me if I had forgotten that I still had a daughter left who needed me. But, you see, I no longer believed that I or anyone else could make any difference in the world. Stephen and Eleanor would get along with or without me. I didn't matter. There was no God of order and cause. Only chaos, cruelty, and whim.

When it was clear to Stephen that his dear wife Amy had turned from an asset into a liability, he sent me to an institution, far away from everyone, where I could safely be forgotten. In time, I grew to like it there. I had no responsibilities at all. And if there was foulness and bedlam, it was no worse than the outside world.

There came a day, however, when they dressed me in a suit of new clothes and stood me outside the big glass and metal doors to wait; they didn't say for what. The air smelled good. It was springtime, and there were dandelions sprinkled like drops of fresh yellow paint across the lawn.

A car drove up and a pretty young woman got out and took me by the arm.

"Hello, Mother," she said as we drove off down the road. It was Eleanor, all grown up. For the first time since Rosie died, I wondered how long I had been away, and knew it must have been a very long while.

We drove a considerable distance, to a large suburban house, white, with a sprawling yard and a garage big enough for two cars. It was a mansion compared to the house in which Stephen and I had raised her. By way of making polite small talk, I asked if she were married, whether she had children. She climbed out of the car looking irritated. "Of course I'm married," she said. "You've met Jason. And you've seen pictures of Sarah and Elizabeth often enough." Of this I had no recollection.

She opened the gate in the picket fence and we started up the neat, stone walkway. The front door opened a few inches and small faces peered out. The door opened wider and two little girls ran onto the porch.

"Hello," I said. "And who are you?"

The older one, giggling behind her hand, said, "Don't you know, Grandma? I'm Sarah."

The younger girl stayed silent, staring at me with frank curiosity.

"That's Elizabeth. She's afraid of you," said Sarah.

I bent and looked into Elizabeth's eyes. They were brown, and her hair was shining blond, like Rosie's. "No need to be afraid of me, my dear. I'm just a harmless old woman."

Elizabeth frowned. "Are you crazy?" she asked.

Sarah giggled behind her hand again, and Eleanor breathed loudly through her nose as if this impertinence were simply overwhelming.

I smiled. I liked Elizabeth. Liked her very much. "They say I am," I said, "and it may very well be true."

A tiny smile crossed her face. She stretched on her tiptoes and kissed my cheek, hardly more than the touch of a warm breeze, then turned and ran away. Sarah followed her, and I watched them go, my heart dancing and shivering. I had loved no one in a very long time. I missed it, but dreaded it, too. For I had loved Delia and Rosie, and they were both dead.

The first thing I saw when I entered the house was Chelichev's *Cat in Glass*, glaring evilly from a place of obvious honor on a low pedestal near the sofa. My stomach felt suddenly shrunken.

"Where did you get that?" I said.

Eleanor looked irritated again. "From Daddy, of course."

"Stephen promised me he would sell it!"

"Well, I guess he didn't, did he?"

Anger heightened my pulse. "Where is he? I want to speak to him immediately."

"Mother, don't be absurd. He's been dead for ten years."

I lowered myself into a chair. I was shaking by then, and I fancied I saw a half-smile on the glass cat's cold jowls.

"Get me out of here," I said. A great weight crushed my lungs. I could barely breathe.

With a look, I must say, of genuine worry, Eleanor escorted me onto the porch and brought me a tumbler of ice water. "Better?" she asked.

I breathed deeply. "A little. Eleanor, don't you realize that monstrosity killed your sister, and mine as well?"

"That simply isn't true."

"But it is, it is! I'm telling you now, get rid of it if you care for the lives of your children."

Eleanor went pale, whether from rage or fear I could not tell. "It isn't yours. You're legally incompetent, and I'll thank you to stay out of my affairs as much as possible till you have a place of your own. I'll move you to an apartment as soon as I can find one."

"An apartment? But I can't…"

"Yes you can. You're as well as you're ever going to be, Mother. You only liked that hospital because it was easy. Well it costs a lot of money to keep you there, and we can't afford it anymore. You're just going to have to straighten up and start behaving like a human being again."

By then I was very close to tears, and very confused as well. Only one thing was clear to me, and that was the true nature of the glass cat. I said, in as steady a voice as I could muster, "Listen to me. That cat was made out of madness. It's evil. If you have a single ounce of brains, you'll put it up for auction this very afternoon."

"So I can get enough money to send you back to the hospital, I suppose? Well I won't do it. That sculpture is priceless. The longer we keep it, the more it's worth."

She had Stephen's financial mind. I would never sway her, and I knew it. I wept in despair, hiding my face in my hands. I was thinking of Elizabeth. The sweet, soft skin of her little arms, the flame in her cheeks, the power of that small kiss. Human beings are such frail works of art, their lives so precarious, and here I was again, my wayward heart gone out to one of them. But the road back to the safety of isolation lay in ruins. The only way out was through.

Jason came home at dinner time and we ate a nice meal, seated around the sleek rosewood table in the dining room. He was kind, actually far kinder than Eleanor. He asked the children about their day and listened carefully while they replied. As did I, enraptured by their pink perfection, distraught at the memory of how imperfect a child's flesh can become. He did not interrupt. He did not demand. When Eleanor refused to give me coffee—she said she was afraid it would get me "hyped up"—he admonished her and poured me a cup himself. We talked about my father, whom he knew by reputation, and about art and the cities of Europe. All the while, I felt in my bones the baleful gaze of the *Cat in Glass*, burning like the coldest ice through walls and furniture as if they did not exist.

Eleanor made up a cot for me in the guest room. She didn't want me to sleep in the bed, and she wouldn't tell me why. But I overheard Jason arguing with her about it. "What's wrong with the bed?" he said.

"She's mentally ill," said Eleanor. She was whispering, but loudly. "Heaven only knows what filthy habits she's picked up. I won't risk her soiling a perfectly good mattress. If she does well on the cot for a few nights, then we can consider moving her to the bed."

They thought I was in the bathroom, performing whatever unspeakable acts it is that mentally ill people perform in places like that, I suppose. But they were wrong. I was sneaking past their door, on my way to the garage. Jason must have been quite a handyman in his spare time. I found a large selection of hammers on the wall, including an excellent short-handled sledge. I hid it under my bedding. They never even noticed.

The children came in and kissed me good night in a surreal reversal of roles. I lay in the dark on my cot for a long time, thinking of them, especially of Elizabeth, the youngest and weakest, who would naturally be the most likely target of an animal's attack. I dozed, dreaming sometimes of a smiling Elizabeth-Rose-Delia, sifting snow, wading through drifts; sometimes of the glass cat, its fierce eyes smoldering, crystalline tongue brushing crystalline jaws. The night was well along when the dreams crashed down like broken mirrors into silence.

The house was quiet except for those ticks and thumps all houses make as they cool in the darkness. I got up and slid the hammer out from under the bedding, not even sure what I was going to do with it, knowing only that the time had come to act.

I crept out to the front room, where the cat sat waiting, as I knew it must. Moonlight gleamed in the chaos of its glass fur. I could feel its power, almost *see* it, a shimmering red aura the length of its malformed spine. The thing was moving, slowly, slowly, smiling now, oh yes, a real smile. I could smell its rotten breath.

For an instant, I was frozen. Then I remembered the hammer, Jason's lovely short-handled sledge. And I raised it over my head, and brought it down in the first crashing blow.

The sound was wonderful. Better than cymbals, better even than holy trumpets. I was trembling all over, but I went on and on in an agony of satisfaction while glass fell like moonlit rain. There were screams. "Grandma, stop! Stop!" I swung the hammer back in the first part of another arc, heard something like the thunk of a fallen ripe melon, swung it down on the cat again. I couldn't see anymore. It came to me that there was glass in my eyes and blood in my mouth. But none of that mattered, a small price to pay for the long overdue demise of Chelichev's *Cat in Glass*.

So you see how I have come to this, not without many sacrifices along the way. And now the last of all: the sockets where my eyes used to be are infected. They stink. Blood poisoning, I'm sure.

I wouldn't expect Eleanor to forgive me for ruining her prime investment. But I hoped Jason might bring the children a time or two anyway. No word except for the delivery of a single rose yesterday. The matron said it was white, and held it up for me to sniff and she read me the card that came with it. "Elizabeth was a great one for forgiving. She would have wanted you to have this. Sleep well, Jason."

Which puzzled me.

"You don't even know what you've done, do you?" said the matron.

"I destroyed a valuable work of art," said I.

But she made no reply.

COYOTE PEYOTE
Carole Nelson Douglas

Award-winning ex-journalist Carole Nelson Douglas's fifty-four multi-genre novels often blend mystery and fantasy elements. Douglas also writes the Delilah Street, Paranormal Investigator, urban noir fantasies and was the first author to use a Sherlockian female, diva Irene Adler, as a series protagonist in the *New York Times* Notable Book of the Year, *Good Night, Mr. Holmes*. Douglas's short fiction has appeared in several *Year's Best* mystery anthologies. See www.carolenelsondouglas.com for more information.

Midnight Louie, feline PI, literary lion, and "Sam Spade with hairballs," has partially narrated twenty-six of her novels, most recently in *Cat in a Topaz Tango*. Douglas first gave voice to the actual Louie, a koi-snagging stray rescued from an upscale Palo Alto motel, in a newspaper feature.

CHAPTER 1
HEAD HONCHO

A lot of folks don't realize that Las Vegas is the world's biggest Cubic Zirconia set in a vast bezel of sand and sagebrush. Glitz in the Gobi, so to speak.

Sure, most everybody knows that the old town twinkles, but that is all they see, the high-wattage Las Vegas Strip and Glitter Gulch downtown. Millions of annual visitors fly in and out on the big silver Thunderbirds, commercial or chartered jets, like migratory flocks of junketing gooney birds equipped with cameras and cash.

They land at McCarran Airport, now as glittering a monument to the Vegas mystique as any Strip Hotel, with shining rows of slot machines chiming in its metal-mirrored vastness.

Most stick to Las Vegas's advertised attractions and distractions: they soak up sun, stage shows, shady doings of a sexual nature and the comparatively good clean fun in the casinos that pave the place. To them, Las Vegas is the holodeck of the Good Space Ship Enterprise in the twentieth century. You go there; it is like no place on earth; you leave and you're right back where you were, maybe poorer but at least dazzled for your dough.

Nobody thinks of Las Vegas as a huge, artificial oasis stuck smack wattle-and-daub in the middle of the Wild West wilderness like a diamond in the navel of a desert dancing girl. Nobody sees its gaudy glory as squatting on the one-time ghost-dancing grounds of the southern Paiute Indians. Hardly anyone ever harks back to the area's hairy mining boom days, which are only evoked now by hokey casino names like the Golden Nugget.

Nobody ever figures that the sea of desert all around the pleasure island of Las Vegas is good for anything but ignoring.

I must admit that I agree. I know Las Vegas from the bottom up, and some in this urban jukebox know me: Midnight Louie, dude-about-town and undercover expert. The only sand I like to feel between my toes is in a litter box, and I am not too fond of artificial indoor facilities at that. I prefer open air and good, clean dirt.

I prefer other amenities, such as the gilded carp that school in the decorative pond behind the Crystal Phoenix Hotel and Casino, the classiest hostelry on the Strip, hence carp so pricey that they are called koi. I call them dinner.

For a time I was unofficial house detective at the Crystal Phoenix and the carp pond was my prime-time hangout. It is always handy to locate an office near a good diner. Location, location, location, say the real estate agents, and I am always open to an apt suggestion from an expert.

I hang out my shingle near the canna lilies that border the carp pond. I do not literally hang out a shingle, you understand. The word simply gets around where Midnight Louie is to be found, and the word on the street is clear on two subjects. One is that Midnight Louie will not look with favor upon any individual messing with his friends at the Crystal Phoenix, whether two- or four-footed. The other is that Midnight Louie is not averse to handling problems of a delicate nature now and again, provided payment is prompt and sufficient.

I am no lightweight, topping twenty pounds soaking wet, and I didn't weigh onto the scales just yesterday either. Yet my hair is still a glossy raven black, my tourmaline-green eyes can see 20/20, and my ears know when to perk up and when to lie back and broadcast a warning. (Some claim my kind have no color sense, but they have never asked us straight out.) I keep my coat in impeccable sheen and my hidden shivs as sharp as the crease in Macho Mario Fontana's bodyguard's pants.

Despite my awesome physical presence, I am a modest dude who gets along well with everyone—especially if every one of them is female—except for those of the canine persuasion.

This is a family failing. Something about the canine personality invariably raises the hair on the back of our necks, not to mention our spines, and makes our second-most-valuable members stand up and salute.

So you can understand how I feel one day when I am drowsing in my office, due both to a lack of cases and a surfeit of something fishy for lunch, and I spot a suspicious shadow on the nearest sun-rinsed wall.

The hour is past six p.m., when Las Vegas hotel pools close faster than a shark's mouth, the better to hustle tourists into the casinos to gamble the night and their grubstakes away. Nobody much of any species is around. Even the carp are keeping low, for reasons which may have something to do with not-so-little me.

So my eyes are slit to half-mast, the sinking sun is sifting through the canna lilies and life is not too tacky... and then, there it is, that unwelcome shadow.

Who could mistake the long, sharp snout, ajar enough to flaunt a nasty serrated edge of fangs, or the huge, long, sharp ears? No doubt about it, this angular silhouette has the avid, hungry outlines of that jackal-headed Egyptian god of the dead, Anubis. (I know something about Egyptian gods, seeing as how a forebear was one of them: Bast. You may have heard of this dude. Or dudette. And you may call me Louie anyway; I do not ride on family connections.)

Right then and there Midnight Louie has a bad hair day, let me tell you, as I make like a croquet hoop and rise to my feet and the occasion. From the size of the shadow, this is not the largest canine I have ever seen, but it is one serious customer, and it does not take a house detective to figure that out.

"At ease!" the shadow jaws bark out, looking even more lethal. "I am just here on business."

I know better than to relax when told to, but I am not one to turn tail and run, either. So I wait.

"You this Midnight Louie?" my sun-shy visitor demands in the same sharp yet gruff voice.

"Who wishes to know?"

"Never mind."

So much for the direct route. I pretend to settle back onto my haunches, but my restless shivs slide silently in and out of my mitts. Unlike the average mutt, I know how to keep quiet.

Above me, a lazy bee buzzes the big yellow canna lily blossoms. I hiccough.

"You do not look like much," my rude visitor says after a bit.

"The opinion may be mutual," I growl back. "Step into the open and we will see."

He does, and I am sorry I asked.

There is no fooling myself. I eye narrow legs with long, curved nails like a mandarin's. I take in eyes as yellow and hard as a bladder stone. The head is even more predatory than I suspected. The body is lean, but hard. The terminal member is as scrawny as a foot-long hot dog and carried low, like a whip.

This dude is a dog, all right, but just barely; no mere domesticated dog, but a dingo from the desert. I begin to appreciate how Little Red Riding Hood felt, and I do not even have a grandmother (that I know of) to worry about.

"What can I do for you?" I ask, hoping that the answer is not "Lunch." I do not do lunch with literal predators.

The dude sidles into the shade alongside me. My sniffer almost overdoses on the odor; this bozo has not taken a bath in at least a week, perhaps another reason I dislike the canine type.

He sits beside me under the canna leaves, his yellow eyes searching the vicinity for any sign of life.

"I need a favor," he says.

Well, knock me over with a wolverine. I am all too aware that the dude I am dealing with is normally a breed apart. He and his kind operate on the fringes of civilized Las Vegas, out in the lawless open desert. Some call them cowardly; others, clever. Certainly they are hated, and hunted. Many are killed. All kill. Among other things.

"I do not do favors for those who practice certain unnatural acts."

"Such as?"

"I hear you and your kin will eat... bugs."

"So will humans," the dude notes calmly.

"That is not all. I also hear that your kind will dine on—" I swallow and try not to let my whiskers quiver—"the dead." Why else was Anubis head jackal of the Underground in ancient Egypt? My visitor looks like a lineal descendant.

"We will, when there is nothing living to eat," he concedes with chilling calm. "In the city, such as we are called refuse managers."

I say nothing, unconvinced.

When sitting this dude looks exactly like an Egyptian statue, and he gazes idly on the lush, landscaped surroundings so different from his usual arid turf. I realize that it has taken some nerve and a good deal of courage for this popular pariah to venture into the very heart of Vegas. Just to see me. Well, Midnight Louie is a teensy bit flattered, come to think of it.

"When did you last," he asks, "partake of a bit of mislaid Big-o-Burger from down the street?"

"That is different," I begin.

"Dead meat," he intones relentlessly. "Someone else killed it, and you ate it." The yellow eyes slide my way. I detect a malicious twinkle. "What about the contents of the cans so feverishly hawked at your kind?"

I am not misled; this dude is about as twinkly as the mother-of-pearl handle on a derringer.

"I do my own fishing." I nod at the silent pond. "So what is your problem?"

"Murder." His answer sends a petite shudder through my considerable frame. I was hoping for something minor, like roadrunner attack.

"Who is the victim?"

"Victims."

"How many?

"Six, so far."

"And the method?"

"Always the same."

"You are talking serial killer here, pal."

"Oh, are we friends?" Another shrewd golden glint. This dude has Bette Davis eyes... when she played the homicidal Baby Jane.

"Business associates," I say firmly. No dude in his right mind would turn down this character.

"Who are the victims?"

"My brothers and sisters."

"Oh."

I do not know how to put it that one—or six—dead coyotes are hardly considered murder victims by the majority of the human population, and, face it, humans run this planet.

For now I know this dude, by type if not name: Don Coyote himself, one of an accursed species, with bounty hunters everywhere ready to clip their ears and tails for a few bucks or just the principal of the thing. It does not take a genius to figure out that any suspects for the so-called crime of killing coyotes are legion.

"If you are so smart," I note diplomatically, "you know that it would be easier to find those who did not kill coyotes than otherwise."

"This case is different," he says sharply. "We are used to the hunters. We have outwitted them more often than not. We survive, if not thrive, and we spread, even while our cousin Gray Wolf clan has been driven to near extinction. We have evaded steel trap and strychnine poison. We are legendary for defying odds. What kills us now is new and insidious. Not just our green young succumb, but those who should know better. This is not the eternal war we wage with both prey and hunter; this is what I said… murder."

"That is no surprise, either. You are not exactly Mr. Popularity around here."

His lips peel back from spectacular sharp white teeth much improved, no doubt, by grinding such roughage as beetle shells and bones. "That is why I seek an emissary."

"Why not try a police dog?"

"Frankly, your kind is more successful at undercover work. Even a domesticated dog"—his tone is more than condescending, it is majestically indifferent; on this subject we agree—"is handicapped. He is assumed to belong to some human, which attracts notice and sometimes misguided attempts at rescue. Your breed, on the other hand, although equally commonplace in human haunts, is known to walk alone by sly and secret ways and is more often ignored."

I shrug and adjust one of my sharp-looking black leather gloves. "Say I was to accept this commission of yours. What would I get?"

His long red tongue lolls out. I cannot tell if he is grinning or scanning the ground for a Conga-line of ants. Antipasto in his book, so to speak.

"I am head honcho around this turf," the coyote ruminates with a certain reluctance, like he is giving away the combination to the family safe. "I keep caches of hidden treasure here and there. If you successfully find—or simply stop—the coyote-killer, I will tell you the whereabouts of one. That would be your payoff."

"How much is it worth?" I demand.

The yellow eyes look right through me. "Beyond price."

"How do I know that?"

"I can only say that humans highly prize these objects."

Hmmm. Coyotes are scavengers of the desert. I speculate on the array of inedible goodies they might run across in the wide Mojave, but silver comes first to mind, perhaps because Jersey Joe Jackson, the high-roller who helped build and bilk Vegas in the Forties, also hid huge caches of stolen silver dollars both in town and out on the sandy lonesome.

Then there are plain old silver nuggets left over from mining days. I am not fussy. Or… maybe jewels. Stolen jewels. I do not doubt for a minute that this wily old dude knows secrets even the wind-singing sands do not whisper about.

I stand and stretch nonchalantly. "Where do I begin?" For a moment I am eye to eye with those ancient, ocher orbs.

Then the dude also rises, and vanishes into the dark at the back of the canna lilies. "Follow me to the scene of the crimes."

CHAPTER 2
HOT TO TROT

It is night by the time we get there. I have forgotten that dudes of this type are always hot to trot and can keep it up for miles. After I showed him a quick exit from the city, we were off through the boonies.

Miles of surly sagebrush have passed under my tender tootsie pads when we finally stop for good. I huff and puff and could not blow down a mouse house at the moment, but I was loath to let this dancing dog outpace me.

Although I pride myself on my night vision, all I can spy are a skyful of stars the wizards of the Strip might do well to emulate for sparse good taste, towering Joshua trees with their thick limbs frozen into traffic-cop positions, and a lot of low scrub, much of it barbed like wire. Oh, yes, and the full moon floating overhead like a bowl of warm milk seen from a kitchen countertop, and, occasionally, the moon-sheen in the coyote's sun-yellow eyes as he gives me mocking glances.

"I forget," he says, "that the city-bred are easily tired."

"Not in the slightest," I pant, hissing between my teeth. "But how can I study the crime scene in the dark?"

"I thought your breed could see despite the night."

"Not enough for a thorough investigation. Where are we anyway?"

"At an enclave of humans away from the city. My unfortunate brothers and sisters ventured near to snag the errant morsel and were cut down one by one."

"Listen, my kind are not noted for longevity either, so I dig the problem. Still, what can I do about it?"

"Perhaps you can interview the survivors."

With that he steps back, braces his long legs, and lifts his head until his snout points at the moon. An unearthly howl punctuated by a series of yips emerges from between those awesome teeth.

So it is that in a few moments I am making house calls on a series of coyote families. While my guide has not stuck around for the painstaking interviews, soon an unsavory picture is emerging: the victims were indeed primo survivors, too savvy to be silently slain in the current manner.

I speak to Sings-with-Soul, the winsome widow of Yellow Foot-Feathers, the first to be found dead.

I no more advocate cross-species hanky-panky than I do bug-biting, but I must admit that Sings-with-Soul has particularly luminous amber eyes and a dainty turn of foreleg, from what I can tell in the dark.

After several interviews, I remain in the dark myself. Unfortunately, although they sometimes run in impressive packs, coyotes mostly hunt alone. The stories are depressingly similar.

Yellow Foot-Feathers did not return to the den after a night's prowl. When Sings-with-Soul left her kits with a friend to go searching, she followed his scent to find him dead, unmarked by any weapon, beside a stunted Joshua tree.

Sand Stalker was out rounding up a delicacy or two for his mate, Moonfinder, and their two helpless kits. In the morning, his body was found a three-minute trot toward the setting sun from Yellow Foot-Feathers'.

Windswift, a two-year-old female, died a four-minute trot away two days later. The same distance further on lay Weatherworn, an elder of the tribe and by far its wiliest member.

"We are used to the high death toll of our kind," Sings-with-Soul tells me with mournful anger, "but these deaths are systematic beyond the bounty hunters' traps and poison, or the so-called sportsmen with guns, or even the angry ranchers who accuse us of raiding their livestock."

I nod. It is not a pretty picture, and I am used to the statistics of my own kind who share the supposed shelter of civilization. Four out of five cuddly kittens born die within a year, often within the environs of a death compound. Still, there is something demonic about these serial slayings. Even in the dark I sense a pattern.

By the wee hours I have settled beside a Prickly Poppy, counting on my choice of plant companion to keep away such night-roving characters as skunks, large furry spiders who are older than Whistler's mother, lizards and snakes, although I would not mind meeting a passing mouse or two, for it has been some time since my last snack.

The coyotes have vanished back into the brush. From time to time they break into heartbroken howls that some might take for the usual coyote chorus, but which I know express rage and sorrow at their helplessness to stop the slaughter.

I wait for daylight, eager to begin investigating for real. My curiosity has been roused, despite myself. As long as I am all the way out here in this desolate wilderness, I might as well earn my tempting coyote cache and maybe keep the young Foot-Feathers kits from the same fate as their father.

Despite the desert chill and forbidding terrain, I manage to doze off. I awake to feel the sun pouring down on me like hot, melted butter, softening my night-stiff bones.

I hear an odd tapping sound, as of someone gently rapping, rapping on a door to rouse me. Confused, I force my eyelids open, preparing for an onslaught of bright light.

In the sudden slit of my pupils I see a sight to curl the hair on a bronze cat—a whole city, a settlement, of buildings against the blatant blue morning sky. I sniff sawdust and stucco. I see pale pine skeletons rising into the sky.

I turn so fast I snag my rear member on a Prickly Poppy. Behind me extends the endless desert I imagined in the dark of last night when I interviewed the coyote crew. Did not their lost ones fall near where we stood, where I stand now?

I turn back to the hub of activity. A banshee saw whines while men with bandannas around their foreheads and sleeveless t-shirts or bare muscled chests as tan as a Doberman move their blue-jeaned legs hither and yon, climbing, pounding, clamoring.

Stunned, I stick to basics. A three-minute trot toward the setting sun. I turn westward and start trotting, allowing for a difference in speed and stride. Indeed, I am soon sniffing a patch of sweet-smelling desert alyssum on which a stronger, sweeter, sicklier scent has settled recently.

The body is gone, no doubt removed by human pallbearers, but the land remembers. Sand Stalker's last stand.

I move on, tracing the path of death and finding the lingering scent where I expect. At no time does my route veer away from the huge clot of buildings under construction. The dead coyotes begin to form a ritual circle around the project, like guardian spirits slaughtered to protect the site.

The head coyote is right. Something stinks in this sequence of events, and it is not merely death.

CHAPTER 3
PEYOTE SKIES

I dust off my topcoat, quell my protesting empty stomach, and stalk casually toward the humans and their works.

Soon I am treading dusty asphalt, walking on roads, however primitive. Beyond the construction site I discover curving vistas of completed edifices—sprawling, two-story buildings big enough to be strip shopping centers, sitting amid fresh-sodded grass. Sprinkler systems spray droplets on the turf like a holy water blessing. After a while I realize that these erections are each single-family homes.

In an hour's stroll I have mastered the place. I am in the midst of Henderson, Nevada, touring its vaunted housing boom. I have heard that this bedroom community just a hop, skip and a commute southeast of Las Vegas was jumping, but never had occasion to see for myself before.

No wonder the coyotes are goners. They were trespassing on some high-end new real estate of the first water. I sit under one of the paired yucca trees that mark the development's entrance to read the billboard, which features colors like trendy turquoise, orange and lavender bordered in a chorus line of alternating jalapeño peppers and howling coyotes.

"Peyote Skies: A Jimmy Ray Ruggles Planned Community" announces angular lettering meant to resemble the zigzags on a Native American blanket. Jimmy Ray's smiling photo discreetly anchors one corner of the sign. Although it is a well-kept secret that I can read, I am having no trouble in looking illiterate as I squint to decipher the tortured script. This is real detective work!

After much study, I know that Peyote Skies is an ecologically engineered environment that imposes no artificial barriers like fences between nature and the community. The words "Sante Fe-like serenity," "untrammeled nature" and "all the amenities" are invoked. No wonder. I have heard that refugees from the Quaker State of California are flocking to places north, south and west of their unhappy home. Apparently, Henderson is providing a haven for escaping excesses.

I stroll the streets of Peyote Skies unquestioned, even unremarked, just as the coyote predicted. Perhaps my dramatic dark good looks seem right at home with the plethora of pastel colors painting every visible surface. Despite my empty stomach, I am soon ready to puke at the amount of dusty orange, lavender and Peyote-Skies turquoise I am forced to digest.

Earlier I had remarked that I was not born yesterday. I am also pretty street-wise, so I know that "peyote" names a blue-green cactus whose flowers produce beads that dry into little buttons of "mescal." Bite into one of these babies and you are soon seeing visions as hallucinatory as the after-dinner mint-colored development before me.

Mescaline's mind-tripping properties were, and are, used for Native American religious rites, but otherwise are strictly illegal. I do not know if the Paiutes around here were, or are, into mescaline, but I do know that less Native Americans definitely are.

As for myself, I take a little nip now and again, but keep off the hard stuff in any form. Obviously, the designer of this mishmash was not so restrained.

The completed houses are occupied but mostly deserted, looking like pages from decorating magazines. Kids are at school, husbands and wives are at work or at play.

I find it macabre that while dead coyotes litter the back fringes of this theme-park development, the front doors and mailboxes bear the colorful image of the howling coyote made ad nauseam familiar of late on jewelry, coffee mugs and fabrics.

Perhaps the surrounding color scheme accounts for the en masse howling, but, like the desert itself, these coyotes are silent, despite their posture. I do not blame them for complaining; my own kind's image has been appropriated for a panoply of merchandise we would not scrape kitty litter over. Humans are especially sentimental about creatures they kill.

Because of the lack of "artificial barriers," I can stroll around these palatial joints unimpeded, although I spot a ton of security service signs and even more discreet warning labels on windows.

The back yards are as manicured as the front, then end abruptly where the desert begins. I move to the verge between green and griege, my sand-blasted pads relishing the cushy carpet of grass. Then a door cracks behind me. I turn to stare. Something small, blond and fluffy is flouncing toward me over the green, barking. I glance to the house across sixty yards of crew-cut Bermuda. It is so distant that Fideaux's high, affected yips are beyond earshot, but I believe I hear a frantic human voice fruitlessly urging the little escapee homeward.

So I show my teeth and hold my place until Fideaux is within pouncing distance. It stops to tilt a head as adorably curly-topped as Shirley Temple's. It sits on its little hind end. It drops its tiny jaw. The big, bad, black pussycat is supposed to be scrambling up a tree or over a fence, but there are only Joshua trees here and they sting like hell, and there is no fence, just desert and the Great Sandy Beyond.

Fideaux's irritating yaps become a whimper.

"You," I tell it savagely, "are coyote meat."

I turn and stroll onto the sand—ouch! Still, it is a dramatic exit. I glance back to see Blondie barreling back to the rambling deck, whimpering for Mommy.

Then I ramble myself, out front to civilization, where I finally hitch a ride on a landscaping truck back to Vegas proper. (Or improper.)

I cannot decide which I am happier to escape: the sere, sharp-fanged desert of cactus and coyote, or the rotted-fruit shades of the faux-Southwest landscape at Peyote Skies.

CHAPTER 4
GHOST SUITE

After taking a dip in the carp pool, I avoid the vicinity and any new visits by strange dudes with odd-colored eyes by heading for a secret retreat of mine. Now that I have scouted the situation, I am ready to do some deep thinking.

Luckily, I know just the place: the ghost suite at the Crystal Phoenix. This is room 711, which used to be a permanent residence for Jersey Joe Jackson back in the Forties, when the Crystal Phoenix was called the Joshua Tree Hotel. Jersey Joe didn't die until the seventies, by which time he was reputed to be a broke and broken man—and worse, completely forgotten.

The empty suite stands furnished as when he died, partly because the current management recognized it as a snapshot of an earlier era that should not be destroyed, partly because certain parties claim to have seen a thin, silver-haired dude dancing through the crack in the door now and again.

I have spent many unmolested hours here in recent years. While I may have glimpsed an odd slash of light through the wooden blinds, I cannot say yea or nay to the notion of a ghost. No one bothers me here, but I have never found the door locked to my velvet touch.

I settle on my favorite seat, a chartreuse-green satin chair that happens to make a stunning backdrop for one of my coloring. I do my best thinking when I look particularly impressive, although I am often accused of simply sleeping at such times.

The silence is as potent as Napoleonic brandy (not that I have ever sampled such a delicacy, but I do have imagination). While I lap it up, my eyes closed and my claws kneading the chartreuse satin, certain surly facts darken my mind.

First, how. The lack of marks upon the bodies suggests poison. The victims' wary familiarly with strychnine, the poison of choice for coyote hunters, suggests another toxin. I do not rule out snakebite. It is possible that the hustle and bustle of Peyote Skies has disturbed nests of venomous critters and driven them to the boundaries of the development, which would explain the neat alignment of the bodies.

Snake bite, however, usually results in swollen limbs, and the survivors detected nothing of the sort.

All right. Say the perpetrator is the usual snake of the human sort. Say some other poison was used that would take in the wiliest coyote.

Why? What is the motive? It cannot be for pelts, because the animals were left where they fell. It cannot be the ancient antipathy of sheep ranchers toward the ignoble coyote, because you can bet that the surrounding land, however vacant at the moment, is all owned by developers like the creators of Peyote Skies. Developments multiply around each other like fire ant mounds, gulping up huge tracts of land.

Round and round I go, mentally retracing the semi-circular path of the coyote corpses, my eyes always upon the grotesque hub of housing hubris and hullabaloo whose boundaries are marked with death.

My contact coyote, who was oddly shy about giving his name, no doubt due to a criminal past, said that nearby families have been warned to avoid the area. However, no number of nightly howls will warn off passers-by, given the wide range of the average desert dog.

More coyotes could die, not that anybody much would notice, any more than anyone has much noted the current crop of dead coyotes. But I have no personal grudge against Don Coyote, and I do have a deep desire to get a piece of a coyote cache.

Odious as the notion is, I must return to the crime scene—and Peyote Skies—and set up a stakeout. Maybe I can talk Sings-with-Soul into leaving her kits with a sitter and keeping me some feminine company. An ace detective can always use a leggy secretary for dramatic effect.

CHAPTER 5
PUPPY BUSINESS

It is no dice on the dame, but I do get the loan of Happy Hocks, a half-grown pup with time on his tail. The head coyote himself is nowhere to be seen. I hope he does not pull this vanishing act when it is time to reward Midnight Louie for successfully concluding the investigation. After being forced to hop a ride on a gravel truck to get to the site, I am not in a good mood.

"Keep down and out of sight when I say so," I instruct the gangly youngster.

"Yes, sir, Mr. Midnight. I want to be a famous crime solver like you when I grow up. I will be as quiet as a cactus."

I doubt it. There is too much vinegaroon in this punk.

We work our way closer to the settlement, Happy Hocks bounding hither and thither among the brush and occasionally running out whimpering to rub his snout in the sand.

"Cat Claw," I diagnose as I survey the particular cactus patch he has just learned to leave alone. "Did not some elder tell you about those spines?"

"Naw, we have to learn some things on our own, Mr. Midnight." Happy sneezes and then grins idiotically.

"Well, stay out of the flora and stick close to me. You might learn something really useful."

He bounds over and keeps me pretty tight company, close enough so I can see him lower his nosy snout to the sand again, snuffle and come up smacking an unidentified insect. It is a good thing I skipped breakfast or I might have lost it right there. I am far from squeamish about the unadorned facts of life, since I have eaten a lot of meals raw in my time, but I draw the line at insects.

I can see that it will be a long day, but as we creep on our bellies toward the completed houses, plain awe quashes a lot of Happy Hocks's more annoying qualities.

"What are these painted canyons, Mr. Midnight?" he asks.

I appreciate a suitably humble tone of address. "Houses, Happy. Modernistic mansions for idle humans with tons of money and a *soup's-on* of social conscience." (I like to expose the young to a little French.)

"Dens, Mr. Midnight?"

"Right. Dens... and exercise rooms and wet bars and state-of-the-art kitchens."

Happy frowns at my laundry list of amenities, being a country boy, but grins again. "Dens. Are there kits inside?"

"Sure. Little kits and big kits."

He frowns again. "Is that green that surrounds the dens some fancy water, for safety?"

"No, my lad. That is a moat of the finest Bermuda grass imported to cushion the humans' bare feet and clipped to permit a few practice golf balls."

"It grows, and they cut it?"

"Strange behavior, I know."

"Can I walk on it?"

I eye the house before us, which is not the one that hosts the obnoxious Fideaux. "I guess it is okay, kid. Just here at the edge, though."

So he trots along the sharp demarcation line between desert and cushy carpet of grass, his long legs pumping on the Bermuda.

"It is cool and soft," he says with another grin.

"But not for you." I gesture him back on the sand with me. If anyone is going to patrol on the emerald plush, it will be the senior member of this team.

Happy Hocks gives a yip only slightly less annoying than Fideaux's and forgets himself enough to bound over to a clump of beaver-tail cactus.

"Watch those spines!" I warn again, beginning to sound like a nanny.

"Look, Mr. Midnight, bonanza!"

I trot over, hoping for a clue. Is it possible the amiable idiot could have stumbled across something important?

I spot a bright patch of tissue-paper on the ground. Orange. Then my less lengthy nose finally catches a whiff of what roped Happy's attention. The paper is a Big-o-Burger wrapper. Nestled at its center is a nice bit of bun, burger and exclusive Big-o-Burger Better Barbe-Q Sauce, which I have been known to sample myself.

Happy politely steps back from his find. "You can have it, Mr. Midnight."

Do I detect a glint of hero-worship in those bright yellow eyes? Certainly it is unheard of for a coyote to share with a dude of another species, and usually even with his own.

My nose tells me that the Better Barbe-Q Sauce is permeating a thick slab of meat, which is cooked but is also indubitably dead. I am about to partake when I recall my conversation with the head coyote about superior species spurning dead meat. I cannot go back on my avowed position, at least not within witnessing distance by any of the coyote clan, so I shake a mitt and mince back from the find.

"Go ahead, kid. I prefer sushi."

"Fish!" he says in disgust, wrinkling his long nose. Happy Hocks nails the remaining Big-o-Burger with one bite.

We continue our rounds, observing the activity. Happy Hocks is full of wonder at the ways of humans. I know their ways and am watching for any that are out-of-the-ordinary.

Not much happens here. Any kids too young to be in school are kept in from the heat and nearby construction dangers. I see faces of my kind peering out from windows, never looking as downcast as I would expect at their imprisoned lot.

Except for the escaping Fideaux, I do not spy any dogs, no loss to me personally, except that this breed must go out, whether free or on lines, to do their disgusting duty. Imagine, leaving such unwanted items in plain view for someone else to pick up and bury! Such vile habits explain why the canine family occupies a lower rung of the evolutionary ladder than the feline.

I express my disdain to Happy, who frowns again.

"But Mr. Midnight, if we of coyote clan were to bury our water and dung we would not know where we had been, or who had been there first. We would have no way to mark territory."

"Who would want such tainted territory?" I mutter.

CHAPTER 6
DESERT ASYLUM

But I get to thinking. Maybe this whole case *is* a matter of marking territory.

In a couple of hours I have toured as much of Peyote Skies as I can stand. I have also had enough of Happy Hocks' prattle. I send the kid home, watching his yellow coat blend instantly with the dung-shaded desert. Our discussion of bathroom habits has definitely colored my outlook.

With relief, I take up a lone outpost under a newly planted oleander bush—no seedlings for these Peyote Skies folks, only expensive full-grown plantings.

Three houses down, workmen hammer, saw and shout. Here all is peaceful. Too peaceful. Although I welcome a world without dogs, I am uneasy at the absence of these popular house pets in this development. The entire outdoors is dogless, except for the undomesticated coyotes, and any of those that came within howling distance of here are dead.

Is Peyote Skies too pristine for dogs? I know some housing developments rule against many things.

Human voices disturb my reverie. I cringe deeper into the oleander shade. A woman exits the house, wearing slacks and sweater in the same putrid shades that saturate the development. Sure enough, a turquoise coyote is howling on her chest.

The man wears a suit, but the color is pale and the jacket is open. "Which sprinkler isn't working, Mrs. Ebert?"

"More than one, a whole line, down by the oleanders."

"Oh, at the edge of the lot."

He walks my way, but he does not see me, because I am dark as dirt and I shut my eyes to thin green slits. His foot kicks at the small silver spikes poking up like lethal flowers through the expensive grass.

"Looks like a line's out, Mrs. Ebert." He bends down to fiddle with a sprinkler, but his eyes are skipping over the edge of the desert so close you can smell the sweet alyssum on the hot, dry breeze. At least coyotes use room deodorizers.

He is big, overweight like a middle-aged busy man will get, with a fleshy face too tan for an office-bound dude. He has thinning brown hair and dirt-brown eyes, sneaky brown eyes. The short hairs on my shoulder blades begin to rise. He acts like he knows someone is watching, but he never notices me, and I am even gladder of that fact now.

His back still to the woman, he reaches into his pocket to pull out something, maybe a handkerchief. Sweat beads on the hairless patches atop his head. His mouth quirks into what would be a grin if he were happy. He looks nervous, intent.

He throws the handkerchief past the oleanders, out toward the desert, as he stands. A good hard throw. Even I know that cloth is too flimsy to carry for a distance like that.

"Just a bum line, Mrs. Ebert. The company will replace it free of charge."

"That's great, Mr. Phelps." The woman expected this, but she makes gratified noises anyway.

"Peyote Skies wants its residents happy with everything." Mr. Phelps is donning a genial face and moving over the thick grass toward the woman. "Jimmy Ray

Ruggles didn't develop this concept from the ground up to let a broken water line turn a band of your Bermuda brown."

"Plus, a broken line could be wasting water," she reminds him.

"Right." I hear his smirk though his broad polyester-blend back is turned to me. "No water wasted here," he says, standing on an ocean of emerald-green grass. "Peyote Skies is a Jimmy Ray Ruggles baby, down to the last leaf of landscaping. It's gotta be perfect."

They smile at each other and amble toward the pale yellow house together. I do not wait to see them enter. I have turned and streaked into the desert.

Not far away I find the orange handkerchief. A stone the size of a catnip mouse lies near it, but it is not really a handkerchief. I take one look and go bounding into the deeper desert at a coyote pace, thinking furiously. I do not like the idea of a new victim dying while I am on the job.

It is easiest to find Sings-with-Soul's den, next to the big stand of coyote cactus, whose gourds are catnip to the clan. With the kits yipping serially in the background, I tell her my problem. Her yellow eyes show their whites.

"I can call, but then what?" she asks me.

"Just get him here. I will think of something."

She assumes a position that uncannily mimics the image on the homeowner's sweater, lifts her head until her yellow throat aims at high noon, and lets loose an ungodly series of yowls.

Sings-with-Soul has Janis Joplin beat by a Clark County mile. My own ears flatten as much as hers, in self-defense. Even the kits quit yipping and join in with falsetto mini-howls. *Ouch!*

Daylight howls seem out of place but I figure they will attract attention. Sure enough, soon coyotes spring out of the drab desert floor as if they were made of animated dust. Frankly, they all look alike to me, so I do not recognize any I met the night before.

One comes slowly. My gut tightens as I recognize my quarry, Happy Hocks. The old dude who commissioned me is nowhere to be seen, and I am not unhappy. I do not have good news.

Once I am the center of a circle of quizzical coyotes (it is a good thing I am not the nervous type), I explain.

"I have discovered who is killing your kin—and how. Unfortunately, Happy Hocks ate some poisoned food."

Heads snap toward Happy, whose own head is hanging a trifle low. His big ears are not as erect as before, and I notice his eye whites are turning yellow.

"I was feeling... tired, Mr. Midnight," he whimpers. "What can I do?"

"Is there anything you do *not* eat around here?" I ask the others.

"There is little coyote clan will not eat, if they have to," a gray-muzzle answers.

"There must be something that you would not touch on a bet, some cactus, some plant, that makes you sick."

Sings-with-Soul's head lifts. "Of course. We were too shocked to think.

An antidote."

"No sure bet," I warn, eyeing the listless Happy Hocks. "I have already thought of oleander, but that is so poisonous the cure could kill as well. Whatever this unknown poison, if we act quickly enough—"

"Alyssum leaves," says the unnamed grizzle-muzzle, "taste hot and harsh."

"Prince's Plume," another coyote offers. "Worse taste!"

"Desert Tobacco," the oldster suggests again. "Paiutes smoked it. Such stink-weed should make this youngster plenty sick."

"I know!" Sings-with-Soul edges away from the big-eyed, big-eared kits watching our powwow. "Brushtail was sick only a week ago after I nipped her home from that plant, there."

We turn as one to regard a modest, foot-high growth covered with tiny dull-green leaves. Small leafless stalks are crowned with seed-beads.

Happy Hocks is nosed over to the plant and watched until he bites off several tiny pods. Meanwhile, grizzle-muzzle trots off, returning with a fragrant bouquet of desert alyssum.

Happy Hocks's muzzle develops a perpetual wrinkle as he downs these desert delights, but his eye-whites gleam with fear.

"Sharp," he comments with a short bark. "Hot. Burning."

I say nothing. The hot burning, I fear, could be the poison working. I have no love for vegetables, but in the interests of science, I nibble a pod. I am not an expert, either, but I have nicked the occasional burger-fragment and I recognize this plant's terrible taste. Ironically, Happy Hocks is having lots of fresh mustard on his death-o-burger.

We watch the poor pup gum down these tough little taste-bombs. Finally his skinny sides begin to heave. I am surprised to see the gathered coyotes politely turn their heads from this unpleasant sight.

When it is over, the dirty work is left to Midnight Louie.

I amble over to examine the remains. In a pile of regurgitated greens lies the fatal lump of meat. It looks fairly undigested. With one sharp nail I paw the meat. After a few prods it falls open along the fault line. Inside lies a metallic powder.

"Bury it," I growl at the assembled coyote clan.

Happy Hocks's hang-dog look lifts. "I think I feel better, Mr. Midnight."

"Keep it that way and, ah, drink lots of liquids and get plenty of rest." What can it hurt?

Amid a chorus of coyote thanks, I flatten my ears and head back to the dangerous turf of Peyote Skies.

I now know the means (if not the brand of poison) and I know the motive. I even know the perpetrator. What I don't know is how to stop him.

CHAPTER 7
SECRET SHADOW

So I shadow him.

This is no big deal. For one thing, my coloration makes me a born shadow, and I have always been good at tailing. For another, Mr. Phelps is all over this development.

Apparently, he is a trouble-shooter for this Jimmy Ray Ruggles. Mr. Phelps inspects deck planking that gapes too much for an owner's aesthetic sense. He orders shriveling bushes replaced. He keeps everybody happy.

And he obligingly confesses to the crime. So to speak.

"My kids are real upset about having to keep Rocky inside," a harried householder in a thousand-dollar suit complains when he buttonholes a passing Mr. Phelps in his aggregate driveway. "We never thought about coyotes running off with our pets. What about stockade fences—?"

"Jimmy Ray wants the development open to the desert; that's the whole point. We're working on the coyote problem. Maybe electric fences."

"What about those dead coyotes on the perimeter? That's not healthy, dead animals so close to the houses."

"We clean up the area as soon as they're found."

"What's killing them? They're not rabid?"

"No, no," Mr. Phelps says quickly. You can see the word "rabid" conjuring visions of damage suits and buyer panic. "Just varmints. Pests. Coyotes die all the time. Old age. Gunshot wounds. Don't worry, sir. As soon as the coyotes catch on that this area is populated now, they'll keep their distance."

The busy man in the suit hops into a red BMW convertible and takes off, looking unconvinced.

Mr. Phelps heads on to the biggest house in the completed section, a white stucco job with a high, red tile roof the size of a circus tent.

I follow, the only free-roaming critter in the complex. The feeling is spooky. At the back of the big house is a circular sun room with floor-to-ceiling windows surrounded by a bleached redwood deck.

Mr. Phelps soon comes out with a man and a woman carrying a kid. These Peyote Skies people sure like their backyards and their desert view.

I stay low in the landscaping and edge close enough to hear every word.

"It's going great, Jimmy Ray." Mr. Phelps' hearty, adman voice gives "phony" a gold-plating.

"What about the pet-killing problem?" the top man asks.

"We'll be rid of all coyotes, dead or alive, any day now. We're trying low-profile electric fences."

The boss-man's face darkens. "That'll ruin the view."

Mr. Jimmy Ray Ruggles is as nice-looking as his picture. Though he is only in his mid-thirties, he even smells rich, thanks to some Frenchy men's cologne. Mrs. Jimmy Ray Ruggles, a slender woman with sun-streaked blond hair, wears Chanel No. 5 with her tennis whites.

She puts down the small girl, whose dark hair suggests that Momma's been in the bleach bottle. The kid is a little doll of maybe four in a pink dress. She grabs onto her mother's shorts and hides behind her.

Mr. Phelps looks nervous again. He glances down the green expanse of lawn to the broad brown swath of desert. Between here and there stands the bright Tinker-Toy construction of a kiddie play set that sports enough swings, slides and monkey bars to outfit a whole playground.

"We're putting the wires real low," Mr. Phelps says.

"The coyotes will jump 'em if they want to come in bad enough."

"Maybe not," Mr. Phelps adds lamely.

I can smell what he's thinking: not if enough of them die. So the boss does not know about this guy's one-man pest-control plan.

Mr. Phelps suddenly bends down and smiles at the little girl. "How are you, Caitlyn? Want Uncle Phil to take you for a swingsy?"

Caitlyn doesn't look too good. In fact, she looks as down in the mouth as Happy Hocks did not long ago. Her dark eyes are as round as two moons in eclipse, and her precious opposable thumb is stuck in her mouth like a lollipop, where it can do no good whatsoever. What I would give for one of those! Preferably two; I am a balanced kind of dude.

"What do you say, Caitlyn?" her mother prods. "Uncle Phil was awful nice to get you that recreation set." Mrs. Jimmy Ray looks apologetically at Mr. Phelps. "She's so shy for her age."

"That's okay." Mr. Phelps is really turning on the hard sell now. "She knows her Uncle Phil is her best friend. Come on, Caitie, upsy daisy."

He swoops the little girl up on one arm, and I can see the fear in her eyes. I myself do not care to be swooped up. As for being forced to swish to and fro at a height in the name of fun... *please!*

The fond parents smile as Uncle Phil leads little Caitie to the swing set.

I slink under the oleanders until I am level with the gaudy swing set, most unhappy. I will not overhear anything good way down here, but I must follow Mr. Phelps until I get something on him that will stick. At least I now know that his dirty deeds are a solo act.

Mr. Phelps lifts the little girl onto the swing seat. Her clinging mitts turn white-knuckled on the chains. He shoves off. She goes sailing to and fro above his head, down to the ground and up again forward and then down and back.

I shut my eyes. This is worse than watching Happy Hocks lose his Big-o-Burger.

Mr. Phelps looks up as Caitlyn swings over him, her skirt lifting in the wind. Her eyes flash by, terrified.

Then he slows the swing.

"Phil!" Mrs. Jimmy Ray Ruggles is calling from the deck.

Mr. Phelps bends down to whisper something to the little girl. Her fingers do not uncurl from the swing chains.

Mr. Phelps goes up the green lawn to the deck. I turn to follow, but something makes me look back at Caitlyn.

The swing is still. She has bent to pick up something from the grass and is setting it in her lap, gazing at it unhappily. Then, as if taking a pill that will make a bad headache go away, she lifts a hand to her mouth.

I scope the entire scenario in a nanosecond. My mind flashes back to Mr. Coyote-killer Phelps, his hands up, pushing the swing. Again I see his open suit coat swinging back, side pockets tilted at an angle. I can imagine something falling out, and down, to the grass, unnoticed.

The little girl, a shy, unhappy kid who is afraid of almost everything. A familiar package, bright orange, with a tasty piece of Big-o-Burger still in it. Maybe she thinks you can swallow fear, push it back down. Maybe some kids will eat anything, just like coyotes.

I am over in a sling-shot.

I leap up to paw the too-familiar orange paper, then to push her hand away from her mouth. She is chewing. Now her eyes grow enormous, and her fear erupts in a scream.

"Mommy, Mommy!"

She is still chewing.

I leap onto her lap (claws in), to rap her cheek.

Some half-chewed food falls to the orange wrapper covering her short pink skirt like a napkin.

She is still chewing in dazed reflex.

I pat her cheek until she coughs out something more.

But I have seen her swallow.

Then they come for me, three running figures.

"Caitlyn!" they shriek.

"*Shoo!*" they shout. "Get away!"

I leap down with the Big-o-Burger wrapper in my mouth, dragging it from the yard.

"Mommy, Mommy!" Caitlyn cries as she is swept into her mother's arms, as the two men in their big shoes come after me.

I could outrun them in the snap of a maitre'd's fingers, but I dare not leave behind the poisoned Big-o-Burger. It is evidence. Uncle Phil knows now that he has to destroy it.

I drag it into the last oleanders between me and the desert, working myself deep into the shrubbery and shadows.

"Jimmy Ray!" Caitlyn's mother sounds annoyed. "I think she ate some of the food that filthy alley cat dragged into the yard. What was it?"

The men's feet stop pounding beside me. "I saw the wrapper," Jimmy Ray Ruggles shouts back. "A Big-o-Burger."

"Can you imagine how long that was sitting around?" she demands. "Oh, Caitie—"

She retreats to the house, carrying the kid.

I see her husband's feet swiveling to follow her.

I see Mr. Phelps' feet moving closer along the oleanders.

I do not need to see his face to know that he looks even more nervous than ever, and angrier. At this moment, Midnight Louie is one should-be dead coyote.

"Phil!" The boss is calling. "Forget the cat. We better get Caitlyn calmed down for a nap. Come up to the house and we'll talk later."

The feet before me do not move and I know why. I am a hunter myself. Uncle Phil wants to destroy—evidence, and me. I do not move. If I must, I will desert my hard-won prize, but not without a fight. This time my shivs are out and my teeth are bared.

Finally, the feet turn and thump away.

I withdraw, but not far. I know what I wait for.

CHAPTER 8
OLE BLACK DEVIL

The moon is out again, full as a tick.

I watch the dark house.

At what must be my namesake midnight hour, a light blinks on upstairs. I edge forward to watch lights turn on through the house, down to the kitchen.

In five minutes, I can hear sirens. The wash of revolving red lights splash the sides of the big white house like gouts of blood. Soon the sirens wail away, fading, but the house stays brightly lit. Out on the dark, unseen desert, coyotes keep the siren heartfelt company.

Dawn is no surprise. I wait.

Around noon, Mr. Jimmy Ray Ruggles comes out onto the deck. He looks even younger in jeans and a rumpled t-shirt. He walks down the lawn, Mr. Phelps a deferential step behind. Mr. Jimmy Ray Ruggles's face is more rumpled than his shirt. I glimpse in his eyes the same fear that filled his daughter's less than a day ago. I know the swing that Mr. Jimmy Ray Ruggles has been riding for the past twenty hours. I want to know what has happened to Caitlyn.

"It was near here," Mr. Jimmy Ray Ruggles says in a weary, angry voice.

"That cat is long gone, with his booty," Mr. Phelps says. Hopes.

"I've got to look. I've got to know what it was, Phil."

Mr. Jimmy Ray Ruggles gets down on his hands and knees to peer under the oleanders.

I am waiting, where I always was.

"By God, the damn cat's still here!" he hisses. "I can see the wrapper too!"

"There won't be anything left."

"Dammit, Phil! They can analyze even little bits, molecules maybe. I've got to know what—" His voice breaks. "That's all right, kitty. I just want the paper."

He sticks his hand under the bush. I see his pale face. I see Mr. Phelps peering over his shoulder, twice as worried.

"Jimmy Ray, that's a big cat. He could have rabies. He could scratch or bite you—"

"I don't care! It's for Caitie." His hand reaches the crumpled orange paper in front of me with the two lumps of mashed food on it.

I sit very still and let him take it. He slowly draws it away, seeping fear. I am sorry that I am such a scary dude.

Then he is gone and Mr. Phelps is staring at me through the spiky oleander leaves with as much hatred as I have ever seen.

"Black devil!" he says like a curse.

I am not sorry that I am such a scary dude after all.

I wait again. I want to know.

But the house is empty and the hours pass. I am hungry, but I wait. When I am thirsty, I slink out to lap up some sprinkler water. Then I return to my post.

The odds are that I will never know, just as they are one hundred percent that I will never tell. But I wait.

I am rewarded at dusk, when the desert sky bleeds a Southwest palette of lavender and peach... and orange... that developers can only dream of.

Two men on the lawn. Lights in the house.

"Tell me," Mr. Jim Ray Ruggles is saying, and I think the iron tone in his voice could force even me to talk.

"Tell you what?" A nervous laugh.

"The dead coyotes. You said you were handling it. How? Phil, how!"

"Jim—"

"It was with poisoned food, wasn't it? And somehow Caitie got into it. Listen, you can tell me now. Caitie will be fine, thank God. She's still unconscious, but the doctors say she didn't get enough poison to cause permanent damage. They hope not, anyway. Listen, I won't blame you. I know you're devoted to Peyote Skies, like I am. Maybe too much. Tell me."

"All right." Mr. Phelps sounds empty. The men walk toward the oleanders, toward me. "I never dreamed, Jimmy Ray—I just wanted to discourage the damn coyotes, and it was working. We haven't found any dead ones since a week ago. I salted the Big-o-Burgers. Somehow, one of the... traps... fell out of my pocket yesterday and I never knew. Caitie swooped it up, and I never saw—"

"Don't you remember? She's always loved Big-o-Burgers," Mr. Jimmy Ray Ruggles says softly.

Mr. Phelps' voice is breaking now, but this theatrical touch does not break Midnight's Louie's heart. "I was going to stop soon."

"But... thallium, Phil, an outlawed poison! With no taste, no smell, a poison that never degrades even though it's been illegal for decades. Didn't you realize it could kill more than coyotes—pets, children? Where on earth did you get it?"

"I own some old houses in town. The carpenters back then used it as rat poison, inside the walls. It was still there. I figured it would fool the coyotes; they're too smart for anything else. I swear to God, Jimmy Ray, if I had known it would hurt Caitie I would have cut off my right arm—"

"I know. I know."

Mr. Jimmy Ray Ruggles has stopped directly in front of me. "I suppose that big ole black cat is dead from it by now, but thank God he fought Caitie for it. Thank God we found him and a sample of the poison so they could treat her."

His shoes turn, then go. Mr. Phelps's do not.

276 • CAROLE NELSON DOUGLAS

"Black devil," he whispers to the twilight air.

I accept my plaudits with silent good grace and finally depart.

CHAPTER 9
TRICKSTER GOD

It takes me a full day to recover my strength, and placate my defrauded appetite. I am satisfied that no more coyotes will be sacrificed on the altar of Peyote Skies, and that the developer's daughter will be well, but I do wish that Mr. Phelps would find the fate he deserves. I fear that the scandal would hurt Peyote Skies too much for even a fond father to pursue the matter.

Then I begin to worry about my payoff. I am, after all, not doing charity work. I dash out to the desert on the nearest gravel truck to find that Happy Hocks is as peppy as ever (alas!) and that these coyote clan types have never heard of the strange old dude who commissioned me.

So I am soon languishing beside the carp pond at the Crystal Phoenix again, feeling that I have been taken in a shell game, when I spot a familiar profile on the sun-rinsed wall.

"I thought you had headed for the hills."

"Foolish feline," the big-eared coyote silhouette answers. "I always keep my bargains. I merely had to insure that you had done as agreed."

"And then some. Where is my reward?"

I watch the shadow jaws move and hear the harsh desert voice describe a site that, to my delight, is on the Crystal Phoenix grounds.

"Once all of Las Vegas was desert," the coyote says, "and my ancestors had many secret places. You will find my cache behind the third palm on the east side of the pool."

"Where?"

"In the ground. You will have to dig for it. You can dig?"

"I do so daily," I retort.

"Deep."

"What I can do shallow, I can do deep."

"Good. Goodbye."

With that terse farewell, me and the coyote call it quits.

I spring for the pool area. I dodge stinking tourists basting on lounges, dripping coconut oil between the plastic strips.

I count off palms. I retire discreetly behind one and dig. And dig. And dig.

About a half-foot down, I hit pay dirt. Coyote pay dirt. Excavating further, I uncover my treasure. Then I sit back to study it.

I regard a deposit of small brown nubs. Of pods, so to speak. Of coyote dung intermixed with a foreign substance: the button of the Mescal cactus, called peyote by the Indians. I have been paid off, all right. In Coyote peyote, both forms. Apparently this big-eared dude thinks that his leavings are caramel. The worst part is feeling that it serves me right for trusting a coyote.

By nightfall I have retreated to the ghost suite of the Crystal Phoenix to salve my wounded psyche. It does not soothe the savage soul to have been taken to the cleaners by a dirty dog. A yellow dog. By Don Coyote. Maybe the mescaline is worth something, but not in my circles. I do not do drugs, and my only vice, catnip, is a legally available substance. As for coyote dung, it does not even have a souvenir value.

As I muse in the antique air of suite 711, I recall that there is coyote, and then there is Coyote. Coyote of Native American legend is also called the Old Man, the Trickster, the Dirty Old Man who is at times advised by his own droppings. It is said that Coyote takes many forms and that to deal with him is always dicey, for he embodies the worst and the best of humankind.

I contemplate that though I have saved coyote clan from an underhanded attack, I have also saved humankind from the ricochet of that attack upon itself, that I have suffered hunger and thorns in my feet, not to mention threats to body and soul, and I have nothing to show for it but coyote peyote.

My self-esteem is so low that I could win a limbo contest dancing under it.

And then I notice that a console across the room has flipped its lid. I have seen that ash-blonde oblong of furniture for many years, and never knew that it had a lid to flip.

By the way the light dances inside the lid, like an aurora borealis, the lid interior is mirrored, and in that mirror is reflected an oval image.

The image flickers eerily, then resolves. Sound issues from the bowels of the cabinet. I sit mesmerized, even when I realize that I am watching a late-Forties-vintage TV set display a perfectly ordinary contemporary television show I do not normally deign to watch—that exercise in tabloid journalism known as "the Daily Scoop," but which I call the Daily Pooper Scooper in my septic moments. Or do I mean skeptic?

Whatever, what to my wandering eyes should appear but a camera-pan across the entry sign to Peyote Skies. An offscreen voice begins saying what a tony development this is, and discusses the rash of coyote poisonings culminating in the tragic poisoning of the developer's daughter. Caitlyn's image flashes across the screen, smiling and happy.

Next I see an image of Mr. Phelps being led away in handcuffs by grim-looking men. *Hallelujah!*

Then Miss Ashley Ames, a most attractive anorexic bottle-blond with bony kneecaps, comes on screen with a breathless narrative.

It seems that little Caitlyn Ruggles's poisoning was considered a tragic mistake stemming from a misguided attempt by a Peyote Skies employee to rid the development of pet-napping coyotes... until the child victim regained consciousness and began speaking of the unspeakable. "Uncle Phil" had been sexually abusing her.

Caitlyn's shocked parents called the police. An investigation revealed that P.W. Phelps, a vice president in the Peyote Skies Company, had indeed been abusing the child, who was beginning to talk of telling.

"It is alleged," Miss Ashley Ames says in a tone that is most delightfully dubious about the "alleged" part, "that he poisoned the half-dozen coyotes to create a pattern in which the 'accidental' death of young Caitlyn Ruggles would be seen as a tragic side effect.

"Had it not been," she goes on, and I can hardly believe my ears, even though they are standing at full attention, "for the lucky chance that a starving stray black cat fought the child for the poisoned piece of a major fast-food chain hamburger, this nefarious scheme would have never been discovered."

I am more than somewhat taken aback by my description as "starving."

The next shot distracts me: Caitlin and her parents all smiles at the Las Vegas Humane Society, adopting a small black kitten. Even the kitten is smiling.

I am smiling. Hell, I suspect that somewhere Coyote is smiling.

In fact, as the ancient television's image and sound fade, I believe I glimpse a silver-haired human dude with mighty big ears vanishing through a crack in the door.

I recall that Jersey Joe Jackson hid a few caches around Las Vegas in his time. And that Coyote never changes, and always does. And that he performs tricks, maybe even with vintage television sets.

The best and the worst of both beast and man himself.

Indeed.

THE POET AND THE INKMAKER'S DAUGHTER

Elizabeth Hand

Elizabeth Hand is the multiple-award-winning author of numerous novels and three collections of short fiction. She is also a longtime reviewer for many publications, including the *Washington Post, Salon, Village Voice* and the *Boston Globe,* and is a columnist for the *Magazine of Fantasy & Science Fiction. Illyria,* her World Fantasy Award-winning novel inspired by Shakespeare's *Twelfth Night* was recently published for the first time in the U.S. Her most recent novel is *Available Dark*, a sequel to the Shirley Jackson Award-winning novel *Generation Loss.*

Hand says: "When I was eight or nine years old, one of my favorite books was Frances Carpenter's *Tales of a Chinese Grandmother*, traditional fairy tales re-told for a more modern, western audience. A few years later I fell in love with Lafcadio Hearn's Japanese ghost stories, especially 'The Boy Who Painted Cats.' 'The Poet and the Inkmaker's Daughter' is an homage to those stories. There are various legends about Japanese bobtail cats, including an origin tale about a cat whose tail caught on fire: the panicked cat ran through the streets, setting houses aflame in its wake. Its descendants to this day have no tail."

Heian Japan

In the reign of she who became known as the Dark Willow Empress, there lived in a far-off city a poet by the name of Ga-sho. He lived as all poor poets do, upon memories and tea-dregs, but what sustained him most of all were thoughts of a certain young woman, a maid to a lady-in-waiting to the Dark Willow Empress. This young woman had no name, at least none that Ga-sho knew of. He had glimpsed her only once, as she followed the litter bearing her mistress along a canal and then over a bridge at the city's edge. The hem of her kimono was spattered with mud and rotten waterweeds, but her face—what he could see of it, anyway, as she kept her head down and her long sleeve held before her cheeks—was exquisite, with skin as fine and white as rice paper and long-lashed eyes like chrysanthemum blossoms. As he stood aside on the bridge to let her pass, he caught the strong fragrance of *kurobo*, sweet incense, trailing her like a warm wind. For this reason, and the beauty of her eyes, in his thoughts he called her Fair Flower.

Ga-sho had inherited a small sum after his father's death, enough to keep a tiny room in the very darkest quarter of the city. Here, before a brazier no bigger than his cupped hands, Ga-sho wrote his poems upon scrolls of rice paper. All of his verses praised Fair Flower's beauty, her gentleness, her devotion and her virtue (though mostly he wrote of her beauty). He did not know that the young woman he loved was in fact bad-tempered and shrill, with a voice like green sticks breaking; that she gambled with the other maids and had amassed a considerable debt, which she had absolutely no intention of paying; that she snored, and her breath often stank of plum wine, even in the morning; that she had for some time now been trysting with a handsome gardener in the Dark Willow Empress's employ; and that she dallied also with the gardener's cousin, and occasionally with the cousin's best friend, who worked in the lower kitchen. (The name they had for her was less flattering than "Fair Flower," and I will not reveal it here.)

No, Ga-sho's poems took none of this into account, and that is perhaps for the best. That which is true often makes for very dull reading.

Poor as he was, Ga-sho kept a cat. She was a fastidious creature, bobtailed as cats of that time and place were, with pale grey eyes and black front paws; not as beautiful as Fair Flower, perhaps, but with far better manners. The most remarkable thing about her was her color: a strange, deep reddish brown, the color of new bronze tinged with blood. Such red cats were considered to have special powers by the superstitious, and were called *Kinkwaneko,* Golden Flower, but Ga-Sho, while a sentimental sort when it came to women, was not particularly superstitious. He called her Clean-ears.

The red cat slept beside Ga-sho and kept him warm at night. In the morning, she gently woke him by nudging his cheek. When the poet ate, he always saved bits of fish for his companion. When he had little money for food, or forgot to eat, Clean-ears would slip silently as a sigh from his tiny room and make her way to the city docks. An hour or so later she would return, bearing a fish, or perhaps a prawn, that she would lay upon the poet's wooden pillow. Always she would politely refuse to dine until he was finished, and in return he was careful to save for her the choicest parts of the head, particularly the eyes, to which the red cat was very partial.

One of the few people Ga-sho could afford to do business with was an inkmaker whose shop was not far from the poet's cramped room. The inkmaker was a poor man himself, but poverty had made him neither kindly nor patient toward those who owed him money. Rather, he was mean-spirited, craven to those with more wealth than his meager savings, and to one person at least he was downright cruel.

This was his stepdaughter, Ukon. He had married her mother under the misprision that she had a small fortune; upon discovering that she did not, he had hounded her to her death (or so it was believed in that part of the city, where gossip ran hot and destructive as the fires that often broke out during the winter months). Ukon's mother was also reputed to have been a fox-fairy, and for several weeks after she died the inkmaker kept a cudgel by his bed, in case her vengeful spirit returned to harm him.

But either because she was not a fairy, or because she feared for her daughter's well-being, the ghost did not appear, and poor Ukon was left alone to her fate. Neighbors could hear her piteous cries late at night when her stepfather beat her—bamboo-and rice-paper walls do little to hide such things—but no one moved to help her. A man's daughter, even a stepdaughter, was his own concern. So, as her father spent his days and nights drinking with his customers and creditors, the brunt of the work of making ink was left to his stepdaughter.

It was Ukon who tended to the small stove where red pine wood and red pine resin were burned, all through the autumn and winter months. It was Ukon who then scraped the resulting soot from inside the stove, placing it in a bowl to which she added fish glue. The fish glue she made herself, begging fish bones from the docks, then boiling them on another stove. It smelled horrible, so she added plum and peony blossoms, and sometimes even sandalwood, if she could afford it. She mixed the fish glue and the soot together on a wide wooden plank, kneading the thick paste until it became soft and pliable as sweet rice cakes, then pressed the soft ink into wooden pattern blocks, square and round and rectangular. But the ink could not be left in the pattern molds, or it would crack as it dried. Ukon had to very carefully remove the blocks of ink, transferring them to wooden boxes filled with damp charcoal. Here the sumi ink would dry slowly, for days or even weeks, and Ukon had to replace the charcoal as it dried. Finally the sumi was dry enough to be wrapped in rice paper and hung to cure for another month, in the little shed in the alley behind the shop where she and her stepfather lived. Only then would Ukon carefully mark each sumi stick with her stepfather's mark, wrap it in fine paper, and pile them all in neat stacks in the rear of the little shop. Her hands and fingers had become so stained by sumi ink that they never washed clean, nor did the rank smell of fish bones ever leave her skin; rather than help her, though, her drunken stepfather only mocked the girl.

"You will never win a suitor," he said disdainfully, staring at her black hands. "I will be lucky if you don't frighten away the few customers we have—"

And he cuffed her fiercely on the cheek, sending her reeling back to where the largest ink blocks awaited cutting.

Now, I have written that no one ever moved to help Ukon, but that is not quite true. Because the girl, poor and miserable as she was, yet possessed a kind heart, and like the half-strangled rosebush that still reaches toward a thread of sunlight, so did Ukon strive toward charity. As there was not a single human being in that quarter as poor and unhappy as she, Ukon's kindnesses by necessity were directed toward other creatures, smaller and even hungrier than herself. So she would rescue crippled crickets trapped in their bamboo cages when the boys grew bored with them and tossed them aside, and save grains of rice to feed half-starved sparrows in the winter snow. And she would secretly feed a cat that often showed up in the alley behind the shop, a small red cat with a puffy bobbed tail like a blossom past its prime. It was drawn like other strays by the smell of rotting fish that rose from the ink shed. But it was smaller than the other cats, and milder-tempered, and Ukon made a point of saving fishtails for it, and fish bones with bits of flesh still adhering to them like hairs to a brittle comb.

It was on one such afternoon, late of a winter day in the Eleventh, or Frosty, Month, that Ukon made one of her furtive forays into the alleyway.

"Ah, *suteneko*," she crooned, stooping to stroke the red cat behind its ears. "Poor *suteneko*, pretty *Kinkwa-neko*—you are so cold! Here—there is hardly anything, but…"

She held out her ink-blackened fingers, and the cat licked the flakes of fish from them gratefully.

"She's not a stray, you know."

Ukon whirled, frightened, and backed against the flimsy wall of the shed. She lowered her head automatically, as she would in deference to any customer, but she also raised her arm, as though to protect herself from a blow.

Peering through her fingers she saw not the threatening figure of her drunken father, but a young man in frayed robes and worn wooden shoes.

The poet, she thought, recognizing him by the ink stains on his sleeves and his hollow cheeks. Slowly she lowered her hand, but remained where she huddled against the wall, heedless of the sleet pelting down on her bare head.

"She stays with me," the poet went on matter-of-factly. "*Suteneko!*" he said chidingly, and bent to pick up the cat. "She thinks you're a stray!"

He stroked her head, blowing into her pointed ears, then looked at Ukon. "I call her *Kuri-ryoumimi*," he said. "Kury-ri."

"Ah." Ukon smiled tentatively "'Clean-ears.'"

The poet smiled back at her. But his smile died as he took in her blackened hands and red face—red and chafed from crying, and still bearing the marks of her stepfather's blows. "I… I was in the shop, but saw no one," he said apologetically. "I need some more ink. But I can come back tomorrow—"

"No, no," Ukon cried, and hurried back inside. "My father is gone on an errand"—in fact, he was drinking at the tavern—"but I will get whatever you need."

She busied herself with finding and wrapping several rectangular blocks of ink. The poet had asked for the cheapest kind, which was all he could afford, but as she began to pull the ink from its shelf, Ukon suddenly hesitated. She glanced over her shoulder to make sure he could not see, and that no other customers had entered the shop. Then she swiftly replaced the inexpensive sumi stick with a chrysanthemum-shaped block of the most expensive ink her stepfather sold, scented with geranium leaves, and tinted a deep vermillion. She wrapped it in a second sheet of rice paper, so that the poet would not see its value and refuse it. Then she hurried back to the front of the shop.

"Here," she said, bowing as she handed it to him.

And as she gazed at him, her face reddened even more, though not from fear or pain. The poet took the sumi ink and stared back at her musingly.

She is nothing like Fair Flower, Ga-sho thought. *There is no fragrance here but the reek of boiling fish guts, and her hands are black as my cat's paws, and her skin is as red as—well, as red as Clean-ears's fur. And everyone says the old man beats her…*

And yet her smile was sweet, her voice low, her gaze gentle. And she had shown kindness to a stray cat….

"Thank you," he said, too quickly, then turned and left.

That night Ga-sho wrote a poem in praise of the inkmaker's daughter. He could not, in good conscience, compare her to a flower, or even a blossoming weed. But the Japanese have many poems that honor cats, and so he began by comparing her to Clean-ears. After some time spent thus, his thoughts began to move from feline virtues to more feminine ones, and he found himself composing verse that (to his own mind, at least) was at least as fine as those poems inspired by Fair Flower. He recited the best of these several times to Clean-ears, who sat washing her paws (which became no whiter than Ukon's palms) beside the lamp.

Red cheek, raven hair,
Her hands night-shaded and raw—
I would know her name!

He took a sheet of paper, withdrew the sumi stick he had bought that afternoon, and unwrapped it.

"Ah!"

The poet's eyes grew wide and wondering. He held up the blossom-shaped ink block, glossy, with a telltale reddish tinge. He felt his cheeks grow hot, and looked furtively aside at the cat, as though to make sure she did not notice his blush.

But the cat was gone. And so, smiling to himself as he ground the vermillion ink on his inkstone and licked the sable tip of his brush, Ga-sho began to record his poem.

Meanwhile, Ukon was waiting up for her stepfather in the back of the shop, where her bed was a thin pallet on the floor. She dared not sleep before he returned; in any event, her thoughts were too full of the young poet to be at rest. So she busied herself tending the small hearth that heated the shop, and removing dry sumi sticks from their rice husks and wrapping them in paper.

It was past midnight when she heard the sound of stumbling footsteps in the alley, followed by the creaking of the door as it was pulled open.

"Father," she called softly, going to greet him.

Her stepfather stumbled into the room, robes awry and his thin hair disheveled. Ukon drew up alongside him, trying to help him keep from falling.

"Lazy bitch!"

He struck at her furiously, but in his drunkenness he went flailing wildly, bashing against one thin wall. Ukon ran to his side, but he lashed out at her again, striking her so that she fell, weeping, by the hearth.

"You have been seeing men in here," he gasped, struggling to his feet. "The old woman next door said she saw that layabout from the next street—"

"He was a customer, most watchful of stepfathers," Ukon pleaded. "You must remember him, he is the poet—"

"Poet! He is worthless, as you are! Whoring like your mother before you!"

But at the word "customer" his eyes had gone to the metal strongbox where each day's accounts were kept. He grabbed it, shaking it; opened it, then glared accusingly at Ukon.

Oh *no!* She covered her face with her hands. Her delight in serving the young poet had blinded her to duty—she had forgotten to get payment for the ink stick!

"Father," she stammered, but it was too late. He began beating her with the strongbox, battering at the poor girl's face and shoulders until she collapsed onto the floor in a heap.

"I will find this poet and kill him," she heard her stepfather mutter thickly as he flung the metal box aside. "That I will..."

Ukon was too weak to do more than pull herself to a corner, watching through swollen eyes as her stepfather lurched out the back door into the alley. But soon sheer exhaustion washed over her pain, as with time the tide will cover a littered beach, smoothing out the soiled sand and, for a little while at least, making the world seem at peace. So it was that Ukon fell into fitful sleep upon the dirt floor, one arm still flung protectively over her poor battered face.

She woke to a low voice calling her name.

"Ukon... Ukon, you must wake!"

She raised her head groggily, the torn sleeve of her robe catching on the edge of a small table, and looked up. In her dreaming she had half-imagined the voice belonged to the young poet.

But as she blinked in the darkness she saw a woman standing before her. She was older than Ukon, her neat coif showing wisps of gray beneath thick black hair lacquer; for an instant, Ukon thought it was her mother. Then she saw that while the woman's pointed face had the same piquance as her mother's, her eyes were a very pale gray, like seawater, and she wore a kimono of deep scarlet silk, a color her mother would never have worn.

"You must come with me," the woman said, calmly but with great urgency. As Ukon began to stammer a question, she raised a hand, its palm smudged as black as Ukon's own. "There is no time—come!"

Ukon got to her feet. Her ears rang from the blows her stepfather had given her, and she thought she could hear another sound, oddly familiar, but the strange woman did not give her the opportunity to look around the shop for its source.

"This way!" she hissed; grabbing Ukon's wrist, she dragged her out to the street. They began running along the narrow way, their wooden shoes sliding in the sleet and dirty snow. As they ran, Ukon began to hear agitated voices behind her, and then a sudden shout.

"Fire! The inkmaker's shop is on fire!"

"Aiie!" With a cry, Ukon stopped and looked back. From the alley behind her stepfather's shop rose a plume of smoke. Abruptly the wind shifted, carrying the smell of burning pine. "He must have overfilled the stove in the shed! I must go—"

"No." This time the woman's voice was a command. Her hold on Ukon's wrist tightened. Her breath as she pulled the girl to her smelled of rotting fish. "Your life there is over. You will come with me now. Do not look back again."

In a daze, Ukon turned and let herself be led along twisting alleys, away from the inkmaker's shop. A great clamor of gongs and bells now arose from the streets, as people signaled that the quarter was in danger of burning; as dozens of men raced toward the shop carrying wooden buckets of water and sand, few noted the inkmaker's stepdaughter hurrying in the opposite direction, a small red cat at her side. Afterward, those who *had* seen her running displayed neither recrimination nor much remorse for her leaving her stepfather to perish in the flames. His cruelty and drunkenness were well-known; the fire, which had indeed started in the shed, was contained to his quarters, and no one else was harmed.

Ukon followed the strange woman to a narrow street where she had never been.

"Here," the woman said, bowing as she gestured at the door. "Here you will find safety."

And before Ukon could protest, or give voice to her questions, the woman was gone. The poor girl stood shivering in the snow, tears once more springing to her eyes, when suddenly the little door slid open, and who should be standing there, yawning and rubbing his face, but the young poet, Ga-sho.

"Why...?" He stared at her in disbelief. Ukon dropped her head, abashed and ashamed, and had begun to turn away when he grabbed her hand. "Don't go! Please, come in. You look half frozen, and"—his voice dropped, and he chuckled—"and look who you've found! Kury-ri, you naughty creature..."

He bent to pick up the red cat, which had appeared out of nowhere to rub against the filthy hem of Ukon's kimono. "Where have you been?"

He held the cat to his breast and looked at Ukon. "She ran off after I saw you—she's been out all night! But please, come in."

And he stood aside so that Ukon could enter.

They did not marry immediately, and for a while there was some mild scandal over the fact that the inkmaker's stepdaughter had found a home in the poor poet's rooms. But the tongues of that quarter soon enough found other tales to wag about, and by the time Ukon and Ga-sho were wed and had a baby due, the red cat had given birth to a litter of kittens of her own.

And, while the strange woman who had saved Ukon was never seen again in that district, for years afterward the descendants of the cat called Cleanears—red-furred, black-pawed, gray-eyed like their mother—were said to be lucky. Because how otherwise to account for the success the poet had, and the long and happy marriage he and Ukon endured? Such things did not come often to the poor people of that time, any more than they do to us today!

In medieval Japan, red bobtailed cats were known as Kinkwa-neko, "Golden Flower." They were thought to assume the forms of beautiful young women, and to help young girls in distress.

THE NIGHT OF THE TIGER

Stephen King

Stephen King needs little introduction. Since the publication of his first novel, *Carrie*, King has been entertaining readers by writing exactly what he wants to write, when he wants to write it. And this includes the occasional short story published in such varied venues as *OMNI*, *Playboy*, *The Magazine of Fantasy & Science Fiction*, *Cemetery Dance*, and *The New Yorker*. He won the O. Henry Award and the World Fantasy Award in 1995 for his story "The Man in the Black Suit."

"Night of the Tiger" is an early and relatively obscure work from the master of horror. With its circus traveling around small town America, the story has a Ray Bradbury feel to it, but with a harder edge.

I first saw Mr. Legere when the circus swung through Steubenville, but I'd only been with the show for two weeks; he might have been making his irregular visits indefinitely. No one much wanted to talk about Mr. Legere, not even that last night when it seemed that the world was coming to an end—the night that Mr. Indrasil disappeared.

But if I'm going to tell it to you from the beginning, I should start by saying that I'm Eddie Johnston, and I was born and raised in Sauk City. Went to school there, had my first girl there, and worked in Mr. Lillie's five-and-dime there for a while after I graduated from high school. That was a few years back... more than I like to count, sometimes. Not that Sauk City's such a bad place; hot, lazy summer nights sitting on the front porch is all right for some folks, but it just seemed to itch me, like sitting in the same chair too long. So I quit the five-and-dime and joined Farnum & Williams' All-American 3-Ring Circus and Side Show. I did it in a moment of giddiness when the calliope music kind of fogged my judgment, I guess.

So I became a roustabout, helping put up tents and take them down, spreading sawdust, cleaning cages, and sometimes selling cotton candy when the regular salesman had to go away and bark for Chips Baily, who had malaria and sometimes had to go someplace far away, and holler. Mostly things that kids do for free passes—things I used to do when I was a kid. But times change. They don't seem to come around like they used to.

We swung through Illinois and Indiana that hot summer, and the crowds were good and everyone was happy. Everyone except Mr. Indrasil. Mr. Indrasil was never happy. He was the lion tamer, and he looked like old pictures I've seen of Rudolph Valentino. He was tall, with handsome, arrogant features and a shock of wild black hair. And strange, mad eyes—the maddest eyes I've ever seen. He was silent most of the time; two syllables from Mr. Indrasil was a sermon. All the circus people kept a mental as well as a physical distance, because his rages were legend. There was a whispered story about coffee spilled on his hands after a particularly difficult performance and a murder that was almost done to a young roustabout before Mr. Indrasil could be hauled off him. I don't know about that. I do know that I grew to fear him worse than I had cold-eyed Mr. Edmont, my high school principal, Mr. Lillie, or even my father, who was capable of cold dressing-downs that would leave the recipient quivering with shame and dismay.

When I cleaned the big cats' cages, they were always spotless. The memory of the few times I had the vituperative wrath of Mr. Indrasil called down on me still have the power to turn my knees watery in retrospect.

Mostly it was his eyes—large and dark and totally blank. The eyes, and the feeling that a man capable of controlling seven watchful cats in a small cage must be part savage himself.

And the only two things he was afraid of were Mr. Legere and the circus's one tiger, a huge beast called Green Terror.

As I said, I first saw Mr. Legere in Steubenville, and he was staring into Green Terror's cage as if the tiger knew all the secrets of life and death.

He was lean, dark, quiet. His deep, recessed eyes held an expression of pain and brooding violence in their green-flecked depths, and his hands were always crossed behind his back as he stared moodily in at the tiger.

Green Terror was a beast to be stared at. He was a huge, beautiful specimen with a flawless striped coat, emerald eyes, and heavy fangs like ivory spikes. His roars usually filled the circus grounds—fierce, angry, and utterly savage. He seemed to scream defiance and frustration at the whole world.

Chips Baily, who had been with Farnum & Williams since Lord knew when, told me that Mr. Indrasil used to use Green Terror in his act, until one night when the tiger leaped suddenly from its perch and almost ripped his head from his shoulders before he could get out of the cage. I noticed that Mr. Indrasil always wore his hair long down the back of his neck.

I can still remember the tableau that day in Steubenville. It was hot, sweatingly hot, and we had a shirtsleeve crowd. That was why Mr. Legere and Mr. Indrasil stood out. Mr. Legere, standing silently by the tiger cage, was fully dressed in a suit and vest, his face unmarked by perspiration. And Mr. Indrasil, clad in one of his beautiful silk shirts and white whipcord breeches, was staring at them both, his face dead-white, his eyes bulging in lunatic anger, hate, and fear. He was carrying a currycomb and brush, and his hands were trembling as they clenched on them spasmodically.

Suddenly he saw me, and his anger found vent. "You!" He shouted. "Johnston!"

"Yes, sir?" I felt a crawling in the pit of my stomach. I knew I was about to have the wrath of Indrasil vented on me, and the thought turned me weak with fear. I like to think I'm as brave as the next, and if it had been anyone else, I think I would have been fully determined to stand up for myself. But it wasn't anyone else. It was Mr. Indrasil, and his eyes were mad.

"These cages, Johnston. Are they supposed to be clean?" He pointed a finger, and I followed it. I saw four errant wisps of straw and an incriminating puddle of hose water in the far corner of one.

"Y-yes, sir," I said, and what was intended to be firmness became palsied bravado.

Silence, like the electric pause before a downpour. People were beginning to look, and I was dimly aware that Mr. Legere was staring at us with his bottomless eyes.

"Yes, sir?" Mr. Indrasil thundered suddenly. "Yes, sir? Yes, sir? Don't insult my intelligence, boy! Don't you think I can see? Smell? Did you use the disinfectant?"

"I used disinfectant yes—"

"Don't answer me back!" He screeched, and then the sudden drop in his voice made my skin crawl. "Don't you dare answer me back." Everyone was staring now. I wanted to retch, to die. "Now you get the hell into that tool shed, and you get that disinfectant and swab out those cages," he whispered, measuring every word. One hand suddenly shot out, grasping my shoulder. "And don't you ever, ever, speak back to me again."

I don't know where the words came from, but they were suddenly there, spilling off my lips. "I didn't speak back to you, Mr. Indrasil, and I don't like you saying I did. I—resent it. Now let me go."

His face went suddenly red, then white, then almost saffron with rage. His eyes were blazing doorways to hell.

Right then I thought I was going to die.

He made an inarticulate gagging sound, and the grip on my shoulder became excruciating. His right hand went up... up... up, and then descended with unbelievable speed.

If that hand had connected with my face, it would have knocked me senseless at best. At worst, it would have broken my neck.

It did not connect.

Another hand materialized magically out of space, right in front of me. The two straining limbs came together with a flat smacking sound. It was Mr. Legere.

"Leave the boy alone," he said emotionlessly.

Mr. Indrasil stared at him for a long second, and I think there was nothing so unpleasant in the whole business as watching the fear of Mr. Legere and the mad lust to hurt (or to kill!) mix in those terrible eyes.

Then he turned and stalked away.

I turned to look at Mr. Legere. "Thank you," I said.

"Don't thank me." And it wasn't a "don't thank me," but a "don't thank me." Not a gesture of modesty but a literal command. In a sudden flash of intuition—empathy if you will—I understood exactly what he meant by that comment. I was a pawn in what must have been a long combat between the two of them. I had been captured by Mr. Legere rather than Mr. Indrasil. He had stopped the lion tamer not because he felt for me, but because it gained him an advantage, however slight, in their private war.

"What's your name?" I asked, not at all offended by what I had inferred. He had, after all, been honest with me.

"Legere," he said briefly. He turned to go.

"Are you with a circus?" I asked, not wanting to let him go so easily. "You seemed to know—him."

A faint smile touched his thin lips, and warmth kindled in his eyes for a moment; "No. You might call me a—policeman." And before I could reply, he had disappeared into the surging throng passing by.

The next day we picked up stakes and moved on.

I saw Mr. Legere again in Danville and, two weeks later, in Chicago. In the time between I tried to avoid Mr. Indrasil as much as possible and kept the cat cages spotlessly clean. On the day before we pulled out for St. Louis, I asked Chips Baily and Sally O'Hara, the red-headed wire walker, if Mr. Legere and Mr. Indrasil knew each other. I was pretty sure they did, because Mr. Legere was hardly following the circus to eat our fabulous lime ice.

Sally and Chips looked at each other over their coffee cups. "No one knows much about what's between those two," she said. "But it's been going on for a long time, maybe twenty years. Ever since Mr. Indrasil came over from Ringling Brothers, and maybe before that."

Chips nodded. "This Legere guy picks up the circus almost every year when we swing through the Midwest and stays with us until we catch the train for Florida in Little Rock. Makes old Leopard Man touchy as one of his cats."

"He told me he was a policeman," I said. "What do you suppose he looks for around here? You don't suppose Mr. Indrasil—?"

Chips and Sally looked at each other strangely, and both just about broke their backs getting up. "Got to see those weights and counter weights get stored right," Sally said, and Chips muttered something not too convincing about checking on the rear axle of his U-Haul.

And that's about the way any conversation concerning Mr. Indrasil or Mr. Legere usually broke up—hurriedly, with many hard-forced excuses.

We said farewell to Illinois and comfort at the same time. A killing hot spell came on, seemingly at the very instant we crossed the border, and it stayed with us for the next month and a half, as we moved slowly across Missouri and into

Kansas. Everyone grew short of temper, including the animals. And that, of course, included the cats, which were Mr. Indrasil's responsibility. He rode the roustabouts unmercifully, and myself in particular. I grinned and tried to bear it, even though I had my own case of prickly heat. You just don't argue with a crazy man, and I'd pretty well decided that was what Mr. Indrasil was.

No one was getting any sleep, and that is the curse of all circus performers. Loss of sleep slows up reflexes, and slow reflexes make for danger. In Independence Sally O'Hara fell seventy-five feet into the nylon netting and fractured her shoulder. Andrea Solienni, our bareback rider, fell off one of her horses during rehearsal and was knocked unconscious by a flying hoof. Chips Baily suffered silently with the fever that was always with him, his face a waxen mask, with cold perspiration clustered at each temple.

And in many ways, Mr. Indrasil had the roughest row to hoe of all. The cats were nervous and short-tempered, and every time he stepped into the Demon Cat Cage, as it was billed, he took his life in his hands. He was feeding the lions inordinate amounts of raw meat right before he went on, something that lion tamers rarely do, contrary to popular belief. His face grew drawn and haggard, and his eyes were wild.

Mr. Legere was almost always there, by Green Terror's cage, watching him. And that, of course, added to Mr. Indrasil's load. The circus began eyeing the silk-shirted figure nervously as he passed, and I knew they were all thinking the same thing I was: *He's going to crack wide open, and when he does—*

When he did, God alone knew what would happen.

The hot spell went on, and temperatures were climbing well into the nineties every day. It seemed as if the rain gods were mocking us. Every town we left would receive the showers of blessing. Every town we entered was hot, parched, sizzling.

And one night, on the road between Kansas City and Green Bluff, I saw something that upset me more than anything else.

It was hot—abominably hot. It was no good even trying to sleep. I rolled about on my cot like a man in a fever-delirium, chasing the sandman but never quite catching him. Finally I got up, pulled on my pants, and went outside.

We had pulled off into a small field and drawn into a circle. Myself and two other roustabouts had unloaded the cats so they could catch whatever breeze there might be. The cages were there now, painted dull silver by the swollen Kansas moon, and a tall figure in white whipcord breeches was standing by the biggest of them. Mr. Indrasil.

He was baiting Green Terror with a long, pointed pike. The big cat was padding silently around the cage, trying to avoid the sharp tip. And the frightening thing was, when the staff did punch into the tiger's flesh, it did not roar in pain and anger as it should have. It maintained an ominous silence, more terrifying to the person who knows cats than the loudest of roars.

It had gotten to Mr. Indrasil, too. "Quiet bastard, aren't you?" He grunted. Powerful arms flexed, and the iron shaft slid forward. Green Terror flinched, and his eyes rolled horribly. But he did not make a sound. "Yowl!" Mr. Indrasil hissed. "Go ahead and yowl, you monster, Yowl!" And he drove his spear deep into the tiger's flank.

Then I saw something odd. It seemed that a shadow moved in the darkness under one of the far wagons, and the moonlight seemed to glint on staring eyes—green eyes.

A cool wind passed silently through the clearing, lifting dust and rumpling my hair.

Mr. Indrasil looked up, and there was a queer listening expression on his face. Suddenly he dropped the bar, turned, and strode back to his trailer.

I stared again at the far wagon, but the shadow was gone. Green Tiger stood motionlessly at the bars of his cage, staring at Mr. Indrasil's trailer. And the thought came to me that it hated Mr. Indrasil not because he was cruel or vicious, for the tiger respects these qualities in its own animalistic way, but rather because he was a deviate from even the tiger's savage norm. He was a rogue. That's the only way I can put it. Mr. Indrasil was not only a human tiger, but a rogue tiger as well.

The thought jelled inside me, disquieting and a little scary. I went back inside, but still I could not sleep.

The heat went on.

Every day we fried, every night we tossed and turned, sweating and sleepless. Everyone was painted red with sunburn, and there were fistfights over trifling affairs. Everyone was reaching the point of explosion.

Mr. Legere remained with us, a silent watcher, emotionless on the surface, but, I sensed, with deep-running currents of—what? Hate? Fear? Vengeance? I could not place it. But he was potentially dangerous, I was sure of that. Perhaps more so than Mr. Indrasil was, if anyone ever lit his particular fuse.

He was at the circus at every performance, always dressed in his nattily creased brown suit, despite the killing temperatures. He stood silently by Green Terror's cage, seeming to commune deeply with the tiger, who was always quiet when he was around.

From Kansas to Oklahoma, with no letup in the temperature. A day without a heat prostration case was a rare day indeed. Crowds were beginning to drop off; who wanted to sit under a stifling canvas tent when there was an air-conditioned movie just around the block?

We were all as jumpy as cats, to coin a particularly applicable phrase. And as we set down stakes in Wildwood Green, Oklahoma, I think we all knew a climax of some sort was close at hand. And most of us knew it would involve Mr. Indrasil. A bizarre occurrence had taken place just prior to our first Wildwood performance. Mr. Indrasil had been in the Demon Cat Cage, putting the ill-tempered lions through their paces. One of them missed its balance on its pedestal, tottered and almost regained it. Then, at that precise moment, Green Terror let out a terrible, ear-splitting roar.

The lion fell, landed heavily, and suddenly launched itself with rifle-bullet accuracy at Mr. Indrasil. With a frightened curse, he heaved his chair at the cat's feet, tangling up the driving legs. He darted out just as the lion smashed against the bars.

As he shakily collected himself preparatory to re-entering the cage, Green Terror let out another roar—but this one monstrously like a huge, disdainful chuckle.

Mr. Indrasil stared at the beast, white-faced, then turned and walked away. He did not come out of his trailer all afternoon.

That afternoon wore on interminably. But as the temperature climbed, we all began looking hopefully toward the west, where huge banks of thunderclouds were forming.

"Rain, maybe," I told Chips, stopping by his barking platform in front of the sideshow.

But he didn't respond to my hopeful grin. "Don't like it," he said. "No wind. Too hot. Hail or tornadoes." His face grew grim. "It ain't no picnic, ridin' out a tornado with a pack of crazy-wild animals all over the place, Eddie. I've thanked God mor'n once when we've gone through the tornado belt that we don't have no elephants.

"Yeah," he added gloomily, "you better hope them clouds stay right on the horizon."

But they didn't. They moved slowly toward us, cyclopean pillars in the sky, purple at the bases and awesome blue-black through the cumulonimbus. All air movement ceased, and the heat lay on us like a woolen winding-shroud. Every now and again, thunder would clear its throat further west.

About four, Mr. Farnum himself, ringmaster and half-owner of the circus, appeared and told us there would be no evening performance; just batten down and find a convenient hole to crawl into in case of trouble. There had been corkscrew funnels spotted in several places between Wildwood and Oklahoma City, some within forty miles of us.

There was only a small crowd when the announcement came, apathetically wandering through the sideshow exhibits or ogling the animals. But Mr. Legere had not been present all day; the only person at Green Terror's cage was a sweaty high-school boy with clutch of books. When Mr. Farnum announced the U.S. Weather Bureau tornado warning that had been issued, he hurried quickly away.

I and the other two roustabouts spent the rest of the afternoon working our tails off, securing tents, loading animals back into their wagons, and making generally sure that everything was nailed down.

Finally only the cat cages were left, and there was a special arrangement for those. Each cage had a special mesh "breezeway" accordioned up against it, which, when extended completely, connected with the Demon Cat Cage. When the smaller cages had to be moved, the felines could be herded into the big cage while they were loaded up. The big cage itself rolled on gigantic casters and could be muscled around to a position where each cat could be let back into its original cage. It sounds complicated, and it was, but it was just the only way.

We did the lions first, then Ebony Velvet, the docile black panther that had set the circus back almost one season's receipts. It was a tricky business coaxing them up and then back through the breezeways, but all of us preferred it to calling Mr. Indrasil to help.

By the time we were ready for Green Terror, twilight had come—a queer, yellow twilight that hung humidly around us. The sky above had taken on a flat, shiny aspect that I had never seen and which I didn't like in the least.

"Better hurry," Mr. Farnum said, as we laboriously trundled the Demon Cat Cage back to where we could hook it to the back of Green Terror's show cage. "Barometer's falling off fast." He shook his head worriedly. "Looks bad, boys. Bad." He hurried on, still shaking his head.

We got Green Terror's breezeway hooked up and opened the back of his cage. "In you go," I said encouragingly.

Green Terror looked at me menacingly and didn't move.

Thunder rumbled again, louder, closer, sharper. The sky had gone jaundice, the ugliest color I have ever seen. Wind-devils began to pick jerkily at our clothes and whirl away the flattened candy wrappers and cotton-candy cones that littered the area.

"Come on, come on," I urged and poked him easily with the blunt-tipped rods we were given to herd them with.

Green Terror roared ear-splittingly, and one paw lashed out with blinding speed. The hardwood pole was jerked from my hands and splintered as if it had been a greenwood twig. The tiger was on his feet now, and there was murder in his eyes.

"Look," I said shakily. "One of you will have to go get Mr. Indrasil, that's all. We can't wait around."

As if to punctuate my words, thunder cracked louder, the clapping of mammoth hands.

Kelly Nixon and Mike McGregor flipped for it; I was excluded because of my previous run-in with Mr. Indrasil. Kelly drew the task, threw us a wordless glance that said he would prefer facing the storm and then started off.

He was gone almost ten minutes. The wind was picking up velocity now, and twilight was darkening into a weird six o'clock night. I was scared, and am not afraid to admit it. That rushing, featureless sky, the deserted circus grounds, the sharp, tugging wind-vortices, all that makes a memory that will stay with me always, undimmed.

And Green Terror would not budge into his breezeway.

Kelly Nixon came rushing back, his eyes wide. "I pounded on his door for 'most five minutes!" He gasped. "Couldn't raise him!"

We looked at each other, at a loss. Green Terror was a big investment for the circus. He couldn't just be left in the open. I turned bewilderedly, looking for Chips, Mr. Farnum, or anybody who could tell me what to do. But everyone was gone. The tiger was our responsibility. I considered trying to load the cage bodily into the trailer, but I wasn't going to get my fingers in that cage.

"Well, we've just got to go and get him," I said. "The three of us. Come on." And we ran toward Mr. Indrasil's trailer through the gloom of coming night.

We pounded on his door until he must have thought all the demons of hell were after him. Thankfully, it finally jerked open. Mr. Indrasil swayed and stared down at us, his mad eyes rimmed and oversheened with drink. He smelled like a distillery.

"Damn you, leave me alone," he snarled.

"Mr. Indrasil—" I had to shout over the rising whine of the wind. It was like no storm I had ever heard of or read about, out there. It was like the end of the world.

"You," he gritted softly. He reached down and gathered my shirt up in a knot. "I'm going to teach you a lesson you'll never forget." He glared at Kelly and Mike, cowering back in the moving storm shadows. "Get out!"

They ran. I didn't blame them; I've told you—Mr. Indrasil was crazy. And not just ordinary crazy—he was like a crazy animal, like one of his own cats gone bad.

"All right," he muttered, staring down at me, his eyes like hurricane lamps. "No juju to protect you now. No grisgris." His lips twitched in a wild, horrible smile. "He isn't here now, is he? We're two of a kind, him and me. Maybe the only two left. My nemesis—and I'm his." He was rambling, and I didn't try to stop him. At least his mind was off me.

"Turned that cat against me, back in '58. Always had the power more'n me. Fool could make a million—the two of us could make a million if he wasn't so damned high and mighty... what's that?"

It was Green Terror, and he had begun to roar ear-splittingly.

"Haven't you got that damned tiger in?" He screamed, almost falsetto. He shook me like a rag doll.

"He won't go!" I found myself yelling back. "You've got to—"

But he flung me away. I stumbled over the fold-up steps in front of his trailer and crashed into a bone-shaking heap at the bottom. With something between a sob and a curse, Mr. Indrasil strode past me, face mottled with anger and fear.

I got up, drawn after him as if hypnotized. Some intuitive part of me realized I was about to see the last act played out.

Once clear of the shelter of Mr. Indrasil's trailer, the power of the wind was appalling. It screamed like a runaway freight train. I was an ant, a speck, an unprotected molecule before that thundering, cosmic force.

And Mr. Legere was standing by Green Terror's cage.

It was like a tableau from Dante. The near-empty cage-clearing inside the circle of trailers; the two men, facing each other silently, their clothes and hair rippled by the shrieking gale; the boiling sky above; the twisting wheatfields in the background, like damned souls bending to the whip of Lucifer.

"It's time, Jason," Mr. Legere said, his words flayed across the clearing by the wind.

Mr. Indrasil's wildly whipping hair lifted around the livid scar across the back of his neck. His fists clenched, but he said nothing. I could almost feel him gathering his will, his life force, his id. It gathered around him like an unholy nimbus.

And, then, I saw with sudden horror that Mr. Legere was unhooking Green Terror's breezeway—and the back of the cage was open!

I cried out, but the wind ripped my words away.

The great tiger leaped out and almost flowed past Mr. Legere. Mr. Indrasil swayed, but did not run. He bent his head and stared down at the tiger.

And Green Terror stopped.

He swung his huge head back to Mr. Legere, almost turned, and then slowly turned back to Mr. Indrasil again. There was a terrifyingly palpable sensation of directed force in the air, a mesh of conflicting wills centered around the tiger. And the wills were evenly matched.

I think, in the end, it was Green Terror's own will—his hate of Mr. Indrasil—that tipped the scales.

The cat began to advance, his eyes hellish, flaring beacons. And something strange began to happen to Mr. Indrasil. He seemed to be folding in on himself, shriveling, accordioning. The silk-shirt lost shape, the dark, whipping hair became a hideous toadstool around his collar.

Mr. Legere called something across to him, and, simultaneously, Green Terror leaped.

I never saw the outcome. The next moment I was slammed flat on my back, and the breath seemed to be sucked from my body. I caught one crazily tilted glimpse of a huge, towering cyclone funnel, and then the darkness descended.

When I awoke, I was in my cot just aft of the grainery bins in the all-purpose storage trailer we carried. My body felt as if it had been beaten with padded Indian clubs.

Chips Baily appeared, his face lined and pale. He saw my eyes were open and grinned relievedly. "Didn't know as you were ever gonna wake up. How you feel?"

"Dislocated," I said. "What happened? How'd I get here?"

"We found you piled up against Mr. Indrasil's trailer. The tornado almost carried you away for a souvenir, m'boy."

At the mention of Mr. Indrasil, all the ghastly memories came flooding back. "Where is Mr. Indrasil? And Mr. Legere?"

His eyes went murky, and he started to make some kind of an evasive answer.

"Straight talk," I said, struggling up on one elbow. "I have to know, Chips. I have to."

Something in my face must have decided him. "Okay. But this isn't exactly what we told the cops—in fact we hardly told the cops any of it. No sense havin' people think we're crazy. Anyhow, Indrasil's gone. I didn't even know that Legere guy was around."

"And Green Tiger?"

Chips' eyes were unreadable again. "He and the other tiger fought to death."

"Other tiger? There's no other—"

"Yeah, but they found two of 'em, lying in each other's blood. Hell of a mess. Ripped each other's throats out."

"What—where—"

"Who knows? We just told the cops we had two tigers. Simpler that way." And before I could say another word, he was gone.

And that's the end of my story—except for two little items. The words Mr. Legere shouted just before the tornado hit: *"When a man and an animal live in the same shell, Indrasil, the instincts determine the mold!"*

The other thing is what keeps me awake nights. Chips told me later, offering it only for what it might be worth. What he told me was that the strange tiger had a long scar on the back of its neck.

EVERY ANGEL
IS TERRIFYING

John Kessel

John Kessel teaches creative writing and literature at North Carolina State University in Raleigh. A winner of the Nebula Award, the Theodore Sturgeon Award, the Locus Award, and the James Tiptree, Jr. Award, his books include *Good News from Outer Space*, *Corrupting Dr. Nice*, and *The Pure Product*. His story collection, *Meeting in Infinity*, was named a notable book of 1992 by the *New York Times Book Review*.

Kessel co-edited *Feeling Very Strange: The Slipstream Anthology* and *Rewired: The Post-Cyberpunk Anthology* with James Patrick Kelly. His recent collection *The Baum Plan for Financial Independence and Other Stories* contains the 2008 Nebula and Shirley Jackson Award-winning story "Pride and Prometheus." About "Every Angel is Terrifying" he says: "The cat was the only survivor of the family in Flannery O'Connor's harrowing short story 'A Good Man is Hard to Find,' so it was natural for me to carry it along into this story. But being a long-time student of cats (and having been the subject of their indifferent gaze in return), I can believe that they have the power to alter reality in metaphysical, if not physical, ways."

Railroad watched Bobby Lee grab the grandmother's body under the armpits and drag her up the other side of the ditch. "Whyn't you help him, Hiram," he said.

Hiram took off his coat, skidded down into the ditch after Bobby Lee, and got hold of the old lady's legs. Together he and Bobby Lee lugged her across the field towards the woods. Her broken blue hat was still pinned to her head, which lolled against Bobby Lee's shoulder. The woman's face grinned lopsidedly all the way into the shadow of the trees.

Railroad carried the cat over to the Studebaker. It occurred to him that he didn't know the cat's name, and now that the entire family was dead he never would. It was a calico, gray striped with a broad white face and an orange nose. "What's your name, puss-puss?" he whispered, scratching it behind the ears.

The cat purred. One by one Railroad went round and rolled up the windows of the car. A fracture zigzagged across the windshield, and the front passenger's vent window was shattered. He stuffed Hiram's coat into the vent window hole. Then he put the cat inside the car and shut the door. The cat put its front paws up on the dashboard and, watching him, gave a pantomime meow.

Railroad pushed up his glasses and stared off toward the woodline where Bobby Lee and Hiram had taken the bodies. The place was hot and still, silence broken only by birdsong from somewhere up the embankment behind him. He squinted up into the cloudless sky. Only a couple of hours of sun left. He rubbed the spot on his shoulder where the grandmother had touched him. Somehow he had wrenched it when he jerked away from her.

The last thing the grandmother had said picked at him: "You're one of my own children." The old lady had looked familiar, but she didn't look anything like his mother. But maybe his father had sown some wild oats in the old days—Railroad knew he had—could the old lady have been his mother, for real? It would explain why the woman who had raised him, the sweetest of women, could have been saddled with a son as bad as he was.

The idea caught in his head. He wished he'd had the sense to ask the grandmother a few questions. The old woman might have been sent to tell him the truth.

When Hiram and Bobby Lee came back, they found Railroad leaning under the hood of the car.

"What we do now, boss?" Bobby Lee asked.

"Police could be here any minute," Hiram said. Blood was smeared on the leg of his khaki pants. "Somebody might of heard the shots."

Railroad pulled himself out from under the hood. "Onliest thing we got to worry about now, Hiram, is how we get this radiator to stop leaking. You find a tire iron and straighten out this here fan. Bobby Lee, you get the belt off'n the other car."

It took longer than the half hour Hiram had estimated to get the people's Studebaker back on the road. By the time they did it was twilight, and the red-dirt road was cast in the shadows of the pinewoods. They pushed the stolen Hudson they'd been driving off into the trees and got into the Studebaker.

Railroad gripped the wheel of the car and they bounced down the dirt road toward the main highway. Hat pushed back on his head, Hiram went through the dead man's wallet, while in the back seat Bobby Lee had the cat on his lap and was scratching it under the chin. "Kitty-kitty-kitty-kitty-kitty," he murmured.

"Sixty-eight dollars," Hiram said. "With the twenty-two from the wife's purse, that makes ninety bucks." He turned around and handed a wad of bills to Bobby Lee. "Get rid of that damn cat," he said. "Want me to hold yours for you?" he asked Railroad.

Railroad reached over, took the bills, and stuffed them into the pocket of the yellow shirt with bright blue parrots, that had belonged to the husband who'd been driving the car. Bailey Boy, the grandmother had called him. Railroad's shoulder twinged.

The car shuddered; the wheels had been knocked out of kilter when it rolled. If he tried pushing past fifty, it would shake itself right off the road. Railroad felt the warm weight of his pistol inside his belt, against his belly. Bobby Lee hummed tunelessly in the back seat. Hiram was quiet, fidgeting, looking out at the dark trees. He tugged his battered coat out of the vent window, tried to shake some of the wrinkles out of it. "You oughtn't to use a man's coat without saying to him," he grumbled.

Bobby Lee spoke up. "He didn't want the cat to get away."

Hiram sneezed. "Will you throw that damn animal out the damn window?"

"She never hurt you none," Bobby Lee said.

Railroad said nothing. He had always imagined that the world was slightly unreal, that he was meant to be the citizen of some other place. His mind was a box. Outside the box was that world of distraction, amusement, annoyance. Inside the box his real life went on, the struggle between what he knew and what he didn't know. He had a way of acting—polite, detached—because that way he wouldn't be bothered. When he was bothered, he got mad. When he got mad, bad things happened.

He had always been prey to remorse, but now he felt it more fully than he had since he was a boy. He hadn't paid enough attention. He'd pegged the old lady as a hypocrite and had gone back into his box, thinking her just another fool from that puppet world. But that moment of her touching him—she'd wanted to comfort him. And he shot her.

What was it the old woman had said? "You could be honest if you'd only try… Think how wonderful it would be to settle down and live a comfortable life and not have to think about somebody chasing you all the time."

He knew she was only saying that to save her life. But that didn't mean it couldn't also be a message.

Outside the box, Hiram asked, "What was all that yammer yammer with the grandmother about Jesus? We doing all the killing while you yammer yammer."

"He did shoot the old lady," Bobby Lee said.

"And made us carry her off to the woods, when if he'd of waited she could of walked there like the others. We're the ones get blood on our clothes."

Railroad said quietly, "You don't like the way things are going, son?"

Hiram twitched against the seat like he was itchy between the shoulder blades. "I ain't sayin' that. I just want out of this state."

"We going to Atlanta. In Atlanta we can get lost."

"Gonna get me a girl!" Bobby Lee said.

"They got more cops in Atlanta than the rest of the state put together," Hiram said. "In Florida…"

Without taking his eyes off the road, Railroad snapped his right hand across the bridge of Hiram's nose. Hiram jerked, more startled than hurt, and his hat tumbled off into the back seat.

Bobby Lee laughed, and handed Hiram his hat.

It was after 11:00 when they hit the outskirts of Atlanta. Railroad pulled into a diner, the Sweet Spot, red brick and an asbestos-shingled roof, the air smelling of cigarettes and pork barbecue. Hiram rubbed some dirt from the lot into the stain on his pants leg. Railroad unlocked the trunk and found the dead man's suitcase, full of clothes. He carried it in with them.

On the radio sitting on the shelf behind the counter, Kitty Wells sang "It Wasn't God Who Made Honky-Tonk Angels." Railroad studied the menu, front and back, and ordered biscuits and gravy. While they ate Bobby Lee ran on about girls, and Hiram sat sullenly smoking. Railroad could tell Hiram was getting ready to do something stupid. He didn't need either of them anymore. So after they finished eating, Railroad left the car keys on the table and took the suitcase into the men's room. He locked the door. He pulled his .38 out of the waistband, put it on the sink, and changed out of the too-tight dungarees into some of the dead husband's baggy trousers. He washed his face and hands. He cleaned his glasses on the tail of the parrot shirt, then tucked in the shirt. He stuck the .38 into the suitcase and came out again. Bobby Lee and Hiram were gone, and the car was no longer in the parking lot. The bill on the table, next to Hiram's still smoldering cigarette, was for six dollars and eighty cents.

Railroad sat in the booth drinking his coffee. In the window of the diner, near the door, a piece of cardboard had been taped up, saying, "WANTED: FRY COOK." When he was done with the coffee, he untaped the sign and headed to the register. After he paid the bill he handed the cashier the sign. "I'm your man," he said.

The cashier called the manager. "Mr. Cauthron, this man says he's a cook."

Mr. Cauthron was maybe thirty-five years old. His carrot red hair stood up in a pompadour like a rooster's comb, and a little belly swelled out over his belt. "What's your name?"

"Lloyd Bailey."

"Lloyd, what experience do you have?"

"I can cook anything on this here menu," Railroad said.

The manager took him back to the kitchen. "Stand aside, Shorty," the manager said to the tall black man at the griddle. "Fix me a Denver omelet," he said to Railroad.

Railroad washed his hands, put on an apron, broke two eggs into a bowl. He threw handfuls of chopped onion, green pepper, and diced ham into a skillet. When the onions were soft, he poured the beaten eggs over the ham and vegetables, added salt and cayenne pepper.

When he slid the finished omelet onto a plate, the manager bent down over it as if he were inspecting the paint job on a used car. He straightened up. "Pay's thirty dollars a week. Be here at six in the morning."

Out in the lot Railroad set down his bag and looked around. Cicadas buzzed in the hot city night. Around the corner from the diner he'd noticed a big Victorian house with a sign on the porch, "Rooms for Rent." He was about to start walking when, out of the corner of his eye, he caught a movement by the trash barrel next to the chain-link fence. He peered into the gloom and saw the cat trying to leap up to the top to get at the garbage. He went over, held out his hand. The cat didn't run; it sniffed him, butted its head against his hand.

He picked it up, cradled it under his arm, and carried it and the bag to the rooming house. Under dense oaks, it was a big tan clapboard mansion with green shutters and hanging baskets of begonias on the porch, and a green porch swing. The thick oval leaded glass of the oak door was beveled around the edge, the brass of the handle dark with age.

The door was unlocked. His heart jumped a bit at the opportunity it presented; at the same time he wanted to warn the proprietor against such foolishness. Off to one side of the entrance was a little table with a doily, vase and dried flowers; on the other a sign beside a door said, "manager."

Railroad knocked. After a moment the door opened and a woman with the face of an angel opened it. She was not young, perhaps forty, with very white skin and blonde hair. She looked at him, smiled, saw the cat under his arm. "What a sweet animal," she said.

"I'd like a room," he said.

"I'm sorry. We don't cater to pets," the woman said, not unkindly.

"This here's no pet, Ma'm," Railroad said. "This here's my only friend in the world."

The landlady's name was Mrs. Graves. The room she rented him was twelve feet by twelve feet, with a single bed, a cherry veneer dresser, a wooden table and chair, a narrow closet, lace curtains on the window, and an old pineapple quilt on the bed. The air smelled sweet. On the wall opposite the bed was a picture in a dime store frame, of an empty rowboat floating in an angry gray ocean, the sky overcast, only a single shaft of sunlight in the distance from a sunset that was not in the picture.

The room cost ten dollars a week. Despite Mrs. Graves's rule against pets, like magic she took a shine to Railroad's cat. It was almost as if she'd rented the room to the cat, with Railroad along for the ride. After some consideration, he named the cat Pleasure. She was the most affectionate animal he had ever seen. She wanted to be with him, even when he ignored her. She made him feel wanted; she made him nervous. Railroad fashioned a cat door in the window of his room so that Pleasure could go out and in whenever she wanted, and not be confined to the room when Railroad was at work.

The only other residents of the boarding house were Louise Parker, a school teacher, and Charles Foster, a lingerie salesman. Mrs. Graves cleaned Railroad's room once a week, swept the floors, alternated the quilt every other week with a second one done in a rose pattern that he remembered from his childhood. He worked at the diner from six in the morning, when Maisie, the cashier, unlocked, until Shorty took over at three in the afternoon. The counter girl was Betsy, and Service, a Negro boy, bussed tables and washed dishes. Railroad told them to call him Bailey, and didn't talk much.

When he wasn't working, Railroad spent most of his time at the boarding house, or evenings in a small nearby park. Railroad would take the Bible from the drawer in the boarding house table, buy an afternoon newspaper, and carry them with him. Pleasure often followed him to the park. She would lunge after squirrels and shy away from dogs, hissing sideways. Cats liked to kill squirrels, dogs liked to kill cats, but there was no sin in it. Pleasure would not go to hell, or heaven. Cats had no souls.

The world was full of stupid people like Bobby Lee and Hiram, who lied to themselves and killed without knowing why. Life was a prison. Turn to the right, it was a wall. Turn to the left, it was a wall. Look up it was a ceiling, look down it was a floor. And Railroad had taken out his imprisonment on others; he was not deceived in his own behavior.

Railroad did not believe in sin, but somehow he felt it. Still, he was not a dog or a cat, he was a man. *You're one of my own children.* There was no reason why he had to kill people. He only wished he'd never have to deal with any Hirams and Bobby Lees anymore. He gazed across the park at the Ipana toothpaste sign painted on the wall of the Piggly Wiggly. *Whiter than white.* Pleasure crouched at the end of the bench, her haunches twitching as she watched a finch hop across the sidewalk.

Railroad picked her up, rubbed his cheek against her whiskers. "Pleasure, I'll tell you what," he whispered. "Let's make us a deal. You save me from Bobby Lee and Hiram, and I'll never kill anybody again."

The cat looked at him with its clear yellow eyes.

Railroad sighed. He put the cat down. He leaned back on the bench and opened the newspaper. Beneath the fold on the front page he read,

Escaped Convicts Killed in Wreck

Valdosta—Two escaped convicts and an unidentified female passenger were killed Tuesday when the late model stolen automobile they were driving struck a bridge abutment while being pursued by State Police.

The deceased convicts, Hiram Leroy Burgett, 31, and Bobby Lee Ross, 21, escaped June 23 while being transported to the State Hospital for the Criminally Insane for psychological evaluation. A third escapee, Ronald Reuel Pickens, 47, is still at large.

The lunch rush was petering out. There were two people at the counter and four booths were occupied, and Railroad had set a BLT and an order of fried chicken with collards up on the shelf when Maisie came back into the kitchen and called the manager. "Police wants to talk to you, Mr. C."

Railroad peeked out from behind the row of hanging order slips. A man in a suit sat at the counter, sipping sweet tea. Cauthron went out to talk to him.

"Two castaways on a raft," Betsy called to Railroad.

The man spoke with Cauthron for a few minutes, showed him a photograph. Cauthron shook his head, nodded, shook his head again. They laughed. Railroad eyed the back door of the diner, but turned back to the grill. By the time he had the toast up and the eggs fried, the man was gone. Cauthron stepped back to his office without saying anything.

At the end of the shift he pulled Railroad aside. "Lloyd," he said. "I need to speak with you."

Railroad followed him into the cubbyhole he called his office. Cauthron sat behind the cluttered metal desk and picked up a letter from the top layer of trash. "I just got this here note from Social Security saying that number you gave is not valid." He looked up at Railroad, his china blue eyes unreadable.

Railroad took off his glasses and rubbed the bridge of his nose with his thumb and forefinger. He didn't say anything.

"I suppose it's just some mixup," Cauthron said. "Same as that business with the detective this afternoon. Don't you worry about it."

"Thank you, Mr. Cauthron."

"One other thing, before you go, Lloyd. Did I say your salary was thirty a week? I meant twenty-five. That okay with you?"

"Whatever you say, Mr. Cauthron."

"And I think, in order to encourage trade, we'll start opening at five. I'd like you to pick up the extra hour. Starting Monday."

Railroad nodded. "Is that all?"

"That's it, Lloyd." Cauthron seemed suddenly to enjoy calling Railroad "Lloyd," rolling the name over his tongue and watching for his reaction. "Thanks for being such a Christian employee."

Railroad went back to his room in the rooming house. Pleasure mewed for him, and when he sat on the bed, hopped into his lap. But Railroad just stared at the picture of the rowboat on the opposite wall. After a while the cat hopped onto the window sill and out through her door onto the roof.

Only a crazy person would use the knowledge that a man was a murderer in order to cheat that man out of his pay. How could he know that Railroad wouldn't kill him, or run away, or do both?

Lucky for Cauthron that Railroad had made his deal with Pleasure. But now he didn't know what to do. If the old lady's message was from God, then maybe this was his first test. Nobody said being good was supposed to be easy. Nobody said, just because Railroad was turning to good, everybody he met forever after would be good. Railroad had asked Pleasure to save him from Bobby Lee and Hiram, not Mr. Cauthron.

He needed guidance. He slid open the drawer of the table. Beside the Bible was his .38. He flipped open the cylinder, checked to see that all the chambers were loaded, then put it back into the drawer. He took out the Bible and opened it at random.

The first verse his eyes fell on was from Deuteronomy: "These you may eat of all that are in the waters: you may eat all that have fins and scales. And whatever does not have fins and scales you shall not eat."

There was a knock at the door. Railroad looked up. "Yes?"

"Mr. Bailey?" It was Mrs. Graves. "I thought you might like some tea."

Keeping his finger in the Bible to mark his page, Railroad got up and opened the door. Mrs. Graves stood there with a couple of tall glasses, beaded with sweat, on a tray.

"That's mighty kind of you, Miz Graves. Would you like to come in?"

"Thank you, Mr. Bailey." She set the tray down on the table, gave him a glass. It was like nectar. "Is it sweet enough?"

"It's perfect, ma'm."

She wore a yellow print dress with little flowers on it. Her every movement showed a calm he had not seen in a woman before, and her gray eyes exuded compassion, as if to say, I know who you are but that doesn't matter.

They sat down, he on the bed, she on the chair. She saw the Bible in his hand. "I find many words of comfort in the Bible."

"I can't say as I find much comfort in it, ma'm. Too many bloody deeds."

"But many acts of goodness."

"You said a true word."

"Sometimes I wish I could live in the world of goodness." She smiled. "But this world is good enough."

Did she really think that? "Since Eve ate the apple, ma'm, it's a world of good and evil. How can goodness make up for the bad? That's a mystery to me."

She sipped her tea. "Of course it's a mystery. That's the point."

"The point is, something's always after you, deserve it or not."

"What a sad thought, Mr. Bailey."

"Yes'm. From minute to minute, we fade away. Only way to get to heaven is to die."

After Mrs. Graves left he sat thinking about her beautiful face. Like an angel. Nice titties, too. And yet he didn't even want to rape her.

He would marry her. He would settle down, like the grandmother said. But he would have to get an engagement ring. If he'd been thinking, he could have taken the grandmother's ring—but how was he supposed to know when he'd killed her that he was going to fall in love so soon?

He opened the dresser, felt among the dead man's clothes until he found the sock, pulled out his savings. It was only forty-three dollars.

The only help for it was to ask Pleasure. Railroad paced the room. It was a long time, and Railroad began to worry, before the cat came back. The cat slipped silently through her door, lay down on the table, simple as you please, in the wedge of sunlight coming in the window. Railroad got down on his knees, his face level with the table top. The cat went "Mrrph?" and raised its head. Railroad gazed into her steady eyes.

"Pleasure," he said. "I need to get an engagement ring, and I don't have enough money. Get one for me."

The cat watched him.

He waited for some sign. Nothing happened.

Then, like a dam bursting, a flood of confidence flowed into him. He knew what he would do.

The next morning he walked down to the Sweet Spot whistling. He spent much of his shift imagining when and how he would ask Mrs. Graves for her hand. Maybe on the porch swing, on Saturday night? Or at breakfast some morning? He could leave the ring next to his plate and she would find it, with his note, when clearing the table. Or he could come down to her room in the middle of the night, and he'd ram himself into her in the darkness, make her whimper, then lay the perfect diamond on her breast.

At the end of the shift he took a beefsteak from the diner's refrigerator as an offering to Pleasure. But when he entered his room the cat was not there. He left the meat wrapped in butcher paper in the kitchen downstairs, then went back up and changed into Bailey Boy's baggy suit. At the corner he took the bus downtown and walked into the first jewelry store he saw. He made the woman show him several diamond engagement rings. Then the phone rang, and when the woman went to answer it he pocketed a ring and walked out. No clerk in her right mind should be so careless, but it went exactly as he had imagined it. As easy as breathing.

That night he had a dream. He was alone with Mrs. Graves, and she was making love to him. But as he moved against her, he felt the skin of her full breast deflate and wrinkle beneath his hand, and he found he was making love to the dead grandmother, her face grinning the same vacant grin it had when Hiram and Bobby Lee hauled her into the woods.

Railroad woke in terror. Pleasure was sitting on his chest, her face an inch from his, purring loud as a diesel. He snatched the cat up in both hands and hurled her across the room. She hit the wall with a thump, then fell to the floor, claws skittering on the hardwood. She scuttled for the window, through the door onto the porch roof.

It took him ten minutes for his heart to slow down, and then he could not sleep.

Someone is always after you. That day in the diner, when Railroad was taking a break, sitting on a stool in front of the window fan sipping some ice water, Cauthron came out of the office and put his hand on his shoulder, the one that still hurt occasionally. "Hot work, ain't it boy?"

"Yessir." Railroad was ten or twelve years older than Cauthron.

"What is this world coming to?" Maisie said to nobody in particular. She had the newspaper open on the counter and was scanning the headlines. "You read what it says here about some man robbing a diamond ring right out from under the nose of the clerk at Merriam's Jewelry."

"I saw that already," Mr. Cauthron said. And after a moment, "White fellow, wasn't it?"

"It was," sighed Maisie. "Must be some trash from the backwoods. Some of those poor people have not had the benefit of a Christian upbringing."

"They'll catch him. Men like that always get caught." Cauthron leaned in the doorway of his office, arms crossed above his belly. "Maisie," Cauthron said. "Did I tell you Lloyd here is the best short order cook we've had in here since 1947? The best *white* short order cook."

"I heard you say that."

"I mean, makes you wonder where he was before he came here. Was he short-order cooking all round Atlanta? Seems like we would of heard, don't it? Come to think, Lloyd never told me much about where he was before he showed up that day. He ever say much to you, Maisie?"

"Can't say as I recall."

"You can't recall because he hasn't. What you say, Lloyd? Why is that?"

"No time for conversation, Mr. Cauthron."

"No time for conversation? You carrying some resentment, Lloyd? We ain't paying you enough?"

"I didn't say that."

"Because, if you don't like it here, I'd be unhappy to lose the best white short order cook I had since 1947."

Railroad put down his empty glass and slipped on his paper hat. "I can't afford to lose this job. And, you don't mind my saying, Mr. Cauthron, you'd come to regret it if I was forced to leave."

"Weren't you listening, Lloyd? Isn't that what I just said?"

"Yes, you did. Now maybe we ought to quit bothering Maisie with our talk and get back to work."

"I like a man that enjoys his job," Cauthron said, slapping Railroad on the shoulder again. "I'd have to be suicidal to make a good worker like you leave. Do I look suicidal, Lloyd?"

"No, you don't look suicidal, Mr. Cauthron."

"I see Pleasure all the time going down the block to pick at the trash by the Sweet Spot," Mrs. Graves told him as they sat on the front porch swing that evening. "That cat could get hurt if you let it out so much. That is a busy street."

Foster had gone to a ball game, and Louise Parker was visiting her sister in Chattanooga, so they were alone. It was the opportunity Railroad had been waiting for.

"I don't want to keep her a prisoner," he said. The chain of the swing creaked as they rocked slowly back and forth. He could smell her lilac perfume. The curve of her thigh beneath her print dress caught the light from the front room coming through the window.

"You're a man who has spent much time alone, aren't you," she said.

"So mysterious."

He had his hand in his pocket, the ring in his fingers. He hesitated. A couple walking down the sidewalk nodded at them. He couldn't do it out here, where the world might see. "Mrs. Graves, would you come up to my room? I have something I need to show you."

She did not hesitate. "I hope there's nothing wrong."

"No, ma'm. Just something I'd like to rearrange."

He opened the door for her and followed her up the stairs. The clock in the hall ticked loudly. He opened the door to his room and ushered her in, closed the door behind them. When she turned to face him he fell to his knees.

He held up the ring in both hands, his offering. "Miz Graves, I want you to marry me."

She looked at him kindly, her expression calm. The silence stretched. She reached out; he thought she was going to take the ring, but instead she touched his wrist. "I can't marry you, Mr. Bailey."

"Why not?"

"Why, I hardly know you."

Railroad felt dizzy. "You could some time."

"I'll never marry again, Mr. Bailey. It's not you."

Not him. It was never him, had never *been* him. His knees hurt from the hardwood floor. He looked at the ring, lowered his hands, clasped it in his fist. She moved her hand from his wrist to his shoulder, squeezed it. A knife of pain ran down his arm. Without standing, he punched Mrs. Graves in the stomach.

She gasped and fell back onto the bed. He was on her in a second, one hand over mouth while he ripped her dress open from the neck. She struggled, and he pulled the pistol out from behind his back and held it to her head. She lay still.

"Don't you stop me, now," he muttered. He tugged his pants down and did what he wanted.

How ladylike it was of her to keep so silent.

Much later, lying on the bed, eyes dreamily focused on the light fixture in the center of the ceiling, it came to him what had bothered him about the grandmother. She had ignored the fact that she was going to die. "She would of been a good woman, if it had been somebody there to shoot her every minute of her life," he'd told Bobby Lee. And that was true. But then, for that last moment, she *became* a good woman. The reason was that, once Railroad convinced her she was going to die, she could forget about it. In the end, when she reached out to him, there was no thought in her mind about death, about the fact that he had killed her son and daughter-in-law and grandchildren and was soon going to kill her. All she wanted was to comfort him. She didn't even care if he couldn't be comforted. She was living in that exact instant, with no memory of the past or regard for the future, out of the instinct of her soul and nothing else.

Like the cat. Pleasure lived that way all the time. The cat didn't know about Jesus' sacrifice, about angels and devils. That cat looked at him and saw what was there.

He raised himself on his elbows. Mrs. Graves lay very still beside him, her blond hair spread across the pineapple quilt. He felt her neck for a pulse.

It was dark night now: the whine of insects in the oaks outside the window, the rush of traffic on the cross street, drifted in on the hot air. Quietly, Railroad slipped out into the hall and down to Foster's room. He put his ear to the door and heard no sound. He came back to his own room, wrapped Mrs. Graves in the quilt and, as silently as he could, dragged her into his closet. He closed the door.

Railroad heard purring, and saw Pleasure sitting on the table, watching. "God damn you. God damn you to hell," he said to the cat, but before he could grab her the calico had darted out the window.

He figured it out. The idea of marrying Mrs. Graves had been only a stage in the subtle revenge being taken on him by the dead grandmother, through the cat. The wishes Pleasure had granted were the bait, the nightmare had been a warning. But he hadn't listened.

He rubbed his sore shoulder. The old lady's gesture, like a mustard-seed, had grown to be a great crow-filled tree in Railroad's heart.

A good trick the devil had played on him. Now, no matter how he reformed himself, he could not get rid of what he had done.

It was hot and still, not a breath of air, as if the world were being smothered in a fever blanket. A milk-white sky. The kitchen of the Sweet Spot was hot as the furnace of Hell; beneath his shirt Railroad's sweat ran down to slick the warm pistol slid into his belt. Railroad was fixing a stack of buttermilk pancakes when the detective walked in.

The detective walked over to the counter and sat down on one of the stools. Maisie was not at the counter; she was probably in the ladies' room. The detective took a look around, then plucked a menu from behind the napkin holder in front of him and started reading. On the radio Hank Williams was singing "I'm So Lonesome I Could Cry."

Quietly, Railroad untied his apron and slipped out of the back door. In the alley near the trash barrels he looked out over the lot. He was about to hop the chain-link fence when he saw Cauthron's car stopped at the light on the corner.

Railroad pulled out his pistol, crouched behind a barrel and aimed at the space in the lot where Cauthron usually parked. He felt something bump against his leg.

It was Pleasure. "Don't you cross me now," Railroad whispered, pushing the animal away.

The cat came back, put her front paws up on his thigh, purring.

"Damn you! You owe me, you little demon!" he hissed. He let the gun drop, looked down at the cat.

Pleasure looked up at him. "Miaow?"

"What do you want! You want me to stop, do you? Then make it go away. Make it so I never killed nobody."

Nothing happened. It was just a fucking animal. In a rage, he dropped the gun and seized the cat in both hands. She twisted in his grasp, hissing.

"You know what it's like to hurt in your heart?" Railroad tore open his shirt and pressed Pleasure against his chest. "Feel it! Feel it beating there!" Pleasure squirmed and clawed, hatching his chest with a web of scratches. "You owe me! You owe me!" Railroad was shouting now. "Make it go away!"

Pleasure finally twisted out of his grasp. The cat fell, rolled, and scurried away, running right under Cauthron's car as it pulled into the lot. With a little bump, the car's left front tire ran over her.

Cauthron jerked the car to a halt. Pleasure howled, still alive, writhing, trying to drag herself away on her front paws. Her back was broken. Railroad looked at the fence, looked back.

He ran over to Pleasure and knelt down. Cauthron got out of the car. Railroad tried to pick up the cat, but she hissed and bit him. Her sides fluttered with rapid breathing. Her eyes clouded. She rested her head on the gravel.

Railroad had trouble breathing. He looked up from his crouch to see that Maisie and some customers had come out of the diner. Among them was the detective.

"I didn't mean to do that, Lloyd," Cauthron said. "It just ran out in front of me." He paused a moment. "Jesus Christ, Lloyd, what happened to your chest?"

Railroad picked up the cat in his bloody hands. "Nobody ever gets away with nothing," he said. "I'm ready to go now."

"Go where?"

"Back to prison."

"What are you talking about?"

"Me and Hiram and Bobby Lee killed all those folks in the woods and took their car. This was their cat."

"What people?"

"Bailey Boy and his mother and his wife and his kids and his baby."

The detective pushed back his hat and scratched his head. "You all best come in here and we'll talk this thing over."

They went into the diner. Railroad would not let them take Pleasure from him until they gave him a corrugated cardboard box to put the body in. Maisie brought him a towel to wipe his hands, and Railroad told the detective, whose name was Vernon Scott Shaw, all about the State Hospital for the Criminally Insane, and the hearselike Hudson, and the family they'd murdered in the backwoods. Mostly he talked about the grandmother and the cat. Shaw sat there and listened soberly. At the end he folded up his notebook and said, "That's quite a story, Mr. Bailey. But we caught the people who did that killing, and it ain't you."

"What do you mean? I know what I done."

"Another thing, you don't think I'd know if there was some murderer loose from the penitentiary? There isn't anyone escaped."

"What were you doing in here last week, asking questions?"

"I was having myself some pancakes and coffee."

"I didn't make this up."

"So you say. But seems to me, Mr. Bailey, you been standing over a hot stove too long."

Railroad didn't say anything. He felt as if his heart was about to break.

Mr. Cauthron told him he might just as well take the morning off and get some rest. He would man the griddle himself. Railroad got unsteadily to his feet, took the box containing Pleasure's body, and tucked it under his arm. He walked out of the diner.

He went back to the boarding house. He climbed the steps. Mr. Foster was in the front room reading the newspaper. "Morning, Bailey," he said. "What you got there?"

"My cat got killed."

"No! Sorry to hear that."

"You seen Miz Graves this morning?" he asked.

"Not yet."

Railroad climbed the stairs, walked slowly down the hall to his room. He entered. Dust motes danced in the sunlight coming through the window. The ocean rowboat was no darker than it had been the day before. He set the dead cat down next to the Bible on the table. The pineapple quilt was no longer on the bed; now it was the rose. He reached into his pocket and felt the engagement ring.

The closet door was closed. He went to it, put his hand on the doorknob. He turned it and opened the door.

CANDIA

Graham Joyce

Graham Joyce is the author of sixteen novels and a collection of short stories. He won the World Fantasy Award for his novel *The Facts of Life*, and has won the British Fantasy Award for Best Novel an unprecedented five times. His work has been translated into more than twenty languages. In 2009, he was awarded the O. Henry Prize for his short story "An Ordinary Soldier of the Queen." He is currently working on the computer game *Doom 4*.

Joyce says: "While I was still trying to get published as a writer I lived on the Greek islands for a while, and I spent six months in Chania on the west of Crete. It had been under Ottoman rule for some centuries, when the name of the town was Candia. While I was there someone led me to a strange nightclub behind the old spice warehouses on the seafront. The person who took me there left the island suddenly and I was never able to find the place again. At the place where I thought it should be an empty building was home to a number of feral cats, and that last detail was what triggered the story."

Candia. It was surely in Candia, with its crumbling Venetian waterfront and its abandoned minarets, and its harbor sliding into the rose-coloured sea further by an inch every day. Just like Ben Wheeler when I first spotted him, with his bottle of raki at his permanent station outside the Black Orchid Café, a misted tumbler forever fixed at some point on the arc between tabletop and bottom lip.

I had just climbed down from the rusting, antiquated bus, the sole passenger to disembark in that dusty square, when I saw him, at a time when I never expected to see again anyone I'd ever known.

His glass of raki arrested itself on its mechanical ascent, and he peered across the rim of his tumbler directly into my eyes. He was sitting at a table on the concrete edge of the neglected wharf. Over his shoulder the sun was punctured on a derelict minaret, spilling lavender and molten gold across the motionless waters of the harbor. He took a sip from his glass, and turned away.

"Wheeler," I called. "Hey, Wheeler!"

On hearing his name he spun round and looked at me again, this time with an expression of incredulity and horror. Then he looked around wildly, as if for egress. For a moment I thought he was actually going to make a break for it and run away from me. I crossed the square to the café and dragged a seat from under the table; but as he showed no sign that he would allow me to join him, I was made to hover.

"Don't you remember me?" I asked.

Before I got an answer a singer struck up in the square. He had a cardboard shoe-box for donations and was singing in that curious, deep-throated and unaccompanied *resitica* of the dispossessed people from the mountains. The sound was of almost unendurable melancholy and sweetness, and the guttural voice resonated along the baked brickwork.

Wheeler put down his glass and hooked his thumbs in his waistband, regarding me with an unblinking gaze. I wasn't fooled. He was clearly nervous. It was as if he had somewhere important to go, but in his astonishment at seeing me there, he couldn't tear himself away.

"So what are you doing here?" I asked.

He eyed me steadily. "I might ask you the same question."

He looked back at the square and stroked the white stubble of his beard. Again I got the impression I was detaining him from something important.

"I've come here to drink myself to death," I joked. At least, it was a truth hidden inside a joke, but he nodded seriously, as if this was perfectly reasonable.

The arrival of a waiter brought a moment's relief. Slow to spot him, Wheeler turned suddenly and fixed the waiter with his extraordinary gaze. The boy shuffled uncomfortably, tapping the steel disc of his tray against his thigh.

"Let me stand you a drink," I suggested.

Wheeler put his hand to his mouth, removing something very small from the tip of his tongue. "Sure." He let his eyes drop. "Sit down. I'll have a beer. Yes, I'll have a beer."

I sat, but I was already beginning to regret this. Ben Wheeler looked terrible. I could see a ring of filth on the collar of his short-sleeved shirt. The hems of his oil-spotted chinos were rolled and his bare feet were thrust inside a pair of rotting, rope-soled espadrilles. When the beer arrived, he slurped it greedily. We sat in a stiff silence for a while, the swelling vocalizations of the *resitica* man the only other sound in the square in the parched heat of the afternoon.

Our paths had crossed briefly in the eighties, when we were both working for Aid-Direct, the notorious London-based charity, three or four years before public scandal closed the outfit down. Wheeler, Director of Fundraising at the time, was a flamboyant character in a double-breasted suit and sixties haircut that looked like it was woven out of brown twill. For some of the serious-minded charity workers he was too fond of champagne, parties and pretty girls, but he could bring in money the way a poacher can tickle trout from a stream. The eighties. New money wanted to log onto charitable causes, not out of any sense of philanthropy, but to clamber aboard the Queen's Honours List. Wheeler obliged by organizing fatcat charity parties, in which city stockbrokers and dealers would be photographed sipping champers from a Page Three girl's shoe, all before writing a cheque.

After one of these all-night jamborees at the Savoy or the Dorchester, a sack of rice or two would end up on a truck bound for Ethiopia or Somalia. At the time I didn't care where the money came from, or how little of it found a way through so long as it assisted me in my plans to change the world. Or rather, I wasn't so naïve as to believe one could change the world, but I did believe it was possible to change one person's world, and that was good enough for me.

I'd only been working for Aid-Direct about six months before accountants were called in. No one was ever told why, but Wheeler was suddenly given an impressive golden handshake. After the farewell party, I got caught in the lift with him. He was smashed.

"Hey," he said that day, "Something I wanna do, 'fore I leave here."

"What," I said, my finger hovering over the lift button.

He swayed dangerously. "Young tart who works in your office. Wassname. Cat-like. Yum yum. Feline." I offered no help, and he supplied the name himself "Sarah."

"What about her?" The lift started its descent.

"Afore I go. Ten minutes wiv Sarah the feline. In the store cupboard. Hey. Ten minutes."

"Good luck."

"No no," he said, brushing imaginary lint from the front of my jacket. "I want you to ask her for me."

"Get out of here!" The lift door opened.

His huge, manicured hand restrained me as I made to step out of the lift. Fumbling in his pocket, he produced a couple of banknotes and stuffed them in my breast pocket. "Ask her."

"Piss off."

More banknotes, stuffed in with the others. "Ask her for me."

Still more. Big denomination. "Just ask her for me." He patted my cheek with his be-ringed paw.

We got out of the lift and I went back to my office, where Sarah was audio-typing. With her lithe figure and her long, raven hair scraped back from her face and tied at the back, Sarah cut a figure like a ballerina. Who wouldn't want ten minutes with Sarah? I did. I'd taken her out a few times. Despite some lavish wining and dining, she'd resisted all my best efforts. Any man who has tried and failed to seduce a particular woman nurses a tiny malice, and I confess to giving way to a disgraceful and sadistic instinct to collude with Wheeler's drunken lust.

I gently lifted one of her earphones. "We need some more envelopes. Can you go get 'em?"

"Now?"

"Please."

"What's the rush?"

She looked at me quizzically as I turned my back. I heard her replacing her headset on the table. The door closed as she went out. Half an hour later she was back, flushed and looking like she'd learned some new wrestling holds.

I caught her eye, but I was the one to look away first. The expression of guilt, shame and humiliation on Sarah's face filled me with self-loathing and regret. She put her headset back on and resumed work, punching so hard on her keyboard I thought it might shatter. It disgusted me that Wheeler had found it so easy to make a whore out of a perfectly respectable young woman, and a pimp out of me. As for the money he stuffed into my breast pocket, I can't even bring myself to repeat how little it was. I only hope Sarah got a lot more.

I waited until Sarah left the office. I heard her heels clacking angrily on the linoleum of the corridor.

That was the last time I'd seen Wheeler. Ten or more years had gone by. Now here he was, washed up in Candia, his face crumbling like a waterfront warehouse and with eyes like the oil-slicked, scummy backwash of the sea. Did he remember that episode in the lift on his last day at Aid-Direct? I doubted it. But then people choose not to remember things. Or they pretend to forget. He put his fingers to his mouth again, plucking from his tongue what I thought was a loose strand of tobacco. Finessing it clear of his fingers, he drained his glass.

"Have another," I offered. My companionable behavior was more to do with my own intolerable loneliness than with any attraction in Wheeler's company. Besides, I was curious.

He shook his head, didn't move. I signaled to the waiter, who brought another beer, and a raki for me. "You heard about the company, after you left?"

A light went on. "You worked at A-D? That must be where I know you from." Recall the episode with Sarah? He barely remembered me.

I reintroduced myself. "William Blythe. I was in the Training department."

"Yes, yes, yes. I remember." Again his hand went to his mouth.

"What did you do after that? After Aid-Direct, I mean."

"Went here. Went there. Here. There."

It was dark by now. The *resitica* singer had gone, carrying away his shoe-box without a single donation. A breeze picked up off the swelling black tide and Wheeler shivered. The water sucked and slopped around the concrete breakers. Laughter carried across the bay from one of the bars, making him look over his shoulder. I guessed he was hungry. "I'm just going to eat," I said.

We went to a small restaurant converted from a spice warehouse in the narrow streets behind the waterfront. I ordered an array of small dishes and Wheeler fell on them like a man who hadn't eaten in days. After a few glasses of resinated wine, he began to drop his guard.

"How long have you lived here?" I asked.

"Some years. Four maybe. Not sure anymore."

"How do you survive?"

He drained his glass and looked at me quite sincerely. "I don't know. I don't do anything. One day runs into another. I'm always hungry, but I survive. And I don't know how." He became distracted, gazing at something across my shoulder.

Then his fingers went to his mouth again, unconsciously plucking something from the tip of his tongue before flicking it to the floor. He looked up at me with a sudden intensity. "Have you ever tried to leave this town?"

The question was absurd. I'd only just arrived. "It's not hard. Tourist buses come in and out every day in the summer months."

He laughed cynically. "Sure. But I'm no tourist. And neither are you. Tell me: where were you before you came here?"

I tried to think, but my mind went blank. He found this amusing. He laughed again and seemed to relax. He returned to his food, and then he did something I haven't seen anyone do in a long time. He picked up an almost empty plate and he licked the sauce clean with his tongue. "Terrific food here!" he said. "What was in that sauce?"

"Knowing this place," I joked, "it was probably a dead cat."

That was the wrong thing to say. Wheeler carefully set down his plate and pushed it away from him, staring at the dish as if it was on fire.

I broke his trance by asking him where he stayed.

He looked confused. "Anywhere. Anywhere they let me stay. Now I have to go."

"Don't," I said. "Have another drink. Look, it's my birthday." It was true, and though Wheeler wasn't first choice for company, I was feeling sorry for myself The popping of a celebration cork is a lonely sound when you're on your own.

Wheeler looked astonished. "You're lying!"

"Why should I lie? September 21st. It's my birthday."

Wheeler stood up. "But that means it's the Autumnal Equinox today!" I shrugged. "And you arrived here today? You don't understand. This could be an opportunity."

"Opportunity?"

"If it really is your birthday, the Shades Club might be open!"

"Shades? Where's that?"

"You haven't been? I could take you there."

I wasn't sure I wanted to go to the Shades Club, wherever it was, whatever it was. But Wheeler insisted. He became more interested in me than at any other point in the evening. But what else had I to do? I had no one to go home to and nothing to detain me. I was ready to be picked up by any foul wind blowing in from the ocean. It was around midnight when I settled the bill at the restaurant.

As we walked across the waterfront, sounds from one of the cafés drifted across the bay, another explosion of men's laughter and the eerie skirling music of the bow of a lira drawn across strings as taut as a man's nerves on Judgement Day.

Wheeler led me behind the crumbling waterfront and into the derelict streets of what were once spice warehouses in the grand trading days of Candia. Damp odours of ancient plaster, brine, spice and exhausted trade breathed along the ratruns of those streets.

Then Wheeler was clambering over a pile of broken bricks. He spotted my hesitation and beckoned me to follow. "It was on my own birthday that I first discovered the Shades Club," he explained. He ducked under a fractured arch and I could see he was heading for the ruined mosque. The moon, obscured by clouds, barely offered enough light to illuminate the needle of the minaret.

In the glory of its trading days, Candia had prospered under four hundred years of Ottoman rule, but the infidel had returned, and the dome of the mosque lay sundered, like a cracked egg laid by some giant, mythical reptile. The minaret sailed defiantly above the mooncast ruins, but the exotic call of the adhan was no more than a ghost. A clump of jasmine growing amongst the rubble breathed a tiger perfume into the night.

I followed Wheeler through a fissure in the tumbled wall, and we emerged in a darkened street. A flight of stone steps descended behind the shadows of the mosque. The anapaest beat of music thudded from below. At the bottom of the steps a malfunctioning red neon light fizzed, spitting the words SHADES CLUB. The letter S flickered intermittently.

The place was almost empty. Two women sat at the shadowy end of the bar, both stirring tall cocktail glasses with a straw, both displaying a lot of leg.

"It's a clip-joint," I said to Wheeler, annoyed. The bar looked like any other place I'd been in where you pay for girls to sip coloured water, and at prices that would frighten a steeplejack.

"No. It's not like that. Sit down, it'll be all right."

I took a stool at the bar. An old-style juke box was grinding out early rock music. Someone behind me was cleaning tables with a dirty rag. I saw the girls give us the once-over, but the sight of Wheeler made them lose interest.

Wheeler surprised me by storming behind the bar and confidently mixing Vodka Martinis. "I'm known here," he assured me. Knowing he was broke, I took out my wallet but he waved it away. "Don't worry, it's free."

Overhearing, one of the girls snorted. "Free. He says it's free. Nothing is free."

The second of the two, the one who'd said nothing, was smiling at me, holding her cocktail glass to her mouth. The bar was lit by soft blue and ruby lights, and she struck me as extraordinarily pretty as she waited for me to come back at her friend's remark. Perhaps because Wheeler had reminded me of the incident, I was struck by how much she resembled Sarah from our days at Aid-Direct.

"You're a philosopher," I said.

Taking this as a rebuff, the outspoken one looked away, exhibiting the attributes of extreme boredom; but the other continued to gaze in my direction.

"You've made a hit," said Wheeler, coming from behind the bar.

"She's nice," I whispered.

Wheeler nearly dropped his glass. "You like her? You mean you really like her?"

I couldn't understand why he was so amazed. I checked her out again. Wheeler's response suggested he regarded her as some kind of reptile. "Doesn't she remind you of…" Wheeler was looking at me searchingly. I decided to let it go.

"She's beautiful."

And she was, at least so she seemed in shadow: long, auburn hair and a china-doll complexion, just a hint of the oriental about her. Wheeler made some sort of gesture to her, because she got off her stool and came over. I got the chance to look at her in proper light.

She was even more striking than my first impression had suggested. It was not until she came over that I realized the two women were wearing some kind of fancy-dress outfits: leotards and sheer black nylon tights. Her eyes were heavily lined with mascara. Wheeler, in a state of some excitement, introduced us, and she slid onto the stool next to me.

"This is Lilly," Wheeler said, and almost from behind his hand he added, "and I think I've found my way out of this town."

I didn't know what he meant, and I didn't much like the way he said it. It reminded me of how little I trusted the man. I thought again of Aid-Direct, and how after he'd gone the depth of his corruption had been made plain. The organization, heavily in debt, collapsed like a house of cards. The executives, those caring-sharing liberal bleeding-heart charity workers began stripping the place before the liquidators came in. Office equipment was driven away by the van-load, the car-pool drained itself overnight, and fabulously inflated expenses were cash-processed before the banks had wind of what was happening. My immediate superior stopped a consignment of rice before it left the docks and sold it on to a wholefood collective, pocketing the proceeds. I have to say that, demoralized, I joined in this feverish stampede.

But I was too busy getting along fine with Lilly to give much thought to Wheeler's odd remark. Lilly and I sensed immediate rapport. I can't remember anything I said to her, or she to me, but we had anchored and the next fifteen minutes melted in a miraculous and sympathetic exchange of thoughts. It was only when I offered to buy her a drink that I noticed Wheeler deep in conversation with the other woman. They eyed me intently. I sensed that they were striking some kind of deal, and that it involved me.

The jukebox went dead. Lilly jumped up to feed it with a coin, and it was only then that I noticed the tail protruding from the butt of her leotard, part of her fancy-dress. The other woman too, had a tail, sitting erect on the stool behind her. As Lilly bent over the juke box to make her selection, the tail swished slightly in the air.

"How d'you make it do that?" I asked, coming up behind her. I was feeling slightly drunk from the cocktail and all the raki I'd consumed earlier. The tail was actually flesh coloured, with a furry collar halfway along its length, and another at the tip, as if the regions between the furred collars had been shaved. I grasped the brown, furry tail-end, which was still swishing gently as Lilly fingered Bakelite buttons on the jukebox, and I squeezed the tip hard.

It was the wrong thing to do. Lilly spun round, slamming into the jukebox. "Don't DO that!" she hissed at me. "Don't EVER do that!"

She was coiled like a spring, her eyes leaking venom. Astonished by this transformation I mumbled an apology.

"I hate it when men do that!"

"Sorry." I looked round for Wheeler and the other woman, but they were gone. So too had the shadowy figure clearing up the tables behind us. Lilly and I were left alone in the bar.

"Where did—"

There was a few seconds of vinyl hiss before honeyed saxophone music started oozing from the jukebox. Lilly's mood was restored, and she sidled up close, enfolding her arms around me. "Come here. Let's dance. I'm sorry I reacted like that. I'm sensitive. Here, dance a little closer."

The bar dissolved around us. I abandoned myself to Lilly's embrace. Her perfume, or maybe it was her natural cassolette, had me inflamed.

An hour later she was undressed in my apartment and I was carefully examining her tail. Her anatomy was normal in every other way. She had the physique of a centerfold, but she also had a tail. This time she let me touch it, but tenderly. She let me stroke it. She let me run my fingers gently along its sinuous curved length.

Three collars of brown tailfur had been left unshaved. These were at the tip, the location of my early offense, in the sensitive middle; and at the coccyx, where the tail joined the body at the base of her spine. The exposed, shaved skin was considerably lighter than the rest of her sallow flesh tone.

"Why do you shave it?" I asked as she stood over me, naked. I marveled at the way she could make it swish lightly from side to side.

She shrugged. "Fashion."

"Sure," I said. "Doesn't everyone shave their tails these days?"

She grew bored with my fascination for her tail, aggressively straddling me and pinning me back on the bed. For the next hour she rolled over me like a heatwave. Her tongue was rough, like a cat's tongue, and the odour of her body was an intoxicant, like the smell of a waterfront spice warehouse in the old trading days of Candia. I abandoned myself to her, and she to me, though all the time I couldn't help wondering how her tail was behaving behind her, or beneath her, or beside her. At the moment of her orgasm I instinctively reached around and grasped it above her coccyx. She gasped, sinking her nails deep into my back and tearing lightly at my skin with her sharp teeth.

When I woke in the morning I somehow expected her not to be there. But she was already awake, her head resting on the pillow. She blinked at me sadly.

"What is it?" I said, wiping away a tear with my thumb.

She wouldn't answer me. She slipped out of bed, dressed hurriedly and then kissed me deeply and passionately.

"I've got to go."

"When can I see you again?" I didn't want to lose her. "Will you be at the Shades Club?"

"Sure," she said rather cynically. "When it next opens."

And she left. I made to shout after her, but there was something stuck to my tongue. I plucked it from my mouth. It was a dark hair. In distaste I flicked it away, but in that time Lilly had gone. My skin tingled in the places she'd bitten me. I had a high temperature.

In the evening I returned to the Shades Club, only to find it closed. The malfunctioning neon sign had been switched off. I couldn't find anyone around the place to ask when it was going to open again. I scoured the town for signs of Lilly, or of Wheeler, or even for the other girl in the bar. Exhausted I returned to my room, where I fell into a hot, feverish sleep lasting some days.

I don't know if this happened to me a year ago, or just the night before last. Time has a way of becoming a concertina, of expanding and diminishing moments in this town. I spend the hours drifting in the streets, returning to the Shades Club of an evening, never to find it open. I ask the waiters at the other bars if they know anything about it. Someone was working there that night I met Lilly, but no one seems able to tell me anything. They regard me sadly, pour me a drink, sometimes they give me a meal.

I've made efforts to get out of this town, but every time I resolve to leave, then I'm distracted, by another hair on my tongue, or an involuntary twitch of my tail muscle. I don't know when the tail first appeared. I woke up one morning and it was there, as if it had always been there. I keep it self-consciously coiled inside my trousers as I go about the town, hoping its movements won't betray me.

But the discomfort of the tail is nothing compared to the hollow ache, the hunger, the yearning to make one moment snap together with another to form a chain of some consequence, some meaning. For I catch myself, washed up on this street or in that club, with no sense of why I came there, or what it is I'm looking for.

I am haunted by the desire to know what I am doing in this place.

I haven't seen Ben Wheeler since that night. I know he struck some kind of a deal involving me, which helped him get out of town. Meanwhile I wait. I wait for the Shades Club to open its door again. I wait for an old acquaintance to turn up at one of the waterfront bars, so that maybe this time I can strike the deal. And every now and then, something appears on the tip of my tongue, a hair, a strand of fur, like something half remembered, or like the first words in a strange, impossible story I'm about to tell. A story about the town of Candia, with its sleepy waterfront, and its lost bars and missing streets, and its ruined temples dedicated to gods glimpsed only once in a lifetime. A story about Candia, the town that couldn't decide its allegiance between the Greeks and the Turks, and so invited its own downfall.

But then a kind of waking sleep washes over me. And I find myself back again in one of the bars on the waterfront, nursing a glass of raki while the *resitica* man decants from his bursting heart in this town of forgotten miracles.

MBO

Nicholas Royle

Nicholas Royle, born in Manchester in 1963, is the author of five novels—including *Counterparts*, *The Director's Cut*, and *Antwerp*—and two novellas—*The Appetite* and *The Enigma of Departure*. He has published around 120 short stories, 20 of which are collected in *Mortality*. Widely published as a journalist, with regular appearances in *Time Out* and the *Independent*, he has also edited twelve original anthologies, including two *Darklands* volumes and *The Tiger Garden: A Book of Writers' Dreams*. The winner of three British Fantasy Awards, he teaches creative writing at Manchester Metropolitan University. He has a black cat called Max.

"Mbo," one of the more visceral and violent stories in this anthology, is a good example of Royle's talent as crackerjack storyteller and brings together two legends.

He says: "Islands are interesting precisely because they are isolated. Evolution can follow a different path. The Javan tiger (extinct), the Tasmanian tiger (widely believed to be extinct and actually a marsupial rather than a cat), the Zanzibar leopard (probably extinct, but you never know). The Zanzibar leopard was smaller than its mainland counterpart and its spots were different, too. A search for evidence of the cat's presence on the island in the 1990s uncovered no trace, but it's hard, when you stand on the edge of the Jozani Forest gazing in, not to imagine the leopard lurking somewhere within."

It was a question of arriving at the right time. You didn't necessarily, for example, turn up at the same time each evening, but juggled various considerations, such as the heat, the number of clouds in the sky, even what type they were, whether they were cumulus or stratus or cirro-stratus—stuff like that. You wanted to turn up just at the right moment, just in time to get a seat and a good view and not a moment too soon. After all, the terrace of the Africa House Hotel was not a place you wanted to spend any more time than you absolutely had to. It

321

simply wasn't that nice.

It wasn't nice partly because you were surrounded by all those people you had gone to Zanzibar to get away from—white people, Europeans, tourists; mzungu, the locals called them, red bananas. White inside but red on the outside, as soon as they'd been in the sun for a couple of hours. Apparently there was a strain of red-skinned banana that grew on the island.

And partly because the place itself was grotsville. In colonial days, the Africa House Hotel was the English Club, but since the departure of the British in 1963, it had been pretty much allowed to go to seed.

But you didn't go there for the moth-eaten hunting trophies on the walls, or the charmless service at the counter, but to sit as close to the front of the terrace as you could, order a beer and have it brought to you, and watch the sun sink into the Indian Ocean. Over there, just below the horizon—the continental land mass of Africa. Amazing really that you couldn't see it, thought Craig. It didn't really matter how far away it was—twenty miles, thirty—looking at it on the map, Zanzibar Island was no more than a tick clinging to the giant African elephant.

Craig ordered a Castle lager from the waiter who slunk oilily around the tables and their scattered chairs. He was a strange, tired-looking North African with one of those elastic snake-buckle belts doing the job of keeping his brown trousers up. Similar to the one Craig had worn at school—8,000 miles away in east London.

He didn't like ordering a Castle, or being seen with one (they didn't give you a glass at the Africa House Hotel). It was South African and everyone knew it was South African. He supposed it was all right now, but still, if people saw you drinking South African beer they'd assume you were drinking it because that's what you drank back home. In South Africa. And whereas it was all right to buy South African goods, it still wasn't all right to be South African.

And Craig wasn't, and he didn't want anyone to think he was, but not so badly that he'd drink any more of the Tanzanian Safari, or the Kenyan Tusker. One was too yeasty, the other so weak it was like drinking bat's piss.

This was his third consecutive evening at the Africa House Hotel and he was by now prepared to let people think he was—or might be—South African. He wasn't staying there, no way, uh-uh—he was staying at Mazson's, a few minutes' walk away. Air-con, satellite TV, a bath as well as a shower—and a business centre. The business centre was what had clinched it. Plus the fact the paper was paying.

Craig slipped the elastic band off his ponytail and shook out his fair hair, brushed it back to round up any strays, and reapplied the elastic. He took off his Oakley wraparound shades and pinched the bridge of his nose between thumb and forefinger. Stuck them back on. Squinted at the sun, still a few degrees above the bank of stratus clouds which would prevent the Africa House Hotel crowd from enjoying a proper sunset for the third evening in a row.

From behind his Oakleys, Craig checked out the terrace: people-watching, with a purpose for once. News of the disappearances clearly wasn't putting these tourists off coming to Zanzibar. Mainly because there wasn't any news. Not enough of a problem in any one country to create a crisis. One weeping family from Sutton Coldfield—"Sarah just wouldn't go off with anyone, she's not that kind of girl"; a red-eyed single mother from Strathclyde—"There's been no word from Louise for three weeks now." It wasn't enough to get the tabloids interested and the broadsheets wouldn't pick up on it until they were sure there was a real story. A big story. No news was no news and, by and large, didn't make the news.

Craig had latched on to Sarah's story following an impassioned letter to the editor of his paper from the missing girl's mother. He was a soft touch, he told his commissioning editor: couldn't bear to think of those good people sitting on the edge of their floral-pattern IKEA sofa, waiting for the phone to ring, weeping—especially not in Sutton Coldfield. But MacNeill, who'd been commissioning pieces from Craig for three years, knew the young man only attached himself to a story if there was a story there. And since he was between desk assignments anyway, MacNeill let him go. On the quiet, like. Neither the Tanzanian government nor the Zanzibari police would acknowledge the problem—too damaging to the developing tourism industry, ironically—so Craig needed a cover, which Craig's sister, the wildlife photographer, came up with.

The Zanzibar leopard, smaller than the mainland species, was rumoured by some to be extinct and by others to be around still, though in very small numbers. One of the guide books reckoned if there were any on the islands, they had been domesticated by practitioners of herbal medicine—witch doctors to you and me. The Zanzibari driver who collected Craig from the airport laughed indulgently at the idea. And Craig read later in another guide book that witchcraft was believed to be widely practised on Pemba Island, 85 kilometres to the north of Zanzibar though part of the same territory. Though if you tried to speak to the locals about it, they became embarrassed or politely changed the subject. But that was Pemba, and the disappearances—37 to date, according to Craig's researches—were quite specifically from Zanzibar Island.

Thirty-seven. Twenty-three women between 17 and 30, and 14 men, some of them older, mid-forties. From Denmark, Germany, Austria, Britain, France, Italy, Australia and the US. Enough of a problem as far as Craig was concerned. He was torn now, he was ashamed to admit, between wanting the world to wake up and make a concerted effort (thereby, hopefully, securing the earlier recovery of Sarah, or Sarah's body, and 36 others) and hoping he would be the first to break the story.

The cover. A naturalist based at the University of Sussex, Craig's brief was to confirm whether or not leopards still lived wild on the island. They'd even put Sussex's professor of zoology in the picture, for a consideration of course which they called a consultancy fee, so that if anyone called from Zanzibar to check up on Craig, they'd find him to be bona fide.

That afternoon, Craig had visited the Natural History Museum, quite the bizarrest of its type in his experience. Glass cases full of birds, presumably stuffed birds, but not mounted—lying down, recently-dead-looking, their little feet tied together with string. Tags to identify them. Their eyes dabs of chalk. In a grimy case all on its own, the bones of a dodo wired up into a standing position. A couple of stuffed bats—the American Fruit Bat and the Pemba Fruit Bat—ten times the size of the swallow-like creatures that had flitted about his head as he'd walked off his dinner the evening before. A crate with its lid ajar: when he opened it, a flurry of flies, one he couldn't prevent going up his nose. Inside, a board with three rats fixed to it—dead again, stuffed presumably, but with legs trussed at tiny rodent ankles. No effort made to have them assume lifelike poses. No bits of twig and leaf. No glass eyes. No glass case. He dropped the crate lid.

Oddest of all: row upon row of glass jars containing dead sea creatures and deformed animal foetuses, the glass furred up with dust and calcified deposits, so you had to bend down and squint to make out the bloodless remains of a stonefish, the huge crab with the image on its shell of two camels with their masters. The conjoined duiker antelopes.

And the stuffed leopard. They hadn't done a great job on it. The taxidermist's task being to stage a magic show for eternity: the illusion of life in the cock of the head, the setting of a glassy twinkle. The Natural History Museum of Zanzibar should have been asking for their money back on this one. You could still see it was a leopard though. If you didn't know, you'd look at it and you'd say leopard. Craig examined it from every angle. This was what he was here to find. Ostensibly. It couldn't do any harm to have a good idea what one looked like.

Up on the terrace, the touts were working the crowd—slowly, carefully, with a lower-key approach than they tended to use down in Stone Town. In Stone Town the same guys would shadow you on the same streets day after day.

"Jambo," they'd say.

"Jambo," you'd reply, because it would be rude not to.

"You want to go to Prison Island? You want to go to the East Coast today? Maybe you want go to Nungwi? You want taxi?"

You ran the gauntlet going up Kenyatta Street and never had a moment's peace when you were around Jamyatti Gardens, from where the boats left for Prison Island, its coral reefs and giant tortoises. He'd read the books all right.

"Jambo." The voice was close to him. Craig sneaked a look around as he necked his beer. A young Zanzibari had moved in on a blonde English girl who had been sitting alone. The girl smiled a little shyly and the youth sat down next to her. "The sun is setting," he said and the girl looked out over the ocean. The sun had started to dip behind the bank of cloud. "You want to go to Prison Island tomorrow?" he asked, pulling a pack of cigarettes from his pocket.

The girl shook her head. "No. Thanks." She was still smiling but Craig could see she was a little nervous. Doing battle with her shyness was the adventurous spirit that had brought her this far from whichever northern market town she'd left behind. She was flattered by the youth's attentions but could never quite forget the many warnings her worried parents would have given her in the weeks before she left.

The tout went through the list and still she politely declined. In the end he changed tack and offered to buy her a drink. Craig heard her say she'd have a beer. The youth caught the waiter's eye and spoke to him fast in Swahili. Next time the waiter came by he had a can of Stella for the girl and a Coke for the tout. Craig watched as the girl popped open the Stella and almost imperceptibly shifted on her seat so that her upper body was angled slightly further away from the boy in favour of the ocean. Maybe she shouldn't have accepted the beer, thought Craig. Or maybe it was old-fashioned to think like that. Perhaps these days girls had the right to accept the beer and turn the other way. He just wasn't sure the African youth would see it like that. Whether he was a practising Muslim—the abnegation of alcohol told him that—or not.

A high-pitched whine in Craig's ear. A pin-prick in the forearm. He smacked his hand down hard, lifted it slowly to peer underneath.

Craig started, then shuddered; never able to stand the sight of blood, whether his own or anybody else's, he had once run out of the cinema during an afternoon screening of *The Shining*. He had fainted at the scene of a road accident, having caught sight of a pedestrian victim's leg, her stocking sodden with her own blood. She survived unscathed; Craig's temple bore a scar to this day where he had hit his head on the pavement.

The mosquito had drunk well, and not just of Craig either. His stomach turning over, he quickly inspected the creature's dinner which was smeared across his arm, a red blotch in the shape of Madagascar, almost an inch long. Craig wondered whose blood it was, given that the mozzie had barely had enough time to sink its needle beneath his skin. Some other drinker's? Craig looked about. Not that of the Italian in the tight briefs, he hoped. Nor ideally had it come from either of the two South African rugby players sitting splayed-legged at the front by the railing.

He spat on to a paper tissue and wiped his arm vigorously without giving it another look until he was sure it had to be clear. The energy from the slap had been used up bursting the balloon of blood; the mosquito's empty body, split but relatively intact, was stuck to Craig's arm like an empty popsicle wrapper.

This bothered him less than the minutest trace of blood still inside the dead insect's glassy skin.

When he looked up, the blonde girl had joined a group of Europeans—Scandinavians or Germans by the look of them—and was eagerly working her way into their telling of travellers' tales, while the young tout glared angrily at the bank of clouds obscuring the sun, his left leg vibrating like a wire. Craig hoped he wasn't angry enough to get nasty. Doubted it—after all, chances were this sort of thing happened a lot up here. The kid couldn't expect a hundred percent strike rate.

Craig gave it five minutes, then went over and sat next to the kid. Kid turned around and Craig started talking.

Ten minutes later, Craig and the kid both left, though not together. Craig was heading for Mazson's Hotel and bed; the kid, his timetable for the following day sorted, having spoken to Craig, was heading home as well—home for him being his family's crumbling apartment in the heart of the Stone Town, among the rats and the rubbish and the running sewage. To be fair, the authorities were tackling the sewage, but they hadn't yet got as far as the kid's block.

The group that Alison, the blonde girl, had joined was approached by another tout, an older, taller fellow. More confident than the kid, not so much driven by other motivations, less distracted—he had a job to do. With her new companions, Alison was not so nervous about getting into the trips business. She wanted to go to Prison Island, they all did; they looked around to include her as the tout waited for an answer, and she nodded, smiling with relief. Turned out they were German, two of them, the two girls, but naturally they spoke perfect English; the third girl and the boy, who appeared to be an item, were Danish, but you wouldn't know it—their English, spoken with American accents, was pretty good too.

"We were just in Goa," said Kristin, one of the German girls. "It is so good. Have you been?"

"No," Alison shook her head. "But I'd like to go. I've heard about it." She'd heard about it all right. About the raves and the beach parties, the drugs and the boys—Australians, Americans, Europeans. It had been hard enough to get permission to come to Zanzibar, especially alone, but her parents had accepted her right to make a bid for independence.

"Ach!" shouted Anna, the second German girl, flailing her bare arms as she failed to make contact with a mozzie. "Scheisse!"

"Where are you staying, Alison?" asked the Danish boy, Lief, his arm around his girlfriend's shoulder.

Alison named a cheap hotel on the edge of Stone Town.

"You should move into Emerson's House," Lief's girlfriend, Karin, advised. "That's where we're all staying. It's really cool. Great chocolate cake…" She looked at Lief and for some reason they sniggered. Kristin and Anna joined in and soon they were all laughing, Alison included. Their combined laughter was so loud they couldn't hear anything else.

People started to look, but, leaning in towards each other, they could only hear their own laughter.

Popo—the kid—picked up Craig outside Mazson's at nine the next morning in a battered but just about roadworthy Suzuki Jeep.

"Jambo," he said as Craig climbed in beside him. "Jozani Forest."

"Jambo. Jozani Forest," Craig confirmed their destination.

They rumbled out of town, which became gradually more ramshackle as they approached the outskirts. Popo used the horn every few seconds to clear the road of cyclists, who were out in the hundreds. No one resented being ordered to make way, Craig noticed, as they would back home. Popo's deft handling took the Jeep around potholes and, where they were too big to be avoided, slowly through them. Most of the men in the streets wore long flowing white garments and skull caps; as they got further out of town, the Arabic influence became less pronounced. The women here wore brightly coloured kikois and carried unfeasibly large bags and packages on their heads. Orderly crowds of schoolgirls in white headgear and navy tunics streamed into schools that appeared to be no more than collections of outbuildings.

Between the villages, banana plantations ran right up to the edge of the road. Huge bunches of green fruit pointed up to the sky, brown raffia-like leaves crackled in the Jeep's draught.

"You look for Red Colobus monkey?" Popo asked without taking his eye off the road.

"I told you last night," Craig reminded him. "Zanzibar leopard. I'm looking for the leopard."

"No leopard here," Popo shook his head.

"I heard the witch doctors keep them."

"No leopard."

"There are witch doctors, then?"

Popo didn't say anything as they passed through another tiny village, crowds of little children too small to be in school running up to the Jeep and waving at Craig, old men sat under a shelter made out of dried palm leaves. The children shouted after them: "Jambo, jambo!" Craig waved back.

"In Jozani Forest…" Popo said slowly, "Red Colobus monkey. Only here on Zanzibar."

"I know," said Craig, wiping his forearm across his slippery brow. "And the leopards? The witch doctors? I have to find them."

"No leopard here."

He wasn't going to get much more out of Popo, that was clear. When the kid swung the Jeep off the road, he reacted swiftly by grabbing his arm, but they had only pulled into the carpark for the forest. He let go of the kid's arm.

"Sorry. Took me by surprise."

Popo blinked slowly.

"No leopard here," he repeated.

The noise of the boat's engine, a constant ragged chugging, made conversation impossible. There was no point trying to make yourself heard, but that didn't stop Lief from occasionally mouthing easily understood remarks about the choppiness of the water, the heat of the sun.

The others—Karin, Anna, Kristin and Alison—grinned and nodded, although Alison's grin was a little forced. Her trip to Prison Island was already going to exact a price, even though it was only supposed to be a half-hour hop: Alison could barely walk through a puddle without getting seasick. As the 25-foot wooden craft took another dive off the top of the next crest, she lurched forward and felt her stomach do the same, only, it seemed, without stopping. She retched, assumed the crash position, fully expecting to be ditched in the drink. It didn't happen. The boat lumbered up the next heavy swell, perched an instant at its arête, and plummeted into the trough. Alison groaned.

The two Danes were chattering excitedly in their own tongue, clearly having a ball. When she looked up, Alison saw Anna and Kristin smiling down at her. "Are you okay?" one of them asked and Alison just managed to shake her head. "It's not far to the island," Anna said, looking forward, but the boat pitched to port, throwing her off her feet. She tumbled into Alison's lap, Alison dry-retching once again.

"Oh God," she moaned. "I can't stand it."

"It's not far now," Lief tried to reassure her, although he was puzzled as to why they had shifted around so much that the bow was now pointing out to sea.

"Where are we going?" Anna asked, of no one in particular, once she had picked herself up off the duckboards.

Now Kristin demanded "What's going on?" as the bow swung around several degrees further to port. Their course could no longer be even loosely interpreted as being bound for Prison Island. "Where are you taking us?" she shouted at the boat's skipper, a lad no more than 18 sat in the stern, his hand on the outboard throttle.

They were now heading into the wind, and spray broke over the bow every seventh or eighth wave. Alison had started to cry, tears slipping noiselessly over green cheeks. Her mouth was set in a firm, down-curved bow, her brow creased in determined abstraction.

Lief rose to his feet unsteadily and asked the skipper "What's going on?" The 18-year-old just stared at the horizon. "We want to go to Prison Island. We paid you the money. Where are you taking us?" Still the guy wouldn't look at him. Lief leaned forward to grab his arm but found himself jerked back from behind. The other African, who had been squatting in the bow, motioned to Lief that he should sit down. The fingers of his left hand were wrapped around the stubby handle of a fisherman's knife.

"Sit," he ordered. "Sit." He looked at the girls. "Sit." He pointed at the wooden bench seats and everyone complied. Now Anna had started to weep as well and was not so quiet about it as Alison.

"Hands," the boy barked, his jaws snapping around the rusty gutting blade and grabbing at Lief's wrists. With a length of twine he quickly tied Lief's hands behind his back before any of the girls had the presence of mind to knock him off his feet while he had his hands occupied and was temporarily unarmed. They would live to regret this missed opportunity.

Anna and Kristin were almost paralysed with fear. Alison was within an ace of throwing herself overboard, believing that to be actually in the water could not be worse than being in a boat on it. Still the boat struck out against the direction of the incoming waves and soon they were all soaked from the spray over the bow. The boat climbed and plunged, climbed and plunged. Alison leant over the side and was quietly sick; she hoped it would make her feel better. It was funny how not even mortal fear could distract her from her seasickness.

Neither, it transpired, could the act of vomiting. If anything, she felt worse, and when the boat slipped around several degrees to port and took the waves side-on, she liked it even less. Each time the narrow craft leaned to either side she thought she was going in—again she considered doing it deliberately. Anna and Kristin were both crying, staring alternately at each other and at Lief, who was ashen-faced. Alison justified her intention to jump ship by interpreting the others' introvertedness as being an atavistic retreat into their original social groupings in the face of extreme fear. They would no more try to save her life than they would that of one of the two kidnappers, she reasoned. How long had they known her? Twelve hours. What kind of bond grew in such a short time? Not a lasting one.

She remembered what her mother had once told her, when they'd taken the ferry to Calais. "Look at the horizon," she'd said. "Watch the land. Don't look at the water." Thinking of her mother only brought fresh tears and looking left at the palm-fringed shoreline of the island some half à mile away made her feel no better. There was no way she would ever be able to swim such a distance, not even if her life depended on it. And seasickness had to be better than either drowning or being eaten by hammerhead sharks—she'd done her homework and mother nature's bizarrest-looking fish was known to nest in several of the bays around Zanzibar.

She leaned forward again in order to sneak a look at the African boy who had gone back to the bow now that Lief was tied up and neither she nor any of the three other girls appeared to be capable of making a move against him and his mate. He appeared to be searching for something on land at the same time as casting quick little glances back at his captives. If she wasn't mistaken, Alison thought he was nervous. She wondered if they could turn that to their advantage. Maybe he was new to this game, whatever it entailed.

"Listen," she addressed the others, "we've got to do something."

The three girls looked up, whereas Lief retreated further inside himself. He looked as if they might have lost him. Were it not for him, they could have all jumped overboard on a given signal and helped each other to shore. But with his hands tied behind his back, Lief would be unable to swim and the logistics of trying to drag him, lifesaving-style, over half a mile even between them seemed insurmountable.

Karin and Anna were still crying; Kristin had stopped and was calmer. "What can we do?" she wondered.

"Hey!" the boy in the bow shouted at them, brandishing his knife.

"We could all go overboard and take Lief with us," Alison whispered. "See if we can make it to the shore. Or we rush one of them, try and overpower him, knock him in, whatever. We've got to do something."

"Even if we jump in, they've got the boat, they would easily catch up with us."

The boat tipped suddenly as the boy from the bow skipped over the wooden cross-seats towards them and, sweeping his right arm in a wide arc, connected with Kristin under her jaw, knocking her completely off balance. Alison watched in horror as Kristin teetered for a second close to the gunwhale, unaware of the seventh wave about to hit the boat on the starboard side. A scarlet stripe had been drawn on her cheek by the boy's knife which had been in his hand when he hit her.

The wave smacked into the side of the boat and she was gone in a flash, vanished.

"No!" Alison screamed, clambering over to that side of the boat and leaning over. Kristin had been swallowed by the waves. Shock, presumably, having rendered her incapable of reaction. She must have taken her first breath only after hitting the water.

"You murdering bastard! You fucking…"

Alison leapt at the youth in her fury, but he grabbed her slender wrists and held her at bay, grinning while she struggled. She tried to kick him but he threw her down on to the bottom of the boat where she scrambled for safety as he leaned down over her threatening with the knife.

"No more," he said.

Kristin's friend Anna had clasped her arms around her knees and was rocking to and fro on her seat, moaning softly. Karin was sobbing, caught between trying to protect Alison and looking after her distracted boyfriend.

When he was satisfied the threat to his and his partner's authority had diminished, the youth returned to his post in the bows, occasionally shouting remarks back to the stern in Swahili. Alison climbed back on to a seat, unable to control a violent trembling which had seized her limbs. She kept visualizing Kristin washed up on the beach: she would appear not to be moving, then would cough up a lungful of sea water and splutter as she fought to regain control of her breathing. When the images were blacked out by another sickening swoop down the windward side of a wave, she knew that Kristin was dead. She might eventually get washed up among the mangrove swamps of south-western Zanzibar, but her bones would have been picked clean by the hammerheads.

The boat shifted around dramatically on a shout from the look-out boy. They were heading into shore. Alison doubted whether Lief would even be able to walk.

Jozani is the last vestige of the tropical forest that had at one time covered most of the island. The Red Colobus monkeys make it a tourist attraction, but the monkeys conveniently inhabit a small corner of the forest near the road, not far from one of the spice plantations. Visitors are taken out of the car park, back across the road and down a track to where the monkeys hang out.

The first monkey Craig saw was not remotely red.

"Blue monkey," the guide said. "Over there," he pointed through the trees, "is Red Colobus."

Craig saw a number of reddish-brown monkeys of various sizes playing around in the trees; leaping from one to another, they made quite a racket when they landed among the dry, leathery leaves.

"Great," Craig said. "What about the leopards?"

The guide gave him a blank look.

"You want see main forest?"

"Yes, I want see main forest." He followed the guide back to the road and into the car park. The tour around the main forest, Craig knew, would only scratch the surface of Jozani.

"My driver can guide me," Craig said, slipping a five dollar bill into the guide's palm. "You stay here. Relax. Put your feet up. Get a beer or something."

The guide looked doubtful, but Craig beckoned Popo across. He walked slowly, with a loose stride, long baggy cotton trousers and some kind of sandals. "Tell him it's okay," Craig said to Popo. "You can take me in."

After a moment's hesitation, Popo talked rapidly to the guide, who shrugged and walked back to the reception area defined by a bunch of easy chairs and some printed information and photographs pinned up on boards.

"Let's go, Popo."

Popo headed into the forest.

They followed the path until Craig sensed they were starting to double-back on themselves. He stopped, pushed his sunglasses up over his forehead and lit a cigarette.

"I think I want to head off the path a little," he said as he offered a cigarette to Popo.

The African took a cigarette, and lit it, the $100 bill folded around the pack not lost on him.

"Do you want to take the whole pack?" Craig asked. "I have to head off the path a little way. Leopards, you know?"

"No leopard here." Popo's hand hovered in mid-air.

"Witch doctors then. You interested or not?" Craig offered him the bribe again and nodded in the direction he wanted to go. Popo took the pack of Marlboro, slipping the cash out from underneath the cellophane wrapper and folding it into his back pocket. Then he led the way into the forest proper. After a few yards he knelt down at the base of a tree. Craig knelt down beside him and looked where the kid was pointing. There were dozens of tiny black frogs, each no bigger than a finger tip, congregating on some of the broader fallen leaves.

"Here water come," said Popo. "From sea."

"Floodwater?"

"Yes. No one come here. Dangerous."

"Good. Let's go on, in that case."

As soon as they hit the sandy bottom, the youth in the bow jumped out and tugged the boat up on to the beach. The kid in the stern pulled up the outboard. Three gangly, raggedy youths walked across the beach to meet them. Alison, Karin, Lief and Anna were forced out of the boat at knifepoint and the two youths exchanged a few words with the newcomers before turning their boat around and pushing off from the shore.

Alison, Karin and Anna had to walk with their hands on their heads to the treeline; Lief's hands were still tied behind his back. His face betrayed no emotion. Alison was amazed he'd been able to get up and walk. As for Alison, her legs had turned to rubber, despite her small relief at being on dry land. Their new captors were also armed and ruthless-looking.

The wind blew through the tops of the palm trees, an endless sinister rustling. But as they trooped into the forest, the palms thinned out, their place taken by sturdier vegetation. The canopy was so high it created an almost cathedral stillness. All Alison could hear now, apart from their shuffling progress through the trammelled undergrowth, were the occasional hammerings of woodpeckers and the screams of other, unknown birds. From time to time, on the forest floor she would spot sea shells glimmering through the mulch. She jumped when she almost walked into a bat, only to discover it was a broad, brown leaf waiting to drop from its tapering branch. She swiped at it and when it didn't instantly fall she went ballistic, swinging her arms at it as if it were a punchball. The party halted and two of the African youths came towards her, their knives at the ready. She peered over the edge of sanity at the possibility of panic, stood finely balanced debating her options, caught between self-preservation and loyalty to the group.

Before she knew what she was doing she had taken flight. One of the youths might have taken a swing at her, the point of his knife flashing just beneath her nose. She couldn't be sure. Something had happened to spur her into action. Action which she instantly regretted, mainly because it was irrevocable and she knew she would never outrun the local boys; also because she had deserted her companions, which according to her own code of honour was unforgivable. Yet she couldn't be sure they wouldn't have taken the same chance. Indeed, by running, she had created a diversion which, if they had any sense, they would exploit.

These thoughts flashed through her mind as she crashed through the forest, her flesh catching on twigs and bark and huge serrated leaves yet she felt no pain. Adrenaline surged through her system. She couldn't hear her pursuers but she knew that meant nothing. These boys would be able to fly. Whatever it took, to render her bid for freedom utterly futile.

As soon as they heard the drumming, Popo became jittery. Craig didn't give him more than five minutes.

"What is it, Popo?" he asked him. "What's going on?"

"Mbo," was all he would say, his eyes darting to and fro. "Mbo."

It was faint, still obviously some way off, but unmistakably the sound of someone drumming. It wasn't the surf and it wasn't coconuts dropping from the palm trees, it was someone's hand beating out a rhythm on a set of skins. A couple of tom-toms, maybe more, the kind of thing you played with your hand, sat cross-legged—whatever they were called. Craig hadn't a fucking clue. As for Popo, he was out of there. Craig didn't even watch him go, back the way they'd come. His hundred bucks had brought him this far, which was all he'd wanted the kid to do.

A mosquito whined by his ear. He brushed it away and walked on, moving slowly but carefully in the direction of the drumming.

He stopped when he heard another sound, coming from over to his right. Another, similar sound, but more ragged, less musical. The sound that would be made, he realised, by someone running. Craig's mind raced, imagining somone running into danger, and he was about to spring forward to intercept the runner, whom he still couldn't see, when he saw hovering in the space in front of him a whole cloud of mosquitoes.

They shifted about minutely, relative to each other, like vibrating molecules, seeming at one moment to dart towards him, only to feel a restraining influence and hang back. Because of the noise of the fast approaching runner he couldn't hear their dreadful whine, but he imagined it.

And the runner appeared, crashing her way through the trees, arms and legs flying—a young girl, the young girl from the Africa House terrace, Craig realised—heading straight for the source of the drumming.

"Hey! Stop!" Craig shouted as the swarm of mosquitoes swung its thousand-eyed head to follow the girl's progress. The whole cloud tilted and curved after the girl. She screamed as they crowded around her head: hardly could she have announced her arrival any more extravagantly. Not that Craig had any idea who or what was responsible for the drumming, nor whether they represented a threat. He just had his instincts.

The girl had a head start on him. He ran as fast as he could but couldn't close on her. Too many long lunches in The Eagle. Too many fast food containers in the bin under his desk. His heart beat a tattoo against his chest. He thrust his arms out in front of him to catch a tree trunk and so managed to stop short as the girl burst through into a wide clearing, the mozzies still shadowing her.

His hand-drums lying scattered at his feet, the drummer rose to his full height—six foot something of skin and bone, unfolding like some med student's life-size prop. He was a white man, although it was impossible to judge his age. His feet and lower legs were bare, but the rest of him was clothed. Craig rubbed his eyes, which had started to go funny. Perhaps the heat and the exertion. The fear, maybe, which he acknowledged for the first time, his pulse scampering. The man's coat constantly shifted in and out of focus, like an image perceived through a stereogram. Either there was something in Craig's eyes obscuring his vision, or some filmy substance, spider's web or other insectile secretion, draped across the undergrowth between him and the clearing. The tall man moved closer to Alison, who shrank away from him. He peered at her with bulging eyes that indicated thyroid disorder. His coat settled organically around his coat-hanger shoulders. Alison screamed and the coat shimmered. She lashed out with her right hand, drew a swathe through the living, clinging coat of mosquitoes. They swarmed about her head for a moment, mingling with the swarm that had aggravated her, before gravitating back to their host.

The man's movements were slow. He seemed to make them reluctantly, as if he had no choice. His face was too sunken in the cheeks and uniformly white to betray any emotion. Stepping back from the girl, he picked up a long bone-white blood-stained instrument from the floor by his drums and strapped it over his skull. The false snout, a foot long by the look of it, wobbled hideously as he approached the girl again. The base of it—the knuckle joint, let's face it, the thing had been fashioned from a human femur—rested against his mouth. He blew through it, a low burbling whistle, at which the mosquitoes became markedly less agitated and settled around him; Alison sank to her knees in a dead faint and he snuffled about her prone body.

Craig was furiously considering what action he could take when a further crashing through the undergrowth announced the arrival of Alison's friends from the Africa House, bound and led by three tough-looking African youths who each mumbled what appeared to be a respectful greeting to the tall man—"Mbo," they each seemed to be saying.

Lief, the Danish boy, had remained unresponsive throughout the trek from the beach. His girlfriend, Karin, was trembling with fear and continuous shock; Anna simply screamed whenever anyone came near her. Two of the youths took hold of Karin and Anna and laid them out flat on the ground. Grabbing lengths of dried palm leaves, they wound them around the girls' ankles, going around and around several times, then over the loop in the other direction between the legs until they were secure. They left the arms. The third African youth swiftly bound Lief's ankles in the same manner. Craig had to strain to see where the three were taken: beyond the lean-to on the far side of the clearing. But what lay hidden there, Craig could not see.

The tall white-skinned man was still inspecting Alison when one of the youths returned and started to bind her around the ankles as well. The man sat down once more upon the ground, his legs becoming dismantled beneath his hazy coat like a pair of fishing rods being taken apart. He picked up his hand-drums and began to play.

Craig took advantage of the noise to retreat a few yards from the edge of the clearing back into the forest. Twenty yards back, he crept around towards the back of the camp. It took him a while, because he had to move slowly to avoid alerting anyone to his presence, but he got there. Then it took him a moment before he recognised what he was seeing, even though this was what he'd been looking for. What he'd come to Africa for.

They hung from the branches of a single tree. Like bats.

Like bats, they hung upside down.

Like bats, or like the poor creatures Craig had seen in the museum in the town—bound, each one of them, at the ankles. Three dozen at least.

Most of them were completely drained of blood, desiccated, like the Bombay duck Craig would always order with his curry just to raise a laugh. Husks swinging in the breeze. Wind-dried Bombay duck. Long hair suggested which victims were female, while bigger skeletons hinted at male—but there was no way of telling with most of the poor wretches.

Nearest the ground hung the recent additions—Karin, Anna, Lief. Craig heard the tall man coming around the side of the hut, before he saw him. The wind was not strong enough to drown out the whining concert of the mosquitoes the tall man wore around himself like so many familiars. His own insectile eyes protruded as he looked at his new arrivals, all strung up and ready for him.

Behind him came two of the youths carrying Alison.

The tall man, wearing his bone nose-flute, took a tiny step towards Anna, whose screams were torn out of her throat at his approach.

I could already smell the coppery tang of blood even before the ancient ectomorph in the coat of mosquitoes prodded the young girl's throat with the sharpened femur he wore strapped to his head.

Craig was ashamed at himself, but couldn't stop the opening sentences of his eye-witness account forming in his mind.

I was smelling the blood he had already spilt. I must have smelled it on him or in the air, because the ground beneath my feet nourished no more exotic blooms than the surrounding forest, for he spilled no blood. This exiled European, this tall, spindly shadow of a man—scarcely a man at all—drank the blood, every last drop. It was what kept him alive. I sensed this as much as deduced it as my eye ranged across the bat-like corpses suspended from his tamarind tree. At the same time I felt a shadow fall across my heart, from which I knew I should never be free, even if I were somehow to effect an escape for myself and the youngsters who had joined the monster's collection.

This was Craig's problem now. The purple prose would die a death at the hands of the paper's subs—but thinking of it in terms of the news story he had come out here to investigate helped him distance himself sufficiently to keep his mind intact, to remain alert. Whatever the odds stacked against him, he still possessed the element of surprise.

While he was still thinking, racking his brains for an escape route, the tall man's head jerked forwards, driving the tip of his bone-flute into the hollow depression of Anna's throat. Blood bubbled instantly around the puncture then disappeared as it was sucked down the bone. Craig forced his eyes shut, fighting his own terror of spilt blood. But he had heard the man's first swallow, his greedy gargle as he tried to accommodate too much at once. Craig had always believed himself the hard man of investigative journalism, hard to reach emotionally—his bed back home never slept two for more than one night at a time—and impossible to shock. His fear of the sight of blood had never been a problem before; he avoided stories which trailed bloody skirts—car wrecks and shoot-outs—not his style.

As he retched and tumbled forwards out of the concealing forest, he knew this was a story to which he would never append his byline: firstly, because he wasn't going to get out alive, and secondly, even if he did, the trauma would never allow him to relive these moments.

Two youths pounced on him, jabbering excitedly in Swahili. A third youth darted into the forest in search of any accomplices.

As the youths bound his ankles, Craig watched the tall man gulp down the German girl's blood. He drank so eagerly and with such vigorous relish, it was possible to believe he completely voided her body of all nine pints. His cheeks had coloured up and Craig thought he could see a change in the man's body. It had filled out, the mosquitoes that clung to him no longer covered quite so much of his grey-white nakedness.

He wondered when his own turn would come. Would the tall man save up his victims, drink them dry one a day, or would he binge? Already, he had turned to Alison, swinging from her bonds as she tried desperately to free herself. She was a fighter. Karin sobbed uncontrollably alongside, and Lief was wherever he had gone to while they were all still on the boat. As Craig was hoisted upside down and secured by one of the youths, he thought to himself it would be preferable to go first. As if sensing his silent plea, the tall man twisted around to consider the attractions of his body over the girl's.

Popo's approach was swift and silent. The first any of those present knew of it was an abrupt cacophony: the crashing of bodies through dry vegetation, the deep-throated growling of hungry beasts, the concerted yells and screeches of our rescuers. Visually I was aware of a black and gold blur, flashing ivory teeth and ropes of saliva swinging from heavy jaws as the leopards leapt.

Popo saved my life at that point—the exact moment at which the old Craig died. It was necessary, if I were to survive. The hard-nosed journalist was as dead as the corpses swinging in the breeze higher up in the tree. He would not write up this story, I would—but not for a long time, and not for the newspapers. It's history now, become legend, myth—just as it had always been to Popo and the men of Jozani.

Those who survived it—and they are few—speak of it rarely. Lief lives quietly, on his own, in a house by the sea in his native Denmark. Karin, his former girlfriend, has returned to Africa as an aid worker. Most recently she has been in eastern Zaire: I saw her interviewed on the TV news during the refugee crisis. I have no contact with either of them. Alison and I tried to remain in touch—a couple of letters exchanged and we met once, in a bar in the West End, but the lights and the noise upset us both and we soon parted. I have no idea where she is now or what she is doing.

I left my reporter's job on medical advice and spent some time fell-walking in South Wales until I felt well enough to return to work, but on the production side this time. I never have to read the copy or look at the pictures—just make sure the words are on the page and the colours are right.

I go to Regent's Park Zoo every so often to look at the leopards. Watching them prowl around their cages reminds me of the moment in my life when I was most alive—when I saw, with an almost photographic clarity, one of Popo's leopards take a swipe with its heavy paw at the bloodsucking creature's midriff. There was an explosion, a shower of blood, Anna's blood. His skin flapped uselessly, transparently, like that of the mosquito I had swatted against my arm on the terrace of the Africa House Hotel.

Popo and his men—witch doctors or Jozani Forest guides, I never found out—untied us and lowered us safely to the ground. Later that evening, after the police had been called and started the clear-up operation, Popo himself took me back to Zanzibar Town in his Suzuki. On the outskirts of town he brought the vehicle to a sudden halt, flapping his hand about his head as if trying to beat off an invisible foe.

"What's up?" I asked, leaning towards him.

"Mbo," he muttered.

I heard a high-pitched whine as it passed by my ear. I too lashed out angrily.

"Mosquito?" I asked.

"Mbo," he nodded.

It turned out I had got the little sod, despite my flailing attack. Maybe it was just stunned, but it lay in the palm of my hand. I was relieved to see that its body was empty of blood.

"We call it mosquito," I said and I shivered as I wondered if we had brought it from the forest on our clothes.

For months later, I would discover mosquitoes, no more than half a dozen or so, among the clothes I had brought back from Zanzibar. So far, they have all been dead ones.

BEAN BAG CATS®

Edward Bryant

Edward Bryant began writing professionally in 1968 and has had more than a dozen books published, including *Among the Dead*, *Cinnabar*, *Phoenix Without Ashes* (with Harlan Ellison), *Wyoming Sun*, *Particle Theory*, *Fetish* (a novella chapbook), and *The Baku: Tales of the Nuclear Age.* He originally made a name for himself as an award-winning science fiction writer but in the mid-1980s he strayed into horror, where he produced a series of sharply etched stories about Angie Black, a contemporary witch, the brilliant zombie story "A Sad Last Love at the Diner of the Damned," and other marvelous tales. But he's never completely given up writing science fiction.

"Bean Bag Cats®," commissioned by me for OMNI Magazine in 1983, is a little of both.

FROM: John J. Finnegan, President
Wake & Finnegan
Marketing Division

TO: David Brooks, Head Copywriter, Creative Projects Department

Okay, son. Where is it? Life Pro Labs is getting a little antsy. They're laying out more cash for this campaign than you know. Show me something rough.

FROM: Brooks
TO: Finnegan

You want it, Boss. It's yours. It ain't been easy trying to figure how to sell a pussy that looks like a strudel. Notes follow:

338

A significant portion of the Bean Bag Cat campaign will obviously be oriented toward urban consumers. A genetically modified, nonambulatory pet will be very attractive to apartment, co-op, and condominium dwellers.

Imagine the numerous possibilities for utilizing what is essentially a live cat without paws or legs. Standard accessory packs should include Velcro grip strips so that the Bean Bag Cat can be placed securely on a sofa arm, chair seat, or any other surface in a limited living space.

Models will initially include the ten most popular feline breeds. BBCs will be available either in kitten or adult format, although the kittens will be hormonally arrested so that they will stay cute for an indefinite product span.

Item: Life Pro Labs says they'll have the growth-curve problem licked in a year or so, and then we'll be able to offer a BBC that the consumer can obtain as a kitten and then be able to watch grow into adulthood in a matter of weeks.

They'll simply have to change the SaniKit attachments. These can be marketed separately as an educational experience for children, emphasizing the lesson of pet care responsibility.

About the SaniKits. Since prospective consumers will obviously realize that the BBC won't be able to get to a sandbox on its own—or at least not at any practicable speed—the campaign will have to mention the SaniKit bags that the pet owner will be obliged to change at a maximum of three-day intervals.

There must be a marketable way to warn owners that failure to observe the maintenance schedule in the Bean Bag Cat will result minimally in feline renal dysfunction, maximally in cat all over the living room. Perhaps research and development can come up with an audible warning such as the low-battery indicator in home smoke alarms. Call them SaniKat Kits, and Life Pro Labs can look forward to a lucrative accessory trade.

Emphasize in the campaign that Bean Bag Cats will purr, lick, nibble, and squirm just like the original model. But they will not scratch furniture, chase birds, or wander around the neighborhood at night.

FROM: Finnegan
To: Brooks

Looks terrific so far. LPL should love it. One problem. Late word from the lab says there's a hitch in the DNA splicing for the kitties. First year's model run will have to be surgically modified from existing stock so as to stay competitive in the marketplace. Will need some glossing. Can do?

FROM: Brooks
TO: Finnegan

No problem. Just like the suicide from drinking varnish: a horrible death but a beautiful finish.

By the by, what have you got for me after I finish pitching the Bean Bag Cats?

FROM: Finnegan
TO: Brooks

A treat.

How do you feel about Modular Dogs®?

ANTIQUITIES
John Crowley

John Crowley was born in Maine on a World War II air base, grew up in Vermont, Kentucky, and Indiana, then went to live in New York City where he worked on documentary and commercial films and began to write novels. He now lives in Massachusetts. He is the recipient of three World Fantasy Awards (including a Lifetime Achievement Award), the Premio Flaiano "Superprize," and an Award in Literature from the American Academy and Institute of Arts and Letters. Prominent in his *ouevre* are the novel *Little, Big* and the four-volume *Aegypt* series. Other works include *The Translator* and *Lord Byron's Novel: The Evening Land*. His most recent novel, *Four Freedoms* was published in 2009.

"Antiquities" is in the tradition of the very popular science fiction, fantasy, and horror club or bar tale, that is, an improbable or ghostly story told around a fire in a gentlemen's club or in a bar. Crowley reports that the central device of the story, the cat mummy mausoleum in Egypt, is actually real, and the story of how it came to England and was sold for fertilizer is also true.

"Antiquities," the oldest story (other than the Lewis Carroll excerpt) in this volume, was originally published in 1977 by Stuart David Schiff in his classic anthology series *Whispers*. It seems dated not at all.

"There was, of course," Sir Jeffrey said, "the Inconstancy Plague in Cheshire. Short-lived, but a phenomenon I don't think we can quite discount."

It was quite late at the Travellers' Club, and Sir Jeffrey and I had been discussing (as we seemed often to do in those years of the Empire's greatest, yet somehow most tenuous, extent) some anomalous irruptions of the foreign and the odd into the home island's quiet life—small, unlooked-for effects which those centuries of adventure and acquisition had had on an essentially stay-at-home race. At least that was my thought. I was quite young.

"It's no good your saying 'of course' in that offhand tone," I said, attempting to catch the eye of Barnett, whom I felt as much as saw passing through the crepuscular haze of the smoking room. "I've no idea what the Inconstancy Plague was."

From within his evening dress Sir Jeffrey drew out a cigar case, which faintly resembled a row of cigars, as a mummy case resembles the human form within. He offered me one, and we lit them without haste; Sir Jeffrey started a small vortex in his brandy glass. I understood that these rituals were introductory—that, in other words, I would have my tale.

"It was in the latter eighties," Sir Jeffrey said. "I've no idea now how I first came to hear of it, though I shouldn't be surprised if it was some flippant note in *Punch*. I paid no attention at first; the 'popular delusions and madness of crowds' sort of thing. I'd returned not long before from Ceylon, and was utterly, blankly oppressed by the weather. It was just starting autumn when I came ashore, and I spent the next four months more or less behind closed doors. The rain! The fog! How could I have forgotten? And the oddest thing was that no one else seemed to pay the slightest attention. My man used to draw the drapes every morning and say in the most cheerful voice, 'Another dismal wet one, eh, sir?' and I would positively turn my face to the wall."

He seemed to sense that he had been diverted by personal memories, and drew on his cigar as though it were the font of recall.

"What brought it to notice was a seemingly ordinary murder case. A farmer's wife in Winsford, married some decades, came one night into the Sheaf of Wheat, a public house, where her husband was lingering over a pint. From under her skirts she drew an old fowling-piece. She made a remark which was later reported quite variously by the onlookers, and gave him both barrels. One misfired, but the other was quite sufficient. We learn that the husband, on seeing this about to happen, seemed to show neither surprise nor anguish, merely looking up and—well, awaiting his fate.

"At the inquest, the witnesses reported the murderess to have said, before she fired, 'I'm doing this in the name of all the others.' Or perhaps it was 'I'm doing this, Sam (his name), to save the others.' Or possibly, 'I've got to do this, Sam, to save you from that other.' The woman seemed to have gone quite mad. She gave the investigators an elaborate and scarifying story which they, unfortunately, didn't take down, being able to make no sense of it. The rational gist of it was that she had shot her husband for flagrant infidelities which she could bear no longer. When the magistrate asked witnesses if they knew of such infidelities—these things, in a small community, being notoriously difficult to hide—the men, as a body, claimed that they did not. After the trial, however, the women had dark and unspecific hints to make, how they could say much if they would, and so on. The murderess was adjudged unfit to stand trial, and hanged herself in Bedlam not long after.

"I don't know how familiar you are with that oppressive part of the world. In those years farming was a difficult enterprise at best, isolating, stultifyingly boring, unremunerative. Hired men were heavy drinkers. Prices were depressed. The women aged quickly, what with continual childbirth added to a load of work at least equal to their menfolk's. What I'm getting at is that it is, or was, a society the least of any conducive to adultery, amours, romance. And yet for some reason it appeared, after this murder pointed it up, so to speak, dramatically, that there was a veritable plague of inconstant husbands in northern Cheshire."

"It's difficult to imagine," I said, "what evidence there could be of such a thing."

"I had occasion to go to the county that autumn, just at the height of it all," Sir Jeffrey went on, caressing an ashtray with the tip of his cigar. "I'd at last got a grip on myself and begun to accept invitations again. A fellow I'd known in Alexandria, a commercial agent who'd done spectacularly well for himself, asked me up for the shooting."

"Odd place to go shooting."

"Odd fellow. *Arriviste,* to speak frankly. The hospitality was lavish; the house was a red-brick Cheshire faux-Gothic affair, if you know what I mean, and the impression it gave of desolation and melancholy was remarkable. And there was no shooting; poured rain all weekend. One sat about leafing through novels or playing Cairo whist—which is what we called bridge in those days—and staring out the windows. One evening, at a loss for entertainment, our host—Watt was his name, and…"

"What was his name?" I asked.

"Exactly. He'd become a student of mesmerism, or hypnotism as he preferred to call it, and suggested we might have a bit of fun probing our dark underminds. We all declined, but Watt was insistent, and at last suborned a hearty local type, old squirearchical family, and—this is important—an inveterate, dirt-under-the-nails farmer. His conversation revolved, chiefly, around turnips."

"Even his dark undermind's?"

"Ah. Here we come to it. This gentleman's wife was present at the gathering as well, and one couldn't help noticing the hangdog air he maintained around her, the shifty eyes, the nervous start he gave when she spoke to him from behind; and also a certain dreaminess, an abstraction, that would fall on him at odd moments."

"Worrying about his turnips, perhaps."

Sir Jeffrey quashed his cigar, rather reproachfully, as though it were my own flippancy. "The point is that this ruddy-faced, absolutely ordinary fellow *was cheating on his wife.* One read it as though it were written on his shirt front. His wife seemed quite as aware of it as any; her face was drawn tight as her reticule. She blanched when he agreed to go under, and tried to lead him away, but Watt insisted he be a sport, and at last she retired with a headache. I don't know what the man was thinking of when he agreed; had a bit too much brandy, I expect. At any rate, the lamps were lowered and the usual apparatus got out, the spinning disc and so on. The squire, to Watt's surprise, went under as though slain. We thought at first he had merely succumbed to the grape, but then Watt began to question him, and he to answer, languidly but clearly, name, age, and so on. I've no doubt Watt intended to have the man stand on his head, or turn his waistcoat back-to-front, or that sort of thing, but before any of that could begin, the man began to speak. To address someone. Someone female. Most extraordinary, the way he was transformed."

Sir Jeffrey, in the proper mood, shows a talent for mimicry, and now he seemed to transform himself into the hypnotized squire. His eyes glazed and half-closed, his mouth went slack (though his moustache remained upright) and one hand was raised as though to ward off an importunate spirit.

"'No,' says he. 'Leave me alone. Close those eyes—those eyes. Why? Why? Dress yourself, oh God…' And here he seemed quite in torment. Watt should of course have awakened the poor fellow immediately, but he was fascinated, as I confess we all were.

"'Who is it you speak to?' Watt asked.

"'She,' says the squire. 'The foreign woman. The clawed woman. The cat.'

"'What is her name?'

"'Bastet.'

"'How did she come here?'

"At this question the squire seemed to pause. Then he gave three answers: 'Through the earth. By default. On the *John Deering*.' This last answer astonished Watt, since, as he told me later, the *John Deering* was a cargo ship we had often dealt with, which made a regular Alexandria—Liverpool run.

"'Where do you see her?' Watt asked.

"'In the sheaves of wheat.' "

"He meant the pub, I suppose," I put in.

"I think not," Sir Jeffrey said darkly. "He went on about the sheaves of wheat. He grew more animated, though it was more difficult to understand his words. He began to make sounds—well, how shall I put it? His breathing became stertorous, his movements…"

"I think I see."

"Well, you can't, quite. Because it was one of the more remarkable things I have ever witnessed. The man was making physical love to someone he described as a cat, or a sheaf of wheat."

"The name he spoke," I said, "is an Egyptian one. A goddess associated with the cat."

"Precisely. It was midway through this ritual that Watt at last found himself, and gave an awakening command. The fellow seemed dazed, and was quite drenched with sweat; his hand shook when he took out his pocket-handkerchief to mop his face. He looked at once guilty and pleased, like—like—"

"The cat who ate the canary."

"You have a talent for simile. He looked around at the company, and asked shyly if he had embarrassed himself. I tell you, old boy, we were hard-pressed to reassure him."

Unsummoned, Barnett materialized beside us with the air of one about to speak tragic and ineluctable prophecies. It is his usual face. He said only that it had begun to rain. I asked for a whisky and soda. Sir Jeffrey seemed lost in thought during these transactions, and when he spoke again it was to muse: "Odd, isn't it," he said, "how naturally one thinks of cats as female, though we know quite well that they are distributed between two sexes. As far as I know, it is the same the world over. Whenever, for instance, a cat in a tale is transformed into a human, it is invariably a woman."

"The eyes," I said. "The movements—that certain sinuosity."

"The air of independence," Sir Jeffrey said. "False, of course. One's cat is quite dependent on one, though he seems not to think so."

"The capacity for ease."

"And spite."

"To return to our plague," I said, "I don't see how a single madwoman and a hypnotized squire amount to one."

"Oh, that was by no means the end of it. Throughout that autumn there was, relatively speaking, a flurry of divorce actions and breach-of-promise suits. A suicide left a note: 'I can't have her, and I can't live without her.' More than one farmer's wife, after years of dedication and many offspring, packed herself off to aged parents in Chester. And so on.

"Monday morning after the squire's humiliation I returned to town. As it happened, Monday was market day in the village and I was able to observe at first hand some effects of the plague. I saw husbands and wives sitting at far ends of wagon seats, unable to meet each other's eyes. Sudden arguments flaring without reason over the vegetables. I saw tears. I saw over and over the same hangdog, evasive, guilty look I described in our squire."

"Hardly conclusive."

"There is one further piece of evidence. The Roman Church has never quite eased its grip in that part of the world. It seems that about this time a number of R.C. wives clubbed together and sent a petition to their bishop, saying that the region was in need of an exorcism. Specifically, that their husbands were being tormented by a succubus. Or succubi—whether it was one or many was impossible to tell."

"I shouldn't wonder."

"What specially intrigued me," Sir Jeffrey went on, removing his eyeglass from between cheek and brow and polishing it absently, "is that in all this inconstancy only the men seemed to be accused; the women seemed solely aggrieved, rather than guilty, parties. Now if we take the squire's words as evidence, and not merely 'the stuff that dreams are made on,' we have the picture of a foreign, apparently Egyptian, woman—or possibly women—embarking at Liverpool and moving unnoticed amid Cheshire, seeking whom she may devour and seducing yeomen in their barns amid the fruits of the harvest. The notion was so striking that I got in touch with a chap at Lloyd's, and asked him about passenger lists for the *John Deering* over the last few years."

"And?"

"There were none. The ship had been in dry dock for two or three years previous. It had made one run, that spring, and then been moth-balled. On that one run there were no passengers. The cargo from Alex consisted of the usual oil, dates, sago, rice, tobacco—and something called 'antiquities.' Since the nature of these was unspecified, the matter ended there. The Inconstancy Plague was short-lived; a letter from Watt the next spring made no mention of it, though he'd been avid for details—most of what I know comes from him and his gleanings of the Winsford *Trumpet,* or whatever it calls itself. I might never have come to any conclusion at all about the matter had it not been for a chance encounter in Cairo a year or so later.

"I was *en route* to the Sudan in the wake of the Khartoum disaster and was bracing myself, so to speak, in the bar of Shepheard's. I struck up a conversation with an archaeologist fellow just off a dig around Memphis, and the talk turned, naturally, to Egyptian mysteries. The thing that continually astonished him, he said, was the absolute *thoroughness* of the ancient Egyptian mind. Once having decided a thing was ritualistically necessary, they admitted of no deviation in carrying it out.

"He instanced cats. We know in what high esteem the Egyptians held cats. If held in high esteem, they must be mummified after death; and so they were. All of them, or nearly all. Carried to their tombs with the bereaved family weeping behind, put away with favorite toys and food for the afterlife journey. Not long ago, he said, some *three hundred thousand* mummified cats were uncovered at Beni Hassan. An entire cat necropolis, unviolated for centuries.

"And then he told me something which gave me pause. More than pause. He said that, once uncovered, all those cats were disinterred and shipped to England. Every last one."

"Good Lord. Why?"

"I have no idea. They were not, after all, the Elgin Marbles. This seemed to have been the response when they arrived at Liverpool, because not a single museum or collector of antiquities displayed the slightest interest. The whole lot had to be sold off to pay a rather large shipping bill."

"Sold off? To whom, in God's name?"

"To a Cheshire agricultural firm. Who proceeded to chop up the lot and resell it. To the local farmers, my dear boy. To use as fertilizer."

Sir Jeffrey stared deeply into his nearly untouched brandy, watching the legs it made on the side of the glass, as though he read secrets there. "Now the scientific mind may be able to believe," he said at last, "that three hundred thousand cats, aeons old, wrapped lovingly in winding cloths and put to rest with spices and with spells, may be exhumed from a distant land—and from a distant past as well—and minced into the loam of Cheshire, and it will all have no result but grain. I am not certain. Not certain at all."

The smoking room of the Travellers' Club was deserted now, except for the weary, unlaid ghost of Barnett. Above us on the wall the mounted heads of exotic animals were shadowed and nearly unnamable; one felt that they had just then thrust their coal-smoked and glass-eyed heads through the wall, seeking something, and that just the other side of the wall stood their vast and unimaginable bodies. Seeking what? The members, long dead as well, who had slain them and brought them to this?

"You've been in Egypt," Sir Jeffrey said.

"Briefly."

"I have always thought that Egyptian women were among the world's most beautiful."

"Certainly their eyes are stunning. With the veil, of course, one sees little else."

"I spoke specifically of those circumstances when they are without the veil. In all senses."

"Yes."

"Depilated, many of them." He spoke in a small, dreamy voice, as though he observed long-past scenes. "A thing I have always found—intriguing. To say the least." He sighed deeply; he tugged down his waistcoat, preparatory to rising; he replaced his eyeglass. He was himself again. "Do you suppose," he said, "that such a thing as a cab could be found at this hour? Well, let us see."

"By the way," I asked when we parted, "whatever came of the wives' petition for an exorcism?"

"I believe the bishop sent it on to Rome for consideration. The Vatican, you know, does not move hastily on these things. For all I know, it may still be pending."

THE MANTICORE'S TALE
Catherynne M. Valente

Born in the Pacific Northwest in 1979, Catherynne M. Valente is the author of a dozen works of fiction and poetry, including *Palimpsest*, the Orphan's Tales series, *The Labyrinth*, and crowd-funded phenomenon *The Girl Who Circumnavigated Fairyland in a Ship of her Own Making*. She is the winner of the Tiptree Award, the Mythopoeic Award, the Rhysling Award, and the Million Writers Award. She lives on an island off the coast of Maine with her partner and two dogs.

She says: "I love the manticore, as one of the composite creatures that generally gets a lot of screentime in games but narrative short shrift. Maybe it's because they're cats, and cats are sort of beyond morality. I spent days and days trying to come up with an origin story for them, something that wasn't: so a lion, a snake, a man and a scorpion walk into a bar... the Upas tree is a real mythological tree, one of the things Darwin actually debunked. I like the idea that a deadly tree could produce deadly creatures—but of course every creature is just trying to find its way."

Sing, oh, sing, of the sun-muscled Manticore! Thundering fleet are their scarlet feet, and great are their echoing roars! No hunter more patient than we, no serpent so sour-tailed as we, no snarling leaps lighter, no long teeth are brighter than ours—than ours!—on the scrub-spotted deserts of home!

Ha! Let us have none of that. Do not sing of us. We do not want your songs. We will sing, and you will listen.

The desert is wide and white and dry as an old bone. We worry it, we gnaw and tear and peel it bald. And we sing when the moon is jumping on the sand like a skinny white mouse, we sing and the saltbush weeps. The oases ripple under our breath, the blue and clear water where the rhinoceros wrangle, where the cheetah purrs and licks her paws, and the Upas trees waver green and violet in the scalding breeze!

They will tell you the Upas is a death-bower. They will call it the hydra-tree of the desert, and warn that if you sleep beneath it for even a night, you may wake, but to no morning man has known. They will say that three hundred soldiers all in bronze and feathers camped beneath an Upas once, to drink from the clear stream that flowed beneath its branches, and that by the time the sun touched their toes all were dead and cold as dinner. This is ridiculous, a fairy tale. But I suppose it is yet not entirely untrue, for the Upas is our mother, and we are enough of death for anyone. And if soldiers camp under an Upas when she is blowing her seed, it is no fault of the hungry kittens that tumble out if they find their supper plump and laid out on the sand.

Look, passersby—though not too closely!—at the radiant Upas, lover of the Sun in his golden bedchamber, her red branches thick and strong as a haunch, thorny and pitted, her green needles far too glossy and stiff to grow in the thirsty desert. Look at her fruit, nestled in the shadowy forks of her knotted trunk, how scarlet and purple, how thick and full of juice! Touch one at your peril, for these gleaming berries are not fruit but eggs, and it is we that grow within them, in the crimson sacs which wax in the blistering scrub-light, full of the peculiar Upas-yolk we drink and drink, which fills our tails with enough poison for a lifetime, until we rip that silk-thin skin and tumble out head first into the water, or soldiers, whichever seems most convenient.

I remember the Upas-milk. It was sweet, like blackberries and blood.

In the fruit-sac we know all things: how the Sun preened on the face of the oasis-pool, how one Upas, though neither the tallest or most beautiful thing in the desert, opened up her branches and grasped the reddening beams for her own. Her wood warmed and the pool rippled—the Sun would not have noticed if his mirror had not been marred. He would have been angry, and scorched the tree for her theft, had not the first Manticore-fruit burst open before him, and if he did not think the little cub with her needle-teeth and her whipping tail and her sky-bright eyes was the most lovely of all imaginable things, and immediately set about to teaching her to sting and roar and sing and kill, all the things he knew. The Upas smiled, and told her sisters how to follow her lead.

After we fall, it is harder to remember these things, to know they are true. But we do our best to love our parents and turn our prayers to the sky and the sand.

It is only unfortunate that we are more or less helpless when the Upas blows us free. No more fierce than little red kittens or infant snakes, blind and wet and mewling. Our tails do thrash quick and sharp in those first hours, indiscriminate, for we have not quite learned to control it when the oasis, littered with palm nuts and antelope-ribs, catches us in green-gold arms. This is when the wranglers come, if they are clever, with their silver tail-caps spangling in the desert light.

I would like to tell you I was reared in the open flats, the white and worried bone, that I tore open leopards and antelope and rhinoceros, that I remember what that tough gray flesh tasted like, and that horn. I would like to tell you that the Sun and I ran together, bounding red-pawed over the saltbush and the pale weeds, that in the warm red rocks I rolled with my legs in the air, scratching and roaring and eating as I pleased. I would like to tell you that the echoes there taught me to sing. I would like to tell you I was happy, and that the Sun was high in the sky.

But the wranglers came with a little silver cap, something like a thimble with buckles and straps, and armored in polished metals splashed with the last desperate strikes of countless kittens, lashed the thing to my barbed tail. My thrashings were dull thuds and sprays of sand, but nothing more. I howled—it is not only the province of wolves. I howled and that did startle them, for the voice of the Manticore is terrible and piercing and sweet, the sweetest and most terrible of all possible voices, like a flute and a trumpet playing together. It is barbed as surely as a tail. I howled and keened, thumping my useless limb against the ground pitifully. They took out wax stoppers and closed their ears to me, and into an amber cage I went, clapped in an amber collar, and gagged in leather to keep me silent.

Tell me again how the Gaselli sing. Tell me that no melodies are lovelier than theirs.

The heights of the amber city made me dizzy. The platforms spiral up and up those impossible cedars, and on the spindly bridges I nearly fainted away, so far below did the ground sway and wobble. They pulled me up with squeaking pulleys and moving flats drawn up with wet ropes. I retched into the muzzle and choked on my own bile. The green branches cut the clouds as I rose and crumbled against the lifting floor and sobbed against the straps which bit into my face until I tasted my own blood with every lurching inch upwards. I hitched and gagged, bewildered, as afraid as any lost beast. But I was close to the sky, so close, and the Sun beat my back fondly.

The amber cage had an amber lock, and there was a girl with an amber key. She kept it on the beads that slung around her like chains, dangling right at the base of her throat. In those days any number of creatures were brought from every hovel and height in the land to delight this creature, whose clear, calm eyes took in everything with equal regard and due. She was dutifully amazed at my fur and my tail, dutifully frightened at my muffled roar, dutifully patted my head and dutifully passed on to the next wonder of nature brought up the trees for her pleasure. She took no joy in any one animal over any other, and her voice was genteel and grateful when she thanked the wranglers for bringing her these miracles and grotesqueries. By the latter, she meant me, and thus I was given my name.

For some weeks she came, dutifully, to visit her menagerie, escorted by wranglers and noble nursemaids and occasionally her father. She played with the pygmy elephant and the wobble-kneed young Centaur whose legs were bound in her absence so that he would never grow to shame her with excess height. She had a Djinn whose smoke had gone out and a fish in a great glass bowl which owed her yet two wishes. Their games were odd and solemn—she sang to them and sat them to tea with amber cups they could not help but break, and scolded them for their manners. She forced their struggling heads onto her breast and all exclaimed it a miracle that her gentleness of spirit and purity of heart could charm the most savage of monsters.

She did not charm me.

After attempting to get me to drink from her dainty cups and sing with her while she did her sewing, she declared with great sadness that the beast she had named in jest was truly a grotesque beyond salvation, and that I should be sent away, for I was surely, in my unfathomable heart, unhappy there. I knew this meant the slaughterhouse or simply being shoved off of the platforms into the narrow spit of sea, but what maiden knows how the world is skewed to spare any testing of her virtue?

When she and her escort had gone, a small, dark shape remained, silhouetted against the doorframe of the wretched zoo. It came into the light, and I saw that it was a girl like the other one, and lost interest—save that she came and knelt by my cage, and, loosing a strand of black beads from her throat, put her own amber key into the lock, and opened the amber door.

"Poor Grotteschi. Do you see these beads? When amber is burned to make resin, this horrible black stuff is left over when the golden oil pours dutifully into the catch. No one wants it. It is garbage. I, too, am what is left over from her, what is thrown away when she has passed over it, what remains in the corners when she has swept by."

She put her hands to the muzzle's buckles and let it loose. By then I had grown, I was the size of a small horse, but the muzzle had never been changed. My jaw would never close quite right again. She did not mind my teeth. She rubbed my chin and my cheeks, wiped at the hardened blood with the hem of her dress. Her name was Hind. She was a good girl, and I slept in her bed from that night on.

Even when I was fully grown, she slept curled between my paws and demanded iron supports for her pitifully delicate bed. Together we snuck into the libraries at night, and she taught me to read from the books kept on the highest shelves, which I could reach for us, stories of lost girls and lost beasts and grotesques like us. She brought me cakes from the kitchens, covered in icing, so much thicker and richer than the mashed and rotten meat of her sister's zoo. When she became more beautiful even than her sister, I used to sing at her window to the men who gathered there to play their flutes or harps. They scattered when faced with my superior songs, and I padded back to Hind and her black beads. I was happy. The Sun was high in the sky. Happiness, when you look back on it, seems so brief, but then, with her, my whole life seemed to pass by under the flitting cedar-shadows. Until the day she ran into our room and slammed the door behind her, her chest heaving under those black beads, her face flushed with tears. I ran to her, and she buried her head in my mane. Finally she drew back and sobbed horribly, a long, broken howl—I remember when I howled that way.

A pearl fell out of her mouth.

Hind begged me to take her away. She promised that she knew how to use the floating platforms, and we could run from Amberabad to another city, where her affliction of pearls might be of some use to us. And so the girl strung with black beads packed her cakes and some few of her precious books and climbed onto my back, proudly astride, as her father had told her over and over not to do.

Someone had poisoned her, having no business in Amberabad but to vex my friend, causing pearls to spit out of her mouth whenever she spoke. Because her father did not like her books or her cakes or her pets. And so we descended together from the city in the sky, through the branches and clouds, onto the long road, and she clung to me all the way down, her long fingers gripping my mane so as not to fall while I bounded off of the last amber plank. I faithfully kept my tail from curling tightly upward, as the recalcitrant thing is wont to do, so as not to hurt her. We stepped onto the thick grass and my friend laughed to feel it, solid ground beneath her. We went into the world, in search of another city, one which would love us and hold us close, one which would be rich and bright and richer still for our walking and singing and laughing in it.

IN CARNATION

Nancy Springer

After living in Pennsylvania for forty-six years and publishing fifty fantasy, horror and mystery novels for adults, young adults and children, Nancy Springer has moved to an unspoiled area of panhandle Florida, where she is very much enjoying the wildlife while completing *The Case of the Gypsy Good-Bye*: An Enola Holmes Mystery, sixth volume of her series about Sherlock Holmes's younger sister. Two of her previous mysteries won the Edgar Allen Poe award.

Springer says of her relationship with felines, "I had no cats as a child because my father didn't like them, and I had no cats as an adult because my husband was allergic to them. His eyes swelled like golf balls. When I wrote 'In Carnation' I had no cats, but perhaps we can attribute the story to some intuition or prescience, because just as soon as I was rid of the husband with the golf-eyeball problem, I acquired five cats, among the first of which was a female named Amazonian Demon Warrior Princess From the Outermost Reaches of Darkest Perdition. She is still with me, and she still rules. I know a goddess when I see one."

She materialized, stood on her familiar padded paws and looked around at an utterly strange place. After every long sleep the world was more changed, and after every incarnation the next lifetime became more bizarre. The last time, a Norwegian peasant woman fleeing "holy" wars, she had come by a long sea voyage to what was called the New World. Now she found it so new she scarcely recognized it as Earth at all. Under her paws lay a great slab of something like stone, but with a smell that was not stone's good ancient smell. Chariots of glass and metal whined by at untoward speeds, stinking of their own heat. Grotesque buildings towered everywhere, and in them she could sense the existence of people, more people than had ever burdened the world before, a new kind of people who jangled the air with their fears, their smallness, their suspicion of the gods and one another.

As always when she awoke from a long sleep she was very hungry, and not for food. But this was not a good place for her to go hunting. It terrified her. Running as only a cat can, like a golden streak, she fled from the chariots and their stench, from the buildings and the pettiness in their air until she found something that approximated countryside. Outside the town there was a place with trees and grass.

And on the grass were camped people whose thoughts and feelings did not hang on the air and make it heavy, but flitted and laughed like magpies. *We don't care what the world thinks,* the magpies sang. *Some of us are thieves and some of us are preachers, some are freaks and some are stars, some of us have three heads and some can't even get one together, and who cares? We all get along. We are the carnival people. Whether you are a pimp or a whore or a queer or a con artist, if you are one of us you belong, and the world can go blow itself.*

A cat is one who walks by herself. Still, *A carnival! Yes,* thought she, the golden one. *This is better. I may find him here.* For she was very hungry, and the smells of the carnival were good. She was, after all, a meat eater, and a carnival is made of meat. The day was turning to silver dusk, the carnival glare was starting to light the sky and the carnival blare rose like magpie cries on the air. The cat trotted in through the gate, to the midway, where already the grass was trampled into dirt.

"Come see the petrified Pygmy," the barkers cried. "Come see the gun that killed Jesse James. Come see the Double-Jointed Woman, the Mule-Faced Girl, the Iron Man of Taipan."

High striker, Ferris wheel, motordrome, House of Mirrors—it was all new to her, yet the feel in the air was that of something venerable and familiar: greed. Carnival was carnival and had been since lust and feasting began. French fries, sausage ends, bits of cinnamon cake had fallen to the ground, but she did not paw at them. Instead, she traversed the midway, past Dunk Bozo and bumper cars, roulette wheel and ring toss, on the lookout for a man, any man so long as he was young and virile and not ugly. Once she had seduced him and satisfied herself, she would discard him. This was her holy custom, and she would be sure she upheld it. A few times in previous lives she had been false to herself, had married and found herself at the mercy of a man who attempted to command her; she had sworn this would not happen again. Eight of her lifetimes were gone. Only one remained to her, and she was determined to live this one with no regrets.

On the hunt, she found it difficult to sort out the people she saw crowding through the carnival. Men and women alike, they wore trousers, cotton shirts, and shapeless cloth shoes. And leather jackets, and hair that was short and spiky or long and in curls. She became confused and annoyed. True, some of the people she saw were identifiable as men, and some of the men she saw were young, but they walked like apes and had a strange chemical smell about them and were not attractive to her.

"Hey there, kitten! Guess your age, your weight, your birthdate?"

The cat flinched into a crouch. Though the words of this New World language meant nothing to her, she could usually comprehend the thoughts that underlay words, and for a moment she had unreasonably felt as if the guess-man's pitch had been directed at her. Narrow-eyed and coiled to run, she stared up at him.

"Yes, Mother! Congratulations." He was facing a pudding-cheeked woman with a pregnant belly. "What would you like me to guess? Name? Age? Date of your wedding day? Yes? Okay. Fifty cents, please. If I don't get it right, one of my fine china dolls is yours."

He was not talking to the cat after all. *Why would he?* she scolded herself. He offered his invitation to the dozens of people walking by. And many of them stopped for him, perhaps because there was a wry poetry in his voice, or perhaps because he was young and not ugly. Slim, dressed in denims and boots, he stood tall though he was in fact not very tall. In front of the booth that marked his place on the midway he took a stance like a bard in a courtyard. Something about him made her want to see his eyes, but because he wore dark glasses she could not. His face was quiet, unexceptional, yet he seemed like one who had something more to him than muscle and manhead.

Not that she needed anything more. It was enough that he was young and not ugly. He would suffice.

She trotted on, looking for a private place to make the change. It would take only a minute.

Within a few strides the familiar musky scent of lust touched her whiskers. Her delicate lip drew back from her tiny pointed teeth, and she slipped under a tent flap. She had reached the location of "Hinkleman's G-String Goddess Revue."

This will do.

Inside, all was heat, mosquitoes, dim light, and the smell of sweating men. Forty of them were crowded in there, watching a stripper at work on the small stage. The golden visitor leapt to a chair back and watched also. No one noticed her. She sat with her long tail curled around her slender haunches, and its softly furred tip twitched with scorn for what she was seeing.

Stupid, simpleminded cow. She uses her body like a club. She does not know how to walk, how to move, how to tease. Her breasts are huge, like melons, and that is all she knows.

The thoughts of everyone in the tent swarmed in its air thicker than the mosquitoes. Therefore the cat quickly knew that the stripper, called a kootch girl, was expected to more than mildly arouse the men, called marks. She knew that the kootch girl's repertory was limited by her meager talents, that the girl was planning to get out of her G-string in order to achieve maximum effect. She knew that several of the marks were thinking in terms of audience participation. She knew that in back of the tent was a trailer where those with fifty dollars might buy some private action later.

The men roared. The stripper was flashing her pudenda. Jumping down from her perch, the cat darted backstage, hot with scorn and anger.

Is that what they call a woman these days? Can no one show them how it should be done?

Backstage were two more strippers, spraying one another's semi-naked bodies with mosquito repellent. Mr. Hinkleman, the owner, was back there also, lounging in a tilted chair, bored, drinking gin between hot hoarse stints in the bally box. Off to one side was a booth with a flimsy curtain, a changing facility, not much used by women who were about to take off their clothes in front of an audience anyway. The golden cat walked into it. A moment later, a golden woman walked out.

"Carrumba!" Mr. Hinkleman, who had seen a lot over a career spanning twenty-three years in the carnival, nevertheless let his chair legs slam to the floor, jolting himself bolt upright. "Hoo! Where did you come from, honey?"

She answered only with a faint smile. There had been a time when she was more fully human, when she could talk. But that ability was a thousand years and four lifetimes gone. And she did not regret the loss. With each incarnation she found there were fewer to whom she wished to speak. Talking meant little but thoughts told her more truth.

"What's your name?"

The level look she gave him caused him to suddenly remember, without any resentment, the training his mother thought he had forgotten years before. He stood up to greet the naked visitor more properly.

"Hello, ma'am, welcome to—to wherever the heck this is. I'm Fred Hinkleman." His hand hovered in air, then went to his head as if to remove an invisible hat in her presence. "What can I do for you? Do you want to be in my show?"

"She don't got but little tits," one of the strippers put in scornfully. The girl from onstage had joined those backstage, and the three Hinkleman Goddesses stood huddled together like moose when the scent of panther is in the air.

"I know how she gets to look glowy like that all over," complained the dark kootch girl who was billed as the Wild Indian. "She just eats carrots, that's all. Any of us could do it. Eat carrots till they're coming out the kazoo."

Fred Hinkleman seemed not to hear them at all. His gaze was stuck on the newcomer. "Tell you what," he said to her. "You go onstage and show the yahoos what you can do. I'll go introduce you right now. What should I call you?"

Her mouth, smiling, opened into a soundless meow.

"Cat? Good. Suits you." He went out, and a moment later could be heard promising the marks "the hottest new talent in the adult entertainment business, the sleek, feline Miss Cat, uh, Miss Cat Pagan."

"Just another pussy," one of the strippers muttered.

She made her entrance onstage. Contrary to the logic of the word "stripper," it is not necessary for one actually to be wearing anything in order to perform. Cat was wearing nothing at all, but that was not what made the already-sated marks go wild and leap up and stand on their chairs in order to see her. It was the way she wore it.

She did not bump or grind or flash for them. All she did was walk, pose, hint at possibilities, and possess the stage as she had once possessed the known world. Dignity clothed her as if in robes of gold. No mark thought of touching her. Every mark knew that the price of going to her afterward would be more than he could afford.

Looking out over them, she knew she could have any one of them—and many of them were young and well built, far more showily muscled than the man in sunglasses on the midway. But no. It was him she wanted. There was something about the way he stood. He had dignity, too.

When she considered that the marks had seen enough, she went backstage and helped herself to clothing: a short strapless red dress with a flared skirt, a wisp of lace to throw around her shoulders, a picture hat. The other Hinkleman's G-String Goddess Revue girls watched her silently and did not try to stop her. Now that she had showed her stuff she was one of them. In the backstage air she could sense their stoical acceptance, and it surprised her. She had expected dislike, even enmity. But these women were carnies. They breakfasted with snake-eating geeks and sword swallowers, they bathed in buckets, camped in mud, and every day they were expected to perform magic, creating glamour out of dirt. So what was one more freak or freakish event to them? If the stranger wanted to show up out of nowhere, that was okay. They had weathered storms before.

"Honeycat, you're a walking advertisement," Hinkleman remarked when he saw her. "Go on, go do the midway. Have some fun."

The kootcher with the melon breasts went along with Cat—in order to be seen with her, Cat surmised, noticing the other woman's thoughts the way she noticed gnats in the air, with only a small portion of her attention. Melons wanted to make the best of a situation. Melons was not unwise.

"Been around the carousel a time or two, honey?" Melons chirped.

Married, she meant. Ignoring her, Cat headed straight toward the Guess Anything stand. Now that she was in her human form, she would make sure that the man there saw her. From her experience she knew this was all that would be necessary. She would smile just a little and look into his eyes, and when she walked away he would follow her as if she led him by an invisible chain of gold.

There was a crowd around the stand. The Guess Anything man was popular. Asked the standard questions concerning age and weight, he was often wrong, always on the side of flattery, and he gave away many prizes. But asked to guess far more difficult things—birthstones, marital status, number of children or grandchildren, home address, the place where a mark went to high school or nursing school or prison—he was often correct, uncannily so. And there was a quiet charisma about him. People stood listening to him in fascination, giving him their money again and again.

At the edge of the crowd Cat waited her turn with scant patience. She was not far away from him; he should see her... Wishing to enjoy his reaction, she felt for his mind with hers and found it easily. In fact, it awaited her. And yes, there was an awareness of her presence in him, but it was unlike any awareness she had ever experienced in a man before. His cognition of her had no lust in it. Despite her lithe, barefoot, red-clad beauty, her appearance did not affect him in that way. Not at all.

"Who's next?" He took the mark's money and handed it to a boy in the stand, a good-looking youngster. His son, Cat knew from touching his mind at that moment. The mother was long dead but still very much missed. He was raising the boy himself.

As the boy made change, his father guessed the mark's age and weight, both incorrectly, then handed over the cheap ceramic prize with a smile. It was a warm, whimsical smile. Amusement in it: the "fine china dolls" were so worthless he made money even when he gave them away. But also something of heart: he liked to make people happy. Cat suddenly found that she liked his smile very much.

"Who's next?"

"Right here, Ollie," Melons said, nudging Cat forward. "Hey, Ollie, this here's Cat."

"I know. We met earlier." He faced her. His smile was wonderful, but he still wore the dark glasses, even though night had fallen. She could not see his eyes.

"Hello, Cat," he said. "Welcome."

Melons said, "She wants you to guess her age, I guess. I don't know. She don't seem to talk none. Cat got her tongue." Melons laughed at her own weak joke, chin angled skyward, breasts quaking. Ollie smiled but did not laugh.

"Some other time I'll guess for her if she wants," he said. "Not right now. I don't think that's what you really want right now anyway, is it, Cat?" His tone was mild, friendly. There was no flirtation in it.

Frustrated, she thought, *I want you to take off those barriers over your eyes. I want to see into them and make you follow me. I want to know you carnally, and I want to know what you are.*

No, his thought replied directly to her thought. *No, sorry, I can't do any of that. Not even for you, milady Cat.*

Back at the girl show tent, an hour later, she found herself still quivering in reaction. This man had made her feel naked, unshielded, exposed in a way that no lack of clothing could ever make her feel exposed. Whoever or whatever he was, he could touch her mind. Perhaps he could even tell what she was—or had been.

Partly, she felt outrage, humiliation, vexation. As much as she had ever wanted any man she wanted him, and he had not responded as he should have. It is no small matter when a fertility goddess is thwarted in lust.

And partly she felt great fear. The deities of the old religions are always the demons of the new. Once in her thrice-three lives Cat had been found out and put to death, while still in her feline form, by burning. She still remembered not so much the horrible pain as the helplessness of her clever cat body enslaved by rawhide bindings, the leaping, ravenous flames of the bonfire, the stench of her own consumed skin and fur. It was not a death she ever wanted to experience again.

Strutting and posing through her next kootch show, she picked out a broad-shouldered, handsome young mark and summoned him with her eyes. As she had wordlessly commanded, he was waiting for her in back of the tent afterward, not quite able to believe what was happening, his mouth moving uncertainly, soft as a baby's. She led him away into the darkness beyond the edge of the carnival, and he did what she wanted, everything she wanted, and he was good, very good. Afterward, she drove him away with her clawed hands. More punishment was not necessary. She knew he would go mad with thinking of her before many days had passed.

She should have been satisfied. Always before she had been satisfied by the simple, sacred act of lust. Yet she found that she was not.

She should have gone away on four speedy unbound paws from that dangerous place where someone had apprehended her truly. Yet she found that she would not.

Confusion take this Ollie person. He has shamed me and he has made me afraid, but he has not yet bested me utterly. We shall see whether he scorns me in the end.

Scorn was perhaps too strong a word, for when she came back to the carnival, walking alone, she found him waiting for her outside Hinkleman's trailer. "I just want to say I'm sorry if I offended you, Cat," he told her aloud. "I didn't mean to."

The words meant nothing to her. But the thought underlying them was clear as tears. *I didn't mean to stir up anger, and I don't want enemies. I just want to be let alone with my son and my sorrow.*

Sentiment annoyed her. She bared her teeth at him, nearly hissing, then passed him and went inside to sleep in the bunk Hinkleman's girls had cleared for her. When Hinkleman came, a few minutes later, to see if he could share it with her as was the kootch show owner's tacit right, she struck at him, leaving four long red scratches across his face. Then she listened in disgust as he comforted himself with the Indian instead. He was aging, potbellied, foul of breath, altogether repulsive. How could he be so goatishly eager while this man who attracted her, this Ollie, was so indifferent?

Men. Hell take them all. So Ollie wishes to be let alone? That will be no heartbreak for me.

Yet the next day when the carnival lights came on at sunset, she went first to the flower stand, and took a blossom—smiling, the old Italian woman gave it to her. Carnies give other carnies what they can. This was a flower like a woman's petticoat, frilled and fringed and fluted, white once but dipped in a stain that had spread from its petal tips along its veins and into its penetralia, blood red. It was very beautiful. Cat placed it in her golden hair. Then she walked the midway in her red dress again, and came to a certain booth, his booth, and stood there staring at him. It was her curiosity, she told herself, that drew her back to him this way. And she knew that partly this was true.

Hello, Cat, he greeted her without speaking and without looking at her.
Hello.
You are the only one I can talk to this way.
You are the only one I can talk to at all.

There was a pause. Then he thought to her very softly, *Yes. Yes, I see. It had not occurred to me, but there is such a thing as being too much alone.*

No, not really. I like being alone.

Still… if you wish to talk sometimes, it is no trouble for me to talk with you.

It would be a way, perhaps, of finding out how much he knew of her. As for the other thing she wanted of him… she still desired it badly, and still felt no response in him. And there was no way in cold frosty hell she was going to ask it of him again. The flower in her hair should have been invitation enough. That and the summons in her eyes.

She made mental conversation as casually as if she were hostessing a court function, chatting with the lesser vassals. *So you comprehend thoughts. When people come to you and ask you questions, then you can find the answers in their minds?*

Yes. And also many things they would not want me to know. Very beautiful things sometimes, and sometimes very ugly. She heard a poet's yearning in his tone of mind. He wanted to take what was in people and make a song, a saga great enough to hold all of it, everything he had heard and learned. But she did not wish to be in his song.

She could not ask him how much he knew of her. Why would he tell her the truth, anyway? He lied constantly.

So whatever questions the marks ask you, you could answer correctly every time.

Yes.

They why do you so often give the wrong answer?

To please them. People like to win. So I let them win sometimes, and then they come back, you see, and try again.

She turned and walked away. Behind her she could hear him as he started ballying: "I can guess your age, your weight, your occupation! Challenge my skill, ladies and gentlemen! Ask me any question. See if I can answer."

Cat made sure she was well down the midway before she allowed herself to think it: *He keeps them coming back. He keeps me coming back.*

And then she thought, *If I win, will it be because he has let me?*
And she thought, *Who is he? What is he?*

But her sense of fear felt eased somewhat. If she did not know those things of him by touching his mind, there was little reason to think he knew more of her.

That night she lay with a mark again, and found that she despised him and what she did with him. "You should charge," Melons told her crossly after the man left. "It's stupid not to charge. You're making it bad for the rest of us." She glared at the kootcher, but she could not have loathed herself much more if she did indeed perform the holy act for pay. Even the thought of how insanity would punish the man for his daring did not comfort her.

The next morning she went to find Ollie in his trailer with his young son. For hours she sat in their kitchen, and conversed in her silent way with Ollie, and had fried trout, fresh caught, for breakfast with both of them. The boy tended to the breakfast, mostly, just as he tended the booth in the evenings, making change for his father, and for the same reason. The Guess Anything man could not do it for himself.

Ollie was blind.

Blind? But—I didn't know!

Hardly anybody does. Keep it to yourself, will you? His smile told her this was a small joke—he knew she could speak to no one. Yet it was no joke. A guess-man is supposed to see, to find clues with his eyes, to surmise, not to know. Anything else is too frightening. Ollie would be out of business if the marks knew the truth.

Of course.

Cat felt at the same time very foolish and strangely lighthearted. So he had never seen her in her red dress, he did not know how golden her hair glowed in the carnival lights, he had never seen the carnation softly bobbing at her temple, he could not see how beautiful she was at all. Yet he had been sorry to offend her. Yet he had greeted her the first time he felt her walk by.

Your eyes—how did it happen?

In the accident.

The fiery tragedy that had killed his wife. Afterward, he had sold his home, quit his job, and started traveling with the carnival. Built a life for himself the way he liked it. Letting people win. Giving them happiness.

Or—touching their minds, and learning all the truth about them, then telling them lies.

There was a pause. Then Cat asked gently, *May I see your eyes now?*

He hesitated only a moment, then reached up and removed the dark glasses. His eyes were not ugly. Really, she had known they could not be ugly. They were gray, misty, and seemed to stare far away, like the eyes of a seer. And his face, without its dark barrier in the way—how could she ever have thought his face was commonplace? It was exquisite, with arched aspiring cheekbones, brows that dreamed.

You are very beautiful.

You—they tell me you are also, Cat. I know—the feel of your mind—it is beautiful to me. It is proud, like a golden thing, a sunset thing.

You knew everything. Right from the start.

A silence. Then he admitted aloud, "Yes. I know."

I do not understand this strange barbaric language. I understand only what I feel in your mind. Which is now a great sadness. You know I want you. But you are still in love with your wife.

I think—I am now only in love with my memories of my wife.

You are afraid, then. You think I would punish you, as I did the others.

No, I am not afraid. Danger is part of the beauty of you. Everything that is beautiful is full of risk.

But when I came to summon you, you did not want me.

I do not know… I am stubborn. Mostly I did not like the way you planned to take me.

You did not want me.

I want you now.

She had won. But perhaps he was letting her win?

The boy, who had finished scrubbing the dishes, smiled in the same winsome way as his father and went outside to wander the carnival grounds, to admire the motorcycle daredevil's new Harley, and watch the roughies play poker, and talk with the Bearded Lady, the Breasted Man, the Wild Woman of Borneo, the Amazing Alligator Girl.

Cat touched Ollie's fine-sculpted face. He leaned toward her, and let her touch guide him, and kissed her.

His body, she found within the next hour, was as beautiful as his face, and as ardent and clumsy as if he were a boy again. It truly had been years since he had given himself to a woman, a verity that made the gift all the more precious to her. She hugged him, she cradled his head in her arms and kissed him, she adored his awkwardness, she felt her heart burst open like a red, red flower into love of him.

Afterward, she was afraid. She was afraid. Love harrowed her with fear. She had sworn never to give her heart to a man again.

He said softly, "The carnival moves on tomorrow."

Yes.

"There is this about a carnival, it takes in all kinds of people. Criminals, whores, freaks, geeks, holy rollers, crap shooters, it doesn't matter, we're all carnies. We all belong. You, too."

Yes. She heard the wistfulness in herself. I *like that.*

"But there is also this, that we're like wild geese, we carnies. We move with the seasons, everything is always changing. We get used to leaving places behind, people behind, losing bits of ourselves. My problem is I look back too much. I've got to learn not to do that."

She no longer cared that he was letting her win. It was his gift to her, this offering of a choice. He knew what she was. He knew that a cat must walk by herself.

And perhaps he hoped to keep her coming back.

But she did not leave him yet. She put on her dress, but lay down again on his bed. A dying blossom fell from her hair. Her fingers interlaced with his. She thought to him quietly, *Guess my name and age?*

Why, Cat?

You said you would guess for me someday.

Okay. Because you want me to. He took a deep breath. Or perhaps he sighed. *Your name is Freyja. Or that is one of them, anyway. You were the great goddess of fruitfulness, you had many names in different places.*

Yes.

Your age? A lot older than I can comprehend. About four millennia?

Yes. Though for most of the time I have slept.

Catnaps. She felt his gentle smile in his tone of mind and knew he would never betray her.

Yes.

She lay silent awhile before she asked him, *Now tell me. What are you?*

Cat. He was both rueful and amused. *I must give you a prize, a little china doll. That is the one question that baffles me.*

Of course. Otherwise she would have been able to find the answer in his mind. *You do not know?*

Milady—I feel that there is a dream I have forgotten. I keep trying to find the words for the song, but they are gone. I truly do not know.

She lay with his head on her shoulder. Stroked his cheek and temple and the side of his neck. At her mercy and in her arms, he succumbed to her touch, he fell asleep, as she wished him to. When that had happened, very softly she withdrew herself and made the change. Her dress lay on the bed now. She, a golden cat, stood by her lover's pillow.

There is magic in the soft, twitching, fluffy end of the tail of a cat. Countryfolk know this and will sometimes cut off a cat's tail to use in their spells. This act is an abomination. The world that no longer remembers the holy ways of the golden goddess is full of danger for a cat.

Freyja curved the end of her tail so that it resembled the heavy head of a stalk of ripe wheat, her emblem. Softly she brushed it across the lidded eyes of the sleeping man.

Odin, my sweet faithless lover, when you awaken you will be able to see again. Give me no place in your song, do not remember me. And hang yourself no longer from the tree of sorrow, beautiful one. Be happy.

Not far away, the carousel calliope started to sound. The cat bounded to the floor, landing softly on padded paws.

There is still time to stay. Will I regret leaving him?

But perhaps there was no such thing as life without regrets. And a strange new world awaited her wanderings. She pushed her way through the loose screening of the kitchen window, thumped quietly to the ground, and trotted off.

The man would live long and bear her blessing. And it was an odd thing, now at last she felt satisfied.

She slipped away, a golden shadow quick as thought, into the silver dusk. But as she went, she felt the song of the carnival flitting on the air behind her, a fey and raucous magpie melody. *We don't care what the world thinks,* the minds of freaks and barkers and vendors sang. *We are old, we have been gypsying around this world for a long time. Come see a splinter of the true cross! Come see the pickled brains of the frost giant Ymir. Come see Napoleon's little finger. Come see a pressed flower from the Garden of Eden, from the Tree of Life.*

OLD FOSS IS THE
NAME OF HIS CAT

David Sandner

David Sandner is Associate Professor of English at California State University, Fullerton, where he teaches Romanticism, Children's literature, Popular literature and Creative Writing. His work appears in magazines such as *Asimov's Science Fiction*, *Realms of Fantasy*, and *Weird Tales*, and anthologies such as *Clockwork Phoenix*, *The Mammoth Book of Sorcerers' Tales*, and *Baseball Fantastic*. He edited *Fantastic Literature: A Critical Reader*, wrote *The Fantastic Sublime*, and co-edited *The Treasury of the Fantastic*.

Sandner comments: "Old Foss was a real cat—Edward Lear put him in his great Victorian nonsense poetry and drew funny caricatures of him. I'm sure Old Foss, like any good cat, regarded all this attention as only his due. Anyone who has read Lear's poetry knows it's very funny, written in a fine high nonsense style that leads directly to writers like Dr. Seuss, and yet it's quite profoundly sad. That sadness seems based in loneliness. My story attempts to have its own high style, to let nonsense loose, and yet to approach Lear's loneliness and his famous friendship with his cat. I wanted to achieve something like that balance Lear achieved—I guess so that I could understand it better because I find it so moving."

> He has many friends, laymen and clerical;
> Old Foss is the name of his cat;
> His body is perfectly speherical,
> He weareth a runcible hat.

"How Pleasant to Know Mr. Lear"–Edward Lear

Old Foss watched the Old Man out barefoot in his nightshirt ranting in the rain; at least the rain had chased away the boys throwing mud and rocks. The Old Man had black stains along his back and a welt on his forehead, not that he noticed. But as night pushed over the town, growing from shadows lean-ing along the ramshackle red tile roofs, darkness spreading like ink across a tabletop, Old Foss knew there were worse things than rain or boys with rocks. Soon, the Jumblies would rise from the water's edge to bring the Old Man to sea in a sieve. And anyone who goes to sea in a sieve, of course, never returns. They sink and they drown.

The rain wept against the glass as Old Foss watched impassively behind the window. The Old Man ran back and forth across the cobbled street, his long white nightshirt soaked and clinging to his ungainly frame, his paunched belly and skinny pale legs. His long bedraggled beard leaked, sloughing off water when he shook his head and bellowed: "Where is my Jumbly Girl?" The Old Man knocked on every door he came to, but no one answered for they knew the old Englishman too well.

At first, when the fugues came on, the locals had only shaken their heads at him, then argued with him in broken English or too fluent Italian, especially when the rain came up fast. They pushed him towards the villa he and Old Foss rented; but when the confusion came upon him he would only look at them uncomprehendingly, or look at their doors long after they had shut them with the oddest expression of thwarted desire, then he would wander away again and knock on another wrong door. For no one could see the Jumblies but him and Old Foss. None could know of his time with his Jumbly Girl but Old Foss and himself. Old Foss and he is how it should be for the Jumbly girl would bring him only death for all her promises. Why couldn't he see that, Old Foss thought crossly, twitching his tail, and was it really so much as all that to love a Jumbly Girl?

The sun reflected blindingly on the sand and burst across the blue water in shimmers and rolling spots of light, like crystal broken on tile, like sparks shooting and spinning into the air from a roaring fire, like nothing the Old Man could capture on his canvas.

"It's like nothing, Old Foss, why can't the poets ever say that? It's like noth-ing we can see or say, like something more than we can know, like less than I can rhyme and more than I can show."

The Old Man dabbed at the canvas anyway with his paintbrushes, trying to somehow put a glimmer of white behind, between, before smears of blue. He swayed his pear-shaped body, shoved into a too tight brown suit, frayed white cuffs showing at the wrists, coat open to display a mismatched plaid vest missing every other button; he moved from side to side considering the canvas from different angles, cocking his head with deliberation. How to capture the certain slant of light, the moment out of joint, when time pulsed below the threshold of meaning before it can be said? He took the painting off its easel, still rickety in the soft sand, and flung it end over end into the sea.

"Old Foss, what shall we do instead? What is it this moment deserves?"

Old Foss, striped orange and black, fat and with a wide, full tail, lay on a red-checked picnic blanket in a way no human would ever know—stretched out backwards almost in upon himself again, only his tail's end moving when a wind ruffled his fur, only his ears listening; he hadn't moved for an hour. It was what Old Foss considered giving the moment its due already. When Old Foss opened his eyes suddenly it was not to answer the Old Man, but to look out to sea after the canvas. He made one mew.

"What's that?" The Old Man turned to look, and his rotund body seemed to deflate and go limp, his mouth slack, opening in a kind of dumb wonder. The Jumblies sailed out of nothing—or from the edge of things, but too fast, sailing out of his discarded canvas, glancing off blinding light to land on the white sand beach, singing sea chanteys, and laughing too loud like prisoners before a gallows or dreamers awakened too soon from perfect dreams.

The Jumblies sailed in a sieve of glinting polished silver with holes and holes and holes that spouted water as they ran before the wind with a mast made of an upright coat-rack and a sail of fine, aged Swiss cheese stitched with red and gold thread.

"This can't be good," Old Foss said.

The Old Man blinked and without taking his eyes from the Jumblies said, "why can I only sometimes understand you? Sometimes you are just a cat and other times a voice, a friend. Why is that, Old Foss?"

"I am always your friend," Old Foss said, "only you are sometimes deaf. I don't know why."

The Jumblies tumbled out and came galumphing up the shore all together, kicking up sand with their bootheels, until they seemed to arrive in a heap before the Old Man and Old Foss, their green gangly arms stuck out at odd angles, eyes peering from the most unlikely spaces, under elbows and over shoulders, and who was who and which was which and how many were there and how did they move all together like that were questions that could not be asked or answered so the Old Man didn't bother. They were pea green except when they smiled, then they shifted to a kind of off-blue. They smiled at the Old Man just then, bluely.

"Will you come with us," they asked, "to the sea in our shining sieve?" They smiled in a beguiling manner with teeth half-sharpened but blindingly white, and shuffled about together in a way that made the Old Man ache with longing to belong to something as they belonged—it was a dream of empathy, that heap of blue inhumanity smiling up at him, of being so close to others that one speaks as another speaks and each knows what is meant, not something else but just that and every word, at last—finally!—meaning what it means and not so many other things, not a tragic failing off to loneliness, to war, to hunger, to darkness, to death.

"We will see such sights as never have been seen by you or any of yours. We will trade baubles with the Keepers of the sixty winds in their caverns beyond the edge of things; we will live where the Bong-Tree grows in the endless summer of the islands of the sun; we will sail beyond the stars, lifted by Phoenix birds into the sky on silver ropes held in their fiery beaks and we will tread the inky darkness until we reach the river of night and dream along its banks of unknown things. What do you say?" There was a pause. "You must say."

"What do I say, Old Foss?" said the Old Man, never turning his eyes from them.

"They are like what should be over the horizon," Old Foss said, "or a poem dreamed but left unfinished; they are desire and loss. Say no. Say no now and turn and run and do not look back."

"Why not go?" the Old Man said. "I wish to, with all my art, my heart, my feet, to go with them."

"Ah," Old Foss said, "but a sieve will only sink and bring you certainly to a place you cannot know now, but death has been visited by others before and will be again and is common enough that we can wait until it finds us without looking for it. I think there are no dreams there."

And the Old Man turned his head to look at Old Foss, then, and it was enough that first time to save him. For Old Foss yawned and was just a cat again. And the Jumblies were just the wind piling sand and unpiling it again back into the sea, a whisper that did not ask, will you come with us?

But when they came again only she came, the Jumbly Girl, in the night when he dreams, where Old Foss could not protect him.

Old Foss paused to wrinkle his nose for the rain he would have to endure. But he loved the Old Man, and the Old Man loved him; the Old Man had found him long ago when he was a lost kitten, and picked him up and took him in and fed him. Some debts, Old Foss reflected, are always still to be paid, no matter what we do.

He dropped to the floor and hurried to see if the front or back door has been left ajar, but no. The windows were all shut up tight for the storm. So it would have to be the hard way, to slip through a crack between here and there, to unravel the world for a moment as only cats know how to do.

I am too old for such things, Old Foss thought; too fat, he reflected, too comfortable, too tired, too selfish, too peevish, too everything.

Out of the world and back into the world again, but outside. No mean feat, Old Foss thought, even for a cat. He ran around the room, reaching out to catch at the frayed threads of the world where he could find them, pouncing, missing them as they seemed to curl around the corners of things into nothing; faster, he thought. He became wild-eyed with the pursuit, chasing the shadows of elsewhere across the hearth, up the wall, around turns that weren't there. Soon, he was tearing as fast as he could around the room, panting with the exertion, until he disappeared.

Then he was there, like being under a rug, in a dark corridor with light poking through the frayed edges to show him where to go. He pushed through, his ears back, mewing with the work of it, until he felt, through one thin patch, the rain. It would have to do; he tore out, nearly running into a wall, running up it instead and stopping only when he reached the top—a red tile roof, wet and slick. He scrabbled for footing indecorously, caught himself, pulled himself upright and looked about, his eyes big, his heart pumping, the rain cold against his fur and already bringing forth a musty smell. He mewed forlornly with self-pity.

But Old Foss from his vantage saw the Old Man receding in the distance like a wave going out at low tide. No, Old Foss thought, no, he's headed to sea.

Old Foss began to run, clattering over rooftops after the Old Man stepping so briskly to meet only death who waited, Old Foss knew, so patient and still below the unceasing heaving of the water.

Once before the Old Man had gone to sea in a sieve with his Jumbly Girl and her eyes of jade to match her skin and her smiles like sweet heartache in blue. Her touch against his cheek was a heart stopped, her voice in his ear a thought to fill immensity. They went indeed to visit with the sixty contending winds, who traded them wine for their baubles brought out of the world, giving a manna-sweet drink called Ring-Bo-Ree for little rings from the noses of pigs or unfinished paintings thrown discarded into the sea, or perhaps for the occasional runcible spoon. They sailed into the shifting thickness beyond the edge of things and were drawn into the sky by fiery birds and dreamed beside the islands of the sun and the night river. And—who knew?—sieves sink more slowly then one might suppose. At least sometimes, when the wind is right to hold them up, perhaps, or, perhaps when one moves too fast to notice one is sinking.

Old Foss had come after him, hiding in the rigging, or under the bundles to trade, watching and waiting.

And one day when the water of night came in too high and no one was left to bail it out and it was too late by far, Old Foss whispered in the Old Man's ear as he dreamed: "Time to come home, for the water's rising. Time to wake up, now or never. Time to dream a little less and live a little more, old friend," and a partial payment on a debt never to be repaid was made.

"Thank you," the Old Man said, when awake and in his bed again, "for surely I would have drowned."

And yet, something was taken from the Old Man too, something taken that can never be returned—what the Jumbly Girl meant to him—and for that there was a new debt, never to be repaid.

"Why did you bother me," the Old Man would say at other times, when the confusion came to him, "why didn't you leave me to drown in peace, in bliss of other things, with my Jumbly Girl?"

For they had tried to keep him:

"Stay," they had told him, despite the rising water, the leaking of the sieve. "Stay and dream with us."

"Come with me," he had said to his Jumbly Girl, "come with me and be my love; we will think of things to do to pass the time, though it will not be this—we will paint unfinished pictures by the shore and hold hands inside the rain. I will write you poems and you will tell bad jokes. It's not this but isn't it something?"

And she agreed to come with him, to meet him in the morning, by the shore of everything, below the sun, beside the night, where the sky birds came to draw them home by silver cords in their fiery beaks, on a raft made of fronds from the Twangum Tree; he and Old Foss waited for her to come from the sieve as it sank in the river of night, but she did not appear.

Somehow, it seemed, in stepping from the sieve to the shore to the raft, he had misplaced her; when he had turned back to hold out his hand and help her out, she was gone.

She never reappeared. And the Jumblies disappeared from the sieve with the morning light, like fog retreating into the sea, but with an ache like when you remember what you thought the world was going to be like when you were young and foolish.

"Come on, Old Man," Old Foss had said, "the sieve is sinking fast."

"Will I ever see her again?"

There is no answer to such questions and he offered none, but the Old Man asked it again, asked it so many times over the years that Old Foss finally said, "I'm sorry, Old Man."

"Oh, I know, it's all right, Old Foss."

But it wasn't.

Old Foss leapt from roof to roof like a young cat with nothing to lose, not a fat old cat with everything at stake. The rain had depressed him, then frustrated him, then made him ironic and bitterly elated. He sang: "How many lives, how many lives, how many more lives for the cat? At least one more, at least one more, and another one after that!" as he leapt across an alleyway and scrabbled onto the roof on the other side. When he reached the edge of town he climbed quickly, nosily, awkwardly down a drainpipe full with leaking water rushing. Leaping off the pipe, he landed badly, quickly looking around, licking his shoulder uselessly in the rain, and walking with what dignity he could muster toward the shore, his orange and black fur matted to his bulging body where it wasn't sticking out ridiculously.

Then he saw the Old Man curled into a ball on the hill, halfway down to the beach, a white blur among the grey of water falling; Old Foss ran to him.

Old Foss whispered in his ear, "Come, Old Man. Time to come in, the water is falling fast and your nightshirt is thin."

"She came to me in my dreams," the Old Man shouted suddenly, his eyes opening wide and wild, "she came to me in my dreams. They've come again in the sieve to take me to sea."

"This would be the last time," Old Foss said. "Wait a little while longer and we will find ways to pass the time—painting unfinished pictures by the shore, or you can pet me by the fire when it rains, or…."

He didn't know what to say. Could he do this to the Old Man again, take him from his Jumbly Girl?

For the Jumblies were by the shore, and the Jumbly Girl was with them. As the rain lessened they came into sight. She was leaving them and wandering up the hill, a ghost in green, her voice on the wind:

"Come with us, come to stay, and we will sail under the sea, and we will never leave but we will never want to…."

Old Foss turned away from looking at her.

I suppose you should go, Old Foss thought, I suppose you could go and I should stay for I only wanted you for myself, an old debt I will never be able to repay. He didn't say it because it hurt too much to say it.

But the Old Man did not turn his head to look at his Jumbly Girl.

She came closer, calling again, "Come, come, come to sea, to the sieve that sinks below the waves until we drown, to the lost worlds below the sun."

But the Old Man did not turn his head.

The Jumbly Girl stopped. "Can't you hear me, love?"

Old Foss dared not turn to look at her again. The Old Man did not hear. He could not see. Old Foss would not give away her presence.

The Jumbly Girl stood, her body heaving, crying Old Foss supposed, but the rain made that indeterminate. That at least was what he tried to tell himself.

The Old Man cried, too, and that he could see despite the rain, for the Old Man beat his breast and tore at his thinning hair, and pulled hard on his frumpy old beard until he pulled the hair out in uneven patches.

"I want to die," the Old Man said, as the Jumbly Girl reached out for him with arms of green embrace, with love forever and ever for him, to death, yes certainly to death but perhaps beyond as well.

"I'm sorry I made a mistake, so long ago," Old Foss said, "that time by the river of night, I should have let you drown. Or maybe you have with me."

But the Old Man didn't hear, or couldn't listen.

Old Foss mewed piteously, wet through.

"Oh, Old Foss," the Old Man said, "look at you, oh, you're wet through."

Old Foss shivered and looked to him like he had looked to him once long ago as a kitten lost in the rain.

"Come on, Old Foss, let's go home," the Old Man said, rising, pulling Old Foss against him, heading back up the hill. "They're not coming after all." He choked on the words. "They're not here."

The Old Man leaned over Old Foss, and Old Foss peered over the Old Man's shoulder to see the Jumblies come in a heap to the Jumbly Girl crying on the hill. They covered her in their love, with their arms at all angles and their boots kicking out, and their eyes green compassion. They smiled a blue benediction.

"I'm sorry," they said to the Jumbly Girl, and turning they all walked, or rolled, or shambled downhill. "I'm sorry," they said together and held her in their arms until they vanished in rain.

"Home again soon," the Old Man said, soothing, but tired like a drunk man sobered by sorrow on his way home again from a lost night on the town, or like a storm-tossed sailor thrown on the shore, wobbling inland to safety.

"It's all right, it's all right, it's all right, Old Foss."

"I'm sorry," Old Foss said.

"There, there," the Old Man said, though he couldn't hear. "It's all right. It's all right."

But it wasn't.

A SAFE PLACE TO BE

Carol Emshwiller

Carol Emshwiller grew up in both Michigan and France and currently divides her time between New York and California. She is the winner of two Nebula Awards for her stories "Creature" and "I Live With You." She has also won the World Fantasy Award for Life Achievement. She's been the recipient of a National Endowment for the Arts grant and two New York State grants. Her short fiction has been published in many literary and science fiction magazines and her most recent books are the novels *Mister Boots* and *The Secret City*, and the collection *I Live With You and You Don't Know It*. A new collection is forthcoming from P.S. Publishing.

Emshwiller says: "I had no special cat in mind. I haven't had a cat for a long time but I like to use animals in my stories in all sorts of ways. We used to have a marmalade cat like this one. Before he was altered, he used to get in a fight every night—came back with torn ears all the time. He went off to college with my daughter where he lived with a batch of students who had a pet rabbit. Then he came back, got fat, and lived a long, lazy life."

It started with a funny feeling in the bottoms of my feet. Something is going to happen. Perhaps an earthquake. That's what it feels like. But perhaps terrorists on the way. Whatever it is, something's coming.

Why did I (of all people), an old lady, get this warning while everybody else is going on as usual? Have I a special talent nobody else has?

But the cat feels it, too. He's been shaking his paws as if they feel exactly like my feet do. He looks at me as if to say: Why don't you *do* something? I tell him, "I will."

It's coming closer. I'm getting out of here before everybody tries to leave at the same time.

Though could it be that I'm just feeling the future in general. Disaster will come to all of us and at my age it can't be that far away. I'll be as dead as most all of humanity already is. Mother… Dad… Dostoyevsky.

But can I take a chance that this tingly feeling is just because of the normal run of things?

If only I knew when. And also who to tell? I'd like company through all this. Not that a good cat isn't company enough and I do talk things over with him, but a person would be nice, too. I can't think of anybody to tell who would believe me or wouldn't just get in my way as I try to leave in search of safety.

That tingly, rattley vibration is getting worse, rising from the ground, up through my feet and rattling my spine. This morning I could even feel it from my fifth floor apartment. I ran for the central hallway. I stood there for twenty minutes. Then I grabbed Natty, put his harness and leash on him, and ran outside and down the block and huddled under a tree. Again I waited. The cat was shaking as much as I was. A sure sign that I'm right. I ran farther but had to stop to catch my breath in a doorway near the park.

Here, in a place where pigeons are always wobbling along, there wasn't a single one. Not one! That scared both of us even more.

I must have looked just how I felt because somebody asked me what was wrong. I said, "Just a dizzy spell is all." I didn't want anybody else to know. I wanted to get out and safely away before any of the others found out something was going to happen.

I check the feelings in my feet again. I feel a rumbling for sure, by now so strong I wonder why everybody doesn't feel it. Well, all the better then, it gives me plenty of time to escape.

A mountain top would be a good place, nothing could fall down on me from up there and water wouldn't reach, but there aren't even any hills around here. I'll head west, though I don't know if there's time, but out in the country will be better than the city. I'll bring all my money and my raincoat.

I go home, eat a big last meal, pack a knapsack with cat food (it'll do for both of us), my vitamins, and go. I bring Natty in the top part of the knapsack. He doesn't mind. He's glad I'm finally doing something.

I ask a taxi driver to take me twenty dollars worth towards the west. He's nice, he takes me even farther. He doesn't care that I sneaked a cat into his cab. I ask him to come with us. We'd like the company. Especially such a nice man and with a cab to ride in. I tell him why I was getting away. I say we should hurry before the roads get too crowded with people trying to escape. He doesn't say so, but I don't think he believes me. He prefers getting back to work.

So I start walking. He drove me a good ways into the suburbs. I never expected to get this far in just one day. Even though I'm still scared, this is all turning out fine. I stand still and check the bottoms of my feet again, and, yes, no doubt about it, danger, though I keep reminding myself that life is just temporary anyway and at my age even more so.

But right now I have to find someplace to spend the night. I don't want to use up any more of my money than I have to. It has to last at least to the Rockies.

I keep walking well into the night. I was hoping to get beyond the little houses and warehouses to farm land, but no such luck. I wanted to sleep in some country place, a forest or a park. Finally I'm too worn out to go on. I drop where I stop. There isn't a bush or a tree in sight, just warehouses, and airplanes keep coming over low. I'm so tired they don't bother me except for waking me up early in the morning. I worried the cat would get scared and run away, but he stayed with me. I keep his leash on most of the time but I don't attach it to anything. He's too old to run off.

So off we go again (after sharing a cat food breakfast). How come nobody else is trying to escape? Most people, are heading into the city as if everything was just as usual. Is this a special talent of mine worthy of study just as animals predict earthquakes? Should I tell a scientist about it before whatever it is happens so that when it *does* happen, I'll have predicted it? How does one find a scientist? And it has to be somebody interested in this sort of study. I would be surprised if I pass a lot of universities along the way. If the danger is as close as it feels, I'll have to hurry and find somebody.

I'm so happy with our progress, I take us to a diner for lunch. Fish for Natty and a hamburger for me.

That night I find a good place, nine feet high, four feet long, three feet wide. What passes for a window. I won't say where, though it mustn't be thought that I'm ashamed of it. Actually I don't think I'm ever ashamed of anything of that nature, not even that I'm getting rather dirty and mussed.

By now I'm far enough not to have to worry about a tsunami, but this is tornado country now. Natty and I keep studying the sky.

Wherever I end up, I would like a small tree. That is, if I can't have a large one. Living in the city I haven't had a tree of my own of any sort since I came here long ago. Also I'd like a nice round lichen-covered rock that heats up during the day and stays hot all evening. I'd like a place to build a fire and a log beside it to sit on. I'd like a nice bed for Natty.

I buy myself a shopping cart to carry stuff like water bottles. I'm getting ready for crossing places in middle America where the rest stops are far between.

I ask for rides in the parking lots, but if I don't get one I just start walking. And I usually don't get one. I don't blame the people; after all I'm dirty and raggedy and my bundles and the shopping cart are bulky and don't fit in anything but trucks. If I saw me humping along with all this junk I'd take me for a crazy person. I wouldn't pick me up either. Even so, now and then I do get a ride. Usually in an old pickup that isn't going far.

I forget how many days it's been, but up to now everything is serene with the world. Of course I'm not getting the news. Maybe a disaster has already happened and I don't know about it, though you'd think people in diners and rest stops would be talking about it. I always read the headlines in the newspapers when I pass by them. (I don't waste money on them.) And you'd think, if the disaster had happened, that my feet would stop sending me all these signals. Natty's, too. Though maybe after one disaster, there might be another right behind it.

Ahead, you can see the road winding up a hill. I dread trying to climb it pushing my cart. But before I get to it, there's a town and I pass one of those little country hospitals. It's right here, handy. I'm going in and have them check my feet. It might be important for them to study me. For omens. Maybe Natty's, too.

I hide my cart behind the bushes near the door.

The lady at the desk asks me if I want a shower first. I did suspect I was pretty smelly by now, but I tell her I'll just get dirty again. "I'm on the road," I say.

"But wouldn't you like to take this opportunity."

I haven't washed since I started on this journey. Just a little bit in the bathrooms at the rest stops.

I know she means the doctor I'm going to see would like it a lot better if I did.

"But what about my cat?"

She lets him come in to the bathroom with me. "Since," she says, "he's on a leash." Then they let him into the doctor's office with me, too.

Everybody is very nice here.

"I want to report my feet. And my cat's feet."

He doesn't believe me about my feet predicting disaster. He doesn't say so, but I can tell.

"Well," he says, "there's plenty of disasters around to predict."

That type of little black mustache he has always intimidates me, but he's quite nice underneath it.

"This is something really, really big. Like a tornado or an earthquake or a gigantic mud slide. Mud as far as the eye can see."

"Where are you living? Are you eating?"

"Oh, yes, and fish, lots of fish. I know it's good for you."

I don't want him to think I'm just an ignorant tramp.

"There's a shelter just down the road if you need help. You can get a free meal there."

"Will they have cat food?"

"Do you have a place to live?"

"But, Doctor, these tingly feelings? It's getting worse. I thought maybe it was important. I thought you'd like to look into it."

"Nothing to worry about. Old people get these odd nerve twinges all the time. Let me give you the address of this place where they'll help you."

I'm worried they might put me away. I'd have to stay here and the disaster might be right in this area and I couldn't escape.

I say I'll go there right away but I won't.

"I'll drive you, if you can wait a bit."

"I don't mind walking."

I have to show him all my money before he finally lets me go. I still have quite a bit. Also I show him my vitamins and my cod liver oil. (Both Natty and I take it.) That impresses him.

At least he doesn't charge me much. But he didn't do anything either, except to tell me I'm fine.

It's going to be too bad... I mean the big disaster... there are so many nice people in the world like these people at the hospital. It's a shame so many of them will have to die. I'm trying to tell them but they won't listen.

I don't go for the free meal, though that would have been nice. I haven't had any vegetables for a long time. But I'm worried they'll stop me. I know it looks bad, an old lady with a big bundle walking—*walking!*—across the country. I'll have to try to think of a good reason for doing it. Maybe for some cause or other like breast cancer. Why didn't I think of that before?

By evening I finally come to the hill. The road climbs back and forth. It's still a wide and sweeping four lanes. This is going to be hard. Dangerous, too. A good place for a landslide.

I struggle on. Not a single good place to rest. Everything on a slant.

A silvery sporty car stops next to me. The top down. It's the doctor. Just the sort of car to go with his mustache. What's he doing way out here?

He says he doesn't like how I look. It's twilight. How come he can see me so well?

He's popped the trunk.

"Put your cart in back."

I step off the road on the rocky down side. He can't follow. Not in the car.

But he's out and is opening the passenger door for me. "I'll drive you."

Thank goodness it's almost dark. And it's even darker in the shadows of the boulders where Natty and I hide. Natty's a talkative cat, but he knows not to make a sound.

The doctor calls a few more times. "I can help."

Exactly what I don't want most is help.

Finally he drives off.

What now? Are they going to be chasing me? Capture the crazy woman? Do I have something else to worry about? Why do they care?

I'm going to walk on through the night. It's safer.

Whenever a car goes by, I hide in the ditch. It's not easy, what with my cart and all. At least you can see the cars coming from a long ways off.

We reach the top of the hill. Now the road will be flat again for a nice long while.

Finally, there in the ditch, I just have to stay and sleep.

In the morning I see there's somebody else walking along, way, way, way ahead of me—by about six miles I'd say. Here the road is so straight and flat and there's so few trees you can see for miles. I think the next hillock is probably about twelve miles away.

Hours pass, but I'm catching up. He doesn't stop to rest. I don't either. What if he, too, has funny feelings? And there'll be safety in numbers. For me at least. Maybe if the doctor sees I have somebody... especially a man... he won't bother me anymore.

I get all shaky with hope. Somebody else, maybe, who knows what I and Natty know. He won't think I'm crazy.

Finally, he sits down. It takes me half an hour to catch up, and then I walk past so as to take a good look first.

We're both elderly. We're both skinny from so much walking. We're both browned by the sun and have chapped lips. We both have big hats. I got mine when I started wondering about crossing the desert.

He stares as I go by. He's wondering about me as much as I'm wondering about him. He has a cart much bigger and sturdier than mine. More like a wheelbarrow, only he's rigged it with a loop around his waist so he can pull it. I wouldn't be surprised if he didn't have a tent. And there's a frying pan tied on top. I'll bet he never hitch hikes. He's got too much stuff.

He's found a nice spot to rest. There's an arroyo and actually a few spindly cottonwoods growing along the banks. Not exactly giving shade. Under the road is a culvert for when there's water in the arroyo. That'll be where he pees.

I turn around and come back.

He looks like a country person... farmer or some such... though by now I may not look like I'm from the city either.

Before I sit down (not too close), I search the sky. Out here you can see a lot of it.

I say, "So far everything is fine."

He doesn't bother answering. It's clear that it is.

We sit silently but I can't tell if it's a comfortable silence or an uncomfortable one.

Natty's the only one who gives a questioning, "Yeow?"

When the man gets up to go on, I do, too. He didn't ask me to come, but he didn't say not to.

It's evening and this was a good spot to spend the night, but off he goes. He may be trying to get away from us. Some people don't like cats.

Is he going to walk all night? I don't dare ask. If I ask he may tell me not to follow.

We go on and on. Towards morning he comes to a group of spindly trees. I stay about twenty yards behind so as not to be a bother. I collapse just off the road. In the ditch so to speak. At least there's enough run-off for there to be bushes all along the road side. Almost like the edges of the rivers. I don't even have the energy to get us our can of cat food.

I wake up late the next morning. To the sound of traffic—if you can call one car about every ten minutes traffic. My feet are tingling even more than before. Whatever it is is coming closer.

I study the sky. Not a cloud in sight. Not a tree either except for the clump where the man camped. He's gone on ahead. He's already a few miles down the road. Maybe he does mind us following but I'm not going to let him get away.

I and Natty eat our cat food and hurry after him. We're faster than he is, what with that big bundle he has to pull.

It's such a nice morning. All along the roadside the rabbit brush is in bloom. A bright yellow. I hum in spite of whatever disasters might be on the way. You don't have to mope around just because your feet tingle and the world is full of depressing things and something really, really big and horrible is about to happen.

Pretty soon we're almost up to where I want to walk—just a few yards behind the man.

So far he hasn't said a single word.

But here's the doctor's silvery car again. I'm not expecting him. I don't have time to even think of hiding.

The old man stops, turns around and watches.

It really does look as if we're together and as if the old man's waiting for me.

I run up and grab the old man's arm.

Before the doctor leans out the window and says anything, I say, "I'm walking for breast cancer. I forgot to tell you."

"But I can help. I can help you both."

"He's walking for breast cancer, too."

The two of us and our bundles and Natty wouldn't fit in the doctor's little car, anyway.

"We don't want to get helped."

One nice thing, the old man is letting me hang on to his bony elbow. I wasn't sure he would, seeing as how he's always walking off without me and without a word.

And then he does talk.

"She's with me."

His voice croaks out as if he never uses it... and I guess he never does.

"Why don't you people go to our shelter? Get yourself cleaned up? Get a rest? How old are you, anyway? I don't want you having a heart attack out here."

The man says, "Young enough to walk all day."

The doctor grabs my other arm, the one holding my cart. Natty is sitting on top of it in his usual spot. He lashes out and the doctor gets four good scratches all along his hand.

I let go of my cart, I can't help it, and it bounces down into the ditch and tips over. I run down to see if Natty is hurt and so does the old man. The doctor doesn't. He's looking at his scratches. What kind of a doctor is that?

But Natty isn't there. I lift up my cart to see if he's squashed underneath it. Then I see him galloping down the road, his leash dragging. If there was a tree anywhere near he'd be up in it.

I should have known. Cats are fast. They hardly ever get hurt.

I leave my cart in the ditch and run down the road after him. Next thing here's the doctor's car right beside me.

"Get in. I'll help you catch it."

It, he says!

I run into the ditch again. And then beyond, into the brush.

The doctor gives up and drives off.

The old man is waiting for me back beside my cart.

"Cats come back," he says.

Nice of him to say so, but we're not anywhere for a cat to come back to.

How will Natty get along without me? And out here in the middle of nowhere.

This changes everything.

"What we'll do," the old man says, speaking slowly and calmly and in that raspy voice of his. "We'll go on a little bit farther and stop where we think he might have run to, and then we'll stay put until we find him."

He gives me an apple. I haven't had one in a long time, but I can't swallow. I take one bite and give the apple back. I know it's valuable.

That man has all sorts of things I didn't know he had. He gets out a little camping stove and makes me tea. I do feel better after that. At least I have more energy to go looking for Natty.

We go down the road a bit farther, calling out. Nothing here but desert. There won't be anything for Natty to drink. And I worry about that leash dragging behind him. And what about hawks?

Every now and then I step off the road and look around. I look into the shadows. By now Natty's a desert cat and knows that it's cooler under things in the shade.

If there's a disaster I want to face it with Natty, and if I escape it, I don't want to escape without Natty.

Maybe this *is* the disaster. At least it's my disaster.

When we settle down for the night, I sleep a bit away from the old man in case Natty is afraid of him. I open a can of cat food and leave it near me. I can't eat my share of it. I feel too bad. I also leave a cup of water. I wonder what sort of creature I'll attract that I don't want. Do rattlesnakes like cat food?

Maybe Natty is dead already. There's always coyotes.

The man and I set up a kind of camp. Just our bundles and his stove and pan. And branch out from there. It's several yards off the road and behind an old tumbled-down wall. Probably the remains of an old stage coach change-of-horses stop. He hasn't set up his tent. No need. It never rains out here.

He not only has apples but carrots, too. Kind of dried out but still good. But

I can't eat.

We wander around calling, kitty, kitty, kitty. We look under every bush. I hope Natty's good at catching lizards. There are a lot of them. Except he's got that leash holding him back.

The doctor drives back and forth twice a day. He must live in the next town from the hospital. He stops now and then and calls out to us that he just wants to help. Once he yells out that at least we're hidden behind that old wall. What does he mean by that?

If he *really* wanted to help he could bring us some bottles of water. We won't be able to stay here much longer.

But the old man says he'll trot back to that town—and he does mean trot—to bring back some water. He'll use my cart because it's lighter. And then we can stay here longer.

After he leaves, I spend the morning in the usual way, calling and looking in the shadows for a dead or dying cat.

And then, that afternoon, it rains. A hard rain. First I think it's *the* disaster but it isn't. I rush out in it calling kitty, kitty, kitty. I'm sopping but I don't care. Only later do I remember to put out cups and the old man's frying pan to collect water.

Then it stops raining and then suddenly flowers! As far as the eye can see—not mud but flowers.

I walk out in it. It smells wonderful. And here's a whole mass of little luminous blue butterflies. I never knew such a thing could be.

Have I been wrong about the disaster all this time? Is it to be something beautiful instead of something bad? A disaster of flowers?

But then I feel a sharp twinge in my feet as if to remind me I'm wrong and there's a big disaster out there just waiting to come down on us all.

I search the sky again.

Except now I don't care. I yell, "Come on tsunami! Come flood and fire, tornado and meteorites."

Nothing happens.

Then I hear the old man coming back. He's whistling. You just can't help it what with all this beauty. He sees me and waves. Calls out, "I have tomatoes and peaches!" It's as if he knew they were things I haven't had since I started on the journey to escape.

But I sit down in the middle of the flowers and start to cry. So many good things and I don't even care.

He sees I won't be able to eat for a while. He puts everything behind our wall and then comes out into the flowers and butterflies—carefully, trying to avoid stepping on flowers—and sits beside me.

After a bit I take a good look at him… a better look than before.

He sits hugging one knee. He's wearing shorts. His legs are hairy, stringy, and knobby, but strong looking. His big hat partly hides his face, but I already know he's an ugly man and needs a shave. His teeth stick out and his chin recedes, his nose has a bump in the middle, but all of a sudden he looks beautiful. Like Natty. Natty's not a handsome cat but I've never seen one I like better.

I say, "Thank you."

He nods—a series of nods, as if, "Yes, yes, yes," and then shakes his head the other way as if, "It's not important."

I wonder what his name is.

I think to reach out and touch his knee—to say something nice but here comes the doctor, his silver car is parked right across from our wall.

He walks toward us, tramping on flowers. Scattering butterflies. He has a bandage on his hand where Natty scratched him.

"I thought you'd be gone on by now. Or at least gone for help."

Oh my God, he has Natty's red leather leash. He's slapping it against his thigh. Then he hands it to me. "Here's your leash."

We've been looking and calling ourselves hoarse and he's had Natty all this time. Or at least he knows where he is. I can just see it, the doctor driving down the road and seeing that red leash and tricking Natty some way. Or, more likely, the leash hooked on a prickly blackbrush.

I grab it and start whipping him with it. He's not ready. He falls backwards into flowers and I keep on lashing at him.

Long as I'm winning, the old man stands there watching, but when the doctor gets up and hits me one good slap and knocks me over, the old man grabs him from behind and holds him. He's shorter than the doctor but you can see in his stringy arms, very strong.

I'm thinking: *My* old man.

The doctor says, "It's…." (*It's* again) "…at the pound back in Wilkerville. Unless it's dead. They don't keep them very long."

I don't even grab a water bottle. I start running—back down the road.

The doctor yells, "Don't be dumb."

We're maybe only seven or eight miles from town and days and days of walking and pushing my cart have made me strong, too. I run on and on.

Pretty soon the doctor's car pulls up beside me. Since the top is down, as usual, I see right away the old man is in the car with him. The old man tells me to get in. If he's there, I guess it's all right. Though maybe the doctor will see that we both end up stuck in what might as well be the pound for people. The car's only a two seater. I have to sit on the old man's lap, his arms around me. It's a nice place to be.

But then a huge dark cloud comes towards us right down the road. Like a huge, huge dust devil. And it's full of flowers! And the sound. Here comes the disaster. Finally. I'm actually glad that something's happening at last. I don't have Natty to hug, but I do have the old man's arms around me nice and tight.

The doctor stops the car and starts putting the top up, but at the last minute the disaster veers away, rises, then dissipates in a rain of flowers. Flowers all over us, wet and fragrant.

We're all out of breath though we haven't done anything but just sit here. We look at each other… even the doctor. I look into the old man's black eyes. And turn away fast. I'm thinking: that's where all his calmness comes from. Down in there somewhere.

Again, I wonder what his name is.

The doctor drives us—much too fast even for the desert—into town.

At the pound they say, "That skinny old marmalade cat? He was an odd one."

"Well, where is he?"

"He got out. Just today. We don't know how he did it."

I always knew he was smarter than most but now I wish he wasn't. I sit down on the curb.

The old man says it. "Smart cat." Then, "He'll come back." …his slow raspy voice. "They always do."

It's a reassuring voice and nice to hear it, but it doesn't reassure me.

The old man sees that. "He *will*!"

The doctor says, "It's a cat, for Heaven's sake. You'll be fine without it."

How dare he? Of course I won't be fine.

I stand up and attack him again. I land two good blows before anybody can do anything.

But he slaps me down.

"The town wants you in the shelter. You're a nuisance and an eye sore. Look at yourselves."

The old man pushes him away and gets punched and falls backwards. That makes me so mad I get up and fight even harder. It doesn't do any good. I'm on the ground again beside my man.

But there's a great yowling and howling and here, off the roof of the pound comes an orange ball of claws, down on the doctor's head. And a terrible racket. I've heard cats can do that, but I never actually heard the sound before.

The doctor tries to run away, but you can't run away from a cat on your head.

He's around the block and out of sight but we can still hear Natty.

We look at each other again, and this time I let myself look… way down in there.

He nods and then I nod.

He takes my hand. (How strong and calloused both our hands are. Like pieces of sandpaper.)

We sit down and wait for Natty to come back.

"You know there is no safe place," he says.

And I say, "I know it."

"And not all disasters are that bad."

And I say, "I know it."

Pretty soon Natty comes swaggering back.

We walk to our things, me with Natty on my shoulder.

"Let's go on."

"Till we get to a nice green place with a river?"

"And trees."

"And a hill to be on top of?"

"And a cottage."

I wonder what his name is.

NINE LIVES TO LIVE

Sharyn McCrumb

Sharyn McCrumb is an award-winning Southern writer, best known for her Appalachian "Ballad" novels set in the North Carolina/Tennessee mountains, including the *New York Times* best sellers *She Walks These Hills* and *The Rosewood Casket*. Her other best-selling novels include *The Ballad of Frankie Silver* and *The Songcatcher*. Her most recent novels are *The Devil Amongst the Lawyers* and *Faster Pastor*, the latter co-authored with NASCAR driver Adam Edwards. McCrumb was named a "Virginia Woman of History" in 2008 for Achievement in Literature. Other honors include: AWA Outstanding Contribution to Appalachian Literature Award; the Chaffin Award for Southern Literature; the Plattner Award for Short Story; and AWA's Best Appalachian Novel. She lives and writes near Roanoke, Virginia.

She says: "The inspiration for 'Nine Lives to Live' was an elderly, dignified Maine Coon Cat, who belonged to a friend of mine. The expression on that cat's face suggested that he disapproved of us, that he outranked us, and that he was not amused. So I started wondering who he used to be. (I want to come back as a groundhog. They eat constantly all summer, and when they get fat, they're cute. Then when the weather turns cold and wet, they crawl into the burrow and go to sleep until it's warm and sunny outside again. And when they wake up—they're *thin*!—People say dolphins are the smartest animals on earth, but groundhogs have things figured out pretty well, if you ask me.)"

It had seemed like a good idea at the time. Of course, Philip Danby had only been joking, but he had said it in a serious tone in order to humor those idiot New Age clients who actually seemed to believe in the stuff. "I want to come back as a cat," he'd said, smiling facetiously into the candlelight at the Eskeridge dinner table. He had to hold his breath to keep from laughing as the others babbled about reincarnation. The women wanted to come back blonder and thinner, and the men wanted to be everything from Dallas Cowboys to oak trees. *Oak trees?* And he had to keep a straight face through it all, hoping these dodos would give the firm some business.

The things he had to put up with to humor clients. His partner, Giles Eskeridge, seemed to have no difficulties in that quarter, however. Giles often said that rich and crazy went together; therefore, architects who wanted a lucrative business had to be prepared to put up with eccentrics. They also had to put up with long hours, obstinate building contractors, and capricious zoning boards. Perhaps that was why Danby had plumped for life as a cat next time. As he had explained to his dinner companions that night, "Cats are independent. They don't have to kowtow to anybody; they sleep sixteen hours a day; and yet they get fed and sheltered and even loved—just for being their contrary little selves. It sounds like a good deal to me."

Julie Eskeridge tapped him playfully on the cheek. "You'd better take care to be a pretty, pedigreed kitty, Philip." She laughed. "Because life isn't so pleasant for an ugly old alley cat!"

"I'll keep that in mind," he told her. "In fifty years or so."

It had been more like fifty days. The fact that Giles had wanted to come back as a shark should have tipped him off. When they found out that they'd just built a three-million-dollar building on top of a toxic landfill, the contractor was happy to keep his mouth shut about it for a mere ten grand, and Giles was perfectly prepared to bury the evidence to protect the firm from lawsuits and EPA fines.

Looking back on it, Danby realized that he should not have insisted that they report the landfill to the authorities. In particular, he should not have insisted on it at six p.m. at the building site with no one present but himself and Giles. That was literally a fatal error. Before you could say "philosophical differences," Giles had picked up a shovel lying near the offending trench, and with one brisk swing, he had sent the matter to a higher court. As he pitched headlong into the reeking evidence, Danby's last thought was a flicker of cold anger at the injustice of it all.

His next thought was that he was watching a black-and-white movie, while his brain seemed intent upon sorting out a flood of olfactory sensations. *Furniture polish... stale coffee... sweaty socks... Prell shampoo... potting soil...* He shook his head, trying to clear his thoughts. Where was he? The apparent answer to that was: lying on a gray sofa inside the black-and-white movie, because everywhere he looked he saw the same colorless vista. A concussion, maybe? The memory of Giles Eskeridge swinging a shovel came back in a flash. Danby decided to call the police before Giles turned up to try again. He stood up, and promptly fell off the sofa.

Of course, he landed on his feet.

All four of them.

Idly, to keep from thinking anything more ominous for the moment, Danby wondered what *else* the New Age clients had been right about. Was Stonehenge a flying saucer landing pad? Did crystals lower cholesterol? He was in no position to doubt anything just now. He sat twitching his plume of a tail and wishing he hadn't been so flippant about the afterlife at the Eskeridge dinner party. He didn't even particularly like cats. He also wished that he could get his paws on Giles in retribution for the shovel incident. First he would bite Giles's neck, snapping his spine, and then he would let him escape for a few seconds. Then he'd sneak up behind him and pounce. Then bat him into a corner. Danby began to purr in happy contemplation.

The sight of a coffee table looming a foot above his head brought the problem into perspective. At present Danby weighed approximately fifteen furry pounds, and he was unsure of his exact whereabouts. Under those circumstances avenging his murder would be difficult. On the other hand, he didn't have any other pressing business, apart from an eight-hour nap which he felt in need of. First things first, though. Danby wanted to know what he looked like, and then he needed to find out where the kitchen was, and whether Sweaty Socks and Prell Shampoo had left anything edible on the countertops. There would be time enough for philosophical thoughts and revenge plans when he was cleaning his whiskers.

The living room was enough to make an architect shudder. Clunky Early American sofas and clutter. He was glad he couldn't see the color scheme.

There was a mirror above the sofa, though, and he hopped up on the cheap upholstery to take a look at his new self. The face that looked back at him was definitely feline, and so malevolent that Danby wondered how anyone could mistake cats for pets. The yellow (or possibly green) almond eyes glowered at him from a massive triangular face, tiger-striped, and surrounded by a ruff of gray-brown fur. Just visible beneath the ruff was a dark leather collar equipped with a little brass bell. That would explain the ringing in his ears. The rest of his body seemed massive, even allowing for the fur, and the great plumed tail swayed rhythmically as he watched. He resisted a silly urge to swat at the reflected movement. So he was a tortoiseshell, or tabby, or whatever they called those brown-striped cats, and his hair was long. And he was still male. He didn't need to check beneath his tail to confirm that. Besides, the reek of ammonia in the vicinity of the sofa suggested that he was not shy about proclaiming his masculinity in various corners of his domain.

No doubt it would have interested those New Age clowns to learn that he was not a kitten, but a fully grown cat. Apparently the arrival had been instantaneous as well. He had always been given to understand that the afterlife would provide some kind of preliminary orientation before assigning him a new identity. A deity resembling John Denver, in rimless glasses and a Sierra Club T-shirt, should have been on hand with some paperwork regarding his case, and in a nonthreatening conference they would decide what his karma entitled him to become. At least, that's what the New Agers had led him to believe. But it hadn't been like that at all. One minute he had been tumbling into a sewage pit, and the next, he had a craving for Meow Mix. Just like that. He wondered what sort of consciousness had been flickering inside that narrow skull prior to his arrival. Probably not much. A brain with the wattage of a lightning bug could control most of the items on the feline agenda: eat, sleep, snack, doze, dine, nap, and so on. Speaking of eating…

He made it to the floor in two moderate bounds, and jingled toward the kitchen, conveniently signposted by the smell of lemon-scented dishwashing soap and stale coffee. The floor could do with a good sweeping, too, he thought, noting with distaste the gritty feel of tracked-in dirt on his velvet paws.

The cat dish, tucked in a corner beside the sink cabinet, confirmed his worst fears about the inhabitants' instinct for tackiness. Two plastic bowls were inserted into a plywood cat model, painted white, and decorated with a cartoonish cat face. If his food hadn't been at stake, Danby would have sprayed *that* as an indication of his professional judgment. As it was, he summoned a regal sneer and bent down to inspect the offering. The water wasn't fresh; there were bits of dry catfood floating in it. Did they expect him to drink *that*? Perhaps he ought to dump it out so that they'd take the hint. And the dry cat-food hadn't been stored in an airtight container, either. He sniffed contemptuously: the cheap brand, mostly cereal. He supposed he'd have to go out and kill something just to keep his ribs from crashing together. Better check out the counters for other options. It took considerable force to launch his bulk from floor to countertop, and for a moment he teetered on the edge of the sink fighting to regain his balance, while his bell tolled ominously, but once he righted himself he strolled onto the counter with an expression of nonchalance suggesting that his dignity had never been imperiled. He found two breakfast plates stacked in the sink. The top one was a trove of congealing egg yolk and bits of buttered toast. He finished it off, licking off every scrap of egg with his rough tongue, and thinking what a favor he was doing the people by cleaning the plate for them.

While he was on the sink, he peeked out the kitchen window to see if he could figure out where he was. The lawn outside was thick and luxurious, and a spreading oak tree grew beside a low stone wall. Well, it wasn't Albuquerque. Probably not California, either, considering the healthy appearance of the grass. Maybe he was still in Maryland. It certainly looked like home. Perhaps the transmigration of souls has a limited geographic range, like AM radio stations.

After a few moments' consideration, while he washed an offending forepaw, it occurred to Danby to look at the wall phone above the counter. The numbers made sense to him, so apparently he hadn't lost the ability to read. Sure enough, the telephone area code was 301. He wasn't far from where he started. Theoretically, at least, Giles was within reach. He must mull that over, from the vantage point of the window sill, where the afternoon sun was marvelously warm, and soothing… zzzzz.

Danby awakened several hours later to a braying female voice calling out, "Tigger! Get down from there this minute. Are you glad Mommy's home, sweetie?"

Danby opened one eye, and regarded the woman with an insolent stare.

Tigger? Was there no limit to the indignities he must bear? A fresh wave of Prell shampoo told him that the self-proclaimed *mommy* was chatelaine of this bourgeois bungalow. And didn't she look the part, too, with her polyester pants suit and her cascading chins! She set a grocery bag and a stack of letters on the countertop, and held out her arms to him. "And is my snookums ready for din-din?" she cooed.

He favored her with an extravagant yawn, followed by his most forbidding Mongol glare, but his hostility was wasted on the besotted Mrs.—he glanced down at the pile of letters—Sherrod. She continued to beam at him as if he had fawned at her feet. As it was, he was so busy studying the address on the Sherrod junk mail that he barely glanced at her. He hadn't left town! His tail twitched triumphantly. Morning Glory Lane was not familiar to him, but he'd be willing to bet that it was a street in Sussex Garden Estates, just off the bypass. That was a couple of miles from Giles Eskeridge's mock-Tudor monstrosity, but with a little luck and some common sense about traffic he could walk there in a couple of hours. If he cut through the fields, he might be able to score a mouse or two on the way.

Spurred on by the thought of a fresh, tasty dinner that would beg for its life, Danby/Tigger trotted to the back door and began to meow piteously, putting his forepaws as far up the screen door as he could reach.

"Now, Tigger!" said Mrs. Sherrod in her most arch tone. "You know perfectly well that there's a litter box in the bathroom. You just want to get outdoors so that you can tomcat around, don't you?" With that she began to put away groceries, humming tunelessly to herself.

Danby fixed a venomous stare at her retreating figure, and then turned his attention back to the problem at hand. Or rather, at paw. That was just the trouble: *Look, Ma, no hands!* Still, he thought, there ought to be a way. Because it was warm outside, the outer door was open, leaving only the metal storm door between himself and freedom. Its latch was the straight-handled kind that you pushed down to open the door. Danby considered the factors: door handle three feet above floor, latch opens on downward pressure, one fifteen-pound cat intent upon going out. With a vertical bound that Michael Jordan would have envied, Danby catapulted himself upward and caught onto the handle, which obligingly twisted downward, as the door swung open at the weight of the feline cannonball. By the time gravity took over and returned him to the ground, he was claw-deep in scratchy, sweet-smelling grass.

As he loped off toward the street, he could hear a plaintive voice wailing, "Ti-iii-gerrr!" It almost drowned out the jingling of that damned little bell around his neck.

Twenty minutes later Danby was sunning himself on a rock in an abandoned field, recovering from the exertion of moving faster than a stroll. In the distance he could hear the drone of cars from the interstate, as the smell of gasoline wafted in on a gentle breeze. As he had trotted through the neighborhood, he'd read street signs, so he had a better idea of his whereabouts now. Windsor Forest, that pretentious little suburb that Giles called home, was only a few miles away, and once he crossed the interstate, he could take a shortcut through the woods. He hoped that La Sherrod wouldn't put out an all-points bulletin for her missing kitty. He didn't want any SPCA interruptions once he reached his destination. He ought to ditch the collar as well, he thought. He couldn't very well pose as a stray with a little bell under his chin.

Fortunately, the collar was loose, probably because the ruff around his head made his neck look twice as large. Once he determined that, it took only a few minutes of concentrated effort to work the collar forward with his paws until it slipped over his ears. After that, a shake of the head—jingle! jingle!—rid him of Tigger's identity. He wondered how many pets who "just disappeared one day," had acquired new identities and gone off on more pressing business.

He managed to reach the bypass before five o'clock, thus avoiding the commuter traffic of rush hour. Since he understood automobiles, it was a relatively simple matter for Danby to cross the highway during a lull between cars. He didn't see what the possums found so difficult about road crossing. Sure enough, there was a ripe gray corpse on the white line, mute testimony to the dangers of indecision on highways. He took a perfunctory sniff, but the roadkill was too far gone to interest anything except the buzzards.

Once across the road, Danby stuck to the fields, making sure that he paralleled the road that led to Windsor Forest. His attention was occasionally diverted by a flock of birds overhead, or an enticing rustle in the grass that might have been a field mouse, but he kept going. If he didn't reach the Eskeridge house by nightfall, he would have to wait until morning to get himself noticed.

In order to get at Giles, Danby reasoned, he would first have to charm Julie Eskeridge. He wondered if she was susceptible to needy animals. He couldn't remember whether they had a cat or not. An unspayed female would be nice, he thought. A Siamese, perhaps, with big blue eyes and a sexy voice.

Danby reasoned that he wouldn't have too much trouble finding Giles's house. He had been there often enough as a guest. Besides, the firm had designed and built several of the overwrought mansions in the spacious subdivision. Danby had once suggested that they buy Palladian windows by the gross, since every nouveau-riche home-builder insisted on having a brace of them, no matter what style of house he had commissioned. Giles had not been amused by Danby's observation. He seldom was. What Giles lacked in humor, he also lacked in scruples and moral restraint, but he compensated for these deficiencies with a highly developed instinct for making and holding on to money. While he'd lacked Danby's talent in design and execution, he had a genius for turning up wealthy clients, and for persuading these tasteless yobbos to spend a fortune on their showpiece homes. Danby did draw the line at carving up antique Sheraton sideboards to use as bathroom sink cabinets, though. When he also drew the line at environmental crime, Giles had apparently found his conscience an expensive luxury that the firm could not afford. Hence, the shallow grave at the new construction site, and Danby's new lease on life. It was really quite unfair of Giles, Danby reflected. They'd been friends since college, and after Danby's parents died, he had drawn up a will leaving his share of the business to Giles. And how had Giles repaid this friendship? With the blunt end of a shovel. Danby stopped to sharpen his claws on the bark of a handy pine tree. Really, he thought, Giles deserved no mercy whatsoever. Which was just as well, because, catlike, Danby possessed none.

The sun was low behind the surrounding pines by the time Danby arrived at the Eskeridge's mock-Tudor home. He had been delayed en route by the scent of another cat, a neutered orange male. (Even to his color-blind eyes, an orange cat was recognizable. It might be the shade of gray, or the configuration of white at the throat and chest.) He had hunted up this fellow feline, and made considerable efforts to communicate, but as far as he could tell, there was no higher intelligence flickering behind its blank green eyes. There was no intelligence at all, as far as Danby was concerned; he'd as soon try talking to a shrub. Finally tiring of the eunuch's unblinking stare, he'd stalked off, forgoing more social experiments in favor of his mission.

He sat for a long time under the forsythia hedge in Giles's front yard, studying the house for signs of life. He refused to be distracted by a cluster of sparrows cavorting on the birdbath, but he realized that unless a meal was coming soon, he would be reduced to foraging. The idea of hurling his bulk at a few ounces of twittering songbird made his scowl even more forbidding than usual. He licked a front paw and glowered at the silent house.

After twenty minutes or so, he heard the distant hum of a car engine, and smelled gasoline fumes. Danby peered out from the hedge in time to see Julie Eskeridge's Mercedes rounding the corner from Windsor Way. With a few hasty licks to smooth down his ruff, Danby sauntered toward the driveway just as the car pulled in. Now for the hard part: how do you impress Julie Eskeridge without a checkbook?

He had never noticed before how much Giles's wife resembled a giraffe. He blinked at the sight of her huge feet swinging out of the car perilously close to his nose. They were followed by two replicas of the Alaska pipeline, both encased in nylon. Better not jump up on her; one claw on the stockings, and he'd have an enemy for life. Julie was one of those people who air-kissed because she couldn't bear to spoil her makeup. Instead of trying to attract her attention at the car (where she could have skewered him with one spike heel), Danby loped to the steps of the side porch, and began meowing piteously. As Julie approached the steps, he looked up at her with wide-eyed supplication, waiting to be admired.

"Shoo, cat!" said Julie, nudging him aside with her foot.

As the door slammed in his face, Danby realized that he had badly miscalculated. He had also neglected to devise a backup plan. A fine mess he was in now. It wasn't enough that he was murdered and reassigned to cathood. Now he was also homeless.

He was still hanging around the steps twenty minutes later when Giles came home, mainly because he couldn't think of an alternate plan just yet. When he saw Giles's black sports car pull up behind Julie's Mercedes, Danby's first impulse was to run, but then he realized that, while Giles might see him, he certainly wouldn't recognize him as his old business partner. Besides, he was curious to see how an uncaught murderer looked. Would Giles be haggard with grief and remorse? Furtive, as he listened for police sirens in the distance?

Giles Eskeridge was whistling. He climbed out of his car, suntanned and smiling, with his lips pursed in a cheerfully tuneless whistle. Danby trotted forward to confront his murderer with his haughtiest scowl of indignation. The reaction was not quite what he expected.

Giles saw the huge, fluffy cat, and immediately knelt down, calling, "Here, kitty, kitty!"

Danby looked at him as if he had been propositioned.

"Aren't you a beauty!" said Giles, holding out his hand to the strange cat. "I'll bet you're a pedigreed animal, aren't you, fella? Are you lost, boy?"

Much as it pained him to associate with a remorseless killer, Danby sidled over to the outstretched hand, and allowed his ears to be scratched. He reasoned that Giles's interest in him was his one chance to gain entry to the house. It was obvious that Julie wasn't a cat fancier. Who would have taken heartless old Giles for an animal lover? Probably similarity of temperament, Danby decided.

He allowed himself to be picked up and carried into the house, while Giles stroked his back and told him what a pretty fellow he was. This was an indignity, but still an improvement over Giles's behavior toward him during their last encounter. Once inside Giles called out to Julie, "Look what I've got, honey!"

She came in from the kitchen, scowling. "That nasty cat!" she said. "Put him right back outside!"

At this point Danby concentrated all his energies toward making himself purr. It was something like snoring, he decided, but it had the desired effect on his intended victim, for at once Giles made for his den and plumped down in an armchair, arranging Danby in his lap, with more petting and praise. "He's a wonderful cat, Julie," Giles told his wife. "I'll bet he's a purebred Maine coon. Probably worth a couple of hundred bucks."

"So are my wool carpets," Mrs. Eskeridge replied. "So are my new sofas! And who's going to clean up his messes?"

That was Danby's cue. He had already thought out the pièce de résistance in his campaign of endearment. With a trill that meant "This way, folks!," Danby hopped off his ex-partner's lap and trotted to the downstairs bathroom. He had used it often enough at dinner parties, and he knew that the door was left ajar. He had been saving up for this moment. With Giles and his missus watching from the doorway, Danby hopped up on the toilet seat, twitched his elegant plumed tail, and proceeded to use the toilet in the correct manner.

He felt a strange tingling in his paws, and he longed to scratch at something and cover it up, but he ignored these urges, and basked instead in the effusive praise from his self-appointed champion. Why couldn't Giles have been that enthusiastic over his design for the Jenner building, Danby thought resentfully. Some people's sense of values was so warped. Meanwhile, though, he might as well savor the Eskeridges' transports of joy over his bowel control; there weren't too many ways for cats to demonstrate superior intelligence. He couldn't quote a little Shakespeare or identify the dinner wine. Fortunately, among felines toilet training passed for genius, and even Julie was impressed with his accomplishments. After that, there was no question of Giles turning him out into the cruel world. Instead, they carried him back to the kitchen and opened a can of tuna fish for his dining pleasure. He had to eat it in a bowl on the floor, but the bowl was Royal Doulton, which was some consolation. And while he ate, he could still hear Giles in the background, raving about what a wonderful cat he was. He was in.

"No collar, Julie. Someone must have abandoned him on the highway. What shall we call him?"

"Varmint," his wife suggested. She was a hard sell.

Giles ignored her lack of enthusiasm for his newfound prodigy. "I think I'll call him Merlin. He's a wizard of a cat."

Merlin? Danby looked up with a mouthful of tuna. Oh well, he thought, Merlin and tuna were better than Tigger and cheap dry cat food. You couldn't have everything.

After that, he quickly became a full-fledged member of the household, with a newly purchased plastic feeding bowl, a catnip mouse toy, and another little collar with another damned bell. Danby felt the urge to bite Giles's thumb off while he was attaching this loathsome neckpiece over his ruff, but he restrained himself. By now he was accustomed to the accompaniment of a maniacal jingling with every step he took. What was it with human beings and bells?

Of course, that spoiled his plans for songbird hunting outdoors. He'd have to travel faster than the speed of sound to catch a sparrow now. Not that he got out much, anyhow. Giles seemed to think that he might wander off again, so he was generally careful to keep Danby housebound.

That was all right with Danby, though. It gave him an excellent opportunity to become familiar with the house, and with the routine of its inhabitants—all useful information for someone planning revenge. So far he (the old Danby, that is) had not been mentioned in the Eskeridge conversations. He wondered what story Giles was giving out about his disappearance. Apparently the body had not been found. It was up to him to punish the guilty, then.

Danby welcomed the days when both Giles and Julie left the house. Then he would forgo his morning, midmorning, and early afternoon naps in order to investigate each room of his domain, looking for lethal opportunities: medicine bottles or perhaps a small appliance that he could push into the bathtub.

So far, though, he had not attempted to stage any accidents, for fear that the wrong Eskeridge would fall victim to his snare. He didn't like Julie any more than she liked him, but he had no reason to kill her. The whole business needed careful study. He could afford to take his time analyzing the opportunities for revenge. The food was good, the job of house cat was undemanding, and he rather enjoyed the irony of being doted on by his intended victim. Giles was certainly better as an owner than he was as a partner.

An evening conversation between Giles and Julie convinced him that he must accelerate his efforts. They were sitting in the den, after a meal of baked chicken. They wouldn't give him the bones, though. Giles kept insisting that they'd splinter in his stomach and kill him. Danby was lying on the hearth rug, pretending to be asleep until they forgot about him, at which time he would sneak back into the kitchen and raid the garbage. He'd given up smoking, hadn't he? And although he'd lapped up a bit of Giles's scotch one night, he seemed to have lost the taste for it. How much prudence could he stand?

"If you're absolutely set on keeping this cat, Giles," said Julie Eskeridge, examining her newly polished talons, "I suppose I'll have to be the one to take him to the vet."

"The vet. I hadn't thought about it. Of course, he'll have to have shots, won't he?" murmured Giles, still studying the newspaper. "Rabies, and so on."

"And while we're at it, we might as well have him neutered," said Julie. "Otherwise, he'll start spraying the drapes and all."

Danby rocketed to full alert. To keep them from suspecting his comprehension, he centered his attention on the cleaning of a perfectly tidy front paw. It was time to step up the pace on his plans for revenge, or he'd be meowing in soprano. And forget the scruples about innocent bystanders: now it was a matter of self-defense.

That night he waited until the house was dark and quiet. Giles and Julie usually went to bed about eleven-thirty, turning off all the lights, which didn't faze him in the least. He rather enjoyed skulking about the silent house using his infrared vision, although he rather missed late-night television. He had once considered turning the set on with his paw, but that seemed too precocious, even for a cat named Merlin. Danby didn't want to end up in somebody's behavior lab with wires coming out of his head.

He examined his collection of cat toys, stowed by Julie in his cat basket because she hated clutter. He had a mouse-shaped catnip toy, a rubber fish, and a little red ball. Giles had bought the ball under the ludicrous impression that Danby could be induced to play catch. When he'd rolled it across the floor, Danby lay down and gave him an insolent stare. He had enjoyed the next quarter of an hour, watching Giles on his hands and knees, batting the ball and trying to teach Danby to fetch. But finally Giles gave up, and the ball had been tucked in the cat basket ever since. Danby picked it up with his teeth, and carried it upstairs. Giles and Julie came down the right side of the staircase, didn't they? That's where the bannister was. He set the ball carefully on the third step, in the approximate place that a human foot would touch the stair. A trip wire would be more reliable, but Danby couldn't manage the technology involved.

What else could he devise for the Eskeridges' peril? He couldn't poison their food, and since they'd provided him with a flea collar, he couldn't even hope to get bubonic plague started in the household. Attacking them with tooth and claw seemed foolhardy, even if they were sleeping. The one he wasn't biting could always fight him off, and a fifteen-pound cat can be killed with relative ease by any human determined to do it. Even if they didn't kill him on the spot, they'd get rid of him immediately, and then he'd lose his chance forever. It was too risky.

It had to be stealth, then. Danby inspected the house, looking for lethal opportunities. There weren't any electrical appliances close to the bathtub, and besides, Giles took showers. In another life Danby might have been able to rewire the electric razor to shock its user, but such a feat was well beyond his present level of dexterity. No wonder human beings had taken over the earth; they were so damned hard to kill.

Even his efforts to enlist help in the task had proved fruitless. On one of his rare excursions out of the house (Giles had gone golfing, and Danby slipped out without Julie's noticing), Danby had roamed the neighborhood, looking for... well... pussy. Instead he'd found dimwitted tomcats, and a Doberman pinscher, who was definitely Somebody. Danby had kept conversation to a minimum, not quite liking the look of the beast's prominent fangs. Danby suspected that the Doberman had previously been an IRS agent. Of course, the dog had *said* that it had been a serial killer, but that was just to lull Danby into a false sense of security. Anyhow, much as the dog approved of Danby's plan to kill his humans, he wasn't interested in forming a conspiracy. Why should he go to the gas chamber to solve someone else's problem?

Danby himself had similar qualms about doing anything too drastic—such as setting fire to the house. He didn't want to stage an accident that would include himself among the victims. After puttering about the darkened house for a wearying few hours, he stretched out on the sofa in the den to take a quick nap before resuming his plotting. He'd be able to think better after he rested.

The next thing Danby felt was a ruthless grip on his collar, dragging him forward. He opened his eyes to find that it was morning, and that the hand at his throat belonged to Julie Eskeridge, who was trying to stuff him into a metal cat carrier. He tried to dig his claws into the sofa, but it was too late. Before he could blink, he had been hoisted along by his tail, and shoved into the box. He barely got his tail out of the way before the door slammed shut behind him. Danby crouched in the metal carrier, peeking out the side slits, and trying to figure out what to do next. Obviously the rubber ball on the steps had been a dismal failure as a murder weapon. Why couldn't he have come back as a mountain lion?

Danby fumed about the slings and arrows of outrageous fortune all the way out to the car. It didn't help to remember where he was going, and what was scheduled to be done with him shortly thereafter. Julie Eskeridge set the cat carrier on the backseat and slammed the door. When she started the car, Danby howled in protest.

"Be quiet back there!" Julie called out. "There's nothing you can do about it."

We'll see about that, thought Danby, turning to peer out the door of his cage. The steel bars of the door were about an inch apart, and there was no mesh or other obstruction between them. He found that he could easily slide one paw sideways out of the cage. Now, if he could just get a look at the workings of the latch, there was a slight chance that he could extricate himself. He lay down on his side and squinted up at the metal catch. It seemed to be a glorified bolt. To lock the carrier, a metal bar was slid into a socket, and then rotated downward to latch. If he could push the bar back up and then slide it back…

It wasn't easy to maneuver with the car changing speed and turning corners. Danby felt himself getting quite dizzy with the effort of concentrating as the carrier gently rocked. But finally, when the car reached the interstate and sped along smoothly, he succeeded in positioning his paw at the right place on the bar, and easing it upward. Another three minutes of tense probing allowed him to slide the bar a fraction of an inch, and then another. The bolt was now clear of the latch. There was no getting out of the car, of course. Julie had rolled up the windows, and they were going sixty miles an hour. Danby spent a full minute pondering the implications of his dilemma. But no matter which way he looked at the problem, the alternative was always the same: do something desperate or go under the knife. It wasn't as if dying had been such a big deal, after all. There was always next time.

Quickly, before the fear could stop him, Danby hurled his furry bulk against the door of the cat carrier, landing in the floor of the backseat with a solid thump. He sprang back up on the seat, and launched himself into the air with a heartfelt snarl, landing precariously on Julie Eskeridge's right shoulder, and digging his claws in to keep from falling.

The last things he remembered were Julie's screams and the feel of the car swerving out of control.

When Danby opened his eyes, the world was still playing in black-and-white. He could hear muffled voices, and smell a jumble of scents: blood, gasoline, smoke. He struggled to get up, and found that he was still less than a foot off the ground. Still furry. Still the Eskeridges' cat. In the distance he could see the crumpled wreckage of Julie's car.

A familiar voice was droning on above him. "He must have been thrown free of the cat carrier during the wreck, officer. That's definitely Merlin, though. My poor wife was taking him to the vet."

A burly policeman was standing next to Giles, nodding sympathetically. "I guess it's true what they say about cats, sir. Having nine lives, I mean. I'm very sorry about your wife. She wasn't so lucky."

Giles hung his head. "No. It's been a great strain. First my business partner disappears, and now I lose my wife." He stooped and picked up Danby. "At least I have my beautiful kitty-cat for consolation. Come on, boy. Let's go home."

Danby's malevolent yellow stare did not waver. He allowed himself to be carried away to Giles's waiting car without protest. He could wait. Cats were good at waiting. And life with Giles wasn't so bad, now that Julie wouldn't be around to harass him. Danby would enjoy a spell of being doted on by an indulgent human, fed gourmet catfood, and given the run of the house. Meanwhile he could continue to leave the occasional ball on the stairs, and think of other ways to toy with Giles, while he waited to see if the police ever turned up to ask Giles about his missing partner. If not, Danby could work on more ways to kill humans. Sooner or later he would succeed. Cats are endlessly patient at stalking their prey.

"It's just you and me, now, fella," said Giles, placing his cat on the seat beside him.

And after he killed Giles, perhaps he could go in search of the building contractor that Giles bribed to keep his dirty secret. He certainly deserved to die. And that nasty woman Danby used to live next door to, who used to complain about his stereo and his crabgrass. And perhaps the surly headweighter at Chantage. Stray cats can turn up anywhere.

Danby began to purr.

TIGER KILL

Kaaron Warren

Kaaron Warren's first novel *Slights* was published in 2009 by Angry Robot Books and released in North America early in 2010, followed by *Walking the Tree* and *Mistification*. Her short story collection *The Glass Woman* contains the award-winning story "A-Positive", now a short film from Bearcage Productions. Her award-winning short fiction has appeared in *Poe*, *Paper Cities*, *Fantasy Magazine* and many other venues in Australia and around the world. Her story "Ghost Jail", which first appeared in 2012, was reprinted in *The Apex Book of World SF* and "The Blue Stream", her second published story, was reprinted in *Dead Souls*. Warren lives in Canberra, Australia, with her family.

Warren writes about the story: "I was angry when I wrote 'Tiger Kill.' I began writing it because I was so disgusted to read that tiger's penis was used as an aphrodisiac. I wondered at the kind of person who would kill an animal like a tiger for the sake of better sex. I researched aphrodisiacs and found there were so many. I also researched the habits of tigers, which is where the idea for the hunter came from. I wanted to show a scene of complete barbarism, in a wealthy, privileged setting. I also wanted to talk about women being used as belongings in that environment."

Tara's gown was so tight she couldn't breathe. Karl would make her leave the dress on, later, when she would lie back and take it.

She followed him into the dining room.

The only other woman at the table laughed like a man and didn't cringe from their crude talk. There were seven men at the table. It was the only table in the room.

Tara noticed the thickness of the linen tablecloth, wondered what it would be like to sleep on. It was changed after every one of the thirty courses. Cutlery and plates didn't clang when collected. A distraction was performed in the corner of the room as the table was cleared each time; a naked woman bending over backwards to grasp her toes; a dwarf gulping beer from a glass taller than he; two children kissing and touching each other intimately; a cat forced somehow into a large bottle, with just enough room to turn around around aroundroundround; a naked man with idiot eyes and an enormous penis which reached, engorged, almost to his fat, pink, hairless nipples, his swollen breasts; a woman with festering cuts who held her arms and legs for display like a fashion model, showing maggots at their chewing work; a tall, oiled, hairless girl scoring herself lightly with a sharp blade till she shone with a thin coating of blood; an old man stamping weakly, a foot in either of two transparent buckets, stamping wine grapes; a man, drawn and gray, dancing a jig, his raised arms revealing hairless armpits, his shrivelled genitals thumping against his thigh, each leap a day less to live.

All these distractions so the diners would not notice that linen leaving. She fingered the material under the table, wishing her knees were bare so she could feel its texture there.

In an avuncular gesture, Karl gave her a ginger lolly, dug from the corner of his coat pocket. To gum her mouth, keep her silent on this important night.

As they talked around her, mouths full of octopus legs, lettuce soup, deep fried salt and pepper periwinkles, china tea, wine, she thought of the story of Little Black Sambo, such a racist story now. Little Black Sambo begged his mother to make pancakes for his breakfast, and she agreed, if he would run to the stall for butter. "Oh, yes," he agreed. Such a treat.

But on the way back he was spotted by the man-eating tigers. They chased him up the tree, and the sun melted his butter all over their heads. This made them angry, so they ran around the tree faster, faster, around, around aroundroundround, trying to make Little Black Sambo dizzy, fall off.

But it was so hot and they ran so fast, the lovely butter yellow fur of them began to blur, as they ran faster. They ran so fast they turned into butter which Little Black Sambo took home to his mother.

"Such lovely butter," she said.

"Oh, yes," he said, as he sat down to his plate stacked high with springy, hot pancakes.

Tara had loved that story as a child; had always wished for that plate of pancakes to be hers. As the next course came out on a sizzling hot dish, she wished again for those pancakes.

Karl took her plate and piled it with the gray flesh. The other woman had not smudged her lipstick. She seemed to suck the food in without using her lips or chewing. Tara watched the woman eat the meat and did not ask what it was.

"Like it?" the men asked Tara one by one. She had not swallowed the single mouthful she had taken. It sat on her tongue. She smiled around it.

They waited for her answer. It was a trick, of course. If she said yes, the meat would be bear, or cat, or human, the naming of which would make her stomach heave. If she said no, it would only be beef, done in a special way, and she would be the foolish one.

Karl would not let her go to the toilet, although the meal went for many hours. It was a test of strength. She thought perhaps the irritation in her bladder could be mistaken for sexual desire, so perhaps that was the purpose.

She swallowed the meat and did not answer the question. The plate was so large it must have carried the entire animal; what could be so fleshy? They ate sago broth with opium and honey, stir-fried ginger, caraway seeds, coriander, carrots, peas, spinach, cabbage, potato and onion. They ate tomatoes stuffed with avocado and truffle and pimento. Each course came out, the table cleaned between each, and the entertainment went on in the corner of the room. The men ordered the servants about loudly, each trying harder to be more demanding. Karl told them such servants were called tigers, once. That ladies' attendants were called pages. The men began to say, "Hey, tiger," to the servants, because it was the only way they would tame such a creature, by giving its name to a servant.

Tara and the other woman didn't call their attendants page.

As the soup was being prepared, the man who claimed to have caught the tigers came to their table. They all knew he was the hunter, and they wanted to hear the story of how brave the tigers were, how the man nearly died.

"The tiger becomes obsessed with the animal it kills. It doesn't leave the slightest taste, will eat the internal organs, the eyeballs, the hooves, the strings and bows of that beloved creature."

The hunter watched Tara, took in her position, her breasts, the colour of her skin.

The hunter moved around the table as he spoke. They ate quails, tossed the bones over their shoulders, and the crackle of the bones seemed to be his jungle floor, his boneyard.

The hunter circled the table, making them twist their necks.

Karl scraped the last of the sauce from the central bowl. Somewhere teeth crunched on gristle.

"The flesh may rot, and still the tiger will stay. Near that meat it will live, sleep, for as long as it takes."

The next course arrived, each person given a different portion, some a little more, some a little less. She watched them stare at each other's plates, and covet that extra mouthful. Asparagus spears with hollandaise sauce, radishes always within reach, and phallus-shaped bread, which they tore with their hands and did not take the time to butter.

"The tiger will not share with any scavenger. A deer may last six days, a buffalo perhaps weeks. Because the tiger has to work so hard, it has to spend its life hunting. So a large kill is like a little holiday. He doesn't want to cut it short."

"So all a hunter has to do," Tara thought, "is watch the vultures overhead, and find that tiger's feast. And there will be an over-fed, rested tiger, protective of his feast, not expecting danger. All a man has to do is take the prey with a full stomach."

Even at just a mouthful of each dish, her belly was swollen against the tight metallic shine of her dress. Her mother had worn a tight dress too, and her grandmother. They wore tight dresses and remained silent, they lived with legs ready to spread and died on a whim.

"Oh, yes. Until the tigers learnt that man knew the habit. Then the holiday was over; just a mouthful, a single meal, from every kill, and then away, to find more food. A tiger needs thirty cattle a year to live. How much do you think a man needs?"

No one knew. They were no longer listening to the hunter. The other woman had begun the story of a recent assignation, how foolish the man had looked. Each man at the table imagined how he would impress her. They became anxious for the Tiger's Penis Soup, wanting its juices, its life-giving, ever-growing goodness.

The hunter pulled a chair behind Tara. She alone was interested in how the tiger died. As the soup reached the table, the man Karl wanted most to impress said, "I've heard that when a man or beast dies, his soul enters his penis. So we gobble the tiger's soul."

The table laughed heartily. Tara opened her mouth wide at Karl's prodding, as if she, too, found this a delight.

She wondered, but did not ask, where the soul of a woman goes.

The soup cost thousands for the nine of them, the rest of the banquet the same again, and then there was the wine. They need two tiger's penises for a tureen large enough for ten. It is rare to find two males together in the wild; they like their space, and their females, to themselves. The soup is considered an aphrodisiac.

The stock is chicken, a fresh chicken straight into the pot, cooked over day-long heat, strained through muslin. Most delicate. The flesh is discarded, given to the cat or used for the spring rolls.

And then the soup was before them, presented in a gold-edged porcelain tureen made by the finest potter. The hunter presented the lid, allowed steam to reach the noses of those at the tables.

"Just the smell," he said, breathing deeply.

"I paid for that steam," Karl's boss said.

To Tara, it smelt like boiled meat.

There was silence as they swallowed the soup. They waited, each mouthful, for the promised erection, the promised desire, and they winked at each other like young boys pretending to have sprouted pubic bush.

Tara swallowed her portion, did not bite the secret ingredients, let them slide down her throat.

Later, she would think of the tiger's penis as Karl pretended virility. It was so long, twisted. She would feel his tiger's dick reaching up through her intestines to her lungs, where it would squeeze, squeeze, would not let her breathe.

The other woman sucked the fingers of the man to her left; the man to her right licked his lips, his chin, his cheeks, with a rough tongue.

"What about the rest of the tiger?" the boss said, "do we get any of that?"

"Oh, no," said the woman serving them. She was a short woman, dressed in heels which made her tall. "That tiger, he's thrown away. No good. Skin with a bullet hole, stained, all that. Once, a tiger would have been all used up, in another time, when people believed such things. His meat would be swallowed for the stomach trouble. His fur used for ladies' clothes. His brain for curing laziness, sure enough. His gallstones to give better vision. And his tail; in the bath, it makes your skin soft.

"His eyes will stop convulsions and all his fangs, his claws, his whiskers, make a powerful love charm." She laughed. "People were so silly. Now, we just take him for his penis, for the soup. And how was it?"

The man opposite Tara gave the waitress a squeeze, a pinch, a wink.

"Just lovely. Lovely."

The next course was brought out, a mountain of batter pieces, holding surprises Tara didn't want to receive.

As Karl reached for another lychee, she realised how big his hands were, like baseball mitts or paws, broad, short fingers, a vast expanse of palm.

The hunter said, "Once the tigers couldn't be caught by taking their food, the hunter would set up a Tiger Kill."

Only she was listening. Only she could hear.

"The hunters tie a nice deer to a tree and wait. They rustle and make noise, because the tiger hears well. He sees well, too, but his sense of smell is poor unless he is hunting the prey of love. If the creature was perfectly still, well-hidden, quiet, the tiger wouldn't find it. Only when the creature tries to run does the tiger leap."

They ate quince tart, pears stewed with ginger wine and steeped with mint, honeycomb with bee's wings still attached, vanilla and chocolate ice cream, then at last the meal was over. The men went to their rooms where women had been summoned. The other woman went with the boss. Tara went with Karl.

He lay on the bed, his stomach a pink balloon. When he shut his eyes, she locked herself in the bathroom and relieved herself.

"Out you come," he said. She could tell by his playful tone he was naked.

Then his tiger's penis was at work, and his fingers were about her throat, he was squeezing, squeezing. She reached for a weapon and grasped his belt, lifting it high and beating his back with a thick thwap. He enjoyed its caress.

She became aware of a figure standing over him. It was the hunter. He raised his club and hit Karl on the side of the head, knocking him off her, away from her.

"Thank you, my dear," the hunter said. She gathered her clothes as he crouched over the body, nestling the penis in his hand. As she left the room, she heard the thud and click so familiar to her; a brother's knife; a father's; a lover's knife.

She closed the door quietly behind her so as not to disturb the hunter at his work.

She didn't use the lift; she wanted to feel the strength of her muscles. As she descended the stairs, she rubbed at her make-up so it ran in streaks over her face, brushed out her curls with spread fingers. The hunter could not be expected to spare her again.

Next time, she would be ready.

SOMETHING BETTER THAN DEATH

Lucy Sussex

Lucy Sussex was born in the South Island of New Zealand and now lives in Australia, where she works as a researcher and writer. Her fiction has won Ditmar and Aurealis awards, and she has been nominated for environmental awards and the International Horror Guild award. Her short stories have been collected in *My Lady Tongue, A Tour Guide in Utopia*, and *Absolute Uncertainty*. She has also written several books for younger readers and an adult novel, *The Scarlet Rider*. She is completing a non-fiction book, *Cherchez les Femmes*, about early women crime authors and detectives.

Sussex says: "I'd never done a Christmas story before, and what better to use as source matter than a visit to the European original of the festival—Germany during Weihnachten, where the Christmas tree began. Pretty much every detail in the story has its origin in real life, like the East European heavy metal band at the airport, the cat by the Rathaus in Arnstadt. I was based in Bremen, and have photographs of the memorial statue, also tourist kitsch. Yet, while I was there I didn't have a chance to read the original Grimm story, 'Musicians of Bremen', although I had a vague memory of it. That kept niggling at me, like sand-grit inside a shellfish. I trust my niggles, they generally persist for a good reason. Back in the Southern hemisphere, in the middle of a hot summer I *did* read the story, and got a surprise. Here was a complex, multi-layered story, subtly-nasty, about such matters as animal rights and aging. It's easy to riff on Grimm by playing up the gore, or the sentimentality. Harder is to be matter-of-fact, realistic, as the original is."

For anything I know it was all due to jetlag, that curious fugue state in which the body has leapt over space and time as if in seven-league boots, with the protesting spirit, or soul, striving to catch up. Or due to the jetlag medication. Or else that I was betwixt and between stages of my life, or thought I was, and my subconscious was trying to tell me different. Whatever the cause, I walked between waking dreams, intermittent hallucinations, in which what was real and what wasn't mingled and merged madly. In the end it didn't seem to matter—I just went with the flow.

It all began in the Sydney International Departures check-in, where the teenage girl ahead of me exclaimed:

"Ohmigod! Tell me I'm hallucinating!"

Gladly, sweetie, I thought. I hadn't slept the previous night and was decidedly on edge, my body on automatic pilot, my mind darting every which way. Terminals always are artificial, in their air-conditioned saccharine blandness, and today this one seemed particularly unreal. That what *seemed* might actually *be* a genuine unreality was a notion I could welcome.

I followed the direction of her pointing, black-varnished finger, to see four figures and a trolley piled high with flight cases. And a part of me that I had resolved to leave behind pawed the ground and said: Aha! A band.

The trouble with music promotion, if you've done it too long, or long enough that it stops being fun, or fannish, is that you automatically categorize market niches. The girl was an obvious Goth. The band was a little more difficult: tatts, black clothes, long hair can indicate anything from stadium rockers to Norwegian Black Metal, who are more trouble than they're worth, as they have an annoying habit of burning down churches. Probably Speed Metal, I decided, as the girl started hyperventilating. Cult-level, if they're at the economy counter. I could guess at the festival they'd just attended and even take a punt at the promoter. My old life pawed at the ground again, raring to start a professional chat, about festival logistics, equipment, transport. Not the least of the fun would have been giving the Goth fangirl the vapours. To her, I was over forty, and thus nigh death—but I could still best her in the catty cunning stakes.

Instead I suppressed the urge, and stood meekly in queue. Was I not en route to a new life, leaving all frivolous, pop-culture things behind? The band passed through check-in, then security without incident. If the Goth fangirl got autographs I didn't see, for I was deep in Duty-free. What can you get a serious-minded man, apart from seriously good drink? Then I stretched my legs for the last time until Changi, a long walk around the corridors with my headphones and German-language CD. The Goth fangirl I spotted in the lounge for Vanuatu, which would surely ruin her graveyard pallor. My flight had been called, I was handing my boarding pass to the Stew, when a bloc of black joined the queue—the band again, clutching tacky outback souvenirs. Not as evil as you like to pretend, I thought. Like most metallists—who upon acquaintance tended to be polite and obliging, the reverse of the Christian rockers.

I have flown so much it has become routine, but even the tedium failed to deaden my jangling nerves. I watched a movie, *The Jane Austen Book Club*, and decided I didn't believe a word of it, apart from Jimmy Smits playing against type as a nice family man. I ate automatically, listened to my tapes again, dipped into my E-book, which was programmed with everything about Germany, from the *Rough Guide* to the Brothers Grimm. The Stews handed out cocoa, started dimming the lights. Outside it was dark, as if we were passing through an interminable tunnel. It was 2 a.m. my time, and there would be light, and an airport, in a few hours. I took a pill, and, just to make sure, chased it with the last of my dinner red wine.

And awoke, with sleeping passengers all around me and my nerves jangling again. My feet, in their airline socks, felt cramped, so I wandered down the aisles. As I neared the back row, the middle aisle, I had a sense of being watched, and traced it to a hulking dark shape, almost entirely muffled by an airline blanket worn like a hoodie. Eyes showed beneath it, large and lustrous. Beside my watcher were several other forms, similarly shrouded in blanket and curled up in the narrow seats like a pet in a basket. I caught only a glimpse of dyed Mohawk protruding. The band, I thought.

It was easy enough to catch my travel dress on a protruding, blanket-clad limb—elbow or knee I don't know, as he overflowed his seat in several directions. As I crouched down to extricate it, the "Sorry", "No I'm sorry" morphed into a whispered conversation. The accidental proximity of air travel can make for unlikely fellow travelers having even more unlikely conversations. But, as I crouched beside him, whispering into the space beneath his hood, and he whispered back in an accent I couldn't trace, it all seemed natural and easy—in retrospect too easy.

In dreams or drug trips, events occur without apparent connection, and very quickly. They cut to the chase, without small talk—and that's what happened here. Within a short time we were getting personal in a mixture of English and German, a language I was still learning.

"Warum?" Why? Why was I traveling?

"Ein mann,"—the truth, just to stave off any possible pass.

"And what sort of man, to take you half the length of the world?"

"Ein musik-mann."

He emitted a soft laugh, breathy, harsh and nasal, and with more wryness than mirth in it.

"Nobody you'd know. He plays classical, and conducts a small avant-garde consort at the Music School in Bremen." I pronounced it the correct German way, Bray-men.

"Donkey," he said.

"I beg your pardon."

"Katz."

"Yes, I'm Jane Katz," I said. Had he been ever a client, in some previous band incarnation?

That laugh again, but less wry than simply pleased. "Donkey, katz," he repeated. "And hund. And rooster."

"Oh," I said, catching on. "Well, Grimm to you too!" I had just read the story, on the E-book, and it was fresh in my mind. On the first day of Christmas my truelove had even sent to me a stuffed toy, the tourist symbol of the city, a donkey with a dog on its back, on the dog a cat, on the cat a rooster. The Four Musicians of Bremen, made in China.

"That's an interesting story, more than it seems. Like most of Grimm."

"It begins with a donkey," I said.

"Too old to work on the farm anymore."

"And rather than die for the only thing valuable left on him, his skin, he gallops away, down the road to Bremen."

"And there I think is an in-joke. Why does the donkey head for Bremen? To be town-musician. Which indicates the Bremen musicians had the reputation of being worse than donkeys."

"Interesting," I said. "He says he can play the lute."

"How can a donkey play the lute?"

I considered this. "With his teeth, like Hendrix. Or using one hoof on the fret, like a bottleneck or slide."

"Vir gut," he said. Very good.

"The hound says he can play kettledrum," I said, leaping ahead to the next character. "Maybe with the stick tied to his tail."

"To show you can teach an old dog new tricks."

"He too has run away, because he is too old to hunt, and his master has nearly beaten him to death."

"Then they meet a cat."

"Wet through and thoroughly pissed-off."

"Escaped from drowning."

"Because she is too old a hunter, even for mausen."

"What does the cat play?"

I thought again. "Probably some kind of string instrument. With those plucking claws."

"They've already got a guitarist."

"Bass, then." I had dabbled at bass, like various girls in '80s bands. When I got beside rather than on the stage I gave it up, but still harboured respect for the bassists I encountered. They were cool cats mostly, especially the jazzers.

"And the last one," he said. "The rooster."

"Crowing as loud as it can."

"The phrase is 'through marrow and bone.' Vir gut, very creepy."

As is your being word-perfect in a story I only just read, I nearly said. Odd little doubts stir below the surface of dreams, but are never expressed.

"His fate is to be made into soup."

"That's farm economics," I said. "Utterly unsentimental and practical. I grew up on a farm." And got as far away from it as I possibly could.

"And so the rooster completes the band," he said.

"As lead singer, with his penetrating voice."

"All of them seeking in Bremen 'something better than death,' as the Esel, the donkey says."

Now that really was creepy. If there is something that everybody fears, and avoids as hard as they can, it is growing old, finding yourself beyond a useful date, and the end nearing. Old boiler, that's what they say of women, only suitable for soup, like Grimm's rooster.

I think at that point I returned to my seat, too unsettled to continue. Next thing I was waking from a totally unrestful doze, with the cabin lights on for the descent into Changi. There I used the free internet, to send a message to Bremen, and because the line about something better than death was really getting to me, some Duty-free but still expensive night cream. At the bar, I encountered the band again, looking thoroughly unslept—and noticed no Mohawks. Nor were any of them particularly big. And, I suddenly realised, whoever I was talking to, he was older, because he kept emphasizing the animals' age. A young man wouldn't do that, they believe they're immortal. Get off that fire escape now, drink this water, no, don't try and snort wasabi… all from days when my promo work shaded into nannying.

Who was my conversationalist of the night-flight? Someone out of the common, certainly unlike the fellow passengers lining up for airport security yet again, in their tracksuits and jeans, the children clutching *Harry Potter*. He must be on the German-bound flight, he spoke German to me. I scanned the line of passengers, but drew a blank.

No matter, I was really tired now. I wrapped myself in blanket, closed my eyes—and kept waking every fifteen minutes or so, all the way to Hamburg. Mein mann had told me of a spot, hidden but known by seasoned travelers, where you could sit in reclining chairs and watch the take-offs. I found it, but still couldn't relax before my connecting flight to Bremen.

The flight was full of German business-folk, who disembarked with their brief-cases, or waited somberly by the carousel for their suitcases. There the strangeness started again: I swear I saw a sniffer dog leap onto the carousel. Oho, a drug bust! I thought, glad this time I wouldn't be getting any client out of trouble. Instead the dog took hold of a suitcase handle in its mouth, and dragged it off the carousel, for the benefit of a man who merely picked it up, and walked away, the dog trotting briskly at his heels. The things they teach seeing-eye dogs these days! I thought.

I found that Germans took dogs everywhere: into department stores, museums, so a dog in an airport soon seemed not so strange. Not as strange as the new country, even with a native guide in the shape of the musik-mann. How to describe him, except in terms of the stereotypes of love, of race? He was tall, blonde, blue-eyed, handsome (natch!), earnest, methodical, serious. Reader, I fucked him—as soon as we got back to his tidy apartment. Then I slept, despite my resolve to stay up until I was in sync with the local time. Sex does that to me, even earnest, methodical, serious sex. I woke, to find him dressing for a class he had to teach. Why didn't I come and take a look around the wintermarket while he worked, see the Christmas schmuck (baubles), and drink Lumbaba (coffee with rum)?

So, not long afterwards, I was alone in Germany, in below zero cold, bundled up in woollens, at a Christmas funfair. Here were mistletoe branches, the first time I had seen them in their cold green actuality, there were merry-go-rounds, plywood silhouettes cut into Christmas scenes, gingerbread hearts. It was a festival that said: Be merry and keep the frost giants away!

"Ich möchte ein Kaffee," I said carefully to the man at the Schmaltzküchen. Then, "Danke Schon," when I got the coffee.

It raised my body temperature a notch. But still I felt the chill penetrate the sleeves of my coat, cutting through to the marrow and bone of my forearms. Looking around for something to do, preferably warm, I saw a tour for the historic Rathaus, that's Ratehouse (Townhall) auf Deutsch and in English.

I paid my euros, joined a queue again, of people in padded jackets and woolly hats, usually with technicolour plaits attached, a fashion that was no doubt practical but too hippie for my tastes. Inside was warmth again, and our guide.

The bi-lingual tour was detailed, but told with a light, witty touch. I learnt about the Hanseatic league, Bremen as republic, Bishop Ansgar who evangelized Scandinavia from Bremen, about 1000 years ago. And Sydney town is only two hundred years old, I thought, unless you are Yothu Yindi.

Interesting though the tour was, odd details kept distracting me: the dog that padded along with the tour, as if it too had paid its euros to attend, a gargoyle face squinting from a riot of wooden carving, the wry, nasal laugh of the guide...

"Someone has just asked me about the symbol of the city, the key. It was not like now, where keys of the city are given as honours. Not a symbol of opening, but closure. Medieval cities were walled, against what might attack them from outside the zone of tilled fields and pasture, from robbers to robber barons. The keys were closely guarded, for behind the walls were not tolerant places. They had to be that way, to survive."

I looked properly at the guide for the first time. He was large, male, graying, about my vintage, nondescript almost by intention, as if trying to fit in as precisely as a jigsaw piece.

"Since you're talking about symbols, what about the musicians of Bremen?" I asked.

It was as if the rest of the tour group had vanished, and we were just talking to each other one to one, as we had in the plane.

"They never got here," he said. "They got diverted."

"By the lights of a house in the forest," I breathed.

"And when they looked in the window..."

"They saw firelight and robbers, feasting around a table."

"Their mouths started watering, with the hunger."

"And they slunk back into the dark."

"Discussed what to do."

"And devised a plan."

"They watched and waited until the robbers were drunk, but not legless."

"Then the donkey sank down on his knees, and the dog scrabbled onto his back."

"The cat elegantly leapt onto the back of the dog from her vantage point on a water barrel."

"The rooster swallowed his nerves, and fluttered onto the back of the cat."

"The donkey stood carefully, lifting the pyramid of animals."

"And a monstrous silhouette appeared in the robbers' window, followed by an equally demonic sound, in concert. The donkey brayed."

That laugh again.

The dog, who had been sitting quietly by, ears pricked, emitted a small bark.

"The cat wailed," I said, groping in my linguistic memory for the word. "Das miaoen!"

From the tour group came the final sound in the quartet, a crowing ringtone from a mobile phone. It broke the spell, as the guide sighed, and wagged a finger at the perpetrator. Now he was just a tour guide again, and I was just another tourist, alone in an alien country.

Another day, another place, more disorientation. Mein mann had a free weekend and was taking me on a tour of his favourite Germany. This meant a 6 a.m. start, when I had woken at 2, and lay beside the sleeping six-foot of him, unable to doze, unable to find something to do in a strange flat full of books I couldn't read, appliances of which I was yet to learn the nuances. We caught the ICE, the inter-city express, at the Hauptbahnhof as the sun rose. Gradually the landscape emerged from the darkness: mostly windfarms, and winter-brown woods. We changed at Hanover, changed again at a station I only remember for a tree delineated in ice like a faery toy, a moment of sheer magic despite my fatigue. Then, hours later, we reached Arnstadt, famous for Bach. The tour had been organized methodically, chronologically, Arnstadt being where Bach had his first job, as organist at a Lutheran church.

We stood, boots on frost, and surveyed the memorial statue. "Seated one day at the organ," in the hoary old song. Mein mann was reverent, but I had to suppress a giggle. The young Bach was unmistakably phallic, suitable for a father of twenty. And hadn't he wielded a sword, too? He reminded me of the young Keith Emerson but I knew better than to share that thought, especially with the man with whom I would be sharing my life. We entered the Neuekirche, and my irreverence continued, for the interior was like a white and gold wedding cake, even the organ. Can I have a cake like that? I very nearly said. We would have to get married, if I was to stay in Germany, rather than pursue a long-distance romance. He had the steadiest income—I was the alien immigrant, seeking the keys to the city, to let myself into the warmth and the firelight.

The walled cities were not tolerant places, I remembered, from the tour guide's talk. I shivered. He misunderstood, and put his wool-clad arm around me. A warm misunderstanding, in which I could luxuriate for the moment, as we stood like bride and groom in the middle of a white and gold church.

We had lunch in the Musician's Café (of course!): kaffee, schwarzbrot, tagessuppe (daysoup—soup of the day, and vegetarian, for unlike my escort I didn't fancy the chicken broth). In the pearly-grey winter light I watched a stocky white cat skirt the Arnstadt Rathaus, appropriate given the bi-lingual pun.

"I have an appointment for the early afternoon. Musical."

Of course, I thought.

"While I'm away, would you like to see the Puppenstadt?"

"Dollhouse?" I said, after a moment's translating thought.

"Famous. From Bach's time."

Whatever you say, I thought. He could have suggested I go ice-skating on the nearest pond, such was my passive desire to please. But a dollhouse, when I was neither childish nor twee? What did he think of me?

Unexpectedly, it captivated—eighty or so rooms in glass cases, a German principality in miniature, compiled by the childless and widowed Princess Auguste Dorothea, a plump and amiable lady from her portrait. Well, it beats music promotion as an achievement, I thought. I moved among the cases, nose almost touching glass, reading the details of a lost time, musicians, maids, weavers, bakers, dancing bears and all. Behind me came and went a tour group, German old age pensioners, and their guide. Someone lingered, I was aware of the presence, but was otherwise intent on a miniature replica of the Princess's Audience room. The detail extended to a pet monkey—and was that also a cat?—lurking by the folds of her brocade silk skirt.

"Would you like to go in?" said a voice behind me, one with which I was becoming very familiar. A hand moved briefly into my peripheral vision, holding between finger and thumb a tiny key.

"To the dollhouse world? Is it any different from the medieval walled cities?"

"The eighteenth century was more civilized," he said. "The Princess was fond of her court musicians and her pets. But observe the man selling rat traps, the dancing bear"—polar, made of real white fur—"and the old beggarwoman."

"We might come to that yet." Such a fear, to be alone, and old, poor and friendless. I shivered again.

"Imagine," he said, "if I stand at the window, the dog on my back, and you, Katzwoman, between dog and rooster, and we open our mouths and make the biggest cacophany we can—"

"To scare away the dollhouse folk, like we did the robbers," I breathed. "Miaoen!"

My mew was soft, but it seemed shockingly loud in the silence of the museum, somehow augmented, by the laugh behind me, the bark of a dog, even that ringtone cockcrow again: hee-haw-arf-meow-cock-a-doodle. As if the glass before me were water, a surface to shimmer with my breath, it shook. I suddenly found myself not outside, but *within* a 1700s provincial audience room, crouched at the foot of a throne upholstered in yellow silk, around me Chinoiserie wallpaper and marquetry furnishings.

The monkey and I were face-to-face. I bared my teeth at it, hissed, and it slunk away. Then I did what any cat would do, jumped up and settled myself in the best seat in the room, the princely throne with its soft yellow silk, underneath a matching Austrian blind of a canopy.

"And what is your decree, Princess Catwoman?" said the face in the glass, occupying one wall of the audience room.

I waved one paw airily.

"Release the monkey from its chains, also the bears, take the horses out of their harness, and ban all rat catchers, except me!"

"Vir gut," said the voice behind glass, laughing again. The glass quivered and the vision reversed, so that I stood once more gazing into the audience room, with its static doll-princess, monkey, and cat.

"What are you?" I said. "Some kind of animal liberationist?"

"I can hardly be anything but," he said, his voice a trailing thread of sound, ending in silence. I turned and found myself alone. The mobile mein mann had given me rang in my pocket, a Bach fugue. It was time to go.

The next few days passed in snapshots, images of a fairytale tourist German Christmas. Dinner that night was at the Goldene Sonne, where generations of the Bach family had an annual musical meet, and we slept in the hotel above, all to ourselves. Sex was 6/10, from my continuing tiredness perhaps, or else some unacknowledged sense of disapproving Bach family ghosts. To the Lutheran Church the next day, to hear Bach's organ being played, although I nearly nodded off during the sermon. Back to Bremen in the train, snow having fallen so that the countryside was almost over-the-top picture postcard, except for the windfarms. Left alone the next day, I watched German TV, and found it equally trash culture as elsewhere. Feeling very brave, I walked from the Neustadt (new town, typically a name hundreds of years old) along the riverside, all by myself.

I wanted to see the famous statue of the Musicians of Bremen, cast in bronze. It was polished keen by tourist hands, and I touched it too, first the katz, then the donkey, but felt not warm hide and hair, but cold metal. I waited, as tourist happy-snappers came and went, as if listening for a distinctive breathy, braying laugh. Nothing happened; and I consoled myself with some glühwein, drunk in a booth while the Christmas revelers all around slapped backs, dispensed Christmas cheer—to everyone except me, it seemed.

Night, and I put on what I had of winter glam, and went out with mein mann, to see his consort perform. Avant-garde meets with rock music at some junctures, especially at arts festivals—and thus ageing lady rock promoters meet serious classical music dudes. I knew my Steve Reich, my Phil Glass, even if I preferred my beloved Sonic Youth. Why did the performance then seem a cacophony dressed up as art, not even with the honest purpose of frightening some robbers away from their ill-gotten gains? Not to mention that I really did fall asleep during the "quiet movement". Result, in the freezing wind outside, a blazing row, luckily for any relationship grudge sheet largely conducted (by him, berating) in German. Under different circumstances I might have stomped off angrily, but in sub-zero temperatures, in a foreign country, I had no choice but to follow him meekly home, to his home.

By next morning we had sort of made it up. He ate salami for breakfast (German habit, bad as Vegemite) and we took another train, off to Lübeck, where Bach had walked all the way from Arnstadt to hear Buxtehude play. How young, how fannish, I thought, but did not say. The ICE was crammed with Germans, their suitcases and Christmas parcels, all last-minute panic as they headed back home to the volks for Weihnachsfest. We changed trains, as we had on the way to Arnstadt, but this time in a major city. I had missed my essential morning coffee, to make the train, and was decidedly blurry, not-with-it. As we waited outside the coffee booth, I said:

"Where are we?"

His face said: she doesn't know? "Hamburg, of course."

"Oh," I said, suddenly locating a culture point I recognized. "Where the Beatles honed their art!"

And then stopped cold, as his expression changed from condescending amusement to naked disgust. So you think that of me, what I have done, what I adore! With a psychic jolt, as of a train coupling, my jetlagged spirit or soul caught up with me, and with it came my senses. I knew then, that I had made a huge mistake: had I really believed true love was possible with a stranger who was my musical opposite?

"Snob," I shouted, a word identical in English and German. From around us came answering shouts, an approaching roar of song, even what sounded like gunfire. Feet tramped, a whistle sounded, and police in uniforms, with batons and guns, surged into the station. On the next platform a train pulled in, full of football fans, singing lustily and setting off firecrackers. The police flowed to meet them, and within moments there was a riot going on, not only on the platform, but between us lovers-no-more, as last night's row flared again. This time I gave as good as I got, in words with Germanic roots, four-letter, cutting, nasty and final.

Dramatic exit time, like a bow in front of a curtain. I turned on my boot heels and stepped into the larger chaos of the riot. I've survived mosh pits at festivals, I know how to move through trouble unhurt. Not so the fan to one side of me, who stumbled, and got a kick to the head, dislodging his beanie. As the riot eddied around us, I pulled him upright, lest he be trampled.

He looked near-stunned, blood tricking down from his Mohawk, dyed in the team colours. I did what I usually did, when I had a client in strife, led him towards the edge of the riot, then out among the watching passengers, and towards a safe stillness. Somehow along the way we acquired a police dog. I looped a finger through its collar, and as a scuffle neared us took a step sideways, and down a flight of stairs. Perhaps the dog led, perhaps I did, as we step-stumbled down towards a local service platform, containing only a few scattered passengers and their parcels.

A train pulled in, and automatically we entered. It chugged away back in the direction of Bremen, as the looming clouds released their snow, and we passed through empty farmland, small station after small station. The track dived into woodland, and in its centre stood a deserted station, the smallest so far. The dog barked, pulled at my coat skirts with its teeth. I heaved my dopy charge upright again, and we disembarked in the swirling snow, nobody following us out into the cold. The fan bent, scooped up a handful of snow, and rubbed it on his head. It seemed to revive him, and he lurched towards the exit. I could hardly abandon him—so I followed, as did the dog, wagging his bristly tail.

Waiting under the overhang of the station roof was a large grey donkey, whom the fan embraced around the neck, then used, as he had me, as a walking support.

So out we stepped into the snow, the four of us, through a village, decorations and Christmas candelabras at each window, like an advent calendar. Within a few streets the village petered out, and our paws, hooves, runners, and boots stopped scrunching snow, instead fell silent among the rag-rug of damp pine-needles in the forest. The fan walked free now, but I stumbled on a tree root, went headlong, knocking the heel off my boot. The dog bent over me, panting, the donkey lowered its velvet muzzle as if in concern, and the fan lent me a hand upwards. I wobbled, and he scooped me up as easily as he had the snow, depositing me on the back of the donkey. This is not Nazareth, I thought, and I'm definitely not a pregnant Mary. Nonetheless I rode on donkey-back through the forest to a clearing, in which stood what looked like a converted stable, or barn.

I know the donkey nudged the door with its muzzle and it swung open, I remember that, but the next moments are unclear. Somehow I went from riding on a hard hairy back to being carried bride-style, in a man's arms, over the threshold. I got deposited in a hearthside chair, and there followed a flurry of movement, as a fire was lit. I pulled off my wet boots, set them on the ashy hearthstone to dry. The fire caught, streaks of orange shooting up the chimney, and I slid onto the hearthrug. It was littered with straw and pet hair, but I lay on it, luxuriating in the warmth. The dog settled beside me, sighed, and went to sleep. After a moment I closed my eyes too.

Hours later I woke after the first proper sleep in a week. The early winter dusk had come, and with it had come Christmas, celebrated on the Eve in Germany. The fire illuminated a table, set for the feast, and a Christmas tree laden with bling. I couldn't see the fan anywhere, but the dog still snoozed beside me, paws twitching. In the chair on the other side of the hearth sat the Rathaus guide.

"You are Esel," I said.

A smile and nod.

"Tell me what happened next with the story," I said. "So the Bremen musicians drove the robbers out?"

"And the four animals ate their feast and took over the house."

"Did the robbers ever come back?"

"They sent a scout, to reconnoiter. In the dark, only to get scratched by the cat, kicked by the donkey, bit by the dog, and near deafened by the rooster. So he ran off wailing of witches with long talons, men armed with knives and clubs, whatever his fears made believable."

"Unlike an animal insurrection," I said. The fire was furnace-warm now, too much for my woolens. I sat up, and as I did saw perched in the rafters a rooster, with—surely not—what looked like a band-aid on its comb.

"Donkey, hund, hahn… Vo sind die katz?"

"She has nine lives. She might go and live in another one for a while, but always comes back."

Reader, we spent Christmas together, snowed completely in till almost the New Year, in freak winter weather conditions for that part of the country. We talked, prepared excellent meals with Esel, drank glühwein, got to know each other. Nothing more, I wasn't leaping into anything rash again. We listened right through a large collection of vinyl and DVD, then the musical instruments emerged. Esel, could he play slide guitar! And I plunked away cautiously on bass. Hahn hung from the rafters and sang football songs in a mean imitation of Robert Plant. Hund was shy, some drummers are like that, but every now and then he would pad down to the cellar studio, from which would arise the sound of drums, played like a fury.

Just when all the food in the house was exhausted except for a box of chocolate mice, the villagers arrived with a snowmobile and dug us out. And, because I could leave then, cat-contrary, I didn't.

One upon a time the Grimm brothers collected an oral story, tidied it up for print consumption, but left the message intact. Strip it down, and the story is about finding a haven, or of being diverted from your path, most fruitfully. I went to marry a classical musician, and ended up living with a rock band. Nothing I hadn't done before, in my wild youth, an old life of mine, to which I had inevitably returned.

"How does the story end?" I asked Esel, as we watched the New Year's sunrise, coiled up together, under a geological strata of blankets. "So they lived happily ever after?"

"No, that's not what the story says."

"What, then?"

He lay back, thinking. "Everything prospered so well with the quartet."

"That's good!"

"That they did not forsake their situation."

"How very formal those Grimms were!"

"Not the very last line. It ends with: 'And there they are to this day for anything I know'."

There are two ways to write what happened. First is a romantic tale: on the way to what I thought was the love of my life, but in reality was a flingette, I met on the plane a gent more congenial to my tastes, musical and otherwise. Then I encountered him again, while he was doing emergency tour guide work, and found that I could survive a snowed-in Christmas with him and his band-mates. They could even use an experienced rock promoter.

Second is something stranger: life in a continuous Grimm's tale, with a bunch of musical shape-shifters.

It could even be both.

For anything I know.

DOMINION
Christine Lucas

Christine Lucas lives in Greece with an assortment of spoiled cats. A retired Air Force officer and self-taught in English, she likes to explore in her writing overlooked parts of fantasy worlds, especially the lives of the animals that dwell in them. Her work has appeared in several print and online magazines, including *Renard's Menagerie,* the *Footprints* anthology, *Expanded Horizons, Murky Depths,* and *Andromeda Spaceways Inflight Magazine.* She is currently working on her first novel.

Of her story, Lucas says: "A few years ago, I was doing some research on the history of cats for a related article, when I stumbled across a Hebrew myth. According to it, there were no cats in the Garden of Eden. They were created later, aboard Noah's Ark, to help control the vermin population that threatened to overrun the vessel. To me, the obvious conclusion was this: when God gave Man dominion over animals, cats were not included in the deal.

"Furthermore, close observation of any cat will make it clear that cats possess Knowledge of Good and Evil. Just watch them when they shred the toilet paper or knock over your potted plant. They know they're not supposed to do that. They just don't care. And then the pieces clicked together. Man has no dominion over them, and they come with the forbidden knowledge. Their creator could only be a trickster, shaping them after its own image. And my kitty Spitha swears that every word is true."

On the morning of the Seventh Day, the Garden of Eden was calm and peaceful. The Serpent stretched. She had to fix that. Perfection was very, *very* boring.

She crawled through the tall grass to the pride of lions sunning their fur in a clearing by the Euphrates' bank.

"Hey, did you know what lambs are made of? Meat. Fresh and juicy meat. Why would they be made of meat if you weren't supposed to eat them? Go on, give it a try," she whispered to a lioness, her scaly tail pointing at a herd grazing close by. She had never liked lambs.

The lioness rolled over, her amber eyes half-closed. "Too hot to run. The lambs don't bother me, so I don't bother them." She yawned and continued her nap.

Disappointed, the Serpent moved on to a brown bear eating berries by the river.

"There are fat fish swimming in the water," she told him. "Juicy, writhing salmons and carp, filled with nutrients for great fur. And they taste much better than berries."

The bear looked up, his muzzle smeared with juice. "But I like berries. Why should I get wet and harass the carp?"

By noon, the Serpent was annoyed. None of the Garden's animals had humored her. God's last creations, the furless bipeds, seemed promising, but she hadn't dared to approach them. According to the sparrows' gossip, *He* had made the male after His own image. And judging by His blatant preference for lambs, the outcome couldn't be good. Curled around the Tree of Life, the Serpent decided that Creation needed fun—mischievous—creatures. She had watched Him do it from clay with the humans. How hard could it be, especially with the aid of the forbidden fruit? Across the grove, the man scratched his crotch, watching the clouds. It couldn't get any worse than *that*.

She gathered a pile of soft soil from around the roots of the Tree of Life and curled around it, kneading and shaping to the best of her abilities. Perhaps the humans' opposable thumbs had indeed some merit. It took her the better part of the afternoon, but she finally stretched and inspected her handiwork.

The creatures looked good: one male and one female, for all creatures needed a mate in life and an accomplice in mischief. She had made the male bigger and thick-headed, with fast claws and toxic urine to leave his mark all over Creation. The female was more delicate, but faster and fierce when defending her litter. The Serpent lashed her forked tongue and hurried up the Tree of Knowledge. The full moon was ascending and she hadn't finished.

She grabbed a fruit and squeezed it over the creatures, anointing them.

"I give you knowledge of Good and Evil," she whispered, and a sudden breeze shuffled the foliage around them. The clay animals trembled, the mud turning to fur and flesh. "I give you sight to see through the dark hours of the night and through the darkness of souls. May the moon be your ally, may the sun warm your fur. Tread fast, tread soft, and knock down all fragile objects in your path."

She breathed in and spat at them. "I give you free will, your choice either poison or cure. Whatever divine spark lays in me, I share it with you."

A tremor ran through the Garden. She rubbed a fruit from the Tree of Life on them, and dried clay fell off, revealing soft fur underneath.

"Cats, I give you Life. Go forth and multiply. Do it often, do it loudly, until your offspring overruns Creation."

The kittens blinked and sniffed the air. Their eyes glowed, reflecting the moonlight. When they noticed each other, she held her breath. Their eyes grew huge, their backs arched and their tails stood rigid, upright and fluffed up. Bolder than her ginger mate, the calico kitten dared a sniff of his muzzle. A shy lick followed the sniff, and in no time they were curled together, grooming each other. Soon, they grew bored of grooming and started chasing each other's tails.

Perfection isn't always serious.

The kittens stalked unsuspecting fireflies, shredded leaves, and clawed their way up onto the branches of the Tree of Life. The Serpent lay belly up beneath it, laughing herself breathless. It was almost dawn when the kittens, exhausted, climbed down. They curled by the Serpent's coiled body and fell fast asleep, their whiskers and tails twitching in dreams of hunt and mischief.

True perfection is never boring.

The next morning, the Serpent sunned her scales, watching the kittens play. She'd have to feed them soon. They'd probably manage to catch bugs or even a frog on their own, but she'd rather keep them from hunting until they were old enough to defend themselves. And, hopefully, hunt decent prey, like lambs.

A sudden movement caught her eye. Barely turning her head, she spotted the human female hidden among the thick bushes a few paces away. Wide-eyed, mouth agape, Eve watched the kittens play. The serpent lashed her forked tongue and stifled a snicker. Behold the solution to the kittens' feeding problem.

"Come closer, Eve."

Eve licked her lips. She walked out of the bushes, each step slow and cautious. She reached out to touch the kittens.

They fluffed up and arched their backs. The calico growled and showed sharp little claws.

Eve pulled back her hand, her brow furrowed. "Why is it doing that?" She turned to the Serpent, her eyes moist. "Why doesn't it like me?"

"Perhaps it's hungry." She tilted her head toward a nearby plain. "There's a herd of cows grazing over there. Perhaps if you brought them some milk they'd let you pet them. They are very soft, you know. And they purr."

Eve blinked. "What is 'purr'?"

"Purr is bliss," she replied and watched Eve hurry to the nearest cow. The purring had been her greatest idea. It overpowered the opposable thumb any time.

By noon, the kittens had warmed up to Eve. She brought them milk and they rubbed their backs against her legs, played with her hair and curled on her lap, purring.

Half-asleep, the Serpent lay content under the Tree. Her work was complete. She had created perfection and found a guardian for the little ones. At the threshold of a dream, a male voice somewhere close awoke her.

"Eve, where are you?"

Eve's gaze darted from the napping kittens in her lap to the source of the voice and back. The calico stretched and curled tiny paws over her face. Eve's shoulders slumped.

"I must go. Adam needs me."

The Serpent stretched her neck. She couldn't let her leave—not yet. Not for *him*.

"Why does he need you?"

"Um, to gather fruits, and comb his beard, and—"

The serpent rolled her eyes. "Can't he do that on his own?" *What's the point of having an opposable thumb if you don't use it?*

"Yes, but—"

"The kittens need you more," she hissed. "They can't milk cows."

Eve glanced over her shoulder. "I suppose I could stay a little longer."

"WHAT IS THIS?"

His voice was thunder and lightning and Eve fell face down on the ground. The kittens started from their nap with a hiss and climbed up the Tree of Life. The Serpent remained calm and stretched her upper body, certain she saw Adam's ratty face hidden in the bushes at the back.

Amidst a host of angels and seraphim, their Lord God appeared before them.

"What have you done?" He turned his fiery gaze to Eve. "Have you not a mate, woman? Go to him. He has been looking for you everywhere, sick with worry."

Eve stood up and hurried away.

He turned to the Serpent. "Call them down."

She snickered. "Even if I do, they won't obey. I forgot to include obedience when I made them."

God raised an eyebrow. "Of course you did." He stroked his beard and then waved at one of the seraphim. "Bring them before me, so I can inspect the full extent of the Serpent's insubordination."

The seraph flew to the kittens perched upon a branch. "Follow me to your Lord God."

Their eyes grew wide, fascinated by the incessant flutter of the seraph's six wings. The calico outstretched her forepaw to catch one. She licked her whiskers, wagged her behind and lunged at the slowly retreating seraph. A heartbeat later, the ginger kitten followed her.

Amidst hisses and a cloud of torn feathers, the unfortunate seraph flew to its master's feet. An archangel hurried to its aid and managed to detach the berserk kittens from the torn wings.

The kittens stood at God's feet, and He leaned over them. The ginger kitten was busy chasing a floating seraph feather, while the calico seemed mesmerized by God's beard. She attempted to paw one of the long white tendrils, but the feather caught her eye and she went after that instead.

"Insolent," He said.

"I call it free will."

The kittens now chased each other around God's feet, oblivious to the imminent danger.

He frowned. "I gave Man dominion over all creatures. They *should* obey him."

"Kittens didn't exist at that time. They are excluded from the deal."

"They will only disrupt peace. The fruit is forbidden for a reason."

"You said not to eat it. You never said anything about other uses."

His frown deepened. "Semantics." He waved to His host. "Lucifer, escort the creatures out of Eden."

"No!" She darted forward, placing herself between kittens and archangel. "They'll never survive outside."

"They are not defenseless. You should know that, being their creator." His voice was firm but not unkind.

She hung her head. "But they are just babies…"

God signaled to Lucifer, who stood shifting his weight from one leg to another. "Well?"

Lucifer bit his lip. "My Lord God, they will not come."

The kittens cowered at the roots of the Tree, a multicolored bundle of hissing fur. God turned to the Serpent.

"They will listen to *you*." The promise of flood and fire now lurked in His tone. "See to their needs, but escort them out."

Defeated, she nodded. "But will they endure? You're omniscient. Please, tell me."

He tilted His head sideways. "So be it. This I tell you: they will be revered as deities and hunted as demons. Often my mortal servants will know them to be not of my making. They will deem them evil, drown them in water and burn them with fire."

"And you will do nothing to stop them?"

"I do not advocate their actions, and they will not go unpunished." He smirked. "What happened to your support of free will?"

"It has gone with the kittens."

The Serpent escorted the kittens through the wilder lands to a secluded oasis. They'd have fresh water there, and trees to climb on, and unsuspecting frogs and birds to hunt. But they'd be alone, easy prey to all the dangers that lurked outside Eden.

Back in Eden, she could no longer sleep in peace, her dreams now tormented by images of the kittens suffering. She had to find them a guardian, to shelter them in the eons to come. Had He not said, "*See to their needs?*"

Come morning, she climbed up the Tree of Knowledge and grabbed a fragrant fruit, then headed to the clearing where the humans dwelled.

"Eve! I have something for you."

TIGER IN THE SNOW
Daniel Wynn Barber

Daniel Wynn Barber lives in Denver, Colorado, where he teaches history at Englewood High School. Barber and his wife, Patricia, have two grown sons, Sean and Joel, and a lunatic cat named Phoebe. After suffering wounds in the Vietnam War in 1969, Barber was sent to Fitzsimmons Army Hospital in Denver, fell in love with Colorado, and promptly abandoned his native Minnesota for a life in the Mile High City. While teaching and parenting have been his passion for the last twenty years, he hopes to find time to return to writing—a fire that was lighted in him many years ago, and whose flame has never died. His only other story was published in *Bringing Down the Moon: 15 Tales of Fantasy and Terror* in 1985.

Asked about the inspiration for "Tiger in the Snow," he relates: "When I was a kid I had this tremendous fear of lions. I'm not sure where this fear came from, but lions stalked me in my dreams. When I would walk home late at night from a friend's house, I just knew that a lion was out there, following me home, lying in wait. I was reminded of this fear years later when, as an adult with a child of my own, I was walking home from the milk store, in the dark. It was snowing and for some reason I thought of the old lion fear. The story was shaping up nicely by the time I reached home. Why I changed from a lion to a tiger is still something of a mystery; but I think it may have been the beauty of the contrast created by the image of a tiger's orange and black against the stark purity of a world turned white with fresh snow. Or perhaps I still couldn't confront the lion fear, and using a tiger was safer."

Justin sensed the tiger as soon as he reached the street. He didn't see it, or hear it. He simply... sensed it.

   Leaving the warm safety of the Baxter's porch light behind him, he started down the sidewalk that fronted State Street feeling the night swallow him in a single hungry gulp. He stopped when he reached the edge of the Baxter's proper line and looked back wistfully toward their front door.

Too bad the evening had to end. It had been just about the finest evening he could remember. Not that Steve and he hadn't had some fine old times together, the way best friends will; but this particular evening had been, well, magical. They had played *The Shot Brothers* down in Steve's basement while Mr. and Mrs. Baxter watched TV upstairs. When the game had been going well and everything was clicking, Justin could almost believe that Steve and he really were brothers. And that feeling had never been stronger than it had been this evening.

When Mrs. Baxter had finally called down that it was time to go, it had struck Justin as vaguely strange that she would be packing him off on a night like this, seeing how he and Steve slept over at one another's homes just about every weekend. But this evening was different. Despite the snow, home called to him in sweet siren whispers.

Mrs. Baxter had bundled him up in his parka, boots, and mittens, and then, much to his surprise, she had kissed his cheek. Steve had seen him to the door, said a quick goodbye, then hurried away to the den. Funny thing, Steve's eyes had seemed moist.

Then Justin had stepped out into the night, and Mrs. Baxter had closed the door behind him, leaving him alone with the dark and the cold and… the tiger.

At the edge of the Baxter's property, Justin glanced around for a glimpse of the beast; but the street appeared deserted save for the houses and parked cars under a downy blanket of fresh snow. It was drifting down lazily now, indifferent after the heavy fall of that afternoon. Justin could see the skittering flakes trapped within the cones of light cast by the street lamps, but otherwise the black air seemed coldly empty. The line of lamps at every corner of State Street gave the appearance of a tunnel of light that tapered down to nothingness; and beyond that tunnel, the dark pressed eagerly in.

For a moment, Justin felt the urge to scurry back to the Baxter's door and beg for sanctuary, but he knew he should be getting home. Besides, he wasn't some chicken who ran from the dark. He was one of the Shot Brothers. Rough and ready. Fearless. Hadn't he proven that to stupid Dale Corkland just the other day? "You scared?" old zit-faced Corkland had asked him. And Justin had shown him.

At the corner, Justin looked both ways, although he knew there wouldn't be many cars out on a night like this. Then he scanned the hedges along a nearby house, where dappled shadows hung frozen in the branches. Excellent camouflage for a tiger—particularly one of those white, Siberian tigers he'd read about.

He kept a close eye on those hedges as he crossed the street. Snow swelled up around his boots and sucked at his feet, making it impossible to run should a tiger spring from behind the mailbox on the far corner. He stopped before he reached that mailbox, listening for the low blowing sound that tigers sometimes make as they lie in ambush. But all he heard was the rasping of his own breath ("You scared?") Yes. Tigers were nothing to be trifled with. They were as dangerous as the ice on Shepherd's Pond.

Justin had stared at that ice, thinking about the warm weather they'd had the past week. Then he had looked up at Dale Corkland's face, three years older than his and sporting a gala display of acne. "You scared?" And Justin had shown him.

But that was then and this was now; and weren't tigers more merciless than ice? Oh, yes indeed.

Justin gave himself a good mental shaking. He tried to summon those things his father had told him at other times when this tiger-fear had come upon him. (Don't he such a baby.) At night, when he would awaken screaming after a tiger nightmare. (It was only a dream.) Or when he felt certain that a tiger was lurking about the basement. (There are no tigers in the city. You only find tigers in the zoo.)

Wrapping himself snug in these assurances, Justin tramped past the brick retaining wall at the corner of State and Sixteenth without so much as a glance toward the spidery line of poplars where a tiger might be hiding. He rounded the corner and marched on. Heck, he had walked this way dozens of times. Hundreds, maybe.

But tonight the usually comfortable features seemed alien and warped out of reality under the snow, and finding himself in this strange white landscape, Justin suddenly felt the tiger-fear return. It bobbed up and down within him until he could almost feel the tiger's nearness, so close that the hot jungle breath seemed to huff against his cheek.

He was half-way down the block when he saw a shadow slip effortlessly from behind the house two doors up. It seemed to glide dream-like across the snow, then disappear behind a car parked in the driveway. It was just a shadow, but before it had vanished, Justin thought he caught a hint of striping.

There are no tigers in the city.

Justin watched and waited—waited for whatever it was to show itself. He even considered turning hack, rerouting around Rush Street, but that would put *it* behind him.

Come on, he scolded himself. You only find tigers in India. Or the zoo. *Or behind parked cars.* Nonsense. Tigers don't stalk kids from behind parked cars in the middle of an American city. Only little kids let themselves be scared by shadows in the night. Not one of the Shot Brothers. Not a kid who had dared the ice on Shepherd's Pond. Not a kid who was only two years away from attending Rathburn Junior High, where you get to keep your stuff in your own locker and change classrooms every hour and eat your lunch out on the bleachers. Kids at Rathburn didn't go whimpering and whining because they saw a shadow in the snow—probably thrown by a branch moving in the wind.

But there is no wind tonight.

Justin swallowed hard, then started forward. He walked slowly, never shifting his gaze from the tail light of that parked car. If only he could see around it without getting any nearer. If something were crouching back there, it would be on him before he could cover the first five feet. And then…

…teeth and claws, tearing and slashing.

You scared?

You bet.

When he had drawn even with the driveway across the street, Justin stopped. Two more steps, maybe three, and he would see if his father and the kids at Rathburn Junior were right, or if tigers do indeed lie in wait on winter streets. Of course, there was still time to turn back.

Perhaps it was the idea of turning back that propelled him forward. If he were to retrace his steps, he would never know; but if he looked and saw no tiger behind that car, then the tiger-fear would be banished, and he wouldn't see them anywhere. Not in bushes. Not behind trees. Not between houses. Just three steps, and he could lay tigers to rest forever.

Justin took those three steps the way he had walked out onto the ice on Shepherd's pond. Old zit-faced Corkland had dared him, and he had faced it.

One—two—three.

He turned and looked.

Nothing. Nothing behind that car but an old coaster wagon lying on its side. No tigers. No lions, bears, werewolves, or boogie-men. Just an old wagon. His father had been right all along.

He covered the last block and a half with steps as light and carefree as those of a June day, when the air smelled of new-mown grass and the sun baked your skin brown. But, of course, it wasn't June, and as he sprinted up his porch steps Justin realized that he had reached home without a moment to spare. He could scarcely see his breath at all. Much longer out in the icy cold and he thought his lungs might have frozen solid.

As he stepped into the familiar warmth of his own house, he heard voices coming from the living room. It sounded as though his folks were having a party, although the voices seemed rather subdued—much the way they sounded on bridge nights when the evenings began quietly, but noisied up as the hours grew old.

Justin tip-toed down the hall, thinking it wise not to interrupt. And as he passed the living room, he caught a snatch of conversation. It was a man speaking, "…bound to happen eventually. They should have put up a fence years ago. I've a good mind to…"

"Oh, for God's sake, Gordon," a woman said. (It sounded like Aunt Phyllis.) "This isn't the time."

That was all he heard before hurrying to his room.

When he flipped on the light, he was greeted by all the treasures which reflected his short life in intimate detail. The Darth Vadar poster, the Packers pennant, the Spitfire on his dresser, the bedspread decorated in railroad logos.

And one new addition, sitting in the corner on great feline haunches.

For the briefest instant, Justin felt the urge to run—to flee into the living room and hurl himself into his mother's arms, as he had done so many times in the past. But as he stared transfixed into the tiger's huge, emerald eyes, he felt the fear slipping from him like some like dark mantle, to be replaced by the soft and gentle cloak of understanding.

"It's time to go, isn't it?" he said in a voice that was low, but unwavering.

The tiger's eyes remained impassive, as deep and silent as green forest pools. Warm pools that never froze over, the way Shepherd's Pond did.

In his mind, Justin heard again the pistol crack of ice giving way beneath him, and he felt the chill water closing over his head. It really hadn't hurt that much, not the way he would have thought. Not much pain, just a moment of remorse when he realized he wouldn't be seeing his folks anymore—or Steve...

...had it all been a dream, this last wonderful evening together with Steve? Would Steve even remember?

Justin looked at the tiger, searching its peaceful face for the answer; but those fathomless eyes kept their secrets.

"Did you follow me tonight?" Justin asked.

Whiskers twitched as the tiger's muzzle wrinkled into a slight grin.

"Yes," Justin said softly. "I thought it was you. You've been following me all my life, haven't you?" He turned to close his bedroom door, and when he turned back, the tiger was crouching to spring.

THE DWELLER IN HIGH PLACES

Susanna Clarke

Susanna Clarke lives in the medieval city of Cambridge, England, and is the author of the multi-awardiwinning, bestselling novel about English magic, *Jonathan Strange & Mr Norrell*. She also has written a series of short stories about magic, set in seventeenth- and early nineteenth-century England, most of them collected in *The Ladies of Grace Adieu and Other Stories*.

"The Dweller in High Places" is about a young girl who makes an unlikely friend in the attic of her boarding school. The story was originally produced for the BBC. This is its first print appearance.

To begin with then, my name is Lucy Manners and I am twelve years old. Last summer my older sister, Tiz, married Mr. Rainworth. It was a sad change for me because Tiz and I used always to be together. My brother, Gowland, is with Lord Wellington in Spain, fighting the French. So when January came Papa said he was tired of my long face and he sent me to school to Mrs. Hackett's in Great-Titchfield-Street.

On the first day two girls approached me. I was pleased, thinking to make new friends, but I soon discovered that that was not their intention. Instead they called me skin-and-bones, said that my muslin was frayed and my shoes were old-fashioned. There was no end to my faults according to Emmeline Twist and Amelia Froggett, and not content with calling me names, they tried to make me afraid with silly stories about ghosts.

"Oh! Have you not heard?" said Emmeline, "The school is haunted by a mad teacher who was turned out of her place by Mrs. Hackett!"

"She lives in one of the attics," added Amelia. "Sometimes you can hear her speaking in foreign languages and sometimes she will call to you down the chimney."

"And," said Emmeline with great satisfaction, "those girls who she speaks to die before the week is out!"

"I do not believe it," I said. "Who has died? No one at all I expect."

One bleak and windy Thursday Mrs. Hackett gave Emmeline and Amelia and me a long list of German verbs to learn. I had no wish to sit with them, so I climbed up to the top of the house, to a room beneath the attic. I had not been there long when I heard a noise from overhead—a soft, irregular thumping. I barely had time to consider whether or not I was frightened when a starling tumbled down the chimney and began to fly about the room, battering itself against the walls.

A voice hissed down the chimney. "Englishman! Englishman! My bird has flown down! Fetch it up if you please!"

I thought this a little rude. Nevertheless I called politely up the chimney, "I beg your pardon, ma'am, but what do you want it for?"

"Foolish question!" cried the unknown lady. "To eat it of course!"

I opened the window in the hopes that the bird would fly out. Then I ran out of the room and up to the attic. It was very dim, with just one skylight that let in the wind and the rain. It smelt of dead things. Something crunched beneath my foot; I looked down and saw that there were little bones, as of birds and mice, scattered over the floor. A dark shape was moving in the dimness. I could not at first make it out, but then I saw a woman's face and my heart fell to the bottom of my stomach. *Her face was at the wrong end of her.* It was at the bottom of the dark shape and her chin was no more than an inch or two from the floorboards.

I thought I would faint.

Suddenly she stepped into the shaft of gloomy light and I saw that she was not a woman at all. She was a lioness for the most part. She had besides, a pair of bedraggled wings and a sweet, but anxious face. Her human breasts were modestly covered with a ragged blue shawl and her hair had been put into curl papers long ago and never taken out; it was full of knots and tangles. She was altogether such a wretched sight I could not help but pity her from my heart.

We stared at one another. Her lion's tail went from side to side thoughtfully.

"I beg your pardon, ma'am," I said, "but are you not a sphinx?"

"No," she said, airily. "I am *the* Sphinx. Egyptian sphinxes are many, but the Greek Sphinx is only one."

"Oh!"

There was a little silence.

"I wonder, ma'am," I began timidly, "if I might comb your hair for you? It certainly needs it and it is a thing I love to do."

She gave a haughty little nod.

So I pulled a comb from my pocket and began. Her hair was exactly the sort I liked best—a soft, golden colour with a natural curl.

"Good maids are hard to come by," I said. "The same for monsters as for human ladies, I suppose."

"Monsters!" she cried, indignantly. "Who do call you a monster?"

"I beg your pardon, but you have the body of a lion and the face and breast of a woman. And…"

"What nonsense you talk! The world is full of monsters, of which you are certainly one—a fact I would usually be too polite to mention, but you drive me to it. A lion is a sphinx's body with a cat's head on top—which is a very horrid thing. Man is worse. In man the beautiful head and breast of a sphinx are defiled by the arms of a nasty ape and legs like a forked parsnip." She shuddered. "Ughhh!"

There was a whirr of wings in the darkness. Her head whipped round.

"Bird," she said. "Starling. They are not a bit kind. They call me spiteful names."

"Oh!" said I. "I know what you mean. There are two ignorant, ill-bred girls here who do the same to me."

"Bite them in two," she suggested.

"I do not think Mrs. Hackett would like it if I did that and, anyway, my mouth does not open so far."

"Mine does," she said with much satisfaction.

Despite her quarrelsome nature we became friends that day and whenever Mrs. Hackett set me work to do by myself, I would run up to the top of the house and climb out of the skylight on to the roof and there we would sit companionably together. She loved to be in high places looking down at everything. If ladies or gentlemen rode along Great-Titchfield-Street on horseback, she would peer over the parapet and mutter, "Centaurs. Nasty creatures."

One day as I was combing her hair, I said, "How did it happen, Sphinx, that you came to London?"

"Oh, that is easily told. I came in a ship attended by handsome young mariners. It was all arranged by a Frenchman called M'sieur Fauvel. You see, Lucy, M'sieur Fauvel lives in Athens and it is his task to purchase the most beautiful Greek carvings and sculptures and send them back to France. Imagine his dismay when he discovered that a Scottish lady and gentleman, Lord and Lady Elgin, had arrived in Athens for the same purpose! Furthermore Lady Elgin was a great favourite of the Sultan of Turkey (who governs Athens). M'sieur Fauvel was obliged to watch as great treasures (which ought in his opinion to have adorned Paris) were shipped away to his enemies in London. So he came to me and made me a present of the blue knitted shawl and begged me on his knees to come to London to persecute its citizens. Which, of course, I was glad to do."

"Good God!" I exclaimed. "But how will you do that?"

"I will ask them riddles and when they cannot answer I will strangle them."

"Oh! Don't!" I cried. "Please don't. I mean why should you? It is not as if M'sieur Fauvel's present was particularly nice. I can bring you a much prettier shawl than that shabby old blue thing."

"It is not a matter of presents," she said with dignity. "I am the Throttler. I am the Questioner. I am the Guardian of Dark Doors. I am the Dweller in High Places. I am a Blight upon Man."

"Well, if you say so, dear. It really doesn't sound very nice. But if I remember the tale of Oedipus correctly, he guessed the answer to your riddle and you were obliged to throw yourself down and dash yourself to pieces."

The Sphinx yawned. "Yes. Oedipus did claim that, did he not?"

"When will you begin? In London, I mean?"

"Any day now," she said and began to lick her paw.

Privately I did not think she was quite so industrious as M'sieur Fauvel had hoped when he chartered his ship.

She had no great opinion of Mrs. Hackett's methods of teaching. "I do not think you are learning anything useful, Lucy. Fortunately I know many wise teachers. My brother Cerberus—he who guards Hell—will fetch up dead people to tell you all their secrets. And then there is Lamia—a delightful girl with the most elegant green-scaled tail! Oh, you will dote upon her! She will show you how to pluck your eyes out of their sockets and put them back in again!"

She never explained to me why she thought this would be useful.

One day in late February when it was near to sunset, I said, "Sphinx dear, you know that I am very fond of you and that I wish you would stay in London. But if you continue in your plan to ask the citizens riddles, then I think you must ask me first and let me save London if I can."

"You know that if you give a wrong answer then I must begin by strangling *you*," she said.

"Yes."

"Do you think you are so much cleverer than the rest of London?"

"No, indeed! I don't think I am clever at all. But I know you, Sphinx, and perhaps that will help."

"Very well."

My heart thumped like anything. She was silent so long that I grew even more nervous and could not help saying, "Is it going to be the one about the creature that goes upon four legs in the morning, and two legs at noon and three legs in the evening, because if so…"

"Certainly not! No, I have it. Ready?"

"Yes, Sphinx dear."

"My first is a person that is praised to the skies,
But I shall not praise him for I hate his lies.
My second means comfort for travellers who weary
Of roads harsh and stony, a journey so dreary.
But now enters Lucy her city to save,
With a smile that is cheerful and a heart that is brave."

I thought for a moment.

"Well," I said. "Someone that is praised to the skies is a hero. And I know how much you hate heroes because they always try to make themselves seem important by exaggerating their exploits. And, by the bye, Sphinx, did I ever tell you, that the French Emperor, Napoleon Bonaparte, is considered to be very heroic? And so I think it is a little contradictory of you, dear, to be doing his work for him. As for the second part, well, a place that gives comfort to travellers is an inn." I began to cry—I could not help it. "And so put together they make 'heroine'. And it really is kind of you to say that I am one. And I am really very, very sorry to make you dash yourself into pieces."

The Sphinx smiled. "Clever girl," she said, and then gave my face a lick with a pointed pink tongue—which I suppose must be a Sphinx's kiss.

And then she leapt off the parapet, down, down to Great-Titchfield-Street.

And, oh!, what nonsense that old story of Oedipus is! For the Greek Sphinx has eagle's wings and how could a winged creature fall to her death?

Up, up she rose again with slow beats. London was sombre and dark beneath her, like a city of graves and mysterious spirits—which sounds rather dreadful, I know, but I was glad of it, for it was the very thing to please her. The last I saw of her she was above the silver ribbon of the Thames turning east towards Greece; and all the red-and-gold glory of the sunset was reflected upon her, the Dweller in High Places.

HEALING BENJAMIN

Dennis Danvers

Dennis Danvers has published seven novels, including *New York Times* notables *Circuit of Heaven* and *The Watch*, and near-future mystery *The Bright Spot* (writing as Robert Sydney). Recent short fiction appears in *Strange Horizons*, *Orson Scot Card's Intergalactic Medicine Show*, *Lady Churchill's Rosebud Wristlet*, *Space and Time* and *The Magazine of Fantasy & Science Fiction*.

According to the author, "Healing Benjamin" has a dual inspiration: A much-beloved cat named Nyneve, who he had raised from kitten-hood to near nineteen years old. And he wrote this story while facing the inevitable decision of having to put down his aged dog, Alice, who was suffering from serious arthritis at fifteen. Danvers says, "I get deeply attached to animals, and their short life spans can make that painful, but these two animals I count among the most treasured friends in my life. Writing 'Healing Benjamin' helped me put that pain out there and deal with it with both laughter and tears."

> There is something in the unselfish and self-sacrificing love of a brute, which goes directly to the heart of him who has had frequent occasion to test the paltry friendship and gossamer fidelity of mere *Man*.
>
> —Edgar Allan Poe, "The Black Cat"

I got the healing touch when I was 16 years old kneeling over my dying cat Benjamin in my bedroom. He was trying to crawl under the bed to die, but I wouldn't let him, hauling him out and wrapping my body around him, my forehead pressed against his. He was a year older than me. He'd been there my whole life. I couldn't imagine life without him. He stopped breathing, his heart stopped, and I prayed for him, though I rarely prayed then, and I never pray now, squeezing him, imprinting my will on him, picturing him raised from the dead, alive and well. I didn't know what else to do, sobbing, absolutely heartbroken, torturing myself with Joan Baez singing "Old Blue" on the stereo:

…Old Blue died and he died so hard
Shook the ground in my backyard
Dug his grave with a silver spade
Lowered him down with links of chain
Every link I did call his name
Here Blue, you good dog you
Here Blue, I'm a-coming there too!

Benjamin stirred under my hands, his heart beating hard and steady against my palm. I released him, and he rose and walked to the door, his tail erect. He wanted to go out. An hour later, he wanted back in, and he was hungry. He looked good. He looked real good.

I took him to a vet after his healing to get him checked out. I didn't take him to his regular vet, Dr. Diderada, who Ben had been going to since he was a kitten, figuring he'd never believe this was the same half-blind stiff-legged neutered tom living on borrowed time he'd basically given up on a week before. I told this new vet Ben was a stray I was adopting, and he guessed him to be about four, in perfect health. All the vets over the years guessed him to be about four, in perfect health. That's 28 in cat years, not a bad year for me. Benjamin seemingly picked an age he liked and stuck with it. I, meanwhile, kept getting older. I quit taking him to the vet years ago, having exhausted all the convenient ones. Ben was over it, and I couldn't see spending the money to be reassured semiannually that my cat was immortal. He never even had an ear mite or a flea, as if even the insect world knew he was operating under a special dispensation.

Thirty years later, I was 46, and I still had Benjamin. I'll do the math for you. He was 47. That's 329 in cat years. Even if you gave him nine lives, that made each one more than 36 years. No. Benjamin was not a normal cat.

Back when Ben was 17, my parents readily believed Dr. Diderada had resurrected him with some good vitamin supplements. They were wish-upon-a-star, somewhere-over-the-rainbow kind of people, but even they wouldn't believe a 47-year-old cat. After I left home, I didn't see them on my own turf very often, but I always lied and said Ben was a new cat. They thought I was odd for naming every cat Benjamin, but they already knew I was odd—I was their son. It helped that Ben was a fairly generic gray tabby with white boots and a nondescript meow. My ex-wife Penny knew Ben for seven years, living with him for five, but she never noticed he never aged. She wasn't a cat person. She wasn't any kind of animal person I ever discovered. She liked watching monkeys in the monkey house, but that's not the same, is it? I know it sounds weird, but that's one of the reasons we broke up. I just couldn't be with somebody who didn't like animals. When it came down to it, she didn't like people all that much. Which makes sense—people are animals, smart worrisome animals, but still animals.

Anyway, she peacefully coexisted with Ben, and he was never an issue. I never dated anyone else more than a year or so, and nobody who spent much time around Ben. Then at 46, I started going out with Shannon. That didn't last long—the just going out. Our third date started Friday at four—she took off work an hour early—and ended Tuesday at noon. I told Benjamin it was the closest to a resurrection I'd experienced in my life, and maybe it would help me understand him better. He pointed out, however, that death was a necessary precondition of resurrection. He played dead and sprang back to life, a favorite trick of his, flicking his smartass tail. I've always talked to Ben. He hasn't always answered.

For some time, Shannon and I had been practically living together, shuttling back and forth between our houses, but she preferred my place because Benjamin lived there. Benny Boy, as she called him. If he'd been a man, I would've been insanely jealous. To say they hit it off is to say Juliet was sort of into Romeo. He was equally passionate about her.

This was all good. She loved me too, Benny Boy's lifelong companion and confidante, the cleaner of the cat box, the keeper of the can opener, not to mention healer extraordinaire. But then she started asking questions. "Isn't he due for a checkup? Shots or something?"

I made the mistake of just putting her off, and then she saw a little reminder card from one of Benny Boy's many vets in my mail, this one saying he was at least eight years overdue on just about everything. So she called and made an appointment. That's kind of how Shannon was, which was one of the many things I liked about her, except insofar as it pertained to Benjamin, because I'd always figured that sooner or later reality was going to catch up with me. It was like I made a deal all those years ago that I couldn't handle my cat dying right then, but Some Day there'd be no choice, and it would hurt even worse when it finally came. But somehow, if I could just keep his death and persistent life a secret, nothing had to change.

"How old is he?" Shannon asked when they met. About four, I said, never anticipating I'd be caught in my convenient lie. So how could he be eight years behind in his shots? I feared every step I took down this road with Shannon meant Some Day was coming soon. But I couldn't stop myself. I couldn't stop her. Benjamin, closed up in his carrier, in his stoic, dignified way, neither stopped nor started, but was carried along by the tide of events—and by his carrier of course—to the vet.

Ben enjoyed crowded veterinary waiting rooms, the more crowded the better. He delighted in the spectacle. This day, there was a special treat, a harlequin Great Dane lurching about out of control, his suited keeper helpless to stop him from sticking his great nose in the random crotch, body-blocking anyone coming in the door, terrifying every animal in the place—and I'm including humans as animals—except Ben who watched from inside his carrier, purring, purring, the deep rumbling purr I know as laughter. Ben enjoyed watching foolishness. He saw a lot of it at his age.

"He's so calm," Shannon marveled, peering inside his carrier, stroking his untroubled brow with her finger, keeping a wary eye on the Dane. "Is he always this calm?"

"Oh yes," I reassured her, and then we were next, and she wanted to go in too, and how could I refuse?

After a lengthy examination, the vet, a kind, fatherly gentleman, maybe a decade older than Ben chronologically, but a mere child in cat years, broached the subject cautiously. He looked over the end of his reading glasses, up from Ben's near-empty record of perfect health. "According to our records, I last examined Benjamin 12 years ago?"

I couldn't lie, not with Shannon beside us scratching Ben's head with both hands the way he likes, waiting for my answer. "Yes."

"Which makes Ben"—he looked back at the record— "19?" He couldn't quite keep the incredulity out of his gentlemanly voice. Shannon's hands froze on Ben's noble head. All eyes were on me. Even Ben's.

Ben and I had liked this guy, so we stuck with him for three years. The math checked out. He was the last. Ben was 35, ready to do without vets—the shots and the thermometer up his ass anyway. He found the rest interesting. At least I wasn't dealing with Ben's first vet. No bluff possible there. "That's right," I said.

"Would—Would you mind leaving Ben for a few tests? An hour or so? No charge, of course."

Ben gave me an unmistakable look. *No fucking way* is a precise translation. "I'm afraid not," I said.

"Why not?" Shannon asked. She'd done a little math of her own. In her reality, Ben was six, tops, and of course, he looked four, as always.

"Nothing's wrong with him, right?" I asked the vet.

He shook his head no. "Quite the opposite. He's the healthiest cat I'll see this year. This *is* the same cat?"

I considered lying, but couldn't imagine explaining the lie to Shannon in some way that wouldn't sound sick or pathetic. "Yes. Same cat."

"He's the healthiest 19-year-old cat I've ever seen—and we don't see that many. There aren't even any tartar deposits on his teeth." He bared Ben's teeth, pointing with a ball point pen at the gleaming fangs, an indignity Ben graciously endured.

"I know. I think he's had enough for one day." Ben chimed in with a low moan, that if you know anything about cats means his patience is spent, and you're in immediate peril from the aforementioned fangs and the hooked razors that sprout from each paw on demand, the envy of every badass who ever lived. The vet got the message immediately, putting him back in the carrier with a fistful of treats.

I wasn't looking forward to the ride home. No well-timed moan was going to get me out of this one.

There was a moment, when Shannon was already in the car and I was about to put Ben in the backseat, when we were alone. I put his carrier on the roof of the car and pretended I was having trouble finding my keys, though I didn't think Shannon was paying any attention to us. She was staring out the windshield with a determined look on her face. Ben and I spoke in low tones through the bars of his carrier door, our faces inches apart. The traffic flowed by behind me, ignoring me and my cat.

"What do I do?" I asked. "She'll never believe you're 19."

"Tell her my real age," he said.

"You think?"

"I know."

"But I can't prove you're 47. She'll never believe me."

"Proof doesn't matter. You'll see. She senses I'm no ordinary cat. We have a special bond."

"Oh please. Does she sense you're a manipulative little eunuch?"

"For a cat, I'm not so little." He laughed at his own joke. Cat humor, very sly.

I put him in the middle of the backseat, so he could see out the front like he likes, got in, immediately started the car, and put it in gear.

"How can Ben be *19*?" Shannon asked.

We were parallel parked, my eyes glued to the side mirror, waiting for a break in the traffic. Following Ben's advice—I'd never known him to be wrong—I told her. "He's not," I began, "he's 47." I pulled into traffic.

There were certain advantages to telling the tale while driving. I wasn't expected to make eye contact; a brisk, even telegraphic style was perfectly acceptable; and she wasn't inclined to interrupt, argue, or question while I was waiting to make a tricky left turn across a steady torrent of oncoming traffic. The downside was I didn't have a clue how she was taking it until we were back at my place, and I turned off the engine and looked over at her. You might think she would've refused to believe me, end of story, but Shannon wasn't like that. Neither was she some wacko flake who believed any madness I spouted just because she loved me.

"Okay," she said. "I want to figure this thing out." She turned to Ben and looked at him through the bars. *Has Benny Boy been keeping secrets from his Shannon?* He looked right back. Hell. What did I know? Maybe they did have a special bond.

It was early yet, and Shannon had me dig out Ben's vet records, and while I was making breakfast, she called every vet he'd ever been to. The second one was dead and gone, the third seemed to have left town. She made appointments with the rest, booking Ben solid for the day. I wondered if he figured on this when he told me to tell her the truth. I certainly hadn't. I checked my credit card balance, and we were off.

I got pretty good at telling the story economically. I left out any mention of prayer as such—there were no priests on our itinerary, only men of science. It was amazing how many incredulous vets remembered Ben. It was the no tartar thing that seemed to impress them most. All of them, however, dismissed immediately the possibility of a 47-year-old cat and denied there was any way he could be the *same* cat despite the resemblance. One guy got pissed off, like I had something to gain by paying an exorbitant fee for ten minutes of his time to tell him a story I knew he'd never believe. Was he an idiot? Couldn't he see I was doing it for love? Most of the vets were nice, cutting looks at Shannon—*Are you crazy too? Shouldn't you be getting him help?* Shannon just wanted the facts. She examined the records of Ben's perfect checkups with care, except the pissed-off guy's; he threw us out before she got the chance.

Ben's first and favorite vet, Dr. Diderada, interestingly enough, seemed to come closest to believing my story. He was last on Shannon's itinerary. He probably should've retired years earlier. He had a distracted, dreamy quality, like an old cat. He gave us pretty much the same lecture the others had—why it was impossible for a cat to be 47—and certainly not one in Ben's condition. But this time there was something quixotic about the narrative, some sense that among all the dead and dying cats there *might* be one who lived forever and never grew old, but of course, you couldn't expect a scientific professional to speak openly of such a creature.

He bent down, looking Ben in the eye, scratching Ben's trembling chin with his index finger, in a beckoning motion, as if he hoped to lure the true cat out into the open. "Some cats are special, aren't they Benjamin? The world is their oyster." The combination of the chin scratch and the mention of oysters—one of Ben's favorites, especially fried—proved irresistibly seductive, and a resonant rumble issued forth from deep inside him so intense it made the gleaming examining table hum like a struck tuning fork, and both Diderada and Ben smiled like the Buddha. The walls behind them were plastered with lurid posters of cat anatomy, the color of rare roast beef. A plastic cat skeleton on a stand smiled too.

Shannon turned away, whispering, "I'll wait in the car," and hurried out.

"Lovely woman," Diderada said.

Last stop on Shannon's fact-finding expedition was a visit to my folks, the only witnesses to Ben's resurrection I knew how to contact. Any angels who may or may not have been in attendance had steadfastly refused to reveal themselves over the years, and my official policy toward them was blissful ignorance. I managed a cranky ignorance most of the time. I never achieved blissful, though I avoided, for the most part, totally pissed off. Still no angels, no answers. I loved living with Ben, but I didn't like living with an unfathomable enigma.

Mom and Dad loved Shannon, of course, and didn't mind at all that she'd called that morning to invite us to dinner. They were also quite delighted to see Benjamin. After their last cat Angelina died at 16—toothless, blind, and with daily IVs—they'd decided to forego cats indefinitely, but they missed having a feline presence about the house.

As I mentioned before, my parents weren't into grappling with reality. They slept under a pyramid and wanted to believe that breathing exercises and dietary supplements and the well-placed crystal would keep them forever young, though down deep they knew better. As much as they liked to flirt with the flaky, they proved immediately resistant to the notion that *this* Benjamin was the same cat who moved out almost 30 years previously. Metaphorically, spiritually, teleported, time-warped, reincarnated, alien-abducted, cloned, whatever the hell, *maybe*; but not literally the *same* cat living his life ever since, one day at a time, a few months past his 47th birthday. That would be crazy.

Ben, who'd had a half-dozen thermometers shoved up his ass already that day, was not overly invested in the proceedings until dessert. He rubbed up against Mom's legs while she was whipping cream, and when she was done, he stood on his hind legs, his forepaws extended in supplication, and "danced" (an awkward stumbling turn from the usually graceful Ben) and she gave him the beaters. I pointed out they used to go through this identical ritual when I was a kid—Ben got *both* damn beaters then too—but Mom insisted it didn't prove anything, that any cat would do the same.

Shannon maintained an aloof silence during all of this, only asking an occasional question, clarifying some detail, never venturing an opinion herself. Over dessert, Mom suggested a therapist she knew. "I went," Dad said. "I had suicidal thoughts." He popped a strawberry in his mouth. "Not anymore!"

He told us about his "crisis"—which as far as I could tell consisted of realizing that we all grow old and die. He acted like this would be news to us young people, though he was the one who said, "You're only as old as you feel, right?" Wrong. Clearly the man had forgotten Angelina. Dad now took antidepressants to make him feel good, guzzled various mood-altering teas Mom bought from websites, and he felt like a new man. I kind of missed the days Dad smoked pot in the basement and thought I didn't know, while I experimented widely. I'd often speculated that some bizarre conjunction of chemicals in my body expressed in my breath and tears might have affected Ben in some inexplicable way to resurrect him. Might as well believe in fairy dust. God's will? Divine Plan? Come *on*. He's a cat. And if he had a mission on this earth other than enjoying himself with the least possible bother, God failed to inform him of it. *Go forth and lick both beaters, my chosen one.* I didn't think so.

"Maybe you're supposed to be figuring it out for me, Jeffrey," Ben said once. "You're the one who cares about this religious crap." It was true, but I couldn't figure it out. What possible use could God have for a cat who had so little use for Him? I've always wanted to believe but never quite pulled it off except for transitory spasms of awe—what most people call agnosticism. If Ben made God more likely, he also made it more likely that He's totally batshit nuts. Give me agnosticism any day. And if I wanted something to believe in, my folks always had something new on offer. This time it was some mini-messianic therapist with a nimble prescription pad. My folks were almost becoming conventional.

Shannon was no more interested in hearing about Dad's rebirth than I was, so we didn't linger after dessert. At the door, Mom put the therapist's number in my shirt pocket and gave it a little pat. I couldn't begin to describe how swell that felt at my age.

Shannon asked one more time, holding him up as Exhibit A, snoozing in his carrier, his face and forepaws sodden from the post-whipped-cream cleaning he'd given himself, "But this does look *exactly* like the Benjamin you remember, right?"

"Yes, dear," Mom said. "But it can't be, can it?" She gave my shirt pocket another pat to let Shannon know she held her responsible for getting her crazy son to a therapist as soon as possible. I would sooner have gone to Dr. Diderada than any therapist my parents would've recommended.

Shannon was silent all the way home to my place, staring out the window at the night streets like she was a stranger in town feeling homesick. Every once in a while something would snag her vision, and she'd turn and follow it like she'd never seen it before.

I could only imagine what was going through her mind. How did you keep sleeping with a guy who thinks his cat is immortal? How did you let him rub your feet, make you breakfast, adore you, write you bad poetry, without doing something once the miraculous cat was out of the bag? Flee, fix it, lock me up, *something*. She loved me, loved my cat, even claimed to like my parents. But did she sign on for me being flat-out crazy? I couldn't imagine so.

I halfway expected her to say she was going to get in her car and drive home, sleep at her place tonight, think things over, dump me tomorrow. Not Shannon.

When we were inside with Ben, she kicked off her shoes, pulled him out of his carrier, and cradled him in her arms, nuzzling his face. She put her whole body into it. It was kind of erotic, actually. "Benny Boy, I wish you could talk," she said. He just purred like there might be something to this only-as-old-as-you-feel thing. Then she set him down and watched adoringly as he sauntered down the hall to the bed where he slept every night and half the day.

She poured herself a glass of wine. "Want one?"

"Sure."

She poured. A lot. She drank. "I believe you," she said. "I can't see you having some weird serial cat fetish. Showing up at all those different vets with different cats over a twenty year period is just too strange—and for what? So you could convince me now? It has to be the same cat. It has to be Ben. It's the only thing that makes any sense. Dr. Diderada thought so. Don't you think?"

I couldn't believe Ben was right again. I shook my head in wonder. "I did. He said he didn't, but there was something… It was like no time had passed. I was five, I think, the first time I remember seeing Diderada with Ben. He gave me a lollipop when he gave Ben his treat, but Mom wouldn't let me eat it. Sugar was poison."

"I bet you were adorable."

"I was afraid you'd think I was crazy. *I'd* think I was crazy if I hadn't been there."

She laughed, shaking her head. "It was a miracle. A blessing." She looked me in the eye. "Have you ever tried— You know—"

"No. No way. Once was enough. Once has been more than sufficiently weird enough. I couldn't deal with it. At first I tried to convince myself it wasn't Ben who came back that night, but even if an identical cat who acted just like him showed up then, he'd still be 30—210 in cat years."

She made a face, unhooked her bra, and pulled it out her sleeve. She hung it on a chair back. "I thought they changed that. That because of medical advances, it's more like five to one."

"150 then. Looks 20. What's the difference? He doesn't age. I can't explain it."

"So he's just stayed exactly the same all these years?"

"Not exactly. He looks the same, but he changes, experiences new things, learns…" I almost said evolves, but I stopped myself. I'd said too much already.

"Like what?" She poured more wine for herself. I hadn't touched mine.

"Uh. Just things in general."

"Give me an example. One thing he does now he didn't do when he was 17."

There were dozens of simple things I could've recounted, but I couldn't think of a single one of them. They were all blotted out by the enormous eclipsing mass of what I didn't want to say: *He talks.* Would I then go on to explain he's fluent in English, speaking softly, in a half-whisper, like a breathy purr. Not really built for speech, it took him awhile to perfect his technique. He understood what I said long before he talked back.

Would I go on to explain he reads voluminously, has a passion for discussing politics, and expresses his political opinions in unique ways, like pissing and shitting on every Hummer foolish enough to park on our block.

Should I then tell her the first time he met her he told me, "She's the one for you, Jeffrey"? That would've been way too Son of Sam, don't you think? Ben suggested from the beginning, and I'd always agreed with him, that any mention of his linguistic abilities to anyone would be a very bad idea, and he'd never spoken clearly in the presence of others except for a stray word or two, easily explained away as a fluke. He was convinced if word ever got out he could talk, he'd be jailed for all eternity or until they finally carved him up to discover his secrets. He's always had a flair for the melodramatic, but I'm afraid he was right on this one. But how could I not tell her? At that moment, Ben walked back into the kitchen. He gave me the look, the same look he gave me when Dr. Whatsit who started all this with his frigging reminder card wanted to do tests.

"He tells me when his box needs changing," I offered. "He has a—a special meow."

She picked up Ben and cuddled with him. "Is that right, Benny Boy? To what do we owe the honor of your company?" She looked over his purring head at me. "I just realized. You've lived your *whole life* with him." I wasn't sure what all she meant by that, or what it might mean to her, nor did she care to elaborate. "I'm going to bed now." I followed her into the bedroom. She put Ben in his usual place, stepped out of her jeans and left them lying on the floor, pulled back the covers and crawled into bed beside him. She was asleep in moments, the two of them breathing in unison.

I got into bed on Ben's other side.

When I turned off the light, he scolded me in a soft sing-song, "You almost *told* her."

"Oh fuck yourself, Ben."

"Neutered, re-mem-berrrr?" He chuckled softly, enjoying his own humor, enjoying his endless life.

I lay awake listening to them snore together like an old married couple, wondering how these revelations were going to affect our lives, then drifted off. I dreamed Shannon was in a terrible accident, and I healed her, but when she woke up, she no longer spoke, not a word, and she blamed me. You could see it in her eyes, lonely and furious and afraid.

In the morning, Shannon came right to the point. "Jeffrey," she said. "Would you help Aubrey?"

Ben, returning from a crunching good time at the cat food bowl, jumped onto the sofa, and flicked his tail—*Careful*.

Shannon's younger brother Aubrey was in a car wreck five years earlier at the conclusion of a high-speed chase involving drugs—both in his person and in the trunk of the car—and he'd been in a persistent coma ever since. Until that moment, he was a mere fact of her existence from before I knew her, like the name of her childhood dog or where she went to high school. She never went to see him. He was as good as dead. There'd be no point. Not until now. Now there'd be a point. "You mean—"

"Heal him. Like you did Benjamin."

"I didn't *do* anything to Benjamin. It was just a weird one-time thing."

"How do you know? You've never tried to do it again. I can't *believe* you've never tried to do it again."

There was a light in her eyes that made me uncomfortable. This wasn't just about Aubrey, who everyone in her family pretty much agreed was an obnoxious little shit whose final, completely typical screw-up was not to have the good sense to die when he had the chance. "Believe it. Listen Shannon, I think this is a really bad idea."

"But this is my brother. You could save him. I know you could."

"Let me think about it, okay? I have to think about it."

"Okay. How long do you need?"

Some counselor once told impatient Shannon it was okay to ask for clear time limits—deadlines—if it would help her wait more patiently. I'd gotten used to it. She was much more patient with a deadline than without. But this was different. I hadn't been able to figure this thing out in 30 years—how it happened, why it happened, how I felt about it, anything at all—and she wanted to know how long I *needed*? Longer than I had obviously. "Tomorrow. Tomorrow night after dinner. I'll cook. I have a Rachael Ray recipe I want to try with that chicken."

"You sure it's still okay? It's been in there a while."

"I just bought it a couple of days ago. It'll be fine."

"You don't think I'm being selfish for asking you to help Aubrey?"

"Not at all. How could asking to help somebody else be selfish?"

"If I wasn't thinking about how it might be hard for you. I don't want you to do anything you don't want to do, Jeffrey. I love you. You know that?"

"Absolutely."

"Okay then. Tomorrow after dinner." She sipped her coffee. "So you watch Rachael Ray every day?"

"She's on when I break for lunch. What can I say? She's hot. You're going to love this chicken."

To tell you the truth, I couldn't remember Rachael Ray's recipe exactly, but it involved some chopped herbs and garlic and olive oil slathered on chicken parts which were then baked. I recalled the close-up of Rachael Ray's hands slathering breasts and thighs. She was always using her hands. I loved it. I'm a whole bird man myself, but I liked the concept. I figured baked was good, so I wouldn't be standing over the stove while we were having this discussion. I didn't expect Shannon to wait until after dinner to bring it up. My tarragon plants looked like they were up to a chicken-size harvest, and I threw in a little white wine, some chopped mushrooms, a dash of nutmeg, some salt, lots of black pepper and crushed garlic, and (of course) extra-virgin olive oil. It made a fine green goop.

I'd decided to say no to Shannon's request that I attempt to resurrect Aubrey. Here was my reasoning: Most important, I suppose, was my gut said no. This was no surprise. It'd been saying no loud and clear for 30 years now—no wavering. But with Shannon's petition, I'd been forced to rationally examine what I thought about it—in other words, to come up with some likely sounding reasons to validate my gut. If your mind doesn't work like that, more power to you, and hurray for rationalism and all of that, but for me reason lives to serve the gut. In this case, it was persuasive as usual.

First, I doubted I could do it. When Ben came back to life, I *really* wanted it to happen. I'd never willed anything so strongly before or since. As for Aubrey, I could *try* to want his resurrection because Shannon did—though she seemed to have gotten along fine without him in the time I'd known her—but it wasn't happening. Deep down, I felt if Aubrey were going to make a move, it should be in the other direction. So if my will and desire had anything to do with whatever process brought Ben back to life, there was little chance of success with Aubrey.

Assuming I was able to bring him back to life, the questions just began. Ben regressed from being a dying seventeen-year-old to (by all appearances) a four-year-old, and had remained unchanged for 30 years and counting. Would Aubrey, who had his accident at 26, find himself a permanent six-year-old? What effect would five years of unconsciousness have had on him? And as Ben pointed out, death is a necessary precondition of resurrection. Technically speaking, Aubrey wasn't dead. He was in that huge gray arena known as, "as good as dead." Even my silly father had casually described himself thus over dessert the previous night—but there's no such thing, is there? A prescription and some psycho-babble away from a cure isn't *dead*. Nothing's as *good* as dead. Dead is unique, no known therapy or cure.

But let's just say, everything were to go perfectly. Aubrey awakens from his deep sleep a new man of sound mental faculties who lives a long fruitful life and dies at a respectable age like the rest of us, a credit to his species, despite his previous sociopathic tendencies, having seen the light or whatever revelation the resurrected are privy to, and has been utterly transformed by the experience. Did I *really* want to be the guy who raised him from the dead? I wouldn't make it out of the hospital before they'd be doing tests on me, driving me out to the cemetery to see what I could really do. No thanks.

I didn't know why Ben came back to life and continued to live. I hadn't a clue. Until I figured that out, that's as far as it went. God might have a plan, in which case I was sure I couldn't do anything to screw it up, lacking any clear instructions otherwise, but if God had no plan, I didn't feel obliged to come up with one other than the status quo: Everyone dies. That's the way things are. Except for Ben.

Would I get a chance to say all this to Shannon after she hears no? Would it matter to her? Would I lose her? That's all I cared about: I just didn't want to lose her. I knew I should care about her brother, but to me he was an extra out of an old movie with Genevieve Bujold. I couldn't bear to lose Shannon, however. As Ben prophesied, she was the one for me. Trouble was, she had just one tiny little favor to ask, and I couldn't do it.

And there she was, coming in the kitchen door with a bottle of wine, a half hour early, as I should've known she would be, and here I was with my hands dripping garlic, olive oil, and tarragon, anointing the chicken inside and out, lost in thought, reasoning and seasoning. If I could only manage to throw the bird in the oven before Shannon rushed straight to The Issue, we could talk while it baked.

She kissed my cheek, careful to avoid my slathered hands, and opened the bottle of wine, giving a half-hearted account of her day. Traffic was lighter than usual, she claimed, to explain her early arrival. I pretended to believe her.

Ben, who'd shown up to observe the preparations the minute I took the chicken out of the fridge, didn't even glance her way. He was seated on a stool, eye level with his share of the bounty, the bag of innards I always gave him—liver, heart, gizzard—laid out on the cutting board awaiting preparation once the bird was in the oven. He liked them sautéed in butter and garlic with a splash of Worces-tershire, devoured them like a lion on the veldt, if the lion had a chef. I kept the neck for making stock. I didn't treat him to such delicacies often. He liked the Chow, he claimed. "I think they put something in it," he said. "It's highly addic-tive. Perhaps some extract of cat nip." Ben's always had a serious nip habit, but we all must have our vices, I suppose.

Shannon poured, laughing at Ben's rapt attention to my labors. She scratched the top of his head, and he lifted it to press against her hand, arched his back to her touch, as her hand glided firmly down his back, but his eyes never left the prize. "I hope you washed your hands," Shannon said. She held my glass to my lips to give me a sip of wine, careful once again to avoid my glistening green hands and the oily bird. "I'll put your glass over here." She set it on the counter out of the way and took the stool next to Ben's. "So have you thought about Aubrey?"

Damn. "Of course. Let me get this in the oven first, okay? Then we can talk."

"Okay." She idly petted Ben a few strokes, growing pensive. She wrapped her hand around his tail, and he slowly pulled it through, like a napkin through a ring. "It must not be yes. If it was yes, you'd just go ahead and tell me."

As I recalled, the deadline was *after* dinner. I didn't count on being elbow deep in dinner when she arrived. "I'm almost done here. I just need to get this stuff off my hands and get the bird in the oven."

"Why won't you do it?"

"Can this wait *five* minutes?"

"I suppose so. I've waited five years. We all have. I just can't believe you won't…"

I body-slammed the chicken on the counter and splattered oil and tarragon everywhere. "Believe it! No! The answer is no! I don't even know I can *do* anything!"

"You've never even tried!" She touched my oily hands.

It was an eerie moment, her ivory hand laid upon mine as if it weren't smeared with goop, oblivious to the globs clinging to her beige silk blouse. I felt like the Swamp Thing. Somebody loved him too, as I recall. I looked into Shannon's eyes, and there it was again. The light. She wanted me to try out my powers more than she wanted to save her brother. Let's face it. Some brothers aren't missed. But people wait their whole lives to witness a miracle. "Is that what this is all about? You just want to see me *do* it?"

"Certainly not." She almost persuaded herself. She didn't even come close to persuading me. Quite the contrary. It was too much. Years of guilt and mystery and feeling like a freak, and now the love of my life wants me to perform like a dolphin jumping through a hoop—while the saved, the eye of the storm, the miracle kitty, isn't even watching, waiting only to eat some dead bird's heart, cooked the way he likes.

"It is, isn't it? It's driving you crazy. A gen-u-ine miracle. Your boyfriend—with messianic gifts. How cool is that? Here. You want to see?" I scooped up Ben's innards waiting to be sautéed and shoved them deep inside the bird, grasped its oily breasts in both hands and waggled it in her face, then held it aloft, clamping my eyes shut, filling my mind with visions of a perfect chicken pecking celestial corn, or whatever it is they peck, cackling its head off, or maybe that was me. Shannon backed away in terror, knocking over her stool. I squeezed harder, imagined more vividly, willed more forcefully. "Come on you little fucker, live! *Live! Live!*"

And then I felt it, a squirming, writhing wriggling in my hands, and the bird broke loose, erupted from my grasp and hit the countertop, skittering wildly, huge drumsticks pumping footless oiled extremities across Formica. It was amazing how fast the fucking thing could go under the circumstances. Headless, it darted back and forth unpredictably, careening from coffee pot to toaster oven to food processor to bread machine, ricocheting off each white surface with a slimy green stripe. I lunged for it, caught a drumstick, but I couldn't hold on. It hit the floor with a sickening smack and kept running. Then out of nowhere, an airborne Ben landed on its back, digging his claws in deep. Nothing could slip from his grasp. He opened his jaws wide and sank his fangs repeatedly into the bird's thighs and chest, tearing away huge hunks of flesh and swallowing them whole, but still the bird struggled. The battle raged on, with the thing writhing to get free until Ben had consumed all but the bones. He stuck his head deep into the chest cavity, pulled out the still-beating heart, and devoured it in one bite.

There was a huge clatter behind me, and Shannon screamed again. She'd already screamed several times, as I recall. It was the stockpot lid hitting the floor. The goddamn neck was trying to leap out of the stockpot like a fish. I grabbed a long fork and harpooned it, tossing it to Ben on the floor, who polished it off in no time. No problem. I had plenty of stock in the freezer.

Ben was covered in green goop, as was I. The Swamp Thing and his Swamp Cat. The floor was a slimy, glistening extra-virgin olive oil lagoon. *Dear Rachael Ray, I tried your chicken recipe and wasn't entirely pleased with the results…*

I knelt down and started washing off Ben with a wet towel. He was jazzed, purring like an outboard motor, a prizefighter who'd miraculously gone the distance and defeated the champ against all the odds. Usually he preferred to clean himself, but the prize was worth any indignity. It wasn't every day he scored an entire six-pound bird for his personal consumption. Shannon and I would have to go out for dinner, I was thinking, or there was always takeout. I was in a tiny bit of denial.

I'd been avoiding looking at her, though that must be her I heard whimpering. Finally, I looked up from my sopping, wild-eyed cat, still hyperventilating, his stuffed gut swelled out like he was pregnant. She was standing in the corner by the kitchen door, backed into the coat rack, still holding an umbrella cocked like a baseball bat. She'd picked it up when the reanimated chicken was headed right for her, before Ben leapt to the rescue. "Still want me to heal your brother?" I asked. In retrospect, not the best thing to say.

She looked at the umbrella as if she had no memory of how she came to be holding it. Judging from the look of terror on her face, she remembered, perhaps too vividly, what had just happened—the bizarre battle that had raged at her feet—two immortals in a battle to the death.

Ben took a step toward her. "It's okay, Shannon," he said. "It's dead now."

She threw down the umbrella and dashed out of the house. Her car started seconds later and roared off, tires squealing. I'd never known Shannon to drive like that.

"Don't worry," Ben said. "She'll be back."

"Yeah. What woman can resist us?"

The aroma of tarragon and garlic and death hung heavy in the air. I should mop it up, I thought, but I couldn't face the prospect of reliving the moment just yet. The one for me, the love of my life, was gone. Ben had wandered off and was licking the floor. Maybe he can make himself sick licking up the residue of this disaster, I thought. But that's right. He never gets sick. *Remember-r-r-r?*

"I'm going out," I announced.

Ben knew not to say a word.

I walked over to the barbecue place and had chicken that tasted like vinegar and smoke, fire and brimstone. I drank cheap beer and listened to a steady stream of country and western whine, guy after guy pleading for their lovers to forgive them their sins, hanging on to enough hope to manage three chords and a catchy plea built around some outrageous conceit, but none of their desperate hope was contagious, and I remained hopeless. These guys strayed, lied, drank, whatever—typical fucked-up guy stuff. None of them had ever resurrected a six-pound roaster as a clearly hostile act in the midst of a rational discussion. No. At some point, the weirdness has to set off deeply rooted survival alarm bells to head for the hills and not look back. I didn't know how anyone could just work around something like the ride Shannon had been on ever since she was just trying to help and made Ben an appointment at the vet.

Somehow I knew this time, maybe for the only time, I was right and Ben was wrong. Shannon wasn't coming back. I started crying, and the manager came over to tell me I had to leave. I couldn't believe it. I ate his bad food, listened to his sad songs—whose composers would be out of work if they couldn't rhyme die, lie, and good-bye with cry, cry, cry—and now he wanted me to leave because of a few *tears*? I could've done a whole lot worse than tears. I had a good mind to find his walk-in and resurrect his entire inventory, set it loose in the dining room to run amok in his crappy sauce, but of course, I didn't. Wouldn't. Ever again.

Benjamin and a chicken—that's it. My healing career was over.

All attempts to locate Shannon failed. She left town that night apparently, and nobody ever heard from her. Nobody who would tell me, anyway.

A few years later, Dad died, and Mom died the year after that. I held out some hope that Shannon might show up at their funerals, but of course she didn't. Aubrey died, unplugged by his parents apparently. I read the notice in the paper. I lurked nearby in the cemetery, but only the parents and the preacher were there.

When I came home after, even Ben finally admitted we were never seeing Shannon again. "I'm sorry," he said. "I should never have surrendered to my predatory instincts."

"It's not your fault. You're a predator, for christ's sake. It was my fault. I had no business bringing that chicken back to life."

He nodded in somber agreement. "True. True."

We missed her terribly, but we rarely spoke of her. It was too painful for us both.

My parents had left me a modest inheritance, which I invested in the stock market. After weeks fine-tuning voice recognition software so Ben could use the computer, I turned the portfolio over to him, and in no time he'd made us wealthy enough to retire and travel. We went everywhere. If Ben had read about it, he wanted to go there, and if he wanted to go, we usually went, and if we went, I never regretted it. We went to incredible places. We went to ordinary places made incredible by the wonders Ben knew we'd find there.

I soon discovered that if you have enough money, you can take your cat anywhere, especially when you get older. People put up with things from old people, probably figuring they haven't got too long. An old man denied his desires by some heartless gatekeeper may have missed his last chance. What sort of old age might such a heartless individual expect when it comes his time to travel about pathetically with some old cat in a carrier, when the sign clearly says NO ANIMALS ALLOWED? What? An empty building? Do you think homo sapiens aren't animals? What then are they, I'd like to know! Oh yes, by the time I'm 84, I can take my cat anywhere.

Trouble is I'm too sick to go anymore.

We've come to rest in Catemaco, a lovely town on a beautiful lake in Mexico, that teems with cats and *brujas*—witches—and is a favorite town of ours. We've rented a place with a balcony overlooking the lake. The fishermen still fish with hand-tossed nets from small one-man boats. I like to watch them at dusk, casting their nets into water and sky the color of burnished copper. The fish are delicious, embedded with cloves of garlic and fried whole.

They're only a memory to me now. I can't keep anything down. Everything tastes like ashes anyway. The doctor has come and gone. He's said there's nothing to be done to save me. He could admit me to the hospital, so that I might be more comfortable, but when I said I would be more comfortable here watching the fishermen with my cat, he bowed, in deference to my age I suppose, and said he understood.

Benjamin, who's befriended both cats and witches here, has returned with a woman named Hermalinda who brews teas for us both. He has broken his long silence with her, and she has agreed to come see to our needs. "Will it cure me?" I ask Ben of the tea she's brewing. I'm surprised I can smell it. I haven't smelled anything in a long while. I've had to give up cooking.

"Of old age," Ben replies, but I've forgotten what I just asked him.

"I'm afraid," I confess to my old friend.

"I know," he says. "Everything will be all right. I'll be joining you. Walk like an Egyptian." He laughs at his cat humor, very sly, but I don't get it. I wonder what

Hermalinda is brewing for him. Probably nip. It's always the nip with him.

Hermalinda props me up in bed so that I might look out the balcony at the copper waters, the fishermen's nets like women's fans opening and closing, leaving behind a glistening spray of memories. She holds the cup to my lips. It tastes of cloves and juniper. She patiently gives me the whole cup, sip by sip. The last sip is sweet, like honey, like roses.

She sets a saucer on the floor for Ben and quietly slips out the door. Ben quickly laps up his tea and jumps onto the bed, spry as ever, pushing my frail hands apart and inserting himself once more in my grasp. I can feel him through my skin, thin as paper, his heart beating, hard and steady, through my fingertips. "Good night, Jeffrey." He purrs softly, and my hands tingle. I remember the tune from so long ago, centuries in cat years:

> *...Old Blue died and he died so hard*
> *Shook the ground in my backyard*
> *Dug his grave with a silver spade*
> *Lowered him down with links of chain*
> *Every link I did call his name*
> *Here Blue, you good dog you*
> *Here Blue, I'm a-coming there too!*

Ben stops purring, and a moment later, his heart stops, and he's gone just like that. He's tricked me—knowing where he leads, I'll follow—fleeing the unbearable emptiness of this world without him—he's shown me the way. Some Day has finally come.

Everyone dies. Even Ben.

For me.

THE PUMA
Theodora Goss

Theodora Goss's short stories and poems have appeared in a variety of magazines and anthologies. Many of them are included in her short story collection *In the Forest of Forgetting* and the poetry anthology *Voices from Fairyland* (2008). With Delia Sherman, she coedited the short story anthology *Interfictions*. She has won the World Fantasy and Rhysling Awards for her short fiction and poetry.

Goss says: "As I'm sure is obvious, I was inspired by *The Island of Dr. Moreau*, which I was reading at the time. But I've had an interest, for a while now, in characters who don't get to speak. For example, the female monster who is destroyed in *Frankenstein*. She's absolutely crucial to the plot, but she doesn't get to say anything. The puma in *The Island of Dr. Moreau* is like that. She's crucial to the plot (she is, after all, the one who kills Moreau), but she never gets to say anything or achieve full "humanity" in Moreau's terms. She also happens to be the only important female character in the story, although in an early version there was actually a Mrs. Moreau, who was written out during the revision process. I'm particularly interested in these female characters who don't get to speak, on whose silence the story in a sense depends. If they spoke, I think the story would be different… So I like to give them a voice, to give them their own stories and see what they would have to say for themselves. I'm sure that in an obscure way I was also influenced by my favorite cat story of all time, H.P. Lovecraft's 'The Cats of Ulthar,' which is also a revenge story and a story about how powerful cats are. My cat, for example, adds her insightful criticism by chewing on the edges of my manuscripts…"

"Mr. Prendick, there's a lady here to see you."

I must have jumped, because I remember my knee banging into the desk. In the years since I had moved to this obscure corner of England, where even the trains did not come and I could walk over the hills for hours without seeing a human face, I had received only one visitor, the local vicar. There must have been something in my speech, perhaps even in my face, that agitated him, because he would not stay for dinner, and he left without urging me to attend services in the small stone church where he preached, in the valley below. I was sorry to see him leave. He had seemed like a reasonable man, although his inquisitive brown eyes and pinched face, a probable indication of early poverty, reminded me of a lemur. In all that time, I had never been threatened with a visit by anything that could remotely be described as a lady.

"A what?' I wondered what Mrs. Pertwee meant by a lady, exactly. Perhaps one of the female parishioners who lived in the village that surrounded the stone church, with its post office, pub, and collection of six or seven houses, coming to solicit for some missionary society to help our savage brethren.

"A lady, Mr. Prendick. She—" Mrs. Pertwee hesitated. "She calls herself Mrs. Prendick."

I tripped over the chair. The next day, Mrs. Pertwee had to wash the spot where my fountain pen had sputtered on the carpet with strong soap.

She was waiting for me in the parlor, a sanctuary that Mrs. Pertwee only entered to do whatever housekeepers customarily do to horsehair sofas and china ornaments. I had not used the room since renting the cottage, and had seen no need to alter it.

She was heavily veiled.

"Edward," she said. "How nice to see you again."

We are divided beings. One half of me had known that it could not logically be she. The other half had known that no one else in the wide world could claim to be my wife. That other half had been right. I could not mistake her voice, almost too deep for a woman, with a resonance to it, as though she were speaking from the depth of her throat. Like a viol.

"You look better than when I last saw you, on the island."

"Catherine."

"So I have a name now. Did you forget it when you wrote this?" She held up a copy of my book. The book I should never have written, that my alienist had urged me to write. "Did you forget that we all had names? What a terrible liar you are, Edward."

"Let me see your face," I said. The veil was disconcerting. I needed to know, for certain, that she really was speaking to me, that this was not some sort of hallucination.

She laughed, like an ordinary woman, and lifted her veil.

When I had last seen her, her face had been seamed with scars, the remnants of Moreau's work. Now, her face was perfectly smooth. The high cheekbones were still there, the nose aquiline, the best I think that Moreau ever created. The eyes yellow and brown together, like Baltic amber. The tops of her ears were hidden by her hair. Were they still pointed? She noticed me looking, laughed again, and pulled her hair back. They looked completely human. I am a scientist, and no judge of female beauty. But she was the most beautiful woman I have ever seen.

"How did you…"

"Walk with me, Edward." She indicated the French doors, which opened onto the garden. Her gestures were unnaturally graceful. "Let's reminisce, like old friends. Eventually, I'll have a favor to ask of you. But first, I'll tell you what I've been doing with myself for the last few years. Since, that is, you left me to die on the island."

"I didn't leave you to die."

"Didn't you?"

I followed her into the garden. It was an ordinary autumn day, the sky gray above us, with clouds blowing across it, and a herd of sheep like clouds in the valley below. I could see a dog driving them, first from one side of the herd and then the other. Somewhere, there was a man, and it was at his whistle that the dog ran to and fro. What dogs had done, and men had done, and sheep had done, for a hundred years. A quintessentially English scene.

"To what fate, exactly, did you intend to leave me?"

Her voice took me back to another scene, an entirely different scene. The southern sunlight on Moreau, lying in the mud, flies crawling over his shirt where the linen was stained red.

"The Puma," said Montgomery. "We have to find her."

"How did she do this?" I felt sick, mostly I think with shock. I had never, somehow, imagined that Moreau could die. Certainly not like this.

He pointed to Moreau's head. "She struck him. Look, the back of his skull is smashed in. Probably with her own fetters. She must have torn them out of the wall. Damn."

As a word, it seemed completely inadequate.

We followed her trail easily enough. She was heading, not toward the village of the Beast Men, but toward the sea. I wondered for a moment if she might try to drown herself, as I had tried to drown myself, my first few days on the island. But Beast Men did not do such things. They killed others, not themselves. It took a man to do that.

"There she is." Montgomery gestured with his gun.

She stood, up to her hips in the water. She looked at us, then shook herself, flinging spray from her wet hair. She walked toward us. So might Aphrodite have walked when she rose from the sea. But this was an Aphrodite with skin like gold rather than ivory, and the eyes of a beast. Everywhere, her body was covered with fresh scars.

"My God," said Montgomery. "So that's what he's been hiding from me."

"Hiding?"

"For a month, he wouldn't let me into the laboratory. He said the process was working at last. And look at her. She's his masterpiece. Poor bastard."

"I killed the one with the whip," she said. Her voice reverberated, like waves in a cavern beneath the sea. "Will you kill me for what I have done?"

"We will not kill you," said Montgomery. "It was not right to kill him, but we will not punish you for it."

"Have you gone mad?" I whispered to Montgomery. I aimed, but Montgomery caught hold of my arm.

"Can't you see what he did to her?" he whispered. "The man was a brute."

"It was right to kill him, and it gave me pleasure," she said. She walked out of the sea, like a statue of burnished gold.

With that unprepossessing statement began our time with the Puma Woman.

Her scars faded, but they remained visible all over her face and body. She looked like a South Sea islander, marked with cicatrices.

Montgomery took her to live with us, in the enclosure. He gave her his bedroom and slept in mine. We cleaned out the laboratory, releasing whatever still had its own form, killing the results of Moreau's experiments. We had food, guns, and M'Ling, Montgomery's favorite Beast Man, to guard us at night. We planned to wait until the next supply ship came, and then—what? I assumed that we would leave the island, leave Moreau's abominations to their own fate. But what about her? Montgomery seemed to have become particularly attached to her. She walked around the enclosure in one of his shirts, tucked into a pair of his trousers tied at the waist with rope. She looked like a gypsy boy.

She walked so quietly that I never knew, until she spoke, that she was beside me. When I launched one of the boats to go fishing, she would suddenly appear, help me push off, and leap into the boat. Montgomery would stare at us from the shore, with one hand on his gun belt. I didn't want her with me, but what was I supposed to do, push her into the water? She would sit, silent, and stare at me with her golden brown eyes—a woman, and not a woman. No woman could have sat so still.

It was Montgomery who named her Catherine. "Catherine, get it?" he said. "Cat-in-here. There's a cat in here!" He had been drinking. He watched her cross the enclosure, so lightly, so silently, that she seemed to walk on her toes. I did not like the way he looked at her. Perhaps he had initially been disgusted by the Beast Men, as I had been when I landed on the island, but he had long ago grown accustomed to them. They seemed to him human, and natural. I suspect that if you had set him down in the middle of London, he would have exclaimed at the deformity of the men and women who passed. She was Moreau's finest creation. Montgomery had always had his favorites among the Beast Men: M'Ling, Septimus, Adolphus. What did he think of her?

It was he who taught her to shoot, to read the books in Moreau's collection. As she learned, he answered all of her questions, first about the island, then about the world from which we had been isolated, and finally about Moreau's research. If we had been rescued then, I think he would have taken her with him. I imagined her scarred face, her long brown limbs, in an English drawing room. But it seemed to me, sometimes, that she had a preference for my company. And sometimes at night I would imagine her as I had first seen her, rising from the sea like Aphrodite, fresh from her kill.

Once, sitting in the boat, she said to me, "Prendick, how large is your country?"

"Much larger than this island, but smaller than some countries."

"Like India?"

"Yes, like India. Damn Montgomery. What has he been telling you?"

"That your English queen is the Empress of India. How could a country as small as yours conquer a country as large as India?"

"We had guns."

"Ah, yes, guns." She looked at her own complacently. "So, like on this island, it was a matter of guns and whips."

"No!" I tossed a fish with bright orange scales into the basket. "It was a matter of civilization."

"I see," she said. "You taught them to walk upright and wear clothes and worship the English queen. I would like to see this English queen of yours. She must have a long whip."

What were the Beast Men doing all this time? With the control that Moreau had exercised over them gone, they reverted to their natural behaviors. The predators formed a pack, with Nero, the Hyena-Swine, at its head. They moved to the other side of the island. The others stayed in the village, with Gladstone, the Sayer of the Law, to organize what vestiges of government they retained and Adolphus, the Dog Man, to organize their defense. Septimus, the jabbering Ape Man who had been the first Beast Man I had met in my initial flight from Moreau, attempted to create a new religion for them, with various Big Thinks and Little Thinks, but the others would have none of it. Montgomery thought that we should give them guns, but I refused. His sympathy for them angered me. Let them all perish, I thought, and let the earth be cleansed of Moreau's work.

So we went on for several months. It was, I later realized, a period of calm between the killing of Moreau and what came after.

She walked through the garden, stopping once to touch a lily with her gloved hands. "Your native English flowers," she said, "have many admirers. But have you seen anything more beautiful than this? The original bulb was brought generations ago from the slopes of the Himalayas. It flourishes in your English soil."

"Where did you learn botany?" I asked her.

She did not answer, but walked ahead of me, over the fields, up the hill, so quickly that I had difficulty keeping up with her. At the top of the hill, we looked down on the valley, with its English village sleeping under the gray sky.

"Would you like to hear what happened after you abandoned me on the island?"

I nodded. I looked at her again, sidelong. What had she done, to become what she was? She had a way of moving her hands when she spoke that was charming, almost Italian, although no woman could have had her fluidity of movement. Her grace was inhuman.

"I lived in the cave we had shared. I kept track of the time, as you had taught me. I had a gun, but no bullets, and anyway there were only a few of his creatures left on the island. You think that I cannot say his name, but I can—Moreau, the Beast Master. It was burned into my brain, remember? Doubtless it will be the last word I say before I die. But that will not be for a long while yet.

"You wrote that the Beast Men reverted to their animal state. What a liar you are, my husband! You know that would have been an anatomical impossibility. But you do not want your English public to know that after Montgomery's death, after the supplies were gone, you feasted on men. Oh, they had the snouts of pigs, or they jabbered like apes, but they cried out as men before you shot them. Do you remember when you shot and ate Adolphus, your Dog Man, whom you had hunted with, and who had curled up at your feet during the night?

I looked down at the valley. She was bringing them all back, the memories. My hands were shaking. I lifted them to my mouth, as though they could help with the wave of nausea that threatened to engulf me.

"They were animals."

"So too, if your friend Professor Huxley is right, are you an animal. As am I. You are startled. Why? Because I mentioned Huxley? I have done more things than you can imagine, since I left the island. I too have taken a class with Professor Huxley, whom you described so often. Your descriptions of his examinations served me well. He thought, of course, that the questions I asked him after his lectures were theoretical. He was delighted, he told me, to find such a scientific mind in a young lady. He did not know that I had been created by a biologist. I cut my teeth, as you might say, on the biological sciences. Or had my teeth cut on them."

During our time together on the island, after the death of Montgomery, I taught her about the origin and history of life on earth. We looked at geological formations, examined and cataloged what we found in the tidal pools, or the birds that roosted on the island. There were no species native to the island higher than a sea-turtle that laid its eggs there, but we studied the anatomy of the Beast Men we shot, discussing their peculiarities. I explained to her what Moreau had joined together, how pig had been joined to dog, or wolf had been joined to bear. I even, eloquently as I thought then, showed her what Moreau must have intended, where the beast became the man.

"You feasted on them too."

"They were my natural prey. If I had still been the animal Montgomery bought in a market in Argentina, I would have hunted them without thought, without scruple. But I'm getting ahead of myself. For months, I was alone. I reverted, not in appearance but in behavior. I hunted at night, ripped open my prey, ate it raw. After I thought all of Moreau's creations were gone, I lived on what I could find in the tidal pools—fish when I could catch them, clams that I smashed open on the stones. I dug for turtle eggs. I was half starved when the *Scorpion* came. There was nothing left on the island but some rabbits and a Pig Man that had somehow managed to escape me, and rats that I could not catch in my weakened state. They would have devoured me eventually.

"It was searching for the remains of the *Ipecacuanha*. The captain took particular care of me. He thought I was an Englishwoman who had been captured by pirates, and brutally treated. I have to thank you, Edward, for teaching me to speak so correctly! I did not realize, when I imitated your accent, that I was learning to sound like a lady. Montgomery's cruder accent would not have suited me so well. I told the captain that I had lost my memory. He took me to Tasmania, where the Governor treated me kindly, and a collection was taken up for me. Imagine all those Englishmen and women, donating money so that I could return home, to England! It was a great deal of money, enough for my voyage to England and a surgeon, a very good surgeon, to complete what Moreau had left undone.

"After the surgery, I had no more money, and money is necessary in this civilized world of yours. But I found that men will pay money for the company of a beautiful woman. And I am beautiful, am I not, Edward? I should be grateful to the Beast Master. I was his masterpiece."

She smiled, and I did not like it. Her canines were still longer than they should have been. Sometimes, when we lay together, she had bitten me. I wanted to believe she had done so by accident, but had she?

"And so I began to study. In this England of yours, a woman cannot attend universities, but she can attend scientific lectures. She can read at the British Museum. And if she is beautiful, she can ask as many questions as she wishes, and important men are flattered by her interest. I would venture, Edward, that I am now more knowledgeable about biology than you are. I intend to put that knowledge to use. But I need your help. I have come here," her hand swept to indicate the hills around us, the birds that were flying above, the clouds floating against the gray sky, "with the most vulgar of motives. I require money. You see, I have a particular project in mind. The surgeon who repaired me, who erased the scars that Moreau had left, is a Russian émigré, a Jew driven out of his country by religious persecution. How fond your species is of persecutions! For two years I have worked with him, learning everything he could teach me. I am now, he has been generous enough to say, even more skilled than he is. Your women who are agitating for the vote believe that they should have professions other than marriage. I too wish to have a profession. I propose to follow in my father's footsteps and become a vivisector."

I stared at her. Gazing over the hills, with the wind whipping her skirts back and tossing her veil, she looked like the figurehead on the prow of a ship. But where was she headed? Moreau's work had brought us once to disaster. Was she now truly planning to continue what he had begun?

After his death, the more peaceable Beast Men had developed the habit of coming to the enclosure to trade what they grew in their gardens for our flour and salt. Twice a week they came, crowding into the enclosure, like an English market crossed with a menagerie, or a Renaissance painting of some level of Dante's Inferno.

Montgomery should have noticed that Nero and the Wolf-Bear Tiberius had entered the enclosure. M'Ling should have been guarding the gate, but his attention was elsewhere. The Beast Men had begun adopting our vices, for which Montgomery was in no small measure to blame. He had taught them the use of tobacco, which he traded for food, and to pass the time he had whittled a pair of dice, with which they gambled for onions, turtle eggs, whatever the Beast Men had brought to trade. That morning, M'Ling was gambling with the Beast Men.

"Why does she carry a whip?" I heard the shout and went to the window. I usually avoided these market days. I still found it disconcerting to be in the company of so many of Moreau's creations.

Montgomery stood by the door of the storeroom, which held our barrels of tobacco, flour, biscuits, salted meat. Next to him stood Catherine, dressed as he was, with a gun in her holster and a whip tucked into her belt. All around stood the Beast Men with the goods that they had brought, and in the back, close to the gate, stood the Hyena-Swine.

"She is one of us, one of the made. Why does she carry a gun? Why does she carry a whip? Let her join her own people."

The Beast Men stood, staring, and I could see the inquisitive look in their eyes.

"Why does she not come to us?" said Catullus, the Satyr. "We have few females. Why does she not come to live in our huts, and work in our gardens, like the other females?"

"Yes," said the Ape Man. "Let her live with us, with us, with us! She can be my mate."

Then others spoke and said that she could be their mate as well.

I could see Montgomery looking puzzled. He had been up late drinking, the night before, and was still nursing a hangover. He could not understand this rebellion among the usually peaceable Beast Men. From where he stood, he could not see the Hyena-Swine.

I could see Catherine's hand on her gun.

The Beast Men began arguing among themselves, each claiming her. Moreau had never made enough Beast Women, and they were constantly trying to lure the ones they had away from each other. One pushed another. Soon there would be a fight.

I stepped through the doorway, into the enclosure.

"The Master, who has gone to live among the stars, and watches you from above, has intended her for another purpose. She will not be any of your mates. She will be without a mate, but will bear a child that will perpetuate your race. That is the purpose for which he has created her. She will be the mother of a new race of men. Bow to her, who is dedicated to such a high purpose!"

They stared at me.

"Bow!" I said, raising my gun. I could see the Hyena-Swine slinking through the gate.

One by one, reluctantly, they inclined their heads.

"Hail to the Holy Mother," said the Ape Man. He had always been sillier than the rest.

"Well then," I said. "You may continue to trade. There will be no punishment today, despite your disobedience."

That night, Montgomery lit the bonfire. He lit it every night. If there was a ship sailing within sight of the island, we did not want it to miss us. Sometimes the Beast Men came and danced by the light of the bonfire. "A regular corroboree," Montgomery called it.

"Catherine," he called, after the fire was lit. I could see him standing in the enclosure, with the full moon behind him, larger than it ever is in England. "Come to the dance. There's a regular crowd of them tonight."

"Not tonight," she answered. "Tonight I wish to speak with Edward."

"Damn Edward. Come on, Catherine." I realized that he had already started drinking, or perhaps had never stopped.

I did not hear her answer, but he shouted, "All right then, damn you!" And then I heard the gate crash shut.

"He's gone," she said a moment later, standing in my doorway.

"What did you want to speak to me about?"

She came closer. She had a smell about her, not unpleasant but particularly, I thought, feline.

"Do you think he had a purpose for me?"

"Who?"

"Moreau. You can see that I'm made—differently from the others. My hands—he must have taken particular care."

Her hands were on my shoulders. I could feel her claws through my shirt.

"Am I not well made, Edward?"

I looked down into her eyes, dark in the darkness. I don't know what possessed me. "You are—divinely made."

Where my shirt was open, she licked my chest, then my neck. She was almost as tall as I was. I could not help remembering Moreau's neck, torn open.

He had done his work well. Standing on an English hillside, watching her with her veil blown back by the wind, I shuddered at the memory of her brown thighs, with a down on them softer than the hair of any woman.

She smiled at me, and despite my sweater and mackintosh, I felt cold.

We were lying together in a tangle of sheets when we heard the shot.

"Get your gun," she said.

We ran out, me in my trousers, she in Montgomery's shirt. As we passed the storeroom, she disappeared suddenly, then reappeared with an ammunition belt over her shoulder.

On the beach, around the bonfire, Beast Men were dancing. There was a throb in the air, and after a moment I realized that it was a drum. Someone—it looked like the Sayer of the Law—was keeping time while the Beast Men turned and leaped and shook their hands in the air, and shouted each in his own way—some like the grunting of a pig, some like the barking of a dog, one caterwauling. I will never forget that sight, watching from the shadowed dunes while the Beast

Men capered together and the Puma Woman stood, with her gun in her hand, the ammunition belt slung over her shoulder, at my side.

"The fire is larger tonight," she said. "What are they burning?"

I looked again, more carefully. "The boats!" They had not been large enough to carry us away from the island, but they had at least been tangible signs that escape was possible.

Without thinking, I ran among them. "Damn you to hell! Damn you all to hell! What beast among you—"

One of the Beast Men turned toward me. I started back with a cry. He was wearing a mask that made him look like a gorilla. But the eyes behind it were Montgomery's. The other Beast Men stopped, stumbling into one another in confusion.

"What the hell—"

"I'm the—the Gorilla Man. See?" He began to caper about, with the stooping gate, the hanging arms, of a gorilla.

The other Beast Men laughed. I could see the firelight on their teeth.

"Drunk! You're all drunk! It's disgusting—"

"Come on, old stick-in-the-mud Prendick. Old hypocrite Prendick. Having your fun with the Cat. I deserve some fun too, don't you think?"

"Come on, Montgomery," I said. I tried to grab him, but he swung at me, punching me in the mouth. He could have hit harder had he not lost his balance, but I tasted blood. And then I saw a gleaming pair of eyes, and then another, staring at me. The Wolf-Bear was there, as was the Hyena-Swine, and with the instinctive reaction of a predator, the Hyena-Swine leaped at me.

I heard a crack. The Hyena-Swine fell at my feet. Then another crack, and another, and more Beast Men fell. They began screaming, running toward the darkness of the jungle. I thought I would be deafened by the cacophony or crushed as they ran. But the last of them vanished into the jungle, and suddenly there was silence. I was still standing, alone. At my feet lay the body of the Hyena-Swine. Beyond him lay M'Ling, a Wolf Woman, one of the Pig Men, and the Gorilla Man, Montgomery.

"You killed him," I said.

"He became one of them," she said, out of the darkness.

I did not answer. Silently, I turned, intending to walk back to the enclosure. It was a mass of flames. I heard a scream that I thought might come from one of the Beast Men, until I realized that I was the one screaming. For the second time that night, I began to run.

We saved nothing. There was nothing left to save. We had lost our supplies, and worse, we had lost the rest of our bullets. After the ones that Catherine had taken ran out, our guns would be useless.

"One of us must have overturned the lamp," she said. She was, as always, perfectly calm. The only evidence I had seen of her anger had been Moreau's throat, or what was left of it.

What could I say to her? If I had overturned the lamp, it had been by accident.

But she, so agile—could she have done it deliberately? I hated her then, more than I had hated Moreau. If I thought I could have, I would have killed her. But I did not want to die Moreau's death, to be buried, or worse, on that island of beasts that looked like men.

When I remember it now, I realize that I must have overturned the lamp. Montgomery had burned the boats to revenge himself upon me, but she had no use for revenge. Her motives were always simple, logical. What she wanted, she obtained directly, not with human indirection. Although she looked and laughed at me like an English lady, she still thought with the mind of a beast.

And so began the longer part of our stay on the island. Montgomery's body we burned, but the other bodies… She was a predator, and slowly, unwillingly, I fell in with her ways. We hunted together, and with practice my vision became keener, although never, of course, equal to hers. I insisted on cooking our food, although she laughed at me. I would not watch her when she ate it fresh from the kill. We drank from the stream, sucking the water up. Our clothes grew ragged and hung on our brown hides. I lay with her in the cave we called our home, hating her, hating what I had become, but unable to leave her. Even now, I remember her touch, the rasp of her tongue on my skin, the gold of her eyes as she stared down at me and said, "What are you thinking, Ape Man?"

"Don't call me that!"

She would laugh and push her nose against me like a cat that wants to be stroked, and make a sound in her throat that was neither a purr nor a growl.

One day, I was walking along the beach, scavenging what I could, crabs, clams, seaweed. We were using our bullets judiciously, but they were beginning to run out. Soon we would be reduced to hunting like beasts. I would become like her. I saw something floating toward me. A sail! But the boat reeled, like a drunken sailor. It was the boat I have described in my book, with the captain and the first mate of the *Ipecacuanha* sitting aboard, dead. This might be my only chance to escape the island. If I died on the ocean, at least I died as a man.

I stepped into the boat. I was certain, then, that I would never see her again.

"Perhaps," she said, "you would like to know in what way you can help me."

A light rain had begun. Her veil caught drops of moisture, like a spider's web.

I turned away. I did not want to know, and yet I could not stop listening. As a scientist, and a man, I wanted to know what she intended.

"I would have liked to bear children myself. But I cannot. You and I proved that, did we not, Edward? Would you have liked that, to have had children with me? What would they have been like, I wonder? Moreau took away my ability to breed with my kind, and could not give me the ability to breed with yours. Even Dr. Radzinsky was not able to give me that, although he tried. Somewhere, there is an incompatibility that goes beyond the anatomical. Perhaps someday your scientists will find it, and then we will be able to create a true race of Beast Men. But I am impatient. I want my children to flourish and populate the earth. Surely a natural desire, according to Mr. Darwin.

"Here, in England, I will create a clinic, to revive and perfect Moreau's research. But my clinic will be no House of Pain. We will incorporate all the technological advances of the last decade—and the educational advances, since my clinic will also be a school. Think, Edward! My children will be educated along the latest scientific lines. Educated to be the inheritors of a new age."

"What makes you think that I would finance such a—such a mad scheme? Is it not enough that Moreau did it once? Why would you wish to create such abominations yourself?"

"Not abominations. Look at me, Edward. Am I an abomination?"

I did not know how to answer.

"You will finance my mad scheme, as you call it, for three reasons. First, because you are a gentleman, and a gentleman cares about his reputation. If you do not provide me with the financing I require, I will inform your English press. There are two laws, Edward, that all civilized men obey: not to lie with their mothers or sisters or daughters, and not to eat the flesh of other men. You have broken the second of those laws."

"Why should I care what the public thinks of me?"

"Because there will be inquiries. And because nothing will be proven, people will think the worst. You will become notorious. Wherever you go, people will follow you, to interview you, to take photographs. Imagine the newspapers! 'What Mr. Prendick the cannibal had for breakfast. How it compares with human flesh.' But second, you are a scientist. What I am proposing is an experiment. I will bring pumas from the Americas, young ones, less than two years old. Fine, healthy specimens. I will operate on them in stages, changing them gradually. Allowing them, at each stage, to become accustomed to their new forms. Educating them. There will be no pain. There will be no deformity. My children will be as beautiful as I am."

I grasped at straws. "Your plan is impossible. You will never be able to build a clinic like that in England. Where would you hide? There is no part of the countryside that is uninhabited, no place obscure enough that your work won't be observed. You will be found out."

She laughed. "I do not propose to put my clinic in the countryside. No, my clinic will be in the heart of England, in London itself."

"But surely the police—"

"There are parts of London where the police never go. Parts where the inhabitants speak a babble of language, and everything you want to purchase is to be had, from a girl fresh from the English countryside to a pipe of opium that will give you distinctly un-English dreams. I have become familiar with them over the last few years. Do not worry about the practicalities. Those I have thought of already."

"And third—I did tell you there are three reasons—you are a follower of Mr. Darwin. Consider, Edward." She turned again to look at the valley below. "The operation of natural selection is necessary for evolution. Without selective pressure, a species stagnates, perhaps even degenerates, reverting to atavistic forms. How long has it been since selective pressure operated on the human species? You have killed all your predators. How many men are killed by wolves or bears, in Europe? You care for your poor, your sick, your idiots, your mad, who give birth to more of their kind, filling your cities. Your intelligent classes, who spend so much of their energy in their work, do not breed. This is not new to you, I know. You have read it in Nordau, Lombroso. Your very strength and compassion as a species will be your undoing. You will grow weaker by the year, the decade, the century. Eventually, like the dodo, you will become extinct. That is the fate of mankind. Unless…"

"Unless what?"

"You once again introduce a predator. That is what I'm offering you, Edward. Selective predation. A species that I create, to feed off the weakest among you, to make humanity strong."

She was mad, I thought. And I think so still. But there is a kind of reason in madness. Moreau had it, and as she claimed, she was Moreau's daughter. He too had the directness, the simplicity, of a beast.

I have not seen her since that day on the hillside. The money I send her is deposited into a bank account, and where it goes from there, I do not know. Do I believe that the creatures she creates will strengthen rather than weaken mankind? I do not know, but she has never lied to me. It takes a man to do that.

There was a fourth reason that she did not mention. Perhaps it was kindness on her part not to mention it. But I do not think that, in all her interactions with men, she has learned kindness. Surely she must have known. Sometimes at night I still think of her, her fingers twining in my hair, her legs tangled in mine, her lips close, so close, to my throat. I do not think I loved her. But it was a madness that resembled love, and perhaps I am still mad, because I have not refused her. She must have known, because as she stood in the doorway, ready to depart, as respectable as any English lady, she stepped close to me and licked my neck. I felt the rasp of her tongue.

"Goodbye, Edward," she said. "When I am ready, not before, I will invite you to my clinic, and you can see the first of our children. Yours and mine."

Yesterday, in the post, I received her invitation. Will I go? I have not decided. But I am a scientist, cursed with curiosity. I would like to see what she creates and whether she is, indeed, a worthy successor to Moreau.

Editor's Note:

I hesitate to publish this manuscript, left to me by my late uncle, Edward Prendick, because credulous members of the public may connect it with the series of brutal murders that is currently taxing the ingenuity of Scotland Yard. However, Professor Huxley, my uncle's former teacher, has asked me to publish it as an addendum to my uncle's manuscript of his time on the island. I believe the conversation it records was a hallucination. It must be remembered that my uncle's health was severely affected by the shipwreck that left him the sole inhabitant of an island in the South Seas, and that at the time of his death, he was attended by an alienist. I am satisfied that the cause of his death was natural. Heart failure can strike a comparatively young man, and even if we give no credence to the fantastical occurrences that he claimed to have witnessed, my uncle must have suffered a great deal. It is true that upon the execution of his will, his fortune was found to be significantly diminished. However, there are a number of possible explanations for the state of his affairs, and we should not draw conclusions before the investigation into his death is complete. I hope the public will do justice to the memory of my uncle, who, although disturbed in mind, was a man of intellectual promise before the shipwreck that embittered him toward mankind. And I hope the public will dismiss the ridiculous fancies of Fleet Street, and assist our police in catching the perpetrator of the Limehouse Murders.

—Charles Prendick

461

Night Shade Books Is an Independent Publisher of Quality SF, Fantasy and Horror

FEATURING STORIES BY

LAIRD BARRON

RICHARD BOWES

GLEN HIRSHBERG

MARGO LANAGAN

JOE R. LANSDALE

MIRANDA SIEMIENOWICZ

WILLIAM BROWNING SPENCER

MARGARET RONALD

NICHOLAS ROYLE

JOSELLE VANDERHOOFT

AND MANY OTHERS

THE BEST
HORROR OF THE YEAR

VOLUME **ONE**

EDITED BY ELLEN DATLOW

ISBN 978-1-59780-161-4, Trade Paperback; $15.95

An Air Force Loadmaster is menaced by strange sounds within his cargo; a man is asked to track down a childhood friend... who died years earlier; urban explorers delve into a ruined book depository, finding more than they anticipated; residents of a rural Wisconsin town defend against a legendary monster; an orphan returns to a wicked witch's candy house; an unanticipated guest brings doom to a high-class party; a teacher attempts to lead his students to safety as the world comes to an end around them...

What frightens us, what unnerves us? What causes that delicious shiver of fear to travel the lengths of our spines? It seems the answer changes every year. Every year the bar is raised; the screw is tightened. Ellen Datlow knows what scares us. The twenty-one stories and poems included in this anthology were chosen from magazines, webzines, anthologies, literary journals, and single author collections to represent the best horror of the year.

Night Shade Books Is an Independent Publisher of Quality SF, Fantasy and Horror

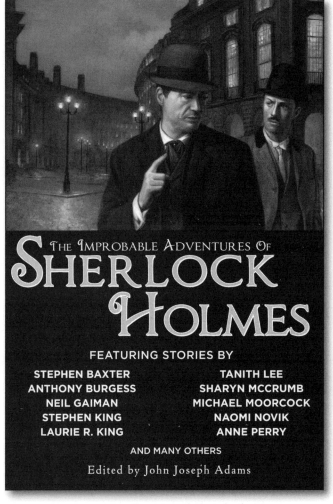

THE IMPROBABLE ADVENTURES OF
SHERLOCK HOLMES

FEATURING STORIES BY

STEPHEN BAXTER   TANITH LEE
ANTHONY BURGESS   SHARYN MCCRUMB
NEIL GAIMAN   MICHAEL MOORCOCK
STEPHEN KING   NAOMI NOVIK
LAURIE R. KING   ANNE PERRY

AND MANY OTHERS

Edited by John Joseph Adams

ISBN 978-1-59780-160-7, Trade Paperback; $15.95

Sherlock Holmes is back! These are the improbable adventures of Sherlock Holmes, where nothing is impossible, and nothing can be ruled out. In these cases, Holmes investigates ghosts, curses, aliens, dinosaurs, shapeshifters, and evil gods. But is it the supernatural, or is there a perfectly rational explanation?

In these pages you'll also find our hero crossing paths with H. G. Wells, Lewis Carroll, and even Arthur Conan Doyle himself, and you'll be astounded to learn the truth behind cases previously alluded to by Watson but never before documented until now. Here are some of the best Holmes pastiches of the last thirty years, twenty-eight tales of mystery and the imagination detailing Holmes's further exploits, as told by many of today's greatest storytellers, including Stephen King, Anne Perry, Anthony Burgess, Neil Gaiman, Stephen Baxter, Tanith Lee, Michael Moorcock, and many more. The game is afoot!

Night Shade Books Is an Independent Publisher of Quality SF, Fantasy and Horror

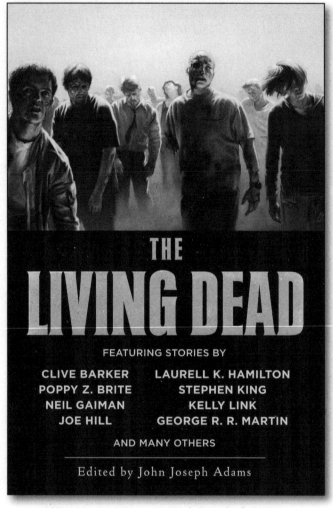

ISBN 978-1-59780-143-0, Trade Paperback; $15.95

From *White Zombie* to *Dawn of the Dead*; from *Resident Evil* to *World War Z*, zombies have invaded popular culture, becoming the monsters that best express the fears and anxieties of the modern West.

Gathering together the best zombie literature of the last three decades from many of today's most renowned authors of fantasy, speculative fiction, and horror, *The Living Dead* covers the broad spectrum of zombie fiction, from Romero-style zombies to reanimated corpses to voodoo zombies and beyond.

"When there's no more room in hell, the dead will walk the earth."

Night Shade Books Is an Independent Publisher of Quality SF, Fantasy and Horror

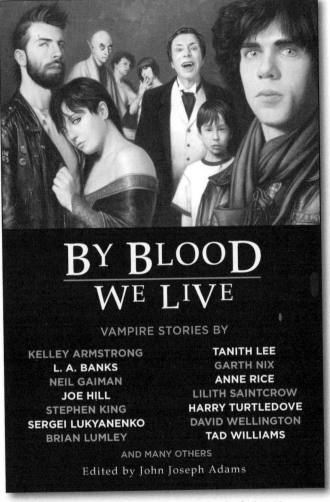

BY BLOOD
WE LIVE

VAMPIRE STORIES BY

KELLEY ARMSTRONG   TANITH LEE
L. A. BANKS   GARTH NIX
NEIL GAIMAN   ANNE RICE
JOE HILL   LILITH SAINTCROW
STEPHEN KING   HARRY TURTLEDOVE
SERGEI LUKYANENKO   DAVID WELLINGTON
BRIAN LUMLEY   TAD WILLIAMS

AND MANY OTHERS

Edited by John Joseph Adams

ISBN 978-1-59780-156-0, Trade Paperback; $15.95

From Dracula to Buffy the Vampire Slayer; from *Castlevania* to *True Blood*, the romance between popular culture and vampires hearkens back to humanity's darkest, deepest fears, flowing through our very blood, fears of death, and life, and insatiable hunger. And yet, there is an attraction, undeniable, to the vampire archetype, whether the pale, wan European count, impeccably dressed and coldly masculine, yet strangely ambiguous, ready to sink his sharp teeth deep into his victims' necks, draining or converting them, or the vamp, the count's feminine counterpart, villain and victim in one, using her wiles and icy sexuality to corrupt man and woman alike...

Gathering together the best vampire literature of the last three decades from many of today's most renowned authors of fantasy, speculative fiction, and horror. *By Blood We Live* will satisfy your darkest cravings...

Night Shade Books Is an Independent Publisher of Quality SF, Fantasy and Horror

DRAGON STORIES BY

PETER S. BEAGLE   MERCEDES LACKEY

HOLLY BLACK   CHARLES DE LINT

ORSON SCOTT CARD   GEORGE R. R. MARTIN

URSULA K LE GUIN   ANNE MCCAFFREY

DIANA WYNNE JONES   GARTH NIX

AND MANY OTHERS

Edited by Jonathan Strahan

ISBN 978-1-59780-187-4, Trade Paperback; $15.95

Dragons: fearsome fire-breathing foes, scaled adversaries, legendary lizards, ancient hoarders of priceless treasures, serpentine sages with the ages' wisdom, and winged weapons of war.

Wings of Fire brings you all these dragons, and more, seen clearly through the eyes of many of today's most popular authors, including Peter S. Beagle, Holly Black, Orson Scott Card, Mercedes Lackey, Charles De Lint, Diana Wynne Jones, Ursula K Le Guin, George R. R. Martin, Anne McCaffrey, Garth Nix, and many others.

Edited by Jonathan Strahan *(The Best Science Fiction and Fantasy of the Year, Eclipse)*, *Wings of Fire* collects the best short stories about dragons. From writhing wyrms to snakelike devourers of heroes; from East to West and everywhere in between, *Wings of Fire* is sure to please dragon lovers everywhere.

Night Shade Books Is an Independent Publisher of Quality SF, Fantasy and Horror

SYMPATHY FOR THE DEVIL

STORIES OF THE DEVIL BY

ELIZABETH BEAR   KELLY LINK
HOLLY BLACK   CHINA MIÉVILLE
MICHAEL CHABON   CARRIE RICHERSON
CHARLES DE LINT   CHARLES STROSS
STEPHEN KING   SCOTT WESTERFELD

AND MANY OTHERS

Edited by Tim Pratt

ISBN 978-1-59780-189-8, Trade Paperback; $15.95

The Devil is known by many names: Serpent, Tempter, Beast, Adversary, Wanderer, Dragon, Rebel. No matter what face the devil wears, *Sympathy for the Devil* has them all. Edited by Tim Pratt (*Hart & Boot & Other Stories*), *Sympathy for the Devil* collects the best Satanic short stories by Neil Gaiman, Holly Black, Stephen King, Kage Baker, Charles Stross, Elizabeth Bear, Jay Lake, Kelly Link, China Miéville, Michael Chabon, and many others, revealing His Grand Infernal Majesty, in all his forms.

Thirty-five stories, from classics to the cutting edge, exploring the many sides of Satan, Lucifer, the Lord of the Flies, the Father of Lies, the Prince of the Powers of the Air and Darkness, the First of the Fallen... and a Man of Wealth and Taste. Sit down and spend a little time with the Devil.

Ellen Datlow has been editing short science fiction, fantasy, and horror for almost thirty years. She was co-editor of *The Year's Best Fantasy and Horror* for twenty-one years and currently edits *The Best Horror of the Year*. She has edited or co-edited many other anthologies, most recently *The Coyote Road* and *Troll's Eye View* (with Terri Windling), *Inferno, Poe: 19 New Tales Inspired by Edgar Allan Poe, Lovecraft Unbound, Digital Domains: A Decade of Science Fiction and Fantasy,* and *Darkness: Two Decades of Modern Horror.*

Forthcoming are *Naked City: New Tales of Urban Fantasy, The Best Horror of the Year Volume Two, Haunted Legends* (with Nick Mamatas), *The Beastly Bride,* and *Teeth* (the latter two with Terri Windling).

She has won multiple awards for her editing, including the World Fantasy, Locus, Hugo, International Horror Guild, Shirley Jackson, and Stoker Awards. She was named recipient of the 2007 Karl Edward Wagner Award for "outstanding contribution to the genre."

For more information, visit her website at www.datlow.com